THE COMPLETE SERIES

USA TODAY & WSJ BESTSELLING AUTHOR

SIOBHAN DAVIS

Printed by Amazon

This paperback edition © February 2023

Say I'm the One © April 2021

Let Me Love You © May 2021

Hold Me Close © June 2022

ISBN-13: 9798375922027

Editing by Kelly Hartigan (XterraWeb) editing.xterraweb.com

Cover design by Shannon Passmore www.shanoffdesigns.com

Cover photograph by Michelle Lancaster www.michellelancaster.com

Cover Model: Brodie

Formatted using Vellum

SAY

I'M

THE

ONE

USA TODAY & WSJ BESTSELLING AUTHOR

SIOBHAN DAVIS

PROLOGUE
VIVIEN - NOW

THE LIMOUSINE DRAWS to a smooth stop outside the entrance to the renowned movie theater in L.A., and the crowd whoops and hollers, the raucous noise clearly audible even through the barrier of the car. The fans' excitement has reached fever pitch this week, and I have struggled to sleep most nights as the weight of expectation bears down on me. I'm grateful to my amazingly talented makeup artist for disguising the glaring dark shadows under my eyes and the pale tinge to my skin.

If I survive this night without puking or fainting, I'll consider it a win.

The usual doubts race through my terrified mind, almost crippling me with anxiety. Am I doing the right thing in ripping my chest wide-open, exposing the vulnerabilities of my heart for the entire world to see?

My breath oozes out in anguished spurts, and I place a hand over my heaving chest, rubbing the tightness there, willing my heart to calm down before I give myself a coronary.

Warm, familiar fingers intertwine in mine, and I cling to his hand like the lifeline it is. "Breathe, Viv. You've got this," he says.

I turn to face him, discovering his piercing blue eyes are already locked on mine. Squeezing my hand, he smiles, his gaze full of love and adoration. I release a shuddering breath, as my pulse slows down, comforted by the reassuring look on his gorgeous face and the firm grip of his hand in mine. Reaching out, I cup his cheek, welcoming the feel of his stubble as it grazes against my palm. "I couldn't do this without you. I would never have even gotten to this point without your support." Tears prick the backs of my eyes as I think of everything we have endured to get here.

So much pain. So much heartache. So much turmoil.

"I love you," he murmurs, resting his hand over mine on his face. "And I will always support you. *Always*." He pulls my hand around to his lips, placing the softest kiss against my palm. Tingles emanate from my hand, all the way down my arm, and

3

his touch helps to soothe my frayed edges. "But you would have gotten here without me because you are so incredibly strong. I'm in awe of you." Lowering our hands to the seat, he leans in, pressing a delicate kiss to the corner of my mouth that is at odds with the usual possessive way he kisses me. "I'm so proud to call you my wife, and no matter what anyone else thinks, I'm proud of how far you've come. Fuck anyone who disagrees." His fingers gently trace the curve of my jawline, careful not to dislodge my makeup. "There will always be haters. We know that. But who cares what they think? This isn't about them. This is about you. About us."

The crowd screams louder outside, and I know it's time.

"He would be so proud of you too, Vivien. Wherever he is, I know he's watching this and cheering for you just like I am."

I can only nod over the messy ball of emotion clogging my throat. I need to get a grip because tonight is about celebrating love and life and cherishing every single moment. Reliving the past will be painful. I have no doubt it will be emotional—not just for me—but I refuse to shed any more tears. Tonight, I will draw a line under the past. I'm determined to stop beating myself up for being happy. I know it's what he would want. Tonight is about finally finding the last sliver of closure I need to fully move on.

I owe it to myself, to my family, and to this man waiting patiently at my side— above everyone, I owe it to him.

Flinging my arms around his neck, I inhale the musky scent of cinnamon, vanilla, and lavender as I cling to his body, permitting his warmth and solid masculinity to infuse me with renewed determination. "I love you," I whisper in his ear. "So damn much."

"I will never tire of hearing those words leave your gorgeous lips," he says, waggling his brows in his usual flirtatious manner. "And you can show me just how much later, but right now, we need to get out of this car before we start a riot."

"I can do this," I say, holding my shoulders back and tipping my head up. It's not like this is my first rodeo. However, it *is* the first time I'm attending a premiere for a movie I wrote and coproduced.

"You were born to do this," he adds, pressing a kiss to the back of my exposed neck. A slew of shivers cascades down my spine, and an ache pulses between my thighs. His touch still lights a fire inside me, even after all this time.

"Wait for me," he says, curling his hand around the door handle.

"Always." I blow him a kiss as he opens his door and exits the car. The screaming elevates a few decibels, and my lips tug up at the corners. I'm not surprised his legions of fans have turned out to catch a glimpse of their idol. I'm granted a temporary reprieve as he closes the door, waving to the crowd, before rounding the back of the car. Scooting closer to the door, I smooth a hand down the front of my pretty pink and silver Dior gown, drawing a brave breath as I wait for him.

He opens my door with a flourish, extending his hand and helping me to my feet. The crowd roars their approval, and we turn around on the sidewalk, holding hands while waving to the thousands of men, women, and children lining the cordoned-off road as far as the eye can see.

My eyes lower to the charcoal-colored sidewalk before us that encompasses a part of the Hollywood Walk of Fame, instantly finding the coral-pink terrazzo five-point star rimmed with brass that houses Reeve's name. I remember how proud he was the day he was honored with it. How proud *I* was to see the culmination of all his childhood dreams etched so permanently into history.

More well-wishers adorn the red carpet on both sides of the covered entrance as he leads me forward. Some hold signs, professing their love for Reeve. Other placards express love for Dillon. Up ahead, hanging back just inside the open doorway of Grauman's Chinese Theatre, are my parents along with my agent, Margaret Andre; the head of Studio 27, who produced the movie; and the studio's overworked publicist.

My husband's hand is steady on my lower back as we walk along the red carpet, smiling and waving. Excitement prickles in the air, helping to drown out my lingering nerves.

"Murderer!"

"Slut!"

The words slam into me like bullets, pushing through skin and tissue and bone, embedding deep in my heart and twisting my soul into knots. Acid churns in my gut, and bile pools in my mouth as I grip my husband's arm tighter. The noise of the crowd fades, and all I hear are those taunts echoing on repeat in my brain. Panic surges through my veins, replacing the life-sustaining blood flow with liquid ice.

"Ignore those bitches," my husband says, circling his arm around my shoulders and pulling me in close to his side. "Someone's head is going to roll for this," he adds through clenched teeth.

Scuffling breaks out on my right as security guards force their way through the crowd to reach the two women hurling obscenities and accusations my way. But I don't hear anything else. I'm numb to everything going on around me, having retreated to that safe place in my head where no one can hurt me.

He hustles me through the open door, past my concerned parents and a clearly distressed studio publicist. My back hits the wall, and heat rolls off him in waves as he leans into me, his palms resting on either side of my head. Cocooning us in our own little bubble, he says, "Talk to me." With gentle fingers, he tips my chin up, forcing my gaze to meet his worried one. We stare at one another, unspoken sentiments passing between us, and the hypnotic depths of his ocean-blue eyes reel me out of the desolate space in my head.

I clear my throat as I press my hand to his chest, the rhythmic beating of his heart grounding me in the moment. "I'm okay. It's not like this is anything new."

"How the fuck did they pass security clearance to get that close to you?" he seethes. "I'm going to shove that prick Rawling's balls down his throat until he chokes." Rawlings is the head of security at the studio, and we've had our fair share of run-ins with him over the past year.

"You'll have to get to him first, and I already called dibs," my dad says, appearing behind my husband.

"Darling, are you okay?" Mom asks, bundling me into a hug.

"I'm good. A few crazies aren't going to ruin tonight."

"That's my girl." Mom presses a kiss to my temple.

"We're so proud of you, princess," Dad says, tucking Mom in under his arm. At six-four he towers over her five-foot-four-inch frame, but they always look like they were made for each other. My parents just celebrated their thirty-seventh wedding anniversary, something exquisitely rare in Hollywood these days. One only needs to look at the adoring way they stare at one another to know theirs is an epic kind of love. The type that weathers any storm because the bond is far too strong to break.

After chatting with some studio heads and members of the cast and crew, we make our way into the famous theater, taking our seats in the front row as we wait for everyone to pile in.

When the large room is full and the doors have been closed, James, the head of the studio, stands in front of the curtain with a microphone in his hand.

Discreetly swiping my hands along the armrests of my chair, I give myself a silent pep talk. No one is forcing me into speaking, but it's something I feel compelled to do. My husband leans into me, planting his lips to my ear. "You're going to nail it." He kisses my cheek and squeezes my hand.

"I feel like I might pass out any second," I whisper truthfully. There is a reason I never wanted to follow Reeve or my mom into acting—I don't like attention and I hate the spotlight. I have always been more comfortable behind the scenes.

"If you do, I'll be there to catch you," he says, peering deep into my eyes. "I'll always catch you, Viv."

He has more than proven that in recent times. "I'm hoping it won't be necessary anymore."

Before he can reply, James calls me forward as applause breaks out around the room. I rise, exchanging a smile with my parents before I stride toward the head of the studio, holding my head up high, projecting confidence even if I'm a basket case on the inside. James kisses my cheek before passing me the mic. I scan the room as a reverential hush descends over the proceedings.

Exhaling deeply, I wet my lips and begin. "Thank you all so much for being here tonight." My voice trembles a little, but I'm not embarrassed to show emotion. "There were several moments in the past few years where I didn't think we would make it to this point. I don't mind admitting I had significant moments of doubt. Moments where I questioned my sanity and whether I could do this. Without the support of my husband, my parents, and my friends and the patience and under-standing of the studio, I would not be standing before you right now. On my darkest days, they reminded me of why this story needed to be told."

Tears well in my eyes as I rake my gaze over my loved ones seated in the front row. Their presence gives me strength, their love fuels my courage, and their endless support makes me feel like I could climb any mountain, overcome any challenge, because they believe in me. Just like he did.

"I have had to sit back and suffer while so many lies were told—to the point where I could barely find the will to get out of bed some days. When I started writing this story, it was for me. For my children. So they would someday know the truth. I never intended for it to see the light of day. But the world deserves to know the truth too."

My smile is wide as I continue. "This is the story of a Hollywood prince, an Irish rock star, and the girl who loved them both. A girl who never wanted the spotlight but found herself thrust into it anyway. This is a story filled with secrets and lies, drenched in heartbreak and pain, but it's also a lesson in forgiveness and redemption and finding the strength to go on when life seems insurmountable."

My eyes wander to my husband. He looks so handsome, so strong, and so proud as he sits upright in his seat, giving me his undivided attention. Pride glimmers in his eyes along with powerful emotion. Tonight is as hard for him as it is for me. I hate that I've hurt him and that we'll be revisiting some of the most painful moments of our history tonight. But I'm not the only one who needs full closure.

I keep my eyes fixed on my husband, hoping he feels the outpouring of love seeping from my every pore. I will never love anyone as much as I love him. "Most of all, it's a story about true love and how love has the power to salvage a broken soul from the wreckage of life." My eyes scan the room one final time. "This is the story of my life."

CHAPTER 1

Senior Year of High School

"ANY NEWS YET?" Audrey asks, coming up alongside me as I stare at my cell, willing it to ring.

I shake my head, chewing on the corner of my lower lip. "Not a word, and I'm starting to freak out."

"You know how long these things take." She opens her locker as students fill the hallway behind us. "I'm sure lover boy will call the minute he gets out of the meeting."

After stuffing some books in my bag, I close my locker and lean my head back against it. "He wants this part so bad. He'll be devastated if they don't offer it to him."

"He'll bounce back," Audrey says, slamming her locker shut. "Remember how upset he was last year when he didn't get the *Riverdale* part, but he got over it pretty quick."

Eh, yeah, no, he didn't. Reeve was upset and plagued with self-doubt for months after getting to the final round of auditions and then being rejected. It's been a pattern these past few years, and while my boyfriend is one of the most focused and most determined people I know, continuous rejections are starting to chip away at his confidence. I do my best to bolster his spirits. To remind him how amazingly talented he is, and when that fails, I distract him with my lips and my hands and my body.

It's a tough job, but someone has to do it.

"Don't let his laid-back attitude fool you. He beats himself up like crazy with every rejection. He's so hard on himself," I admit, tucking strands of my long dark hair behind my ears as I push off my locker, walking alongside Audrey.

We head toward the exit, and I'll be glad to see the back of Blackrock Prep today. I honestly thought this day would never end. Time seemed to drag by, slowing to the point where the world was barely turning. Checking my cell every few minutes didn't help, but I've been on tenterhooks all day, wondering how Reeve's meeting with his new agent and the studio heads went. From the feedback he has received so far, we know the casting director loves him, but the movie director has a few concerns.

"If it's meant to be, he'll get the part." Audrey loops her arm through mine and her emerald gaze pins me in place as we walk. "He's way too talented to be overlooked for long."

"Hollywood is crammed full of talented actors who never make it," I remind her. "But Reeve has the trifecta. Talent, looks, and determination, and I just know he's going to make it."

"I'm sure your parents would help too."

"Help with what?" Alex says, materializing on Audrey's right, injecting himself into the conversation, as usual.

"Reeve's career." Audrey stretches up to peck her boyfriend on the lips.

"They would be happy to help, but he wants to do it by himself, and I respect that." It would be easy for Reeve to use my mom's star power or either of our fathers' connections to get a leg up in Hollywood, but he wants to earn roles on his own merits, and I can relate. While I'm still not totally decided on whether I'll go the writing or costume design route, whatever I choose to do, I want to do it myself, without any interference or help from my parents.

"Fuck." Alex drags one hand through his sandy-blond hair, and I swear I hear a collective swoon from the girls in the vicinity. To the legions of adoring fans who worship the ground he walks on, it doesn't matter that Alex and Audrey have been dating exclusively for the past two years. As our illustrious QB, he has garnered plenty of admirers, in the same way Reeve has. Reeve and Alex are easily the two hottest guys in our private school, and hordes of drooling girls would kill to be in my, and Audrey's, shoes. "He didn't get the part?" Alex asks, holding the double doors open for us.

"I don't know. I haven't heard from him yet," I say, stepping outside into glorious sunshine. Although L.A. in late September is generally warm and sunny, we've had an unusual spell of extremely hot weather this week. We're all hoping it extends to the weekend so we can go swimming at the beach.

Alex slings his arm around Audrey's shoulders as we descend the steps to the sidewalk. A pang of longing hits me square in the chest when he brushes her glossy red hair to one side and plants a trail of little kisses along her neck. I didn't get to see Reeve last night after school, and I'm suffering major withdrawal symptoms. It's the same any time we are separated for more than a day. We have been joined at the hip for so long I cannot even fathom ever living my life without him in it.

An icy shiver crawls up my spine, and I shake the hideous thought from my stupid brain. If there is one thing I'm sure about in this life, it's that Reeve Elon Lancaster was made specifically for me and we will love one another every single day for the rest of our lives. Okay, so that's two things, but I'm just as sure about both.

"Three o'clock," Alex says, briefly lifting his mouth from his girlfriend's neck.

I whip my head around, spotting Reeve parked at the curb, leaning back against his Porsche with his arms folded, looking hotter than any guy has a right to be. My gaze does a slow perusal, from the ground up, and a deep ache pulses between my legs. He dressed the part today, wearing tight, black, ripped jeans that cling to his long, lean legs and toned thighs, fitting snuggly against his crotch in a way that has me licking my lips and squeezing my thighs together. His black button-down shirt is stretched tight across his muscular chest, highlighting the extra definition in his torso and biceps.

Reeve wanted this part so badly he changed his appearance to better suit the role of Camden Marshall. Cam is the hero in *Cruel Intentions*, the first book in the best-selling *Rydeville Elite* series, a firm favorite with fans of dark high school bully romance.

Reeve has been working out like a demon for this part, and his shoulders and chest are broader, he's now sporting an impressive six-pack, and his arm porn is to die for. His hair has been dyed a darker shade of brown to disguise his natural blond highlights. Normally, Reeve wears his hair long on top but styled back off his face. Now, the longer parts of his hair are artfully styled in messy waves and the sides have been shorn much tighter with a zig-zag line in the skin fade. He even wore brown contacts over his natural blue eyes to complete the transformation.

My man is hot, no matter what look he's rocking, but I've got to admit he is sexy as fuck right now, and I'm ready to jump his bones like a demented oversexed kangaroo.

Reeve watches me ogling him, but his expression is giving nothing away, and fear spirals through me, sprouting anxious goose bumps all over my arms.

"You waiting for an invitation?" Alex asks, grabbing my backpack. "He looks tense as shit. Go cheer him up."

I stride toward Reeve, picking up speed and flat-out running when he loses control of his emotions and an ecstatic grin spreads across his mouth. "You got it?" I shout as I approach, and he can't contain his grin as he nods. "Oh my God!" I scream, throwing myself at him and wrapping my legs around his waist. His arms automatically slide under my butt, holding me in place as I pepper kisses all over his face. "I'm so proud and so happy for you, Reeve." I slam my lips onto his, and he holds me tight against his body as we devour one another. I moan into his mouth when his tongue glides against mine. His assured strokes submerge every part of my body with fiery heat that has nothing to do with the weather and everything to do with how much my boyfriend turns me the fuck on.

"I need to be inside you," he groans into my ear, and lust coils in my belly.

"Your dad's still away, right?" I ask though there is really no need. Simon Lancaster is rarely home anymore. It's like he's forgotten his son even exists, and I want to beat the shit out of him for his neglectful treatment of his only child. But it's old news, and Reeve is used to his father's lack of regard for him by now. That's not to say it doesn't hurt him. Of course, it does, but he's gotten better at ignoring the harsh truth of his reality. The fact is, Reeve's dad checked out of his life the minute he was born, which coincided with the moment his beloved wife, Felicia Lancaster, left this world.

I don't understand how Simon can ignore the only part of Felicia that still survives. Shouldn't he want to cherish and love his son because he's all that is left of his wife? Instead, he's married to his work, and his son is an afterthought. If my parents hadn't stepped up, Reeve's childhood would have been an isolated and lonely existence.

I press myself tighter against him, clinging to him fiercely, kissing him passionately as I funnel all the love in my heart into him.

"Jeez. Get a room," Alex says, his smug tone underscoring his words, and we reluctantly break our hungry lip-lock.

"I fully intend to," Reeve replies, while I unwind my legs from his slim waist. He snakes his arm around my back, keeping me flush against him as I rest my head on his chest.

"Does this mean you got the part?" Audrey asks. Warmth spreads across my chest at the obvious delight in her voice.

"I did." Reeve straightens up, beaming from ear to ear. "I got it."

Audrey squeals, shoving me aside so she can hug my boyfriend. She's lucky I love her like a sister and I know she has zero interest in my man. "That is awesome, Reeve. I'm glad to see all your hard work has paid off."

"Congrats, dude." Alex raises his arm, his fist clenched, and they do some elaborate manly handshake. "You deserve it."

I snuggle into Reeve's side, pressing my lips to his neck and sighing.

"Party at my place tomorrow night," Reeve says, waggling his brows. "We've got some celebrating to do." His hand slides down over my jean-clad ass as he leers. "And I intend to start the celebrations right now." He squeezes my ass before his lips melt against mine. His kiss is urgent and demanding, and I feel it all the way to the tips of my toes.

Alex snorts. Audrey laughs, and I squirm on the spot, my body tingling in delicious anticipation.

Abruptly, he rips his lips from mine, digging his hands into my hair. "If I don't stop, I won't be responsible for my actions," he rasps. His lust-filled eyes roam over my body like a sensual caress, and he's not the only one having trouble with self-control.

I'm seconds away from begging him to fuck me.

"Let's get out of here." I nip at his earlobe. "I want to reward you for being the sexiest, hottest, most-talented actor on the planet."

"What about *my* reward, babe?" Alex nuzzles his nose into Audrey's neck.

"You have to do something to earn a reward," Audrey quips, quirking a brow as she tucks her hand into the back pocket of Alex's jeans.

"I think I deserve a reward for that thing I did with my tongue in the supply closet at lunch." He winks, and I laugh as my bestie's cheeks flush pink.

"You got action in the supply closet at lunch? I'm jealous." I fake pout.

"Don't be jealous, babe. I have some tongue tricks of my own," Reeve says before plunging his tongue into my ear.

I shriek, jumping away from him. "That's not the kind of tongue action I was after."

"I know exactly the kind of tongue action you want." He grips my hips, hauling me against his hard body. "Get your delectable butt in my car, and I'll show you that much quicker."

My panties flood with liquid warmth, and my legs almost go out from under me. "I drove this morning, so I'll have to follow you in my car."

Reeve tilts his head to the side, eyeballing his best friend as they silently converse.

Alex flips his palm out. "Hand the keys over, princess. I'll drive your car home, but you owe us."

"Thanks, man." Reeve raises his fist for a knuckle touch.

"I'll call you later to make plans for tomorrow," Audrey says, as Reeve opens the passenger door of his Porsche.

"Cool." I give my bestie a quick hug as Reeve takes my bag from Alex. "See you guys, later."

I climb into Reeve's car, and he shuts the door before running around and sliding in behind the wheel. Leaning over, he kisses me again. "I still can't believe it. It feels surreal. Like I'm dreaming."

I pinch his arm.

"Ow!" he exclaims, but he's smiling.

"Believe it, babe. You're living the dream and you're going to be a star. The world is going to go nuts for Reeve Lancaster, and I'll be cheering for you every step of the way."

His expression sobers a little, and his eyes flood with adoration as he cups my face. "I couldn't have done it without you, Viv. I know I drove you insane rehearsing the audition scenes, over and over again, but you pushed me to deliver the best possible performance, and it showed."

"I love running lines with you, and you're wrong." My lips glide softly over his. "Your true natural talent shone through, and that's what won you the part. Don't let anyone take the credit for your achievement. All I did was support you, just like you support me with my dreams."

He rubs his thumb along my cheekbone, eliciting a wave of delicious tremors across my skin. Even the slightest touch does the most amazing things to me. "Your belief in me is everything." He presses a firm kiss to my brow. "*You're* everything."

"I will always believe in you, Reeve. I've always known you are destined for greatness. I've never had any doubt."

"I fucking love you so much, Viv." I'm surprised to see tears glistening in his eyes. "Sometimes I don't think you realize just how much." His hands land on my hips.

I press my forehead against his and clutch his ripped arms. "I know, baby, because I feel it too."

Sometimes I wonder if this is normal. If this is what it's like for most couples. Because the intensity of my feelings for Reeve are impossible to put into words. He has been a part of my life for as long as I can remember, and our souls are so entwined I can't tell where he starts and I end. He is the oxygen that fills my lungs. The blood that pumps through my veins. The energy that fuels my body. I feel incomplete when we're not together, and I am only truly whole when his essence is wrapped around mine. My skin prickles with awareness whenever he's close, and my heart swells to bursting point the instant he steps into a room.

I never thought it was possible to be so attuned to another human being, but we are connected in ways I cannot logically explain. "What we share is more than love,"

I whisper over his lips. "More than life. It transcends everything that humanity knows about existence."

"That is beautiful," he murmurs, brushing his lips against mine. "Just like every other part of you."

We stay like that for an indeterminable amount of time, just holding one another. Existing in our own little part of the universe, sharing everything without saying a word.

We are both smiling when we separate, and contentment settles deep in my bones. I am so happy right now I could scream.

"This is just the beginning," he says, starting the engine. "Everything we have dreamed of for our future is starting to come true." He rubs my thigh as he glides out onto the road. "Everything is going to change now, babe. Just you wait and see."

If only I'd known how prophetic his words would turn out to be, though not at all in the way Reeve had implied.

CHAPTER 2

"OH, GOD, REEVE. YES! RIGHT THERE." I fist my hands in his hair as his tongue feasts on my pussy like I'm the most exquisite filet from the best Michelin-starred restaurant. Throwing my legs over his shoulders, he continues to work me over until I'm a quivering mess of cells writhing on his king-sized bed. "Holy fuck. You are getting so good at that," I pant, pushing strands of my messy dark hair out of my hazel eyes.

"We aim to please." He smirks as he kicks his jeans to one side before crawling over me.

"We?" I quirk a brow as I push up on my elbows.

He grips his long, hard, straining length. "My cock and I."

"That should be a movie."

"I'm pretty sure there's some porn out there with that title," he says, lining his erection up at my entrance. He holds still, hovering over me. "You okay?" he asks, like he always does, and my heart swells, like usual.

"Get in me already," I demand, sliding my hands over the dips and curves of his abs.

"So bossy and so greedy." He grins, driving inside me in one confident thrust.

I close my eyes, as my limbs melt into the bed, savoring the feel of him inside me. Every time we have sex, I feel like we couldn't get any closer, and I'm always wrong, because each time gets better and better.

"Fuck, Viv," Reeve says, slowly moving in and out of me. "How do you feel so incredible?" Leaning down, he kisses me slow and deep, and my fingers sweep over the velvety-soft hair at the nape of his neck.

"I'm glad we waited until the time was right," I purr into his ear, bucking my hips as he rocks in and out of me. Reeve is always so careful with me. Making love to me like I'm the most precious thing in the world. I'm usually the greedy shrew begging him to go faster, thrust harder.

"It was more than worth the wait." He plants a slew of drugging kisses along my neck.

Reeve and I have been best friends since we were little kids. His mom was my mom's best friend, and both sets of parents were close. When Reeve's mom, Felicia, died giving birth to him, his dad struggled to cope, so my mom stepped in, making sure Reeve was a part of our family, including him so he wouldn't be left out or made to feel lonely on nights when his father worked late and he only had the staff and his nanny for company. Gradually, Reeve spent more and more time at our house. He even has his own bedroom, which my parents updated as he grew older.

My earliest memories all include Reeve, and he's been an intricate part of my life. First as my best friend, and then as my boyfriend.

We made things official when we were fourteen, but we had shared some spine-tingling kisses before that. Things were hot and heavy for a long time until we decided to lose our virginity to one another a few months before my seventeenth birthday. Reeve would have taken the plunge earlier, but I was nervous, and I didn't want to disappoint my parents who had asked us to slow things down. Legal age of consent is eighteen in Cali, but neither of us could wait any longer. I'm lucky my parents are so progressive and they trust us. Mom helped me to get on the pill, and she regularly subjects us to safe-sex lectures. While she lets me sleep over at Reeve's house on weekends, she has a strict no-fraternization policy during the week, which we both respect.

My cell vibrates on the bedside table, but I ignore it, getting lost in the sensations my guy is conjuring from my pliable body. Reeve quickens his pace as my legs wrap around his back, and I dig my heels into his gorgeous ass. His mouth lowers to my chest, and he lavishes attention on my breasts as my cell continues to vibrate.

"You need to get that?" he asks, while sucking on my nipple.

"Nope, and don't you dare stop." I reach over and switch my cell off.

My hands roam his back as he pivots his hips, thrusting harder inside me, and I arch my spine, moaning as I feel another orgasm building. Sinking my teeth into his shoulder, I suck on his skin.

"Don't mark me," he warns, panting as he plunges inside me. "Remember I've got more auditions next week."

"No fair." I pout, wishing I could leave my mark on him so the actresses he's testing against next week understand he is all mine.

Reeve's cell vibrates in the pocket of his pants, and we groan.

"I'm nearly there," he says, sitting back a little so he can thrust into me at the right angle. He rubs my clit as he rocks into me. "Let's come together."

I almost burst into song, but I don't want to ruin the moment, and I'm too lost to the heavenly waves of bliss cresting all over my body to care about anything but my climax. I scream out his name as I succumb to pleasure, and he fills my pussy with his hot cum.

"Damn," he says, collapsing on top of me. "Why can't lover be a professional career choice because I'd love nothing more than to spend my days in bed giving you endless pleasure."

"Don't tease me like that." I trail my hands up and down his arms as he slowly pulls out of my body. I miss him instantly.

16

"Love you," he says, resting his head on the pillow beside me. He threads our fingers together before lifting them to his mouth and kissing my knuckles.

"Love you too." I kiss the tip of his nose and palm his cheek. "Have I told you how proud I am of you?"

His handsome face lights up with obvious joy. "You might have told me a time or one hundred," he admits, brushing his lips against my neck.

A shiver works its way through me, and my greedy pussy pulses with renewed need. Twisting onto my side, I press my body against his so we are skin to skin and perfectly aligned. "I think I'm addicted to sex with you." Grabbing his ass, I thrust my pussy against his semi-hard cock. Either that or the ticking clock leading to our impending separation is looming large, demanding I take everything I can before he has to leave.

"Ditto, babe." He fondles my breasts, softly tweaking my nipples, and they are so hard they could cut glass. "Hold that thought," he adds, grabbing his jeans off the floor. He removes his vibrating cell, flashing me the screen. It's my mom. "Hey, Lauren." Reeve puts her on speaker. "Were you looking for us?"

"I don't want to think about why it took you so long to answer your phone," Mom replies. "Do we need to have the safe-sex conversation again?"

"Mom!" I screech. "You have lectured us enough, and we're always safe."

"As much as I adore children, I'm not ready to be a grandmother yet."

I slap my palm against my forehead. "Mom, seriously?"

Her laughter trickles down the line. "I'm calling to invite you both to dinner. Can you be here in a half hour?"

Although we are neighbors, all houses in North Beverly Park are built on at least two to three acres of land, so it still takes ten minutes to walk between our houses. Considering we are both currently naked and smelling of sex, thirty minutes to shower, redress and get home is cutting it close unless we drive.

I frown, stretching out on the mattress and stifling a yawn as I consider legitimate excuses that Mom will buy. We usually eat takeout in bed while watching movies on Friday nights unless there's a party. I can't remember the last time we ate dinner with my folks on a weekend night, and I'm really not in the mood to get out of this bed.

"We sure can," Reeve says, as I prepare to open my mouth and decline her invitation.

"Great, we'll see you then," Mom says before hanging up.

"Ugh." I snuggle into the pillow, pulling the sheets around me. "Why did you have to say yes? I was planning on giving you celebratory sex all night long."

Reeve rolls his eyes. "Now she tells me." He yanks me up onto his lap. "You can make good on your promise after dinner."

I wrap my arms around him, burying my face in his neck. "Deal."

"Congratulations!" Mom squeals, enveloping Reeve in a big hug. "I'm so happy for you, honey." Her long black hair is loose, tumbling in lush thick waves down her back.

Tears stab my eyes as I take in the lavishly decorated dining room. I don't know how Mom pulled it off so fast, but there are balloons, streamers, banners, and a giant cake that looks like it would feed forty people, not four. Dad pours Cristal Champagne into flutes, and I help him to hand them out. "Don't get used to it, princess," he warns, as I take a sip of the delicious bubbly amber-colored liquid. "Only because this is a special occasion."

"Chill, old man," I tease. "It's not like I haven't been drinking champagne at movie premieres since I was fourteen."

My parents are one of Hollywood's golden couples, and attending industry events was the norm for Reeve and me growing up. Mom has won several Oscar nominations and awards for her acting, and Dad's trophy collection isn't too shabby either. Last year, he took home the Golden Globe *and* the Oscar for best director. What's even more noteworthy is the fact they are happily married and they genuinely adore one another. They manage to have successful careers and a successful relationship, and that's not an easy feat in Hollywood.

They are my idols, and I look up to them in so many ways.

"That had better be a joke, young lady," Mom says, finally letting Reeve go. Her vibrant green eyes pin me in place, and I know she's semi-serious.

It's not a joke though. Those events can get crazy, and Reeve and I always found a way to sneak some champagne. As we've gotten older, my parents have let us drink on special occasions, but it's strictly one glass. I'm sure they know we drink when we're out with our friends, but they don't hassle us about it too much.

My dad squeezes Reeve on the shoulder as he offers his congratulations. I give Mom a quick hug. "Thanks for doing this."

"Has he even called him?" she whispers.

I shake my head, and she sighs. "Felicia would be so disappointed in Simon," she adds, careful to keep her voice down so Reeve doesn't overhear. "This is a big milestone in Reeve's life, and his father should be here."

"He should, but I can't say I'm surprised. He always lets him down."

I hate Simon Lancaster.

I really do.

Even when he is around, he's absent. He's cold and selfish, and Reeve is usually an afterthought to him. Simon is a few years older than my mom but a few years younger than my dad, and he's still a very handsome man. As head of Studio 27, one of Hollywood's most reputable production studios, Simon Lancaster is a busy man and a desirable catch. If he's not burning the midnight oil, he's bumping uglies with his latest fuck buddy. I haven't mentioned it to Mom—as I'm fearful she would stop me from staying over at Reeve's—but we have regularly run into naked women roaming the house at all hours.

It disgusts me and upsets Reeve, and anyone who upsets my love is an automatic addition to my shit list.

"A toast," Dad says, drawing Mom and me back into the conversation.

I walk to my boyfriend, wrapping my arm around his back as his arm encircles my shoulders. My parents mirror our position, and we raise our glasses. "To Reeve. May your star shine bright and your career ascend dizzy heights."

We all clink glasses.

"We're so proud of you, Reeve," Mom adds. "Not just for winning such a prestigious role but for the man you are becoming. It's been a pleasure watching you grow up."

A messy ball of emotion clogs my throat as my parents shower my boyfriend with love.

I definitely won the parent lottery, and I couldn't be more grateful for all the ways they have nurtured and protected me while still giving me space to make my own choices and decisions. More than that, they have set the best example in the beautiful way they love one another. My whole life, I have aspired to a love like theirs, and I know I have found that in Reeve. It's remarkable in any situation, but especially with the industry we've grown up in where constant affairs and quickie divorces are the norm.

My parents are true role models, and I love the relationship I have with them. Sure, they piss me off at times, all parents do, but I wouldn't trade them for the world.

"Thank you so much," Reeve says, his voice sounding choked up. He waves his hand around. "Not just for this but for everything."

"You're family," Dad simply says, running a hand through his brown hair. Strands of gray have appeared lately, and I love that he's not hiding them. It only makes him look more distinguished, and more handsome, though I could be biased. Some of the staff carry steaming plates of food into the room as we talk. "You're as much our son as Vivien is our daughter. There will always be a place for you at this table and in our home."

I swipe at the errant tears leaking out of my eyes, while Reeve steers me over to the table.

"Can I adopt your parents?" he whispers, holding my chair out for me. "I don't think I can wait until we're married to make it official."

I smile, kissing him softly before claiming my seat.

"I'm hearing a lot of buzz about your movie," Mom says a few minutes later when we are all seated and diving into a gorgeous steak dinner.

"Me too," Dad says, in between bites. "It'll be interesting to see how the public at large engages with a darker young adult movie."

"It's going to push boundaries, for sure." I take a sip of my sparkling water. "I hope they remain true to the books. They are so good." When Reeve first auditioned for the role a couple of months ago, I bought all the books in the *Rydeville Elite* series, and I literally could not put them down.

"Me too, and from what I've seen so far, they seem determined to remain as authentic as possible. I'm hella excited to play this part."

"Cam is such an asshole in *Cruel Intentions*," I say, cutting my steak into bite-sized pieces, "and he is so different from you. It will definitely stretch you out of your comfort zone."

"That's one of the reasons I wanted the part so bad."

"Is the contract for one movie only or with an option for more?" Mom asks.

"One with the option of another two," Reeve confirms. "And the author has written more books about other couples, so if it proves popular, it could turn into a franchise and keep going for years."

"Be careful you don't get pigeonholed," Dad warns. "Look at how much Robert Pattinson struggled after the *Twilight* franchise."

"Jon." Mom drills a look at Dad. "Don't rain on Reeve's parade." She smiles across the table at my boyfriend. "That would be a great problem to have, and you are young enough and talented enough to break out of any mold."

"If it comes down to it, I would value your advice." Reeve places his silverware down on his empty plate.

"We are always here for you," Mom says. "And my offer to talk to Margaret still stands." Margaret Andre is Mom's long-term agent, and she is well-respected and well-known in the industry. She comes from a long line of Andres who worked in the industry, and she only takes on a select number of clients. Mom had offered to speak to her on Reeve's behalf last year when he ditched his old agent, but he wanted to find new representation himself. While I don't like Bianca Remington—Reeve's new agent—I can't deny she has pulled out all the stops for him. As long as she has his best interests at heart, I can tolerate her surgically enhanced resting bitchface.

"Thanks, Lauren, but I'm happy with Bianca right now. You should have seen her in the negotiations this morning. I can see how she has earned her rottweiler reputation."

"Have they cast your leading lady yet?" Dad asks.

Reeve shakes his head. "They are having trouble casting Abby. They have rejected all the girls I tested with. However, there is someone they are talking to currently who they are very interested in. I'll be filming a few scenes with her next week to see if we have chemistry."

He mentioned he had to shoot some additional scenes next week, but he never mentioned it was only with one actress. "Who is she?"

"They haven't said. It's all hush-hush for now."

"It must be someone with star power," Mom says. "Someone the studio is desperate to sign."

Reeve shrugs. "I don't care as long as it's someone I can work with, someone who will add value to the production and challenge me to deliver the best performance I can." He turns to face me. "I was hoping you could run lines with me this weekend."

"Of course. You know I'm always happy to run lines with you."

He pecks my lips. "Thanks, babe. You're the best."

CHAPTER 3

"IS SHE HOT?" Nate inquires, waggling his brows. "And how many sex scenes do you have with her?"

Music shakes the windows, filtering out of the open door as the DJ Reeve hired for the party spins tunes in the ballroom where most of our classmates are currently drunk off their asses, or high as kites, or a mix of both.

I roll my eyes as I take a swig of my vodka cranberry. What is it with guys and sex on the brain? Though I really shouldn't be criticizing considering the marathon sex session Reeve and I engaged in last night after we left my parents' house.

"He doesn't know who she is," Audrey replies, swatting the back of Nate's head. "Don't you ever listen?"

A loud splash is followed by giggles and screaming as someone jumps in the pool. Inside Reeve's house, the party is in full swing, but we've retreated to the covered patio to talk without shouting for a while.

"For fuck's sake." Reeve shakes his head, glaring at the two guys and three girls cavorting in their underwear in the swimming pool.

"I'll handle it," Alex says, standing.

Reeve made it clear there was no going in the pool tonight. It's not like it's the height of summer, even if we did get to spend a large portion of our day on Santa Monica Beach.

"So, who is she?" Nate asks again, leaning forward on his elbows.

"Come on, bro," Zeke coaxes. "You know we're gonna find out eventually."

"I don't know," Reeve protests, sliding his arm around my shoulders. I scoot in closer on the rattan couch, snuggling into his side. "And even if I did, I couldn't say anything. I had to sign a watertight NDA, so these lips are sealed."

"But you get to fuck her, right?" Nate asks, his eyes glimmering with mischief.

"You're an idiot." I shake my head. "He's playing a part, and most sex scenes on movie sets are very clinical. Trust me, there is little that is sexy about it." At least, that's what my parents have always said. It's not like I've had a front-row seat or anything.

"Rawr." Nate curls his fingers at me. "Look at your claws coming out."

I flip him the bird. "I'm confident in my relationship and my mad sexual skills. Just ask Reeve. I practically rode him to death last night."

Reeve spits beer all over the tile floor. "Babe. Tell the whole fucking world, why don'tcha?"

I shrug, feeling brave thanks to Mr. Grey Goose flowing through my veins. "I'm not ashamed, and maybe he'll shut up about you fucking your leading lady now."

Truth is, I'm not loving the idea of Reeve performing some of these scenes with another woman. But it's par for the course when you're an actor, and I'll just have to get used to it. The last thing I want is any of my insecurities to impact Reeve's performance. This part is a big deal for him. This role could catapult him onto the world stage, and having a successful acting career is something he has craved for as long as I've known him. I won't do anything to jeopardize his potential or do anything to add to his stress levels, so I'm trying to pull my big-girl panties on and accept it's just part of his job.

I stride across Reeve's father's study in my tight-fitting black dress and stiletto heels, growling as I put my face up in his, fixing him with an angry look. "I've had enough of you for one day," I snap, glaring at him. "Get lost, Cam."

"I thought you were made of stronger stuff," he coolly replies.

I glare at him some more, forcing my body to shake with rage.

Reeve pulls the hood of his hoodie down off his head, stepping into me. His chest brushes against mine, and his eyes glimmer with challenge. My body floods with warmth, and I'm struggling to project the anger Abby demonstrates in this scene. Reeve is so fucking hot wearing Camden's skin, and I'm already salivating.

"Viv." Reeve eyeballs me, and I try to shake all lustful thoughts from my mind.

"Sorry. I'll focus." Planting my game face on, I take a step back, per the script.

Reeve closes the gap between us immediately, running the tip of his finger across my exposed collarbone, eliciting a rake of fiery tingles that makes my toes curl. "The more you fight me, the more I enjoy this," he whispers, pressing his mouth to my ear. "So, keep fighting me, sweetheart. Nothing turns me on more."

Oh God. Nor me!

See, this is why I could never be an actress. I'd never be able to wear another character's skin and ignore my own emotions and reactions. But I'm supposed to be helping Reeve, so I work harder to dampen my desire.

"Fuck you, Cam." I shove him away, stalking to the couch and dropping down on it. In this scene, Abby gets into her car and Cam slides uninvited into the passenger seat. "What the hell do you think you're doing?" I bark as Reeve sits on the couch beside me.

"Coming with you. Unless you already know the way to Lauder's place?" He looks around, as if he's admiring the car interior.

"No, and no. Get out."

"Make me." He slants me a sexy, lopsided grin that is supposed to infuriate me, but all it's doing is turning me on more.

Fishing my pepper spray out of my purse, I uncap the lid and aim it at his face. He reacts fast, pinning me to the couch with his fingers curled around my hand, trying to pry the canister out of my grip while I pretend I'm trying to press down on the button.

We wrestle for several minutes—me trying to get it to explode in his face and him trying to get a hold of it—and it's the hottest type of foreplay. I gasp when his hips press against mine and his hard length rubs against me.

Fuck me. Please.

He wraps his fingers around my wrist, and I yelp as if I'm in pain. Reeve throws the canister on the floor and straddles me. I bite back a moan as my hips lift of their own volition. I can barely remember the script, because I'm so freaking aroused my brain has turned to mush.

"Cuss at me and try to fight me off," Reeve whispers in my ear, and I whimper. I let a string of expletives loose as I fight him, while simultaneously battling with the almost insurmountable urge to shove my hand into his boxers and grab his erection. I emit a frustrated scream.

"I can do this all night, so feel free to keep fighting me."

Oh, yes, Cam, Reeve, ugh. Keep fighting me because this is getting my juices going like you wouldn't believe.

Remembering my part, I buck against him, raising my free hand to slap him, but he grabs both my hands over my head as he presses his body down on top of me. Lust slams into me, and I'm losing the battle. My core aches, my panties are soaked, and my nipples are trying to poke a hole through my lace bra.

Reeve straightens up until he's sitting on my lap, and his hungry eyes latch on to my chest. I try to remember I'm supposed to hate him, not want to strip him naked and bounce on his cock.

When his mouth brushes the sensitive skin just under my ear, I pant and groan, writhing underneath him. Reeve rocks his groin against mine, while he keeps my wrists elevated over my head, and from the familiar lusty glint in his gaze, I can tell he's struggling to stay in the role too. That makes me feel better, if a little guilty.

I'm supposed to be helping him, not making it more difficult.

He thrusts slowly against me. "How is it I crave the thing I hate most?" he whispers, his mouth moving to my jaw. "How do you do that? Make me want you when I despise you?"

"If you discover the answer, please enlighten me," I rasp, keeping my eyes shut.

"Open your eyes, Abigail." He peppers my jawline with kisses, and I'm on the verge of spontaneous combustion. My eyes blink open, and I stare into his beautiful face. Conflict rages in his eyes, as it's supposed to. "I think you've been put on this Earth purely to torment me," he whispers, letting my wrists go so he can wind his hands into my hair. "I need you to hate me."

"Oh, trust me, I'm already there." It almost pains me to say those words to the love of my life, even if they're not true.

"Not nearly enough," he whispers, kissing the corner of my mouth.

"What do you want from me, Cam?" I whisper back.

23

He kisses the other corner of my mouth, and I'm hanging on by a thread here.

"*Everything*, Abigail. I'm going to take everything." Reeve slams his mouth to mine, gripping my head in his large palms, and all bets are off.

He must think so too, because it's like a race to see who can remove clothing faster, and in record time, he's driving his cock inside my naked body as we fuck like wild animals on the floor of his father's study.

"Oh my God." Reeve wipes an arm across his sweaty brow as we sit on the floor, leaning back against the couch, after the hottest sex of our lives. "That was insane."

"Insanely hot." I grin at him.

"If this continues, I'm seriously screwed for rehearsals next week."

The edge slices off my euphoric post-coital high. "If any of your rehearsals end up with hot sex on a floor, you won't just be screwed, Reeve, you'll be fucking dead the second I get my hands on you."

He chuckles, leaning his head on my shoulder. "You know I was talking about us running lines."

"Hmmm."

"Babe?" He lifts his head, swiveling around until he's sitting cross-legged in front of me. His brow puckers. "You know you have nothing to worry about, right?"

I crick my neck to loosen the suddenly tight muscles. "I know I'm being ridiculous, but I don't like the thought of you doing that scene with anyone but me."

"Then maybe you should audition?" He arches a brow.

I crank out a laugh. "Funny, but no. I would suck. I think I've just proven that."

"I happen to like how you suck." His lips curve at the corners, and my eyes automatically lower to his crotch.

"You really do like how I suck, huh?" I play along, watching his dick harden.

"Baby." He grabs his boxers, pulling them on, chuckling as I pout. "We need to talk about this, and I can't do that if we're both naked." I dress in my underwear as he continues. "I don't want you to worry. You know I only have eyes for you. You're the love of my life, Viv," he adds, pulling me onto his lap.

"I know that, Reeve, but it's not just this scene. Abby and Cam have this epic, explosive kind of love, and you'll really need to inhabit his persona to pull it off in a way that will justify the plot and pay homage to the character. You'll need to be passionate with her. That's what worries me."

"I know how to separate my personal feelings from my role. It will only be acting, babe."

"It's not you I'm worried about. It's whoever they cast as Abby." I chew on the corner of my lip. "I still want to punch Marnie Gibson for shoving her tongue down your throat during *Romeo and Juliet*," I admit, my fists clenching as I recall how she used to paw at him during rehearsals. Everyone knew we were in love, and Reeve told her time and time again to cut it out, but she loved pushing my buttons, and we almost came to blows on several occasions. She still smirks at me whenever I pass her in the hallway, and I still want to throat punch her until I wipe the smug grin off her face.

Reeve has taken a leading role in every school play, but that was the only part that required him to kiss his leading lady. I was jealous as fuck, and it doesn't bode well. I hate that I'm worrying, because I trust him completely and it shouldn't be a big deal. I need to trust in him and our love and accept this is the way it will always be.

He tucks my hair behind my ears, dotting kisses along my cheeks. "Her breath smelled like rotten farts, and I almost puked every time I had to kiss her." He grimaces, and I grin, his words helping to ease some of my tension. He cups my face, locking eyes with me. "It wouldn't matter if they cast Gal Gadot opposite me. I'd still have zero interest. You are all I see."

I purse my lips. "Now I know you're lying. I've seen you drooling over her. Don't deny it."

"That was the Wonder Woman costume, and trust me when I say every red-blooded male got hard watching that movie."

"Gross." I place my hands on his shoulders, exhaling loudly. He looks troubled now, and I'm not doing this to him. I just need to get over myself. "It's fine, Reeve. Don't mind me." I kiss him softly. "I know I can trust you. I'm just being silly."

"You *can* trust me." Lifting my hand, he kisses the soft skin on my wrist. "You can trust me one hundred percent."

I do trust him, but I have a sixth sense it's not him I'll have to worry about.

CHAPTER 4

I BURY my head in my hands, tossing my cell on the couch in my living room. "Ugh. Why her? Of all the actresses in the world, why did they have to cast Saffron Roberts as Abby?"

"It sucks, babe," Audrey says. "I hate it and Reeve isn't even *my* boyfriend."

Lifting my head, I exhale heavily. "I'll just have to grin and bear it. It's not like I can do anything about it, and I understand why they hired her."

Saffron starred in a couple of popular Netflix movies. She's beautiful and a decent actress. But they are a dime a dozen in L.A., and if it wasn't for her scandalous affair with a high-profile married film director, she would not be so famous.

Usually, the woman fares unfavorably in such situations, but the director's wife made a statement saying they had an open marriage, even alluding to a threesome with her husband and the then twenty-year-old actress. Saffron signed with a new agent and PR firm, and for a time, you couldn't turn on the TV or scroll through social media without seeing her pretty face. Roles have been pouring in, and she's now being touted as one of the future stars of the big screen.

"I get that she has an edgy vibe that works with the plot, but I still think it's risky," Audrey says, and I love how loyal she is.

I stand, stretching to loosen the kinks in my shoulders. "I hate thinking of Reeve kissing, touching, and faking sex with her, but I'll just have to get over it. The truth is, it's a good thing for the movie that she's come on board. It means more investment and more publicity. I want Reeve to succeed, and I trust him. It's her I don't trust."

Audrey kicks her shoes off, pulling her knees into her chest. "She might not be as bad as we think. You know how the media twists things."

"True," I agree, feeling a little guilty for instantly hating her. I've seen how the media has twisted things with my parents over the years. How they have made innocent hugs and kisses on the cheek seem more. How they have tried to manipulate the truth to suit their own agenda. Saffron has never publicly commented on the affair, so, for all I know, it might not have even happened. "Reeve said she was great. Friendly but professional and very excited for the project."

The door bursts open, and the guys come in, laughing and shoving each other. "Hey, babe." Reeve reels me into his arms, kissing me slowly, and I melt into his arms.

"Fuck, you're all so nauseating," Nate drawls, and we break apart the same time Alex and Audrey do.

"Then maybe you should stop hanging out with us." Audrey slants him a fake sugary-sweet smile. I know he gets on her nerves, but he's on the football team with Alex, and their families are super close, so he's always hanging around.

"Or get yourself a girlfriend," I suggest. Nate isn't my type, but he's a honed slab of muscle, and he's not ugly. I know he has his fair share of willing bed partners, but he needs a personality transplant if he expects any of them to stick around for a relationship.

"What an awesome idea." He rocks back on his heels. "I was just telling Reeve he should introduce me to his sexy co-star."

Saffron was papped entering the studio last week, so the PR people issued a press release the second she signed on the dotted line, confirming her and Reeve for the parts. Now everyone knows, and it's becoming real. The books are popular, and social media is going crazy right now with talk of the movie.

Audrey snorts with laughter, while I try to curb the jealous fluttering in my chest.

"Unless you plan to fly to the East Coast, you can forget that plan," Reeve says, rubbing a soothing hand up and down my back. "I told you we're filming in Boston and other parts of Massachusetts."

"I'm sure you can invite her to come and party with us sometime." He waggles his brows.

Over my dead fucking body.

"I don't think you're her type," Reeve says, and I frown. *How the hell would he know her type, and why does it even matter?*

"Reeve's right," Audrey cuts in, leaning her head back against Alex's chest. "You're not rich enough. Old enough. Or powerful enough. Unless you've got something she can gain, she won't even give you a second glance."

"I didn't realize you were so judgmental," Reeve says. "And you shouldn't believe everything you read online. She's a nice girl and really fucking talented."

Audrey purses her lips, and an awkward silence engulfs the room. I don't disagree with my bestie, even if we are being a little judgy. What bothers me is how quickly Reeve jumped to Saffron's defense. It's not like he knows her either.

"I'd still do her," Nate says. "I've never had any complaints about Woody," he adds, grabbing his crotch.

We all burst out laughing, and it helps to offset the growing tension.

"Butthead is throwing a party on the beach tonight," Reeve says. "You want to go?"

"Sure." I could use a drink or ten after the press announcement today.

"Let's grab dinner at The Shack first," Alex suggests, and we all nod, agreeing to meet in an hour.

"Feeling better?" Audrey asks, as we dance in front of the fire. Butthead may be a butthead, but he sure knows how to throw a proper beach party. It helps that this strip of beach is private and his palatial home is behind us. It means we have access to toilets and chilled drinks, and the line of chimineas spread out on the sand was kindly supplied by his parents so we don't freeze our asses off.

"Much," I agree, shimmying my hips to the pulsing beats pounding from the free-standing speakers. "I just need to get out of my head. This is such an amazing opportunity for Reeve, and I've got to quit the jealous girlfriend routine."

"It's human to be jealous. All week, I've been imagining what it would be like if it was me and Alex, and I wouldn't like it one little bit."

We bump hips, and I throw my hands around her neck, smacking a kiss to her cheek. "I don't like it either, but this is going to be Reeve's life, and I have to deal. He's my one true love, and I'm his, and no one or nothing can ever change that."

Whoops and hollers ring out, and I whip my head around in the direction of the guys. They're sitting on fold-up chairs around a fire, drinking beers and laughing over something on Nate's cell phone.

Audrey loops her arm through mine. "C'mon. Let's find out what's so entertaining."

We amble to the guys, stumbling a little and giggling. I've lost count of how many vodka shots I've downed, but I feel carefree and happy, so I don't care, even if I will have the mother of all hangovers tomorrow. Reeve reaches his arms out, pulling me down onto his lap, and I go willingly, draping myself around him and pressing my face to his neck. I inhale deeply, comforted by the minty, citrusy scent of his cologne. Brushing my lips against his neck, I silently rejoice when he shivers and his dick hardens under my ass.

"Give me that," Audrey says, and I tilt my head, watching her swipe the cell from Zeke as I press feather-soft kisses against Reeve's neck. "What the actual fuck?" she shouts, glaring briefly at Reeve and then Alex. She throws the cell at Zeke before jabbing her finger in Alex's chest. "You better not have been looking at those photos."

Alex shrugs, sliding his arm around the back of his girlfriend's waist. Audrey shoves his arm away. "Babe, relax. It's no different than watching porn, and you already know I do that."

"It is fucking different when you're ogling naked pictures of Saffron Roberts."

Reeve's body stiffens as I lift my head. "Wait. What?"

She sends me a sympathetic look. "They are nudes that were released last year when news of her affair hit the headlines. Apparently, one of her exes took them and cashed in on her popularity."

What an asshole thing to do. For a brief second, I feel sorry for her until my jealousy rears its ugly head again. Grabbing Reeve's face, I tilt his chin up so he's looking at me. "Did you look at those photos?"

"No." He vigorously shakes his head. "And I told them it was a bad idea."

"You would say that," Nate cuts in, his tone scoffing. "You'll get to see her goods in the flesh. You should look at the pics so you can tell us whether she looks better in real life," he adds, cupping his groin, "because I've got to tell you, my cock is dying to slide between those monster tits and fuck the shit out of them."

Audrey pours her beer over Nate's head, and I could kiss my bestie. I'm a generous C-cup, and I've never felt like I'm lacking in the boob department, but there is no way you would refer to my breasts as monster tits, and I hate how Nate's words have me feeling a little inadequate.

"What the fuck?" Nate hops up, mopping the beer on his face with the edge of his shirt as he shoots daggers at my friend.

"You deserve that and more," Audrey retorts, looking and sounding completely unapologetic.

"Viv." Reeve's fingers gently grasp my chin as he reclaims my attention. "Ignore them. They're being idiots." He brushes his lips against mine. "I didn't look at them because I've no desire to see. You're the only naked woman starring in my dreams."

But for how long?

―――――

"Baby." His breath fans across my overheated cheeks, rousing me from sleep. Reeve dusts light kisses all over my face as I yawn, rubbing sleep from my eyes as I sit up in my dark bedroom, pressing my back against the headboard. Pain flares, and cramps twist my belly into knots. I whimper, brushing matted strands of my brown hair off my sweat-slickened brow, as I bend over.

"Here," he says, lifting my tank and pressing the warm heated pad to my lower stomach.

"Why are you here?" I ask over a groan. "Has the press conference been canceled?"

He switches on my bedside lamp, and I squint as my eyes adjust to the light. "No, it's still early, but I wanted to stop by and make sure you were okay first." He hands me a glass of water and drops a prescription pill into my palm.

"Fuck, I love you." I pop the pill, and swallow it with water. "Does every boyfriend keep track of his girlfriend's cycle, or are you a god among men?" I tease.

He puffs out his chest, grinning. "Pretty sure I'm a god among men, but I try to be modest."

I fling my arms around him, squeezing him tight. "Thank you. I love you so fucking much."

"Love you too, babe." He pulls back the covers, gesturing at me to lie down. "Now, go back to sleep. You have another hour before you have to get up. Get Max to drive you to school, and I'll be back in time to collect you." Max is my family's driver, and he usually ferries me around if Reeve isn't available. However, I've been trying to drive myself more places since getting my license last year.

Snuggling down under the comforter, I keep the heated pad against my cramping stomach. Reeve tucks me in before kissing me softly on the lips. "See you later."

"Good luck," I call out after him. "I'll be watching."

"Reeve asked me to give you this," Alex says, setting a paper carton down on the table in front of me. Despite popping another prescription pill just before lunch, I'm doubled over with stomach cramps. It's the same every month when I get my period. Some months, I have to actually stay in bed because the pain is so freaking bad I can't function. Mom took me to see her ob-gyn, and she said there is nothing wrong. Unfortunately, I'm just one of the female population who struggles with chronic period pain.

I pop the lid on the carton, unable to contain my smile, as I inhale the chicken noodle soup.

"Thank you." Alex must have gone to my favorite deli to pick up Reeve's order, and I'm grateful.

"You're welcome. Reeve says I'm to watch you eat every bit." His eyes lower to the tray of uneaten food in front of me.

Normally, I love the food in the cafeteria. Our private school employs highly skilled chefs to create a variety of balanced healthy meals, and the options are diverse and always delicious. But I struggle to stomach any food the first couple of days of my period. Reeve and I usually ditch the cafeteria those days to go to the deli by ourselves. I was tempted to go alone today, just to avoid the gossip, but I don't have my car. Audrey would have come with, but I figure it's best to just get it over and done with.

Anyone that wasn't aware Reeve has landed a career-making role is now in the know, thanks to the press conference that aired a half hour ago. It's all anyone is watching on their phones, and if I have to listen to one more comment about how beautiful Saffron Roberts is and how gorgeous Reeve and Saffron look together, I *will* punch someone.

Nate opens his mouth—to spout some stupid crap, no doubt—and I slap my hand over his lips, silencing him. I cannot deal with his crap today of all days. "Nope." I level him with a dark look. "I do not want to hear any shit from you today. Not unless you want to be bitch slapped and kneed in the balls."

Alex chuckles, and I shriek when Nate licks my palm.

"Eww." Whipping my hand back, I wipe it down the front of my jeans. "That was gross."

"Is it wrong that your little threats turn me the fuck on?" Nate asks, winking as he brings a bottle of water to his lips.

I roll my eyes, biting the inside of my cheek as pain slices across my lower belly. I wince, rubbing my stomach as I look wistfully at my soup. I'm not sure I can even stomach soup today.

"Want me to rub that for you?" Nate asks, leaning in closer and pinning me with a suggestive look.

"Not if you want to keep your head on your shoulders," Alex coolly replies. "Don't think you can hit on Viv just because Reeve will be leaving in a few months. I've already told him I've got his back."

Audrey rolls her eyes and shakes her head. We share a "boys are ridiculous" look. I don't know whether I should be insulted or pleased. "I don't need a babysitter," I mumble, dunking a spoon in the soup.

"And it's not like Reeve has anything to worry about," Audrey cryptically adds, as I sip my soup contemplating the same thing.

CHAPTER 5

THE MONTHS FLY BY, and I wish I could slow them down. We both submit our applications to UCLA, Christmas comes and goes, and before we know it, it's mid-January and Reeve's eighteenth birthday. I organize an epic party for him, and he surprises me with a weekend away on our own at Big Bear Lake. We take to the slopes, go sledding, and toast s'mores in front of the large open fire in the luxury cabin Reeve rented before making love for hours, getting lost in one another, pretending like we're not going to be separated in six short weeks.

"It sucks you'll miss graduation," I say the week before Reeve is due to leave for Boston. It's Friday evening, and we're walking hand in hand through the gardens at the rear of my house.

Mom is an avid gardener, and even though we have a full-time gardener on the staff, she designed and planted our rose garden herself. There are over forty different species of roses. Large blooms and small blooms in an array of different colors. Pink, purple, peach, white, red, yellow, orange, ivory, multicolored, and she even has lavender roses. They are the prettiest shade, and they have a fresh floral fragrance with a hint of spice that I adore. I didn't even know lavender roses were a thing until Mom planted them, and now they are my absolute favorite flower.

"You know I'd be there if I could, but the schedule is too tight." His smile is wistful as we pass the large oak tree with the swing. As kids, we loved hanging out at this tree. Our initials are even carved in the bark, alongside my parents' initials. Back then, we had this massive playground, treehouse, and obstacle course Mom had built specifically for us. I have many fond memories of summers spent outside, swimming and messing around in the pool, and countless hours spent playing on the swings, the monkey bars, slides, and the zipline.

Those were fun times.

I should have protested when Mom had it all removed. Insisted she keep it for our kids, but Mom is always remodeling the house and the gardens in between movies.

"Hey." He tugs on my hand when I don't respond. "You're not mad, are you?" His brow puckers, and I shake my head.

"Not at all. I understand, Reeve, and it's fine." He doesn't look convinced. "Honestly." I give him my biggest, most reassuring smile, and his shoulders relax. While he has done enough to graduate early, I was still hoping he could make it back for the ceremony, but he can't, and that's that. Ironically, shooting wraps four days after graduation, which is a little frustrating. "I'm so glad you got time off for prom. I couldn't attend without you." I swing our conjoined hands as we walk the cream stone path through the massive rose garden.

"There's no way I'd miss seeing you in that dress you're making." He flashes me a cheeky grin.

I slam to a halt, narrowing my eyes at him. "You'd better not have been peeking at it." I've gone to great trouble designing my own gown for prom. I am making Audrey's too, and we want to keep them a secret until then. I'm really looking forward to seeing the look on Reeve's face when he sees me in my own creation.

"Babe, I value breathing." He playfully swats my ass. "I even close my eyes and race past your studio door anytime I'm at your house."

"I've trained you well," I tease, tugging on his hand as we start walking again.

"I don't need to see it to know you're going to be the most beautiful girl there."

Be still my heart. Stretching up, I kiss the underside of his jaw. "Thank you, but you know you're probably biased."

"I'm only speaking the truth." He presses a kiss to my temple. "I hate that I can't be here for your eighteenth birthday, but I will make it up to you this summer. I promise."

I hate he's missing my birthday too. It will be the first time ever that one of us has missed the other's birthday. But I'm trying not to be selfish, so I've told him not to worry about it. I know Reeve would be there if he could. At least we'll be able to make up for lost time during summer break.

Reeve's shooting finishes at the end of May, and the movie isn't scheduled to release until January, meaning he will have a few months off before we start college and before the promotional tour commences. I'm not sure how he's going to juggle school with his promo duties, but we'll cross that bridge when we come to it. "I'm so happy we'll have the entire summer together," I say, drawing circles on the back of his hand with my finger.

"There may be some reshoots in August," he warns, tightening his hand in mine. "But other than that, the summer is all ours."

"I can't wait."

He stops at the lavender rose bush, removing a pair of pruning scissors from his back pocket. I beam at him as he examines the flowers, looking for the perfect rose. I study his gorgeous face, memorizing the light smattering of freckles along his strong nose, the angles of his high cheekbones, the beautiful curve of his tempting lips, and the endless depths of his stunning blue eyes. Reeve is beautiful, and he steals my breath every time I look at him. I trace my finger across the flat beauty mark over the right side of his lip. "Has Lipgate been resolved yet?" I inquire, arching a brow.

"Nope. Honestly, it's ridiculous. They can cover it with makeup for filming, and I don't see why it's such a big deal."

"I'm glad Bianca is fighting them on this." I trace my finger back and forth across the mark I love as he continues scanning the roses. "Studios have too much say in actor's lives as it is. So what if you have a beauty mark? It's absolutely perfect on you, and it never did Enrique Iglesias or Cristiano Ronaldo any harm. Both have had amazing careers, and I'm sure they had asshole PR people demanding they get theirs removed too."

He tweaks my nose, grinning. "You've really given this a lot of thought, huh?"

"I might have googled it after you told me they were making a big deal of it. I thought my research might help if they were still being stubborn about it."

Turning around, he threads his fingers through my hair. "I love how you always wade into battle on my behalf. It's sexy as hell."

"*You're* sexy as hell." I press my lips to the small, neat mark. "And you're perfect exactly the way you are. I don't want any asshole director or ambitious publicist trying to force you to change."

"I spoke with your mom, and she told me to stick to my guns. They can't insist on it because it wasn't part of the contract. She gave me some good advice."

"I'm glad you have her. Even with what I know of the industry, it seems especially crazy right now." The public interest in celebrities is extreme. They want to know every aspect of their personal lives, and privacy is a rare commodity. I'd be lying if I said I wasn't worried about what that means for Reeve and me. I'm a private person, and I deplore the thought of anyone delving into my life just because I'm Reeve's girlfriend, but my parents have warned me it's going to happen.

He removes his fingers from my hair, glancing at the roses as he speaks. "Bianca wants me to hire my own publicist. She says things are going to get insane pretty fast."

"I'd say the six million new followers you have on Insta and TikTok already attest to that fact. And that's before you've even filmed this movie."

"I know." Sighing, he stares up at the darkening sky. "The level of interest is scaring me a little, to be honest."

I place my palm on his chest and peer into his eyes. "In what way? Isn't this what you've always wanted?"

His Adam's apple bobs in his throat. "I've always wanted to *act*. To perfect my art and be the best performer I can be. All this interest in me, in my personal life and my appearance, concerns me. I don't want that to overshadow my work, you know?"

I nod, because I do. We've already had a few paparazzi following us around, and I know the level of interest is going to explode in the coming months. It's not that either of us is unfamiliar with this aspect of the business. Our parents are famous, and there are always asshole photographers following us around on family outings; however, it's rare for paps to take more than a passing interest in us when we are out alone.

Until now.

I hadn't properly considered what Reeve's blossoming career and notoriety would

35

do for me, and it's only adding to the anxiety I feel knowing he is this close to leaving for three months. "I guess it will just take some adjustment," I say, pushing my own worries aside to reassure him. "It's part and parcel of the life of an actor. You're young, hot, and talented as fuck. Of course, there will be media interest and attention from fans."

"At least I have you to keep me grounded." He reels me into his body.

"Don't worry, I'll tell you if you start behaving like a dick with a swollen head." I run my fingers along his chest and stomach, tracing the dips and curves of his abs through his thin shirt. Reeve has been working out like crazy these past few months, and he has massively transformed his body. His arms and shoulders are even broader now, and his six-pack almost looks painted on it's that perfect.

"I'm going to miss you so fucking much." Reaching out, he cuts the stem on a rose.

"Pfft." I stand on my tiptoes and brush my lips against his. "You'll be having too much fun living the dream to miss me. Meanwhile, I'll be stuck with boring classes, annoying teachers, and Nate McAndrews irritating the shit out of me every second of every day." The guy has not let up about Saffron, and I seriously want to rip out his vocal cords so he can no longer speak.

Reeve hands me the rose, and I lift it to my nose, closing my eyes and inhaling the familiar spicy aroma.

"I don't know how Alex puts up with that idiot," he says, as I blink my eyes open. "He is seriously getting on my last nerve." A muscle ticks in his jaw.

"I don't want to talk about Nate." I slide my free hand between our bodies, stroking my fingers along the length of his cock through his jeans, loving how quickly he hardens underneath my touch. "We have much better things to do with our time, right?"

Reeve grabs my hand, pulling me back along the path. "I like the way you think." He shoots me a sexy grin, and his eyes flare with need as we race toward the house and the privacy of my bedroom.

CHAPTER 6

"COME HERE, BABY," Reeve says, opening his arms, as I hastily swipe at the silent tears streaming down my face. "Please don't cry. It's killing me."

"I'm sorry," I choke out, crawling into his lap in the back seat of the car. "I swore I wasn't going to cry, but my tear ducts obviously didn't get the memo."

"It's only three months, not forever. I'll be home for prom before you know it."

I clasp his face in my hands. "I'm so damn proud of you, Reeve, and really excited for you." I might be devastated at the prospect of so long without him, but it isn't a lie.

He rests his forehead against mine. "I needed to hear that, because I'm scared shitless. What if I fuck this up?"

I ease back so I can see him. "Are you kidding me? There is no way you can fuck this up. We've been running lines religiously from the moment you got the part, and even I could recite Cam's lines in my sleep. You've got this, babe. You are going to kill it."

His lips crash against mine in a heated kiss that is laced with desperation and fear. I moan as his tongue plunders my mouth, rocking my pelvis against him, wishing there was time to make love to him again. We have been inseparable and insatiable these past few weeks, yet it still isn't enough. "I love you," he says, pulling me into a hug. "I love you so damn much. Don't forget that." He bands his arms around me, squeezing me tight, and I close my eyes, drinking in the feel of him against me.

"I won't," I promise, resting my head on his hair and clutching his shoulders tight.

"I mean it, Viv." He lifts me off his lap and onto the seat. "Things are going to get crazy, but nothing matters to me as much as you do. You are my entire world, and that will never change."

"Stop it." I swat at his chest as more tears spring from my eyes. "Stop being so damn romantic. So damn perfect, because it just makes our separation even harder."

The door opens, and Simon Lancaster pops his head in. "It's time," he tells his son, and I'm surprised to see his features soften when he looks at me.

"Just give us one more minute," I plead, reaching for the wrapped package on the floor.

Simon nods, closing the door.

"Open it on the plane." I hand the sparkly silver-foil package to Reeve. I bought him a Louis Vuitton messenger bag to hold his script and notes, his phone charger, water bottle, and whatever else he needs with him on set. And I framed a selfie of us from our weekend at Big Bear. In the photo, I'm sitting on Reeve's lap with my arms around his neck, and we're naked underneath the blanket wrapped around us. We are looking deep into one another's eyes, love radiating between us in the adoring way we are staring at each other. It was as if the outside world ceased to exist. There was just us in that moment, and the photo beautifully captured that sentiment.

I framed a copy of it for myself, and it takes pride of place on my bedside table. I want Reeve to be the last thing I see before I place my head on my pillow at night and the first thought on my mind when I wake each morning. I'm hoping the photo will do the same for him.

"I left a gift for you on your bed."

My lower lip wobbles as I struggle to keep my emotions in check. Reeve is always thoughtful, and he makes me feel so cherished. I think, no, I *know*, that is my dad's influence, because he sure as hell didn't pick up any romantic gestures from his own father. My dad dotes on my mom, and he spoils her rotten. I know Reeve's noted it all, and he treats me with the same devotion, love, and respect.

We share a soft lingering kiss before we reluctantly climb out of the car. My heart aches painfully in my chest as I watch the last of Reeve's luggage being stowed on the Studio 27 private jet. The studio producing the movie has arranged transport to collect Reeve from Logan International Airport and take him to the hotel he'll be calling home for the next six weeks. Thereafter, they are filming on location in different parts of Massachusetts, and he'll be living between his trailer and temporary hotels.

"Good luck, son," my dad says, pulling Reeve into a hug. "We're rooting for you."

"Enjoy the experience, honey," my mom says, wrestling Reeve away from my dad. She kisses both his cheeks, one at a time, while taking his hands in hers. "And I'm only a phone call away if you need me. I know from personal experience how daunting it can be, so call any time, day or night."

It's not Reeve's first time on a movie set. We hung around different sets all the time as kids. Plus, he has had some small walk-on parts in a few popular TV shows over the years, and he nabbed a decent part in a Netflix movie last year. But this is the first time he's the lead actor in a big-budget Hollywood production that has already garnered massive interest, and the pressure is real; the responsibility is intense.

"Just focus on the work," his dad says, awkwardly shaking Reeve's hand. "Don't let anything distract you."

Reeve nods, and my heart falters when he reaches out to hug his father. Simon's hands hang at his sides, and pain rips through my chest as I watch my boyfriend with his arms around his father, knowing he's silently pleading for him to hug him back. I almost cry out in relief when Simon lifts his arms and embraces him.

How can it be so difficult for him to love his son?

Reeve is an amazing guy, and he has never given him any trouble. He's put up with his father's long absences and pitiful womanizing. Plenty of other guys our age would resort to alcohol or drugs or sex to cope with the internal pain, but Reeve has channeled all his emotions into his acting, taking something negative and turning it into something positive. I'd like to think I've helped too, but I can't take much credit. Reeve is strong and so determined.

I know part of his desire to succeed is the hope his father will one day look at him with pride.

Every time he tells me this, I struggle not to break down and cry.

Simon Lancaster has every reason to be proud of his son now, and I don't know why he denies him that truth.

Mom bundles me in her arms as we watch father and son hug, and I cling to her like a limpet. This is emotional, on many different levels, and I'm barely holding it together. Their embrace is not a long embrace, but it's an embrace all the same, and I'm glad Simon could do this one thing for him.

"You've done well, Reeve," Simon says, when they break apart. "Your mother would be so proud of you."

I shuck out of Mom's arms, wrapping mine around my boyfriend, feeling his body shudder as those words sink bone-deep.

"We're *all* proud of you." Mom squeezes his shoulder.

"You need to board the plane, or it will have to leave without you." Simon shoots me an apologetic look.

"I love you," Reeve rasps, holding me so tight I can scarcely breathe.

"I love you too," I cry, uncaring that our parents are witness to this.

Grabbing my face, he plants a hard kiss on my lips. "Stay strong, babe."

I nod, sniffling.

He kisses me again before pulling away, striding toward the steps leading up to the private plane with my gift tucked under his arm.

"Be epic, babe," I call out after him. "And know I'm cheering for you every step of the way."

He turns around and blows me a kiss. I jump up, cradling it in my hand, and he smiles.

A heavy pressure sits on my chest as I watch his dark head disappear into the plane, and it feels like my heart is shattering into a thousand pieces. The steps retreat, and the door closes, taking my love away from me. An errant sob escapes my lips, and I'm struggling to breathe normally over the massive lump clogging my throat.

In a surprising move, Simon circles his arm around my shoulders, giving me a comforting squeeze. He probably thinks I'm a complete basket case, and I'm sure my parents think I'm overreacting.

But as I watch the plane take off, flying my boyfriend to the other side of the US, I can't help worrying that everything is changing, and not for the better. I *am* proud of Reeve, and excited for his career, but there's this kernel of doubt, taking up space inside my head and my heart, trying to prepare me for a future we haven't planned.

I can't explain it.

Maybe it's a sixth sense or it's paranoia, but it's enough to have me trembling with fear and twisted into knots. I sincerely hope we are strong enough to weather whatever storm is on the horizon, because I already know that things will not be the same by the time he returns.

And it's those thoughts that keep me up all night in the immediate aftermath of his leaving.

CHAPTER 7

TUCKING my hands under my head, I turn on my side, staring at the photo of Reeve and me with a tight pain in my chest. The pain is always there. It never goes away. It's like this dull, constant ache in my chest, serving to remind me that half of my heart is over two and a half thousand miles away in Boston.

These past five weeks have been the longest five weeks of my life. I knew this would be hard, but it's even harder than I imagined. I only get to speak to Reeve for a few minutes each day because he's usually exhausted by the time he gets back to his hotel room at night. Early morning calls are a no-no thanks to the three-hour time difference. Between the grueling twelve-hour days on set and his daily two-hour workouts with the personal trainer the studio hired for Reeve and a couple of the other male actors, he is crazy busy, and he doesn't have much downtime.

I don't complain. I wait patiently in my room with my cell in my hand every night at eight to hear his voice. Some nights, he's high on the scenes they filmed that day, and I just sit and listen to his exuberant voice. Other nights, he's too tired to even speak, so I regale him with news of my day.

He tells me he loves me and misses me, and he sends flowers every Monday morning, wishing me a great week. I sent him a care package last week filled with his favorite snacks, a Stella Adler acting book, a sketch I drew of the *Rydeville Elite* book covers, a funny "Yoda Best Actor" mug, a towel with "Future Oscar Winner" written on it, and a batch of homemade chocolate chip cookies. Mom taught Reeve and me how to bake cookies when we were eight, using a recipe handed down in her family through the generations, but it's been years since either of us has baked cookies.

I'm feeling nostalgic and a little fragile, and maybe it is my subconscious wanting to remind Reeve of our history.

The cast has been hanging out on set and in their hotel rooms, and they post pics regularly on social media. I know it's a way of building buzz for the movie, but my stomach lurches every time a new photo is shared when I see Saffron sitting and laughing beside Reeve. She's *always* right by his side, and even though there are no obvious signs of anything between them, it still twists my stomach into knots.

Jealousy is not a new emotion for me. For years, girls at school have chased Reeve, but it never bothered me too much, because I knew he had no interest in them and I was secure in his love. It should be the same now, because he has done nothing to elicit these lingering fears in my mind. But I can't help how I feel. Saffron is beautiful and talented, and she's experiencing the start of what I know will be a wild ride with Reeve. I can't help feeling my boring stories of mundane life in L.A. are highlighting all the ways in which Reeve and I are on different paths.

My fingers curl around the diamond-encrusted silver locket hanging around my neck, and I hold it tight, needing to remind myself he loves me. I have to stop being jealous and trust in my man and our love. I pop the locket open, and tears prick my eyes as I stare at the picture of Reeve and me. It's another photo taken that weekend at Big Bear. Only this time, we're in bed, hugging and laughing, with our arms wrapped around one another. This was Reeve's going away gift, and I laughed when I realized how in sync we were with our parting gifts. I haven't taken the locket off for even a second, and it helps to have some physical proof of his love.

A knock sounds on my door, and I lift my chin as Mom pokes her head into my room. "Good morning, birthday girl," she coos, smiling as she steps into the room. Dad follows her, holding a ginormous bouquet of flowers.

"Happy birthday, princess." Dad hands the bouquet to me as I sit up in the bed.

"Thanks, Dad. These are beautiful." I bury my face in the gorgeous flowers, smiling when I spot a few lavender roses.

"I would like to take the credit, but I think Reeve might have something to say about that." He chuckles as I rip the card from the small envelope, reading the message from my boyfriend.

Happy 18th birthday, baby. I wish I could be there to smother you with birthday kisses, but I am there in spirit—can you feel my lips worshiping your mouth? Love you always. Miss you, Reeve.

I swipe at the tears that automatically pool in my eyes.

"No tears." Mom hands me a tissue. "If anyone gets to cry today, it's me." She sniffles, and her eyes well up.

"Don't cry, Mom." I reach out and envelop her in a hug. "I'll never stop the waterworks if you start."

She eases back, clasping my face in her hands. "I can't believe you are eighteen. It seems like it has happened in the blink of an eye."

Dad sits on the other side of Mom, leaning in to kiss me on the cheek. "You have given us so much joy, Vivien. You were the miracle we prayed for, and no parent could ask for a better daughter. You are the sweetest, kindest, most beautiful girl with a big compassionate heart, and we are so very proud of you."

"You forgot intelligent and talented," Mom says, laughing softly as she brushes tears from her cheeks.

Emotion weaves around my heart, and it feels fit to burst. I know how much

Mom and Dad wanted kids and how difficult it was for them to conceive. Then Mom had a succession of miscarriages before getting pregnant with me. They tried for more kids after I was born, but she never got pregnant again. I think, if it wasn't for Reeve, and the fact he's like a surrogate son, they would have adopted. Warmth spreads across my chest as I wrap an arm around each of my parents. "If I'm all that, it's because I had the best role models. Thank you for being the best parents a girl could have."

"Lord." Mom waves her hands in front of her beautiful face. "It's entirely too early for all this emotion." She laughs again while tucking strands of her lustrous black hair behind her ears. "We thought we would take you to breakfast."

"That sounds wonderful."

"Maybe you can drive us in your new car." Dad hands me a rectangular black box. His hazel eyes—so similar to my own—sparkle with happiness and excitement.

My heart is pounding as I open the box, squealing when I see the Mercedes-Benz keyring. "No way!" I lift excited eyes to my parents. "You didn't get me a Mercedes AMG GT!"

Mom winks, and her green eyes are tearing up again. "We did."

I clamp a hand over my mouth. "Oh my God. This is too much." We have a garage full of cars and SUVs outside, but my parents know I've been salivating for an AMG since I got my first permit. I never thought in a million years they would get me one, because they are careful not to spoil me too much. They have instilled in me the value of money, and I know how fortunate I am to have grown up not wanting for anything. "So much for not spoiling me," I murmur, unable to contain my grin.

"It's a special occasion, and we figure if you enjoy driving it we'll see more of you once you leave for UCLA." UCLA isn't far from my parents' house, and even with the shitty L.A. traffic, the daily commute would be manageable. However, Reeve and I want the full student experience, including living away from home. We plan on finding accommodations close to the campus, and we'll start actively looking as soon as Reeve is back home.

"You guys are the best." I squeeze my parents before jumping up to get dressed.

My sadness at Reeve's absence is relegated to the sidelines as I drive my parents to breakfast in my brand-new car.

My heart is swollen with emotion, and my hand shakes as I hold my cell, watching Reeve's very public, very romantic, birthday message for the umpteenth time. He posted it four hours ago, and it's already had over two million views. I have lost count of the number of times I've watched it, and my eyes turn watery every single time.

As well as flowers, he sent me a massive box filled with gifts, including a diamond-encrusted heart bracelet to match my locket, a stunning black and gold Chanel purse, a bunch of Victoria's Secret lingerie that made me blush, and a stunning Charlotte Tilbury makeup set. I nearly keeled over when I opened the box, and I'm blown away by how much thought and effort he went to for my birthday.

I would trade every gift just to have him in my arms for the night, but he has still managed to make me feel like the most treasured woman on the planet, and it goes a long way toward dispelling the jealous doubts I've been harboring.

"Man, Reeve's so pussy-whipped I'm embarrassed for him," Nate supplies from somewhere behind me.

"Shut the fuck up." Audrey flips him the bird. "I'm trying to listen."

"Babe, you're starting to give me a complex." Alex props his butt on the edge of the couch in our living room. Outside, the band is getting set up in the massive marquee Mom had erected on the grounds of our house. I had considered renting a club in downtown L.A. for my party, but I don't want any paparazzi sniffing around. Plus, if we had the party in a club, we'd be forced to drink soda all night. We have stashed a supply of beer and vodka in the garden, and the rents have promised to leave us to our own devices once the music starts, so that's when the party will really start.

"If it means you raise your game, I'm not sorry I'm obsessed with Reeve's message." Audrey winks at her boyfriend, moving the recording back to the start so we can watch it again.

Reeve is shirtless, sitting cross-legged in gray sweatpants on his hotel bed, looking so fucking gorgeous, I wish I could transport there through my cell and jump his bones. His hair is damp, and a few beads of water cling to his ripped upper torso confirming he's not long out of the shower.

Is it weird to be envious of those little water droplets? Because I am.

I can almost hear the collective drooling of females as he flashes a wide grin at the camera, showcasing his perfect set of teeth as he talks.

"Hey, guys. Today is a very special day, because on this day eighteen years ago, the most important person in my life was born." He holds up a baby picture of me, and if it wasn't so cute, I'd yell at my mom for sending him that. Audrey grips my hand as we watch and listen together. "I wouldn't be the man I am today if it wasn't for this gorgeous, smart, funny, compassionate, loving woman," he adds, replacing the baby picture with a picture of us from his birthday in January. Our arms are around one another, and we're smiling at the camera. "Have you ever loved someone so much it physically pains you to be apart from them?" he asks, rubbing a hand across his impressive chest. "As much as I am loving bringing Camden Marshall to life, I am missing my baby so much."

He leans in closer to the screen, and hearts are breaking all over the US. "I love you, Viv. You are the best thing to ever happen to me, and I don't even care that the guys are going to give me shit for this." He blows me a kiss, and I melt onto the couch. "You are my world, and I wish I could be there to hug you and kiss you. Only twenty-seven days until I see you again. I can't wait. Till then, have the happiest of birthdays, my love." He blows me another kiss before ending the recording, and I flop back on the couch with the biggest smug grin on my face.

CHAPTER 8

"YOU SO NEED to up your game, Alex." Audrey attempts to scowl at her boyfriend, but she's wearing a dazed dreamy expression that I suspect isn't much different from mine. She leans in, pressing her mouth to my ear. "I really don't think you have anything to worry about. He just professed his love for you in front of the world, and there's no denying the sincerity of his message. Honestly, I think I'm half in love with Reeve now myself."

I laugh, nudging her in the ribs as I start scrolling through the comments. "That had better be a joke. Hands off my man." I'm smiling as I read through the fan messages, but it doesn't take too long for my smile to fade. A lot of the messages are swooning, mentioning how romantic Reeve is, and how lucky I am, but there are nasty comments too from girls who think I'm not pretty enough for Reeve, and there are a few comments stating Reeve should be with Saffron and not with me.

My good mood evaporates, and a familiar pain spreads across my chest.

"Don't read them." Audrey snatches my cell, slipping it in my purse. "They're just jealous hos."

We head out to the marquee after that, and I force myself to relax and enjoy the party. Everyone I invited from school is here, and now my parents have left us alone, the alcohol is flowing, and we're working up a sweat on the dance floor. The band is amazing, and I'm having a great time until stupid Nate McAndrews opens his big mouth. "Hey, sexy," he says, throwing his arm around my shoulders. "How come Reeve deleted the video?" he asks, his beer breath fanning across my face.

"What?" I shout in his ear, sure I must have misheard him.

"It's gone from all his profiles." He arches a brow. "You didn't know?"

I have tried calling Reeve several times, but he's obviously working late. I sent him a pic of me in the sexy black lace bra and thong set he sent me, as well as a picture of me in my party dress. I designed and made the black minidress with a gold and emerald trim that brings out the green flecks in my hazel eyes. The dress is short, emphasizing my long legs. I left my hair down and styled it in soft curls, just the way Reeve likes it. Mom hired her makeup artist to do our makeup, and I asked her to use the makeup Reeve bought me. It might seem silly, but it makes me feel closer to him.

I hate that I haven't actually spoken to him yet, and my birthday will officially be over in three hours, but I know he'll call or message me whenever he can.

"It's true," Audrey says, showing me her phone. Reeve's Insta profile is displayed on her screen, and the video post is nowhere to be seen. "Maybe he spotted the nasty comments and took it down."

That must be it, I think as my cell vibrates in the pocket of my dress. My lips pull into a smile, and a relieved breath escapes my mouth when I see it's my boyfriend. "Hang on a sec," I shout into the phone, rushing across the marquee. "It's loud as fuck and I can't even hear myself think."

Reeve chuckles, and the sound does funny things to my insides.

"That's better," I say, as soon as I'm outside. The cooler air is like a balm to my hot skin, so I don't mind the slight breeze wafting around me. "Hey, baby," I purr. "I miss you."

"I miss you too, and I wish I was there."

"Thank you so much for my flowers and the gifts, and that video message was beautiful. I tear up every time I look at it."

"I sent it to you privately since I was forced to take it down from social media," he admits, adding, "I hope you don't mind."

"What do you mean you were *forced* to take it down? By who? Did Bianca make you do it?" I knew there was a reason I took an instant dislike to his agent.

His sigh trickles down the line. "It wasn't Bianca. It was Cassidy. She's been hired to handle PR for the movie, and she threw a massive hissy fit."

"Why?"

There's a pregnant pause. "I guess it doesn't look good I have a girlfriend."

Unease slithers through my veins. I'm not stupid. I've been expecting this, but it still hurts. "Oh," I quietly say.

"It's probably for the best. Some of the comments were nasty. The last thing I want is you becoming a target for crazy bitches."

Loud music mixed with noisy chatter fills the line, and I frown. "What was that?"

"Someone just opened the door."

"Opened the door where? Aren't you at your hotel?"

"We're at a club. We worked late tonight, and a few of us decided to go out for drinks." Reeve is the youngest of the main acting crew with most of his costars being in their early twenties and legally able to attend clubs and drink alcohol. I am guessing the PR person pulled some strings to get Reeve in, and I'm sure his costars are sliding a few beers his way.

"Dude," a male says in the background. "We're going to head back to the hotel bar."

"Okay," Reeve says.

"Wait. Is that your girlfriend?" another guy says, and there's a few seconds of muffled talk.

"Happy birthday, Vivien," the stranger says down the line.

"Thanks. And you are?"

A deep chuckle tickles my eardrums. "I'm Rudy. Hasn't Reeve told you anything about me? I'm offended, man," he says, clearly talking to Reeve. "And here I thought we had the bromance of the century."

"Don't sweat it, Rudy," I say. "He's told me all about you, including how you enjoy pranking everyone on set." Rudy had a main role in a popular Netflix show last year, and he's garnered quite a following. With his blond hair, blue eyes, flirtatious manner, and jokey personality, he is the perfect choice to play Jackson Lauder. And just like Camden and Jackson are friends in the *Rydeville Elite* books, Reeve and Rudy have become close too.

"Did he tell you about the lube in his sneakers?" Rudy asks, clearly smothering laughter.

I giggle. "He did, and he also told me how you swapped the sugar for salt and put toothpaste in his shampoo."

"I still owe you for that," Reeve says, sounding distant. "Give me that."

"My turn," a high-pitched clearly feminine voice says, and I gulp over the sudden lump in my throat.

"Hey, Vivien. It's Saffron. Happy birthday! Did you like the lingerie I helped Reeve pick?"

What?!?! All the blood drains from my face, and I'm grappling for a response that doesn't involve me screaming at her to stay away from my man.

"Viv?" she asks, and my natural instinct is to snap that she has no right to call me that.

"You went shopping with Reeve?" I finally manage to say, trying to ignore the anxious fluttering in my chest. My heart is racing so fast I can feel it thudding against my rib cage in panic.

"We did it online one night after work. That photo he has by his bed is so sweet. You make a cute couple."

Words are spoken in the background, but she must have her hand over the phone because I can't hear. Or maybe the sirens blaring warning signals in my head are drowning everything out.

"I've got to go, but I'm so looking forward to meeting you. Buh-bye," she says, as I fight a full-body shiver and narrowly resist the urge to throw up the vodka shots I've consumed.

"Hey, it's me," Reeve says, sounding a little sheepish.

And so he should. "Why was she in your hotel room, and were you in hers?" I hiss.

"Babe, calm down." His cool tone only pisses me off more.

"You let her choose lingerie for me?" My voice elevates a few notches as anger comingles with fear and hurt and a ton of other emotions.

"It's not as bad as it sounds."

"I'm glad you realize how bad it sounds," I snap, pacing back and forth across the lawn.

"Don't overreact, Viv."

And that's like waving a red flag in front of a bull. "Don't tell me not to overreact! You know how I feel about her, and yet you spend time with her in a hotel room and let her pick an intimate gift for my birthday. How the fuck do you expect me to react?" I shout.

"I can't talk to you when you're like this." He lowers his voice. "How much have you had to drink?"

"How much have you?" I retort.

"Our car is here. I have to go. We'll talk again tomorrow when you've calmed down."

The fucking nerve of him to try to turn this back around on me. I have every right to my feelings, and he should be bending over backward to apologize. "Reeve. Don't you dare hang up on me."

"I love you, Viv. We'll talk soon. Go back to your party."

There's a click and then silence. I stare at my cell in utter shock and disbelief. Rage simmers in my veins as my brain struggles to comprehend how my boyfriend just hung up on me mid-argument.

CHAPTER 9

"HEY." Audrey tugs on my arm, her brow creasing with worry. "What's wrong?"

"Nothing," I lie, flashing her a fake smile. I can't tell her now as I'm liable to burst into tears, and I refuse to cry at my party or give the salacious crowd any ammunition for gossip. "I need more vodka. I'm way too sober right now." Nothing sobers a person like emotional anguish. I need to numb the pain and silent my screaming mind.

Two hours later, I've accomplished my mission, and I can barely stand up straight as we dance to the intoxicating beats the DJ is playing. "You need water," Audrey says, when I stumble into her. The room spins as she grabs me and leads us off the dance floor.

"He's probably fucking her right now," I slur, swiping at the tears leaking from my eyes.

"You need to tell me what's going on," she says, guiding me toward our table.

"That fucking bitch picked my lingerie." Anger rips through me as my brain latches on to another thought. "I bet she chose my purse and makeup too."

"Hold up here a sec." Audrey stops walking, turning around so she's facing me. "Are you telling me Reeve got *Saffron Roberts* to buy your birthday gifts?"

I nod, and tears prick my eyes again. God, I'm such a basket case, and I need to get myself together.

"Oh, babe." Her expression floods with sympathy. "I get why you're pissed. I would be too. But I'm sure it doesn't mean anything other than he's a thoughtless moron."

"I don't want to talk about him," I whisper. "It hurts too much." I stumble as nausea swirls in my gut, bending over while I clutch my stomach. "I don't feel so hot."

"Let's get some water into you." She helps me into a chair, scowling at the almost empty table. Her eyes scan the heaving dance floor, looking for Alex, no doubt.

"You." She jabs her finger in Nate's direction. He's slumped over the table across from me, and I'm betting he feels about as good as I feel.

"Go away, Rey," he mumbles, giving her his middle finger.

"Watch our birthday girl while I'm at the bar. I'll grab you a bottle of water too," she adds before pressing a kiss to the top of my head. "Stay put. I'll get some water and some food. I'll be right back."

I nod before closing my eyes. Everything swims, and nausea twists in my gut, so I whip my eyes open, blinking excessively to clear the spiraling dizziness from my head, and try to focus my blurry vision.

Warmth ghosts over my skin as a body presses against my thigh and an arm encircles my shoulders. "It's okay, babe," Nate slurs. "I'll look after you."

I'd snort if I wasn't so drunk. "I don't need anyone to look after me. I can look after myself," I lie, struggling to keep my eyes open. The room is out of focus—the mass of bodies dancing and making out on the dance floor is a mess of wriggly shapeless forms.

"You look sad," Nate slurs. "Why d'you look sad? No one should be sad on their birthday."

I'm barely aware as my face is tilted around. Nate's features are fuzzy as he stares at me. Wet lips glide against mine, and for a few seconds, I'm confused until I realize Nate fucking McAndrews is kissing me. I swat at his chest, feebly pushing him away. "Get off me!"

"What the actual fuck?" Audrey shouts, depositing stuff on the table before yanking Nate away from me. He falls to the sticky wooden floor, cussing like a sailor. "You need to crawl the fuck away like the slithery snake you are before I stomp all over your manhood with my Jimmy Choos," Audrey threatens, looming over him.

Pain darts through my skull, and I wince, cradling my head in my hands. Nausea swims up my throat, and I gag. "Audrey," I moan. "I'm gonna be sick."

Ignoring the asshole on the floor, she helps me to stand, circling her arm around my back and practically dragging me out of the marquee. Alex appears, cursing when he sees the state of me. "Fuck. Reeve will have my head for this. I promised I'd look out for her."

"Reeve can kiss my ass," I murmur before bending over and emptying the contents of my stomach into the nearest bush. Audrey holds my hair back as I violently vomit until there's nothing left to expel. I slump against her while pawing at my sweat-slickened overheated skin, needing to strip out of my clothes and crawl into bed until I fall into a coma. "Bed," I mumble. "I need my bed."

"I've got you," Alex says, scooping me up into his arms. My eyes shutter, and the world turns dark.

A dull pounding in my skull rouses me from slumber the following morning, and I whimper as I turn over in the bed and my stomach twists painfully. My lips are dry, my tongue is glued to the roof of my parched mouth, and the lingering scent of puke invades my nostrils, making me gag.

"Oh God. Are you going to be sick again?" Audrey asks as the bed dips.

I force my eyes open, wincing at the bright light filtering through the open curtains. "I don't think so," I croak, but I really need to pee and erase this vomit taste from my mouth. Pulling myself upright in the bed takes colossal effort, and my body feels like it's done ten rounds with Amanda Nunes in the ring. Glancing down at myself, I notice I'm in my underwear. Sight of the sexy bra and thong brings everything to the surface, and a sob rips from my mouth.

"Hey." Audrey rubs my arm. "It's going to be okay."

I turn to face her with glassy eyes. "What happened? How did I get here, and why are you in my bed and not Alex's?"

She yawns, before sitting up against the headboard. "What's the last thing you remember?"

"Getting shitfaced and dancing. After that it's a blur."

"You were completely trashed, so Alex and I got you out of there. You puked your guts up in the garden, and I decided to stay with you. I was worried you might puke in your sleep. Alex stayed in one of the guest bedrooms." She averts her eyes, plucking at the comforter.

"What aren't you saying?" I ask, because I can tell she's concealing something.

"Go freshen up, and we'll talk when you come back."

I have no energy to argue, so I grab some clean pajamas from my drawer before entering my en suite bathroom. I pee, brush my teeth, and rinse with mouthwash before hopping in the shower. I take my time washing away the excesses of the night while I contemplate everything that happened. Resting my forehead against the tile, I let the warm water cascade down my back as pain infiltrates every nook and cranny of my body.

I can't believe Reeve let Saffron choose my birthday gifts. I'm convinced she had a hand in more than just the lingerie. Reeve has never bought me makeup before, and I'm sure that was her handiwork too. I feel ill thinking about the picture I sent him of me in the underwear. Ugh. I wish I could take it back. As soon as the marching band stops playing the samba in my head, I'm taking the lingerie and makeup out back and burning all of it. How could he let her choose such intimate items for me?

Tears stream down my face, mixing with the water, and my heart hurts so much I'm in immense physical pain. My tears turn into full-blown sobs, and then Audrey is there, turning off the shower and wrapping me in a towel. I slump to the floor of my bathroom, pulling my knees up to my chest as I cry. "How could he do this?"

"You need to talk to him."

I have no idea where my cell is or if he even tried calling me back. "It's not just the gifts," I sob. "It's also how he went out partying with his friends and almost missed talking to me on my birthday. I thought he hadn't called because he was working really late, but he was out drinking and laughing with his new friends, and I was just an afterthought."

"You don't know that." Audrey gently towel-dries my hair. "Reeve loves you, Viv. Look at everything he did yesterday to prove it to you."

"It doesn't matter now," I deadpan as my tears dry up. "He ruined everything. None of it means anything now." I rub at my nose as I turn to face her. "He told me I was overreacting, and he hung up on me." Tears pool in my eyes again. "He has never done that to me. Ever." Shock splays across her face, and it's good to know I'm not the only one who thinks this is out of character for my boyfriend. "He's changing," I whisper. "He's already changing, and I don't like it."

A knock at the door interrupts us. "Viv," Alex calls out. "Is Audrey in there with you?"

"I'm here," Audrey replies.

"You need to get out here. There's something you need to see, and Reeve has been trying to get a hold of you, Viv. You need to call him."

Audrey slips out of the room to talk to her boyfriend while I finish drying myself. I get dressed and drag a comb quickly through my hair before tying it into a messy bun on top of my head. It will be a mass of tangles, but I don't care. It's not like I have plans to do anything today except wallow in my bed, watching sad movies and eating my body weight in ice cream.

When I open the door, Alex and Audrey are arguing in hushed tones.

"What's going on?" A new layer of anxiety settles on my chest.

Audrey's tongue darts out, wetting her lips, in a clear nervous tell. "You need to be sitting for this, babe."

I crawl into my bed, tucking my knees to my chest and pulling the covers up over me. "What is it?"

Audrey moves up beside me while Alex sits on the edge of the bed, wearing an odd expression.

She squeezes my hand. "You don't remember, but that idiot Nate put the moves on you last night."

I blink profusely, tugging at my ears, sure I must be hearing things. "What?" I fix her with an incredulous expression.

"He kissed you as I was coming back to the table. I saw it go down. You were out of it, and he was wasted, so I have no idea if it was intentional or not, but he kissed you and…you didn't push him away immediately."

Horror washes over me. "I would *never* kiss Nate or any other guy," I shriek. "Never." My eyes fly to Alex's, understanding now why he was giving me a funny look. "I love Reeve, and I have no desire to kiss anyone else! I know Reeve and I were fighting, but I would never do something like that to hurt him. Never. You've got to believe me," I plead.

"I believe you," Alex says, his shoulders relaxing a smidgeon.

"I was drunk off my ass, and it must have taken a few seconds to register with me," I continue, grappling to understand how I let this happen. My hands clench into balls. "I am going to kill Nate!"

"You really are," Alex adds, holding his cell out to me. "Because someone recorded it and it's all over social media."

CHAPTER 10

"NO. NO, NO, NO, NO." I clasp a hand over my mouth as I stare at the recording in horror. When I find out who did this, they are going to wish they had never been born. It looks so bad, because it's been edited to just show the kiss, so you can't tell that I'm trashed and completely ignorant of what's going on. It's also recorded in slow motion so it looks like the kiss lasts way longer than it did. Audrey saw it go down, and she says it lasted about five seconds, max, yet this makes it look like we shared a long, lingering kiss.

What's worse is they tagged Reeve on the post, and the barrage of angry comments and vile insults pours more salt on the ugly wound. I look up at Alex. "Please tell me he hasn't seen this?"

His lips pull into a grimace, and his eyes shine with sympathy.

Oh my God. What must Reeve be thinking? My stomach heaves, and I race into the bathroom, reaching the toilet in the nick of time. I dry retch, my empty stomach contorting painfully as I try to expunge my fear.

"Come on, babe." Audrey helps me up after I slump over the toilet bowl. "Rinse your mouth out, and come back to the bedroom. You're going to call Reeve and fix everything."

Like a zombie, I brush my teeth, staring at my washed-out complexion in the mirror. I look like death warmed over. My hair is a knotty, damp mess on top of my head. I have dark circles under my eyes, my lips are cracked, and my hazel eyes have lost all their sparkle. I look as hollow as I feel.

I trudge out to my bedroom, silently accepting the bottle of water from Audrey. "Do you want us to stay here while you call Reeve?" she asks, and I notice she found my cell and has plugged it in. It vibrates with a succession of notifications.

"He probably won't be able to take the call," I say, noticing it's after noon which means it's three in Boston. "He'll be in the middle of filming."

She gets up to leave. "Stay." I grab her arm.

"I'm going to see about breakfast." Alex rocks back on his heels.

Audrey nods, and he exits my bedroom as I pull my big-girl pants on and scroll through my notifications. I have thousands of tags on social media, and I'm not even going to look at them. "Wow. You have a million new followers," Audrey says, looking over my shoulder.

"It's not anything good, I assure you." I open my inbox, looking at all the missed calls from Reeve. They start from three a.m. my time, which means he must have seen the recording first thing when he woke up. I'm too chicken to listen to all the messages, but I need to know what I'm dealing with, so I open his last one, left at eight a.m. my time, putting it on speaker. I have no secrets from Audrey, and, frankly, I need her support to listen to this. She puts her arms around me, and I rest my head on her shoulder.

"For fuck's sake, Vivien, answer your damn phone!" Reeve's frustration bleeds into his tone. "I can't believe you did this. You didn't even give me a chance to explain before you sought comfort from Nate of all fucking people! Do you know how stupid you made me look?! I look like a fucking idiot pining for you, posting how much I love you, and a few hours later, everyone sees you kissing that asshole. You have made me look like a damn fool!" he yells, and I flinch. "I'm so fucking disappointed in you." There's a pregnant pause, and his rapid breathing is the only sound. It's unlike Reeve to curse so much, and it's an indication of how angry and upset he is. I hate that I've done this to him, but he's not entirely blameless either. "Do I even know you at all?" His voice cracks a little, and while it's a relief, I'm also consumed with guilt that I've made a bad situation worse. I shouldn't have gotten drunk and lost control like that. I should have waited until today and called Reeve to talk about what he did. Now, it's a million times worse, and not only have I made him look foolish, I've just garnered a whole army of angry Reeve fans. "I've got to get back, and I don't have another break. Call me tonight." Air whooshes out of his mouth. "Or don't. I…I…I can't deal with this right now."

The message ends abruptly, and I toss my cell aside, folding my arms around Audrey, needing her comfort.

"He's angry."

"No shit, Captain Obvious," I deadpan. "I'm angry too. At him. At Nate. At me."

"Nope." She grabs my arms, and I straighten up. "You have done nothing wrong. *Nothing.* You hear me?"

"I shouldn't have gotten trashed."

She cocks her head to one side. "It didn't help, but he hurt you. I get wanting to drown your sorrows, and if you hadn't been drunk, Nate's lips wouldn't have come even close to yours. But it's not your fault that he took advantage of you. And it's not your fault some asshole recorded it and tried to stir shit. Just like it's not your fault Reeve got that bitch to choose your birthday gifts or hung up on you."

"This is such a mess." I wrap my arms around my middle. "What am I going to do?"

"We're going to get dressed, have breakfast, send Alex over to beat the shit out of Nate, and then we're going to make calls and find out what little idiot posted that recording and get them to take it down."

"I have a better idea," I say, standing. "I'm going to talk to Mom. Her publicist has a guy they use to remove stuff from the internet. I bet he can help, and it'll be quicker than us playing Holmes and Watson."

"Okay. You go talk to your mom and I'll find Alex and get breakfast on the table."

"I'm sorry this has happened to you, honey, and of course I'll help, but you'll need to toughen up." Mom wipes at the moisture on my cheeks. "I don't mean that to sound cold. I know you feel things deeply. Reeve does too. But you must develop a thicker skin, because it's only going to get worse. There will be haters and people who would love nothing more than to take you down and break you two up. You can't give them that power."

"How do you do it?" I ask.

"I don't look at the nasty comments or read any of the rumors on those horrid gossip sites. When I'm confronted with it face to face, I kill the person with kindness. It usually throws them off sufficiently to silence them. But most importantly, I trust your father and let our love build a protective wall around me that no one can tear down. I know we've been doing this a lot longer, and we're rock solid now, but we have been where you are now, and it's not easy." She clasps my hands in hers. "Open communication is key. You need to get a hold of Reeve as soon as you can and talk to him about it. Get it all off your chests, and you'll both feel better."

"Thanks, Mom." I let her envelop me in her arms.

"I hate seeing you so upset, and do we need to have a talk about alcohol consumption?"

I shake my head. "Trust me, I learned that lesson the hard way."

"Go and eat breakfast with your friends while I make a few phone calls. I'll have that recording removed within a few hours and details of the culprit."

"I love you, Mom." I squeeze her tighter.

"I love you too."

A few hours later, Mom finds us in the sunroom, listening to music and chatting. I left a tearful message for Reeve promising to call him later once he's finished filming, and Alex went over to Nate's house and roughed him up a little. He's been blowing up my phone too, but I blocked him. According to Alex, the kiss was his pathetic attempt at cheering me up because I looked sad.

"It's gone," Mom says, depositing a tray with iced tea and cookies on the coffee table. "And the person who posted it has been sent legal correspondence. He'll be shitting his pants for months," she adds with a knowing smile.

Alex barks out a laugh. "Remind me to never get on your bad side, Mrs. Mills."

"Don't hurt my daughter, or Audrey, and you don't have anything to worry about, Alexander."

"Who was it?" I ask, and she falters.

"I think it's best you don't know. It's been dealt with."

I rise, facing her. "Mom. Have you forgotten what high school is like? This is all anyone is going to be talking about next week in school. I need to know who's behind it; otherwise, I look like an even bigger fool."

"If I tell you, you have to promise you won't do anything." Her eyes roam over my head to Alex and Audrey. "That goes for you two as well."

I don't like lying to my mom, but I need to know who did this, and I can't make promises I'm unsure I can keep. Right now, I want to throttle whoever did this with my bare hands. "We won't do anything," I lie, looking her dead straight in the eye.

"It was Randy Jennings," she confirms, and Audrey and I share a puzzled look as I wrack my brains to visualize the guy she's talking about.

"Shit."

Audrey and I whip our heads around to Alex.

"You know him?" Audrey asks.

Alex nods. "He's Tyson's twin brother." Tyson plays on the football team with Alex.

"Why would he want to stir shit?" It's not like anyone that goes to our illustrious private school would need to do it for money. I was expecting it to be someone who hates me and wants to split me and Reeve up, so this makes no sense.

Alex purses his lips, and frowns, as he considers it. His eyes darken a few seconds later before they find mine. "He's dating Marnie Gibson. She's behind this."

"Who is Marnie Gibson?" Mom asks.

"She played Juliet against Reeve's Romeo," I remind her.

"Ah, now it makes sense." She's aware of how badly Marnie was crushing on Reeve. How she kept shoving her tongue into his mouth during the kissing scenes, and how she waged a campaign of war against me for a solid year, until Reeve reported her for harassment to the principal and she was given a warning.

"Can we use this to get her poisonous ass expelled this time?" Audrey asks, looking as angry as I feel.

"I doubt it. It was a private party, and it's not like she forced Nate into kissing me." I turn my head toward Alex as an unwelcome thought lodges in my mind. "Does she have anything on Nate? Was this a setup?"

He shakes his head. "I really don't think he was put up to this. Everyone knows he has the biggest hard-on for you."

Mom clears her throat, sending Alex a pointed look.

Red heat creeps up Alex's neck and onto his cheeks. "Apologies, Mrs. Mills. I kind of forgot you were in the room."

"I think that's my cue to leave." Mom kisses my cheek. "Don't do anything about this. You only have a few weeks until you graduate. Don't let that little bitch ruin it for you. The best revenge you can get is to fix things with Reeve and present a united front. Ignore her at school, which will annoy her to no end." It is good advice and, hopefully, once this burning desire to rip her limb from limb subsides, it is advice I can take.

CHAPTER 11

I'M SHAKING with fear as I press the button to call Reeve later that night. He doesn't answer, and I'm fearful he's avoiding me. Curling into a ball on my bed, I clutch my cell in my hand, trying to talk myself off a ledge. He's probably just running late, and he'll call me back as soon as he can. Ten minutes later, my cell vibrates, and I quell the urge to hurl my dinner when I see his gorgeous face flashing across the ringing screen. Rubbing a hand over my queasy tummy, I answer his Face-Time call.

"I'm sorry," we both say in unison, and it helps to alleviate the tension gnawing at my insides.

"Viv," he whispers, and my heart hurts when his tortured blue eyes turn glassy and his handsome features contort with pain.

"I didn't kiss him!" I plead, sitting upright on my bed. "I would never do that, not even when we've been fighting. I was drunk. Audrey had gone to get me some water and Nate was the only one at the table. He was drunk too and he thought I looked sad so he kissed me."

Alex has spoken to his friend numerous times today, and he is convinced Nate didn't mean it maliciously. He was just acting his usual stupid self.

"I am going to punch that slimy bastard in the face until he no longer resembles himself," Reeve says, a muscle clenching in his jaw.

"I think Alex already beat you to it."

"Remind me to thank him."

"Nate is an idiot. You know I have zero interest in him, and he'd kiss any female with a pulse."

"Don't try to lighten this," Reeve snaps, rubbing at his temples. "Nate has the hots for you, babe. Everyone can see it but you."

"Whether he does or not doesn't matter. I don't have the hots for him, so you don't need to worry."

"And that's exactly what I've been trying to tell *you*." He lies down on his side, and I wish I was there so I could snuggle into his chest and feel the warmth of his strong arms around me. "You have nothing to worry about with Saffron. *Nothing*. Even if she did have feelings for me, which she doesn't, I have zero interest in her."

I don't think it's the same thing, but saying that will only prolong the argument, and I really need to make things right with my boyfriend. However, I do need to tell him this. "I think you're wrong. I think she has set her sights on you, and let's not forget she has a history of stealing other women's men."

"Baby, please, believe me when I say you couldn't be more wrong." He sits up, looking earnest as he comes closer to the screen. "I have told her point-blank how much I love you. She knows you're *the one*, and she's happy for me because she's my friend, in the same way all of my costars are my friends. Honestly, I couldn't have asked for a better crew. We all get along famously, and there are no airs or graces, especially with Saffron. If we weren't in this situation, I think you would really like her and you two would be good friends."

I bark out a bitter laugh. I can't help it. Are all men this blind? "I can safely say that will never happen."

He closes his eyes briefly. "Viv, I need you to listen to me and listen good. She's twenty-one, and I'm eighteen. I'm like her little brother."

A little brother she kisses, touches, and fakes sex with on-screen.

I instantly think of "Drivers License" by Olivia Rodrigo. She apparently wrote the song about her messy breakup with her boyfriend who left her for an older woman. As the lyrics bounce around my head, they couldn't be more apt.

"I know she's not interested in me like that because she's told me," Reeve continues, when I don't comment, "and she's fucking the thirty-year-old assistant director."

I get what he's implying—that she's only into older dudes. But Reeve refuses to see what I see. It's not their age. It's their status and influence in Hollywood. Frankly, I would've thought an assistant director was beneath her, but he must be serving some purpose. I could continue pressing my point, but it's not going to get us anywhere, so I focus on the crux of the matter.

"It hurt knowing she picked my gifts," I quietly say, lying down on my side and tucking my knees into my chest. "It really hurt, Reeve. How could you do that?"

His face contorts in a fresh wave of pain, and his eyes glimmer with remorse. "I didn't stop to think about it. I wanted to buy you lingerie, but I was bombarded by all the choices, and I was struggling to pick things you would like. She offered to help, and I accepted without thinking it through."

"You know me better than anyone, Reeve. Whatever you would've chosen for me would've been perfect." Pain rattles around my chest. "And girls know that helping someone's boyfriend with a gift is a no-no. Especially something so intimate. Unless it's the girl's bestie and there's an established friendship between friend and boyfriend like with you and Audrey." If Reeve needed help, why didn't he call my best friend?

"It wasn't intentional, babe, and the last thing I ever want to do is hurt you. I swear."

"I believe you. It's her motives I don't trust."

He exhales heavily, and silence fills the distance between us in more ways than one.

"I was going to burn the underwear," I admit after I can't take the heavy silence any longer. "But I couldn't bear to destroy such beautiful garments. However, I can't wear them either. I'm going to return the unworn items to you so you can get a refund."

"Babe, please, don't, I—"

"I can't wear things some other woman picked out for me, Reeve," I hiss, rubbing at my temples. "How would you feel if I got Nate to help me choose gifts for you? Would you ever be able to look at them without seeing his face?"

Silence engulfs us again, and my heart is so tormented it feels like it's cracking apart.

"That was low, Viv, but I get the point. Send it back to me, and I'll return it." He worries his lower lip between his teeth. "You had better send the makeup back too," he adds, and at least he has the decency to look ashamed.

He won't be able to get a refund on the makeup after it's been used, so I'll just toss it or see if Audrey wants it. "Not the purse or the bracelet?" I inquire, because I have to be sure.

He shakes his head. "She wasn't involved at all in those purchases."

I nod, averting my eyes, because I'm not sure I won't cry. While he deserves to know how much he has hurt me, I'm aware of the stress he's under, and I never want to add to it. I want to draw a line under this and try to put it behind us. Yet it's easier said than done. I thought talking to him would make me feel better, but I'm just feeling sadder.

"Vivien. Look at me, babe."

I lift my troubled eyes to the screen.

"I'm sorry, Viv. I just wanted to make your birthday special, and instead I ruined it. If I hadn't upset you, you wouldn't have gotten drunk and that degenerate wouldn't have put his toxic lips on you."

"Why were you like that on the phone last night?" I ask, because he needs to know the way he spoke to me was also upsetting. "If you had just talked to me, this could've been avoided. And how could you hang up on me knowing I was upset?"

"I didn't have the privacy to talk to you properly about it, and the guys were leaving and calling for me. The few beers I had probably didn't help either. I don't know what else to say except I'm sorry and it won't happen again."

As apologies go, it's lukewarm, at best, but I'm done talking about this. I'm emotionally exhausted from thinking about it all day, and I want to move forward and pretend like it never happened. "We have both made mistakes," I say, reaching out to touch the screen. "But this won't define us. Let's agree to put it behind us and not let anything like this happen again."

"I love you, baby. So, so much, and it's killing me being away from you. Especially now. If I was there, I would hold you in my arms all night, kissing you and making love to you until I'd banished every single doubt and every molecule of pain I have caused."

I needed that reassurance, and a layer of stress lifts from my shoulders. "I miss you like crazy, Reeve. It's so much harder than I thought it'd be." Tears spill down my cheeks as I can no longer keep my emotions trapped inside.

"I know, babe. I know. But we are nearly at the halfway point, and I'm going to see you in less than a month for prom."

"I can't wait." I manage a smile through my tears. "Just promise me one thing, Reeve."

"Anything, my love."

"I don't want her in your room with you alone or you in hers. The thought of it makes me ill."

He places his hand over his heart. "I promise she won't be in here unless the guys are with her. Same goes for her room. If that's what you need to feel reassured, I can give you that."

"Thank you."

"I love you, Vivien Grace Mills. You are my heart. My soul. My world." He blows me a kiss. "Please never doubt my love. It will always only be you."

His words soothe the remaining frayed edges of my soul, and I sink into the bed, feeling lighter than I have all day. "I love you too, Reeve, in all the same ways. Let's never fight like this again."

"Amen to that." He smiles, and his entire face lights up, heating me from the inside out. We chat for a few minutes about normal stuff before ending our call, and I fall asleep dreaming of him, grateful it's all blown over and that everything is going to be all right.

My cell rings, waking me from slumber, and I'm instantly awake the second I see his face light across my screen.

"Are you on the plane?" I ask, forgoing a greeting.

"Viv. About that."

The edge to his tone has me on instant alert, and I jerk upright in bed, smoothing a hand over the tight pain spreading across my chest. "No, Reeve. Please don't say what I think you're going to say."

It's the morning of prom, and he had a flight booked for noon eastern time, which is around now. It's due to land just after three, and I was planning on surprising him at the airport.

"I'm so sorry, baby, but I'm not going to be able to make it after all."

"Why?" I rasp, swallowing painfully over the messy ball of emotion clogging my throat.

"Something weird happened overnight. The last few shots we filmed yesterday were corrupted, so the director called us in this morning to reshoot them. I tried to get out of it, but it's not possible. We're on a really tight schedule, and there are no other gaps to reshoot them. I'm so sorry, baby. I'm as devastated by this as you are."

I can tell he's upset, and it's not like this is his fault. If he could get out of it, I know he would because he's been looking forward to prom as much as I have. "I hate this. It's so unfair," I say.

"I know. The guys were giving me crap because I was on the verge of tears, but I'm really upset. I don't want to miss tonight, and I would happily trade a limb if it meant I could be there. For years, I have dreamed of holding you in my arms all night at prom. I had booked a suite at Chateau Marmont as a surprise, and I was looking forward to ravishing your body all night long. I'm so sorry, Vivien, more than I can even say."

"I don't want to go without you, and I hate that prom is ruined for us, but this isn't your fault, Reeve. There isn't anything you can do, so don't feel guilty." I shrug, even though he can't see me. "It is what it is." My voice is dead, devoid of the excitement I woke up feeling.

The truth is, it's not just about prom. I really need to see Reeve. To feel his arms around me. To have his mouth worship mine. To join our bodies and relive our connection in the most intimate of ways. I need to prove to myself that we truly are okay because the last few weeks have been hell on Earth.

Not only have trolls been targeting me online, spreading nasty lies and leaving disgusting comments on everything I post to the point where I have stopped posting anything, I've also been subjected to ongoing rumors, popping up daily on gossip sites, about Saffron and Reeve. Insiders on the set are allegedly reporting how their explosive on-screen chemistry has spilled over into their personal lives and they are hot for one another. Other reports claim he's a free agent having dumped me after I cheated on him with one of his friends.

Reeve continues to tell me to ignore it. That it's all par for the course, and that none of it is true, but it's hard when I'm confronted with it all the time. Bitchy girls in school love taunting me with the rumors, stuffing copies of articles into my locker and leaving them pinned to the windshield of my car. But the pretend do-gooders are worse; those girls profess sympathy and offer their help while not so subtly sliding their digs in. And Marnie Gibson has been getting on my very last nerve, but I'm taking Mom's advice and pretending she doesn't exist, even though I'd love to take a baseball bat to her head.

I've tried not to labor the point during the brief daily calls with Reeve, because I don't want to come across like the needy, clingy, scared girlfriend I'm turning into. If you had told me two months ago this is who I would become, I would have laughed in your face. I'm terrified because I know the worst is yet to come, and it already feels like I'm losing myself and like I'm losing Reeve.

"Viv. Baby, are you still there?"

"Yes. Sorry. I'm here," I quietly confirm.

"I want you to go to prom. Please don't stay at home alone. You know you can go with Alex and Audrey, and they will ensure you have a good time. And I need to see photos. I've been imagining seeing you in, and out of, that dress for months."

I know he's putting on a front for me, and I want to reassure him, but it's challenging when I feel so empty inside. I genuinely don't know if I have the strength to wear a mask and look like I'm having a great time when my heart is torn to shreds, and I'm missing the other half of my soul so badly it feels like I'm slipping into a dark abyss. I know how melodramatic I sound, but it's the truth.

Reeve and I have always done everything together.

I don't know how to exist without him.

I'm sure shrinks the world over would have a field day with that statement, but I'm not going to deny I feel helpless and directionless without him by my side. I didn't realize I had become so dependent on him or that I would flounder so deeply without his guiding light. I know it's not a healthy thing. That I need to exist separately from my relationship and assume my own identity and my own path in life.

Suddenly, I'm embarrassed by my own thoughts. I'm a talented, smart, independent, beautiful woman, and I don't need my boyfriend to survive. Yes, I will miss him to the very depths of my soul tonight, but I can't let his absence destroy another special night. I owe it to myself to go to prom and have the best possible night.

"I'll send you pictures, and I'll try my best to enjoy prom even if I'll be missing you every second of every minute of the night."

CHAPTER 12

I PLANT a wide smile on my face as I pose beside Audrey while Alex snaps a few pics. Mom already took some at the house, which I sent to Reeve, and he replied with a quick message telling me I looked gorgeous and he was proud of me. I almost broke down in tears when the stunning corsage he ordered was delivered. He chose white roses decorated with pretty diamante stones encased with red ribbon. Little swatches of greenery add an extra bit of color, and it looks elegant on my wrist.

"You two are, hands down, the hottest babes in the room," Alex says, sliding his cell in the pocket of his dress pants. "I'm no expert, but you did a fucking amazing job with the dresses, Viv. You are very talented."

"Thanks, Alex." I am really pleased with how both dresses turned out. I'm wearing a high-necked, sleeveless, figure-hugging, floor-length red dress. It's a pretty classic design except for the few sequined strips—around my neck, edging my breasts, and running from the curve of my hips to the floor—and the open back which show-cases my skin and a subtle hint of side boob. Audrey opted for a halter-neck gown in deep purple with a fitted top and full skirt. Alex is wearing a tie in the same color, and he and Audrey make a striking couple.

"I know you've decided to major in English rather than costume design, but I totally think you should set up a side business designing dresses," Audrey suggests, taking a sip of the spiked punch.

I'm sticking to nonalcoholic cocktails because I want to avoid another drink-fueled disaster. "I'm considering doing a costume design course after I graduate with my degree," I confess, but nothing is set in stone. I'm passionate about writing *and* dress designing, and while it makes sense that I'll build a career in the movie industry, I'm still exploring all my options.

"Do you think they did all this for Reeve?" Alex waves his hands around the extravagant ballroom.

"Probably," Audrey agrees.

Prom is being held in a top five-star hotel, and the prom committee spared no expense transforming the ballroom into a Hollywood-themed backdrop. It's so cliché, and the irony isn't lost on me either. Walking the red carpet, getting accosted by "paparazzi" as we arrived, being surrounded by movie props, a large golden Oscar trophy, and the myriad of classic movie posters framed around the walls all serve to remind me of *my enemy*. Because that's who Hollywood represents to me tonight.

Hollywood has stolen my Prince Charming, and I'm like a lost Cinderella wandering aimlessly around the room while everyone around me parties hard. I'm trying to put a brave face on, but I'm struggling. Watching couples sway on the dance floor is especially difficult, because that should be Reeve and me. "You two should dance," I say, swiping Audrey's drink. I push her toward Alex. They open their mouths to protest, but I don't give them the opportunity. "Go on. I don't need you to chaperone me all night." I flash them my brightest smile, only letting it go once they have hit the dance floor and they are satisfied I'm not going to fall apart.

I glance at my cell, grateful it's almost eleven. I'm hoping I can make my escape in an hour or so and retreat to the sanctity of my bedroom. Removing my locket from underneath the top of my dress, I rub my fingers over it, wishing it was a genie's lamp and I could summon Reeve as one of my three wishes.

A guy from the football team approaches and asks me to dance, but I decline, like I've declined the other couple of guys who asked me. While most everyone came with a date, a lot are just friends, and it's clear there are plenty of single guys on the prowl. Even if it was innocent, there is no way I'm dancing at prom with anyone but Reeve.

I danced with Alex earlier when he stepped in for Reeve after we won prom king and queen, only because it was expected. I honestly couldn't care less about the award. It's meaningless without my boyfriend. However, I am still wearing my crown so I don't come across as a total Debbie Downer. While I promised Reeve I would try to have a good time, sticking to that promise is challenging. It's hard to enjoy myself when he's not here and I'm missing him so much.

"Hey, Viv. Want to dance?" Nate asks, approaching me with a cocky smile.

"Go away," I snap, not even looking at him.

"C'mon, Viv. I've said I'm sorry. Are you going to avoid me forever?"

Sighing, I turn to look at him. "I've told you I forgive you, but we can't be seen together. You know I have a spotlight on my head right now, and I won't do anything to cause issues for Reeve or give the trolls another reason to hate me. Even talking to you is freaking me out," I admit, scanning the room to ensure no one is recording us. My paranoia has reached new levels in the past few weeks.

"That's no way to live your life," Nate says, and I don't disagree.

"It's the way things are."

"I hope he appreciates all you sacrifice for him." There's an edge to his tone I don't like. Nate has always been jealous of Reeve, but I didn't realize part of it was connected to me.

"I love him, and I'd do anything for him," I say, grabbing my purse from the table. "Now, if you'll excuse me, I need to use the bathroom."

I exit the ballroom into the swanky hallway and make my way to the ladies' restroom. After attending to business, I touch up my makeup and wash my hands before heading back out. Only another hour and I can make my escape.

Hands wrap around my eyes from behind, and I shriek as a hard body presses up against me.

"Don't scream," he says, in that husky voice of his. "It's only me."

My heart is jackhammering against my rib cage as he releases his hands, and I spin around in his arms. Butterflies roam free in my chest as we come face to face for the first time in two months. Happy tears leak from my eyes as I fling my arms around Reeve's neck, squeezing the living daylights out of him. His large hand lands on my lower bare back as he holds me close. Familiar citrusy notes wrap around me as we cling to one another, and I close my eyes, savoring the feel of him against me, letting his warmth sink bone-deep, eradicating all the heartache.

Sweeping my hair to one side, he buries his face in my neck. "I've missed you so much, baby," he murmurs while planting feather-soft kisses in that sensitive spot just under my ear.

"Reeve." My tone is breathy as I angle my head, granting him better access, while my hands roam his back through his suit jacket. "I have missed you so damn much. It's been the worst pain."

"I need to taste you," he says, lifting his head. Emotion seeps from the hidden depths of his ocean-blue eyes before he clasps my face in his firm hands and his lips collide with mine. Grabbing his jacket, I tug him close as he makes love to my mouth in a desperate marriage full of longing and lust and pain. I willingly open my mouth when his tongue prods against the seam of my lips, demanding entry. He presses his erection against my stomach, and I moan into his mouth when his tongue tangles with mine in an erotic dance I feel all the way to the tips of my toes.

We fall back against the wall, grinding against one another as we kiss like we'll never get to kiss again. Desire floods every corner of my body, and my panties are wet with need for him. My heart is swollen with love, and everything feels right in my world again.

This is what I've needed.

What we've *both* needed.

Reeve's touch and his scent and the comforting solidity of his hard body moving against mine remind me we belong together and I should never doubt this connection we share.

"I don't have much time," he rasps against my mouth.

"How long?" I inquire, briefly ripping my lips from his.

"My car will return in ninety minutes."

"Then let's make every second count," I say, grabbing his hand and pulling him into the wheelchair accessible bathroom.

Reeve locks the door, and when he turns around, I'm on my knees, reaching for his zipper. "Jesus, Viv."

"I need to taste you too." I peer up at him while I lower his zipper and pull his dress pants down.

"Fuck. You look beautiful, Viv." Yanking his boxers down to his knees, I lick the crown of his cock, soaking up the precum on offer. Reeve hisses as his back slams against the door, and he spreads his thighs a little wider. "I'm dying for you, baby," he adds. "You have no idea how much."

I lick a line up each side of his hard cock, lapping and nibbling on his velvety-soft flesh before I take him into my mouth and suck hard. His hands are gentle in my hair as he holds me to him while I show him how much I'm dying for him too. "Viv. I'm not going to last long, and I need to be inside you."

He helps me to my feet, and I lean back against the sink as I bunch my dress up to my waist. I don't care if it wrinkles. I need him inside me more than I need air to breathe. Removing his pants and boxers, he stalks toward me as he strokes his straining length. "I love you," he says, wrapping one of my legs around his waist and pushing my lace panties to one side. He lines his cock up at my entrance. "And I wish I had all night to show you how much."

"You're here, Reeve." I run my fingers through the stylish layer of stubble on his cheeks. "That's all the proof I need."

He slams into me in one powerful thrust, and I cry out as he fills me with his love. Our kisses are passionately frantic as we fuck with an edge that's new. I sit up on the counter, so Reeve can pound into me harder, placing both my legs around his trim waist, rocking my hips forward to meet his thrusts. "Oh God, Reeve," I pant, in between kisses, "you feel so freaking good." My orgasm is building fast, my neglected body rejoicing in our reunion.

"Fuck, Viv. I want to stay buried inside you forever. This feels incredible." Reeve holds my hips steady as he drives his cock into my pussy, plowing into me like he's trying to embed himself so deep I never forget the feel of him as he lays claim to me in all the ways that count.

My climax consumes me without warning. I hit my peak and fall over the ledge, shaking and crying as I cling to him while wave after wave of pleasure rolls through me. Reeve grunts, shouting my name when he finds his own release, spilling his hot seed inside me.

"Wow," I whisper, holding him tight as his head drops to my shoulder. "I think we needed that," I add, grinning. Sex with Reeve has always been amazing, but that was something else.

"I love you," he says before welding his lips to mine. This kiss is softer, sweeter, and I'm drowning in sensation as he worships my mouth, reassuring me of our love with every glide of his lips. Slowly, he pulls out of me, reluctantly breaking our kiss. "I would love nothing more than to spend my time balls deep inside you, but it's prom, and I believe I promised you some dancing." He stares adoringly at me, and my heart does cartwheels behind my rib cage.

"You did." I'm smiling as I fix my panties and my dress while Reeve tucks himself back into his pants. "You look gorgeous," I say, watching him through the mirror as I smooth my hair into place and tidy my makeup. His broad shoulders fit snugly in the tailored black Armani suit, and the red tie looks vibrant against his crisp white dress shirt.

"Stop stealing my lines," he purrs, circling his arms around me from behind. "You are stunning, Vivien Grace. More beautiful than any mere mortal. You are a goddess among women."

Reaching back, I run my fingers through the longer strands of his hair. "Thank you." My eyes glisten with emotion as I twist around in his arms. "Thank you for being here. I can't express how happy I am to see you."

"I'm sorry our plans were ruined." Lifting my hand to his mouth, he kisses my knuckles. "And I wish I could stay all night, but I had to beg the director to give me a few hours off."

"I don't care." I place my hand on his chest, right over his heart. "I'll take whatever time I can get with you."

He dots kisses all over my face before his lips brush against mine. "I hate being separated from you." He bundles me into his arms. "It's the worst form of torture."

"I know," I admit against his chest. "It's been killing me too."

He rubs his nose against mine. "You're my home, Viv," he whispers.

"I know what you mean." I softly cup his handsome face. "Everything feels right when you're with me."

He eases back, smiling as he takes my hand. "Then let's make the most of our time, because it's got to last us another month before I'm back home." His gaze treks up and down my body. "Damn, Viv. You're breathtaking, and that dress is exquisite."

His words and his loving gaze paper over the cracks in my heart, and I'm dancing on air as we make our way into the ballroom and out onto the dance floor. Our classmates call out and reach for Reeve, but he has single-minded determination, and he stops for no one. Alex plonks Reeve's crown on his head, and we grin at one another like lovesick fools as we dance. Reeve lavishes me with his undivided attention, twirling and spinning me around as we dance and laugh and revel in being back together. His lips don't stray far from mine, and we cling to one another through the more romantic songs. It's everything I had hoped prom would be and more.

All too fast, our time is up and Reeve needs to leave.

I go with him in the car, because it gives us more precious minutes together, and we make out like demons on the back seat, enjoying every second.

His father's private jet is ready and waiting on the runway when we arrive at the airport, and we hold tight to one another until time has run out. I swipe at the silent tears streaming down my face as he walks away from me and I wonder if I'll ever get used to the long separations.

CHAPTER 13

"CONGRATULATIONS, HONEY," Mom says, enveloping me in her arms. My graduation cap tilts sideways on my head, but Dad fixes it.

"I want a photo of the two of you." He gestures for us to pose. "Say cheese, princess."

I laugh, snaking my arm around Mom's shoulders as she holds on to my waist. We smile for a few pics, and then Dad swaps with Mom. Audrey approaches with her parents and her two younger sisters, and my bestie takes some shots of the three of us before I return the favor. Then Mom takes some solo shots of me, as well as some with my friends.

We made plans to enjoy a celebratory meal with Audrey's family and Alex's family, but we separate to travel to the restaurant in our own cars. En route to the steakhouse, I post a group pic with our friends on social media, tagging Reeve and mentioning how much we miss him today.

"Have you heard from Reeve?" Audrey asks, as we settle into our chairs at the restaurant.

I shake my head, and waves of my long dark hair tumble over my shoulders. "I had a message when I woke up, and he sent me flowers, but I haven't spoken with him yet." The time difference and his early starts are a real pain.

"Only four more days and it'll all be over," my bestie says, hugging me. "We're going to have the best summer."

"We are, and I can't wait."

I laugh as Nate lets out a loud battle cry before jumping from the large speaker resting on the temporary stage, hurling himself into the packed crowd. He is such an idiot, and I wonder if he'll ever grow up.

69

Butthead is hosting our graduation party, but this time the action is largely taking place indoors because his parents have moved to Greece for the summer, giving him free rein of his palatial home. Some people spill out onto the beach, drinking and skinny-dipping, but the DJ has been set up inside, and that is where most of my classmates have gravitated.

I drink my vodka cranberry while I take a breather from the dance floor. I chuckle to myself as I watch Audrey and Alex dirty dancing in the middle of the packed crowd. Alcohol sloshes through my veins, and I'm nicely buzzed yet still in control of my faculties. I keep an eye on the time and my cell, hoping Reeve isn't too late calling me tonight. I'm desperate to speak to him, having really missed him at graduation today. I don't like thinking about all the milestones Reeve is missing, because it just gets me depressed. Instead, I'm trying to focus on the fact he'll be home in four days, we have all summer together, and then we'll be starting UCLA. Finally, things are falling into place, and I'm excited for this next phase of our lives.

Extracting my cell, I open my Insta, to check my graduation post, because I'm clearly a glutton for punishment. "What the fuck?" I blurt, squinting at my screen in confusion.

"What's wrong?" Alex plonks his butt on the stool beside me.

"My graduation post is gone."

"What do you mean gone?" He arches a brow while swigging warm beer from a red cup.

"I mean it's disappeared. Gone poof." I rub a tense spot between my brows.

"How does a post just disappear?" he asks, smiling as Audrey makes her way toward us.

"That's what I'd like to know," I murmur, as a sense of unease slithers over my skin.

"Do you know anything about my missing graduation post?" I ask Reeve when he calls twenty minutes later. I've been mulling over ideas and quietly stewing since I discovered my post was gone.

"I didn't know anything until after the fact," he says, immediately on the defensive, which instantly pisses me off.

"What did Cassidy do?" I bark, because I've no doubt the stuck-up hyper-ambitious publicist hired by the studio is behind this.

Tension oozes between us down the line.

"I'm disgusted, Viv. I just want to put that out there first, and I've already ripped her a new one. It's not going to happen again."

"Spit it out, Reeve." I flee the house and walk around the corner in search of somewhere more private to have this argument, because I sense one brewing.

"She had someone hack into your account and remove it."

"She *what*?!" I screech. "She has no right to do that! I'm going to sue her fucking ass. The studio too. Who the hell do these people think they are?" My free hand is clenching and unclenching at my side, and I have an almost insurmountable urge to punch something.

"I get you're pissed. I am too. It's the closest I've ever come to wanting to hit a woman, but we can't do anything about it."

"You can't, but I can!" I pace back and forth on the stone path that runs alongside Butthead's house. No one is back here, and the noise from the party is muted.

"Babe. You can't. Not without it affecting me."

"You're almost finished filming," I remind him.

"There are still reshoots, promo, the premiere, and the potential of more movies. You know this, Viv." I do, but I've been languishing in denial, trying to avoid that possibility because I know what it means for our plans, and I can't deal with more disappointment. "I can't do anything to rock the boat, and that means you can't either."

I lean my head back against the wall, close my eyes, and sigh.

I hate these people.

I hate this side of the industry.

And I hate that I have no choice, because I won't do anything to jeopardize Reeve's future career even if there is a part of me that prays the movie tanks so he doesn't get offered more films with Saffron Roberts.

Yes, I know I'm a selfish, jealous bitch and Reeve would be so hurt if he was privy to my inner thoughts and feelings. I suffer enormous guilt every time it enters my mind, but the thought of Reeve spending more time with that woman sends me spiraling into a pit of anxiety. Honestly, if it happens, I'm not sure we'd survive.

"What was her objection this time?" I ask, in a resigned tone. "You weren't even in the photo with me."

He sounds tired when he speaks. "You tagged me."

"So, are you saying I can't tag my boyfriend in posts now?" I stuff my clenched fist in my mouth to stifle the scream begging to be set free.

"No. You can't." He lowers his voice. "They don't want any ties linking us together. They need me to appear to be single."

My stomach drops to my feet, and a heavy pressure settles on my chest. "I think they'd put a bullet through my skull if they thought they'd get away with it."

"Don't say that! Of course, they wouldn't. It's just semantics."

"It's not just semantics, Reeve. Don't insult my intelligence."

"I don't know what you want me to say here, Viv." I visualize him throwing his hands in the air. "This is my career, and we both know this bullshit is the norm in the industry."

"I know all that, but you can't let these people manipulate every aspect of your life, Reeve! Are you really sure this role is worth it?"

He sucks in a gasp, and I instantly know I've said the wrong thing. "You know how much this part means to me, Viv. This is one of the biggest studios in the biz. This role will make or break my career. I thought you supported me, but I'm beginning to wonder if that's really the truth."

"Now you're being unfair. Of course, I support you, but I didn't realize I'd have to become your dirty little secret!" My voice raises a few levels as anger rears its ugly head.

"Babe, c'mon. You know it's not like that. Who cares what anyone else thinks? You know I'm yours and you're mine. As long as we're solid, it doesn't matter what the press says."

"It matters to *me*, Reeve." I slap a hand over my aching chest. "Do you think this is easy for me? To have people say I'm not good enough for you? That *she's* more deserving of you? Now, I can't post about us, or talk about us, because I have to pretend like I'm not your girlfriend? In what realm do you ever think I'd be okay with that?"

"It's not going to be forever, and we know the truth, as do our friends and the people who matter. Everything else is industry bullshit, but it's a necessary evil."

"What happened to the guy who spoke so eloquently about wanting to be known for his acting ability not his celebrity status? What asshole has been whispering shit in your ear, hmm, Reeve?"

"I was naïve to think one existed without the other," he says, in a clipped tone. "I have a role to play on-screen and off of it."

"God, Reeve. Do you even hear yourself? You're already indoctrinated." I shake my head, disgusted that he can't see my point of view at all.

"I'm doing what I need to do to establish my career!" he shouts, and I'm taken aback by the venom in his voice. Reeve has rarely raised his voice to me, and we don't fight very often. These past three months, I estimate we have fought more than we've fought in years. It's draining. More than that, we are drifting apart, and I don't think he even feels it. Or he's pretending like it isn't happening, or maybe he just doesn't care.

"Well then, you continue doing that. Continue putting yourself first Reeve, because you're so good at it." Then I do something I swore I'd never do—I hang up on him and switch off my cell. Fuck him and his selfishness.

Dragging myself out of bed the following morning, I try to think of a plausible excuse to get me out of meeting Audrey at the yoga studio for our regular class, but I know she's not going to let me get away with it. I drank way too much after I hung up on Reeve last night, and I'm paying for it now. Big-time. As much as it'll be torture attending class with a monster hangover, it should help to sweat the last of the alcohol from my system, so I grab a quick shower, change into my workout gear, and race out the door to meet my bestie.

"Man, that sucked balls," I admit, as we sit in the café across from the yoga studio after our class has ended. "I honestly thought I was going to vomit during the revolved downward-facing dog."

"You did look a little green," Audrey agrees, smothering a smile.

"I feel better now, so it was worth the pain and suffering." I smile at the waitress as she drops our salads and smoothies on the table. "Thank you."

"Have you heard from Reeve yet?" Audrey asks, picking up her silverware.

I shake my head. "Nope, but he never calls early. Besides, I should probably call him first. I shouldn't have hung up on him."

"Are you sure you want to deal with all this shit, Viv? It's already gotten complicated and the movie hasn't even released yet. It's going to get nuts next year, and, honestly, I'm concerned about you. I've seen the comments online, and you don't deserve that shit. I'm pissed Reeve isn't doing more to protect you."

"I'm going to talk to him about it this summer. Arguing over the phone is getting us nowhere."

"What will you do if he gets offered the other two movies?" she tentatively inquires in between mouthfuls of chicken.

"Cry, most likely," I admit, carefully cutting up my chicken. "But ultimately adapt. Attending UCLA with Reeve has been my dream for years, but if I have to go it alone, I'll survive." I reach across the table, patting her hand. "At least, we can be UCLA widows together." Alex wasn't offered a place to play ball at UCLA, like he had hoped. Competition is fierce, and it was close, but they passed on him. So, he's moving to Boston College to play for the Eagles.

"Isn't it coincidental that our boyfriends may both end up in Boston while we're still in L.A."

"They couldn't have planned it better, even if they'll have little time to catch up with their busy schedules."

"I have something to tell you." Audrey wipes the corner of her mouth with her napkin.

I take a sip of my green smoothie while I wait for her to tell me her news.

"Alex and I have decided to break up at the end of the summer."

She could've told me she murdered someone in cold blood, and I wouldn't be any more surprised. "Why?" Those two are rock solid and so good together.

"Neither of us wants to spend our four years at college pining for one another. We have seen how hard it's been on you and Reeve, and we don't think we can cope with the long-distance thing."

My mouth opens and closes as I grapple for the right words. "I don't know what to say, except I hope our situation hasn't forced you both into making this decision."

"We were already discussing it. What you've gone through just reinforced our thought process."

"I don't know how you can be so…blasé about it."

She sets her silverware down, gulping. "Trust me, I'm not. I'm trying to put a brave face on and accept it. Every time I think about him not being there, I tear up, and every time I think about him being with other girls, I want to throw up. But I don't want to spend my time at college worrying about my boyfriend. I trust Alex. I really do, but he's going to play for the Eagles, and women will be throwing themselves at him. I don't know how you deal with the girls already fawning over Reeve. I couldn't do it, and while I know Alex isn't going to be dealing with it at the same level, I worry it'll end up breaking us up anyway. At least this way, we can part as friends, enjoy college, and when it's over, if we are meant to be, we'll find our way back to one another."

"It feels like the end of an era," I truthfully admit. "It's always been the four of us, and now we're all separated."

"I know, but I prefer to look at it like the start of a new era." She stabs a piece of chicken with her fork, popping it in her mouth.

"Do you think Reeve and I should break up if he gets offered the other two movies?"

Audrey almost chokes on her food, and I pour her a glass of water from the jug on our table, handing it to her. She gulps back a few mouthfuls and composes herself. "Jesus, Viv. Don't do that to me while I'm eating!"

"Sorry."

"I can't answer that. Only you and Reeve can decide what to do about your relationship, and we don't want to influence you guys. Your relationship is different. You've been in each other's lives forever, and you have this unshakeable bond. If anyone can weather a few stormy years, it's you two."

I squeeze her hand. "Thank you for saying that, but it really doesn't feel like that right now. To be honest, I'm upset at how quickly we seem to be drifting apart."

"No one said love was easy, and I bet everything will be okay the minute he gets home."

I'm mulling over Audrey's words when she goes to the bathroom, so I don't see the woman with the pink-tipped hair approaching until she's slid into the booth, occupying my best friend's seat.

I jerk my head up, shock splaying across my face. "Bianca! What are you doing here?"

"I was in the neighborhood and thought we could have a little chat."

Bullshit. She obviously tracked me down. I purse my lips and fold my arms across my chest, already knowing I'm not going to like this little chat. "Say what you came here to say."

She offers me a tight grin, and her skin is stretched so taut it's a wonder her face doesn't split in two. Gossip sites put her at mid-forties, but I'm betting she's older. It's hard to tell under all the cosmetic surgery and thick makeup. Not that it's uncommon in L.A. My mom is the anomaly, while someone like Bianca Remington is more the norm. In a city full of fake women, my mom truly stands out. Lauren Mills has chosen to grow old gracefully, and the surgeon's knife has never touched her flawless porcelain skin. It's just another reason to admire Mom.

Reeve's hard-ass agent is wearing one of her signature power suits in black with a rich red silk blouse. A string of pearls rests around her smooth neck, and I briefly imagine choking her with them. If she gives me shit, I might very well be tempted.

"You're a smart girl, Vivien. You've grown up in the industry, and I've no doubt your mother has told you how things work. To put it bluntly, you're holding Reeve back. He's spending too much time worrying about upsetting you and not enough time focusing on his career. If you truly love him, you will let him go."

"Loving Reeve means I will be there to support and encourage him every step of the way. I will ensure he isn't manipulated by people who profess to have his best interests at heart, when all they care about is lining their own pockets on the back of his success." Take that and shove it up your bleached asshole.

Her haughty smile aggravates the hell out of me, and I'm having a hard time containing my anger. "I don't care what you think of me. You're insignificant." She flicks a piece of lint off the sleeve of her jacket before standing. "I came here as a courtesy, but I couldn't care less if you get your little lovesick heart broken." She leans down, and the overpowering scent of Chanel almost knocks me out. "Reeve is going to be a huge star, and he has no room for a girlfriend." Her gaze rakes over my bare face, my tight ponytail, colorful workout clothes, and sneakers. "At least, not one like you." She straightens up before delivering her closing shot. "Act like a stage-five clinger if you want, but mark my words, by this time next year, you will be nothing but a distant memory."

CHAPTER 14

"WELL, WHAT DID SHE SAY?" I ask when Reeve rejoins us at the pool. His dad is away again, so we've spent the first week of summer break hanging out at Reeve's house. Reeve is recharging his batteries after an intense three months of nonstop work, and I'm enjoying chilling out after exams and graduation and just being with Reeve. Waking up every morning wrapped in his strong arms is the best remedy, and gradually, all the frustrations of the past few months are slipping away.

Audrey and Alex are presently frolicking in the pool, while I'm stretched out on a lounger, sipping the homemade lemonade Mrs. Thompson, the housekeeper, left in the refrigerator for us.

"She admitted it but won't apologize." Bending down, he pecks my lips before collapsing on the lounger alongside me.

I snort. "That sounds about right. Bianca is a piece of work." I didn't want to accost Reeve with the details of his agent's nasty little chat with me the instant he came home, so I left it a few days before finally mentioning it last night. He was fuming, and he left her a heated voice message, demanding she return his call, yet he's only just managed to speak with her. Either that demonstrates where he fits on her priority list or she was giving him time to cool down.

"I've told her if she pulls a stunt like that again I'm terminating my contract." He swipes his beer bottle off the ground and brings it to his lips.

Sitting upright, I remove my sunglasses so I can look him in the eyes. "I thought you were going to terminate it now." At least, that's what he said last night when he lost it after I told him every horrid word she'd said to me.

He grimaces before swinging his legs to the side and reaching out for my hands. "I can't, babe."

I mirror his position, and our knees touch. "You can. You know Mom already spoke to Margaret and she's interested in signing you. She is the best in the industry, and your career will be in safe hands with her."

"I can't walk away from Bianca now, Viv." His eyes blaze with excitement, and my stomach dips.

"What don't I know?"

"They've just offered me a contract for the next two movies!" Flames of delight dance in his eyes while that uneasy feeling in the pit of my stomach churns faster. "Bianca is negotiating terms, but it's looking like a done deal. I'm sorry, babe. I know you don't like her, and I'm not happy she was rude to you, but I can't change representation in the middle of all this."

"They've decided to make more movies in the series already?" I ask, struggling to share his excitement amid the pain eviscerating me from all angles. "The first movie has only just wrapped, and it's not premiering until January."

"The studio commissioned reports from industry analysts who predict outcomes, and all the indicators point to this movie being a massive success. The buzz has been steadily building since the news first broke of the adaptation and it's showing no sign of slowing down." He can't contain his grin, and I hate that I can't be happy for him because I know what this means for us.

"When does filming start?"

"November, and then we'll be taking a break to promote the release before shooting restarts again next May."

"So, it's definitely going ahead?" I try to mask my distress, but his smile fades, confirming I'm hiding nothing.

He rubs circles on the back of my hand with his thumb. "The second movie definitely is. While I'll sign a new contract, which includes both films, there is an opt-out clause with part payment if the first movie doesn't perform as expected at the box office."

"And when would the third film begin production?"

"Provisionally November of next year with a break for promotion of the second film, and then it will resume in April of the following year."

That would be the end of the spring semester of our sophomore year. Between promotion and filming, Reeve is going to be extremely busy in the next two years. "What about UCLA?" I ask, even though I already know the answer.

"Babe." He pulls me over onto his lap, snaking his arms around me. "I'm not going to UCLA." He tilts my chin up with his finger. His features soften when he spots the upset on my face. "I know we had it planned, and I hate that I'm disappointing you, but this opportunity is too big to turn down. We both knew this was a possibility. Please say you understand?" he pleads.

My chest heaves as I struggle to phrase this in a way that doesn't come across as selfish. "I know it's a massive opportunity for you, Reeve, and I *am* proud of you. You clearly impressed them, not that it's a surprise. You're destined for greatness. I still stand by that, but I can't help feeling disappointed because thinking about college was basically the only thing that got me through these past three months." I hook my arms around his neck. "You've already missed out on so much, and now you're going to be gone for the next two years, and I'm scared." Tears cloud my eyes, but I don't disguise them. I want him to see how difficult this is for me. "I'm scared what this means for us. We will barely see one another."

Taking my wrist, he presses a soft kiss on my delicate flesh. "Do you love me, Viv?"

My brow puckers. "What kind of stupid question is that? Of course, I love you!"

"And I love you." He laces our fingers together. "I know it's been rough, but we'll get better at it. It's been a big adjustment is all. Besides, you'll probably be having too much fun to miss me."

"Like you?" I snap, as my emotions get the better of me.

A muscle clenches in his jaw, and he drops my hand. "Don't be mean, Viv. You know I missed you like fucking crazy. If you think I'm out partying every night and hardly thinking about you, you are sorely mistaken. It's a lot of hard work. I'm up at six every day, and I fall into bed exhausted at midnight. The schedule is punishing, and we had little downtime. It's not as glamorous as it might seem."

I slide off his lap and sit beside him, worrying my lip between my teeth. Bile fills my mouth as I prepare to speak my mind. I don't want to even think about this, let alone put a voice to it, but it needs to be said. "Would it be easier if we weren't together?" Swallowing over the painful lump in my throat, I peer deep into his baby blues. "Is Bianca right? Are Audrey and Alex? Should I let you go so you can focus on your career?"

"No, Viv. Jesus, no." He lies down, tugging me on top of him. "That is the last thing I want." Clasping my nape, he pulls my face to his. "I can't do this without you," he whispers, brushing his lips across mine. "I don't want to be without you. I know it will be hard, but not having you in my life would be infinitely harder." Tears swim in his eyes. "I hate that you think I'd want that. You're the love of my life, Viv. You're my soul mate and the only woman I want by my side until the day I die. That hasn't changed, and it's never going to." Banding his arms around me, he rests my head on his hot, bare chest. "Please don't leave me," he whispers. "You're the one true constant in my life. The only one who fully understands me. The only one who loves me unconditionally. I can't lose you, Viv. I couldn't exist without you."

I lift my head, brushing his tears away. "You're all that for me too, Reeve, but I need you to promise me something."

"Anything, babe." He traces his fingers up and down my spine.

"If that changes, I need you to be honest with me."

"Always, Viv, but I know my heart, and nothing will change."

I place my hands on his chest, looking him straight in the eye. "This is going to be a true test of our love, Reeve, and let's not pretend like the last three months have been smooth sailing. We both know it's been anything but. We won't survive unless there is total transparency between us, especially if I have to pretend I'm not your girlfriend." I almost choke on the words. "I don't like it, and I still think you should stand your ground, but it's your career, your decision, and I'll do my best to support you, but you need to be truthful with me."

"I will. I promise." He kisses me softly. "It's going to be okay, Viv."

I wish I shared his optimism.

The rest of the summer passes in blissful peace, and it's just like old times. We spend most days at the beach or hanging out by the pool. At night, we go to the movies or head out for dinner, and there are always several parties to attend. Some paparazzi show up, on occasion, but, for the most part, they seem to have forgotten about Reeve for now. I know it won't last. I know as soon as the promo starts, things are going to ramp up overnight, but I'm trying not to think about it. To just enjoy being with Reeve and our friends. We have slotted seamlessly back into our easygoing relationship, as if the pain of our separation was a figment of our imaginations.

In the end, Audrey and I decide to take a dorm on campus, and I'm grateful I'll get to share the college experience with my bestie. It helps to soften the blow of Reeve's absence.

Most of the undergraduate dorms are in the northwest part of UCLA, called the Hill, and we manage to secure a two-bedroom suite with a private bathroom and living space. It's not huge, by any stretch of the imagination, but it's got everything we need. Reeve and Alex came shopping with us, and we picked up lots of things that will help to make the space homey. Reeve will be gone filming reshoots—starting from next Monday—but he'll be back in time to help us move into our dorm in three weeks.

The guys surprised us this week with a mini vacay to Laguna Beach, renting a fabulous five-bedroom house that is right on the beach. The four of us arrived four days ago, and we've spent our days exploring the different beaches, coves, and tidal pools and filling our days with sunbathing, swimming, snorkeling, and surfing. At night, we've dined out and returned to our place to enjoy some drinks on the gorgeous deck facing the beach, sipping cocktails under the stars while the gentle ebb and flow of the ocean provides a soothing backdrop to our conversation. It's hella romantic and just what the doctor ordered.

Reeve and I have taken midnight walks on the gorgeous sandy shore each night, holding hands and stealing kisses, and it's exactly what we need to remind us of what we have before we are forced to go our separate ways again.

It's Thursday night, and the guys are grilling steaks and chicken out on the deck while Audrey and I prepare salads in the large fully-equipped kitchen. "What's this Rudy guy like?" Audrey asks, while we slice tomatoes and dice onions side by side at the counter.

"He seems like a good guy, but I've only spoken to him a few times. I know Reeve hit it off with him almost immediately and he's his closest friend on the set." Rudy is due to arrive soon along with Nate, and he said he might bring a couple of others from school. Reeve wasn't keen on Nate joining us, but his parentals just announced they are getting a divorce, and Alex says he's really messed up and he could use a few days away. It sounds like a recipe for disaster, if you ask me, but he has been on his best behavior since the night of my eighteenth birthday, and like it or not, he's Alex's friend.

The doorbell chimes, and I set my knife down, padding to the front door in my silver flip-flops. I quickly check my reflection in the hallway mirror, to ensure I'm presentable.

Unlike the nights we glammed up for dinner on the town, I haven't made much of an effort with my appearance tonight. There didn't seem much point since we're just entertaining at home, but I still want to look nice. So, I'm wearing a short white summery dress with thin straps, my hair is wavy and running loose down my back, and I'm only wearing a touch of lip gloss and mascara. Satisfied I'll do, I march to the door and swing it open.

I'm immediately swept up into a set of strong arms and twirled around. "Hello, beautiful," Rudy says, swinging me around once more before planting my feet on the ground. "Wow. Reeve wasn't exaggerating. You're gorgeous." He dazzles me with a stunning smile as he rakes his gaze over me.

Warmth spreads up my neck as I return his smile. "And you're every bit as charming as Reeve told me you would be."

"Don't believe everything those two tell you," an unwelcome female says. "They are thick as thieves on set and always up to mischief." I work hard to keep the smile plastered to my face when Saffron—carrying two large suitcases—appears behind Rudy, but it's difficult when your arch-nemesis shows up without warning.

What the fuck is she doing here? If Reeve knew about this and purposely didn't tell me, there will be hell to pay.

CHAPTER 15

I HATE TO ADMIT IT, but Saffron is even more beautiful in real life, even if she's heavily made up and wearing the tackiest designer dress with matching wedge heels. Her long jet-black hair is thick, glossy, and smooth, her complexion is flawless, her big, blue eyes draw you in, and she has enviable curves in all the right places. I'm taller than her, even in my flip-flops, but what she lacks in height she makes up for with confidence. Her tight-fitting red minidress leaves little to the imagination, and her large boobs are almost spilling out of the top.

I understand some of the vitriol I've seen directed at her online by fans of the series. While she has Abby's dark good looks, she doesn't have the lithe, small-chested, dancer's body as described in the books. It's clear the studio decided to take a gamble on displeasing the die-hard *Rydeville Elite* series fans in the hopes Saffron's notoriety and sex appeal will endear her to the wider audience. She also has a loyal, core following of her own who defend her to the nth degree anytime anyone accuses her of being miscast.

Holding her head up high, she flashes me a toothy smile, and I have a sudden urge to rip every strand of hair out of her head. Without warning, she digs her elbow into Rudy's side. "Thanks for leaving me with the luggage, doofus."

"Dude, you never…" Reeve's voice trails off as he strides down the tiled hallway toward us. His eyes widen as he whips his head to look at me. Panic is etched across his face, and I'm glad he knows this is a problem. "Saff, what are you doing here?" he asks, rubbing the back of his neck.

Saff? Are you fucking kidding me?! Anger mixes with hurt at the obvious familiarity between them.

"Surprise!" Rudy says, his eyes bouncing between me and Reeve as he suddenly realizes he might have made a boo-boo.

Dropping the cases on the floor, Saffron flings her arms around Reeve's neck, and I dig my nails into my palms while grinding my teeth to the molars. "Aw, don't pretend like you didn't miss me," she says, as Reeve quickly shucks out of her embrace.

I move over to him, slinging my arm around his waist. Reeve's arm automatically encircles my shoulders, and I suction myself to his side while trying to restrain from snarling at the bitch who is still standing way too close to my man.

"You two are so cute; bucking the trend for childhood sweethearts," she says, grinning.

"What trend is that?" I ask, tightening my hold around Reeve.

"Most high school sweethearts split up by the time they graduate." She keeps the fake smile glued to her face while she stares at me.

"I think you'll find that's bullshit, and couples who get together in high school are less likely to divorce than couples who meet under other circumstances." According to the report I read online, less than two percent of couples who marry are high school sweethearts, but they stand a higher chance of success than couples who didn't meet in high school. Not that I'm admitting I googled this shit during dark moments a few months ago when I was beginning to doubt if Reeve and I would last the distance.

"Sounds like someone has done their research." She plants her hands on her hips, licks her lips, and smiles at Reeve. "What about you, movie star? Have you done your homework?"

Movie star. Blech.

"Knock it off, Saff," Rudy says.

She laughs, tilting her head to the side and bracing me with a wide smile. "Relax, Rudes. Viv knows I'm just teasing."

"My name is Vivien. Only my close friends call me Viv," I say through gritted teeth, digging my nails into Reeve's side.

"My bad." She pats my arm in a condescending fashion before looping her arm through Rudy's. "Let's get this party started. I'm in dire need of a drink."

They wander off toward the kitchen while I drag Reeve into the nearest room, which happens to be the study, and shut the door.

"What the fuck is she doing here?" I hiss, pacing the hardwood floor while blood boils in my veins.

Reeve throws up his hands. "I didn't invite her. I swear. This is all Rudy's doing."

"I want her to leave," I say, fisting handfuls of my hair. "I already cannot stand her, and there's no way she's ruining the last three days of our vacation."

"Viv." Reeve stalks toward me, reeling me into his arms. "I know you don't like her, and I understand why, but maybe this is a good thing."

I arch a brow, because surely, he's not that stupid?

"I can't kick her out, babe. She's my costar, and it would cause tension between us on set. I know she's a big flirt, but she flirts with everyone. She's not interested in me, I promise." He clasps both sides of my face. "She's fun, and if you give her a chance, you'll see that."

"I very much doubt it." I know her sort, and whether Reeve wants to believe it or not, she wouldn't think twice about screwing him, girlfriend or no girlfriend. "And it's not just whether she wants you. She spent months kissing and making out with you on set." Even the thought of her hands or her lips anywhere near Reeve sends me

82

into a blind rage. I don't know how I'm going to sit through the premiere and not want to hurl.

"Viv, you seriously can't hold that against me? It's my job, and it meant nothing to either of us." He cocks his head to the side, examining my face.

I know I'm being irrational. I know actors and actresses have to act intimate with costars to play parts. I've seen my mom in sex scenes on the big screen and while it always makes me squirm, I know it's not real. But this is Reeve, and the reality of him doing this is very different than the idea of it. "I know you were acting, Reeve, and I know I'll have to get used to it, but I can't help how I feel." My eyes fill up. "I hate thinking of her with you like that. It makes me sick, and I really don't need my nose rubbed in it."

"Do you think I like being around Nate knowing his lips have touched yours and he most likely jacks off to visions of you on your knees?"

"Reeve!" I swat his chest. "Firstly, eww." A full-body shudder works its way through me. "And secondly, it's not the same thing."

"I don't like that he's here, but I put my feelings aside because Alex is worried about him."

Now, I feel selfish. Which I'm sure is the point.

"Baby." He bundles me against his chest, holding me tight. "You have nothing to worry about. *I love you.* I don't know what else to say or do to show you she means nothing more to me than a friend." He tilts my face up to his. "Do you honestly think I would jeopardize our love for anyone or anything?"

"No, but she doesn't care about our history. She just wants to fuck you."

"Viv. She's got a boyfriend. She doesn't want me like that, and even if she did, it wouldn't matter when I don't want her. I only want you."

He's saying all the right things, so why am I struggling to believe it? I sigh, resting my forehead on his chest. Am I overthinking this? Am I reading more into it and tying myself into knots for no reason?

"Look at it like this," Reeve continues, dotting kisses into my hair. "Let her see us together. Let her see how much we are in love. Let her see how I can't keep my hands off you and how I have eyes for no one but my sexy girlfriend."

"Okay," I reluctantly concede. "But if she's rude to me, she's out of here."

"Scout's honor, babe." Reeve lowers his mouth to kiss me. "Your happiness is my sole focus, Viv, but it would be good if you could find a way to make your peace with her because I'm going to be working closely with her for the next couple of years, and having my costar and my girlfriend at odds will really stress me out."

I know I'm never going to warm to Saffron Roberts, but I vow to try to get along with her. Or at least to pretend—like she's clearly doing—for Reeve's sake.

Reeve stays true to his word, and he's an attentive boyfriend the entire weekend. He barely leaves my side, and he ensures he's close to me whenever Saffron is around so she has little opportunity to deliver any sly digs. Saffron loves the sound of her own voice, and she enjoys regaling us with stories of her escapades. Her voice grates on my nerves, and every second in her company only confirms my initial opinion of her.

Nate has been hanging off her every word and following her around like a little lost puppy, but I'm actually glad he's here, because he's helping to keep her distracted.

It's Saturday night, our last night at Laguna Beach, and we decide to enjoy some drinks at the house before hitting a club later. Audrey and I went all out with our outfits and our makeup, and we're both wearing little black dresses with high heels. I've consumed a few vodka cocktails, and I'm nicely buzzed, sitting on top of Reeve's lap as we chat outside on the deck.

"So, *Vivien*," Saffron says, enunciating my name like she has been since Thursday night when I ripped into her for calling me Viv. "I didn't have you down as a screamer, but judging by the sounds coming from your room last night, I'm guessing movie star has learned a few moves."

She winks at Reeve, and he smirks. I barely resist the urge to thump him. I detest how she calls him movie star, and I'm not fond of her insinuation that Reeve has somehow picked up new skills. I will admit I've been fucking Reeve into a virtual coma these past two nights, purposely screaming and moaning louder than normal to ensure she hears. It's juvenile but satisfying.

Tossing my hair over my shoulder, I fix her with a smug grin as I run my fingers through Reeve's hair. He's had to leave it longer on top and shorter at the sides for his role, and I enjoy having more hair to tug on when we're having sex. "My Reeve has always had mad skills in the bedroom. He knows how to keep me happy. Isn't that right, baby?" I purr before pressing my lips to his.

"But you've only ever slept with each other, right?" she says, snuggling under Nate's arm. I hope to fuck that's an educated guess—that Reeve didn't confide in her how we lost our virginity to one another. Nate stares at Saffron like he's just won the lottery. Idiot. Still, if he keeps her occupied tonight, I might start having nicer thoughts about him.

"And your point is?" I ask, running my fingers up and down Reeve's arm.

"Variety is the spice of life, and you don't know what you're missing until you've tried it." She rubs Nate's thigh, and the growing bulge in his shorts makes me gag. "I never thought I'd enjoy fucking a woman, but it was an enlightening experience."

Rudy laughs, Reeve spits his beer out, Alex's eyes pop wide, and Nate's mouth hangs open.

"Is this the wife of the director you were having an affair with or a different woman?" Audrey asks, her voice carrying an edge.

"You shouldn't believe everything you read online," Saffron replies, smirking a little. "Our three-way relationship was entirely consensual, as was the information we leaked to the press when it came to a natural end."

"You leaked details of the affair?" I blurt, disbelief evident in my tone. Considering how she's already shown herself to be a media-hungry whore, I don't know why I'm surprised.

"Of course." She moves her hand up higher on Nate's thigh. "It put my name on the map, strengthened my brand, and led to tons of new roles. There is nothing like a bit of salacious gossip to get everyone talking about you."

"I'm more interested in you getting it on with this chick," Rudy says, waggling his brows. "I want deets." He makes a rude hand gesture, and the guys all laugh.

"We never got it on alone. It was always when her husband was there. She liked watching him fuck me, and he liked watching us fuck each other with our fingers and our tongues. I fucked her with a strap-on once while he watched. Another time he fucked my ass while she ate me out. Then this one time, she fucked him with the strap-on while he fucked me. It was hot while it lasted, but I'm not really into pussy. I'm all about the D."

She says this while eyeballing me, and I'm uncomfortable with her attention, her obvious experience, and complete lack of shame. If I didn't dislike her so much, I might admire her sexual confidence. I think I'm adventurous if I ride Reeve reverse cowgirl style or he takes me from behind.

"Aw, you're blushing. It's so cute." She laughs at my discomfort.

"Saff. Don't be mean," Reeve says, and I'm glad he called her on it.

"Maybe you need to learn a few new skills, movie star," she replies, winking at Reeve before knocking back a few mouthfuls of beer.

"I don't understand why any couple in their situation would want to leak the details to the press. What did they get out of it?" Audrey asks, and I could kiss her for redirecting the conversation.

"More willing bed partners," Saffron replies. "And it didn't harm Bryan's directorial career either. Sex sells," she adds, like we haven't heard that one before. "Reeve understands that. Don't you, movie star?" She licks her lips while her hand moves to cover Nate's crotch. Nate groans, nuzzling into her neck as he pulls her in tight to his side.

Reeve almost chokes on his beer, and his eyes pop wide in alarm.

Saffron smiles sweetly at me, but she's like a viper waiting to deliver the fatal strike. "It's why he readily signed his new contract agreeing to fake a relationship with me."

CHAPTER 16

JUMPING OFF REEVE'S LAP, I storm into the house, even though I know I'm playing right into that bitch's hand. But I can't stay outside because I'm liable to either break down in tears, strangle Saffron Roberts, or murder Reeve. She carefully timed that reveal to cause maximum damage, just as Reeve has to leave to film reshoots with her. I hate that woman like I have never hated anyone before in my life.

"Vivien!" Reeve races after me, and I ignore him, striding toward our bedroom as murderous rage infiltrates my veins. "Viv. Baby, stop." Reeve grabs my arm and pushes me up against the wall, crowding me with his body.

"Let me go, you fucking asshole. I hate you!" I shout. I don't need to ask if it's true, because I was witness to the panicked look on his face before his costar spilled the beans.

"No. We need to talk about this. Look at me, Viv." He grips my chin, forcing my angry gaze to meet his worried one.

"You lied! You already fucking lied after just promising me you would always be open and honest!" I shriek.

"I was going to tell you tomorrow when we got home, I swear."

"Your words are empty, Reeve. The same as your promises."

"I knew this would piss you off, so I was trying to find a way of breaking it to you that would cause the least amount of pain."

I bark out a laugh. "Don't pretend you care about my feelings. You're more worried about upsetting that ho than you are about hurting me."

"That is not fucking fair or true." He slams his hand into the wall, and I'm glad I'm not the only one who is angry. "It was a condition of the contract, Viv! I told Bianca I wouldn't sign it unless that clause was removed, but the studio refused."

"That's bullshit, Reeve, and you know it. You're the star of this movie. The fans are already going crazy for you. If this movie is going to be as big as predicted, there's no way they can recast Camden Marshall. You have leverage, Reeve. You're the one with the power in this situation. All you had to do was tell them that clause was a deal breaker, and they would've conceded. I bet that bitch Bianca has been filling your head with crap because this feeds into her agenda too," I fume.

"This is bigger than me, Viv. Fans of the series aren't happy that Saffron has been cast as Abby."

"I don't disagree," I snap.

He continues, ignoring my little outburst. "It's an issue if they don't get on board. While Saff has her own loyal following, the series fans could make or break this movie."

"More bullshit," I hiss. "This isn't a PG-13 movie. The main target audience will be adults, and most adults don't give a crap about stuff that's said online. And what does some fans objecting to Saffron's casting have to do with you agreeing to a fake relationship?"

"The studio believes the fans will come around if they think we're in a real relationship. That it'll cement us as Abby and Cam. Ultimately, it's for the greater good of the movie. That's why I agreed, and I got it modified so we only need to hint at a relationship in public. It won't go beyond a few fake dates, some holding hands, and suggestive looks. I won't have to kiss her. I made them take that out."

"Well, that makes it all okay then!" I yell. I shove at his chest, but he's a solid wall of muscle. "Get the fuck away from me. I can't even look at you right now." I shove him again, and I'm seconds away from beating him with my fists.

"I'm not budging until we fix this."

I snort, balling my hands into fists at my sides. "The only way you can fix this is to get that fucking contract modified."

"You know I can't do that. Please, Viv." He rests his forehead against mine. "Please don't make a big deal out of this."

"Are you for fucking real—"

"Oops, sorry." Saffron tugs on Nate's hand as she pulls him past us in the hallway. "I didn't mean to interrupt."

"I'm sure you didn't," I scoff.

"Leave us the fuck alone, Saffron," Reeve snaps, and I'm glad he's not hiding his anger from her. Maybe all hope isn't lost after all.

"We'll just be on our way," she says, ignoring me and mouthing "sorry" at Reeve.

I stare numbly after her and Nate, watching them walk up the stairs, groping and laughing like my world isn't crumbling around me in shattered piles. "I thought she was fucking the assistant director?" I say to Reeve.

"We broke up. He was too old and boring. Younger guys have much more stamina!" she shouts down the stairs, and I flip her the bird, even though she can't see me.

"You mean he served his purpose and you're chasing the next victim who can help your brand?!" I roar up the stairs at her.

Reeve can deny it all he wants, but I know she has her sights set on him. Pity he's too fucking blind to see she's already laying the groundwork, and I hate how much she's coming between us. I'm so frustrated I could scream, and I'm mad at my boyfriend for sucking me into all this drama. I shove his shoulders again. "Get off me. I mean it, Reeve. If you don't step back, I will not be responsible for my actions. Right now, I hate you. I hate you with the heat of a thousand suns." My anger gives way to pain. "How could you agree to this?" I cry. "You didn't even consult me about it. We used to discuss everything, and you never made decisions that impact me without my input." I shake my head as tears stream down my face. "What happened to me grounding you, huh?"

"What happened to you supporting me?!" he shouts, eventually pulling away from me.

"I have always supported you, Reeve."

He harrumphs, flattening his back against the wall across the hallway. "All you have done since I got this role is bitch and whine. I have never given you any reason to doubt my loyalty, yet you hurl accusations at me all the time. I can't handle your insecurities, Viv. Do you have any idea of the stress I'm under? I don't need this shit from you. You know it's not real. It's part of the industry." He pushes off the wall. "For fuck's sake, more than half the so-called relationships in Hollywood are fake. It means nothing, Viv. It's part of the role, and I am getting sick of repeating myself."

"If I'm that unsupportive, you know what to do," I challenge, rubbing my tears away and straightening my shoulders. We stare at one another across the hallway, and there may as well be an ocean between us.

"I don't want to break up, Viv," he eventually says, walking toward me. He takes my hand and links our fingers together. "I love you, but you've got to find a way to deal with this."

"And if I can't?" I don't know how to reconcile this new development with my own wants and needs.

He shrugs, looking sad, and we don't need to articulate it.

I wrench my hands from his, briefly closing my eyes as pain lances me on all sides. "I'm calling a car to take me home," I say after a few tense minutes of silence.

"No, Viv. Please don't do that."

"I can't be around that bitch another second."

"I'll come with you," he offers.

"I don't want you to." I eyeball him, letting him see the full extent of my devastation. "I need some space to think."

"Don't do this, baby. I don't want to leave for reshoots when we're arguing."

"You should've thought of that before you lied to me again."

I walk off, and this time, he doesn't follow me.

"Hey." Audrey steps into my home studio the following day, and I stop my sewing machine, setting the piece of multicolored fabric down on the table.

"You're back." I swivel around in my chair.

Audrey props her butt against the edge of the table. "How are you feeling today?"

I shrug. "Hurt. Scared. Confused."

"He gave Saffron hell this morning at breakfast before we all went our separate ways."

"It's too little, too late. I never thought Reeve would be such a pushover, but he's letting all these horrible people manipulate him."

"He explained a little on the car ride home, and he's as upset as you are over everything."

My anger flares again, and I dig my nails into my thigh. "That's just not good enough, and I'm not buying it. If this movie is going to be as big as predicted, there's no way they would go ahead with the other films without their leading man. Reeve holds all the cards, not the other way around. He didn't have to agree to this. He *chose* to." Leaning back, I kick my bare feet up on the table. "It was that bitch, Bianca. She was the one who pushed this. All Reeve had to do was talk to my mom or talk to Margaret Andre, and they would have given him good advice."

"Reeve wants to do things by himself. He doesn't want to run to your mom and be accused of nepotism, and I really think getting his dad to notice him is the driving force behind a lot of this."

"He told you that?" I know how desperate Reeve is to be a success in the hopes his father will sit up and take notice of him.

"He got really drunk last night after you left, and before you ask, no, he didn't seek her out or spend any time with her when you were gone. She fucked Nate, or at least that's what Nate said this morning. Anyway, the three of us stayed out on the deck drinking until the early hours. Reeve spilled his guts to me and Alex. He was a mess, babe. He's terrified of losing you, and he was crying his heart out. It was hard to witness and not feel some compassion."

Slamming my feet to the ground, I jump up. "So, it's like that. You've switched teams now?"

"Jesus, dramatic much?" She pins me with a stern look, planting her hands on her hips. "Do not ever accuse me of that shit. I am always, *always*, on Team Vivien. One hundred fucking percent, no matter if you turn into the world's biggest bitch."

My shoulders relax as I exhale heavily. "Sorry. I'm a mess too," I admit, plopping back into my chair. I rest my elbows on my knees and prop my head in my hands. "I don't want to lose him, but how do I hide in the shadows while he pretends that bitch is his girlfriend?" I sniffle, fighting tears. I am so sick of crying because of that ho's interference. "I can't do it, Rey. I just don't think I can do that."

Kneeling in front of me, she takes my hands in hers. "I don't envy you this decision, but I will support you no matter what you choose to do."

"What would you do?"

"I can't answer that, Viv, because we're different people and I don't have a Reeve in my life. He's more than just your boyfriend. He's your best friend. Your family. He's a part of every happy memory you have, and I know that won't be easy to walk away from, even if that's what you decide to do for your sanity."

"I love him so much," I cry. "I really do, but he's changing, and I don't know if I like the person he's becoming."

"He's still the same Reeve underneath it all. You're not the only one struggling to adjust. I don't think he's doing this deliberately to hurt you, but he has been cowardly and secretive, and that shit's definitely not cool."

"I can't bear the thought of the entire world believing they are in this epic romance. I think the media coverage will break my heart, but if I let him go, then what's to stop him from starting something real with her?" This is the crux of my dilemma. "If I walk away, I'm handing Reeve to her on a silver platter, and I might lose him forever."

"I'd love to refute that, but I can't," she says, reclaiming her seat. "I saw her watching him all weekend. She's a good actress, I'll give her that, but a woman knows."

"I know she wants him. I'm just not sure if it's because she would get a kick out of stealing him from me, whether she genuinely has feelings for him, or she just sees him as a means of elevating her star power higher."

"I doubt she feels anything for him. It's about what he can do for her career, and I've no doubt she would love to stick the knife in your back. You two traded barbed insults all weekend, and you've definitely laid down the gauntlet now." Audrey tucks her lustrous red hair behind one ear. "If there is anything positive to come from the weekend, it's that Reeve did see what you've been saying. He was not one bit happy with her when she left for the airport with Rudy."

"Maybe her plane will crash, and problem solved," I deadpan.

Audrey laughs. "Maybe you shouldn't say stuff like that. You don't want the bad karma."

"Fuck karma. If it existed, that manipulative bitch would've already gotten what's coming to her."

Reeve doesn't call or make an appearance, and that only adds to my foul mood. I'm being unfair, because I told him I need space and he's not a mind reader.

Or maybe he is.

"Knock, knock," he says in my ear, as I'm hunched over my sewing machine later that night.

"Oh my freaking God!" I shriek, slamming a hand over my chest, willing my pounding heart to slow down. "Don't creep up on me like that. You nearly gave me a coronary."

"I did knock, but you clearly couldn't hear me." He tugs on my earbuds.

I turn around, and his doleful expression mirrors my own. His Adam's apple bobs in his throat as we stare at one another. "I know you probably still hate me, but I'm flying out tomorrow for two weeks, and I can't leave without trying to make things right."

"I don't hate you," I say, in a quiet voice. "Sometimes, I wish I could. It might make things easier."

"I couldn't bear it if you hated me, Viv. I hate that you're hurting and it's my fault. I'm hurting too," he adds, taking my hand and pulling me to my feet. "I don't want any of this, and it's killing me inside."

Sighing, I wrap my arms around him, closing my eyes as I rest my head on his chest. The steady thrumming of his heart is comforting. "I just don't see how we can make this work, Reeve."

"Walk with me?" he asks, and I find myself nodding.

We don't talk as he leads me out of the house and down to the rose garden. It's clearly much later than I thought, as it's pitch-dark out, and we only have the garden lamps to light our path.

I suck in a gasp as we near our tree, spotting the large tent that wasn't there this morning. A myriad of twinkling lights is hanging from the inside of the tent, which has been erected over a temporary wooden floor. The roof of the tent is clear, offering a perfect view of the nighttime sky. Scented candles mix with the perfume of roses wafting in the air as we step inside. A comfortable bed has been set up, adorned with tons of soft cushions, behind a small table and two chairs. A bottle of champagne is chilling on ice, and my tummy rumbles appreciatively as the aroma of hot pizza hits my nostrils. "What's all this?"

"I thought we could sleep under the stars, in one of our favorite places, and remember everything we mean to each other." His eyes fill up with tears. "I can't lose you, Viv. If that's where your mind is at, I'll pull out of the production. They can sue me for breach of contract. I don't care anymore. None of it will matter anyway if I lose you."

"Reeve." I fling my arms around him and we hug each other tight. "You can't do that. Your career would be over before it's begun."

"You matter more than my career, and maybe I had begun to lose sight of that, but not anymore. I'll give it all up for you, if that's what you want."

One part of me screams yes, but I know I can't ask him to do that. I can't ask him to give up everything for me. That would drill the final nail in our coffin some day when he came to resent me for forcing him into a life that is less than what he desired. "I would never ask you to give up your dreams for me, Reeve, but I am asking you to consider my feelings before you make decisions that impact me. Don't shut me out. Let me be involved. No more secrets."

I press my mouth to his, and he readily opens for me. So many emotions are swirling through my veins as we kiss, but for the first time in twenty-four hours, I have some clarity. I can't lose Reeve. He is the other half of my soul, which is why the pain cuts so deep.

Reeve deepens our kiss, holding my body flush against his, as he reassures me with his lips and his tongue. I don't know if I'm strong enough to do this, but I'm not giving up without at least trying, and I'm not going down without a fight.

CHAPTER 17

AUDREY and I have settled into our dorm, and we're making new friends and coming to grips with our classes and assignments, so I don't have too much time to pine for Reeve. He spent most of September and October auditioning for other roles, and buzz is definitely building for him in Hollywood. November sees the start of filming the second *Rydeville Elite* movie, but they begin heavy promotion for the first movie in early December. You can't turn on the TV or open social media without something popping up about the impending release.

"Have you seen this?" Audrey looks at her phone as we're gathering our stuff to head home for Christmas break.

"You know I shut down all my social media accounts, so no." Since stuff started appearing online about Reeve and Saffron potentially "dating," the level of hatred toward me from the Saffhards—Saffron's die-hard fans—escalated to such an extent I had to remove myself altogether from social media. While some of Reeve's fans came out in support of me, most were shipping Reeve with his costar and trolling me like crazy. All that shit is depressing, and I'm taking what steps I can to protect my mental health and my sanity.

"*Reeveron,*" Audrey says, in a scathing tone, and I stop folding my sweaters to stare at her. "That's what the fandom is calling Reeve and Saffron."

"Great, they have a ship name. Totally awesome." Sarcasm drips from my tone.

"This sucks." She slings a comforting arm around me.

I rest my head on her shoulder. "It does, especially when I barely get to speak to him these days." Reeve is on an international tour at the moment, so between our busy schedules and the time difference, it's virtually impossible to find time to talk. We're communicating mainly via messages, but he's coming home for three days over Christmas, and I can't wait to see him.

"Are you holding up okay? Will you see Alex at Christmas?"

"It's harder than I thought it would be, and I don't know." She chews on her lip as pain flares in her eyes.

"What's happened?"

Tears flood her eyes. "I think he's already found a new girlfriend."

"No way." I shake my head. "I can't see Alex in a new relationship already. I saw his face the day you two said goodbye. He was devastated."

Her fingers fly over her screen. "Look." She thrusts her cell in my face. "See that blonde? She's in a few of his photos, and she's hanging off him in every single one."

I scroll through the photos, examining them closely. "All this proves is Alex has groupies. See how she's draped over him?" I point to the image on the screen before flicking to the next one. "Sure, he's smiling at the camera, but he's not touching her. She's touching him." She's a fuck buddy, most likely, but I'm not saying that out loud because I don't want to upset my bestie, and Audrey has been a rock for me this past year.

"It doesn't matter anyway." She wipes her tears with the sleeve of her sweater. "We broke up, so he's free to date, and I can't get pissy about it. I just didn't think it would hurt this much."

I bundle her into a hug, and she sobs into my shoulder. "We're a sorry pair," I admit when we break apart. "And I know exactly what we need. Movie night at my place with ice cream. Your parentals aren't home until tomorrow anyway, right?"

She bobs her head, and I loop my arm through hers. "It's settled then. We're heading to Chez Mills."

Christmas comes and goes, and I didn't get to spend much quality time with Reeve since he was so exhausted and sleeping all the time, thanks to Mr. Jet Lag. However, at least I got to sleep beside him and derive what little comfort I could.

The past three weeks have flown by, and now it's the night of the premiere. I hate that I'm dreading it, but it's nothing like how I imagined it would be. In all my dreams, I was on Reeve's arm as we greeted his fans on the red carpet, just like I've seen my parents work the crowd at Mom's premieres. My reality couldn't be any further removed from that fantasy.

"Oh, Vivien," Mom exclaims entering my room, her eyes popping wide as I turn to face her in my dress. It's a strapless lemon chiffon gown with intricate silver diamante- beading over the corset top and dotted around the full skirt. The hem is longer at the back while it's shorter at the front to highlight my lower legs and the gorgeous silver sandals on my feet.

I designed and made the dress myself, aiming for understated elegance. For two seconds, I'd considered creating a spectacular gown that would ensure I was the talk of the night, just to rub Saffron's nose in it, but that's like something she'd do to try to steal my thunder, and I won't sink to her level. Besides, drawing attention to myself would only backfire on Reeve, and he went to huge efforts to get me into the premiere. Bianca and the studio were hell-bent on excluding me, but everyone knows Reeve and I grew up together and our families are super close, so it's not inconceivable that I'd be there, even if we are supposedly broken up.

"I'm really wondering if you should have gone the design route in college because your talent is incredible." Mom examines the intricate beading.

"I couldn't agree more," Marlena says, standing back to admire the job she did on my hair and makeup. Again, I opted for simple. My hair is gently pulled away from my face with a few carefully placed diamond clips, and it flows in soft waves down my back. Marlena focused mainly on my eyes, creating a sultry smoky look, and she finished it off with nude lips and a light blush on my cheeks. "You look stunning, Vivien. Like a bona fide Hollywood princess."

"Thank you." I squeeze her hands. "If I look stunning, it's because you worked your magic, as usual."

Marlena spins around to Mom. "And this is why you two are my favorite clients. You must be so proud of your daughter. It's rare to meet such genuine people in this business."

"You're a sweetheart," Mom tells her, giving her a quick hug. "Just like my daughter and that wife of yours."

"Where is my better half?" Marlena asks.

"Carole went to load up the car. She said she'd meet you outside."

"Have a great night," Marlena says, waving as she strides toward my door. "And tell Reeve I said congratulations."

"I will, if I see him," I mumble under my breath.

"Aw, honey." Mom threads her fingers in mine. "I hate that we have to enter through the back like thieves in the night, but Reeve knows we are there, and it's our support he needs."

"I'm trying to be less selfish, but it's hard. I hate that I can't walk the red carpet with my boyfriend on his big night. Even worse, I hate that *she* will be hanging off his every word, fueling the rumors and getting one over on me at the same time."

"You have his heart," Mom reminds me. "Something she will never have." Her expression softens. "And Reeve will die when he sees you in this creation. It's perfect, Vivien. Truly perfect. Regal and sophisticated, yet not too ostentatious. No one can accuse you of trying to upstage that attention-seeking madam."

I grin despite my anxiety. Mom always knows the perfect thing to say to settle my frayed nerves. "You look incredible, Mom," I say, admiring the white silk Ralph Lauren gown. It's a classic figure-hugging design, and the material clings to Mom's enviable curves. It dips low at the front, showcasing her cleavage, but it's still classy and elegant. Mom has paired it with diamond studs in her ears and a matching bracelet and necklace.

"Wow. I'm going to be the envy of every man at this premiere tonight," Dad says, entering the room. "You both look beautiful." He kisses us gently on the cheeks, careful not to mess up our makeup. "This is for you from Reeve." Dad hands me a small black velvet box.

"No crying," Mom warns, spotting the emotion building in my eyes.

I pop the lid on the box, gasping at the gorgeous diamond earrings. My chest swells as my heart soars at the physical confirmation of his love. While I don't need or want expensive gifts, it is the thought that counts. I know that sounds cliché, but it's the truth. Just knowing he was thinking about me on his special night warms all the frozen parts of me. This is the Reeve I know, and I cling to that sentiment as we make our way to the limo and travel to the theater, because I know I'm going to need that reminder to survive this ordeal.

"Don't make a scene, Mom." I grab her arm to halt her forward trajectory. "I'm fine to sit here," I lie, struggling to maintain my composure. I knew I wouldn't be seated at the front, but shoving me into a seat by myself in the very back row of the theater over in the corner was not anticipated. If Bianca wanted to remind me of my place in Reeve's life, she's found a good way of driving the point home. My heart hurts. I'm in actual physical pain, and I don't know if I'm strong enough to do this. Maybe it would've been better for everyone if I had bowed out, but I want to be here to support him. Even if he won't see me hidden away like I'm an embarrassment.

I know Reeve would have requested I be seated with my parents, but no one in this town would dare relegate Lauren and Jonathon Mills to the shadows. They have no issue in disrespecting their daughter though.

"Absolutely not," Dad says, scrubbing a hand over his chin. "Take my seat for now while I find someone to fix this."

Mom extends her hand, and I clasp it as we walk down the center aisle to my parents' seats, which are about ten rows from the front. "This isn't good enough," Mom says, as we sit down. "Reeve should've ensured you were looked after."

"I'm sure he trusted it to someone else and they let him down."

Mom opens and closes her mouth in fast succession.

"What?" I can tell something is on her mind.

She shakes her head. "It can wait. Let's just try and enjoy the night."

I spot Simon Lancaster, Reeve's dad, talking to a couple of men in suits a few rows in front of us, and I'm glad he showed his face. All week, Reeve has been terrified he was going to pull out of attending. Noticing my attention, Simon waves to Mom and me, and we nod our heads in his direction.

Seats fill up fast, and there's still no sign of Dad or the main cast members. A large crowd turned up to greet them, and I'm betting they are still outside on the red carpet giving interviews, signing autographs, and posing for photos with the fans. I've deliberately avoided checking the coverage on my phone, because I don't want to witness Reeve and Saffron faking it for the public. I feel sick enough as it is.

"Hey." Dad materializes at the end of our row, crouching down. "There's nothing that can be done. They are at full capacity. I could make a scene, but that would force someone else to be moved, and I didn't think you'd want that, honey," he says to me.

"I wouldn't." I stand. "It's fine. Don't worry about me." I'll just go lick my wounds in the corner.

"Sit back down, Vivien. I'll take your seat. You stay with your mom."

"But Dad—"

"No buts, honey. No one puts my baby in the corner."

I bark out a laugh despite the pain slicing through my chest. "So cheesy."

"But so true. And it removed that sad look from your face." Leaning in, he kisses me on the cheek. "I'll be having words with that young man of yours later. This is not acceptable."

I shake my head. "No, Dad."

"I agree, Vivien. I'm disappointed in Reeve," Mom says.

"Don't say anything to him tonight, either of you. Please," I beg. "This is his big night, and I don't want to ruin it by upsetting him or arguing with him."

"As you wish," Mom says. "But this isn't right. I haven't said anything before now, because I didn't want to interfere, but Reeve isn't treating you right, and that isn't okay with me or your father. Frankly, we expect more from him."

"This isn't the time, Lauren," Dad says, as the main cast members appear at the entrance doors. "Enjoy the movie," he adds before turning around to walk back up the steps.

My heart thuds painfully behind my rib cage as Reeve and Saffron approach. She has her arm linked through his, and she's whispering animatedly in his ear. He's laughing at something she says, and I swear I feel the rupture splitting my heart into two. Reeve looks so handsome in his custom-made Armani suit. Saffron looks like a slut in a monstrous red silk and lace dress that leaves little to the imagination. If the top was any lower, you'd see her nipples.

"Hey, Viv." Rudy stops, leaning down to kiss my cheek. "You look beautiful."

"Thanks, Rudy. This is my mom, Lauren."

Rudy kisses Mom's hand. "I'm a big fan, and it's an honor to meet you."

"Thank you. This is an exciting night for all of you. We're looking forward to seeing the movie," Mom diplomatically replies.

"Lauren, Viv." Reeve stops to say hi with the clinger suctioned to his arm like she's a bloodsucking leech. Her glowing smile falters a little when she sees me beside Mom, but she recovers fast.

That bitch. She must have had something to do with the seating arrangements.

"Oh my God, it's so amazing to meet you, Lauren. You're my biggest inspiration, and I just adore you," Saffron gushes.

Mom gives her a tight smile but doesn't reply, glancing away, and that's as good a snub as anything she wishes she could say. I have never loved my mom more than I do in this moment. She always has my back, unlike some I could mention.

Saffron's eyes glint with malice as she leans into Reeve, placing her hand on his chest and peering up at him like he hung the moon.

I want to rip her hands away and pummel my fists into her face until I reveal the ugly monster hiding behind that beautiful exterior. I swear she must have been put on this Earth to test my self-control. Gripping my armrests tightly, I latch on to my anger, because it's better than letting the hurt take control.

The smile drops off Reeve's face when he sees my expression. "You go on," he tells Saffron.

"Okay, baby," she croons, pulling his head down and moving her lips toward his. Mom clamps her hand down on my arm to hold me in place. If she kisses him, all bets are off. I don't give a flying fuck how much trouble I'd land Reeve in.

Reeve turns his head, and her lips caress his cheek instead. Giggling, she shoots me a victory smile. "Don't be too long. It's just about to start. I can't wait for everyone to see what amazing chemistry we have." She walks off, grinning like she's the master of the universe. In her fucked-up brain, she probably thinks she is.

So much for no kissing and offering the public only hints of a relationship. It seems to have gone from zero to sixty in the blink of an eye.

Intense pain settles on my chest, as if someone has taken a baseball bat to my heart. My insides are tied into knots, and acid churns in my gut. I'm glad I couldn't stomach any dinner, because I'm pretty sure I'd have puked it back up. I wish I hadn't come now, and I'm tempted to leave, but I won't give that bitch the satisfaction.

"All that girl is missing is a scarlet A strapped to her chest," Mom says, drilling Reeve with a harsh look I would not like to be on the receiving end of.

"I'm sorry about that. I know she's a lot to handle."

"I hope you know what you've gotten yourself into, Reeve, and I'm not the one you should be apologizing to."

Reeve quickly glances around before mouthing "I'm sorry."

I can barely look at him, let alone speak. Reaching into my purse, I hand him the card I made for him. Our fingers brush in the exchange, and his touch sends tremors shooting up my arm, like always. However, it offers none of the usual comfort. His hand twitches, and while it's only a subtle gesture, it's enough to tell me he still feels our connection too.

I wonder if she ignites sparks in him, or if her touch makes his skin crawl like one look at her does to me.

"You look beautiful," he whispers, glancing around to ensure no one is paying too much attention. "Do you like the earrings?" he adds in another whisper.

I nod. "Thank you. You look hot," I croak, barely managing to get the words out.

An awkward silence descends, and I hate this. Even strangers would have some polite words to say, but I've got nothing. There's a distance between us for the first time ever, and I have no clue how I can close it. The lump in my throat is so painful I'm almost choking on air.

Cassidy, the studio's obnoxious PR person, rushes up to Reeve, whispering in his ear.

"I've got to go, but I'll see you at the after-party," Reeve says, shooting me another apologetic look. I nod tersely, watching him walk away with a horrid ache in my chest.

Mom takes my hand, holding it tight. "You don't have to deal with this. Just say the word, and we'll leave."

I squeeze her hand back. "Thanks, Mom, but I came here for Reeve, and I'm staying to support him." Whether he deserves it is another matter entirely.

CHAPTER 18

I GRAB another flute when a waiter passes by, depositing my empty glass on the table beside us. "At least there's free champagne," I deadpan, taking a healthy glug of the expensive amber-colored liquid as my eyes scan the packed hotel ballroom. My parents are doing the rounds, leaving me and Audrey to our own devices. While Reeve wasn't able to secure a ticket for my bestie to the premiere, he scored her an invite to the after-party. Thank god, because there's no way I would have attended without her. "Maybe if I drink enough, I can erase the image of Reeve with that bitch from my mind." I should probably lower my voice, but I'm beyond the point of caring.

The movie was good, but it's blatantly obvious Reeve is the star. His performance was utterly magnetic, and I am so proud of him. He nailed it completely, enough to become the latest hot commodity in Hollywood. Directors will be hammering his door down after tonight. Reeve's performance was so masterful I forgot who he was a lot of the time because he wore Camden Marshall's skin with effortless ease. However, I couldn't forget it was Reeve during the sex scenes. I had to close my eyes and not look after the first one almost killed me.

"She truly is shameless." Audrey glares daggers into Saffron's back. The bitch hasn't left Reeve's side, and my patience is in short supply. We've been at the after-party for over an hour, and Reeve hasn't come near us, apart from a fleeting hello when the main cast members arrived. He's the man of the moment, and everyone wants to speak to him, but it's like he's completely forgotten I'm here, and I'm getting sick of being an afterthought. If you had asked me a year ago if Reeve would ever treat me like this, I'd have laughed in your face.

My loving, attentive, protective boyfriend exists now only in my memory.

And I'm sad.

So sad and lonely.

"Fuck her," Audrey says, spotting the forlorn expression on my face. "When karma comes for her, we'll celebrate."

"Are you going to talk to Alex?" I inquire, needing to stop thinking and talking about Saffron fucking Roberts. Subtly, I jerk my head to the side where Alex is congregated with a couple of guys from our old high school. I've watched him sneak longing glances at Audrey when he thinks no one is looking, so I don't understand why he hasn't approached her yet.

"Probably not. Our last conversation at Christmas didn't go too well."

Alex and Audrey had met for coffee over the Christmas break, and they ended up having a massive argument when Alex confirmed he was sleeping with the blonde. They're not dating, just fucking, but the distinction doesn't matter to Audrey. It still hurts that he could move on so fast when they parted out of necessity, not because they had fallen out of love.

For a while, I wondered if Reeve and I should adopt Alex and Audrey's strategy, but it's clear it doesn't matter how you play it when feelings are involved. My bestie thought she could cut ties amicably and maturely and it wouldn't hurt. Technically, Alex hasn't done anything wrong, and apparently, guys find it easier to engage in no-strings-attached sex. But I honestly don't understand how you can switch off your feelings so quickly. You couldn't convince me Alex no longer loves Audrey. From the way he can't take his eyes off her tonight, it's clear she still owns his heart. Yet he wasted little time climbing into bed with another woman.

Men are such confusing bastards.

After a half an hour, and another glass of champagne, I have reached my limit, and I need to get out of here before I do something I regret. "Want to ditch?" I ask my bestie, and she eagerly nods.

"I was ready to ditch the second we got to the hotel."

"I'm just going to the bathroom. Can you find my parents and tell them we're leaving?"

She agrees, and I exit the ballroom, heading toward the ladies' restroom.

After attending to business, I step out of my stall to discover Saffron Roberts waiting for me. "I'm surprised you managed to peel yourself off Reeve. Clinging to his coattails makes you look desperate and pathetic," I say, my tongue much looser, thanks to the alcohol sluicing through my veins. I know she staged this little meet and greet, and I want to get the first shot in. "It's clear to everyone he's the star of the show, and you're destined to linger in his shadow."

She laughs, and it's a haughty, shrill sound that grates on my nerves. I wash my hands in the sink to keep them occupied so I don't do something reckless—like strangle her.

"The only person slinking into the shadows is *you*." She pins me with a smug look I instantly want to wipe off her face.

"I hate to disappoint you, *Saff*, but I'm going nowhere."

"It won't be up to you," she retorts.

"It sure as fuck won't be up to you." I wipe my hands on a paper towel before we face off. Even in her skyscraper heels, I am still taller, and I derive immense satisfaction in towering over her diminutive frame.

"Didn't anyone ever tell you not to underestimate your enemies?"

"I'm glad you're openly admitting the truth, and I'm not threatened by you." That latter part is a semi-lie, but I'll never admit it to her. I'm not threatened by Saffron, per se. It's what she represents and how easily she has injected herself between Reeve and me. I've begun questioning how strong our relationship really is, if it's crumbling this fast at the first sign of trouble.

She steps closer, prodding her finger into my chest. "You should be."

I shove her finger away. "Reeve loves me. He has loved me his entire life. You will never compete with that."

"He might think he loves you, but it's only because he's known no different. I mean, look at me and look at you." Her scathing gaze roams me from head to toe, obliterating the last of my patience.

"Exactly. Reeve would never choose a skank like you over me, but continue to daydream, you delusional bitch." I move to sidestep her, because I'm done breathing the same toxic air as her, but she grabs my wrist, halting me.

"I'm going to enjoy taking him from you, and I'm going to rub it in your face in the most public way." Her nails dig painfully into my skin as she twists my wrist, and I attempt to wrench my arm back, but she's got hidden strength I can't shake off. "You're such a stuck-up prissy princess. I bet you've been handed everything on a silver platter. Reeve included. Consider this my gift to you. It's time for a wake-up call, and I'll get enormous pleasure delivering it."

I stomp on her foot, digging my stiletto heel into her flesh, enjoying the murderous scream she emits as she finally drops my hand. My wrist is throbbing, and I cradle it against my chest. "You don't know me, and you don't know Reeve."

Her eyes narrow, her jaw tenses, and she glares at me with such unrestrained loathing, I take an automatic step back when she advances on me. Prickles of awareness dance over my skin, and I rein my anger in, because she's unpredictable right now. She looks like one hell of a scary bitch, and I wonder if I haven't under-estimated her, in part. The evil glint in her eyes sends a spike of fear shooting through me. She is shaking with visible rage, and I wonder if she isn't more than a little unstable. "I know he was hard during every single sex scene. I know the moans we both made when he thrust his giant cock against my pussy during filming was real."

Her words poke holes in my fragile heart, and she continues digging in the knife.

"Reeve is *mine*." She shoves at my shoulders, and I stumble a little. "He might not have accepted it yet, but he wants me as much as I want him. He is mine. Not yours. *Mine*. You don't fucking deserve him. I do!" she yells. Her eyes dart wildly around the place, and something is definitely off. Scrutinizing her more closely, I can tell she's on something, because this mania isn't like her. She's been nothing but cold, calculated disdain in all our previous encounters.

Saffron paces the tile floor, and I bite my tongue, some inner voice of self-preser-vation warning me not to push her any further. "I will be the one wearing his ring and having his babies. *Me*, not you!" She jabs her finger in the air, waving it at me. "It will take minimal effort to dispose of you, so either back off or prepare to be defeat-ed." She laughs as I edge toward the door. "You'd do well to be afraid of me, bitch," she threatens. "You don't know where I've come from. The people I know."

Feeling braver now I've reached the door, I level a parting shot. "I know your crazy is showing, and if you think I'm keeping this conversation a secret from Reeve, you are truly delusional."

She lunges for me, and I open the door, racing out into the corridor, slamming headfirst into a familiar warm solid chest. Reeve's citrusy scent wafts around me, and I grab him, grateful he's here. "Oh my God, Reeve. Thank God."

Saffron comes barreling out of the bathroom, slamming to a halt and crumpling to the floor the instant she sees him. "She attacked me!" she shrieks, clutching her foot and sobbing.

"You have got to be kidding me." I shake my head in disgust. "You really are a piece of work."

"Viv. What the hell is going on?" Reeve asks, his blue eyes turning stormy as his gaze bounces between us. Sighing, he pries my hands off his chest and takes a step back, glancing anxiously over his shoulder, fearful of an audience.

My heart dips to my toes when I realize he's more concerned about being seen than my feelings. Exhaustion washes over me, mixing with emotional lethargy, and I speak quietly, just wanting to get out of here. I don't have the strength or stamina to deal with this anymore. "I can explain, but she hurt me first."

"Dude, what's going on?" Rudy asks, materializing behind us.

"Can you get Saff out of here?" Reeve asks, glancing over my head at his friend. "I need to talk to Viv in private."

Rudy walks around us and helps Saffron to her feet. She lets out a pained sob, clinging to him like a legit damsel in distress. "I don't know if I can walk," she cries.

Anger resurfaces, waking me the fuck up. "You had no trouble chasing me out of the bathroom," I hiss.

"That's enough!" Reeve snaps, rubbing a spot between his brows.

"Baby." Saffron reaches for Reeve, but he moves back.

"Go with Rudy," he barks, glaring at her. "And I don't care how fucking sore your foot is. If you go out there and make this into *anything*, I'll walk."

A muscle clenches in his jaw, and her lower lip wobbles, as tears leak freely from her eyes.

Man, I've got to give it to her. She can turn on the waterworks at will. Pity she didn't invoke some of those acting skills on the screen. She was a lukewarm Abby at best, and I can't imagine the die-hard series fans will be happy at all with her lackluster performance.

"Please, Reeve. This wasn't my fault," she pleads, reaching for him again. "I did nothing wrong. You've got to believe me."

"Fuck off, Saff," Reeve snaps, and I'm silently fist-pumping the air. Maybe he's finally seeing the light where his costar is concerned. It's about damn time.

Rudy half-carries Saffron down the hallway, and I release a relieved breath the second she's out of sight.

"Ow," I cry, as Reeve grabs my sore wrist, pulling me into the nearest room, which is a small office of some sort. "You're hurting me."

He loosens his tight grip, turning my wrist over and examining the raised, red nail imprints on my skin.

"She did that, and I only stabbed her with my heel because she wouldn't let go of me."

102

"What the fuck is going on, Viv?" Reeve drops my hand, dragging his fingers through his hair as he steps away from me.

I quickly explain what happened, telling him everything she said, word for word.

He shakes his head. "I know you two don't like one another, but lying about it doesn't help."

What the actual fuck? "I'm not lying," I yell. "Why would I do that?"

"Maybe because you want to ruin things for me? God knows you're trying hard to suck all the enjoyment out of this experience." He slams his fists down on the desk, and I jump, unused to seeing Reeve so angry and wound up. "You couldn't just give me one night without all this shit? You didn't even congratulate me! I am so sick of the two of you in my ear, and it's got to stop!" he shouts.

Forcing my pain aside at his hurtful words, I latch on to my anger instead. "What the fuck do you think I've been doing all night? I was sidelined so you could have your moment in the spotlight with her. You haven't even spent five minutes with me, so when the fuck was I supposed to congratulate you?! When Reeve?" I throw my hands in the air. "She's been clinging to your side all night, and I've put up with it even though my heart feels like it's being ripped apart. Do you have any idea how hard tonight has been for me, you selfish self-absorbed prick?"

"*I'm* selfish?" he roars, putting his face all up in mine. "That is fucking rich, coming from you. Your selfishness is ruining my career!" His eyes roll back in his head, and I step back, horrified as realization dawns.

"You're on something. You did drugs with her!" I clamp a hand over my mouth. "My God, Reeve. What is she doing to you? What are you doing to yourself?" Reeve is notoriously anti-drugs, having seen how it's destroyed the careers of many people in Hollywood. I just can't believe how quickly he has let go of all his beliefs and his morals. How easily he has let himself be manipulated by the lifestyle and the people around him who profess to care for him but only care for themselves.

"So, what if I did?" He shrugs. "We all did a line after the premiere. It's not a big deal."

"Maybe not to you. But it is to me." I move toward the door. "I don't even know who you are anymore, Reeve."

"I could say the same thing to you."

"Then I guess we both know what to do." Without saying another word, I exit the room, feeling like someone has taken a machete to my heart.

CHAPTER 19

I WAKE THE FOLLOWING MORNING, after a sleepless night crying into my pillow, determined to end things with Reeve permanently. Pain eviscerates every part of me even thinking the thought, but I don't see how we can continue with the way things are.

Reeve shows up that night, with flowers and apologies, promising me he'll do better. He swears he'll stop taking drugs and make more time for me. When he begs me not to break up with him, to give him a chance to make things right, I concede. I still love him so much, and I can't bear the thought of losing him, but I'd be lying to myself if I didn't admit that bitch played a part in my decision-making process. If I break up with Reeve, I'll be making things easier for Saffron. She'll be waiting in the wings to console him, and he'll get sucked even deeper into her orbit.

I don't want that for him, because she's poison and she'll only bring him down.

But I'm also not going to let her steal him from me. We have invested years in one another, and I'm not letting some psycho bitch trample over our history and destroy our plans for the future. I need to trust Reeve loves me and believe our love is strong enough to withstand the next couple of years and come out stronger for it.

The months pass, and I throw myself into college life to avoid confronting the gaping hole Reeve's absence leaves in my heart. He is crazy busy between auditions, promotion, and filming, and we barely talk more than a couple of times a week. I haven't seen him since January, and we weren't together for our birthdays again, which sucked. Pictures of Reeve, with Saffron, blowing out candles on his birthday cake made the front page of almost every magazine and newspaper, forcing me to confront the fact the world believes they are dating and that he and I are no more.

It sickens me, and my heart physically aches all the damn time. Yet, I don't voice my fears to Reeve anymore, because I'm sick of sounding like a broken record.

Freshman year of college ends, and I vacation in Europe with Audrey for the entire summer break. Reeve's career is on the up and up, and he has landed another couple of high-profile roles. He's filming a new movie with established actors all summer in Australia with no break, which means I won't get to see him.

At least he's not with that conniving bitch. Saffron is occupied filming in the US, so I am able to relax a little. Speculation about the state of their relationship is rampant online, along with anticipation for the next *Rydeville Elite* movie. Reeve now has forty million followers on social media, according to Audrey. I avoid looking at any posts or media commentary. I prefer to languish in ignorant bliss, even if my overactive imagination loves torturing me on a near constant basis.

I return to my parents' house in August for a week, before college resumes, and Reeve makes a surprise appearance, much to my delight. We stay holed up in his house for the week, catching up. Paparazzi follow his every move these days, and fans turn up in the most obscure places, so hiding out is our only option. We can't be seen together, but I'm not complaining. Having Reeve to myself is something I've desperately craved.

I'd like to say it helps, but there's a massive void between us, and even sex can't bridge the gap. For the first time ever, there's a disconnect in our relationship, and it's breaking my heart. Everything I believed I had mapped out for my future is in flux, and I'm drowning in a sea of uncertainty. I should talk to Reeve about it. The old Vivien would've had no qualms in broaching the topic, but I can't form the words to open such a conversation, and I think Reeve is the same. We avoid talking about the elephant in the room, but I wonder how long it will be before one of us cracks.

"What're you going to do?" Audrey asks when we meet up at our new apartment a few days before classes resume. Neither of us could bear to return to the dorms, so we found a plush, spacious, two-bedroom penthouse that is only a ten-minute walk from campus.

"I don't know." I sigh, flopping down on our new leather couch. "I'm in limbo, and it feels like my life is on hold."

Audrey sinks onto the multicolored rug on the floor, sitting cross-legged as she faces me. "It does get easier. You know I struggled at first without Alex, but I'm over it, and we've managed to resume our friendship."

"Do you still love him?"

She drums her fingers on her chin as she stares into space. "I don't know. There are definitely still feelings there, but I'm reluctant to dig too deep because what's the point?" She shrugs. "I've accepted we can't be together, and I'm having fun hooking up with random guys. I'm not ready for anything heavy with Alex or anyone else."

Audrey had a few casual romances this summer, and while I have no genuine desire to kiss anyone but Reeve, I'll admit I was envious. I'm starved for human touch, and I'm not just talking about sex. I miss Reeve's arms around me and the adoring way he used to pepper my face with kisses, and I absolutely hate sleeping alone. It's worse now I've just had a week's reminder, and I'm missing him as much as I did at the start.

"Do you think I should end it with Reeve?"

She shrugs. "I think you should do whatever it takes to be happy." She scoots closer, taking my hands. "I don't want to see you moping again this year. These are the best years of our lives and you should be enjoying college more than you are. I hate seeing you so unhappy."

"I still love him, Audrey," I quietly admit. "Sometimes, I wish I didn't, because it would make the decision easier."

"I know." She nods, squeezing my hands tighter.

"The thought of letting him go kills me." I wrench my hand from hers, rubbing it across the sudden tight pain in my chest. "But it feels like I'm slowly dying inside. We might be technically together, but we're not really. It feels like I've already lost my boyfriend, because I hardly ever get to see him, and our phone calls are tense and filled with all the things we aren't saying. I think we're both clinging on by our fingernails."

"I'm sorry, babe. I wish I had a crystal ball and I could tell you what to do, but it's got to be your decision."

"I know." Leaning on my side on the couch, I slide my hands under my face. "I can't imagine my life without Reeve in it, and I'm counting down the days until he's finished with these wretched films."

"The last movie doesn't premiere for a year and a half. That's a long time to hang on when you're miserable."

"He'll finish filming with her by next summer, so it's only a year. I feel I owe it to my relationship to go the distance."

She tosses her long red hair behind her shoulders. "Don't hate me for saying this, but are you sure you're hanging on for the right reasons?"

I purse my lips, urging her to continue with a nod, though I'm sure I know what she's going to say.

"Are you sure this is about love and not about one-upping that bitch?"

"You mean would I cling to Reeve if I didn't love him anymore purely to spite that slut?"

She nods.

"If I didn't love him, I would let him go. But I do love him, Rey. I've thought of nothing else for months, and he's the love of my life. That hasn't changed, even if I'm so mad at him sometimes I could scream. And yes, you're right, I'm also afraid to cut him loose and send him running straight into her arms."

"It's a valid concern, but you've got to put yourself first, Viv. That's what Reeve is doing. Just promise me you're making the right decisions for you."

"I'm trying to, but honestly, I think I'm a little depressed. I'm not sure I'm in the right frame of mind to be making the best decisions for me."

Audrey climbs onto the couch and hugs me. "You're going to get through this, and I've got your back."

"Love you." I hold my friend tight. "I couldn't have gotten through this past year without you."

"You supported me too. That's what friends do."

"You need to call Reeve," Audrey says, plonking into the seat beside me in the cafeteria, wearing a furious expression. It's mid-November, and our sophomore year is well underway by now. I was the first to arrive at our usual lunch table, and our other friends are still standing in line at the counter.

"What now?" I ask, sighing in resignation. I know the angry look she's sporting doesn't mean anything good.

"I know you don't want to be shown these things, but I'm keeping an eye on them for a reason." She hands me her phone, and I almost vomit up my salad as I read the bold headline.

ARE REEVERON ENGAGED?

"It's bullshit," I reply in a dead tone, handing her cell back to her. I have zero interest in reading what supposed insiders on the set have to say. It's ridiculous how easily the public has believed all the lies despite not a single photo existing where Reeve and Saffron are kissing off-screen. I know, because Audrey checks daily, and it would make front page news if such a photo existed.

"I know that," she whispers, clicking out of the article and glancing around to ensure no one is listening. She moves her lips close to my ear. "But is it *fake* bullshit? Is this what they're forcing him to do now?"

I bury my head in my hands as my train of thought catches up to hers. "Fuck."

"Let's get out of here," Audrey suggests, smoothing a hand up my back.

I lift my head, willing the sudden throbbing pain in my skull to disappear. "If it is orchestrated, and Reeve has agreed to this, it's game over. There is only so much pain a heart can endure."

"If Reeve has agreed to this insanity, he can kiss my friendship goodbye," she agrees.

I can't even bear the thought of him going along with this. Hasn't he humiliated me enough?

With a heavy heart and equally heavy feet, I drag myself out of the cafeteria and return to our place to call Reeve.

"Fuck this shit," I say six hours later when Reeve still hasn't returned any of my calls or texts. He must've seen the gossip online by now, or someone has at least told him. It's blowing up all over the internet, and I'm at my wit's end. "I need to get drunk. Let's go to a party." The great thing about college is there's always a party somewhere. "I'll call Danny. He'll find us one to go to."

Danny is an English major like me, and we met during our first month of freshman year and became instant friends. When we met, we just clicked. Danny's that kind of friend. I held back a little at the start, fearful he was looking for something more than friendship. Until I found him kissing a guy, he confirmed he was gay, and I knew there was nothing to worry about. Reeve knows about him, but they have never spoken or met, because as far as Danny is concerned, I'm single. He knows about my past with Reeve, and I've played on my broken heart to extract myself every time he tries to set me up on a blind date. I hate lying to all my friends but especially Danny since we're the closest.

It's just another example of how Reeve's career has impacted my life and forced me to become someone I'm not sure I even know these days.

Audrey and I meet Danny and his latest boyfriend, Lawrence, at one of the frat houses a few hours later. I've been knocking back vodka at our place, and I'm already drunk, but I couldn't care less. Reeve is clearly avoiding me, and I'm done with that selfish prick.

The party is already rocking, and we waste no time entering into the spirit of things. Usually, I hate warm beer out of red cups, but tonight, I'm draining them like they're lemonade. I desperately need to numb the destructive thoughts screaming in my head.

Audrey and I dance, flirting up a storm. Normally, I shove guys away when they approach me at parties, but tonight, I let them feel me up a little. Yet it does nothing to stem the flow of pain coursing through my veins. I draw a line at kissing any of them or doing anything else, wishing I could be like Audrey and take a hottie upstairs to bump uglies. I guess it's a good thing I haven't completely lost my moral compass, even if I have compromised my soul all in the name of supporting my boyfriend.

"Hey, babe." Danny appears, extracting me from the arms of a guy with dangerous wandering hands. The room is spinning, and my vision is blurry as I slump into my friend's arms. "Time-out." Danny circles his arm around me, walking us over to an empty couch in a quieter corner. "Sit down, drink some water, and tell me what's wrong."

I throw back my head, laughing bitterly. "Fuck, Danny. I wouldn't even know where to start."

"At the beginning, babe. Start at the beginning."

His concerned expression touches me, and I'm just so tired. Of all the drama. The unnecessary heartache and pain. Of keeping everything locked up inside because I need to protect all of Reeve's secrets. My inebriated state has loosened my tongue, but I still know what I'm doing when I drop my walls, tear through all the lies, and tell him everything that's been going on with Reeve and me. Including how his so-called relationship with the bitch is fake and how she attacked me and I retaliated the night of the premiere.

Tears are streaming down my face, and I'm hiccupping my way through part of my explanation, drawing inquisitive glances from several people, but I've gone beyond the point of caring. Danny holds me tight, ushering reassurances in my ear as I spill my guts. I break down in his arms as almost two years' worth of pain seeps out of me like poison. I hear how pitiful it sounds. How pathetic it makes me seem to have put up with this shit and to still love him. But there's a certain freedom in telling my friend. Briefly, I wonder if I should have seen a therapist, because letting the words fall from my tongue is cathartic, even if I'm sure I'll regret it tomorrow.

After locating Audrey, Danny walks us both home, tucks me into bed, and leaves water and two pain meds by my bed before saying his goodbyes. I'm barely coherent at this point, and my eyes are closed, but I've a sense that he lingers, watching me from my doorway before making his exit.

CHAPTER 20

"BABE. WAKE UP." Audrey shakes my shoulders, and I pull a pillow over my face in a feeble attempt to drown out the drums playing a furious rhythm in my head.

"Go away." I swat at my bestie. "There's a death march hammering in my head, and I need to sleep for eternity." I'm not ready to face this day yet, and I want to wallow in ignorance for a little longer.

"It's after twelve, and I can't keep this to myself any longer. Your phone is going crazy, and your mom called me. She's threatening to come over here."

"What?" That claims my attention. Whipping the pillow off my head, I whimper as pain rattles through my skull. My tired limbs protest when I pull myself up against the headboard. Pushing strands of knotty hair from my eyes, I work hard to focus my vision until Audrey appears less blurry. "She can't see me like this. She'll freak!" Mom knows I drink alcohol, but she's always cautioning me to drink sensibly. She would be utterly ashamed if she saw the state of me right now.

"I think that ship has sailed," she cryptically replies, handing me a mug of steaming coffee. "Drink this though you'll probably need something stronger."

"If it's more bad news, I don't want to know." I blow on my coffee before taking a sip. "I can't handle anything else right now."

"This can't wait, because I'm pretty sure the instant we step foot out of this apartment we'll be accosted by paparazzi."

All the blood drains from my face, and I clasp my hands around the mug, trying to siphon some of the warmth. Cold infiltrates every nook and cranny of my body, and I shiver, drawing the obvious conclusion. "It's true? He actually got fake engaged to that bitch?"

"No, babe." Audrey crawls up beside me, mirroring my position. "I spoke to Reeve earlier when he called for you, and he vehemently denies there is any engagement. Real or fake. Seems it was just tabloid speculation."

"You spoke to him? He called?" He never calls in the mornings when he's on set since they have super early starts. Filming on *Sweet Retribution*, the third *Rydeville Elite* movie, began a couple of weeks ago, but the filming won't be complete until next spring, because they'll have to stop to do promo for *Twisted Betrayal*, the second movie, which is releasing in January.

She gives a terse nod of her head, and an ominous sense of dread washes over me.

"What is going on?" I ask. I might as well get this over and done with.

"There is no easy way to say this, so I'm just ripping the Band-Aid off." She slides her arm around my shoulders. "Danny sold you out, Viv. He recorded everything you told him last night on his cell, and it was posted online a few hours ago. Clearly, someone doctored it to make it sound like you're a bitter ex mouthing off because the love of your life just got engaged to someone else."

I throw up all over my bed as the mug slides from my hands, splashing the already destroyed comforter and drenching the hardwood floor. Audrey is still speaking, but I don't hear the words. I'm too busy losing my goddamn mind as my world comes crashing down around me.

Somehow, Viv manages to get me into the shower, and I tilt my head up, letting warm water stream down my face while I shiver from a coldness that emanates from my soul. I don't cry, and that's a first. Either I used up all my tears last night or I'm numb to it at this stage. I lather my body with shower gel and shampoo and condition my hair, as if on autopilot.

Audrey turns off the water, holding a large towel out for me. "Your parents are on their way. I couldn't hold them off any longer," she explains, as I tuck the soft towel around my body.

"It's okay." Tucking a towel around my head, I stare at my pale reflection in the mirror wondering when exactly I turned into this vampire-like version of myself. My collarbones jut out, confirming I've lost weight without even noticing. Bruising shadows attest to many sleepless nights, and my eyes have lost all their spark.

I look like I'm as dead on the outside as I am inside.

I could blame Reeve for this.

I *do* blame him for this.

But I blame myself more.

I've let myself get beaten down. Made excuses for him time and time again, and yet I'm the only one suffering the consequences.

Audrey watches with concern in her eyes as I brush my teeth, cleanse my skin, and comb my damp hair. "I need to call Reeve," I say.

"Don't." She hands me my underwear, a pair of jeans, and a T-shirt. "He was pissed earlier when I spoke to him. You should let him calm down."

"It won't matter." I get dressed and head back out to my bedroom. Fresh sheets adorn my king bed, and the window is open, clearing the noxious smells from the room. Audrey is such a good friend, and I'd be even more lost without her.

"He's so fucking selfish, and he deserves to stew. I'm not sorry I ripped him a new one earlier, and I'm not sorry for interfering. I realize now I should've staged an intervention months ago." Audrey grabs my shoulders. "Viv, are you listening to me?"

I nod, but I'm strangely devoid of feeling inside. It's a welcome change, and I cling to the numbness like it's a second skin.

"Dump him," she continues. "He's changed—and not for the better. He's so self-ish, and he even had the nerve to accuse you of cheating. He's lucky he's hundreds of miles away because I could happily kick his ass."

I cock my head to one side. "Why would he accuse me of cheating?"

"That asshole Danny took photos of you dancing with guys last night, and he posted them along with the video."

"He really did a number on me. Why? Why would he do that to me?" I ask, sitting down on my bed while I plug my cell in to charge.

"I'd like some answers too, but his cell has been deactivated. I managed to get a hold of Lawrence, and he swears he knows nothing. He went over to Danny's dorm this morning, but he's disappeared. Looks like for good. All his clothes are gone apparently."

"He was paid to do this," I surmise, logging on to one of the main gossip sites.

"Don't look at that," Viv pleads, attempting to snatch my cell.

"I need to see how bad it is." I watch the video without flinching or passing comment. Like I'm a bystander and the drunk broken girl sobbing her heart out on the screen is some stranger and not me. The photos are pretty damning, and they don't show me in a positive light, so I can kind of see where Reeve is coming from. Except he should know better. No matter how broken I am, I would never cheat on him.

I scroll through the nasty comments until Audrey grabs my phone and shoves it in her pocket. "You're not reading any more of that poison. People are assholes. Especially those bitchy Saffhards."

"They want me dead," I say, in a monotone voice. "One girl said I should slit my wrists." I peer off into space.

A sob rips from Audrey's mouth and she leans down, hugging me. "Viv. You're scaring the shit out of me right now, babe. Those people are scum of the Earth, and you're not to read any more of that crap."

My cell rings, and I grab it out of her pocket before she can stop me. Reeve's face lights up the screen, and I press the button to accept his call. Audrey cusses, shaking her head.

"Viv?"

"It's me."

"What the actual fuck is going on with you? I can't believe that video." He wastes no time laying into me. "I have never seen you like that! If you wanted to hurt me, you've definitely succeeded. Did you cheat on me last night?"

I laugh at the irony, and once I start, I can't stop.

"Vivien, what the hell? Stop laughing. This is fucking serious. You've landed me in a world of shit today. This will damage my brand and my rep." He goes on in a similar vein, but I tune him out, watching Audrey whisper into her cell while sparing me troubled glances as she paces the floor in my room.

"Viv. Are you still there?" Reeve snaps.

"Are you done?" I ask, in a flat tone, lying prostrate on my bed and staring at the ceiling.

"No, I—"

"I'm not in the mood to argue today," I say, cutting across whatever he was going to say. "And I give zero fucks how this impacts you. That bitch of a costar or that bitch of a PR person or that bitch of an agent orchestrated this whole situation, and I'm done pandering to all of you. I am done being the punching bag." My lower lip wobbles, and my voice quakes as all the emotion I've been fighting resurfaces. "I am done coming last all the time." I exhale heavily. "I am just fucking *done*," I shout. "Do you hear me? I'm done, Reeve. Fuck you. Fuck Saffron. Fuck Cassidy, and fuck Bianca. Fuck you all." Tears spill down my cheeks, and I'm openly crying now. "Don't call me again," I say before hanging up.

"Oh, Vivien." Mom rushes into my bedroom, and I fall apart in her arms. "I'm so sorry, honey. Shush. It's okay. You're okay." She presses kisses into my hair, while rubbing my back. "We're here, and we're going to make it all go away. I have people working on getting the photos and the video removed. Your father is talking with Douglas Simmonds about security for you on campus, and he called in a favor with the LAPD, and all the paparazzi have been cleared from the front of your apartment building."

"Thank you," I sob against her chest. I'm so grateful she is here and my parents are stepping in to help because I badly need it.

"Maybe you should come home for a while."

I shake my head, brushing the tears off my face. "No. I'm done hiding myself away. I've done nothing wrong, except get drunk and trust the wrong person."

"You were clearly set up." Her jaw pulls tight. "And I'm going to find proof and hang them out to dry."

"We already know who it is, Mom, and I doubt they left tracks. Let it go. I just want to get on with my life and put it behind me."

Mom and Audrey trade a worried look. Mom kisses my temple, while holding me close. "At least come home for the weekend. Let us look after you, and if you want to come back to campus next week, we won't stop you."

I take Mom's advice and return home with them. I end up staying for the weekend and the following week, letting my parents fuss over me while I try to pick up the shattered pieces of my life. Reeve has been regularly calling my cell and the house, but Mom told him, in no uncertain terms, that I need space, putting a halt to all communication.

I insist on returning to UCLA on Sunday night. I have exams approaching, and I meant what I said about not letting anyone force me into hiding. I've taken some time out to begin the healing process, even meeting with a therapist, and now it's time to resume my life.

I know I'll be under a spotlight when I return to campus, and I'm not looking forward to it. I'm sure I'm the butt of many jokes—the pitiful ex-girlfriend crying over the movie star who has moved on—but it will die down in time. Especially now the recording and photos have been removed from the internet. I don't know exactly what my parents have done, but whatever it is has ensured there is no more press coverage of me. Mom's IT contact was able to confirm the origin of the recording, and there's a warrant out for Danny's arrest because it's illegal to record and share a private conversation without consent in California.

No wonder he fled. He must've known this would happen. Which begs the question—Why did he do it? I know he was at UCLA on a scholarship and his family isn't wealthy, so I can only guess that he needed money badly. Why else would you throw away your future?

I exchange heated words with my father when he tries to force a full-time bodyguard on me before I leave for my apartment on Sunday night. I know my parents are worried sick because of the hatred and bullying online. Tons of abusive letters and a few death threats have been sent, but Mom intercepted my mail, and her assistant, Moira, has been going through it, sending anything suspicious or concerning directly to the police. "Dad, I know you mean well, but I'm not returning to campus with a bodyguard shadowing my every move. This is already going to be hard enough without drawing extra attention to myself."

"Your safety is our only concern, Vivien."

"Didn't you say campus security has tightened procedures and they'll be keeping a closer watch on me?" Dad is an alumnus, and he's close friends with Douglas Simmonds, the current UCLA president. Dad went straight to him the day all the shit went down, and I know these new security measures are because of his timely intervention. Normally, I hate using my parents' connections to my advantage. But on this occasion, I'm not complaining.

"That's not enough. It's——"

"Perfectly adequate, Dad." I stretch up and kiss his cheek. "I promise if I feel threatened or anything serious happens I will let you assign a bodyguard to me then. Remember, most students on campus are not keyboard warriors. Those nasty bitches online are fans of the series and idiots who ship Reeve with Saffron. Lots are teens with nothing better to do. I doubt I'll have much trouble on campus, but if I'm wrong, I promise I'll tell you."

They reluctantly agree, and I return to our apartment sans bodyguard.

CHAPTER 21

THE FIRST WEEK back is a little rough, but I keep my head down and try to ignore the attention. Whispering and finger-pointing are the norm, along with a few taunting comments, but it quickly dies down, like I predicted. A few girls try to befriend me, purely to get information about Reeve, but I'm on to them immediately. Something I hadn't predicted is guys hitting on the crazy broken girl, yet it happens. Most of them think it'll raise their profile to be seen with me, and others want to be able to say they've dated Reeve Lancaster's childhood sweetheart.

We live in crazy times, that's for sure.

Exams start next Monday, so I throw myself into studying, and it helps to distract me from the mess in my head. Reeve sends me daily texts telling me he's sorry and he loves me, but I don't respond, even though it's hard to ignore him knowing he's in pain too. My head and my heart hurt too much, and I'm not ready to talk to him yet. I need to try and figure out what it is I want. I still love him. I think I probably always will, but I don't know if love is enough anymore. For now, I'm focusing on my exams, and there'll be plenty of time to talk to Reeve when he's home at Christmas.

I return to my parents' house on the weekend, because being home comforts me right now. Which is a bit weird, because home also reminds me of Reeve. Reliving cherished memories hinders as much as it helps. Maybe I'm one of those girls who gets off on the whole pleasure-pain thing. Or I just like torturing myself with all the what-ifs. I don't know. I imagine my head is a therapist's worst nightmare right now —or maybe a wet dream—so don't expect me to figure out the inner workings of my mind or my heart any time soon.

Everywhere I turn, I'm accosted with memories of the boy I have loved since I was a little girl—it soothes the ache *and* adds fuel to the fire.

Audrey has a hot date with this new guy she's seeing, and I wanted to give her the apartment to herself, so coming home this weekend killed two birds. God knows my bestie has earned it, putting up with me and my mood swings these past few months. She seems to like this guy, and I hope it works out for her.

At least one of us should be happy.

I rise early on Saturday morning and have breakfast with Mom before locking myself away in our home library to study. Needing to work out the tension wracking my body, I attend an evening yoga class at our usual studio in downtown L.A. After the class ends, I hang back to shower and change, having already decided to pick up food from Mom's favorite restaurant on my way home.

My parents have been so good to me lately, and I want to do something nice for them. I'm planning to surprise them with a romantic candlelight dinner tonight. I already told them not to eat, and I set the table in the small dining room before I left, locking the door and taking the key so they don't peek. Rose petals are scattered across the table, and an abundance of scented candles—which I intend to light when I return home with the food—fill the room. Chilled champagne is already hidden in the back of the refrigerator.

I'm smiling to myself, imagining my parents' faces, as I step outside the studio. Darkness has descended, and it's pitch-black as I walk through the narrow alleyway toward the parking lot where I left my car.

I haven't gone far when someone shoves me forcefully from behind. Startled, I scream, arms flailing as I lose my balance and face-plant the ground. My head slams off the asphalt, and I almost black out. Stars swim behind my bleary eyes as pain ricochets through my aching skull. Bits of debris cling to my sore cheek, and I whimper. Something heavy presses down on my lower back, and alarm bells ring in my ears as adrenaline courses through my body. I attempt to use my hands to force myself upright, but the pressure on my back is solid and my limbs are weak and uncooperative.

"Stay the fuck down, whore," an unfamiliar female says, her voice bristling with malice. All the fine hairs on the nape of my neck stand at attention, and blood thrums in my ears as I struggle to clear my mind and think of a way out of this situation.

Savage pain shoots through my fingers and up my left arm as someone stands on my hand. A scream rips from my throat, and tears leak involuntarily from my eyes as pain slams into me.

"Shit. Shut her the fuck up before someone hears," a different female says.

Several pairs of hands flip me over, and something coarse is shoved into my mouth. Blinking my eyes open, I stare up at the girls looming over me with mounting panic. This can't be happening. There are five of them and they're young. No older than sixteen, maybe seventeen. They are all wearing jeans and boots, and their sweaters are official merchandise I recognize, confirming my worst fears.

These girls are Saffhards, and they clearly hate my guts. I have no idea how they found me, but something tells me this wasn't a coincidence, because they were obviously lying in wait for me.

A big girl with long black hair sets her booted foot on my chest, pressing down in a way that constricts my breathing. My heart is racing superfast as fear spreads through me like quicksand. "Leave Reeveron alone!" she hisses, pressing the full weight of her foot down on my body. Although I'm in pain, instinct kicks in and I thrash about, trying to use my legs to get at her, but it's a feeble effort at best. Throbbing pain rattles around my skull and the back of my eyes, my hand aches, and I can scarcely breathe with the pressure on my chest.

She laughs as she spits in my face. Before I can wipe her saliva off, another girl grabs both my hands, binding them roughly with rope. A fresh wave of pain spreads up my arm as she tightens the rope around my wrists. My screams are muffled against whatever they shoved in my mouth, and I'm struggling to breathe as the bitch with her foot on my chest digs in deeper.

Pain sears through my right side as another girl kicks me in the ribs. "You're a pathetic bitch clinging to Reeve like that. He doesn't want you."

"He loves Saffron," a girl with stringy blonde hair says, kicking my other side.

"As if Reeve would ever love an ugly bitch like you," a skinny girl with dark curly hair says. Crouching over me, she drags her nails down my right cheek.

"We need to hurry up," the bitch with her foot on my chest says. "I'm not going to jail for this slut."

Pain covers my upper torso in a blanket of agony as they all kick me. The skinny bitch yanks on my hair, and it feels like my scalp is on fire. They laugh as my muted screams echo faintly in the eerie quiet of the vacant alley. Tears stream from my eyes, and I try to stay awake, to not succumb to the darkness, but as they continue to kick me, I lose the fight and pass out.

CHAPTER 22

MY CHEST BURNS, and searing pain hammers at my skull, as I slowly regain consciousness, immediately wishing I could return to my previous pain-free ignorant slumber. Blinking my eyes open, I cry out, wincing at the brash glare of the overhead fluorescent light in the strange room. The rhythmic beeping of a machine elevates in intensity, sending a fresh wave of piercing pain through my head. I whimper as urgent footsteps come closer. "Ms. Mills? I'm Nurse Watts," a woman says as cool fingers press against my wrist. "Stay with me for a few minutes, and then you can go back to sleep."

"We're here, Vivien," Mom says.

I force my eyes to remain open, avoiding looking directly at the harsh overhead light. "Mom," I croak. "Everything hurts."

Her worried face hovers over mine. "I know, honey, but it's going to be okay."

Dad pops up beside her. "You gave us quite a scare, princess." Tears fill his eyes, and I want to reach up and hug him, but it feels like I'm superglued to the hospital bed.

"I know you're anxious to talk to your daughter, but she still needs rest," the nurse says.

I angle my head to look at her, moaning as intense pain batters my skull and the backs of my eyes.

"You have a concussion, Vivien, so any sudden movements should be avoided." Her warm brown eyes are kind as she leans over me. "Your vitals look good, so I'm going to give you some more morphine." She gently pats my hand. "Sleep. Your parents will be here when you wake up."

I don't remember falling asleep, but I do. When I wake, Mom is asleep in a chair by my bed, and Dad is holding my right hand.

"How are you feeling?" he whispers, not wanting to wake Mom.

"Thirsty," I rasp.

With huge tenderness, he props the pillows behind my head and elevates the bed before dropping some ice chips in my mouth.

"You're awake," Mom says. Her voice is drenched with sleep as she rubs her eyes.

"What happened?" I ask, opening my mouth for more ice chips.

"What do you remember?" Mom stifles a yawn while she dabs a damp cloth against my sweaty brow.

"Being shoved from behind and hitting my head hard. Then these girls, high school age, took turns kicking me. They were Saffhards, and they enjoyed hurling insults while beating the shit out of me. I guess I blacked out after that."

"God, Vivien." Mom's cries bounce off the walls in the semi-dark room, and I flinch, groaning as the sound sends stabby pains shooting through my skull. Thank fuck someone dimmed the lights. "Sorry, honey." Mom sniffles and wipes the moisture from under her eyes. "We thought it was a random mugging, but this is so much worse." Her anguished eyes move to my father. "This was a targeted attack, Jon! She could've been killed."

"Why wasn't I? Did someone interrupt them?" I ask, praying they are locked up in police custody. I want to see them imprisoned for assaulting me. I'm not one of these do-gooder types who forgives them because they're young and impressionable. Fuck that shit. They are old enough to know right from wrong, and they should be made to pay. Otherwise, how will they learn not to do this again? Giving girls like that a get out of jail free card will not serve them or society well. They need to learn there are consequences for beating up innocent women and that you can't believe everything you read online.

"Unfortunately not," Dad confirms. "The owner of the yoga studio found you when she was heading to her car."

"They just left you beaten, bloody, and unconscious in the alley," Mom sobs, more quietly this time.

"I'm okay, Mom." I try to reassure her, because I hate seeing her so upset, but, obviously, I'm not okay. I'm the very furthest from okay a person can be.

"You have a concussion, three broken fingers, a broken wrist, and several fractured ribs, Vivien. They scratched your face and pulled out clumps of your hair. That is not my definition of okay."

"Lauren." Dad cautions her with a soft look. "Vivien is alive, and she'll heal. We'll leave no stone unturned until we find who did this." Dad presses a light kiss to my brow. "Could you identify them?"

"It's a bit of a blur, but I think so. I can definitely identify the girl who stood on me. I think her face will be imprinted in my nightmares for a long time to come."

"She stood on you?" Mom gasps, pressing a shaky hand to her mouth.

"Yes. She held me down so the others could kick me."

Mom buries her head in her hands, openly sobbing, and it's killing me. Physically and emotionally. Using my eyes, I gesture to Dad to comfort her. He rounds the bed, holding Mom as she softly cries into his shirt.

The dull pounding in my head is not as bad as the pain I felt when I woke the last time, and the fiery pain in my chest is dialed down to where it's manageable, but it still feels like there's a dead weight resting on my upper torso, making my breathing labored. Glancing down, I notice the cast on my left hand and wrist for the first time, grateful it's not my writing hand.

"Wait," I say, panic bubbling to the surface. "What day is it? How long have I been out? What about my exams?" I blurt.

"It's Sunday night," Dad confirms, and my mouth opens in horror. "Stop freaking out. I spoke with Doug, and he's arranged it so you can take your exams online later this month or in early January, whenever you feel up to it. You just need to complete them before you return for the spring semester."

Air expels from my lungs in grateful relief. "Thanks, Dad."

"Just focus on getting better," he replies.

"Does Reeve know?" I quietly ask.

Mom's eyes narrow. "He knows, and I'll be having a stern conversation with him when I see him."

"This isn't his fault, Mom."

"The hell it isn't," she hisses. "His behavior has led directly to this. He never should've agreed to that bullshit contract. His actions have placed you directly in harm's way, and I'm done biting my tongue. I don't know what's gotten into that boy, but this is not the Reeve Lancaster I helped to raise. I am so disappointed in him."

"He's beside himself with worry," Dad adds. "And he'd be here if he could."

I close my eyes, unable to deal with the usual emotional turmoil thoughts of Reeve invoke when I'm in so much physical pain. "Does the media know?" I ask, even if I'm not sure I want to know the answer.

"Yes. Unfortunately. News of your attack has been widely reported."

"Well, that's swell," I drawl, forcing my eyes open. "What about Audrey?"

"Audrey was here earlier, but we sent her home to get some sleep. She'll be back tomorrow after her exams," Mom confirms.

"You should go back to sleep, princess. It's late."

As if on cue, I yawn, and the instant I close my eyes, I fall back asleep.

When I wake the next morning, faint beams of light are filtering into the room through gaps in the blinds, causing me to wince.

"Viv. I'm here." Reeve's voice is low, laced with pain and a tinge of remorse. My good fingers twitch, and the touch of his hand is warm in mine.

Gulping over the messy ball of emotion clogging my throat, I turn to face my boyfriend, whimpering as a fresh wave of pain pounds in my skull. Fuck. This hurts like a bitch.

"Baby, I'm so sorry." He plants his lips on the back of my hand as tears fall silently down his face. "Sorry this happened to you, and sorry I wasn't here immediately. I got here as soon as I could. The plane ride was the most excruciating journey because I was terrified, Viv." He lifts our conjoined hands to his cheek, nuzzling into me. "You were still unconscious when I got on the plane, and I didn't know what I'd find when I arrived."

His sobs fill the quiet room, and it appears Mom and Dad have made themselves scarce.

"I was so scared you were dead, Viv. Scared I would never get to hold you again or tell you how much I love you. Scared I wouldn't get the chance to apologize for all the ways I have let you down. Scared I wouldn't get an opportunity to make up for all the wrongs."

My chest heaves painfully, and I'm struggling to breathe over my injuries and the emotional cocktail sloshing inside me. I don't have the mental capacity to deal with this right now, but I am glad he is here. "Your fans hate me, Reeve. They want you with her, and it seems they'll stop at nothing to make that happen." Tears stream down my face, and I'm in so much pain, on so many different levels, and I just want it to stop.

Loving someone should not hurt this much.

"Your parents filled me in," he explains, as his tears dry up, replaced with anger. "I know this is my fault. I haven't prioritized you or your needs, and I've been a selfish asshole, but it stops now." Determination glimmers in his eyes. "I'm going to make this up to you." With deliberate tenderness, he briefly touches my injured cheek. "They will pay for what they did to you, and I'm going to make sure no one ever touches you again."

That sounds like a tall order, and while I want to believe his pretty words are sincere, in recent times Reeve has a habit of promising me things he fails to deliver.

***

"Oh my God," I hiss, ducking my head into my chest and squeezing my eyes shut to avoid the glare of the camera flashes as Reeve wheels me out of the hospital in a wheelchair. Pain accosts me on several fronts, and I grip the arms of the wheelchair tight while gritting my teeth. Mom and Dad flank me on either side as we head toward the waiting Lincoln Navigator. Reporters shout questions at me, and pain rattles around my skull, protesting the noise elevation. There must be at least one hundred reporters here, and TV station vans line both sides of the road outside the hospital. Thousands of Reeve's adoring fans are being herded behind temporary barriers, and several police officers are doing crowd control. It's complete chaos, and it's playing havoc with my sore head.

"This is insane," Mom says, shooting daggers at Reeve. "I think your presence here is doing more harm than good."

I want to tell Mom to stop, because Reeve is damned if he does and damned if he doesn't in her eyes at the moment, but I'm in too much pain to form words.

"I'm going to fix it," he reassures her, scooping me out of the chair and carrying me into the back seat.

"See that you do," Mom warns, while Reeve buckles me into my seat belt.

He claims the seat beside me, and I lean my head against his shoulder, closing my eyes as the driver cautiously edges out of the hospital and onto the main road. I drift off to sleep almost immediately, and when I wake, Reeve is carrying me into my bedroom.

Mom helps me into clean pajamas while Reeve makes himself scarce. I'm yawning as I crawl under my comforter, grateful to be back in my own bed. I was only in the hospital for three days in total, but it felt like longer, and there is no place like home. "Do you want me to ask him to leave?" Mom inquires, perching on the edge of my bed.

"He's come all this way for me, and he has to leave tomorrow to get back to the set, so no. It's not worth the fight. Besides, I want him here." I'm not going to question the right or wrong of it, but I need Reeve, and I'm glad he came home for me.

Her lips pull into a tight line, but she nods, holding back her real thoughts. I'm sure I'll hear them at some point, but I'm glad it's not now. "Reeve is getting you something to eat, and then you should try to sleep. The LAPD will be here in the morning to take your statement. They wanted you to come downtown, but after the fiasco leaving the hospital, your dad managed to convince the detectives it would be better to conduct your interview here."

"Thanks, Mom. For everything."

She pats my arm. "You're our daughter, Vivien. We'd do anything to keep you safe." Her expression turns more somber. "Changes will need to be made. A bodyguard is nonnegotiable now. It's the one thing Reeve and I wholeheartedly agree on."

I nod, because I'm not going to turn down protection after what happened. Those Saffhards are crazy bitches, and I don't want to be on the receiving end of their hatred again. I will make whatever changes are necessary to keep myself safe.

She points to a pill bottle and a glass of water by my bed. "Don't forget to take your pain meds after you eat. You have to take them three times a day for the next week, and then we can start weaning you off them."

"Okay," I say, as Dad and Reeve appear in the room.

Mom helps me to sit upright, as Reeve places a tray table over my lap.

"It's good to have you home, princess." Dad drops my hospital bag on the floor by the wall.

"It's good to be home, Dad."

My parents leave, after sending Reeve blatant warning looks, gently closing the door behind them. I sip my chicken noodle soup while Reeve watches me, stretched out beside me on my bed. There is so much we need to say, but I can't go there. Not when the pain of my concussion is still so debilitating and all I want to do is rest. For now, I'll accept the comfort his presence brings without beating myself up over it.

After finishing my soup and bread, I snuggle under the covers as Reeve sets the tray to one side, lying down beside me. He laces his fingers in mine, leaning in to press a gentle kiss to my lips. He scoots closer, and I rest my head on his chest, welcoming the familiar steady thrumming of his heart. His fingers gently touch my hair, and when he is holding me like this, everything feels right in my world again.

I know it's an illusion.

A fantasy bubble.

At some point, I'll need to return to reality, but not yet.

My eyes fight to stay open as soothing darkness beckons to me like a tempting lover. "I love you, Viv," Reeve whispers, pressing a feather-soft kiss to my damaged cheek. "I know I've done a piss-poor job of showing you recently, but I'm going to do better. Almost losing you has put everything into perspective. I can't lose you, Viv. I won't. You're the other half of my soul, and nothing matters more to me than you."

I drift to sleep with his words lingering in my ears.

When I wake, it's the middle of the night and Reeve is crouched over me, softly sweeping hair back off my face. "I've got to leave, baby," he whispers. "But I meant everything I said. I know we need to talk too, and I promise we'll do that when I come home for Christmas." He leans in, kissing me tenderly. "Don't give up on me yet. Let me make this right, and everything will go back to the way it was. I promise."

I don't see how things can go back to the way it was, but I'd like to think we can find a way to move forward and put the recent past behind us. "How?" I ask, needing to know how he intends to make this right.

"I've hired my own publicist, and I'm issuing a video statement later today. When I return to the set, I'm telling the studio I'm publicly 'breaking up' with Saffron." He makes little air quotes with his fingers. "And I'm setting her straight too. I know she harbors ideas of us, but I'll tell her again that it'll never happen."

"That will only make her more determined," I mumble. Saffron is the type to thrive on the chase. I have no doubt, if she ever managed to win Reeve's heart, she'd tire of him fast.

"It doesn't matter. I love you. I know I've let her come between us, and it ends now."

I want to believe him so badly, but the truth is, I'm struggling to accept his pretty words as gospel. I'll need to see it to believe he is sincere this time.

CHAPTER 23

"HEY, BABE." Audrey strolls into my bedroom the next evening, looking gorgeous in skinny jeans and an off-the-shoulder black-and-silver-striped sweater. Her gorgeous red hair is tied up in a ponytail, and a light camouflage of makeup covers her flawless skin.

"You are glowing. I take it the date went well?"

She beams. "It did. I really like Troy."

"I'm happy for you."

"That's not why I came though." She carefully crawls up beside me. "I wanted to check up on you, and you need to watch the video statement Reeve put out earlier." She hands me her cell. "I think your boy has finally pulled his head out of his ass."

Lowering the volume a little, I press play on the recording and settle back to watch it. Reeve is in his bedroom at home, so he clearly recorded this before he left for the airport earlier today.

"Hey, guys. I know you have all seen the reports of what happened to Vivien Mills, and I want to officially comment." His Adam's apple bobs in his throat, and he looks tired as he drags a hand through his hair. "Girls who profess to be fans of mine, of Saffron's, and the *Rydeville Elite* series were responsible for the assault on Viv, and that's not cool. Not cool at all." Tears well in his eyes. "These girls scratched her face, pulled out clumps of her hair, and left her with broken bones, and that is not fucking acceptable." His chest heaves as he pauses for a second. "Viv has done nothing to deserve the kind of hatred that has been leveled her way, and I should have spoken out sooner."

He rubs a hand across his chest, staring at the camera with pain evident in his eyes. "Vivien Mills is the love of my life, and if you hurt her, you hurt *me*." He slaps a hand over his chest. "So please stop. Stop with all the hatred. Leave my girl alone. And if you are one of the girls who attacked her, please come forward and turn yourselves in, because I promise you will be apprehended and brought to justice. Make it easier on yourselves and fess up now."

His features soften as he blows a kiss to the screen. "That's for you, babe. I love you, Viv. Feel better soon."

The recording ends, and I silently hand the cell back to my friend.

"He'll get in trouble for that," she surmises, as we stare at the ceiling.

"He will. He's broken the terms of his contract, but they won't fire him. He's the star. They'll just hit him in the pocket."

She stares at me curiously. "I thought you'd be happier about it. He has finally put those rumors about him and the bitch to rest."

I turn my head to face her, ignoring the stabbing pain the motion induces. "I *am* happy he's done that but…" I trail off, unable to articulate the turmoil waging a battle inside me.

She squeezes my hand. "You're confused."

I nod. "I am. I love Reeve. I really do, but I'm so sick of it all. I'm exhausted, and I'm in pain, and I'm struggling to feel anything…concrete. Maybe his statement will help, and the shit will die down, or maybe it will only enhance the interest in me." I shrug. "The fact remains he will still have dealings with her until the last movie premieres, and I know she won't go away easily. I'm not sure I'm strong enough to handle more of it, yet the thought of permanently ending things with Reeve makes me ill. I don't want to lose him, but I'm not sure us being together is healthy for me either. I'm a mess, Rey."

"I think anyone would be after everything you've endured. You don't need to decide anything now, and maybe things will be clearer when you spend time with him at Christmas."

"Maybe." I exhale heavily, feeling the weight of everything pressing down on me.

"How did it go with the police?"

"I made my statement, and a police artist drew a few sketches. I told them I believe they are all under eighteen, and once I thought about it, I realized they're not from Cali either. They had accents I couldn't place. Anyway, the police can't issue the sketches because of their age, but they will put them into their system and see if anything comes up. Everything points to it being a setup, so I'm not holding out much hope they'll find them."

"What do you mean?"

"I mean someone knew where I was. It wasn't my usual yoga class, yet those girls were waiting for me. The police informed me someone hacked into the cameras outside the studio and across the street and wiped the footage from Saturday before they could access it."

"Holy shit." Audrey's eyes pop wide.

"I told them I believed it was Bianca, Cassidy, or Saffron who orchestrated this either with or without the studio's permission, and they looked at me like I was crazy. As if something like this is outside the realm of what Hollywood would do to ensure the success of a franchise."

"Did you tell Reeve about your suspicions?" she asks, idly plucking at the comforter.

"No. I know he appears to have seen the light, but I'm not sure he'd buy into my theory, and things will already be difficult enough for him on set in light of his statement. Plus, if I'm correct, he's going to feel huge guilt for not believing me. I didn't want to put that on him until, or *if*, I get proof."

"I wouldn't hold my breath," Mom says, appearing in the room with a dinner tray. "Sorry, I wasn't eavesdropping. Your door was open." She sets the tray on my lap.

"It's fine. I wasn't saying anything you didn't hear earlier."

"Can I get you some dinner?" Mom asks Audrey, and she shakes her head.

"I ate in the cafeteria, so I'm good." She tilts her head to the side, eyeballing Mom. "You think they've covered their tracks too well to be caught?"

Mom nods. "We're not dealing with amateurs. Our best bet is finding those girls, but I'm guessing they have made them disappear and made it worth their while to keep quiet. We've hired a PI to try to locate them, and that's our best chance at finding justice for Viv."

Two weeks later—eight days before Christmas—Audrey shows up, clutching a crumpled letter in her hand. "It's from Danny," she excitedly says, thrusting it into my chest. "The student who took over his dorm found it under the bed when he moved in."

I trace my finger over my name, scrawled in Danny's messy handwriting, before ripping open the envelope and reading his words.

"What does it say?" Audrey asks, impatience peppering her tone.

"That he's sorry. He didn't want to betray me, but his dad is ill with cancer, they don't have medical insurance, and when someone showed up on campus offering him two hundred K to spy on me, he couldn't turn them down."

"That rat bastard."

"Did you know his dad was sick?" I lift my head briefly from the letter.

She shakes her head. "He never said a word to me."

"Nor me." A veil of sadness washes over me. "If he had just told me, I could've given him the money. One of the charities my parents spearhead is for this very thing. They distribute millions every year to people with illnesses who have no insurance."

"Does he say who paid him?"

I shake my head as I finish reading the rest of the letter. "He signed an NDA, and he can't disclose any of the details because he doesn't have the money to give back anymore."

"I can't believe he was such an idiot! You were a really good friend to him, and he must've known if he'd told you the truth you would have done everything in your power to help his dad."

I carefully fold the letter, placing it back in the envelope. I'll get Dad to deliver it to the cops. "All of it is connected to those damn movies. I wish Reeve had never gotten the part."

"I can't believe the lengths they have gone to. All to try and split you two up? It's disgusting. They can't get away with it." She paces the room, clenching and unclenching her fists at her sides.

"Well, unless we can find Danny or any of those girls, they will."

"At least you can show Reeve that letter. Maybe then he'll start coming around to your way of thinking."

Reeve returns home three days before Christmas, but I'm busy completing my exams online, so we don't get to spend time together until Christmas Eve, when he surprises me with a romantic candlelit meal at his house. After a gorgeous lobster and steak dinner and some expensive champagne, we retreat to my bedroom. Mom refuses to let me out of her sight at night, even though I'm feeling a lot better in the weeks since the attack. My concussion is more like a niggly occasional headache now, and the scratches and bruising have completely healed. My ribs still ache like a bitch, and I have another two weeks in my cast before it's removed, but the doctors are pleased with my progress, and I should be fully recovered by the time I return to UCLA. I'll need physical therapy for my wrist and fingers, but other than that, I should be fine.

Reeve makes love to me for the first time in months, and the careful way he cherishes and worships me, ensuring I'm not in any pain, brings tears to my eyes. I've missed this closeness between us. The way he clings to me like I'm his entire world has been missing from our intimate moments this past year. Although we still have a lot to discuss and things to work through, I feel like we might have turned a corner, and we might be through the worst of it.

How very wrong I end up being.

"You look beautiful," Reeve says, appearing in my doorway the following morning. He returned home earlier to shower and change before coming back with his dad for Christmas lunch. Spending Christmas Day with the Lancasters has been our tradition for as long as I can remember. Yet, this was the first year Mom asked if I wanted to rescind Reeve's and Simon's invitation. Although my parents are pleased Reeve is trying to make amends, they are still in overprotective mode, and any potential risk to my recovery is approached with caution.

Unfortunately, Reeve falls into that category.

Now I'm feeling better physically, I am better prepared to tackle my emotional needs, and I'm determined to enjoy the holidays and get things back on track with my boyfriend. The new year is a fresh start. A clean slate. And an opportunity to reset things with Reeve.

"Thanks. You don't look so bad yourself." My gaze appreciatively roams his delectable form, approving of his ripped dark jeans and blue button-down shirt. His smooth jawline is devoid of the stylish stubble he wears to play his role, and he looks more like my Reeve. That helps to reassure me.

Striding across my bedroom, he quickly closes the gap between us. Careful not to hurt my injured hand, he reels me into his arms. My black, gold, and red dress swirls around my thighs as he holds me close, leaning in to kiss me. The urgency of his kiss surprises me, because he's been extra gentle with me since the attack, and there's an undercurrent of desperation that concerns me. I ease back a little, frowning. "What's wrong?"

"Nothing is wrong." He smiles, but it seems off.

The edge slides off my euphoria. "Just tell me."

"It's nothing."

I pin him with a warning look. Has he forgotten how well I know him? "Don't lie to me, Reeve. I don't want to get into all our shit on Christmas morning, but I don't want you keeping more secrets from me. Something is obviously on your mind, so spill."

"Saffron keeps messaging me," he admits, sighing. "I've told her nothing will happen between us, and I can't hang out with her anymore, but she's not giving up without a fight." He kisses the tip of my nose. "She's going to be difficult. I'm sorry."

Acid crawls up my throat. "I'd like to say I'm surprised, but I'm really not. She's a scheming bitch, and she's not going to let you go easily."

Reeve winds his fingers through my hair. "You know I love you, Viv, right? No matter what she says, you know you're the only one I love."

Raw fear shimmers in his eyes, sprouting goose bumps all over my arms. "Are you telling me everything?"

His Adam's apple jumps in his throat as he nods, not making eye contact, and my stomach lurches painfully.

He's lying.

I'm about to call him on it when Dad pops his head in the door, telling me it's time to leave for church. We're not a very religious family, but we attend mass at our local church every Christmas Day.

After church, we return to the house, and I help Mom with the dinner. Christmas and Easter are the only times of the year when Mom sends the staff home for the holidays and we have to fend for ourselves. I actually love it. Cooking a Christmas feast with Mom is one of my favorite things, and we always drink mimosas and chat while we're getting everything ready. The men enjoy some drinks in Dad's study while we are slaving away, but they know they're on cleanup duty. We are all about equality in this house.

Conversation is flowing freely around the table as we eat our sumptuous dinner, but I notice Reeve is hardly eating anything, toying with his food and looking distracted. I place my hand on his thigh under the table and whisper in his ear. "What's wrong?"

"I need to talk to you," he whispers. His knee taps on the floor as his cell vibrates in his pocket.

"We're in the middle of dinner, Reeve. It'll have to wait," I whisper back. Butter-flies run amok in my chest as I take in his pale complexion and the tiny beads of sweat forming on his brow. "What did you do?"

"Not here." He wipes his damp brow. "Please, can we go to your room to talk?"

"Turn on the TV," Mom suddenly shouts, surprising us all. Her eyes drill into Reeve as she clutches her cell to her chest. "Turn on E-News, Jonathon," she commands, in a voice that tells him not to question or challenge her.

"It meant nothing," Reeve whispers, clutching my hand. "Just let me explain."

The panicked expression on his face matches the mounting hysteria in his tone.

Dad looks between Mom and me as he holds the remote out in front of him.

"Turn it on, Daddy." I know this is going to hurt, but I won't shy away from the truth.

"No!" Reeve jumps up, holding on to my hand. "Don't look at that. Please, Viv. Come with me and I'll explain." He already knew this was going to happen, and yet he said nothing. Looking at him, I wonder if I know him at all anymore.

I wrench my hand from Reeve's, turning around so I'm facing the TV mounted on the wall behind us, just as Dad turns on E-News.

The headline bores a hole in my skull, and my heart instantly cracks into a million broken shards.

REEVERON HOT KISS! WE'VE GOT THE EXCLUSIVE VIDEO THAT PROVES THEIR LOVE IS REAL!

CHAPTER 24

"BABY, please. Don't look at that," Reeve pleads again, dropping to his knees in front of me. "It looks worse than it is."

I don't know how that is even possible.

Ignoring him, I stare in a state of numbed shock as the hideous recording plays. It's at some club, in Boston, I'm assuming, and while it's dark, you can clearly make out Reeve's and Saffron's features. I spot Rudy and a few of the other cast members drinking and dancing in the background. Christmas decorations hang from the ceiling and adorn the walls, confirming it was a recent night out. Most likely, just before he left Boston for the Christmas break.

Silent tears stream down my face as I watch them kissing. It's no chaste kiss either. Their arms are wrapped around one another as they lock lips, and they are devouring one another like it's a new Olympic sport.

Pain races through every part of me, and I'm struggling to breathe. I sway on my feet when I stand, clutching a hand to my mouth as I rush out of the room. Reeve calls after me, chasing me down the hallway. "Vivien! Stop, please! Let me explain! I love you!"

I slam to a halt at those three little words and spin around to face him. "Stop fucking lying!" I scream, my entire body shaking as rage takes control. "Stop saying you love me when your actions prove you don't! How could you do this to me?" A sob rips from my chest, and my upper torso aches. While the pain from my concussion has subsided and my broken ribs are healing, I'm still in physical pain, and the additional heartache is most unwelcome. "Haven't you humiliated me enough?"

"I was high," he blurts. "It was stupid. I never should've taken molly, but everyone was doing it. Filming was over. I was coming home to you, and I was happy." The words tumble from his mouth in desperation.

I bark out a bitter laugh. "Yeah. I saw how happy you were." I slam my unbroken hand into his chest, shoving him. "How long has it been going on, and have you fucked her?" I bend over, clutching my stomach as my half-eaten dinner threatens to make a reappearance. "Oh God. We had sex last night." We never use condoms because I'm on the pill, and I never thought Reeve would cheat on me. "That slut is probably riddled," I shout. "Now I'll have to get tested!" The thought of that additional humiliation ignites a fresh layer of pain.

"I didn't fuck her, and that was the only time I've kissed her. I swear."

I throw my hands in the air, swallowing bile. "Like I believe a single fucking word coming out of your lying mouth!" I scream.

"Baby. I know you're upset. I'm upset too. I'd never taken molly before. It made me horny as hell, and she pounced on me when I was wasted. I didn't push her away at first, because I was confused. I thought she was you!" He puts his hands on my shoulders, beseeching me with his eyes.

He's upset? He has the fucking nerve to say that to me after what he's done?! Shoving his hands away, I swipe at the hot tears running down my cheeks, vowing this is the last time I'm crying over Reeve Lancaster.

"As soon as I realized who I was kissing, I pushed her away."

"A likely fucking story." In the distance, I spot our parents holding back but listening to every word.

Reeve pulls out his cell, handing it to me. "Call Rudy if you don't believe me. He'll confirm it."

As if his best friend on set wouldn't cover for him! He really must think I'm an idiot if I'd believe that. I thrust his hand away. "I don't care if he does. I don't care if you were high. You promised me you were done with drugs, but that was obviously another lie, and it's not an excuse." I rest my head on the wall, and my body shakes as I flounder.

I'm drowning in soul-splitting pain.

Suffocating under an avalanche of hurt.

Torn between rage and gut-wrenching heartache.

"I'll quit the movie," Reeve quietly says, cautiously approaching me again. "They can sue me. I don't care."

"What about your career?" I hiss, lifting my head and staring straight at the wall. I can't look at Reeve. It physically pains me to look at him now.

"I don't care about my career!" he cries. He puts his hand on my back. "I only care about you."

Shucking out of his hold, I carefully wrap my one good arm around myself, as if that will keep the shattered pieces of my psyche together. "You don't care about me. If you did, you would've pulled out a long time ago. You only care you got caught."

"That is not true."

I harrumph, turning to face him. "It seems you need a little history lesson, so let me enlighten you. From the very start, you have refused to see what is blatantly obvious. That bitch, Bianca, and Cassidy have conspired to make my life miserable. They're behind it all, I'm sure of it, but you still don't believe it. That"—I point back toward the dining room, where the TV is probably still playing—"was carefully timed to inflict the worst pain on a day that should be special. A day that will now be forever tarnished for me. But I'm sure you'll find some way of defending that bitch and blaming the press. Or better yet," I say, gnashing my teeth. "Why not turn it around on me? Because you're so good at that!" I scream.

Out of the corner of my eye, I spot my dad physically restraining my mom. I love how readily she wades into battle on my behalf, but this is one fight I need to finish myself.

"Go on!" I roar. "Tell me how selfish I am for not supporting you! How much I'm adding to your stress because I won't get with the program and endorse your so-called fake relationship!" I'm really hitting my stride now, and months of pent-up frustration pours out of my mouth. "I am the only one who has suffered for your dreams. *Me!* Not you!" I place a hand over my heart. "I have been humiliated and vilified at every turn. I was attacked, and I know that bitch orchestrated it, and there you go kissing her in public without any regard for my feelings! You did that days after professing undying love for me and promising to fix everything! I have tried to love and support you, but you continuously shut me out. You refused to accept Mom's help. You refused to believe me. *Me!* The person you profess to have loved for nineteen years. Instead, you believe that conniving slut. You—"

"It wasn't that I didn't believe you, Viv," Reeve pleads, cutting across me. He grabs fistfuls of his hair. "You were so irrational when it came to her that it made it difficult for me to believe it wasn't jealousy driving your behavior, but I see it now."

"Well, that makes it all fucking right then, doesn't it?!" I screech, poking my finger in his chest again. "Tell me one time I was irrational!? One time I said something that hasn't turned out to be true?" I plant my hands on my hips, daring him to challenge me.

"Rehashing that shit won't do either of us any good."

A derisory laugh escapes my mouth. "Bullshit. You can't think of even one thing because you know I'm right!"

"I'm not disagreeing with you!" he yells, and I see red.

"Don't you dare shout at me, you two-timing bastard! You have no right! I'm entitled to my anger! *I'm* the one who looks like a goddamn fool in front of the entire world. Not you or that man-stealing whore! So don't you fucking shout at me." I slam my fist into the wall, beyond angry at this point. "Ugh." Dad releases Mom, letting her run toward me. I hold out my hand. "Stay back, Mom. I'm getting this all off my chest, and then Reeve is leaving."

She stops running, leaning against the wall, concern etched upon her face.

"This isn't on me," I continue, in a more even tone. "This is all on you. You've messed up everything, *movie star.* Your selfish pursuit of your dreams at all cost has destroyed what we once shared."

"No, Viv. Please don't say that. We can get through this. I will do whatever you want to make this right. Anything. I'll do anything, but I can't lose you. Please, Viv, I'm begging you." He drops to his knees, clutching my legs and clinging to me.

God, how did we end up here? Both of us destroyed and hurting.

I shake my head, as a wave of sadness washes over me. "You've already lost me, Reeve. I might as well be single, because I never see you. I'm lonely, and I'm heart-sick, and I can't do it anymore."

"Vivien. I love you. I know I've fucked up, but please give me another chance." Easing back, he lifts one knee and removes a box from his pocket. He pops the lid, and I don't know whether to laugh or cry. "I was planning to ask you to marry me tonight. It's always been you, Viv. Deep down, you know that. Don't let her come between us anymore than she already has. I'm begging you. Please forgive me, and say you'll be my wife."

This is crazy. Even if things hadn't blown up today, how could he feel we were in a place where it was right to propose? Our relationship has never been so broken. Hurt infiltrates every nook and cranny of my body, and I wonder if your heart can physically break? Because it feels like mine is. I stare at him through blurry eyes, forcing words out over the anguished lump in my throat. "There was a time I would have jumped into your arms and screamed yes, but we are so far removed from that now." Sorrow fills my chest as I glance at the stunning princess-cut diamond engagement ring that would be perfect if I wasn't so devastated by his betrayal. "How could you even consider asking me to marry you when our relationship is in tatters?"

"We've lost our way, but we'll get it back. I'm still committed to you, and this was my way of proving it. I wasn't expecting us to get married any time soon, but I hoped you would see how much I love you and know I'm still serious about spending the rest of our lives together."

Just kill me now.

"This is the action of a desperate man. It's nothing more," I whisper, drowning in pain and sorrow. "I don't even understand why you claim to want me anymore."

"Because I fucking love you!" he yells. "I made a mistake. Lots of them, but my love for you has never wavered. Not once. You're the other half of my heart and soul, Vivien. Please say you believe that? Please, baby. Please, please, believe me. I can't lose you. I'll die without you."

I clutch the wall behind me, incredulous that he's stooping to emotional blackmail. My heart is in shreds, and I can't tolerate much more. Can't he see that? "I don't believe it, Reeve," I croak, sniffling. "I don't believe a word that comes out of your mouth anymore. I can't marry you. I *won't* marry you, so put that ring away."

I can't bear to look at it. It's the physical representation of all my shattered hopes and dreams. Although the ring is truly stunning, it's ugly to me because it embodies everything I've lost. My heart is obliterated, and I'm amazed it's still able to beat in my chest.

My anger is fading, replaced with utter devastation and a hopeless sense of inevitability. "Actions speak louder than words, Reeve. And your actions confirm I don't matter."

"I'll put out another statement. I'll tell the world it was a mistake. I'll stop taking drugs. I'll pull out of the movie." Hysteria filters through his voice as realization dawns. He's grasping at straws now, throwing everything at it, because he knows he can't talk his way out of this. Staggering to his feet, he repockets the ring with the saddest look on his face. Seeing it hurts me, but he doesn't deserve any sympathy, and it's not my place to console him anymore. My place in his life is dead and buried, and I can't allow myself to get sucked in any longer.

This must end now.

Even though it'll kill me to say these words, I know this is the way it has to be. "You have pushed me away, downplayed my feelings, scoffed at my concerns, and let yourself be manipulated. We should have broken up like Audrey and Alex and protected our past because everything is tarnished now. All my memories include you, Reeve. Every single memory I have of my childhood, you are in it, and now they are all tainted!" I cry as heartfelt pain surges through my veins. "She hasn't just stolen you from me. She's stolen every good memory. I will never be able to look at our past with anything but pain in my heart."

"She hasn't stolen me, Viv. I don't want her. I only want you." Resignation is clear in his strained tone. He knows I mean this. That there is no way to come back from this.

"I thought we meant everything to one another. I thought you were the one person I could trust with my life. But you've trampled all over my heart. You have shattered my soul and broken my spirit. I hate who I've become." I gulp over the painful lump in my throat as I cut myself open and bleed in front of him. "I don't even know who I am anymore. I'm in so much pain, and I'm so lost, and you didn't even see. You didn't see or you chose to ignore it."

He hangs his head, and it's telling how he's stopped trying to defend himself.

Exhaustion weighs heavy on my shoulders, and my knees feel like they could buckle. I have reached my breaking point, but I need to get this last bit out, because it's the first step in starting to properly heal. "What if the roles were reversed and you were the one in my shoes? Have you ever considered that? How hurtful would it be if I were the one parading another man around in public as my boyfriend, shunning you and relegating you to the shadows in case anyone discovered the truth? Being victimized online and attacked when you have done nothing, abso-fucking-lutely nothing, but try to be a supportive partner? How would it feel to watch me kissing another man in public, knowing the entire world is watching and laughing at you for being such a gullible fool to believe I was faithful?"

I wrap my arm around my waist as pain lays siege to my body. "You cheated on me with her." It all boils down to that. Tears roll down my face again. "You have publicly betrayed me. Slain me as skillfully as if you'd taken a sword and sliced me wide-open."

Tears cascade down his face too, and his shoulders are slumped as he stares dejectedly at me.

"It's time I put myself first," I say, straightening up. "I need to protect my heart and my sanity, and you're just not good for my health. I can't be with you anymore."

"No, baby." He takes a step toward me, but I shake my head, warning him to stay back. "Please, Viv. Please give me one more chance."

"You're all out of chances, Reeve. I don't want to be with you. I don't want to see you or speak to you. I want you out of my life," I add, sobbing. This shouldn't be so hard. He cheated on me in front of the world. Cutting all ties shouldn't feel like it's killing me, but it does.

"I think it's time for you to go, Reeve." Mom steps up, pulling me into her arms. I cry into her chest, clinging to her like I used to do when I was a little girl and I'd skinned my knee, needing the comfort only a mother can give.

"I'm sorry, Viv. More than you can know. I'll give you some space, but I'm not giving you up."

"You don't have a choice." I lift my head, pinning him with bloodshot eyes. "You gave up on us a long time ago—you just didn't realize it."

Simon walks forward, rubbing the back of his neck. "Thanks for dinner, Lauren, and I'm sorry for all of this."

Mom stares at Reeve's dad with narrowed eyes. "Perhaps, if you were around more for Reeve, he wouldn't feel like he needs to sell his soul to be a success just so you'd be proud of him. You're not innocent in this either, Simon."

Dad walks up, circling his arms around both of us, and I've never been more grateful for my parents' love and support as I am now. I know this is going to be one of the most painful things I have ever done. I'm going to miss Reeve more than I can describe. But as he walks out the door with his father, I know there can be no going back.

Reeve and I are over, and there is nothing he can say that will ever change my mind.

CHAPTER 25

IN THE TWO weeks that follow, I barely venture out of my house. Media vultures have camped outside the main gates to North Beverley Park, hoping to catch a glimpse of Reeve or me. The only time I left was to visit my ob-gyn to get tested. Thankfully, the tests came back clear, but that doesn't prove or disprove Reeve's claims.

Despite asking for space, my ex is bombarding me daily with gifts, flowers, and notes, and I've had to switch off my cell because I can't read any more of his pleading messages. I asked Mom to deliver the flowers and gifts to a local nursing home and to tell him to stop sending them. Before he left to resume promotion for *Twisted Betrayal*, he dropped by my house a few times, but my parents are steadfast in honoring my wishes, and they turned him away each and every time.

I want him to stop—I *need* him to stop—because I meant what I said, and he's only making it harder.

Audrey is furious with him. She called and ripped into him for doing this to me. Reeve issued a public apology, but I refuse to watch it. My emotions are veering all over the place, and I can't let myself be swayed. I'm experiencing the full gamut of emotions, and I have days where I can barely get out of bed I'm crying so hard and days when I'm so freaking angry I want to punch the wall until I bleed. Other days, I want to punch myself for being such an idiot. For letting it go on so long. For believing all his lies. For missing him, because I do, and that's the most pathetic admission.

Most of all, I'm sad. So unbelievably sad.

I'm glad I completed my exams before Christmas because there's no way I'd be in the right state of mind to focus on anything right now. My heart is broken, and I've never experienced such crushing pain, such devastating loss, such debilitating anger.

"Your dad has hired you a bodyguard," Mom says three days before I'm due to return to UCLA. We're in the kitchen, seated at the breakfast table, enjoying homemade muffins and freshly squeezed orange juice. "And if the media interest doesn't die down, we can assign more."

"I'm sure it'll be fine," I say, knowing nothing of the sort. "Dad told me he spoke to Doug, and campus security will be on the case too."

"I'm worried about you." She reaches across the table to take my hand. "Have you thought any more about seeing a therapist?"

"You and I both know there's no way I'd get in and out of a therapist's office without someone discovering it and reporting it. I'm already a laughingstock. Let's not make it worse." She opens her mouth to argue, but I go on, not giving her an opportunity. "I just need time, Mom. Time to process all my feelings. Time to lock Reeve and all our memories into a box and throw away the key."

"Oh, honey." Tears pool in her eyes. "That's not going to be easy. He's been such a huge part of your life. He was your best friend growing up before he was anything else. I really wish you'd consider therapy. It will help."

"I know you're worried, but you need to let me do this my way and in my own time. I can scarcely get out of bed some days as it is."

"And that's why you should seek help."

Getting up, I round the table and pull her into a hug. "Mom, I love you, and I love Dad and everything you are doing for me, but you have to let me handle this my way. I'm going to focus on my studies, go to physical therapy now my cast is off, resume yoga, design dresses, hang out with my bestie, and do everything I can to heal myself," I say, barely pausing to draw a breath.

She smiles up at me, tucking a piece of my hair behind my ear. "You are so strong, Vivien Grace Mills, and you make your father and me so proud to be your parents." Her face floods with compassion. "I know you're hurting, and I wish I could take your pain away. But you will get through this. It might get rougher before it gets better, and if you need us, for anything at all, you only have to ask."

Mom pulled out of a new role she was preparing to take because she didn't want to leave L.A. and me behind.

Reeve should take a leaf out of Mom's playbook.

That's what true selfless love looks like.

I tried persuading her to change her mind, but she wasn't having any of it.

"Sometimes, I wish I was a million miles away, someplace no one knew me where I could heal in private without everyone knowing my business," I murmur.

"I'm sure we could arrange a sabbatical with UCLA if you wanted to defer this semester and go someplace," Mom suggests, and a light bulb goes off in my head. My eyes widen as possibilities open. I'm not sure I can make it happen at such short notice, but I'm damn well going to try. "I have an idea. Where's Dad?"

Mom arches one elegant brow. "He's on set today, but you could call him. You know he'll make time for his princess."

"Are you very sure this is what you want to do, honey?" Mom asks a week later as Dad carries the last of my luggage from my bedroom down to the hallway.

"I'm sure." I smile, and it's the first genuine smile I've had on my face in weeks. "I know it's all happened superfast, but this feels like the right move."

"I hate the thought of you being so far from home when you're not in a good place." Her brow puckers with worry. I know she'd love to beg me not to do this, but Mom will never interfere in the decisions I make for my life. I'll be twenty in April, and it's time I started living independently of my parents…and Reeve. I need to prove to myself that I can survive without him. That life will go on and it will get better.

"I promise I will see a therapist," I remind her. "It should be easy to go about my business unnoticed in Dublin."

At least, that's the plan. From the research I've done online, Ireland sounds like the ideal place to hide until all the interest in me dies down. Though I refuse to think of it as hiding. It's more akin to self-preservation. I'm taking time for myself, to heal, away from the fishbowl that is my current life in L.A. I'm nervous but excited too.

I'm thrilled at the prospect of studying at Trinity College Dublin, one of the world's most renowned and reputable colleges. Established in 1592, it boasts prestigious alumni. I will be joining the likes of Oscar Wilde and Samuel Beckett as an English literature student, and I'm giddy at the prospect of exploring all that wonderful Irish heritage and legendary Irish charm.

"I'm proud of you, princess." Dad reels me into a smothering hug. "We're going to miss you so much, but I think this is wonderful. Your mom does too. She just can't help worrying."

"I can't, but your dad is right, as usual." Mom wraps her arms around both of us, and we indulge in a group family hug that helps to warm all the frozen parts of me. "And maybe we could visit?" she asks when we break our embrace.

I bite on my lower lip. "Lauren and Jonathon Mills showing up in Dublin might get reported, and I'm trying to keep a low profile. But we'll see," I add when Mom's face drops. "Look at the positives." I squeeze her hand. "You can take that role now." They hadn't recast it yet as they were begging Mom to reconsider so my decision works out best for everyone.

Dad glances at his Patek Philippe watch, as the door opens and our driver starts grabbing my bags. "If you still want to drop by Reeve's house, you'll need to hurry. We'll be leaving in thirty minutes."

I nod, gathering my courage and taking a deep breath. "I'll go now, but I think I'll walk." I can work up the nerve to face him without breaking on the way over. It gives me an excuse to say what I want to say and leave, and if my resolve cracks, I have the ten-minute walk back to compose myself.

"Honey. Are you sure this is wise?" Mom asks.

"I can't leave the country without telling him, Mom."

"You don't owe Reeve anything, Vivien." Mom folds her arms, and I wonder if she'll ever forgive him.

Reeve hasn't just lost me.

He's lost my parents too.

Considering my parents virtually raised him, it's no small matter. From what I can see, Simon Lancaster is still keeping his son at arm's length. Reeve has lost his support system, and I'd be lying if I said I wasn't worried about him. I'm betting he never stopped to consider that before he took molly and made out with that bitch.

And, just like that, my anger is back.

I've had moments of weakness, where his words and his gestures have almost broken through the fragile walls I've erected around my heart. Then I remember that video—and how everyone knows he cheated on me—and I lose any remaining compassion for my ex.

A tight pain spreads across my chest, and I rub at it, willing it to go away. It hurts so much to call him that. I still can't believe he threw everything we had away for *her*. It's like the nineteen years we shared meant nothing to him, and I don't think I'll ever forgive him.

"Honey." Mom gently grips my shoulders. "You can write him a letter, and I'll see he gets it."

I shake off my melancholy. "No, it's okay. I'm going to speak with him."

Mom still looks uncertain. Dad circles his arms around her waist from behind, and I hate that the loving gesture pierces me straight through the heart. Reeve used to do that to me. Most likely he was subconsciously copying my dad, and I wonder if every time I see a couple engaged in PDA it will feel like someone is tearing strips off my annihilated heart. "Let Vivien do what she needs to do. Besides, I think Reeve needs to know. Otherwise, he may chase after her."

Like hell will he come anywhere near me. I'm doing this for my sanity. To get away from him and the media attention. If the hottest new movie star suddenly appeared on the streets of Dublin, I'm sure the Irish people would sit up and take notice, and my cover would be blown.

Reeve is not ruining this fresh start for me. I won't let him.

With fresh determination, I stride with purpose toward his house.

CHAPTER 26

MY HAND SHAKES as I press the bell, rocking back on my heels at Reeve's front door. It's strange to be waiting to be admitted when I'm used to having a key and letting myself in at all hours of the day and night.

The housekeeper opens the door, her eyes widening when she spots me.

"Hi, Mrs. Thompson. Is Reeve home?" I know he's here, because the premiere is tomorrow night and he texted me last night to tell me he was home. He begged me to attend it with him, but I told him a firm no. How the fuck could he expect me to walk the red carpet with that bitch? I'd be up on a murder charge before the end of the night. It's a moot point anyway. We're broken up, and I won't be walking any more red carpets with Reeve. The thought saddens me, but there's no going back now.

He also asked if we could talk, so he'll probably be ecstatic to discover I'm here.

"Hello, Vivien." Her smile is laced with pity, and I loathe it. I know she means well, but I hate that everyone knows he cheated on me. I force out a tight smile, and she steps aside to grant me entry. "Mr. Lancaster is here. He's eating breakfast in the sunroom if you'd like to join him."

"Thank you." Stepping inside, I set my key down on the hallway table. Won't be needing that anymore. Acid churns in my gut, and my heart jackhammers behind my rib cage as I walk through familiar hallways and rooms. Stopping outside the door to the sunroom, I wipe my clammy palms down the front of my skinny jeans, willing my thumping heart to slow down. I close my eyes and breathe deeply, trying to compose myself. Briefly, I consider fleeing, because now I'm here I don't know if I can do this. I could write him a letter in the car on the way to the airport and avoid seeing him.

A subtle whooshing of air as the door opens confirms it's too late to make an escape. Drawing a brave breath, I open my eyes, coming face to face with the man who broke my heart into itty-bitty pieces.

We stare at one another, and it's painful beyond belief. Tension bleeds into the air, mixing with the usual spark of electricity. Where once our connection comforted me, now all it does is exacerbate the agony. I dig my nails into the sides of my jeans to ignore the almost insurmountable urge to wrap my arms around him. Physically, my body still needs to get with the program. Reeve is breathtakingly handsome, even with punishing shadows under his eyes, a thick five-o'clock shadow, and the anguished expression etched on his face. His gorgeous blue gaze drills into mine, and his eyes turn glassy with emotion.

"Viv," he whispers. "You came." A hint of a cautious smile tugs up the corners of his mouth as he reaches for me.

Taking a step back, I avert my eyes and shake my head, gulping over the lump clogging my throat. Every part of me is in agony. Pain ravages me from the inside, and I wrap my arms around my torso, silently coaxing myself to just say my piece and get out of here.

"I miss you," he adds, shoving his hands in his pockets and leaning against the door frame. His accompanying sigh is heavy with emotion.

Reinforcing the walls around my heart, I lift my chin and pull my shoulders back, letting my arms drop to my side. I'm not going to fall apart in front of him again. "I miss you too, but it changes nothing."

His smile disappears. "Why are you here then?"

"I came to tell you I'm leaving."

He frowns, straightening up a little. "Leaving? Leaving for where?"

I had considered being vague, but I know Reeve. His stubbornness is legendary. If I don't tell him, he'll make it his mission to find out, and I can't have him showing up in Ireland unannounced.

"I'm moving to Dublin, Ireland. My plane leaves at noon."

Shock splays across his face, and he just stares at me for several tense seconds. Dragging his hands repeatedly through his hair, he asks. "How? Why? For how long?"

"UCLA has a transfer program with Trinity College Dublin. It's usually for junior year students, but Dad knows the president, and he made it happen for me. I'm going to complete my sophomore spring semester there." Normally, I hate relying on my parent's contacts. I like to be as independent as possible and to achieve things on my own merits. But this is a unique situation, and there is no way I would be leaving if Dad hadn't pulled strings and Doug Simmonds hadn't personally arranged it with Trinity.

Reeve's face drops, and he scrubs a hand over his stubbly jawline. "You're going away for five months?"

He says that like it'll be any different than last year when I barely saw him at all. It won't make any difference to Reeve whether I'm in L.A. or Ireland or Timbuktu. "At least. If I like it, I'll probably stay during summer break too," I explain. Audrey said she'll come visit me this summer if I'm still there. "As for why, I think that's obvious. I need to heal, and I can't do that in L.A. I need to go someplace the media won't find me. I need to leave all the noise behind."

"Leave me behind, you mean," he says in a pained voice.

I wet my dry lips, refusing to hide the truth even if I know my words will hurt him. "Yes. I can't put you and our relationship behind me when your face is everywhere and reminders of you are everywhere."

He grabs my hand, and the familiar tingling across my skin hurts so damn much. "Viv. I love you. I don't want to lose you. I don't want her. I've never wanted her. I only want you."

I yank my hand back, tucking both hands under my arms so he can't pull that maneuver again. "I don't want to leave on bad terms, Reeve. I will never forget what you did, but maybe one day I can find a way to forgive you. You're a free agent now. You can be with her with a clear conscience." It kills me to say that, and the thought of him being with her permanently might very well do me in, but I'll be thousands of miles away, blissfully ignorant, and that's the way I prefer it. Setting him free will ultimately help to set me free too, so that's why I'm doing this.

"Viv, please, just *hear* me. I don't want her," he blurts. "She means nothing to me and you're everything." He grabs fistfuls of his hair. "You're fucking everything, Viv." Tears stream down his face, and it's so hard not to comfort him, but I can't get drawn back in.

"You made a lot of mistakes that hurt me, but I don't want to hold on to the hurt and the pain. I don't want our relationship to be defined by our final days. I hope someday to be able to look back and remember the good times, because there were a lot of those." I am nowhere near ready to face that, but in the future, I hope the pain will ease and I can cherish the happy times and remember Reeve the way I want to remember him.

"This isn't the end, Viv. Please, baby. I can't lose you."

I exhale heavily, rubbing my throbbing temples. "Reeve, stop. Please stop. I can't do this again. You're making this harder." I drag in deep breaths as I fight to maintain the tenuous hold on my emotions. "I didn't want to leave without telling you in person, and now I've told you." I turn to go, and he pulls me into his arms.

"Please, Viv. Please don't say it's the end. It's not the end. It can't be. I'm not going to stop fighting for you."

Wracking sobs rip from my chest as I wrench myself from his arms. The scent of his cologne, the feel of his strong arms around me, the warmth emanating from his masculine body—it's all too much. I can't take it, and Mom was right. I shouldn't have come here. It's undone the little progress I've made in the intervening weeks since our breakup.

"If you love me, you won't fight, Reeve. You'll do this one thing for me," I sob, backing away from him. "Look what you've done to me! I'm destroyed." I openly cry, done pretending. "I'm so lost and in so much pain. Please just let me go. Let me go, and don't come looking for me. Don't contact me, because clinging to what we had won't help either of us," I whisper.

"I hate what I've done to you. What I've done to *us*, and I will get you back because I love you too much to let you go forever." He clasps my face in his hands, brushing my tears away as his fall. "But I'll give you space. Take whatever time you need. I'll wait for you."

I shake my head and remove his hands. "No. I don't want any loose ends. We are over, Reeve."

Determination glints in his gaze. "Not for good, Viv. Never for good."

"I don't know what the future holds, but I can't go to Ireland with things hanging in the air. The past two years of my life have been spent in limbo waiting for you, and I can't do it anymore. For my sanity, I need a clean break. If you love me, you'll stop fighting my decision. You need to let me go. I can't heal otherwise."

He opens and closes his mouth a few times before speaking. "Okay, if that's what you want, but this isn't goodbye, Viv. Only goodbye for now."

His stubborn determination knows no bounds. He can believe what he wants, because it doesn't matter. This is over, and I'm done letting his choices dictate mine. I won't be making any promises, and I'm done arguing. "I need to go, or I'll miss my flight."

"Take care of yourself. I'll be thinking of you."

My eyes lock on his. "I'm not saying this to hurt you, but I'll be trying not to think about you at all."

"I deserve that." His sad eyes drop to my chest. "You're not wearing your locket."

"It hurts too much to look at it, and I meant what I said about a clean start."

He takes a step closer, peering deeply into my eyes. "Someday, I'm going to correct my mistakes and win back your heart. I won't stop until I prove I'm worthy of your love again."

I can't respond to that, and I need to get out of here before I throw caution to the wind and take everything back. Reeve has always been a true romantic. He always has the right words at the right time. But loving words and promises aren't enough to extinguish the deep-seated pain of his betrayal. Still, I came here to leave things on an amicable footing, and I'm determined to do that. I cup his face one last time, and he leans into my touch. "Be happy, Reeve. That's all I've ever wanted for you."

With one last look, I walk off, grateful that he doesn't chase after me.

The next part of the story takes place in Ireland. There is a glossary at the front of this book you can refer to, which includes some explanations of local words/phrases and Irish/Gaelic pronunciations. We phrase some things differently, so if some of the Irish characters' dialogue seems a little odd, that is why!

CHAPTER 27

THE FLIGHT LANDS in Dublin at seven a.m. local time, and as I disembark, I promise myself I'm leaving my tears and my melancholy behind on the plane. The nighttime flight helped, but I found it hard to sleep with the eight-hour time difference and the fact my broken heart took a severe beating earlier today. Having Audrey say goodbye at LAX was a disastrous move too. Leaving my bestie behind only added to my distress.

I spent the first two hours of the ten-and-a-half-hour flight trying to fight tears and the next two hours trying to disguise my sobs from the other passengers. Being in first class helped, and the Aer Lingus flight attendant was super sweet and attentive when she noticed I was upset. Still, it's embarrassing, and I need to get a grip. I'm just lucky no one on the plane seemed to realize who I was.

I'm yawning as I move through passport control, but I perk up as I get my first proper look at Ireland through the large windows as I walk with other passengers toward the arrival hall. Gray skies and rain peer back at me, and it's kind of reassuring. If everything about Ireland is as expected, I think I'll really enjoy my time here.

Out in the arrivals area, I scan the space, my eyes inspecting all the cards held aloft until I spot one that says GRACE MILLS. As an extra precaution, I've decided to use my middle name here. Just in case any locals or visiting tourists make the connection. Pushing my luggage cart toward the rotund man in the ill-fitting black suit, I battle a sudden rush of butterflies.

I can't believe I'm here.

That I've really done this.

Excitement combines with nerves as I approach my driver. His name tag says Micheál, which I'm assuming is a Gaelic name.

"Hi. I'm Grace Mills."

"Howya, love. Aren't you a right looker?" Grabbing my hand, he vigorously shakes it.

"Ugh…" I'm at a loss for words.

"I'm Micheál," he says, pronouncing it like Mee-haul. "I'll be driving ya to your swanky apartment building in town." He winks, but it's not leery in the slightest. He gives off jovial grandpa vibes that have me instantly relaxing. "Good flight?" he continues, taking control of my luggage cart without asking.

"Yes," I lie, because I'm sure he doesn't want to hear how I spent half of it crying over my cheating ex and nursing my broken heart.

"First time in Dublin?" he inquires, waving to another couple of drivers as we walk off, heading into a plexiglass tunnel.

"First time in Ireland," I confirm. Audrey and I had planned to visit when we were in Europe last summer, but we never made it.

"Well, you're in for a treat. What part of America are you from?"

He talks fast, and his accent is so thick that I have to wait a few seconds for my brain to process the words and decipher his question. "Los Angeles."

He whistles under his breath, nodding at me. "I took one look at ya, and I just knew you were a Hollywood princess."

My eyes startle wide, and panic races to the surface at the thought my cover might have already been blown. Maybe I'll just say California in the future, because I don't want to lie and have to keep track of what I'm telling people. Remembering to say my name is Grace will be challenging enough.

He chuckles heartily as we head across the dark, chilly parking lot. A full-body shiver works its way through me, and I can already tell reports about the cold winter weather were not unfounded. I sense a shopping trip in my near future.

"Relax, love. It's only a figure of speech. I've heard all the birds in Hollywood are real beauties and they all want to be actresses." He stops at a black Mercedes car with a yellow taxi sign on the roof. He continues talking while he opens the trunk, and I glance at the other cars around us, spotting a lot of brands I'm familiar with. "Is it true they all have fake knockers?" he asks.

I blink profusely, staring blankly at him. I thought they spoke English in Dublin, but I'm completely confused and second-guessing myself.

He chuckles at the expression on my face. "Plastic tits," he explains.

Ah, now I'm getting the gist. "It's true a lot of women in Hollywood are fans of cosmetic surgery." Not this gal though. I plan to grow old gracefully, like Mom.

"I've only been to America once," he adds, swiftly stacking my suitcases in the trunk. "I brought me missus and the kids to Orlando, when me missus was me mot. It's a fecking fantastic place."

He might as well be speaking Gaelic. For all I know, he is. I stare blankly at him again, and he chuckles as he opens the back door of the car for me.

"I always forget you Yanks speak differently. Me missus is me wife."

"Good to know. Thank you." My smile is genuine, because it's easy to respond naturally to his friendly manner.

Removing a photo from his wallet, Micheál leans back to show me. "That's my Maureen, and my three boys. She's still a looker, even after all these years." His chest swells with pride.

"You have a beautiful family," I agree, handing the photo back to him.

He talks nonstop throughout the journey from Dublin Airport to the city center, changing subjects seamlessly and barely pausing for a breath. Traffic is heavier than I was expecting but it's not as bad as L.A. His driving skills leave a lot to be desired, and he's constantly switching lanes, honking his horn, cussing, and shaking his fist when other drivers try to cut in front of him.

By the time we reach the brown brick and glass high-rise I'll be calling home for the next few months, my heart is in my mouth from the stress of his crazy driving and he's given me a summary of his life story and a list of places I need to visit. "Home sweet home, love," he says, pulling into an underground parking lot under the Capital Dock Residence building. "This place is the perfect location," he adds, maneuvering into a vacant spot by the doors that lead to the elevators. "You're right beside the Liffey, and it's only a ten-minute walk to Trinners. You're slap bang in the heart of the city with access to all the shops, pubs, and restaurants. You'll have a grand ole time in our fair city."

"Thank you so much, Micheál." I lean forward, handing him a fifty-euro bill as a tip. Mom's assistant Moira booked everything, and I know he's already been paid for the journey.

"Jesus, love. You can't be giving me that. It's too much."

"Trust me. It was worth it for the wealth of knowledge I've gleaned on the journey here. You should be a tour guide," I quip, climbing out of the car.

"Maybe I missed my true calling." He waggles his brows while unloading my suitcases.

He insists on coming inside with me, and between us, we manage to get all my luggage into the small elevator. Or lift, as Micheál keeps calling it.

Micheál whistles under his breath as we step out of the elevator into a large lobby. "Would you get a look at this place?" he says, looking awestruck as he glances around. "This is how the other half live."

A tall, slim woman with dark hair pulled back in a ponytail steps forward to greet me. She's wearing a navy skirt suit with a white blouse and holding a clipboard. "Ms. Mills?" she asks, extending her arm for a handshake.

"That's me." I shake her hand.

She smiles, flashing a set of beautiful white teeth. "I'm Ciara, the manager on duty today. I'm delighted to welcome you to Capital Dock Residence, and I hope you'll enjoy your stay with us."

"You're in capable hands now, love." Micheál grabs my hand, pressing a card into my palm. "Enjoy your time in Ireland, and if you need a taxi, I'm yer man." I wave him off while Ciara arranges for someone to take my luggage up to the penthouse apartment.

Ciara gives me a quick tour of the communal areas, which includes a resident's lounge, a game room, business suite, small cinema, and a decent-sized gym. We don't venture outside, because the rain is plummeting down now, but she points out the landscaped gardens and courtyards, and maybe if I'm still here in the summer, I can make use of the outdoor space. She confirms I'm booked and fully paid until the beginning of June and all the utilities are included in the monthly rental payment.

She escorts me up to my apartment, and I'm blown away by the gorgeous, large, spacious two-bedroom, three-bathroom penthouse complete with a small rooftop garden. Sophisticated interior design and modern furniture are the main features of my new home, and I couldn't have asked for anything better. I know it's a world away from the average student accommodations, and I'm lucky. I would've taken a place on campus, but *Trinners* doesn't have many accommodations, and there were no vacancies. Walking to the large floor-to-ceiling windows, I inhale deeply, already feeling a layer of stress lift from my body.

This place is perfect.

Just perfect.

My smile expands as I press my nose to the glass, rain pitter-pattering against the window. The views over the River Liffey and Dublin City Center are spectacular.

Ciara shows me how to work the appliances, use the shower, and regulate the heating. She laughs when I crank the thermostat to the max, feeling decidedly chilly even though the apartment isn't cold. I'm guessing it'll take this Cali girl some time to adjust to the vastly different climate in Ireland.

After she leaves, I do a little dance and emit a squeal before exploring the rest of my new home.

I make a quick call to my parents since I know they are waiting up to hear from me. I texted them when I landed on Irish soil, and I had planned on calling them from the taxi, but Micheál and his enthusiastic banter ended that plan. I FaceTime Mom and Dad, giving them a quick tour of my new place, thanking them profusely for organizing all of this and asking Mom to email me Moira's address so I can send her an Irish care package as a thank-you.

Stripping off my clothes in the bigger of the two bedrooms, I take a blistering-hot shower before changing into yoga pants and a top. Yanking my wet hair into a messy bun on top of my head, I flop down on the bed and open the Irish cell phone Moira organized for me. It wasn't necessary. I could've just used my US one, but I like the idea of switching off my main cell and forgetting about all the shit I've left behind.

My parents and Audrey are the only people I need to stay in contact with, so I shoot them a quick text ensuring they have my new number. Briefly, I contemplate messaging Reeve from my US cell, but I think better of it. I need to cut ties, and it's best to start out how I mean to go on. It's hard though, because I'm used to sharing everything with him without even thinking about it. It's second nature to call him or message him, but I guess I'll eventually break the habit.

I spend a couple of hours unpacking all my stuff and hanging it in my closet. Then I dress more warmly in boots, jeans, and my thickest sweater, grab my jacket, and head out to explore. My inability to sleep properly on the plane is affecting me now, and I need to keep busy to stop myself from falling asleep. Classes start in three days, and I need to have reset my body clock by then. I'm determined to stay awake for as long as possible today.

The instant I step outside, I'm accosted by a blast of cold air I feel deep in my bones. "Holy shit," I mumble to myself. "There's cold, and there's Ireland." At least the rain has stopped, which is a bonus. Pulling up Google maps, I follow the sidewalks to Grafton Street. Ciara said it's the best place to shop, and she suggested I try Brown Thomas, a high-end department store.

I have to walk past Trinity College on the way, and I can't resist taking a peek. I'm wearing the biggest smile as I pass under Trinity's famous granite campanile—

the iconic bell tower. Superstition says anyone passing under the campanile when the bell chimes will fail their exams, so apparently, many students refuse to walk under it.

I'm determined to be strong and brave.

To emerge from the wreckage of my heartbreak like a new woman, and from now on, I'm going to laugh in fate's face.

With that in mind, I walk back and forth under the bell tower for several minutes, gathering plenty of inquisitive stares from the men and women walking across the campus.

Taking out my phone, I snap a ton of pics as I stroll among the impressive gray stone buildings, admiring the exquisite architecture. The campus is pristine and clearly well-maintained. Ghosts of students past seem to hover around me, and the air vibrates with the history of the surroundings. My glee elevates with every step I take, reaffirming the decision I made to come here.

Something about this place feels so right.

It's an unshakeable feeling.

Like fate has brought me here for a reason.

Laughing at myself, I resist the lure of the library and the *Book of Kells* continuing my way to Grafton Street. The pedestrianized street is only a few minutes' walk from the campus, and it's bustling with people. I stop outside Bewley's Café to listen to some of the musicians busking in the street, soaking up the electric atmosphere.

My tired body gains a new lease on life as I explore my new city.

I purchase some warmer clothes in Brown Thomas, organizing delivery direct to my apartment building. Then I spend an enjoyable afternoon strolling through the park at St. Stephen's Green, feeding the birds, and wandering through quirky little side streets. When my stomach rumbles, reminding me I haven't eaten anything since the plane, I step into my first Irish pub.

Bruxelles is just off Grafton Street, and it's a traditional Irish pub known for its live music and great food. Pulling myself up onto a stool, I examine the menu, ordering the beef stew because I'm fucking freezing and I could use something hot to warm me up. Micheál told me I should sample the black stuff, aka Guinness, but I'm not sure I could stomach it today, so I opt for a glass of wine, purely because I can. In Ireland, the legal drinking age is eighteen, which is an added bonus.

I do some grocery shopping on the return journey, almost collapsing with exhaustion by the time I make it back to my new abode. It's only seven p.m. and still way too early to sleep. So, I figure out how to use the Nespresso coffee machine and make myself a double espresso before logging on to the Trinity College student portal and downloading my class schedule.

I give up the fight a couple of hours later and crawl into bed, too tired to remember my heartache.

Waking up the following morning, I'm disorientated for a few seconds until I remember where I am. I glance at the clock, surprised to see it's ten a.m. I slept for a solid thirteen hours, which has got to be a new record for me.

Nausea swims up my throat as I wonder what went down at the premiere last night. Grabbing my cell, I press it against my chest as I try to talk myself out of checking the internet. All the thoughts I'd so successfully blocked yesterday resurface, and I think I might be sick. My mind unhelpfully conjures up images of Reeve and

Saffron pawing at one another on the red carpet, dredging up the visual of them kissing that is forever imprinted in my brain, and a sob rips from my chest.

Why did I tell Reeve he was a free agent?

Why did I say he was free to be with her with a clear conscience?

Why did I leave?

Tossing my phone on the bed, I sit up, burying my head in my hands as I cry. Pain rips through me like a tornado, flattening everything in its path. Intense longing washes over me, and I wish Reeve was here. I wish he was experiencing all the wonders of Ireland alongside me. I wish that I wasn't alone, but I'd better get used to it, because we're not together anymore. I won't be sending him any of those pics I took yesterday or sharing details of my first day in a new country, because that's not who we are to one another anymore.

Losing Reeve impacts my life in so many different ways, and it's learning how to exist on my own that is my biggest challenge.

One I'm not sure I'm strong enough to accomplish.

Maybe I was too hasty in walking away from him.

Too quick to discount his declarations of love.

"Oh God," I cry out, rolling into a ball on my side. "Make it stop!" I scream to the empty room. "Please make this pain stop!"

My cell pings, and I snatch it up, desperate for a distraction. It's a message from Audrey. She must be out partying if she's still up this late.

You said you didn't want to know, but I'm your best friend, and I know you're tearing yourself apart wondering what happened at the premiere. Reeve wasn't with her. He looked tense in all the photographs, and he kept his distance as much as possible. He left the after-party early, and he was alone. If it helps, he looked utterly miserable. According to reports, she was hanging off Rudy all night. So, dry your tears. Remember I love you and I miss you so much already. Be brave, and go shape your own destiny.

CHAPTER 28

MY LEGS ARE SHAKING with nervous anticipation as I enter the lecture hall for my very first class at Trinity. Ironically, it's American literature. Though I will be taking classes in Irish writing, postcolonial literature, Shakespeare, and the Middle Ages too. I am also attending some classes in film studies, because the degree program here is a joint majors course. The syllabus this year has a big focus on screenwriting, so it wasn't a hard sell.

Choosing a middle row in the center section of the room, I claim a seat and take out my iPad, notebook, and pens. There aren't many people here yet, but the class doesn't start for fifteen minutes. I wanted to be early in case I got lost, but it's not a difficult campus to navigate.

Gradually, the room fills up, and sounds of laughter and noisy conversation reverberate around me. There are a couple of guys sitting at the end of my row, shooting curious glances my way, but I'm alone until a petite girl with a strawberry-blonde pixie cut and a stud in her nose plops down in the seat beside me.

"What's up?" she says, smiling at me as she removes her chunky wool coat, placing it on the back of her seat. Leaning down, she stuffs her scarf into her bag.

"Hey." I return her warm smile with one of my own.

She pulls a notepad and pen out of her bag. "I was scared shitless I'd miss the start of class. I'm sure you've heard Professor Chalmers biting the head off me for being late before."

"Actually, I'm new here. This is my first day."

Her pretty blue eyes spark with intrigue. "You're American?"

"I am. I'm from L.A." I've decided not to lie about that.

"I've always wanted to visit L.A, but with five kids in the family, money for trips to America wasn't plentiful in our house." She cocks her head to the side, smiling again. "I'm Aisling, by the way. But everyone calls me Ash."

"Grace. Nice to meet you."

"What other classes are you taking?" she asks, and I pull out my schedule, showing it to her.

"Deadly. We've got a few classes together. I can show you around, if you like?"

"That would be awesome."

She flashes me a grin, crossing her booted feet at the ankles. "I could listen to your accent all day."

I laugh. "I could say the same thing." Her voice is more lyrical and less guttural than Micheál's but not quite as refined as Ciara's. It's obvious that like the US, dialects and speech patterns are different depending on what part of Ireland someone is from.

Our conversation comes to an abrupt end when the professor enters the room and the lecture starts.

Ash and I have the same classes this morning, which is a godsend, because it means I don't have to wander aimlessly around campus. At lunch, she takes me to the Buttery, one of the dining options on campus, and I meet some of her friends.

"Grace is from L.A.," Ash tells the two girls and two guys.

"How come you're at Trinners?" the pretty girl with red hair asks. I think Ash said her name is Catriona.

"I go to UCLA, and they have a transfer program with Trinity. The opportunity came up to spend this semester here and I jumped at the chance."

"Who's your new friend, Ash?" someone with a deep voice asks, and I whip my head around, trying not to stare at the hot guy standing beside Aisling. With his nose ring, eyebrow piercing, skull tattoo, and brown faux hawk with white-blond tips, he's about as far removed from the stereotypical Irish male image in my head as you can get. His black jacket is open, revealing a wrinkled Muse T-shirt which clings to his broad chest and toned abs. Shredded jeans and scuffed boots complete the look, and there's no denying he's a good-looking guy. Several girls in the vicinity blatantly check him out.

Ash folds her arms and glares at him. "So, you're talking to me now?"

He narrows his eyes at her while scrubbing a hand along his unshaven jaw. "I'm not a morning person. You know that. You also know the session went on late last night, so stop annoying me."

They've clearly got history, and from the heated way they are staring at one another, it seems pretty tempestuous.

Ash huffs as she turns to me, jabbing her finger in the guy's direction. "This dumbass is Jamie." She looks up at him, fixing him with a tight smile. "Dumbass, this is Grace."

"Hey." I jerk my head in acknowledgment, offering him a small smile.

"You must be new because I'd never forget a face like yours," he says, waggling his brows and licking his lips. Intense brown eyes drill into mine, and I squirm in my seat.

"I just moved here from the US."

He rakes his gaze over me, from head to toe, and heat creeps up my neck. Are all Irish guys this blatantly obvious? "Bring her on Friday," Jamie says to Aisling. "We can show her how we like to party in Ireland."

His smirk is suggestive, making me even more uncomfortable. I'm not that naïve to think he's awed by my beauty. More like my newness is a novelty. Along with the fact I'm from overseas. Guys are the last thing on my mind, and this one screams trouble with a capital T. He's also rude and arrogant, and neither are traits I admire in a man. Plus, there's some history with Ash, and I have zero desire to get in the middle of that. I like my new friend, and this jerk isn't going to get in the way of our burgeoning friendship.

Ash rolls her eyes. "Shut up talking shite, Jay. You're an idiot." A scowl crawls across her pretty face, and she sits up straighter in her chair. "Here comes your tramp. Do us all a favor and fuck off."

A sexy blonde saunters toward us wearing leggings and a long off-the-shoulder sweater that skims her upper thighs. Thick black liner rims her big blue eyes, and her lips kick up in amusement as she loops her arm through Jamie's. "I thought we were meeting the others at Yum Thai?"

"Which one are you banging this week, Aoife, or do I need to ask?" Ash says, eyeing the woman with clear contempt.

"Who says I'm only banging one of them?" Aoife smirks, leaning her head against Jamie's shoulder. He wraps his arm around her waist while continuing to stare at Ash.

"Charming," she tells her before turning the full extent of her disgust at Jamie. "I hope your dick falls off."

Aoife eyes me suspiciously from her perch on Jamie's shoulder, and I school my features into a neutral line as I maintain eye contact.

Jamie tugs at his eyebrow piercing while smirking at Aisling. He leans his face in closer to hers and lowers his tone a little. "Sure, you do, Ash."

She huffs out a sigh. "Get lost, Jay. I'm busy." A brief flash of pain spreads across her face before she hurriedly hides it.

Straightening up, Jamie brushes Aoife's hair off her shoulder, leans in, and presses a kiss to the corner of her mouth. "It seems I'm busy too." He winks, licking his lips again, and I'm liking this guy even less with every passing minute.

Aoife turns into him, flinging her arms around his neck. "Your place or mine?" she purrs, licking a path along his neck.

Gross.

Aisling lowers her eyes to the table, and I notice her hands are gripping her chair tight. I clicked instantly with Ash this morning when we met, but it's this moment right here that tells me we're going to be great friends.

Reaching under the table, I squeeze her hand.

Jamie and Aoife wander off without saying goodbye, and it's good riddance. Neither seem like nice people.

"He's a wanker," Catriona says. "And you can do so much better."

"Don't tell me you're sleeping with him again?" Ash's tall dark-haired friend asks.

She vigorously shakes her head. "I'm not. I learned that lesson, but it's not like I can avoid him, ya know?"

"Who is he?" I inquire, watching the couple disappear through the far door of the restaurant.

"Jamie is one-quarter of Toxic Gods and my brother's best mate."

I quirk a brow. "Toxic Gods?"

Bending over in her seat, she rummages through her bag. "It's a fucking stupid name. I keep telling Dil and Ro to change it." She pulls out a pack of cigarettes and stands. Lifting one shoulder, she asks, "Keep me company outside?"

We leave our stuff at the table with the others and head outside to the smoking area. Fuck, it's cold, and I'm regretting leaving my new coat on the back of my chair. Wrapping my arms around myself, I try to ward off any shivering. I'm silent as I watch Ash pull a few long drags of her cigarette. "Shit, sorry. You want one?" She holds the pack out to me, and I shake my head.

"I don't smoke."

"Good for you." She draws a few more drags, blowing smoke circles into the frigid air. "I've tried to give it up, but I have no willpower. It's hard to go cold turkey when you hang around the live indie rock scene as much as I do. Most everyone smokes."

"So Toxic Gods is the name of a band?" I surmise.

She nods. "Crap name, but the guys are great. Destined to be stars if Dillon would take it seriously for five fucking seconds."

"And Dillon is?"

"One of my brothers."

"How many do you have?" She mentioned there were five kids at home previously.

"Four, ranging in age from twenty-seven to eighteen."

"Holy shit. That's a lot of testosterone under one roof!"

"You've no idea. Cursing and smoking are only two of the bad habits I picked up from them."

I step aside to let a few people pass by. "It must be kind of nice too. I bet they're protective of you," I say, automatically thinking of Reeve. No one got away with bullying me at school because Reeve would give them hell if they even looked funny at me.

"They are. Mostly Dillon. We were only one year apart in school, and we've always been the closest. My little brother Ronan is in the band with Dillon, and he stays at their apartment in Temple Bar on the weekends, so I'm getting closer to him too. They can be clowns at times, but it's good to know they have my back." Throwing her cigarette butt on the ground, she stomps it out with her boot before linking her arm in mine. "C'mon. Let's get you inside before you freeze your arse off."

I don't see Ash for the rest of the afternoon as we're in different classes. She invites me to go for a drink with her and her friends later, but I decline because I've got my first physical therapy appointment this evening. I've lost a lot of strength in my left hand since the attack, and I need to work on building it back up again. My natural go-to distraction is designing and making clothes, and I need both hands in full working order ASAP. So, I've booked a few sessions each week with a physical therapist, and I plan to go shopping for a new sewing machine and supplies this weekend.

The rest of the week goes fast, and I'm enjoying my classes and hanging out with Ash and her friends. They have welcomed me with open arms, and it's nice to meet genuine down-to-earth people with no agenda who accept me for who I am.

So, when they ask me to go for a drink with them on Thursday night, I agree this time.

We start off at the Pav, the bar on campus, before walking to Grogan's, a local bar that is popular with students and an older crowd. Ash goes to the bar to order drinks with the others while Catriona and I nab the only vacant table in the corner. "Wow, this place is like a throwback to the sixties." I remove my coat and scarf and sit down on a low stool with a blue velvet seat. Wooden panels adorn the lower section of the art-covered walls. Patterned carpet that has seen better days covers the floors while old-fashioned lights hang from the white ceiling. There is no music playing, and the only melody in the place is the lyrical hum of many Irish voices. The place is packed. "Is it usually this busy?" I ask, peering at the eclectic local art on the walls.

"Yeah. It's a popular pub, and Thursday night is a popular night to go out in town."

"This one's on me," Ash says, placing a glass of Guinness down on the table in front of me. "I didn't get you a pint in case you can't stand it. The barman added a dash of blackcurrant. I find that makes it more drinkable." She claims the stool beside me, and the others join us. She clinks her beer bottle against my glass. "Bottoms up!"

Gingerly, I take a sip, letting the taste linger in my mouth for a few seconds before taking another.

"Well? What's the verdict?" she asks.

"It's an acquired taste, for sure, but not altogether bad." I don't think I'll be drinking much Guinness while I'm in Ireland, but I can manage this glass. I ask Ash to take a pic of me with it so I can send it to Audrey later. She has demanded I document everything.

After drinking half the glass, I change my mind. It sits heavily in my stomach, like I've just eaten a bowl of stew, and I need something more refreshing to cleanse my palate. They all tease me when I push the rest of my drink toward one of the guys and head to the bar to order a vodka cranberry.

"So, what's your story?" Ash asks a little while later when we're talking alone. "Do you have a boyfriend back home in L.A.?"

Stabby pains shoot through my heart, and bile churns in my gut. It's a harmless question. A normal one. One I'm sure I'll get asked again and again. But it instantly sends me drowning in an ocean of grief.

"Shit, sorry. I didn't mean to pry," she says when my face clearly conveys my emotions.

"It's okay." My watery smile says otherwise. "I had a recent breakup. It's still pretty raw."

"Were you guys together long?"

"Yeah. Over five years as a couple but longer as best friends." I circle my finger around the rim of my glass. "We were neighbors, and our families were close. His mom died giving birth to him, so he basically grew up at my house." I'm deliberately keeping the details vague on the off chance she knows any of Reeve's background and makes the connection.

"Shit. That's rough."

"Yup." I take a large mouthful of my drink.

"The guy must be a dope to let someone like you go."

I think so, because I doubt Reeve will ever find anyone who loves him as much as me. But I can't let my mind go there. I'm still way too fragile and the last thing I want to do is burst into tears in front of my new friends, and then have to explain. I'm not ready for explanations yet, if ever. "What about you?" I ask, desperately wanting to change the subject. "Are you dating anyone?"

"I'm not seeing anyone. I was going out with this guy from school for a few years. During sixth year, he broke my heart, and I swore off boyfriends after that." I know from my research that sixth year in Ireland is the equivalent of senior year in high school. She looks off into space with the saddest expression on her face. "Anyway, Trinners has been great. I've been embracing my inner slut and sleeping with different guys, but I run a mile if any of them look for more. I had to commute from home during first year here, which made it hard to get with guys, but I'm living in a studio flat close to my brothers' apartment this year, so I have more freedom."

"I'm getting a feeling you and I might be kindred spirits," I tell her, because it's clear she's suffering the aftereffect of heartache. Maybe she'll have some tips for how to repair the fractures in my heart.

CHAPTER 29

I SURVEY the pile of clothes covering my bed and the floor while I stand in my black lace underwear in front of the mirror in my bedroom, no closer to making a decision. I have no clue what to wear. Glancing at the time on my cell, I curse out loud in the empty room. I tap out a quick message to Ash, asking her for help, and then I pad into my en suite bathroom to apply a full face of makeup. I don't normally wear much makeup, but it's my first proper night out in Ireland, with a bunch of new people, and I feel like I need armor.

I'm straightening my long dark hair when my cell pings with a new message.

Keep it casual but sexy. Jeans with a crop top and heels.

Inspecting the items surrounding me, I choose some ripped black jeans, black and gold Armani high heels, and a black lace crop top I've never been brave enough to wear. The sheer lace design covers my arms and my upper body, but my bra will be clearly visible underneath. The V-shaped hem exposes a decent amount of my midriff, but as I examine my reflection in the mirror, I know I look hot.

Gulping back nerves, I down a vodka shot for courage before I grab my coat and purse, lock the door, and leave to meet up with Ash.

She's waiting for me outside Trinity, and we walk up Grafton Street, meeting the others outside the mall before we walk to the venue. "This place will be mad," Ash warns me as we approach the bar. "Whelans is known for live music, and it's always packed at the weekends. Toxic Gods have played here before but usually upstairs. Tonight, they're playing in the main room, so it's going to be wild."

We follow the others into the deceptively large bar, and I'm accosted by a blast of heat and noisy chatter from the crowded room. Ash may be pint-sized and slim, but that doesn't stop her from charging her way through the busy room. I spot Jamie's distinctive faux hawk as we approach a long L-shaped seating area in the corner. A scratched mahogany table is in the middle of the space with red leather seating against the wall and a bunch of freestanding high-backed wooden chairs in front. A group of guys and girls are already seated, but there's just enough room for us.

"What's up, assholes," Ash says, leaning down to give a one-armed hug to a guy with messy dark hair and startling blue eyes.

"Sis. You made it." Muscular arms wrap around Ash as he squeezes her tight.

"Where's Dillon?" she asks, straightening up and looking around.

"In the jacks," a guy with long brown hair and matching brown eyes says.

"Come sit here," Jamie says, patting his thigh and arching a brow at Ash.

"Over my dead body," she replies.

The guy she was hugging—who I'm assuming is her youngest brother Ronan—lifts his eyes to meet mine. His mouth turns up at the corners as he gives me a quick once-over. Unlike when his buddy Jamie did it the other day, his inspection is respectful, and it doesn't make me squirm. He's cute in an innocent boy-next-door kind of way. Unlike the guys surrounding him, I see no visible ink or piercings.

"Aren't you going to introduce me?" He jerks his head in my direction.

"If it isn't my favorite sister," someone says in a deep husky voice from directly behind me, cutting across the conversation. "About time you showed up."

All the tiny hairs on the back of my neck lift, and warmth races over my skin. Heat rolls off the newcomer in waves, and I feel it even through my heavy coat. My heart hammers against my rib cage, and all my senses are on high alert.

Ash spins around, thumping him in the upper arm while I stand rooted to the spot, watching their interaction out of the corner of my eye. "I'm your only sister, clown, and that joke's getting real old."

"Is this the Yank?" he asks, and Ash thumps him again.

"Be nice, Dillon," she warns, as I slowly turn around.

Shock splays across his stunning face as our eyes meet for the first time. Panic slams into me, and I'm temporarily horrified at the thought he might have recognized me. Prickles of awareness dance over my skin as every cell in my body sizzles with an instant connection. I'm only a few inches short of six foot in these heels, but Dillon still towers over me. He must be six two or three, at least. Broad shoulders stretch across a tight black T-shirt that clings to his impressive chest and abs. Ink covers both arms, and he has an eyebrow and nose piercing. A silver chain circles his neck, and he's wearing a cluster of leather bands on one wrist and a few silver rings on one hand.

But that's not the most striking thing about him.

Bleach-blond messy hair tumbles in waves over his forehead, and the sides are shorn tight. With high cheekbones, a sharp jawline, and a stylish layer of stubble coating his chin and cheeks, he is fucking gorgeous. Piercing bright green eyes stare intensely at me from behind long thick black lashes. Electricity crackles in the small space between us, and I know I'm staring, but I can't drag my eyes away. Heat blooms in my cheeks as I blush.

I have never had such a visceral reaction to a guy before, and it's unnerving.

The initial shock I registered has faded from his face, replaced with a look that is borderline angry. A muscle pops in his jaw, and I instinctively step back, the backs of my thighs hitting the side of the table, rattling it. Glasses clink, and drinks slosh over the table.

"Watch it," Jamie snaps, eyeballing me. "Or the next round's on you."

"Stop complaining," Ash says to Jamie while tugging on Dillon's arm. "A little drink got spilled. Big deal."

Dillon is glaring at me, his fists clenching and unclenching at his sides, and I'm feeling hugely uncomfortable.

Ronan gets up, shoving Dillon aside. "You're being rude." He drills him a pointed look.

Ash snorts. "Are you even surprised?"

"I'm Ronan," he says, smiling at me. "Ash and Dillon's brother, but please don't hold that against me."

"Grace." I smile back at him. "Nice to meet you."

Dillon's eyes narrow. "Why are you here, *Grace?*" he spits out, staring at me like my presence personally offends him in some way.

"Ash invited me," I say, purposely projecting my voice and standing taller, even as I gulp over the anxiety traveling up my throat. Dillon's single-minded focus, dark stare, and strange intensity intimidate me. I'm pretty tall for a girl, so it's rare I feel small or an urge to cower, but I'm feeling both things now. He has this larger-than-life presence that is scary as much as it's intriguing. Ash told me there is only a year separating her and Dillon, but somehow, he seems older.

His lips curl into a sneer. "In Ireland," he clips out.

I frown. "What does it matter why I'm here?"

"Just answer the question," he barks, his eyes darting all around for a few seconds before he refocuses that all-consuming lens on me again.

"I don't owe you any explanation, and is this how you always treat new people you meet?"

"I'm suspicious of anyone who comes into my sister's life," he says, leaning his face in closer to mine. "Especially nosy Americans."

"Wow. Generalize much?" Crossing my arms over my chest, I glare at him. What the hell is his problem?

"You're pissing me off now, Dil." Ash grabs his arm, yanking him back.

"Fact." Ronan agrees.

"What's going on?" a familiar blonde says, coming up behind Dillon. It's the same girl who was with Jamie in Trinity on Monday—Aoife.

"Nothing," Dillon grits out, his jaw clenching. Slinging his arm around Aoife's shoulders, he sinks onto a chair beside Jamie, pulling her down on his lap. She paws at him, whispering something in his ear.

Air oozes out of my mouth in grateful relief now his attention is diverted. My limbs loosen as a layer of tension evaporates.

"Don't mind him," Ash says. "He's an overprotective idiot, and his bark is worse than his bite."

"Sometimes," Ronan drawls.

"Why would you need protection from me?" I ask Ash, confusion clear in my tone. "Have you guys had a bad experience with Americans in the past or something?"

"Honestly, don't take it to heart," Ash says. "Dillon is…complicated."

"He's a grumpy prick," Ronan says. "But it's nothing personal. He's angry with the world most days." He flashes me a dazzling smile. "Forget about him. Tell me more about you. What part of the US are you from?"

I'm grateful for the subject change, even if talking about myself gives me a major case of the heebie-jeebies these days. I'm a little on edge, praying someone doesn't recognize me and out me to my new friends. Yet I don't want to lie. I can be vague and fudge the truth. That way, if my identity is ever revealed, I can still look my friends in the face. "Los Angeles."

His eyes widen. "Really?"

I nod, instantly warming to him. He's the polar opposite of his brother and as friendly as his sister.

"My dream is to emigrate to L.A. and make it big on the music scene. We're good enough to make it, if we can just catch a break."

"You'll realize quickly both my brothers have extremely healthy egos," Ash says, steering me toward the opposite end of the table.

"I got us some drinks," Catriona says, patting the comfy leather seat beside her. "Sit with me."

Noticing the pile of coats and jackets on the window ledge behind our table, I unbutton my coat, folding it and my scarf and placing it on top of the existing mountain.

"Holy fuck. You look smokin'," Ash says, grinning.

Feeling eyeballs on my back, I turn around, meeting Dillon's heated stare. Slowly, his eyes rake over me from head to toe. It's as if he's peeling off my clothes, leaving me naked and exposed to his hungry eyes. I squeeze my thighs together as desire coils low in my belly, and my heart is thumping wildly in my chest. Aoife narrows her eyes, scowling in my direction when she notices Dillon's attention has strayed. Her arms wrap more possessively around his neck, but he's not showing her any attention.

Out of the corner of my eye, I see Jamie and the guy with the long hair staring at me too, and I'm wondering if it was a good idea to wear this top after all. I'm not sure I'm ready for attention from the opposite sex, even if a part of me is thrilled at their reactions.

My chest heaves as Dillon's eyes linger on my black bra, and my mouth is suddenly dry.

"Wow. You're beautiful," Ronan says, admiration evident in his gaze and his tone. His words break the hypnotic spell I was in, and I wrest my gaze from Dillon, focusing on Ash's younger brother. "If all the women in L.A. look like you, I'm even more determined to make it there someday." He waggles his brows.

"Most of them *don't* look like me," I supply. "I think there are more blondes with fake tits in L.A. than any other place in the world."

"I'd really love to chat to you about it," he adds, as I maneuver my way around the table, flopping down on the seat beside Cat.

"Not now." Ash nudges her brother aside so she can claim the last seat beside me. "We're here to have a good time. Grace can talk to you about L.A. another time."

"I'm happy to talk to you. Maybe you and Ash could come over to my place for lunch sometime, but just understand I know nothing about the music scene in LA," I admit, curiously eyeing the pink concoction with floating strawberries in the large wineglass. "What's this?" I ask, turning to face Cat.

"Pink Gin with 7UP. It's delicious. Try it."

I'm more of a vodka girl, but I take a sip, instantly liking the sweet, fruity, refreshing taste. "This *is* good."

"It's too sweet for me," Ash says, bringing a bottle of beer to her lips.

"I still feel like pinching myself being able to openly drink," I admit, even if I'm luckier than most because at private industry parties back home no one bats an eye if I drink.

"You can't drink in America?" Ronan asks. He's leaning against the wall, sipping a beer.

Someone hasn't done their homework. "Legal age is twenty-one, and they're strict." I'm not sure how the music industry works, but if it's anything like Hollywood, I think he'll get by.

"That's fucked in the head," Ronan replies.

"Changing your mind?" I tease, taking another mouthful of my drink.

"Nah. I'll just have to get a fake ID." He grins, lifting the bottle to his mouth.

A shrill whistle rings out, and we whip our heads to the end of the table. Jamie, Dillon, and the guy with long hair are standing, eyeballing Ronan.

"Sound check," Dillon says, gesturing him forward.

"You're hanging around to watch our set, yeah?" Ronan asks.

"Sure." I give him a reassuring smile, purposely ignoring Dillon. I don't need to look to know his eyes are fixed on me, because I feel his penetrating gaze crawl over every inch of my skin.

The guys wander off with Aoife trailing behind them.

"What's up with Aoife?" I ask, when they have disappeared.

"She's the band's main groupie." Ash purses her lips as she confirms my suspicions. "She's banged them all except Ronan. He's got more sense."

"For now," Cat says. "If they make it big, it will be harder for your little bro to maintain that innocence."

Ash almost spits beer all over the table. "Ronan might not get with girls as much as the others, but he's far from innocent. Trust me, I learned that lesson the hard way."

"I'm sensing a story." I smile over the rim of my glass, tossing my hair over my shoulders.

"My parents own a farm in County Wicklow, and let's just say my brothers know how to make good use of the various barns and sheds around our property. I've walked in on all of them getting up to no good with girls at least one time." She visibly shudders. "I don't have to worry about it with Shane and Ciarán anymore. Shane is engaged and Ciarán has a long-term girlfriend. Despite what I just said, Ronan is a sucker for love, and he's not into casual sex. He's had his fair share of girlfriends. Dillon is a hound though. He gets with a lot of women. And I mean *a lot.*"

"I can see that." I bite down on my lower lip, looking off into space.

"Oh God. No. Not you as well," she groans, shaking her head.

Heat creeps into my cheeks. "I've sworn off men, but that doesn't mean I'm blind. Both your brothers are hot, but Dillon has this presence about him that is hard to ignore. I have no trouble believing women drop at his feet."

Just not this woman.

"It's true, and the fact he's a total asshole seems to work in his favor. I'd like to say I don't understand it, but my ex had that dickhead vibe too, and I fell for him so fast."

"Let's not go there." Cat slurps her drink as she looks at Ash. "Mixing talk of that prick with alcohol never ends well."

We leave our table fifteen minutes later to move to the room where Toxic Gods is playing. It's a dimly lit square room with scuffed wooden floors, a DJ box at one end, and a small stage at the other. On the very left of the room is an elevated seated section. Aoife and a couple of other girls are already sitting at the top tables, and they ignore us as we enter the reserved area.

Claiming seats in the middle, away from the groupies but close enough to have a good view of the stage, we settle down with our drinks. The room slowly fills with most of the crowd standing in front of the stage. I sneak glances at the band as they warm up. Dillon is out front, at the microphone, and he has a guitar slung around his shoulders. Ronan is on drums. Jamie and the other guy are either side of Dillon, and both have guitars strapped to their bodies too.

"Who's the guy with the long hair?" I ask Ash, as we wait for the band to start.

"Conor Pierce. He's the lead guitarist. He and Dillon write all the songs."

"How long has the band been together?"

"Dillon set the band up when he was fifteen. Conor and Jamie were in his year in school. They had a different drummer, but he dropped out last year when he moved overseas. Ronan stepped in then though my parents weren't exactly happy about it."

"How come? I thought your parents were supportive," Cat says.

"They are. It's just he's young, and he's only sitting his Leaving Certificate in June. They want to make sure he gets it so he has options. Ronan couldn't give two shits about school, and if he had his way, he would've dropped out last year, but my parents refused." Ash finishes her beer, waving the waitress over. "Ronan hates being at school all week while the rest of the band are living the rock and roll lifestyle in town."

"June isn't that far away," I say. "And I can understand your parents' logic."

"What can I get ya?" the waitress asks, whipping a pen and pad out of the pocket of the black apron she's wearing.

"How about shots?" Ash asks, glancing between me and her friends. We all nod, and she orders sambucas just as the music starts.

Ronan pounds out a rhythm on the drums, quickly joined by Conor and Jamie, and then Dillon steps forward, cradling the mic and closing his eyes before he bursts into song. I'm instantly mesmerized by the gritty carnal edge to his soulful voice and the way his body moves fluidly to the beat of the music. His black shirt molds to his gorgeous physique, and the muscles in his lower arms and biceps flex and roll as he caresses the mic, pouring his heart and soul into the song. His ripped black jeans hug muscular thighs, and it's clear Dillon works out. He's bulkier than the others without looking too ripped.

His eyes snap open, scanning the crowd briefly before flitting directly to me. From the quick way he found me, it's clear I wasn't the only one sneaking peeks during the sound check. Lyrics flow from his gorgeous mouth, thick with emotion as he pours everything into the song. His eyes don't stray from mine as he stares pointedly at me. Butterflies scatter in my chest as we maintain eye contact, and a thrill sweeps through me.

Our shots arrive, and I immediately grab one, not waiting for the others before I knock it back. I desperately need a diversion from Dillon's electric stare. He has this magnetic charisma, this energy, that just sucks you in. I hate that I'm drawn to it, powerless to avoid his gaze, and I wonder what it says about me.

Reeve is still front and center of my mind.

My heart is ripped wide apart, and I have plenty of festering wounds.

Grief and turmoil are my constant companions.

So, it will be a long time before I can entertain the notion of another man. And that's why this weird connection I feel with Dillon is freaking me out a bit.

We order more shots, and I'm buzzing. High on alcohol and the vibe in the room. The crowd is going crazy. Singing along with Dillon as they play a mix of covers and original music. After a while, we push out into the crowd to dance. Emptying my mind, I close my eyes and let myself get swept up in the music. Dillon's gritty raspy voice wraps around me like a sensual caress, and I could listen to him sing for eternity.

We return to our seats after a few songs, ordering more shots, as we settle in to watch the end of the show. I try not to stare at Dillon, especially when I notice Aoife shooting daggers in my direction, but it's hard to avoid his hypnotic pull. I'm not the only one fixated on him. Most every woman in the place is ogling him.

The other guys are hot too, and I'm sure they have their fair share of admiring fans, but it's crystal clear that Dillon O'Donoghue is the main attraction. Talent oozes from his pores, and it seems so effortless. He is the bona fide definition of stage presence. He was born to be up there. Born to entertain. He has the crowd eating out of his hand, and a line of scantily clad women are pushing for pole position at the front of the crowd, desperately trying to claim his attention.

While I like music as much as the next person, I'm no expert. I know little about musical genres; I just know I like what I like. When Ash said the band was an indie rock band, I wasn't sure what to expect. Maybe something hardcore like ACDC but not this. Toxic Gods is giving me major U2 vibes. They have the same edgy, rock feel but with a unique sound. Dillon's vocals are as enigmatic and distinctive as Bono's, and he has the same charisma and stage presence.

Ronan might have come across as a little arrogant earlier, but he wasn't wrong. Toxic Gods is fantastic, and if they catch a lucky break, I imagine things will really take off for them.

CHAPTER 30

I WAKE the following morning with the hangover from hell, grateful I declined Ash's invite to continue the party back at the band's apartment. It was almost two a.m. when we left Whelans, and I was smashed. Spending time in close confines with a prickly Dillon didn't appeal to me, and I'm glad I still had my wits about me. He didn't speak to me the rest of the night, but he stole glances at me anytime he wasn't preoccupied with shoving his tongue down Aoife's throat.

The buzzing of the door has me crawling out of bed, groaning. Covering my body with my robe, I pad to my front door, stifling a yawn as I check the peephole.

A jolly man with a big belly smiles at me when I open the door. "Good morning, Ms. Mills. We have a delivery for you." He thrusts a clipboard at me, as I glance at the large box on the ground. "Just sign there." He points to a space at the end of the page. I scribble my signature while he carries the box inside, depositing it on the kitchen counter.

After he leaves, I stare at the brown box for a few seconds wondering what it could be. Ripping the envelope off the top, I remove the small card, startled to discover it's a gift from Reeve.

I'm pissed he's somehow gotten his hands on my address. Sending gifts, while thoughtful, isn't going to help me to forget him. I'm guessing that's the point. I contemplate not opening it, but curiosity gets the best of me. As well as a brief note, he's enclosed a gift card for CLOTH, a specialist fabric shop near Grafton Street. My hands tremble as I unwrap the sewing machine with tears coursing down my face, both hating and loving his thoughtful gesture.

God, Reeve.

A sob rips from my mouth as my fingers trail along the smooth edge of my new machine.

This reminds me so much of the sweet boy I loved, and it's killing me. The loss hits me anew, and my heart hurts. So freaking much. Pain lashes me from all sides until I can barely breathe.

Why did he have to betray me and destroy what we had?

Why, why, why? I don't think I'll ever understand.

Resting my head on the marble counter, I give in to my grief, openly crying. My pitiful cries bounce off the lonely walls of my apartment, adding to my misery. I cry until I've exhausted all my tears and my throat feels scraped raw. The backs of my eyes sting, and I rub at the tightness in my chest. My head is still pounding, and my stomach sloshes uneasily at the memory of all the alcohol I consumed last night.

Unable to process this multitude of emotions while I'm feeling like death warmed over, I pop a couple of pain meds and crawl back into bed.

Waking a few hours later, physically, I feel better, but emotionally, I'm crippled. I lie in bed, going back and forth over whether I should message Reeve to thank him. In the end, I decide not to. I know if I message him it'll only open a line of communication, and I can't undo all my good work. However, I *can* send him a thank-you card in the mail. I doubt he'll write back, so that way I can appease my conscience without any unwanted complications.

I head to CLOTH after I get dressed and order a ton of supplies to be delivered to my apartment. Then I grab takeout on my way home and perch my butt in front of the fire to watch a movie.

I settle into my new life over the next few weeks, doing my best to keep busy because it helps to distract me from my heartache. I go to my classes and attend physical therapy a few times a week, and I've even had a couple of sessions with a therapist. I join the team at the *Trinity News*, Ireland's oldest student-led newspaper, as a contributing writer. I'm trying to cram activities into every spare hour, so I don't have too much time to think, but the nights are the hardest. If I've nothing planned, I usually work out in the gym in my building for a couple hours, draw some designs, and chat with Audrey or my parents until it's time for bed. Other nights, I go out to eat or catch a movie with my friends, and we usually do a bit of a bar crawl on Thursday nights, but I've avoided all social interaction involving Toxic Gods. I don't think being around that scene or Dillon is what I need in my life right now.

But I'm so damn lonely, and I'm not sure I like living by myself.

Being here alone gives me too much time with my thoughts, and those are the hardest nights. Nights when I cry myself to sleep, feeling a physical ache at Reeve's loss. Despite strong temptation, I haven't checked social media, and I can't deny I have gleaned some sense of inner peace from shutting out all that noise.

I miss Reeve so much. I hate admitting it, and I hate myself for missing someone who humiliated and betrayed me, but I don't know how to force myself to not miss him. All I know is I want it to stop. I'm tired of feeling like this. Sick of missing someone who didn't appreciate or respect me. Fed up of my happiness being tied to his existence in my life. I know it takes time to heal, and I can't move on until I'm ready, but I wish I could press the fast-forward button and wake up happy again with all the pain left in the past and a bright outlook for the future.

With that in mind, I decide I need to do better, so I invite Ronan, Ash, and Catriona over for lunch at my place on Saturday.

Cat can't come as it's her sister's birthday, so I set the table for three, heat up the butternut squash soup to accompany the chicken salad sandwiches, and move my sewing stuff into the spare bedroom before they arrive so the apartment looks less messy.

"Fucking hell." Ronan whistles under his breath as he stands at the floor-to-ceiling window, staring at the stunning view from my open-plan living space. "This place is sick."

"Ro is right." Ash's eyes are out on stalks. "This place is incredible." She tilts her head to one side. "I don't mean to be nosy—"

"Yeah, you do," Ronan quips, interrupting her. "Nosy is your middle name."

She flips her middle finger up at him before refocusing on me. "I know you have money, because I've seen your clothes and you're the only one who brings an iPad to class, but how wealthy are you?"

"Jesus, Ash." Ronan strides toward us, shaking his head. "You can't ask Grace that."

"It's okay. It's not a secret. My parents are wealthy, and I'm fortunate to have grown up without wanting for anything. Mom organized all this for me," I say, waving my hands around. "I was prepared to live in one of the dorms at Trinity, but they didn't have any vacancies."

"I'd take this place over a dorm room any day," Ash says, arching her back and groaning.

We chat casually as we eat lunch, and I'm enjoying the good-natured banter between the siblings. Ronan fires questions at me about L.A., and I do my best to answer them without giving too much away. He talks animatedly about the band and his plans for stardom. They talk about their crazy family, making me promise I'll visit the farm one weekend. Every so often, Ash straightens her back and stretches her arms up over her head, and curiosity gets the best of me. "What's with all the back stretching?"

"Dillon's lumpy couch doesn't make for the best sleep," she replies. "My back is fucking killing me."

Ronan narrows his eyes to slits. "Try sleeping on the floor in a threadbare sleeping bag."

"I thought you said you weren't crashing there anymore after the last time?" A couple of weeks ago, Ash confided that she walked in on Dillon and Jamie tag-teaming Aoife. She had stayed over after a party at their place and stumbled upon them while taking a trip to the bathroom. She swore she was never staying there again. She clammed up after departing that nugget, but I could tell she was hurt. I want to ask her about her history with Jamie, but I stop myself because I don't want to be a hypocrite. I can't demand she tells me shit about her life when I'm guarding my secrets so close to my chest.

Audrey says I should tell her. That she's proven herself in the month since I've known her, but I'm still wary. Which makes me feel like a bitch because Ash has done nothing to demonstrate she's untrustworthy. I know I have trust issues after what Danny did to me, but Audrey pointed out I can't keep living my life shutting people out. I know not everyone will be like him, but it's hard to trust people when you're the daughter of famous parents and the ex-girlfriend of one of the hottest Hollywood stars. I want to tell Ash, but it feels too soon.

"I didn't see you yesterday to tell you," Ash explains. "I had to move out of my flat. They found a shitload of asbestos in the building, and it's not safe to stay there. I slept on Dillon's couch last night."

"Your brother didn't even offer you his room?" Wow, that guy is an even bigger douche than I thought.

"He did, but there's no fucking way I'm sleeping in his bed. I'd probably get an STD from the sheets."

"Eww." My nose scrunches in distaste.

Ronan chuckles. "I don't think it works like that, sis, and I know Dil's a lazy bastard, but he's not a slob. He does wash his sheets."

"It's beside the point," she says, rubbing her shoulders. "Whether I sleep on the couch or Dil's bed isn't the issue. They don't have room for me, and I don't want you sleeping on the floor every weekend. I need to find a new place."

"Move in here," I blurt without hesitation.

Ash's eyes blink superfast. "What?"

"I have a spare bedroom that's going to waste."

"It's sweet of you to offer, but I can't afford the rent for a swanky place like this." Ash works at a local store a few nights a week, and she mentioned her parents give her a contribution toward her flat, but I know money is tight.

"You don't need to pay anything. The rent is already paid up, and the utilities are covered as part of the agreement. You'd only have to pay for groceries."

"Wow. That is really generous," Ronan says.

"I don't want to sponge off you. It would feel wrong."

I knew I loved this girl for a reason. "Honestly, Ash. You'd be doing me a huge favor. I don't like living alone. It's kinda lonely."

Her eyes carefully examine mine. "You're not just saying that?"

I shake my head. "I swear it's the truth. I would love your company, and the place is big enough that we won't be in each other's way." Reaching across the table, I squeeze her hand. "Please say yes! It would be so much fun."

"Ow," Ash exclaims, pinning her brother with a dark look. "Don't fucking kick me."

"Someone needs to knock sense into you. Take the room, Ash."

I stand. "Come and look at it. Maybe that'll convince you."

They follow me out to the bedrooms, and I open the door to the spare double room. It's not as big as my room, but it's spacious with a king-sized bed, matching bedside tables, and a large closet. It's been tastefully decorated in shades of white, gray, and pink, and it has an en suite bathroom with a shower.

"Oh my fucking god!" Ash squeals as she enters the room. "Are you kidding me?" She spins around, and her eyes are as big as saucers. "Pinch me, Ro. I must be dreaming."

Ronan pinches her arm, and she thumps him in the chest. "I was speaking metaphorically, dumbass." She rolls her eyes, and I grin.

"Test the bed," I say, knowing I've sealed the deal.

"Is this yours?" Ronan points to my sewing supplies. I dumped them on the dresser earlier to clear the dining room table.

"Yep. I like to design and make my own clothes."

"Get the fuck out!" Ash says when she's finished rolling around the bed and groaning appreciatively. She jumps off the bed, walking toward us. Her fingers dance across the various materials. "This is so cool. What kind of clothes do you make?"

"Dresses mainly. I made my own gown for prom," I stupidly admit, and pain spears me through the heart. My face drops as I revisit that night in my head.

Sympathy splays across her face. "You went with your ex?"

I nod. Remembering that night is bittersweet for a heap of reasons now. "I could make you a dress sometime?" I offer, needing to switch topics.

Her eyes widen. "You could make us dresses for the Trinity Ball! It's black tie, and everyone dresses up."

"I read about that. It's in April, right?" If I'm not mistaken, it's the night of my birthday.

She nods excitedly. "It's awesome. You've got to come with us. We usually have pre-ball drinks at someone's place before heading to the campus later that night for the music event. It goes on until the early hours of the morning, and it's completely wild." She tugs on my arm. "Please say you'll come."

"Please say you'll move in." My eyes plead with her to say yes.

"Are you really sure?"

"I am." I don't hesitate to confirm it.

"Then I would love to move in." She flings her arms around me. "This is going to be so fun!"

CHAPTER 31

"REMIND me again why I agreed to this?" I ask, dumping bags of chips into a large white ceramic bowl.

Ash nudges my hip, grinning. "Because you love your new roomie and it's about time you threw a housewarming party. Plus, it's Saturday night. *And* it's Valentine's Day."

God, please don't remind me.

"That's four good reasons," she adds, handing me a vodka cranberry. Her features soften. "I also have a feeling if we hadn't organized this party tonight you'd spend the night crying in your room." Her eyes flit to the large bouquet of lavender roses presently sitting in a vase on the dining table. I need to move them before anyone arrives, because they'll only invite questions I'm not prepared to answer.

They arrived earlier today from Reeve, and I broke down in front of my new roomie for the first time. Tears prick my eyes, and my lower lip wobbles. "Shit." Ash puts her drink down, taking mine and placing it on the counter, before enfolding me in a hug. We're both still in our slippers and pajamas. No one is due to arrive for a couple of hours yet, so we planned to get everything set up and then make ourselves beautiful. Ash is so tiny and she barely reaches my chest, but her hug is solid and comforting, and I need it.

"Sorry," I sniffle, rubbing at my eyes when we break apart. "I hate how fragile I am. It's been eleven weeks, and I'm still a basket case."

"I get it." She hoists herself up onto the marble island unit, dangling her legs off the edge. "It's been almost three years since my relationship with Cillian ended, and it still hurts."

"Ugh. Don't tell me that." I crick my neck from side to side, hoping to loosen my stiff muscles. "If I still feel like this in three years' time, I'll have to be committed."

"It does get easier, but the pain of Cillian's betrayal will always sting."

Leaning back against the counter, I grab my drink and take a sip, wondering if I should have this conversation.

Ash makes that decision for me, continuing without me having to ask. "Our story sounds a little like yours. Cillian was my boy next door. He lived directly across the road from our farm, and we went to the same school. He was Dillon's best friend, so he was always hanging around with us. He was my first kiss at eleven, and we spent a few years messing about before it became serious." She grabs the edge of the island unit, staring off into space as she takes a wander down memory lane. "I lost my virginity to him at fifteen. We were inseparable after that. Fucking like rabbits any chance we could get. He drove me insane half the time, but I loved him," she adds, fixing her eyes on my face. "We argued nonstop, but we shared this real fiery passion, ya know?"

Do I? I know her question is rhetorical, but it sets my mind thinking. I wouldn't call what Reeve and I shared a fiery passion, but it was passion none the less. "What happened?"

Tears pool in her eyes, and she grabs her beer, knocking back a few mouthfuls. I wait patiently for her to continue, understanding how hard it is to relive the past. "He cheated on me with my arch-nemesis." In this moment, I feel her pain as acutely as my own, and I can't believe we have had similar experiences. "This bitch had been chasing after him for years. Cillian and I had fought earlier that night. It was a particularly vicious fight, and he went out partying without me." A lone tear rolls down her face. "He had sex with her, but I didn't find out for six weeks because he was a fucking lying bastard as well as a cheat. Rumors were doing the rounds at school, but he denied them until he couldn't." Anger flashes in her eyes, and I can relate to the lightning-fast emotional switch. "He got her pregnant."

She visibly gulps, and my heart aches for her. I think I would lose my shit if Reeve turned around and told me Saffron was pregnant. My stomach lurches, and I knock back half my vodka in one go, wishing I could scrub that thought from my brain with bleach.

"The chickenshit didn't even have the guts to tell me before that bitch thrust the news in my face."

"I'm so sorry, Ash. I can't even begin to imagine that level of pain."

"I've never been one of those girls who dreams of a big white wedding, but I always imagined my future with Cillian in it. His betrayal destroyed me. Even if I hadn't kicked his cheating ass to the curb, he would've left me. His family are very conservative and extremely religious, and I knew they would force him into marriage."

I almost spit my vodka all over the floor. "He married her?!" She nods. "What the fuck? We're not living in the dark ages. He could've supported the child without marrying the mother."

"Of course, he could, but he let his parents force him into it. They had a quickie wedding two months after I found out she was pregnant." Her chest heaves as more tears shine in her eyes. "Three weeks after that, I tried to kill myself," she quietly adds.

Setting my drink down, I rush over and hug her with tears clouding my vision. "Oh no, Ash."

"I was in a real bad place. In so much pain," she sobs, easing back from my embrace. "She was parading her bump, her wedding ring, and him all over school, and I just couldn't take it." She swipes the sleeve of her pajama top across her damp eyes. "The night before I took an overdose of my mum's sleeping pills, he had come to me, telling me he was sorry but it didn't mean we had to be over. He said he didn't love her and he'd only married her because he had to do right by the baby." She snorts out a laugh. "The dickhead proposed we continue sleeping together and that we could sneak around behind his wife's back. It was the final straw for me. I lost it that night. Threw shit at him. Screamed and roared. Woke my whole family up."

"I can't believe the nerve of him," I fume, angry on her behalf. "Men are assholes."

"Dillon beat him to a pulp the next day while I dumped a load of pills down my throat."

I rub her arm. "I'm glad you didn't succeed. I would never have met you otherwise."

"Dillon found me. Called an ambulance and got me to the hospital in the nick of time. My recovery was rough. I ended up having to defer my Leaving Cert while I took time to heal. I put my parents and my brothers through hell, but I eventually crawled my way out of the black hole, and you will too," she says, draining her beer and jumping down off the island.

I'm understanding Dillon's need to protect his sister from all threats more clearly now. I can imagine finding Ash like that must have been traumatic.

"Can you keep a secret?" I ask, as she grabs another beer from the refrigerator. Ash has trusted me with her story, and my gut is telling me I can trust her with mine.

"I can." She looks me straight in the eye. "But you don't owe me anything. Just because I shared my story doesn't mean you have to tell me yours."

"I want to, but you have to promise you won't tell another soul. Not Catriona or any of your friends and certainly not your brothers."

"I promise you can trust me to be confidential. If you don't want anyone to know, I won't breathe a word."

"I need another drink for this," I say, snatching a second can of vodka cranberry from the refrigerator and dumping it into my glass. At this rate, we'll both be drunk before any of our friends even get here.

We move into the living room, and I glance at the clock on the wall, wondering if there is enough time to explain.

"We can get party-ready in record time, and all the food and drinks are done," Ash says, reading my mind.

I flop down beside her on the leather sectional. "Does the name Reeve Lancaster mean anything to you?" I ask, watching her brow creasing.

"The actor?" she says, still looking confused.

"Yeah." I wipe my clammy hands down the front of my pajama pants. "Reeve is my ex. He's the guy who broke my heart."

Her eyes pop wide, and I can almost see the light bulb going off in her head. She hops up. "No fucking way! You're the girlfriend he cheated on with that tramp Saffron Roberts?"

I exhale heavily. "Yep. That sucker would be me." I take a healthy glug of my drink.

"I don't usually pay attention to Hollywood gossip, but I heard mention of it in an online Facebook group, only because I'm a massive fan of the *Rydeville Elite* series. I didn't see any details though, so I don't know the specifics." Wincing slightly, she adds, "*Twisted Betrayal* is coming to the cinema here in a couple of weeks, and I was actually going to ask you to come see it with me."

"Hard pass," I drawl. "If I never see that bitch's face again, it'll be a happy day."

She sinks onto the couch beside me. "What happened?"

I give her the CliffsNotes version of how it all went down. She listens intently without interruption, reaching out to hold my hand during some of the harder parts. "He's a cheater, a liar, and a coward," she seethes when I tell her about that awful Christmas Day. "I am so sorry you went through that. No woman deserves to be treated like that." She rubs my arm. "I probably shouldn't admit I had a little crush on Reeve at first. But as soon as I heard that stuff online about him being a cheater, he got added to my shit list."

"Mine too."

"Cheating is a deal breaker for me."

"Same here. As soon as it was confirmed, I ended things, even though it killed me."

"You were right," she says.

"About what?"

"We *are* kindred spirits." She slings her arm around my shoulders. "I think you and I were meant to find one another. Maybe together, we can help ourselves to fully heal."

CHAPTER 32

THE PARTY IS in full swing, and surprisingly, I'm having an amazing time. Ash and Cat were in charge of the guest list, and it seems like they invited half the English class from school. Beats pulse out of the sound system in the main room where people are lounging on all available couches and chairs. Others stand chatting in the kitchen, and a small crowd is dancing in the living area. I opened the balcony beside the living room so people can smoke where I can see them, but I locked the door to the roof garden. People are either drunk, high, or a combination of the two, and the last thing I need is someone jumping off the roof pretending they can fly.

I'm talking to a nice guy from our class when tingles of awareness skate across the back of my neck, and I turn rigidly still. A loud cheer goes up, and I don't need to turn around to know Toxic Gods has entered the room.

I adore Ash, and we have meshed well as roomies this past week. I love having her here, and I don't regret my decision. The only downside is her brother. All four band members showed up the Sunday Ash moved in, and I purposely stayed out of Dillon's way, grateful they didn't stay long as they were all hungover as fuck.

I knew they were dropping by tonight after they finished their set at Whelans, so I don't know why I'm suddenly feeling nervous. Butterflies flutter in my chest, and my pulse picks up.

"Yay! You made it!" Ash squeals, racing past me to welcome her brothers.

Slowly, I turn around, finding Dillon's dark gaze already locked on mine. He's wearing his signature black T-shirt, ripped jeans, and biker boots. His almost white-blond hair is a mess of waves falling into his eyes, and I have a sudden urge to run my fingers through it. My heart skips a beat, and blood rushes to my nether regions. Hot damn. Why does he have to look so sexy? And why do I have such a strong reaction to him every time? His lips curve up at one corner, and he cocks his head to the side in a gesture that looks eerily familiar.

Hands wrap around him from behind as a girl with long straight jet-black hair presses herself up against his back. Acid crawls up my throat as I break our intense eye stare, displeased to see the band invited their entourage of groupies to come with. I'm pretty certain Ash would not have invited them. In fact, seeing how much she detests Aoife, I imagine she probably told her brothers they were specifically *not* to come. I don't see Aoife, but she's probably here somewhere. I don't know these girls, and I don't want to pass judgment, but they remind me too much of *her*. Clingy. Manipulative. Bitchy. Ready to turn on any woman who presents a threat.

Shaking off my wayward emotions, I thrust my shoulders back and stride toward them, plastering the biggest smile on my face, determined to be the perfect hostess. Dillon's gaze ensnares me as I approach, and his eyes are superglued to my body despite the girl currently shoving her wandering hands into the front pockets of his jeans. "Welcome," I say, deliberately avoiding eye contact with Dillon. "What can I get you guys to drink? We have beer, cider, wine coolers, vodka, gin, and a ton of different sodas."

"Are *you* on the menu?" Jamie asks, undressing me with his eyes. His comment earns a scowl from the brunette tucked under his arm.

"Do I look like something you can drink?" I retort.

His gaze darts to my crotch. "I can think of some juice I'd love to lap up." His tongue darts out, and he rolls it back and forth in a crude manner.

"You're disgusting."

"Trust me, from personal experience, there's nothing disgusting about it," the brunette at his side says with a smug grin.

"Have you no self-respect?" Ash asks her before making a face at Jamie. "Your taste in women gets worse with every passing day," she adds before knocking back her beer. I make a mental note to ask her tomorrow about him.

"Fuck," Dillon hisses, and my eyes are like laser beams as I flick my gaze to him. "Not yet." Grabbing the girl's wrists, he yanks them out of his pockets. The bulge pressing against the crotch of his jeans is obvious in the extreme, and my stomach sours. I think I'll have to have a quiet word with my new roomie. I can't be around this scene. Not without wanting to hurl. I'm not sure what expression is on my face, but it's enough to have Dillon bark out a harsh laugh. "I think our Hollywood princess is a prude," he says, immediately raising my hackles.

I level him with sharp look. "Just because I don't go around openly groping men doesn't mean I'm a prude."

"Whatever you say, princess." He smirks as he purposely fondles the girl's ass, trying to get a rise out of me.

Planting her hands on her hips, she sends me a withering look. "Where'd you find this stuck-up bitch?"

"She goes to Trinners," Dillon says, as if that explains it.

"Nuff said." Stretching up, she makes a show of kissing him. As if I care.

"What's up, Grace," Ronan says, moving away from Conor and approaching me.

"Hey, Ronan." I give him a quick hug, glad he's here. Ronan is a nice guy, and I can't fathom how he and Dillon are brothers. They look nothing alike, and their personalities are like night and day. Whipping his hand out from behind his back, he presents me with a red rose. "Happy Valentine's Day." He softly kisses my cheek.

Warmth spreads across my chest as I bring the flower to my nose and inhale. "This is so sweet. Thank you."

"Aw, you're so sweet, Ro," the bitch with Dillon says, in a piss-poor impression of my accent. Everyone laughs except for me, Ro, and Ash, and I wouldn't mind bringing all the rest of them up to the roof and helping them to fly.

Straightening to my full height, which happens to be at least three inches taller than the bitch, I pull my shoulders back and look down my nose, pinning her with a dismissive look that conveys how insignificant her words are to me. How dare she come into my house and laugh at me. One more rude comment or snide look, and I'm booting her skanky ass out of my party.

Dillon is watching me with that asshole smug grin of his, and it pisses me off. Why is he always staring at me? He's clearly got zero interest in me, so why does he seem to have difficulty removing his eyes from my face? "What's your problem with me?" I ask, working hard to keep my tone level and a pleasant smile on my face. I won't give him the satisfaction of knowing he rattles me.

"Where would you like me to start?" He arches a brow, and his eyebrow ring pulls with the movement.

"Dil! I swear to God I will fucking castrate you if you don't stop this shit! Grace is my friend, and my roommate, and if you can't be nice, you'll have to leave."

Please leave. I chant it over and over in my head hoping maybe if I say it enough times it'll come true.

"You'd like that." Dillon lights up a joint as he eyeballs me, daring me to challenge him and confirm my prude status in his mind, no doubt. "You'd like me to leave, which is exactly why I won't."

Ash pushes past Dillon's fuck buddy, prodding her finger into his chest. "No smoking in here." Ash yanks him outside, and I watch through the glass as she rips him a new one. It's no less than he deserves.

"You really seem to get Dillon riled up," Ronan says, frowning a little.

"It's mutual. He infuriates me." A part of me is grateful he seems to hate me for some inexplicable reason. Another part of me feels wounded. I know I'm not a bad person. I try to be nice to people, and I don't think I have a shitty personality, so I don't understand why he's taken such a strong dislike to me. At any other time, I couldn't care less. But my ego has taken a recent battering, along with my heart, and having someone react to me with such blatant hostility is upsetting.

"What about me?" Ronan asks, flashing me a cheeky wink. "Do I infuriate you?"

"Not a bit." I loop my arm through his. "You bring me roses and act like a reasonable human being. You could never infuriate me. Now, what can I get you to drink?" I ask, pulling him toward the kitchen where the alcohol is.

A couple of hours later, I've forgotten all about Douchey Dillon. I know he was outside smoking with his friends and the cling-ons a while ago, but I have no clue where he is now. Not that I care. With any luck, he's already left. I've been dancing with Ash, Ro, and a couple of guys from school for the past half hour, and I need to take a breather to hydrate my parched throat. But first I need to pee.

I head straight for my bedroom because I'm sure the main bathroom is a mess by now. Placing my hand on the door handle, I frown as the door opens because I haven't inserted my key yet. Slurping sounds tickle my eardrums as I stand on the threshold, my anger spiking fast. We locked our bedroom doors for a reason, and I have no clue how someone got in here without the key. Fueled by vodka and adrenaline I push into the room, slamming to a halt at the scene in front of me.

Dillon is sitting on the side of my bed with his head thrown back and his eyes closed. The black-haired bitch is kneeling between his legs, sucking his dick. Neither of them has noticed me, and I watch with mounting disgust as she hollows her cheeks, sliding her lips up and down his thick shaft. His jeans are pooled at his feet, and he hasn't bothered to remove his boots.

She lets go of his cock, with a loud popping sound, the second she spots me. "What the fuck do you think you're doing?"

Her words fade into the background as I stare at Dillon's impressively long dick. But that's not what has caught my attention. He has a barbell piercing through the tip of his penis with a diamond-like beading on each end. Holy shit. An ache throbs down below, and stirrings of desire take root.

I've never seen one on a guy.

Well, duh, because I've only slept with Reeve, and he'd rather you cut out his heart than put a needle through his dick.

"Get the fuck out!" she screeches, and I rip my eyes from Dillon's hard-on, lifting my chin up.

His grin is extra smug now, and he spreads his thighs wider, drilling me with that magnetic gaze. "You're welcome to join us, princess. The more, the merrier." He licks his lips, watching my expression, as he curls his hand around his erection and gives it a few quick pumps.

Lust coils tight in my lower belly and my mouth feels suddenly dry as I stand rooted to the spot.

"Get lost, bitch," the girl says, standing and slanting me a look that says she's ready to bring her claws to the party.

Snapping out of it, I race from the room with Dillon's laughter following my every step. Once out in the hallway, I slump against the wall, breathing heavily. My panties are plastered to my body, my skin is flushed, and every cell and nerve ending comes alive in a way it hasn't in a long time. Embarrassment washes over me, and I hang my head until I remember whose room they are in.

Racing back into my bedroom, I grab the girl by the hair, yanking her off Dillon. "This is my room, and my apartment, and you've outstayed your welcome. Get the fuck out!" I hiss.

"Let go of me, you stupid bitch," the girl says as footsteps thud in the hallway outside.

"Jesus," Ronan says, bursting into the room with Ash hot on his heels.

Ash shrieks, turning back around. "For fuck's sake, Dil, put your cock away unless you want to scar me for life."

Dillon chuckles, standing proudly, his hard dick practically winking at me as Ronan drags the girl from my room. She's shrieking like a hyena, screaming she's going to kick me in the cunt—how lovely—but I can't drag my eyes from the manwhore in front of me.

"Liking what you see, princess?" he asks, purposely flicking his tongue out, demonstrating he has a piercing there too.

My body prickles with arousal, and I really need to get him the fuck out of my bedroom. I stare him straight in the eyes. "You're every bit as disgusting as your friend. And stop calling me that."

"Are you decent yet?" Ash asks, still hiding her eyes.

"Nope." Dillon flashes me a grin, showcasing a set of straight white teeth. "I might just stay like this. There's nothing more freeing than being at one with nature."

"I think your brother is an exhibitionist, or he likes trying to shock people," I say, maintaining eye contact. "Pity it won't work on me."

"Get fucking dressed, Dil," Ash snaps. "Or I'm telling Ma you flashed my new best friend."

"You sure about that, *Princess Grace*," he sneers, refusing to respond to his sister. Bending down, he slowly pulls his boxers and jeans up his legs, and I'm grateful he's at least listening to her about that.

"Think what you like about me. I don't care." I shrug, relaxing a little now his cock is safely tucked back in his jeans.

He stalks toward me, putting his face all up in mine. At this angle, I spot a little bump in the center of his nose I didn't notice before. "I think you do care. You want everyone to love you because Mommy and Daddy always told you what a precious princess you were. It bugs you that I can't stand you. That everything you represent annoys the fuck out of me."

"Everything I represent?" I shout, shoving him away from me as Ash races to his side.

"Pretty little princess with her pathetic purple roses in her palace rented with Mommy and Daddy's money," he slurs.

I moved my flowers in here, away from prying eyes, for a reason. Knots twist in my gut as my eyes dart briefly to the framed pictures by my bedside. One photo shows me with my parents, and the second is a pic of Audrey and me from graduation. Did he recognize my mom and dad and that's where his comment is coming from? Fuck, I hope not, because the last thing I need is this jerk learning my true identity. I very much doubt Dillon O'Donoghue would keep it a secret, and there's no way I want to be beholden to him.

A sneer paints his handsome face with an ugly veneer, and I step back as Ash thumps him in the arm, shouting abuse at him. But we're locked in our own little bubble, ignoring our surroundings.

"Wow. That's some fucked-up generalization right there. You know nothing about me. Nothing about my life. And you don't get to come into my apartment and spout this shit at me."

"You think you're so superior, like all arrogant rich wankers," he says, slurring his words again. I don't care if he's smashed. Nothing gives him the right to break into my room and then insult me to my face.

"How did you get in here?" I demand, folding my arms across my chest and leveling him with a stern look.

His smug grin makes an unwelcome reappearance. "I picked the lock."

My mouth hangs open while Ash screams more abuse at her brother.

"Wow. You're really something else."

"I am."

A cocky grin spreads across his mouth, and I've had enough of this guy. "That wasn't a compliment." I turn to face Ash as Ronan comes back into the room. "I'm sorry, Ash. I know he's your brother, but he's a giant bag of dicks, and I don't want him here. I'm not going to be insulted in my own fucking home just because he's got some massive stick shoved up his ass."

"Careful, princess. You've just used up your cursing quota for the year."

"Fucking hell, bro. Stop annoying the girl," Ronan says. "You need to lay off the weed and the booze, man."

"Either that or get a personality transplant," I suggest.

"I'll talk to him," Ash says, sending me a pleading look. "We were coming to get you because we kicked everyone out except our friends. We're up on the roof, and the guys are going to play their guitars. Let me knock some sense into this dumbass and we'll follow you up."

"If he says one more nasty thing to me or he calls me fucking princess again, I'll throw him off the roof and make no apology for it," I warn. I detect a slight curling of his lips, but he smooths them out before I can be sure.

"Come on, Grace," Ronan says, enunciating my name to make a point. "Let's get fucked up."

"Sounds like a plan." Ignoring his asshole of a brother, I link my arm in his, letting him escort me out of the bedroom.

CHAPTER 33

I TURN OVER IN BED, and my arm automatically stretches out, reaching for Reeve. Reality slaps me in the face when my palm grazes cold untouched sheets, and I crash down to earth with a bang. The usual pressure sits on my chest as I blink my eyes open, staring at the stark white ceiling, wondering if I'm destined to live with this soul-crushing pain for the rest of my life. When will it stop?

It's the little things that really get me.

Like waking up thinking I'm still going to find Reeve's warm body curled around mine, his large palm flat against my stomach, his morning wood pressing into my ass.

Squeezing my eyes shut, I ward off tears as I slide out of bed, purposely ignoring the roses that seem to stare at me from the top of my dresser. I fell into bed sometime after five, collapsing into an immediate deep sleep, before I could return them to the living area.

Stripping off my clothes, I stand under the steaming-hot water in my shower, welcoming the sharp sting as it pummels my weary limbs like a thousand fine pinpricks.

Apart from the minor setback with Dillon and that black-haired bitch, last night was an epic success, and I really enjoyed myself. I ended up kicking Dillon out because he insulted me again before we'd even made it to the roof. Ash didn't protest, and from the disapproving look she gave her brother before I shoved his annoying ass out the front door, I could tell she was disappointed in him.

We spent the rest of the night on the roof with the remaining band members smoking joints and singing along to Jamie's and Conor's guitar playing. They assumed Dillon had left with his fuck buddy, and no one corrected them. I thought Ronan would, but he seems to have taken my side, which makes me a little uneasy. I don't want to come between family, and I'm beginning to sense Ronan might be developing feelings for me, which could get awkward. Even if I hadn't sworn off men, nothing would happen. He's cute, funny, smart, and great to be around, but I'm not attracted to him. There's no spark. His gaze doesn't scorch a path along my skin, unlike his older brother's.

After showering and dressing, I exit my bedroom, stalling when distinctive moaning sounds filter out under Ash's bedroom door. The banging of the headboard would be a dead giveaway if Ash's blissful scream hadn't just confirmed it. A man cusses in a deep voice, followed by heavy grunting, and I hightail it out of there.

I thought all the guys left around five, but either Jamie snuck back in or he never left. I've no doubt that's who she's got in there.

I hope Ash knows what she's doing with that guy. He hasn't made the best first impression with me, but he seemed different on the roof last night. More mellow and less assholish. The guys are clearly serious about their music, and we were mesmerized listening to them sing and play guitar. Jamie accompanied me when I sang Sinead O'Connor's "Nothing Compares to You," and I blushed profusely when they all clapped loudly in appreciation. Mom has a beautiful voice, and I inherited some of her talent in that regard, but I don't get the opportunity to sing in front of an audience often.

Jamie didn't seem like a bad guy last night, and it's obvious there are hidden layers to him, but I'm still worried for my friend.

Switching the coffee machine on, I set about making breakfast for three when I hear the others stirring. I'm just plating bacon, toast, and scrambled eggs when the lovebirds emerge, freshly showered. "I hope you're hungry," I say, holding up two plates. "I made breakfast."

I set them down on the table and spin around, bumping straight into Ash. She smacks a quick kiss on my lips, and I'm momentarily stunned. She laughs at the expression on my face. "I was just thinking I could kiss Grace for this, so I thought why the heck not?" She shrugs, sliding into a seat beside Jamie while I try to snap out of it.

Jamie grins. "I think you've shocked your friend into stunned silence."

"That she has," I agree, finally snapping out of it. "Do you make it a habit to kiss all your female friends?"

"Only the pretty ones." She winks.

I distribute mugs of coffee and orange juice before taking my plate to the table. I join Ash on her side, and we joke and laugh about the night while we eat. As I refill our mugs, I decide to risk a question. "So, you two bumped uglies last night, huh?"

Jamie bursts out laughing, slapping a hand on his thigh. "Bumped uglies?" He wipes tears from his eyes. "I think Dillon might be onto something with his prudish princess remarks."

"Jamie!" Ash screeches, glaring at him.

I withdraw my previous charitable thoughts, and I'm tempted to dump the entire contents of the coffee pot over his head. "I was trying to be polite, that's all. I can say fucking, screwing, banging, without blushing. I've had plenty of sex, and I grew up in Hollywood. Trust me when I say there is little I haven't heard or seen."

"Sorry," he says, looking and sounding completely unapologetic. "Maybe it's just a cultural thing, but you're too funny sometimes."

"Uh-huh." I level him with a scathing look as I drop back down on my seat. "So, what's the score?" I ask, my gaze bouncing between them.

"We're friends who like to fuck occasionally," he says, spooning a ton of diabetic-inducing sugar into his mug. "It's no big deal, right, Ash?" He winks at her and I want to punch him in his annoying face.

"Right." Her tight grin is borderline a grimace.

Awkward tension bleeds into the air, and I regret asking my question. Maybe I should have waited until he left and asked Ash on her own. Discreetly, I squeeze her hand in silent apology under the table.

Jamie's phone pings, and he snatches it up, reading his message. "I've got to go." He takes his plate, glass, and mug over to the sink. I watch Ash's crestfallen face out of the corner of my eye while he rinses and stacks his plate in the dishwasher. At least the boy has some manners. He grabs his leather jacket from the arm of the couch before coming back to the table. "Thanks for breakfast, Grace." Shoving his hands in the back pockets of his dark jeans, he fixes me with a cocky look. "I guess I should apologize too."

"You guess?" I arch a brow. "What kind of way is that to apologize?"

A sheepish grin creeps over his face. "I apologize for being a dick to you. Sometimes I let my inner Dillon take too much control."

I snort out a laugh. "I'll say."

Placing his hands on Ash's shoulders, he leans down, whispering in her ear before he kisses her goodbye.

I wait until I hear the front door snick shut before I question her. "What's the story with you two?"

"You heard him," she says, vigorously swirling her spoon in her lukewarm coffee. "We're just friends with benefits—except we're more like enemies most of the time." Her head thuds off the table. "Ugh. I'm such an idiot. I swore I wasn't going to sleep with him again."

"We had a lot to drink last night. And we were smoking."

"That's no excuse," she grumbles, lifting her head.

"How long has it been going on?" I ask, getting up to make a fresh pot of coffee. If it wasn't eleven a.m., and I wasn't already hungover as fuck, I'd suggest we need alcohol for this conversation.

"A while." Air huffs out of her mouth. "Jamie's always been flirty with me, but I never thought anything of it. A, he's a big slut. Almost as bad as my brother. And B, he was one of Cillian's friends too."

"So all the guys hung around together?" I surmise, propping my elbows on the table.

"Cillian and Dillon were best friends growing up, and then they met Conor, Jamie, and Aaron—the old drummer—at secondary school, and they all started hanging out."

"Is Jamie still friends with Cillian?" I know Dillon isn't because he's loyal to his sister.

She shakes her head, and tears glisten in her eyes. "The guys were all disgusted with him. They took my side. None of them talk to him anymore."

I'm glad they supported her. I can't imagine how much harder her situation would be if Cillian was still friends with the band. "So, the Cillian connection isn't an issue."

"Except it is." She climbs to her feet. "I'm not feeling so great. Let's lie down on the sofa."

I grab coffees and waters and join her on the large leather sectional, kicking off my sneakers and stretching my legs out.

"I think I've got a brother's-best-friend addiction. Is there a support group for that?" she jokes.

"There's certainly a lot of romance books where women fall for their brother's friend. I'm not so sure about support groups though." I tuck my hair behind my ears, stifling a yawn. "You can't help who you fall for, and so what if he's Dillon's friend?"

"Dillon made all his friends swear not to touch me after everything that happened with Cillian. I'm strictly off-limits. It didn't bother me at the time because I didn't have feelings for any of Dillon's friends until last summer when something shifted between Jamie and me. There were a lot of heated looks and sneaky touches, and then one night at a party, we had sex. After that, we couldn't keep our hands off one another. We knew Dillon wouldn't approve, so we snuck around for a month until Ronan caught us in the act and he went nuts. He said Dillon would go crazy and it could hurt the band. Jamie told me he couldn't see me anymore the next day."

"I know Dillon's a dick, but do you really think he'd care if you two like one another?"

She rolls over onto her stomach, facing me. "That's the thing, Viv. I don't think Jamie cares about anything but sex. I'm just another warm body to him." Her chest heaves, and pain shimmers in her eyes.

"But *you* care."

Slowly, she nods. "I don't want to. I've tried hard not to, but I do."

"You deserve someone who will fight for you," I say, sitting up and crossing my legs. I grab a large pillow, pressing it to my chest.

"I know I do." She worries her lower lip between her teeth. "And right now, that's not Jamie, but it could be. He's got a lot of issues he's dealing with."

"Yeah. Who doesn't?" I sip from my water wondering if that's just life.

"His older sister died suddenly of a brain aneurysm sixteen months ago. She was his only sibling, and he took it hard. Now, his parents are getting divorced, and he's a bit lost. He's resorted to Dillon's PAW method of coping."

"Do I even want to know?" I ask, tilting my head to one side.

A wry grin appears on her lips. "Pussy. Alcohol. Weed."

"What demons is your brother fighting?"

Ash rests her head on the side of the couch, sighing. "Dillon is battling a lot of inner demons. It's not my place to tell you his story, but he's always had an issue accepting love. It's fucked up, because our parents are amazing. Our house was chaotic growing up, but love was never in short supply. Yet Dillon feels unworthy. He's never had a girlfriend, and I think it's because he's too afraid to get close to someone in case they prove he isn't worthy of being loved."

"That's actually really sad," I admit.

"I know." She sits up, mirroring my position. "I know he's been a dick to you, and I think maybe it's because he feels something for you and he doesn't know how to handle it."

"I—"

"Don't try to deny it, Viv. I've seen the way you look at one another. It's the way Jamie and I used to look at one another before he started pretending I don't exist. I'm not excusing my brother's behavior, and I'll be having words with him, but I think he's floundering a little again, like when he was seventeen. I'm worried about him."

"What happened when he was seventeen?" I blurt, intrigued more than I should be.

"He really went off the rails and it was a bad time for our family." Tears fill her eyes. "All that shit happened with me around the same time."

"You think whatever was going on with him was connected to you?"

She shrugs. "I don't know. Maybe. Cillian was his friend, and he shit all over me. I think Dillon felt responsible, which is ridiculous because the only person at fault was Cillian. I can't even blame that bitch because she was single."

"I'd still blame her. She knew he was with you, and she targeted him. She's not blameless." Like Saffron Roberts isn't blameless. She knew Reeve was in a committed relationship with me, and she still went after him.

"It doesn't matter anymore except for what it did to Dillon. It's like he woke up one morning the spawn of Damien from *The Omen*. He started acting out in a serious way, and he didn't care to hide it. He almost got expelled from school. He was constantly drunk or stoned. He lashed out at everyone. It culminated in him drastically changing his appearance." A grin breaks through her concerned veneer. "When he came home with the piercings, I thought my parents were going to die on the spot. But then he got all the tattoos." She chuckles. "Mum hates them, but she eventually got over it. She just wants to see him happy. I do too, but he's not. The only time he lets go of his demons is when he's on stage. That's the only time I truly see him happy."

"You probably hate me for making him leave last night."

"No. Not at all." She shakes her head. "He deserved it, but I'm going to talk to him because I can't have two of my favorite people not getting along. I can't cut him out of my life, Viv." Her eyes turn pleading. "He's always been there for me, and I need to be here for him now."

"I would never ask you to cut your brother from your life. It's fine. I can make myself scarce if you want to have him over."

"I'm not asking you to do that. This is your home, and I'm just a blow-in. I will fix things. I promise. I'll make him toe the line."

Good luck with that plan. Dillon clearly marches to his own tune, and I doubt anything Ash says will change his mind.

CHAPTER 34

"JUST ONE THING BEFORE WE LEAVE," I say, applying a layer of gloss to my lips. "Don't forget to call me Grace." In the two weeks since I told Ash who I am, she's been calling me Viv at home, and I'm scared she's going to slip up and out me to our friends and the band.

"Can I be honest?" she asks, as she finishes applying eyeliner. She looks at me through the mirror.

"No, please lie to me," I joke, fluffing out the soft curls in my hair.

"I think you should just tell everyone who you are. They will understand why you wanted to keep your identity a secret, and they won't hold it against you."

"I don't want anyone to know, Ash." I lean back against the tile, sighing. "I don't want to see pitying looks in their eyes or give the guys any more ammunition to make fun of me."

"They've really made a bad impression, haven't they?" she murmurs, rubbing some product into her short hair.

"Conor and Ronan haven't."

"Jamie made his peace with you the morning after he stayed over, and Dillon has promised he'll be on his best behavior tonight."

I'll believe it when I see it. "I don't want them to know," I repeat, because this is important to me. I'm still not sure if Dillon saw the photos by my bed, but I guess I'll find out tonight. If he knows who I am, he will need little encouragement to reveal my secrets and embarrass the shit out of me.

"Celebrities aren't a big deal in Ireland, and not many people are up to speed on Hollywood gossip. I honestly don't think anyone will know who you are, and you can trust my friends not to tell anyone. Wouldn't you rather just be yourself?"

"I know you mean well, Ash, but you have no clue the shit I had to put up with in L.A. I'm loving it here because no one knows any of that. I'm not ready to face it, and I'm not ready to talk about it. If I tell everyone to call me Viv, I'll have to explain, and I can't." The words project from my mouth like vomit.

"I'm sorry." She grabs my arm. "I didn't mean to upset you. You're right. I have no idea how bad things were for you before you came here. I just hate that you don't feel like you can be yourself with us."

"I'm still me, Ash. Just because I'm using my middle name and choosing not to tell people about my ex and my famous parents doesn't mean I'm fake."

"I wasn't suggesting you were." She wraps her arms around me. "Can we just rewind the last five minutes and forget I said anything? You look sexy as fuck, and you've finally agreed to come to Whelans again, and I don't want anything to ruin tonight. We're going to paint the town red and wash those dicks right out of our hair."

Eyes bore into my back, and I feel his potent stare without the need to turn around. I knew Dillon was in the bar somewhere, but we've been here for over an hour, and he hasn't shown his face. Jamie is giving Ash the cold shoulder, like usual, and Aoife is hanging all over him. The bitch Dillon was with at our party has been shooting me daggers for the past hour, and I'm close to saying fuck it and leaving.

I only agreed to come out because I know Ash feels torn leaving me at home every Friday night, and I don't want her to have to choose between me and the band.

Personally, I don't know how she can subject herself to this torture every week. I know she comes to support her brothers, but watching Jamie with different girls must be killing her. "How do you stand it?" I ask, taking a sip of my pink gin as I subtly gesture in Jamie and Aoife's direction.

"Alcohol helps. Fucking other guys does too. I haven't done that in a while, so I think it's time I found someone to bang tonight. His behavior reminds me why I need to stay away from him. I slipped up at our party but never again. Watching him with other girls helps strengthen my resolve." She drinks some of her beer. "I've thought a lot about what you said. I *do* deserve someone who would fight for me. If Jamie truly cared, he'd talk to Dillon and make it right. I'm done being second best."

"Amen to that, sister." I raise my glass to her beer bottle, and we say "Sláinte."

I rub the back of my neck, feeling tingles all over from Dillon's intrusive gaze, and I wish he'd focus on one of his groupies instead.

"You do know he's staring at you, right?" Ash says.

"Unfortunately, yes." Giving in, I angle my head to the side, and our gazes connect. My heart skips a beat, like always.

Tonight, Dillon is wearing a tight white T-shirt under a black leather jacket and blue jeans that hug his muscular thighs. The usual chains and bands adorn his neck and wrists. He fiddles with his eyebrow piercing as his eyes drift up and down my body, drinking in my one-shouldered silk pink top, formfitting black leather pants, and kick-ass knee-high boots. I let Ash do my makeup and style my hair, and I know I look good. I haven't missed the ardent stares of men in the vicinity though I've been avoiding making eye contact with anyone. I'm still not ready to cross that bridge.

"Holy fuck, Grace. You look gorgeous," Ronan says, snaking his arms around me from behind, forcing me to break my face-off with his older brother.

"Thanks, Ro." I beam at him while gently removing his arms. He's getting braver, and it's making me uncomfortable. "Where were you?"

"Dillon and I were being interviewed for *Hot Press* magazine. It's a pretty big deal."

Pride suffuses his tone, and I twist around in my chair. "That's awesome."

"I love how you say that," he says, winding his fingers through my hair.

"How did it go?" I ask, squirming a little under his adoring gaze.

"Really well. Since we released our self-produced EP three months ago, buzz has been steadily building. One of the main radio stations played the title track last week, and we got a call from *Hot Press* the next day. They're going to do a feature on Toxic Gods."

"I'm rooting for you guys," I truthfully admit. "Let me buy you a beer to celebrate." I stand.

Ronan shakes his head. "Ladies never buy the drinks."

I glare at him. "Are we living in the dark ages now?"

Holding up his palms, he backtracks furiously. "I meant no offense! I was just trying to be a gentleman."

My angry spurt dies out. "You already are. Me buying you a drink doesn't change that." His smile expands, and I silently curse. I'll have to say something to him before he hits on me. I'm genuinely flattered, and I wish I had feelings for him because he's a decent guy and I know he could help me move on, but I can't force myself to feel things I don't. This has the potential to get messy, and I need to handle it soon.

I'm hanging by the crowded bar, waiting in line to place my order, when a shadow looms over me. Spicy cologne tickles my nostrils, and every nerve ending on my body is on high alert. What the hell is with that? Why do I keep reacting to him like this? "What do you want, Dillon?" I clip out, working hard to keep a neutral tone.

"You to look at me, for starters," he says, pressing his mouth right to my ear.

A full-body shudder works its way through me, and I hate that he most likely noticed. Steeling myself, I turn sideways and look up.

His lush lips part, and air spills softly from his mouth as our eyes engage and the outside world seems to evaporate. Fire kindles in my chest, spreading lower, and I lick my dry lips, wondering if spontaneous combustion is actually a thing. Dillon's eyes drop to my mouth, and electricity charges the tiny gap between our bodies.

This is *not* happening, and I've got to put a stop to it now.

"What?" I croak, averting my eyes.

"Look at me," he growls, tilting my chin up with one of his fingers. Tingles explode across my face, and from the way his jaw pulses, I'd say he felt it too.

"Why?" I challenge, feeling out of sorts and wanting to get the first shot in.

"Because apologies should always be made face to face. Only cowards apologize when someone is looking at their feet."

"Okay. I'll bite." I'm curious to see if this is bullshit to appease his beloved sister or if he's capable of any genuine emotion.

He arches one dark brow. "Didn't peg you for a biter," he rasps, his seductive tone doing funny things to my insides.

"I've been known to bite," I reply, deliberately biting down on my lower lip.

His greedy eyes follow the movement, and my core throbs, reminding me I'm still a sexual being with needs. Needs that haven't been properly fulfilled in months. My little electronic friend doesn't count because there's no substitute for a real cock.

"My sister and Jamie tell me I'm wrong about you." He leans his face in extra close, and I stop breathing, staring into green eyes that look almost green-blue in this light. "Maybe they are right." Grabbing a few stray strands of my wavy hair, he tucks it behind my ear. His fingers brush my earlobe, and I'm close to testing that spontaneous combustion theory.

"Dil." A whiny voice breaks the spell, and we jerk back from one another.

"Not now, Aoife," Dillon grits out, not even looking at the sexy blonde.

"But—"

He turns around, clenching his jaw. "I'm trying to have a private conversation here. I'll talk to you later." It sounds like he's taking great effort to not snap at her.

Predictably, she scowls, throwing me a scathing look before she saunters off, sashaying her hips in an exaggerated fashion. Pity for her Dillon has already turned back around to face me. He opens his mouth to speak just as the bartender calls my attention. Giving Dillon my back, I lean over the counter, shouting my order over the background music. Spinning around, I find Dillon's eyes glued to my ass, and I fold my arms, slanting him a knowing look.

"What?" He shrugs. "If you don't want guys staring at your arse, you shouldn't wear tight leather trousers."

"Was there a reason you accosted me?"

"*Accosted?* That makes me sound like some pervert." He smirks that annoying smirk, and I narrow my eyes at him.

He chuckles, and I'm two seconds from throat punching him. "Aren't you?" It's not like I've forgotten what went down in my bedroom. Even after changing my bed that night and washing the sheets, I still couldn't look at them without seeing him with that skank, so I ended up throwing them in the trash. And let's not forget Ash saw him tag-teaming Aoife with Jamie. Though neither of the guys knows she witnessed that.

Seeing something in my gaze, he loses the grin, fixing me with an earnest expression. "I'm sorry for acting like a giant bag of dicks." He's smothering a smile again, and this time, so am I. His entire face lights up when he smiles—his eyes sparkle and two cute dimples appear in his cheeks—and I'm a goner. It's like being sucker-punched in the ovaries and the boobs at the same time.

"Why did you?" I ask before I can question the wisdom of it.

"I have my reasons."

"And you're not going to share those with me?"

"If it was something I felt you needed to know, I'd tell you." He jerks his head at something or someone behind me, and before I can stop him, he's paid for my drinks.

"You didn't have to do that." I just tore into Ronan for trying to do the same thing.

"Call it a peace offering." The dimples make a reappearance with his flirtatious smile, and I think I'm in trouble.

"I think I preferred it when you were mean to me," I whisper, instantly clamping a hand over my mouth. *What the fuck, Viv?*

"Be careful what you wish for," he cryptically says, winking before he walks away.

CHAPTER 35

"ARE you sure I don't need to bring anything else?" I call out to Ash through my open bedroom door.

"Just your sexy arse, some cash or your bank card, and something to change into for the event tonight. Wear your jacket with the hood. It might rain."

I smile to myself as I reach for said jacket. If there's one thing I've learned about Ireland in the two months since I've been here it's that it always fucking rains. Now we're into March, it should start easing off soon. Or so I've been told.

"Someone looks happy," Ash croons from my doorway.

"I'm excited to do all the touristy things," I truthfully admit. "Audrey can't believe it's taken me this long to visit some of the sights."

"She didn't tell you she gave me shit the last time we talked? Why else do you think I organized today? Your *bestie* is terrifying."

I throw back my head, laughing. "Audrey is fierce. I can't wait for you to meet her next week." I almost burst Ash's eardrums when Audrey confirmed she booked a flight to Dublin during spring break. She's arriving the day before St. Patrick's Day, so her timing is perfect. Ash and Audrey have been chatting up a storm in recent weeks, and it pleases me that they seem to get along.

"I'm looking forward to meeting her. We'll have a blast."

We meet up with Catriona and the guys outside Trinity, heading to a nearby restaurant to load up on carbs for the action-packed day ahead. In order to make the most out of our day, we are spending it mainly in the city center. This evening, we're taking a tour of the infamous Kilmainham Gaol, and then we're seeing The Frames play at The Royal Hospital Kilmainham.

The Frames are an Irish rock band fronted by Glen Hansard, who I know because he won an Oscar for best song for a movie my dad directed when I was a little girl.

"Why didn't Conor come?" I inquire, as we enjoy a delicious full Irish breakfast.

"He was too stoned to get up this early the night after a show," Ronan says, stuffing toast into his mouth.

"Conor's a loner at heart," Dillon supplies.

"And he doesn't like crowds," Jamie adds.

"Wait! What?" I gawk at them. "But he's in a band! A band with big ambitions. How the hell will that work?"

"He gets lost when he's on stage," Jamie explains, tearing a bite out of a crisp piece of bacon. "He barely even notices the crowd most of the time."

"Who says we're a band with big ambitions?" Dillon asks, and there's a familiar edge to his tone. Things have been better since he broke the ice last week, but he barely said two words to me when he and Ronan came for dinner on Wednesday night. I think he's as perturbed by this freaky chemistry we share as much as I am.

Ronan groans, slinging his arm along the back of my chair. Dillon's eyes instantly wander to his brother's arm, and he purses his lips. "Come on, bro," Ronan says. "Don't pull this shit again."

"Sue me for trying to keep things real," he snaps, and Ash glares at Ronan from behind Dillon, making a slicing motion with her hand across her throat.

"Fine, fine," Ronan grumbles. "Let's not mention the war."

"So, what's first on the agenda?" I ask, pushing my half-eaten plate away.

"Not hungry?" Dillon lifts a brow.

"Are you kidding? Did you see the size of that thing? It would feed at least three people."

"More for us," Jamie says, yanking my plate away.

Dillon and Ronan grab some of the food from my plate before Jamie takes it all, and I watch them devour it like they haven't been fed in days.

"They're savages," Ash says, handing over her half-eaten plate.

"Blame Ma," Ro says, cutting into his egg. "She always gave us seconds."

"It's so unfair," Cat says. "I only have to look at that greasy plate, and it goes straight on my hips. You three shovel food into your gobs like it's a national sport, and you all look like that!" She waves her hands in their direction.

"Jesus, Cat." Ash shakes her head. "Their egos are already floating near Mars. Let's not give them bigger heads."

"It's not our fault the lovely Catriona recognizes potent male sexiness when she sees it," Jamie lifts the hem of his shirt, tracing his fingers across his toned abs. "Can't help if the ladies love what we're offering."

Ash's eyes are trained to Jamie's stomach, and he isn't the only one noticing. I kick her leg under the table, subtly moving my eyes in Dillon's direction. She straightens up, coughing. "Come on, slow coaches. Hurry the fuck up. We've got a full agenda."

I insist on getting the check despite my friends' half-hearted protests. Everyone is giving their time today to come with me, and it's the least I can do. I have also organized a little surprise for tonight. One I hope won't backfire on me.

We set off around the city on foot, and I'm glad I wore my trusty sneakers. We visit the GPO, the headquarters of the Irish postal service. It was also the headquarters of the leaders of the Easter Rising, a pivotal moment in Irish history when the Irish tried to take back control of their country from the British. Gunfire was traded, and much of the building was destroyed but later rebuilt. Dillon points out divots in the gray stone pillars where bullets tore into the impressive building. We wander around the visitor center for a bit before we continue our tour.

Next, we head to the National Wax Museum, and they tease Ash and me mercilessly for taking our time in the Irish Writers section. We are escorted out of the building by security after Dillon is caught with his face buried underneath Mrs. Doyle's skirt in the Father Ted Room. I laugh so hard I almost pee my pants.

A guided tour of the Guinness Storehouse and a beer-tasting session follows, and I readily hand my drinks to the guys while I stock up on souvenirs in the store. We visit Christchurch Cathedral before enjoying chicken wings at Temple Bar. Then we take an Uber to a different part of Dublin to visit Croke Park.

We saunter through the museum to learn the history of GAA—Ireland's national sport—before taking a tour of the stadium, but my favorite part is the Skyline Tour. The stunning rooftop walkway is Dublin's highest open-viewing platform offering incredible panoramic views of the city and the sea.

"Wow, this is breathtaking," I admit, stopping at the highest point to admire the view.

"It blows my mind every time I come up here," Dillon says, leaning his elbows on the railing. We're all wearing harnesses, and the others are a few steps ahead, listening to whatever bit of history the tour guide is explaining now. "Do you know anything about Bloody Sunday?" he asks, after a few silent beats.

"Only the U2 song," I admit. Although, all I know is it was Bono's way of venting his frustration at the IRA.

"There are two Bloody Sundays in our past. The one U2 referenced was the 1972 massacre of twenty-six innocent civilians in Derry, which is in Northern Ireland. In 1920, the full island of Ireland was still under British rule, and armed police stormed Croke Park during a GAA match and killed fourteen people, including one of the players, and injured many more. It was retaliation for the IRA's assassination of British intelligence officers known as The Cairo Gang."

"That's awful."

His Adam's apple bobs in his throat, and he looks straight ahead as he continues speaking. "Can you imagine the chaos?" He points at the massive pitch below. "Can you visualize all the crowds in the stands? The players racing after the ball across the field? And then police charge the ground, opening fire." A veil of sadness washes over his handsome features. "If I close my eyes, I can almost hear the screams and the cries as men, women, and children fled for their lives."

"You're passionate about your country's past," I softly say.

"I'm passionate about injustice." His eyes burn with indecipherable emotion as he faces me. "What gives anyone the right to take action which decides another person's fate without their knowledge or permission? Who decides what is morally just and right? And when is it ever right to justify heinous crimes in retaliation for something else? How can people value other lives so flippantly?"

I'm wondering if we're even still talking about the same thing. "It's not right. There are many injustices in the world, and people don't seem to learn from the past."

"Unless they're forced to learn that lesson," he clips out.

I'm not really sure how to respond to that, and I'm not sure I want to get into some big political debate either.

Silence descends for a few minutes, but it's not uncomfortable.

"You should see a match before you head back to the States," he says, doing a complete three-sixty. "The buzz is amazing."

I roll with it. "When does the season run?" I ask, trying to ignore how close we're standing. I can almost feel the heat rising from his body.

"From May to September."

"I'll probably stick around for the summer, so maybe I can catch a game then." I'm loving it here, and it's definitely helping to be away from the press intrusion in the States.

Dillon turns his head to stare at me, drilling me with one of those deep intense looks of his, as if he's looking straight into my soul and discovering all my secrets.

"What?" I ask, worried I might have dried sauce left on my face from lunch.

"Nothing." He offers me a tight smile before turning his head.

I grind my teeth to the molars. "I know you have something on your mind, so just say it."

He looks straight ahead as I stare at the side of his face, noting the tense set of his jaw. He has a gorgeous side profile. Chiseled high cheekbone. Full soft lips I'm sure deliver the best kisses. And a strong jawline coated in a sexy layer of stubble that would feel delicious scraping against my thighs. Arousal swirls in my belly, and I try to focus my thoughts because swooning over a guy like Dillon is only inviting a world of hurt.

His face isn't perfect though. The little ridge on his nose and the small scar over his right eyebrow ensure that. Yet these small flaws only add to his appeal, as well as the conundrum his personality presents.

We've been chatting a lot today, and he's almost like a different person. He's been in great spirits, and he has a wicked sense of humor. I doubt we needed any of our tour guides as his local knowledge and memory for historical facts is incredible. When he's not acting the clown, he's articulate and intelligent, and I'm struggling to see how a guy like this could deem himself unworthy of love. Unless he normally keeps this side of himself hidden, and the hostile angry version I was presented with at first is the mask he usually wears.

"I was expecting you to run back home to your boyfriend the instant exams are over," he says, through gritted teeth, yanking me out of my head.

Panic flares to life in my chest at his words. "I don't have a boyfriend," I croak, glancing around to ensure the others are out of earshot.

"Don't you?" he asks, eyeballing me again.

"Not anymore," I whisper.

His gaze turns dark as his eyes bore into mine. Tension filters into the air, and I swallow the painful lump in my throat to force more words out. "You know who I am."

He nods, and I try to control my errant breathing, gripping the rail and exhaling heavily.

"Breathe," he says, placing his large palm against my lower back. Heat seeps into my body from his touch, even through my clothes. "I'm not going to tell anyone, if that's why you're panicking."

"You're not?" I inquire, raising my worried eyes to his. He shakes his head, looking sincere. "Why not?"

"Because it's no one's business but your own, and I misjudged you at first."

"Did Ash tell you?" I ask because I need to know if she betrayed my trust.

He turns to face me, peering directly into my eyes. I fight the urge to drown in the hypnotic depths of his gorgeous green eyes. "There is one major thing you should know about my sister, and that is she's the most trustworthy person you will meet. I know she told you about Cillian. He took her trust and abused it. She would never do that to someone else."

I instantly feel bad for doubting her for even a second. "I know. And she can trust me too, because I've had my trust abused and I could never do that to another person either."

Lowering my eyes, I lean over the railing, wondering if he's trustworthy or if his words are as flimsy as the air circling around us.

"I saw the photo by your bed, and I recognized your mum. Google told me the rest," he admits.

I rest my head on my hands, ashamed to face him, even though I know I've done nothing wrong. I just don't want to see the pity on his face.

"Don't hide from me," he says, his tone gruff. "I cannot stand people who run away from the truth."

Anger bubbles to the surface as I whip my head up. "You think I'm running from the truth?"

"Aren't you?"

I straighten up, biting the inside of my cheek. "You think you have it all figured out because you've read some shit on the internet, but you don't know anything." My voice rises a few notches, and I work hard to rein my emotions in. Just when I thought Dillon and I were finding common ground and getting along, he has to ruin it with his narrow-minded half-assed assessment.

"Who were the roses from, Vivien?" he hisses, glaring at me in a more familiar way.

"My ex," I bark. "And he's my ex for a damn good reason, but you were right about one thing," I say, jabbing my finger in his hard chest. "It's no one's business but my own."

CHAPTER 36

I TAP my fingers on the wheel as the car idles in the alley across from Christchurch Cathedral where we are waiting for Ronan. Mom's assistant organized a driver's license and a rental for me, but so far, this SUV has been gathering dust in the parking lot under my building. It's about time I took her out for a spin.

Ash is snoring softly from the back seat, barely visible under her comforter. So much for her being my wingwoman. Driving around Dublin city streets has me on edge because I'm not used to driving on the left-hand side of the road. It also feels weird to be behind the wheel in what is our passenger seat. I'm freaking out a little and hoping Ronan isn't as hungover as his sister so he can help. Otherwise, I have no clue how we're getting to County Wicklow in one piece.

The passenger door opens, and Ronan's happy face greets mine. "What's up, Grace," he says, climbing into the seat and slamming the door.

"Ugh." Ash groans from the back seat. "Stop the noise. My head," she mumbles, yanking the comforter up over her face.

Ronan chuckles. "I knew she was overdoing it backstage last night."

"She spent half the night worshiping the porcelain god," I joke. He stares blankly at me, and I giggle. "Throwing up," I explain.

"You Yanks say the weirdest things." He darts in, kissing my cheek. "I cannot thank you enough for last night. I'm still buzzing." He practically bounces in his seat, and I'm glad the risk I took paid off.

At my request, Dad had called Glen Hansard to arrange backstage passes after the event last night. Dad explained my situation, and Glen had no issue keeping my identity a secret. After he won his Oscar, he experienced the scary attention of the world's media, so he understands my need to keep a low profile. He mostly chatted to the guys about music while we shared a few drinks. Ash slunk off to the bathroom with one of the crew, much to Jamie's obvious disgust. I silently fist-pumped the air on her behalf. It's good for him to get a taste of his own medicine.

"What's the best route to take?" I ask, switching on the GPS.

"We'll take the M50. It's the quickest and easiest route out of the city. I figure you'd prefer to drive on the motorway."

Ro babbles away as I slowly navigate my way out of the busy city center. "Glen already messaged Dil this morning to say he downloaded our EP and he's impressed. He still has a few contacts in L.A., and he's going to put us in touch with them."

Taking my eyes off the road for a second, I flash him a smile. "That's amazing. I hope he can help."

"I still can't believe you arranged that. Your dad must be well-connected to set it up."

I fudged my way through an explanation last night. Honestly, I thought the guys might put it together, but I'm grateful they didn't. They were all young—like me—when the film came out, and Glen's movie success wasn't driving their excitement. They are fans of The Frames, and they were focused on the music. "I'm glad it worked out." I need to divert this line of inquiry before I get in hot water. "Are you sure Dillon is okay to drive his motorcycle?"

His brow puckers. "Why do you care when he was such a grumpy prick last night?"

"Your brother might irritate the fuck out of me, but that doesn't mean I want to see him get into an accident." Dillon gave me the silent treatment last night after our little argument at Croke Park, which suited me fine. I stayed with Ash, Cat, and Ro, while Jamie and Dillon kept to themselves. As much as his sullen moody behavior grated on my nerves, I still offered him a ride today. His mom was sweet to invite me to Sunday dinner, and it wouldn't look very gracious to turn up with only two of her children.

I take the exit for the M50, relaxing when we finally hit the highway. According to the GPS, it's pretty much straight all the way from here until we reach Kilcoole.

"Don't worry about Dil," Ro says, the smile dropping off his face. "He knows how to take care of himself."

"He drank a lot last night, and he'd probably be over the limit if the police stopped him." I'm glad I switched to water early in the night. My head and my stomach thank me for it. I knew I was driving today, and I didn't want to turn up to Ash's house looking like something from a zombie movie.

"You seem very concerned about him all of a sudden. Last night, you could barely look at each other." I feel his eyes boring a hole in the side of my face. "Did something happen between you at Croke Park?"

"We had a difference of opinion, and some harsh words were spoken." I shrug, tossing my hair over one shoulder. "It's no biggie."

"If you say so," he sulkily replies, turning his head and staring out the window.

Switching the radio on, I keep the volume low so we don't wake our Sleeping Beauty. We are both quiet as we drive. While I know Ronan is irritated, I'm not prepared to have a conversation about our feelings when we're en route to his house. However, his reaction reminds me I need to have that talk with him soon.

Ash wakes when we take the exit for Kilcoole, yawning loudly as she stretches her arms out over her head.

"How do you feel?" I ask, looking at her through the mirror.

"A little more human."

"You just need to get some of Ma's famous roast beef in ya and you'll feel better." Ro pokes his head through the gap in the console to look at his sister.

"Gawd." Ash rubs her tummy. "The thought of eating turns my stomach."

"Jesus!" I exclaim, slamming on the brakes as a silver and black motorcycle overtakes me just as I'm due to take a left turn. The loud rumbling of the engine accelerates when the motorcycle picks up speed, tilting dangerously to one side as it cuts a sharp corner, racing ahead of us in a scary display of recklessness.

"Fucking Dillon," Ash fumes. "If he kills himself on that thing, Mum will lose it."

"He's a bloody show-off," Ro scoffs.

Passing no remark, I follow the narrow winding roads, driving past rows of tall trees and overgrown shrubbery and bumping along uneven asphalt, until we come to a property bordered by high stonewashed walls.

"Take a right through those gates," Ronan instructs, pointing across me.

I navigate my SUV easily through the wide-open wrought-iron gates, following the long driveway that cuts across massive fields, bypassing impressively large greenhouses. "I thought your farm was a dairy farm," I say, driving slowly as I spot the two-story farmhouse in the distance.

"It is," Ash confirms, "but when Shane graduated with his agricultural degree five years ago, he took over as business manager, and he has made a lot of changes."

"Diversification is critical for a lot of farmers today," Ro continues explaining. "Now we grow organic vegetables and fruit, and we're one of a growing number of flower farmers in Ireland."

"Shane is your eldest brother. He's the one getting married soon, right?" I've tried to memorize all the names, and who does what, so I don't embarrass myself today.

"Someone's been doing her homework," Ro teases.

"I have," I readily admit, easing my foot off the accelerator as we approach the big rustic stone farmhouse. Pulling the car into a spot beside Dillon's motorcycle, I kill the engine. A few other cars are parked in front of the house, confirming the whole family is here for dinner. Wetting my suddenly dry lips, I rub my clammy hands down the front of my knee-length dress, willing my nerves to disappear.

Ronan hops out as a little girl with bouncing brown curls and big blue eyes comes bounding out of the house, quickly followed by two large dogs. The dogs instantly start barking when Ronan scoops his niece into his arms, burying his head in her tummy.

"Welcome to the madhouse," Ash says, climbing out of the back seat as I slide from behind the wheel. She loops her arm in mine. "Don't worry. We don't bite. Expect tons of questions because my family are a bunch of nosy fuckers. My dad will have his head buried in *The Irish Farmer's Journal*, Mum will pile your plate with food and insist you take seconds, and the boys will be rude arseholes because they just can't help themselves."

"Sounds fun," I lie, wondering why the hell I agreed to this.

Throwing back her head, she howls with laughter. "Please can I take a picture of your face right now because it's priceless."

I thrust my elbow into her ribs. "I'll get you back, just you wait and see. I'll drag you to L.A., and you can see what it's like to live in a social media warzone."

"Sunday dinner at O'Donoghues *can* be scary, but I guarantee it's not as scary as L.A. I think you'll survive." Ash winks, dragging me toward the slim woman standing at the door with a welcoming smile on her face. I'm assuming it's her mom—Catherine O'Donoghue. Her silver hair is cut in a blunt bob, tucked behind her ears, and Ash shares her heart-shaped face and button nose.

"My darling girl," her mom says when we reach her, pulling Ash into a big hug. "We've missed you." I hang back, giving them privacy. Ro has already disappeared inside the house with his little niece in his arms, and the dogs have run off someplace.

"Missed you too, Ma." Ash holds on tight, and a pang of envy swells in my chest. Being here makes me miss my parents. We FaceTime regularly, but it's not the same. "Can't breathe," Ash chokes out a minute later. "I know you missed me, but that doesn't mean you should hug me to death."

"You're too thin," she says. "Just as well I made plenty of dinner." Ash's mom turns her attention to me. "You must be Grace. I'm Cath." Reaching out, she reels me into a big hug. "You're very welcome. We've been dying to meet you since Aisling and Ronan told us all about you."

Tears stab the backs of my eyes as I sink into the comforting warmth of her hug. "Thank you for having me. Ash has told me lots about her family and the farm, and I'm excited to visit."

We break our embrace, but she keeps ahold of my hands. "I could listen to you speak all day. I love the American accent."

Ash laughs. "I said the same thing when we first met."

Cath beams at me, stepping aside to let me enter. "Come on inside. Everyone is waiting to meet you."

CHAPTER 37

I STEP into the wide bright hallway with Ash, following her mom past a couple of open doorways until we enter a humongous kitchen. The right side of the large space houses wall-to-wall wooden cupboards and a myriad of kitchen appliances. A double-sided stove-slash-oven occupies prime real estate in the space, and a girl with long strawberry-blonde hair stands in front of it, stirring something in a pot. "This is Fiona, Shane's fiancée and little Chloe's mum," Cath explains, taking my hand and leading me over to the stove.

Eyes bore into me from behind, and my heart does a little skip, which is just pathetic, because it really needs to get with the program where Dillon is concerned.

"Hello," Fiona quietly says, smiling shyly.

"I'm Grace. It's nice to meet you."

"You're a fucking clown," someone with a deep voice bellows from behind us, claiming our attention. "Ma! D'ya see the state of this bleeding idiot?"

Turning around, I lock eyes with an older version of Ronan. I don't know if it's Shane or Ciarán, but he has the same dark curls and piercing blue eyes as his younger brother. He's not quite as tall as Ro, and he's stockier, but I could identify them as brothers from a lineup with no difficulty.

"Leave your brother alone, Shane." Cath leads me toward the long wooden table. "And behave in front of our guest."

"Da. You talk some sense into Dillon, will ya?" Shane says, gesturing wildly to the broad-shouldered man with thick salt-and-pepper hair sitting at the head of the table.

"Knock it off, Shane. You're upsetting your mother," Ash's dad says without glancing up from his paper.

"Un-bloody-believable." Shane throws his hands in the air. "Next time I'll say nothing and let my brother kill himself on that goddamn bike. Am I the only one who cares he's still riding that deathtrap?"

Dillon rolls his eyes from where he's standing against the wall behind the table. He has one knee bent, the sole of his booted foot flat against the wall, and his arms are folded across his muscular chest.

Cath lets go of me, striding toward Dillon. She grabs his stubbly chin, yanking his face down to hers. "What have I told you about driving that bike while you're hungover? You'll give me a heart attack from worrying one of these days."

"Shane is overreacting, like always." Dillon throws an annoyed look at his brother. "I would've come with the others if I wasn't sober enough to drive. I'm not completely reckless."

A guy with reddish-brown hair snorts as he stretches across the table to grab a piece of bread from the wicker basket in the center.

Sadness washes over Cath's finely lined face as she grabs Dillon's cheeks. "Promise me you'll be more careful. Please, Dillon. If anything happened to you, it'd kill us all."

Dillon lowers his arms, reeling his mom into a bear hug. He holds her tight, closing his eyes momentarily. "Ma. There's nothing to worry about. Shane just loves stirring shit."

It didn't sound like that to me. It seemed like his brother is genuinely concerned. From the way Dillon took that corner earlier, I'd say his brother's fears are well-founded.

Dillon presses a kiss to the top of his mom's head while she wraps her arms around him. Her head only reaches the bottom of his chest, and she looks so small and thin circled in his strong arms.

"And you love swanning around town pretending you're god's gift to women," Shane retorts, smirking and flipping him the bird behind their mother's back.

"There's zero pretending involved," Dillon smugly replies as his mom shucks out of their embrace.

"You just need the love of a good woman, Dillon," Shane says, snaking his arm around his fiancée as she leans over him to set some bowls down on the table. Shane pulls Fiona into him for a quick kiss, and it's a sweet gesture.

"Love is for pussies," Dillon replies.

Cath messes up Dillon's hair, shaking her head and fighting a smile. "Language, Dillon. You'd swear you were dragged up in a brothel."

"You should've washed his mouth out with soap more often, Ma," Shane quips.

"Feel like running off screaming yet?" Ro asks, coming up on the other side of me. He casually slings his arm around my shoulders.

"It's fifty-fifty," I tease, watching Dillon's eyes narrow on Ronan's arm.

"Who's that?" a girlish voice asks, and I whip around, grateful when Ro's arm naturally falls off my body.

"This is my friend, Vi—Grace," Ash says, quickly recovering. "Sorry," she mouths, cradling her cute three-year-old niece in her arms.

"Hi, Chloe." I raise my hand for a high-five, and she slaps my palm enthusiastically with her tiny one.

"You speak funny." She eyes me like I'm an alien species she'd love to examine.

"Grace is from America," Ash explains.

Chloe's eyes pop wide. "You're from Disneyland?" she squeals, almost jumping out of Ash's arms. "I'm going to Disneyland after my mommy and daddy marry. On our moonhoney."

Laughter reverberates around the room. "It's honeymoon, little munchkin," Shane says, standing and coming around the table. He lifts his daughter from Ash's arms. "And Disneyland is only one tiny, tiny part of America." Shane hoists her onto one hip, pinning me with a smile. "I'm Shane. Nice to meet ya, Grace."

Ash introduces me to the others then. The guy with the reddish-brown hair is her other brother Ciarán. He works for Microsoft as an IT programmer. The pretty brunette sitting beside him is his long-term girlfriend Susie. She's a local hairdresser. She talks so fast I struggle to understand a word she says, but she's smiley and pleasant and welcoming. Ash's dad Eugene gives me a firm handshake, before returning to his paper. Ash giggles, mouthing "I told you" as she deposits big bowls heaving with meat and vegetables in the center of the table.

"Now we all know one another, let's sit." Cath ushers everyone to the table.

"You can sit beside me," Ronan says, pulling out a chair for me.

Ash rolls her eyes. "Knock it off, Casanova. Grace is my friend, so she's sitting beside me."

"This is like being back at school," Shane says. "Why aren't you staking your claim, Dil?"

"Shut up, Shane," Dillon replies, slathering lashings of butter on a piece of brown bread. "That's enough shit stirring for one day."

"Boys. I won't tolerate this at the dinner table," Cath says, her stern gaze bouncing between both her sons. "Zip it. Now."

"You heard your mother," Eugene says, reluctantly setting his paper aside.

I end up seated between Ash and Ro with Dillon across from me. Oh joy. Dillon's searing-hot gaze drills into me as his mother places a loaded plate in front of me.

"Jesus, Ma." Ciarán shakes his head. "There's enough on that plate to feed two grown men."

"Better to be too much than too little," she says, finishing handing out plates.

My eyes are on stalks at the mountain of food on the table. The bowls in the middle are clearly the infamous second helpings I've heard about. I've no idea how Cath expects me to eat even a quarter of what is on my plate, but I'll do my best, as I don't want to insult her.

Conversation flows freely around the table as we tuck into the gorgeous roast beef dinner. Shane proudly tells me the beef and vegetables all came from the farm, and you can definitely taste the difference. It's absolutely delicious. The meat is succulent and melts in my mouth—testament to Cath's impressive cooking skills. Ash clearly inherited her mom's talent in the kitchen, and I've been content to let her cook every night at our apartment when she offers because my skills are limited in the extreme.

When I compliment the gorgeous colorful bouquet holding court in an ornate vase in the center of the table, Cath informs me the mix of narcissi, roses, and sweet pea all came from their greenhouse. I tell them my mom is a great gardener and we have a rose garden back home. The discussion naturally moves to the flowers Fiona has chosen for her forthcoming nuptials and then into more general wedding conversation.

"How are the wedding plans coming along?" Ash asks her.

"Good," she says, in between mouthfuls of her dinner. "Although I'm a little concerned about the bridesmaids' dresses. They were shipped from New York three weeks ago, and they still haven't arrived."

"I'm sure they'll arrive any day now, hon." Shane squeezes his fiancée's shoulder. "Try not to worry."

"You should see them," Ash says, turning to me. "They are the most gorgeous jade-green color." Ash eyeballs her future sister-in-law. "Grace designs and makes dresses. She made that dress she's wearing, and she's making our gowns for the Trinity Ball."

"Get out! Your dress is gorgeous. I can't believe you made it yourself," Susie says, running an admiring eye up and down my floral-print skater dress. It's pink with a black trim and matching belt, and I teamed it with a white cardigan and black ballet flats.

"I used to make all of Aisling's dresses when she was a little girl," Cath reminisces. "I've still got my old Singer around here someplace."

"I have a Singer back at my house in L.A.," I admit.

"What's L.A. like?" Ciarán asks. "Microsoft asked me to spend a couple of weeks in their Santa Monica offices on training, and I'll be leaving a few days after the wedding."

"Santa Monica is pretty. The beaches are gorgeous, and you'll have to visit the pier."

"Is it true it's hot there all the time?" he asks, and I nod.

"Yep. There are lots of things I love about Ireland, but the cold weather definitely isn't one of them," I admit.

"Is it true all the women have fake boobs and blonde hair?" Cath asks, earning a round of titters from the table. "What?" she says, throwing her hands in the air. "I watched that *Selling Sunset* on Netflix, and all the women look like that!"

"Chrishell isn't blonde," Ro says.

"Her tits are fake," Dillon adds, throwing it out there with casual confidence.

"How the hell would you know?" Ash asks, pushing her half-eaten plate away mid-groan.

"We watched the show at our place, and trust me, they're not real." He waggles his brows, and Shane snorts. Fiona whacks her fiancé on the arm.

"Wow. Did you put your magnifying glass up to the screen?" Ash teases.

Dillon smirks, flashing those dimples I'm such a sucker for. "Are you for real? Do you not see how little they wear on that show?"

"Google's your friend." Ro grins, holding up his cell phone. "Chrishell hasn't hidden the fact she's had boob implants."

"Google isn't always a reliable source of information, you know," Ash says. "You shouldn't believe everything you read online."

"I'm betting you must've met tons of celebrities living in L.A.," Cath says, her eyes lighting up. "I'm not into all that celebrity nonsense, but if I was ever in L.A., I'd definitely sign up for one of those tours. You know the ones that visit celeb homes. I'd love to—"

"I'm sure Grace is sick of everyone asking her about L.A.," Dillon says, rudely cutting across his mother.

"The only celebrity your mother has ever gushed about is Lauren Mills," Eugene supplies, rubbing his bulging belly as he leans back in his chair.

Holy hell.

What are the odds the only celebrity Ash's mom is interested in is my mom? You couldn't make this shit up, if you tried. Nerves fire at me, and I shift uneasily in my seat. Dillon looks over at me while Ash squeezes my knee under the table. Blood rushes to my head, making me lightheaded, and I'm terrified I'm about to hurl up everything I've eaten.

"Why have I never heard about this?" Ash glances between her parents with a frown.

"I used to go see all her movies before I was married and had you lot. Then the farm and family responsibilities took over." Cath shrugs, beginning to clear away the plates.

"Sit down, Ma," Dillon says, standing. "I've got it." He takes the plates from her hand before walking over to the sink.

"You're all too young to remember this," Eugene says, continuing the story, oblivious to my inner panic. "But one of her movies premiered at the Savoy in Dublin, back in the day, and rumors were rife that Lauren was going to be there. We got your nana over to mind you lot, and we headed into town early so we could see her."

"Unfortunately, Lauren had to pull out," Cath says. "Her daughter fell out of a tree and broke her arm. She didn't want to leave her. As a mother, I respected her even more for that."

I remember that day as if it was yesterday. I was six, and Reeve and I had managed to ditch our nanny in the house and sneak outside. Dad had just left to drive Mom to the airport. The workers from the construction company my parents had commissioned to build a treehouse in our back garden had just left for the day, and I wanted to investigate. Reeve tried to talk me out of it, but I was impatient, and I couldn't wait to see. The two-room treehouse was being built between two large trees, and a bunch of scaffolding propped the half-finished structure up. I got halfway up the side of one of the trees when I lost my footing and my balance. I can still remember Reeve's cries and screams as I fell through the air toward the ground. He caught me, and we both fell awkwardly, but he definitely cushioned the blow. I ended up with a broken arm, and Reeve suffered a sprained ankle, but it could've been a lot worse.

"She's a fine mother and a fine actress," Mr. O' Donoghue says, yanking me out of the memory and back into the present.

All the blood drains from my face, and bile swims up my throat. This is what I get for concealing the truth. I feel terrible sitting here, after enjoying this woman's hospitality, not letting her know she's in the presence of Lauren Mills's daughter.

"Grace's surname is Mills," Ronan says. "What a funny coincidence."

And that's my cue to fess up. I'm not going to insult my friend's mother by lying to her. Clearing my throat, I grip Ash's hand under the table. "Actually, it's not really a coincidence."

Ro frowns, and a quiet hush settles over the table. Expectant faces stare back at me.

"You might as well tell them," Dillon says, clawing a hand through his white-blond hair as he resumes his previous position against the wall. His intense gaze settles on mine as he gives me a quick reassuring nod.

"Wait? You know?" Ash's eyes pop wide, her gaze darting between me and her brother.

"He saw the photo by my bed," I confirm.

"So, you two are an item?" Shane asks, pointing between us.

"No!" Me, Dillon, and Ronan say all at once.

Dillon glares at Ronan. Ronan returns it and then some.

"But you said—"

"Shut up, Shane," Ronan and Dillon say in unison, trading more pointed looks.

"My mom is Lauren Mills," I blurt, just needing to get it out. "I'm her only daughter, Vivien Grace."

CHAPTER 38

SHOCKED SILENCE ECHOES around the table with my revelation. "I remember that accident you were just talking about," I blurt, turning to face Cath. "I was six and too impatient to wait for our new treehouse to be built. I was scaling one of the trees to take a look when I lost my footing and fell. I was lucky I didn't break more bones." I'm deliberately leaving Reeve out of the story, because I'm not prepared to get into all that.

"How come Dillon and Ash know? Why didn't I know?" Ronan asks. Hurt splays across his face, and I feel so bad.

"I didn't intentionally leave you out, but I'm sorry if I hurt your feelings."

"Viv came to Ireland to study and to get away from the paparazzi in L.A.," Ash explains. "It's not something she wants to publicize, which is why she planned to keep it quiet."

"I don't believe it," Cath whispers. Her hand is clasped to her chest. "But I see it now. You look so much like her!"

I'm sure she's being polite because my hazel eyes and brown hair are inherited from my dad, but I got my height and my curves from Mom. "I didn't mean to deceive anyone," I quietly admit. "And I apologize if I've caused any offense."

"Oh, honey. No." Cath gets up, giving me a quick hug. "There's no need to apologize. I just wish I'd known Lauren Mills's daughter was coming for dinner. I'd have taken out the fancy china."

The look of regret on her face, combined with her words, breaks the sudden tension, and everyone bursts out laughing.

They ask me a few polite questions after that while I shoot off a message to Mom. She's an early riser, so she should be awake in an hour or two. I plan to call her and put Cath on the phone. I'm sure she'll get a huge kick out of that, as Mom will when I explain.

The rest of the men get up to help Dillon with the cleanup after dinner, and I trail Ash out to the large orchard at the back of her house.

"I had no idea Ma was a closet Lauren Mills fan or I would've warned you," she says, lighting up a cigarette.

"It's okay. At least it's out in the open now. I didn't feel comfortable lying to your family. Especially when they've been so nice to me." I trail my fingers along the bark of the apple trees as we walk between them, wrapping my cardigan more tightly around my torso. A light breeze wafts through the orchard, sending chills down my spine. "I think I hurt Ronan's feelings though."

"Ro needs to toughen up. He's too sensitive sometimes."

"I like that about him. Too often men are told they must be strong. What's wrong with showing vulnerability?"

"You need to speak to him." She slants me a pointed look, before leaning back against one of the trees, blowing smoke circles into the air.

"Speak to who?" someone familiar asks, lifting all the tiny hairs on my arms.

"This is a private conversation, Dil. Butt out."

"Chloe wants you to push her on the swing," Dillon replies.

"C'mon." Ash stubs her cigarette out on the tree, gesturing for me to come with.

"Don't let Shane see you doing that." Dillon smirks. "He'll probably have a heart attack."

"What he doesn't know won't hurt him," she says with a cheeky grin.

"I want to speak to the princess alone," he says, earning an instant growl from me.

"Dillon. Please." Ash harrumphs. "Would it kill you to be nice?"

"I'm trying to play nice, and you're getting in my way." He gives her a gentle shove. "Shoo. I'll escort her highness to you when we're done."

"You're insufferable," I huff, folding my arms more tightly around myself as a blast of cold air sweeps past me, blowing strands of my hair into my face.

"You want me to kick him in the nuts?" Ash offers.

"It's okay. I can handle Dillon," I reply, brushing knotty hair out of my face.

Ash wiggles her fingers, wandering off.

"Is that right?" Dillon lounges against the tree Ash just vacated, crossing his feet at the ankles. The devilish glint in his eye, combined with his lazy, lopsided sexy smile, does weird things to my insides, and I'm questioning my sanity in agreeing to be left alone with him. Honestly, this guy's facial expressions should be outlawed in all four corners of the globe.

"What do you want?" I want to minimize my time out here with him alone. Number one, because I don't trust myself with him, and two, it's fucking freezing and it feels like my toes are turning blue.

"That's a loaded question." Flashing me a panty-melting smile, he lights up a joint, as if he has all the time in the world.

"C'mon, Dillon. I'm freezing my ass off here."

Startled eyes meet mine. He pushes off the tree, stalking toward me, and I gulp at the look of determination on his face. "Hold this." He thrusts the joint at me, and I frown. He cocks his head to one side. "It's not going to bite."

Rolling my eyes, I take it from him, bringing the end to my lips without invitation, inhaling deeply. Amusement glints in his eyes as he shucks his black jacket off. Stepping closer, he takes my free hand, sliding the sleeve of his jacket down the length of my arm. A flurry of delicious tingles spreads along my skin at the feel of his callused fingers against mine. Forgetting how to breathe, I almost choke on the smoke filling my lungs and my mouth, and he chuckles, patting my back until I've composed myself.

"I keep forgetting how precious you are."

His grin is smug in the extreme, and I shove him away, handing the joint back to him. "I'm not some prissy precious princess," I declare, angrily thrusting my other arm into his jacket. I'm too cold to be stupidly proud in this moment. It feels warm, and it smells like him. "And I've told you to stop calling me that."

"Why does it bug you so much?" He hollows his cheeks as he sucks in a long drag. "Your boyfriend calls you that or something?" A muscle ticks in his jaw as he drops down on his butt, pressing his back up against the tree.

Sitting down beside him, I tuck my knees into my chest. "I told you he isn't my boyfriend anymore, and no. If you must know, my dad is the only one who calls me princess, and he says it in a much nicer way than you do."

"I'm sorry," he quietly says. "I know I'm being a dick. It's my default setting."

"I'm beginning to realize that." I hold out my hand for the joint. Ash can drive us back to the city. "Hit me."

He turns his head to the side, and his nose brushes against my cheek, igniting every nerve ending in that part of my face. His eyes probe mine, and I forget how to breathe again. It's becoming a common, concerning problem in his presence. He stares deep into my eyes, and I could get lost in the mysterious depths of his soulful gaze. "You have the most stunning eyes," he admits, his voice husky and threaded with raw sexiness. "You have these little gold and green flecks I've never seen before. They're enchanting." He leans in closer, and our noses bump. His warm breath fans across my cheek, as his heated gaze sweeps over every inch of my face.

"Thank you," I rasp, no longer feeling cold. His spicy scent clings to his jacket, swirling around me, mixing with his minty breath and the citrusy smell emanating from his skin. The overall effect is intoxicating, and I'm in uncharted territory with this guy. I should run a million miles from him right now, yet I can't ignore the instinctual pull to stay close to him.

"Let me try something," he says, and my heart flip-flops behind my rib cage.

Leaning his head back against the tree trunk, he takes a long, slow drag of the joint, closing his lips and trapping the smoke inside. Twisting to one side, he reaches for me. My heart jackhammers in my chest, and butterflies swoop into the pit of my stomach. Long slim fingers touch my cheek, drawing my face in closer to his. He rubs his thumb along my lips before pushing it into my mouth. On instinct, I suck his thumb deeper into my mouth, laving my tongue against his coarse flesh, and his eyes turn a darker shade of green.

He brings his lips closer, his mouth hovering over mine, until there's barely any gap between us. His eyes dip to my mouth, and I squeeze my thighs together as liquid lust gushes to my core. Keeping his gaze locked on my lips, he removes his thumb before blowing smoke directly into my mouth. Gently, he pinches my lips closed, trapping the fumes inside, and I inhale deep into my lungs. The heady scent of Mary J swirls around me, loosening my limbs, my inhibitions, and my tongue.

"More," I whisper, incapable of wrenching my eyes from his gorgeous face. Dillon could be a model with those high cheekbones and that strong jawline. He has a unique edgy look with the hair, his ink, and his multiple piercings. Let's not mention his incredible body, or that fascinating dick piercing, because I'm hanging by a thread here.

I wish we didn't share such a strong attraction, because I already know I can't act on it.

If Reeve decimated my heart, a guy like Dillon O'Donoghue would set fire to it; burning it until only charred fragments remained.

Despite my acknowledgment, and the danger I'm in, my ass refuses to budge. We sit side by side in his family's orchard, under a blossoming apple tree, sharing a joint in companionable silence. After a while, I've forgotten why we're even out here. "How'd this happen?" I ask, softly touching the little ridge on his nose.

"Got into a fight at school. Asshole shoved my face into a wall. Broke my nose in three places."

"Ouch." Having suffered relatively recent injuries, I can almost feel his pain.

"I broke his jaw in two places, so I'd call it even." He shrugs, taking another pull from the almost finished joint. His hand moves to my hip, and he pulls me in closer until our bodies are touching, side to side. Arousal spikes in my blood and drenches my panties. I'm trying to talk myself out of climbing into his lap when his lips brush against mine. It's a teasing touch. The lightest caress, but I feel it everywhere, and I mean *everywhere*. He touches my chin, and I part my lips, letting him fill my mouth with more smoky temptation.

"You have the most flawless skin," he whispers, dotting feather-soft kisses along my cheek while drawing circles on my hip through my dress with his thumb. His touch is electric, and I can't ever remember feeling so turned on from just a few simple touches. Dillon has magic hands and magnetic lips, and I'm slowly falling under his spell, which is *so* not a good thing.

"What are you doing?" I manage to choke out, grappling with the last vestiges of my self-control.

"I don't know," he whispers, pressing a kiss to the corner of my mouth.

Throwing the joint to the ground, he clasps my face firmly in his palms. "I just know I want more of it."

Before I can utter a single word, his mouth crashes down on mine, and my protest dies on my tongue.

CHAPTER 39

"VIVIEN GRACE!" Ash shouts. "Get your tongue out of my brother's mouth and your arse over here now!"

I rip my lips from Dillon's and scramble to my feet.

Shit. Shit. Shit.

That shouldn't have happened, and I'm glad Ash rode to the rescue before the kiss turned more heated.

"Running scared, Hollywood?" Dillon asks, lifting one knee as he smirks in my direction.

"That never happened," I coolly reply, like my heart isn't about to sprout wings and erupt from my chest. "We were stoned, and it was barely a kiss anyway." His lips had only just collided with mine when Ash staged her timely intervention.

Scrubbing a hand over his prickly jaw, he pins me with a cocky look. "If you say so."

"Ahh. I'm going." I stomp off toward his sister, flustered and angry with myself, hating how his dark chuckle follows me through the orchard.

"What in the ever-loving fuck was that?" Ash asks, looping her arm through mine and dragging me away.

"Oh God." I massage my throbbing temples. "I have no clue. It looked worse than it was, and there were no tongues involved."

"I didn't know whether I should interrupt or not," she admits, steering me toward the house.

"I'm glad you did before it turned into a full-on make-out session. Ugh." I rub a hand across my tingly lips. "God only knows where those lips have been." Ash cracks up laughing, and I thump her on the arm. "It's not funny." I tug on her jacket as we reach the door, stopping her from entering. "By the way, I'm stoned, and you're driving home."

"No problem, but you need to have some apple tart first. Mom took out the fancy

217

china." She grins, yanking me into the house, my lips still tingling from that barely there kiss.

———

Shoving my purse at Ash, I squeal, racing across the terminal in Dublin Airport and flinging myself into Audrey's arms. We hug it out for ages, forcing other passengers to walk around us, but I don't care. I've missed my bestie. "I'm so happy you're here."

"Me too. I missed your bony ass."

"I'm feeling left out," Ash says, pouting as I shuck out of Audrey's embrace. "And you're causing a traffic jam," she adds, pointing toward the crowd now streaming through the doors into the terminal.

I make quick introductions, and then we hightail it out of there.

Ninety minutes later, the three of us—plus Cat—are huddled in a corner booth of a swanky bar just off St. Stephen's Green. While I'm keen to show my bestie the traditional pubs we usually frequent, I thought she'd appreciate a classier, more modern bar to start off our mini pub crawl. We can't get too trashed today. Jet lag will kick Audrey in the ass soon, plus tomorrow is St. Patrick's Day. We'll need our stamina for the nonstop party that lasts all day, if Ash is to be believed. "I can't believe the sun is shining," Audrey says, moaning appreciatively as she tastes her first sip of the pink gin cocktail I recommended. "Viv hasn't stopped bitching and whining about the cold and the rain."

I bump her shoulder. "Hey. I haven't complained *that* much."

She bats her lashes at me. "Do you know you?"

I laugh, slurping my cocktail through a straw. "That's been the hardest adjust-ment. I guess I'm a Cali girl through and through."

"I still can't believe you dated he who shan't be named," Cat says, staring off into space with a slightly dreamy look on her face that irritates me.

After Sunday, I decided to bring Cat, Jamie, and Conor into my confidence. They're the main crowd we hang around with, and it didn't seem right anymore not to tell them. The guys couldn't have cared less, especially Conor who pretty much keeps to himself. Cat was shocked, only because she seems to share Ash's *Rydeville Elite* obsession. She's been a little off with me since, but I'm hoping it's only temporary.

I didn't give her a blow-by-blow account of the shit Reeve put me through, but she knows enough to wipe that swoony expression off her face.

"He's been keeping his nose clean," Audrey says. "Reeveron speculation is still rampant, but he's keeping his distance from her. I saw this post he put up the other day. It was clearly about you. He—"

"I don't want to know, Rey," I semi-lie. "I'm finally starting to feel less heartsore, and I'd rather not be reminded of all that crap. Ireland's been good to me in that way."

Sympathy skates across her face. "I'm sorry. I won't say another word."

"Did Viv tell you she kissed my brother last Sunday?" Ash just drops it into the conversation with a faux innocent expression on her face. I was a little worried she might have an issue with this thing—whatever it is—between me and Dillon, but she seems to be cool with it.

"You did?" Audrey squeezes my shoulders. "Good for you, babe."

"I was planning on telling you," I admit, giving Ash the stink eye, "but it wasn't really a kiss."

"Their lips were pressed together, and he had his hands *all* over her," Ash confides, and I glare at her disloyal ass. "I'd call that a kiss."

"Same," Cat agrees, chiming in.

"I was stoned!" I blurt.

"Excuses, excuses." Audrey fails to disguise her grin.

"He irritates the fuck out of me most of the time!" I protest.

"Passionate." Audrey waggles her brows. "Tell me more."

"You'll get to meet both my brothers tomorrow," Ash says. "They're playing a set in Whelans. There'll be music all day and night, and the drink will be flowing."

"You'll be off your tits by six o'clock," Cat supplies.

"I've always wanted to celebrate St. Paddy's Day in Ireland," Audrey says. "This is going to be so much fun!"

"So, what's going on with you and the sexy Irish rocker?" Audrey asks the following morning as we lie side by side in my bed.

"Nothing much." I scrunch the comforter between my fingers. "The kiss really was a non-kiss. He'd only just placed his lips against mine when Ash interrupted."

"And that was a good thing...or not?" she inquires, sliding her hand under her long red hair.

I eyeball my bestie. "I don't know." I worry my lower lip between my teeth. "It scares me."

"Dillon does or the thought of what he represents?" she quietly asks.

I contemplate her question for a few seconds. "Both, I think. He makes me feel things, Rey. Things I can't handle yet. The chemistry between us intimidates me, and I'm terrified that if I let him in, he'll destroy whatever is left of my heart." Tucking my hands under my head, I share my truths with my bestie. "I didn't come here to find another man. I came here to find myself."

"Can't it be both?"

"I don't want to complicate an already complicated situation, and I can't risk my heart again. It's still in desperate need of repair."

"I'm going to be honest, because that's how we always roll." She leans over and hugs me. "I love you like a sister. You know that, right?"

"Yes, and you know that's how I feel too."

"I just want you to be happy, whether that's single, reunited with Reeve, with Dillon, or some other guy."

"Why would you say that about Reeve? You know I—"

"I'm not telling you what to do, Viv, or putting ideas in your head."

"What are you saying then?"

"That you have options, and I will always support your decisions. I've been talking more regularly with Alex," she admits, and my eyes pop wide. "Just as friends," she rushes to assure me. "I'm still seeing Troy, and Alex is casually dating. But he's told me Reeve has reached out to him, and he's making amends, putting more effort into their friendship. Alex said Reeve is missing you like crazy and he's seen the error of his ways. He wants to fight for you, but he's giving you space like you asked."

"I'm not getting back with him." I shake my head. "He betrayed me. The trust is gone."

"I know, babe." She props up on one elbow. "You feel like that now, but I speak from experience when I say you don't know how you'll feel in six months' time, one year's time, or two years from now."

"No offense, Rey, but you can't compare your breakup to mine." I sit upright in the bed, resting my spine against the headboard. "Alex didn't cheat on you in front of the whole world. That's the big difference."

She sits up beside me. "I know, but you and Reeve have a shit ton of history Alex and I don't. That's a big difference too." She scrubs her hands down her face. "Ugh. I'm not explaining this right." She turns her head to the side so we're looking at one another. "Maybe things are completely over between you two, or maybe they're not. But you're here now. In a gorgeous place. You've made new friends. Found a new scene. And you're glowing, babe. You're turning a corner, and I think you should make the most of every opportunity."

"You think I should get with Dillon?"

"I think you should do whatever you feel like doing. You have no ties, no responsibilities, no shithead paparazzi trailing your every move. You're young, free, and single, and you can do whatever you want, do whomever you want," she adds with a naughty glint in her eye.

"One part of me wants to do it, because I know it's the first step in truly moving on, but another part of me is sick at the thought of sleeping with anyone else." I bark out a bitter laugh. "It's ridiculous, right?"

She vigorously shakes her head. "No. Not at all. I can relate, but here's the thing. I didn't start properly moving on until *after* I started dating again. Look at it this way," she adds, pulling her knees into her chest. "Being with someone else is either going to help you to move on or confirm that things with Reeve aren't fully reconciled."

"What if I'm not ready to face that truth yet?" I whisper.

"Then you're not ready." She shrugs. "There's no rule book for this. Just do what feels right. What makes you happy. But promise me you'll try."

"I am trying."

"I'm proud of you, Viv, and I hope you're proud of yourself too. You are stronger than most people I know. To come here after what happened and to pick up the pieces and start over in a new place is huge. Not many people could do it."

"Heartache is a strong motivator. I'm not going to let what happened define who I am for the rest of my life. And no guy is going to determine how I live my life."

"Atta girl." She yanks me into another hug. "Now, let's get up. We've got a parade to see."

CHAPTER 40

"EXCUSE ME," I say, holding the tray aloft as I edge my way through the crowded bar. The walls rattle with heavy beats as bands play on all available stages at Whelans.

"I got it," a man with a familiar husky voice says from behind me, and I almost drop the tray in fright. Dillon chuckles, taking the tray as his mouth presses to my ear. "Do I make you nervous, Hollywood?"

"Don't be stupid," I lie. "As if." I brush damp strands of hair behind my ears. It's hot as hell in here, and I'm glad I took Ash's advice and dressed casually and comfortably in jeans and a green T-shirt. A sprig of shamrock is pinned to my chest, and both Audrey and I have miniature Irish flags painted on our cheeks and green streaks in our hair.

"You're really getting into the spirit of things, huh?" Dillon effortlessly holds the tray overhead with one hand as he rakes his gaze over me from head to toe. Placing his free hand on my lower back, he steers us toward our usual table in the corner. My skin burns from his touch, even through my shirt, confirming what I already know—I'm fucked when it comes to this guy.

I've been mulling over my conversation with Audrey in the hours since we talked, and maybe she's right. Maybe I need to stop freaking out about this attraction and just let nature take its course. It's not as if a guy like Dillon would ever be serious about someone like me. He's a serial fucker, rotating bed partners as often as he changes clothes. He probably just wants to nail the Yank and brag about it to his friends. Maybe I need to take a leaf out of his book and just treat it like a casual fuck with no strings attached. It's only sex. And if it'll help me move forward with my life, then maybe it's worth the risk.

"Earth to Hollywood," he says, glaring at a guy blocking our path. "Where'd you go?"

Hollywood is almost as annoying as princess, but at least it doesn't remind me of how much I'm missing Dad every time I hear it. "This will probably be the only time I'm in Ireland on St. Patrick's Day. I'm making the most of it," I shout to be heard over the noise of the crowd. "You weren't at the parade," I add.

"Aw, did you miss me?" he purrs, straight in my ear, making me jump. Tremors zip up and down my spine, and a throbbing ache vibrates between my legs.

"Like a hole in the head," I joke, as a short, stocky guy wearing an Irish rugby jersey slams into my shoulder while walking past. Beer sloshes onto the floor from the three pint glasses he's carrying. My sneakers skid on the sticky liquid, and I almost take a tumble.

"Watch it, dickhead!" Dillon snaps, glowering at the guy. He slides his arm around my waist, holding me steady. "I fucking hate how every asshole and his mother crawls out of the woodwork on Paddy's Day."

"It's an experience, for sure," I agree, as we reach our table.

Dillon carefully sets the tray down in front of Ash. Audrey quirks a brow at me, blatantly checking Dillon out while I distribute drinks. "I didn't get you a drink," I explain, looking up at him. "I didn't realize you guys had arrived."

"It's fine. We've got to head straight to our sound check."

"Introduce me, Viv," Audrey says, staring shamelessly at Dillon.

"Dillon, this is my bestie from L.A., Audrey. Audrey, Dillon."

Dillon chuckles, murmuring bestie under his breath like it's a naughty word. "What's up?" He jerks his chin in acknowledgment.

"It's good to meet the guy I've heard so much about," she says, and a familiar smirk tilts the corners of his mouth. My jaw slackens, and I make a slicing motion with my hand, cautioning her to quit that shit. Dillon already sports an ego the size of the planet, and he needs no more encouragement.

Pale arms encircle his waist from behind, and I'd recognize those nasty red talons anywhere. It's the skank from that night at my place. Ignoring the rapid beating of my heart and the acid crawling up my throat, I scoot past Ash and Cat, plopping down in the seat beside Audrey.

Dillon extracts the girl's arms from his waist, pushing her off without looking at her. Leaning down, he places his large palms on the table, peering into my eyes. "You're coming up to watch our set, right?"

"We wouldn't miss it," Audrey says. "I can't wait to hear if you're as good as Viv says." Dillon's eyes stretch wide, and, if I'm not mistaken, a slight flush stains his cheeks.

Interesting. Maybe he's not quite as arrogant as I thought.

Behind Dillon, the skank is seething, looking like she wants to rip my head off my shoulders.

"That sounds like a challenge." Dillon's gaze flits between me and Audrey. "And everyone knows I never run from a challenge." Smirking, again, he straightens up, fiddling with his eyebrow ring. "I'll catch you later," he adds, spotting Ronan, Conor, and Jamie draining their beers and standing. He maintains eye contact with me for a few seconds, spearing me with a sexy grin before he walks to the end of the table to join his friends. The skank plasters herself to his side, and he pries her off, crossing his arms as he says something to her. Her head whips around, and she glares at me before storming off into the other room. Good riddance, if you ask me.

"Woah. My ovaries are on fire." Audrey fans her face. "You held out on me," she accuses, narrowing her eyes. "He is so fucking hot and sexy as shit. You should totally climb that tree and ride that pierced cock until he's given you at least four orgasms."

I spit my drink all over the table. I cannot believe she just said that in public. Actually, I can. It's so Audrey.

"Girl, if you don't want him, I'll happily take him off your hands," she adds.

Ash pops her head in between us, looking a little green in the face. "I almost barfed listening to that. Gross, so gross. That's my brother! A sister should never hear that shit!" She visibly shudders, and I laugh.

"Your brother is hot. Both of them are," Audrey says. "You didn't fall off the ugly tree either. Good looks clearly run in the family."

"Sucking up has totally redeemed you," Ash quips. "But you should know both my brothers only have eyes for this one." She jabs her finger in my chest.

"I noticed," Audrey says, as Ash tugs on my arm.

"You should talk to Ro now." Her eyes lift to her youngest brother, and I see he's looking straight at me.

"Now?" I shriek. "As in, just before they go on stage?"

"Yep." She fixes me with a no-nonsense expression. "Ro looked like he was ready to beat the shit out of Dillon just now. He's not blind. He sees the sparks flying between you."

"You don't seem to mind the idea of Dillon and Viv but not Ro and Viv," Audrey says, voicing what I haven't been brave enough to ask. "Why is that?

"Viv isn't attracted to Ro. She's attracted to Dillon," Ash states matter-of-factly. "And Dillon is attracted to her. Oh, he's trying to fight it, but we all see it." Her features soften as she looks at me. "I don't want to pressure you. I would never do that. I just think you two could be good for one another. I'm excited to think Dil might finally have found a girl worthy of risking a relationship for."

I lift my palms as panic bubbles up my throat. "Woah. Let's not get carried away here. We've got chemistry. Right now, that's all it is."

"I hope you explore it, but I'm here for you, no matter what."

"It won't get awkward if anything does happen?"

She shakes her head. "Nope. As long as we agree that whatever happens between you and my brother won't impact our friendship."

"I can get with that plan." I don't know how easy it would be to separate things, but I can try.

"Ro needs to understand he's out of the running," Ash adds. "Please put him out of his misery. He's my little bro and I don't want to see him hurt."

"You know I'd never do that, Ash. Ro is a great friend."

"Tell him that," she says, giving me a nudge. "Please, just tell him."

I know she's right. I also know I've been delaying this talk, because the thought of hurting Ronan upsets me, but I can't let this linger. Whether anything happens between Dillon and me doesn't even matter. Ro needs to know he's a friend and nothing more.

Drawing a brave breath, I approach him just before the band leaves the room. "Hey. Can I talk to you for a second?"

"Sure." A happy smile covers his mouth as he angles his body into mine. "I'll meet you guys up there," he says to the others. Dillon drills me with a look, but I pretend I don't see it. "So, what's up?"

My tongue darts out, wetting my dry lips. Fuck. How do you say this to someone without coming off like a conceited jerk and without hurting his pride as well as his feelings? Shoving my hands into the back pockets of my skinny jeans, I force a shaky smile on my face. "You know you're one of my best friends, right, Ro?"

His eyes examine mine as uncertainty filters into his gaze. "Sure."

"I was so nervous coming to Ireland, but meeting you, Ash, and Cat was a stroke of luck because you've made this experience everything I'd hoped it would be."

"What are you getting at?" He folds his arms across his chest.

I purposely soften my expression and lower my voice. "I value your friendship so much, Ro, but that's all there will ever be between us."

Hurt flickers in his eyes. "Because of Dil?" His voice hums with quiet resignation.

"No." I shake my head, hating to have to say this, but I don't want him harboring false hope. "Because the feelings I have for you are strictly platonic. I'm sorry."

"Don't apologize for how you feel, and it's cool. I appreciate you telling me." He takes a step forward. "Was that it?"

I nod. "Are we okay?" I reach out to touch his arm before thinking better of it.

He smiles, but it doesn't quite meet his eyes. "Of course. Look, I've got to go. I'll see you later, yeah?"

I sigh as he walks off, trudging back to our table with a heavy heart. Grabbing my vodka, I knock back a large mouthful as I slide into my seat. "I hate you for making me do that," I tell Ash.

"It had to be done."

"Yeah. I know." I swallow over the lump in my throat.

"He'll get over it. Ro falls in love every other week. By next week, he'll have forgotten all about you."

I hope she's right.

Alcohol sloshes through my veins, and I'm nicely buzzed as we push our way to the front of the crowd in the upstairs room where Toxic Gods has just started their set. "Over here," Ash hollers, guiding us over to the right, away from Aoife and the other groupies.

My eyes latch on to Dillon as I sway my hips in time to the rhythmic beats of the music. He looks so good up there, wearing his signature black, his clothes already clinging to his toned physique with the stifling heat of the packed room. The Irish flag is wrapped around his slim waist, in a nod to the occasion, and a green bandana is tied around his brow. Apart from that, he's remarkably low-key, but I guess this day isn't as much of a novelty for the locals.

The band rips through a montage of covers and original songs, whipping the crowd into a frenzy. I guzzle water as we dance, wishing I could douse myself in it. Little beads of sweat pool between my breasts and cluster on the back of my neck, and a fine line drips down my spine. Yanking a hair tie off my wrist, I pull my hair into a messy bun on the top of my head, but it only grants light relief.

"He can't keep his eyes off you," Audrey shouts in my ear.

I look up at the stage, finding Dillon's dark gaze already locked on mine. I get a thrill knowing I'm the one he's constantly staring at. Girls are screaming at him, throwing bras and panties onto the stage, and he only has eyes for me. The atmosphere is already electric in the room, but the energy pulsing between him and me is enough to power a nuclear generator. I've caught a few side-eyes from different girls, but I'm careful to keep my distance. The irony isn't lost on me. Maybe I have a type and I'm destined to go for guys other girls want.

I sincerely hope that isn't true because I'm sick of other women hankering after my man.

CHAPTER 41

THE GUYS FINISH their set to the enthusiastic roaring of the crowd. Dillon jumps down off the stage, after passing his guitar to Conor, as the next band is getting ready to rock it out. Women grab at him as he makes his way toward us, but he has singular focus—me.

"Holy shit, babe," Audrey roars in my ear. "He looks like he wants to eat you alive."

I slap her arm. "Not helping!" I'm practically hyperventilating at the hungry glint in his eyes as he heads straight for me.

"Uh-oh." Ash pulls me down, shouting in my ear. "You're in trouble. Just remember to make him double bag it!"

"Ash!" I shriek, as she and Audrey burst out laughing. "I'm not sleeping with your brother!"

Lips brush my ear. "Is that a challenge?" Dillon grabs my hips from behind, tugging at my earlobe, and it's like there's a direct line to my pussy. My core throbs, screaming at me for release, as I push back against his body. He grinds his erection against my ass as his hand slips under my T-shirt. "Well?" he asks.

"Well, what?" I whimper, moving my body in sync with his movements and the music reverberating around the room.

His deep chuckle sends shivers cascading down my spine. "Is that a challenge? Because you know how I feel about those."

"It's...not," I stutter.

Tingles race across my neck when he presses his lips there. "You don't sound sure," he whispers against my overheated skin, and my legs almost buckle.

"I'm not one of your groupies," I say, angling my head so I can see his face.

All playfulness disappears from his face. "I know you're not." His earnest tone goes some way toward reassuring me. "But you can't deny we have chemistry," he adds, sweeping his fingers along my cheek. Jerking his head back, he tosses waves of damp white-blond hair out of his face.

"I won't lie about that." I stare deep into his startling green eyes. "But I'm still not sleeping with you."

He lowers his face to mine until there's only a tiny gap between us. "Yet," he whispers, as his tongue darts out, licking across the seam of my lips.

Gingerly, I lift my hand, trailing my fingers softly across the dark stubble on his chin and cheeks.

"Hmm." Closing his eyes, he leans into my touch as we're jostled from the side. We should probably leave the dance floor, but I don't want to break this connection. I feel like I'm getting a glimpse of the real Dillon, and I like it.

He moves us back a little to where it's less crowded, and he continues to hold me like this, with his chest to my back, as we dance, grinding against one another, uncaring who sees. There is no sign of Ash, Audrey, or Cat, but I'm not worried. I know my Irish friends will look after my bestie, and I'm sure they just left to give us some privacy.

Dillon's hands wander, palming my stomach, lingering on my hips, and gliding up and down my arms as we gyrate together to the sound of our own beat. Nibbling on my neck, he licks a path up and down my sensitive flesh with his hot tongue, and low moans trickle out of my lips. His expert fingers work my body into a tizzy until I'm no longer in control. My head is thrust back on his shoulder, my eyes are closed, my body flush against him, and I've never felt more wanton or more desired. I'm majorly turned on by the sizzling touch of his hands and the feel of his hard-on digging into my back. I'm seriously considering eating my words and dragging him someplace to have my wicked way with him when something cold and sticky unexpectedly hits my face and my upper body, and I scream.

"What the fuck, Breda?" Dillon snaps, as I blink my eyes open, wincing when liquid drips from my eyelashes into my eyes. The black-haired skank smirks at me, holding an empty pint glass in her hand. Looking down, I see my shirt took the brunt of her jealousy. Sopping wet cotton adheres to my stomach and my chest like a second skin. Warm hands grip my upper arms as Dillon turns me around to face him. He curses, glaring at Breda over my shoulder. "Are you okay?"

"I need to go." I attempt to wriggle out of his arms, but he holds me tight, piercing me with a stern look.

"You're not going anywhere."

"I'm a fucking mess, Dillon," I say, in case he's missed the obvious. I bet I'm rocking a great pair of panda eyes, and last time I checked, that shit isn't attractive.

"I have a spare shirt in my bag, and I'll take you to the staff toilets to clean up. She's not ruining your night." He slides his hands down my arms, turning one of my palms over and lacing his fingers in mine. It's a sweet gesture, one I would never have thought him capable of.

"C'mon, Dillon. It was only a joke," Breda says from behind me.

Keeping my fingers locked in Dillon's, I turn around to face her.

"You're a clingy jealous cunt, and I'm sick of your shit," Dillon seethes, fixing her with the full extent of his disgust. "You're not welcome around us anymore, so fuck off."

"You're dumping me for *her*?!" she screeches, waving her hands around like a crazy person. Her eyeballs are rolling around in her head, and she's clearly high as a kite.

"That would imply we were in a relationship, which we aren't," Dillon hisses. "We fucked one time, Breda. *One time*, and it was a big mistake. I've tried letting you down gently, but fuck that shit. You don't get to throw your drink in anyone's face. Grace hasn't done anything to you, and that shit you just pulled is not on. In case it's not clear, I'm not interested in you, now or ever, so back the fuck off before I have you thrown out."

He doesn't wait for her to reply, leading me off the dance floor to a staff door at the back of the room. A burly man with heavy eyebrows and a thickset mustache guards the entrance, but he nods at Dillon, stepping aside to let us enter.

"I'm really sorry about that," Dillon says, glancing worriedly at me as he pulls me along the narrow hallway. A few bodies loiter inside a large room on our left, but no one bats an eye as we pass by.

"It's not your fault your psycho radar is out of whack," I deadpan. Or maybe it is. I don't know. I'm too wet, sticky, and pissed off to care.

"I'm pretty sure it is my fault." He shoots me a sheepish look as he leads me into a small coatroom. Coats and jackets hang off hooks on the wall, and a variety of bags are stuffed into open cubby holes on the other side of the space. "I only brought her to your party to wind you up, and now she's like a dose of bad breath I can't shake." He removes a black duffel bag from one of the holes, dropping it on the ground.

"Nice analogy," I drawl, plucking at the wet material clinging to my flat stomach as he rummages in his bag.

"Here." He thrusts a wad of black cotton at me while bending over his open bag. "These might help too." He hands me a pack of wipes.

I arch a brow, holding the items away from my wet shirt, and he grins. "Don't judge. It gets hot as fuck under stage lights." Straightening up, he claws a hand through his hair. He points over my shoulder. "Toilet is right across the hall. Take as long as you need. I'll be right here."

I knock on the door of the single toilet, to ensure it isn't occupied, before I step inside. The scent of lavender and jasmine floats through the air as I lock the door behind me. From the schedule pinned to the wall, I can see this bathroom has only recently been cleaned.

Stripping out of my wet shirt is harder than it looks. "Ugh." I throw it into the sink, rinsing it under the hot water as I stare at my reflection in the mirror. Yep, I'm sporting a nasty case of panda eyes, and my Ireland face paint is a streaky mess of color on my cheeks. Using a couple of wipes, I scrub my face clean. My purse is downstairs at our table, along with my gloss and mascara, but right now, I couldn't give two shits that I'm wearing no makeup. I am so over this and ready to call it a night.

Thankfully, my bra is only slightly damp, so I leave it on as I use another couple of wipes to clean my stomach, chest, and my arms. After toweling dry, I slide Dillon's plain black tee over my head. Predictably, it swamps me, skimming way below my butt. I twist the material into a knot under my boobs, and it looks more presentable.

Spritzing some of the complimentary spray, I hope it masks the scent of cider that still seems to cling to me. I wring out my ruined shirt, balling it up, hoping Dillon has a spare plastic bag I can put it into. After going to the toilet and washing my hands, I emerge to find Dillon in the hallway waiting for me.

A dark glimmer of lust flits across his retinas as he drinks me in. "Fuck me." He claws a hand through his hair. "You look too fucking good in my shirt." In two seconds, he's across the hallway, pinning me against the wall. His strong, muscular arms cage me in as he leans in close. Too close. Spicy notes of his cologne invade my senses, and I gulp over the lump clogging my throat.

Dillon is gorgeous, and I already know sex with him would be out of this world because he oozes sexual confidence from every pore. But I can't do this to myself again. I can't put myself in another world where girls have ulterior motives and I'm collateral damage. Whatever this is between us ends here. "I need to go," I say, gently pushing at his chest as I avert my gaze.

"Don't do that." His fingers curl around my chin, and he forces my eyes to his. "Don't shut me out. I know you were into it downstairs." His fingers creep up the side of my face. "I promise I'll tone down my default setting if you don't push me away."

His eyes lower to my mouth. A flash of silver glints at me when his tongue darts out to lick his lips. Carefully, he presses his body against me, and my nipples harden the instant his chest touches mine. He rubs his nose against mine, as his fingers caress the side of my neck.

God, his touch does intense things to me, and I'm putty in his hands.

Arousal coils in my belly, and my body is screaming for a release only he can give me. The shirt drops to the floor, and I grip his waist. A needy moan escapes my mouth when his lips replace his fingers on my neck, and he plants a slew of drugging kisses along my traitorous skin. My hips arch against him as raw need courses between my legs. "I know you want this as much as me," he whispers with his lips edging dangerously close to my mouth. "Stop fighting it. Give your body what it needs."

His finger rims the low band of my jeans, and I jolt out of my lust-fueled bubble. "No." I push more firmly at his shoulders. "I can't do this."

He instantly withdraws, stepping back and giving me space. His eyes scrutinize mine. "What are you so afraid of? I won't hurt you. I promise."

I'm horrified when tears fill my eyes. "You shouldn't make promises you don't know you can keep," I rasp, avoiding his outstretched arm as I brush past him, racing along the hallway and out through the exit door.

CHAPTER 42

"I'LL GET IT!" Ash hollers when the bell chimes, bounding out of her room and racing toward the front door of our apartment.

Audrey left yesterday morning, and I've been melancholy ever since. Her trip was too short, and I'm already missing her like crazy.

"Package came for you," Ash says, strolling across the living room toward me. She sets it down on the table. "Wow, I love this color," she exclaims, trailing her fingers along the deep blue satin material bunched around my sewing machine. "I love how there's a hint of purple hidden underneath the blue. It makes it more vibrant."

"I agree, and you have a good eye." I snatch the large brown padded envelope up. "I should have your top finished by tonight so you can try it on and see if it fits," I confirm, reaching for my scissors. Both of us have opted for quite daring dresses for the Trinity Ball. Mine is like a minidress under a full skirt with a slit right up the front and a plunging neckline that ends at my navel. Ash is wearing an emerald-green satin high-necked sleeveless crop top and matching full-length skirt that will look amazing with her strawberry-blonde pixie cut. Both dresses are ball-worthy in a nontraditional way.

Now my physical therapy has ended, and my hand is back to normal, I'm throwing myself into getting the dresses finished early as I'll have to start studying in earnest next month. Exams are only seven weeks away, and I can't believe how fast time is flying.

"It's from Dillon," Ash says, as I cut the opening of the envelope. I arch a brow. "I recognize his handwriting."

I empty the contents of the package on the table, and my heart does a funny little dance. Lifting the shirt I wore on Paddy's Day to my nose, I inhale the fresh lemony scent with a slight lump in my throat.

"Fucking hell. Dil must want in your knickers real bad, Viv." Ash rummages through the myriad of Cadbury's chocolate bars spread across the table, while I put the shirt down and inspect the small box of Lyon's Tea.

A flash goes off, and I whip my head up to Ash. "What are you doing?"

"Taking photos because no one is going to believe my brother is capable of this shit without proof."

"Do not share that!" I level her with my best "don't mess with me" look. "This is super sweet, and you're not going to tease him for it," I warn.

"Aw. You're no fun." She swipes her fingers across the screen of her phone before thrusting it in my face. "Gone. See?"

"Why would he do this?" Dillon doesn't seem like the type to make thoughtful gestures.

"In our house, we believe tea and chocolate can cure all ails." She plucks the box of teabags from my hands. "Dil asked where you were last night, and I said you were missing Audrey too much to come out to party." She perches her butt against the edge of the table. "He avoided the skanks last night too, and I know for a fact he went home alone, straight after their set." Her blue eyes sparkle. "I think my brother likes you. Like *really, really* likes you."

"No need to throw a party," I drawl, spotting the obvious glee on her face.

"Hey." Her expression turns more solemn. "I didn't mean to scare you." She sinks onto the chair beside me. "Is it wrong that I'm giddy over the prospect of seeing two of my favorite people happy together?"

"I'm scared, Ash." I examine my fingernails like they're the most fascinating things. "Even more so after Paddy's Day."

"Tell me this." She props her elbows on the table and her chin in her hands. "If it wasn't for the groupies, would you give it a shot?"

I shrug. "Probably. Yes. I don't know."

"I understand why you're afraid, but Dillon is not Reeve. People think because Dillon's a dick he's a disrespectful jerk, but he's not. Our parents raised all the boys to be respectful of women. Dillon would never let those skanks hurt you or belittle you. He wouldn't make excuses for them or his behavior."

"I believe you, because he defended me and took care of me the other night." When I was lying in bed the next morning, thinking over everything, I realized that. "And he accepted responsibility without me having to say anything. That was Reeve's biggest failing. He always made me feel like I was somehow at fault."

"I know Dillon has gotten with a lot of girls, but he treats them well. He never lies. He is always straight with them, ensuring they know it's a onetime thing. Aoife is the only one I've known him to be with more than once, but he has told her straight up it's just sex. I've no doubt she sticks around, hoping it will become more, but I know it won't. She fucks the others thinking it will make him jealous, but Dillon never cares."

"Why am I different?"

She shrugs, getting up and snatching the tea. "You'd have to ask Dillon that. Now, put your sewing shit away. You're taking a break for tea and chocolate."

232

I send Dillon a quick message thanking him for cleaning my shirt and for the tea and chocolate, and he sends me a brief "You're welcome" message back. Neither of us engages in further conversation over the following week, but he doesn't stray far from my thoughts. Reeve doesn't either. I'm mulling over everything Audrey and Ash have said, and by the time Friday rolls around, I'm ready to get out of my head. Overanalyzing everything is driving me crazy, and avoiding Dillon isn't going to make him magically evaporate from my brain. So, that's how I find myself back at Whelans with Ash and Cat Friday night after swearing I was going to keep my distance last week.

"Is this seat taken?" Dillon asks, looming over me. Their set finished fifteen minutes ago, and we returned to our usual table in the corner, waiting for the band to show up.

"Depends on who's asking?" I cheekily retort, trying not to ogle him too obviously. He's wearing a Guns N' Roses T-shirt today over dark jeans with his usual scuffed boots. His hair is even messier than usual, and my fingers twitch with a craving to run my hands through it. I honestly don't know how I'm expected to keep my hands off him when he always looks good enough to eat.

"What if it's me?" He flashes me that stupidly annoying hella sexy smug grin, and I'm a lost cause.

"You can sit," I relent, discreetly shoving Ash as she pinches my thigh under the table.

"Here." Dillon hands me a glass as he sits down. "You drink pink gin and 7UP, right?"

I nod, accepting the drink. "Thank you." Our fingers brush in the exchange, sending little jolts of electricity zipping up my arm.

"Good set, bro." Ash leans across me for a knuckle touch with her brother. "When are we going to hear these new songs you're writing?"

"You're writing new music?" I inquire.

His lips twitch. "I'm our chief songwriter. What else do you think I do with my days?"

"Watch porn. Jerk off. Bang groupies," I deadpan, shrugging casually.

His chest rumbles with laughter, his eyes dance with amusement, and his dimples come out to play. I'm mesmerized by him. Drawn to him in a way I'm not even sure I felt with Reeve, and we shared an intense connection that spanned years. There is something so familiar about Dillon yet thoroughly unique. I can't explain it. I just know fighting my attraction to him will only lead to more pain down the line.

What if I return home and regret never acting on our chemistry?

"You're staring." He lowers his voice so only I can hear. His thigh brushes against mine, infusing my body with liquid heat.

"You're kind of beautiful," I blurt before I can engage my brain.

"*You're* beautiful, and there's no kind of about it."

My cheeks flush at his compliment, and I see no trace of humor or insincerity on his face. "Thank you," I whisper, dropping my eyes to my lap.

"You act like no one's ever told you you're beautiful before, and I know that can't be the truth."

I tip my chin up, stabbing him with a direct look. "I'm kind of not myself at the moment."

"I kind of want to do something about that." His lips kick up, and I can't help smiling.

"You do?"

He nods.

"Why?"

He purses his lips, taking a moment to reply. "I've never felt drawn to any woman from the first second I met them, like I have with you."

"You were an ass to me," I remind him.

"I was confused, and it scared the crap out of me. Still does." He maintains eye contact as he lifts his bottle to his lips, tipping beer into his mouth. Even the way his throat works as he drinks gets my juices flowing. We have this raw sexual chemistry I'm both keen and terrified to explore.

"That makes two of us," I admit.

"Then I don't see what the problem is." His cheeky grin makes a reappearance. "We can be scared together."

"You don't just want to fuck me?" I ask, and Ash almost chokes on her drink. I turn to face her, rubbing my hand up and down her back as she splutters. I know she's talking with Cat and the girl who's here with Ronan, but she's definitely keeping one ear on our conversation. As if I wouldn't tell her everything later, ad verbum.

Dillon's eyes take a leisurely stroll up and down my body, giving new definition to eye-fucking. He might as well have stripped me bare by the way his scorching gaze mentally undresses me. I flush all over, and I'm sure my cheeks are the color of ripe strawberries. Leaning in, he presses his mouth to my ear. "Trust me, there is no part of me that doesn't want to fuck you."

I jerk back, but he slides his arm around my shoulders, pulling me in closer. "Stop. Fucking. Running," he growls. "I wasn't finished speaking."

"I kind of want to slap you right now," I admit.

"And I kind of want to knock some sense into that beautiful thick skull of yours. So just shut up and listen."

I gnash my teeth at him, wondering how it's possible to want to kill someone and kiss them at the same time.

"You're sexy with a body to die for. I'm a horny twenty-year-old man with sex on the brain twenty-four-seven. *Of course*, I want to fuck you. I want to fuck you so hard you'll be feeling my cock inside you for days. But—" He grips my chin, forcing my eyes to his. "Listen up, Hollywood. This is the important part." I narrow my eyes to slits, glaring at him, but he just chuckles. "I also want to get to know you. I *like* being around you." His Adam's apple jumps in his throat. "Your presence calms me, and I just want to spend time with you."

Ash fails at her attempt to disguise her snort of laughter. I dig my elbow into her ribs and stomp on her foot, hoping she gets the message and butts out.

Dillon blows out a breath before draining the rest of his beer.

My expression softens, matching my insides. Gingerly, I touch his bare arm. His skin is warm to the touch as my fingers stroke the dark hairs coating his muscular arm. Every part of Dillon is gorgeous, but his arm porn is to die for. Shaking myself out of my lustful thoughts, I lift my head, finding his intense gaze waiting for me. Our eyes lock, and our surroundings fade. My heart thumps against my chest cavity, and butterflies swoop into my belly. "I know that was hard for you to say," I rasp, struggling to speak with the heated way he's staring at me.

"It was. This isn't me. I have no clue what I'm doing." He barks out a bitter laugh. "But I'd like to try."

"What exactly are you saying?"

"Go out with me?"

"Like, on a date?"

He nods.

Wiping my clammy hands down the front of my jeans, I remind myself I'm strong and brave. I've promised myself I'm going to go with the flow and see where things take me, so this isn't difficult to concede. "Okay."

His eyes light up. "Yeah?"

I smile, hoping I won't regret this. "Yeah. I'll go out with you."

CHAPTER 43

"DO I LOOK OKAY?" I ask, barging my way into Ash's room without invitation. She's lying on her stomach on the bed with a pen between her teeth and a book opened in front of her. I'm frazzled over my impending date with Dillon and seriously considering canceling it. I need my Irish bestie to talk me off the ledge.

"You look perfect," she says, "though you might want to put your hair up." Her lips twitch, and I narrow my eyes.

"You know where he's taking me?"

"I do." She makes a zipping motion with her finger. "Don't bother asking. These lips are sealed."

All I know is it's an afternoon date, and I'm guessing it's outdoors since Dillon told me to dress warm. "Is it normal to feel physically ill?" I flop down on my back beside her on the bed.

She chuckles. "You'd swear you were never on a date before."

I roll over onto my side, facing her. "Not like this."

Genuine curiosity sweeps over her face. "You didn't get nervous going on dates with Reeve?"

"I did, but it was different. He was my best friend, and I'd known him my whole life. It was more of an excited kind of anticipation. I don't remember my stomach pitching, my hands sweating, or my heart galloping so fast it feels like I'm on the verge of a coronary. What if I throw up on him?"

She roars out laughing. "You're too funny." Seeing my glare, she tries to rein in her mirth. "You'll be fine. Dillon will put you at ease." She pats my arm.

I narrow my eyes. "Don't you know your brother at all? I'll probably want to poke his eyeballs out in less than a minute."

"That's all part of the attraction." She sits up, cross-legged. "I have a really good feeling about you two." Her eyes glimmer mischievously. "Imagine you end up getting married!" She squeals, bouncing on the bed. "Then we'd be sisters for real!"

"Aisling Margaret O'Donoghue," I shriek, whacking her in the chest. "You're not helping with the no-puking situation!"

"I'm sorry." She's trying not to laugh.

"No, you're not." I pout.

"No, I'm not," she agrees, scooting across the bed when I reach to whack her again. "I let my mind run away with me sometimes, but I'm just excited. You two looked so cozy last weekend, and Ro said Dillon's been writing up a storm all week, which is a sure sign he's feeling shit."

"And Ro is really okay with it?"

She bobs her head. "He's fine. I told you he would be. He's officially seeing Zara now."

"Wow. He's a fast worker."

"Told ya. Relax. It's all good. There won't be any need for pistols at dawn."

"You're so weird." I shake my head, grinning.

"But you love me anyway."

I throw myself at her, hugging her tight. "I do. Thank you. I needed that pep talk."

"Just relax and enjoy yourself. Hopefully, my brother won't irritate you too much!"

"I am not getting on that thing," I say, setting foot on the sidewalk outside my building and stalking toward the curb to my date. I plant my hands on my hips and glare at Dillon. He's slouched against the side of his motorcycle, wearing a leather jacket, black jeans, and his usual smirk.

"Scared, Hollywood?" he teases, unfurling to his full height.

"Straight up."

He moves in close to me, looking hotter than any man has a right to. His fingers curl around my chin. "I thought we agreed we'd be scared together. Hmm?"

"There's scared, and there's insanity." I point over his shoulder. "That is insanity. I saw how crazy you are on that thing, and this might be hard to believe, but I'd love to live to see my birthday in eleven days."

He chuckles. "You have such little faith." Leaning in, he presses a lingering kiss to my cheek. "I promise you'll survive the ordeal."

I thump him on the arm, as he turns to the side, frowning a little. "This is no laughing matter."

He sighs, losing the snarky humor. "Vivien Grace." His fingers sweep along my cheekbone. "I promise I will take care of you. I will go slow, and I won't make any risky moves. I've been riding for three years, and I've never had an accident. You can trust me. I swear."

"Trust isn't easy for me."

"I'll bet." He drops his hand, and his pinkie hooks in mine. "I'm guessing you've never been on a bike."

"I haven't."

"Then you've got to do this. It's Saturday. The sun is shining. We'll hit the open road, and as soon as you feel the wind on your back, it'll blow all the troubles from your mind. There is nothing as exhilarating as this." He wraps his hand around mine. "C'mon, Hollywood. Take a risk with me." He presses a kiss to the corner of my mouth. "Live a little," he whispers.

His words could be construed as condescending, but I can tell it's not. "Okay, but don't make me regret this."

"You won't." He looks over my shoulder, frowning.

"What?" I whip my head around, spotting a man dressed in jeans and a navy jacket leaning against the wall by my building. He's wearing shades while he whistles under his breath and scrolls through his phone.

"Is that guy familiar to you?" Dillon asks.

I shake my head, peering into Dillon's eyes. "No, why?"

"I thought I saw him outside Whelans last weekend." He shrugs. "Must be my overactive imagination at work."

Alarm bells blare in my head, and I swallow back bile. Dillon smiles while I cast a shaky glance at the guy, but he's gone. Prickles of apprehension wash over my skin. I haven't noticed anyone hanging around, and I sincerely hope Dillon is mistaken. If the paparazzi have discovered my location, I will legit cry. Especially since I already told my parents I'm staying here until August and Moira is in the middle of extending my rental agreement.

Dillon helps me to put my helmet on, and I climb onto the motorcycle behind him, jumping when he kick-starts the engine, and it roars to life. He grabs my hands, pulling my arms tight around his waist. My body is flush against his, my core pushed up against his ass, and his spicy scent swirls around me when I press my helmet against his back.

Slowly, he inches out into the traffic, carefully weaving in and out of busy city center traffic, until we hit the M50. We pick up speed, and I hug him tighter as we drive toward our destination, enjoying the thrill of being this close to him. I never did get to ask him where we're going, but it doesn't matter. I'm enjoying this a lot more than I thought I would, and apart from fleeting nerves at the start, I'm relaxed and comfortable. Dillon has stayed true to his word, pulling no dangerous maneuvers, and I no longer fear for my life.

Sun beats down on my back, heating me through my jacket, and it makes a welcome change from the cold and the rain. Now we're into April, the weather is definitely more pleasant though still a lot cooler and less predictable than I'm used to.

After a while, Dillon takes an exit off the highway, and we fly down smaller tree-lined roads, passing through a couple of towns, before we hit a sign for Killiney. He slows our pace as we ride over speed bumps in the road before turning right between stone pillars, entering a park. Driving past open fields on both sides, we reach an open-air parking lot at the top, and Dillon slides into a vacant space, killing the engine, and parking the bike.

I ease my helmet off as he does the same. Strands of hair have come undone from my ponytail and I swat wispy hair off my face.

"Surprise. You're alive," he drawls, and I laugh.

"That was actually fun."

239

"Told ya!" He tweaks my nose, helping me off the seat. He unzips his black leather jacket, revealing a wrinkled U2 shirt.

"You love your band shirts," I tease, unzipping my own jacket.

"I'm a rocker." He shrugs. "And I like shirts." He lifts the seat up, removing a Nike backpack. "Bono lives near here."

"Really?"

"Yep. If it's not too late when we leave, I can drive by his place, if you like." He slams the seat down, and it clicks into place.

I shrug, because I'm not really fazed.

A wide grin stretches across his mouth. "I keep forgetting you're not bothered by celebs."

"One of the things I love about Ireland is how relaxed people are about fame. It's a refreshing change."

Slinging the bag over his shoulder, he takes my hand, leading me toward a path. "I hate the thought of fame," he admits, as we walk.

"That surprises me." I admire the gorgeous scenery as we walk up an incline. "Because you own that stage. You have real stage presence. The natural kind. Not contrived. I think that's why you have the audience eating out of your hand. They can't help but be drawn to you."

"When I'm up there, I feel like the truest version of myself, if that makes sense."

I smile at a couple holding two toddlers in their arms as they pass by us. "It does," I tell him, as we walk up gray stone steps. Everywhere I look, I see green. Grass. Shrubs. Gorse bushes. Trees. Plants. No flowers, but it's still beautiful. "I can tell you're happy. Your passion oozes from every pore when you're entertaining a crowd."

"I can't reconcile that with the other side of fame." He pulls me to one side to let an elderly couple pass, draping his arm around my shoulders. On instinct, I lean into his side, pressing my face into his neck, inhaling the citrusy scent of his shower gel. His lips nuzzle my hair, and I can't get over how natural it is being with him like this.

"Is that why you're not keen on moving to the US?" I surmise, when we commence walking again. His hand is solid and warm in mine, and quiet contentment blooms in my chest.

"That's part of it."

I'm quiet for a few beats as I think of how to respond. "I think you're right to seriously contemplate what it'll mean for your life. It would be a shame if you couldn't make it work, because I think you're extremely talented and the band is going places."

"Is it possible to have success on the worldwide stage and hold on to your integrity, do you think? Can you have all this fame but still be yourself? Or is it too easy to get sucked into the machine?" He looks deadly serious as he casts a glance at me. "I know you've seen the nasty side of the industry, so I value your opinion."

Wow, this is some heavy shit for a first date, but I'm glad he's opening up to me. I'm quiet for many seconds as I work out how to explain my thoughts. "It is possible. I've seen it with my parents. There's no denying their love and support kept them true, but as individuals, they are both strong."

He nods, listening intently to my words as we ascend the hill.

"I think you can hold on to your integrity, but you need to be really strong-willed.

240

You'll have people pulling you in all kinds of directions, and if you don't know your own mind, and you can't stick to your resolve, you'll get sucked in. It's that easy." I gnaw on the inside of my mouth, as bile churns in my gut. "Reeve swore he didn't want the spotlight. That it was all about the acting for him. He promised nothing would change, and I believe he meant that. I believe he started out with those lofty aspirations, but it didn't last long. I always thought he was strong, but it all unraveled so fast."

"And he grew up in the business," Dillon says after a few awkward beats of silence. "What hope do a bunch of naïve Irish boys from County Wicklow have?"

"If you ask me, I think it might be easier for you to hold on to your principles. You have a loving family who will help you to stay grounded, and you're going in with your eyes wide-open. The fact you're hesitant because you don't want that side of fame is half the battle. The rest is down to how resilient and dogmatic you can be."

CHAPTER 44

WE DON'T TALK for several minutes, but it's a comfortable silence. I can tell Dillon is deep in thought. In a lot of ways, I completely relate to Dillon's situation. I have never wanted to be famous. I've always been happier staying in the shadows, but Reeve's fame forced me into the spotlight. I thought I was prepared for it. That I'd prepared my whole life for it, but I wasn't. I don't know if it's ever possible to fully prepare yourself for that kind of intrusive invasion.

"Wow," I exclaim when we reach the top of the hill. A large stone obelisk occupies center stage on the grassy incline. Blue-green ocean extends as far as the eye can see on one side with the vast expanse of the Irish landscape on surrounding sides. "What is this place?"

"This is Killiney Hill. It's one of the highest vantage points in County Dublin. Killiney is only a half hour's drive from Kilcoole, and we spent many Sunday afternoons here as kids. Now, I come here when I need to clear the cobwebs from my head." He continues talking as we walk around the obelisk. Pointing at a worn bench tucked under an alcove on the other side of the structure, he smiles. "I've written plenty of songs from that very spot. Sometimes Conor and me grab a couple of sleeping bags, a few bottles of beer, and come up here to write and jam."

"It's a wonder you don't freeze to death," I mumble, shivering as imaginary chills ghost over my spine.

He chuckles. "Us Irish must have thicker skin than ye thin-skinned Yanks."

"Ha! I might have started out like that, but I've definitely developed thicker skin over the past couple of years."

In a surprisingly sweet gesture, he presses a kiss to my temple. "I'm sorry for all you've been through."

"You mean that." I look up at him, and his eyes have that hypnotic green-blue sheen I've noticed in certain light.

"I do." He squeezes my hand, kissing my brow again. "Come on. I know a secluded spot where we can eat lunch."

My eyes are on stalks as we wander around the top of the hill, going up and down various steps and exploring other smaller stone structures that are dotted around Killiney Hill. I make Dillon take a ton of pictures of me to send to my parents and Audrey, and he jumps into a photo, taking a selfie of us in front of the obelisk.

I look at the pic with a warm smile on my face as he holds my hand, bringing us over to a rocky area that faces the Irish Sea. In the photo, our hair is windswept, our cheeks are rosy red, and we're both sporting massive smiles. I'm shocked to see how happy I look. I swallow over the lump in my throat at the thought I might finally be moving on, wondering why I feel joint elation and sadness.

Dillon veers off onto a narrow, bumpy grassy path, guiding me down closer and closer to the edge.

"Is this safe?" I inquire, noticing how there is no one else around.

He chuckles. "You really are a scaredy-pants, aren't you?"

I flip him the bird, and he tips back his head, laughing heartily. The sound warms my bones. "It's fair to say I've led a more sheltered, less reckless existence than you."

His laughter instantly dies, his smile fades, and for a moment, he looks almost… angry. As if I've insulted him. "Did I say something wrong?" I inquire, frowning as he slams to a halt at a small rocky ledge right on the edge of the hill.

He offers me a tight smile that doesn't reach his eyes. "Don't mind me. I'm a moody fucker."

"I've noticed," I deadpan, even though I know he's deflecting. "At least you're self-aware. There's a lot to be said for that."

"Trust me, I'm well aware of all my failings," he cryptically replies. My brow puckers as I watch him unpack a red-and-black-plaid blanket and some food and drink from his bag. Muscles flex and roll in his shoulders and back as he lays the blanket out flat on the rock, and I get the sense he's silently berating himself for something. "Come sit." He pats the blanket. "I promise it's safe." He sits down first, his long legs dangling off the edge.

Cautiously, I sit down beside him, ignoring the rapid pounding of my heart.

"I've got chicken, tuna, or ham," he says, opening a Tupperware box.

They all look delicious, made with a variety of different breads, filled with various lettuce and dressings.

"This is delicious," I say, after I've devoured a chicken sandwich and a tuna one. "What deli did you get it from?"

He smirks, and I'm glad to see the previous strained look is gone from his face. "Deli O'Donoghue."

My eyes pop wide. "You made these?"

"Don't look so shocked. I have many talents." He waves his hands in front of my face. "These hands are *very* skilled." His tone and expression are suggestive in the extreme, and a lick of arousal flows through my veins.

"They've had enough practice, I'm sure," I murmur.

He brushes a few stray strands of hair off my brow. "Does my history with women turn you off?"

Do I like thinking of him with other girls? No. And I really don't like the whole Aoife situation. However, everyone has a past, and I don't want to hold that against him and ruin things between us before they've even started. "A little, if I'm being honest. But you can't change your past any more than I can change mine."

"Would you want to?" He seems genuinely interested in my response.

"That's the million-dollar question." I stare out at the Irish Sea, wondering if I would change things even if I could. Tilting my head to the side, I stare at him. "If I could erase the last couple of years, I would, but before that, everything was perfect. In a lot of ways, it's easier to cling to the hurtful stuff, to let my anger override my other emotions. It's easier to forget about the good times, but there were lots of good times," I quietly admit, absently rubbing crumbs off my thighs as I stare at my lap.

"What's he like?" he asks, and I jerk my head up. "I'm guessing everything reported isn't true."

"It's not. Reeve isn't a bad person, and I know he loved me. I guess he just lost his way."

"That sounds like polite bullshit." He hands me a bottle of water.

"I need to believe he was manipulated and tricked into following the path he did, because the other reality is too hurtful." I release a shaky breath. "If he knew what he was doing, it means he didn't care that he hurt me, and that thought is unbearable." Tears sting my eyes, and I wish I could rewind to ten minutes ago and not start this conversation.

"I'm sorry. I don't mean to upset you." Dillon circles his arm around my shoulder, pulling me in closer, and I rest my head against him. "I'm just trying to understand."

"How much of a basket case I am?" I ask, half-laughing, half-crying.

"How badly he damaged your heart and whether there's any hope for an impatient asshole like me."

I lift my head and turn into him, draping my arms around his shoulders. "He hurt me, but I'm not some fragile broken doll you need to walk on eggshells around."

He clasps my face in his hands. "I already know that, Viv. I just don't want to rush you when you're not ready. You'll need to set the pace because the very last thing I want to do is hurt you too."

"I think you're a liar, Dillon O'Donoghue."

All the blood drains from his face, and his Adam's apple jumps in his throat.

Easing back, I inspect his face closely, wondering why my words have evoked such a reaction. Maybe he's realizing how vulnerable he's made himself today, and he's uncomfortable. That must be it. "Remember, we're going to be scared together." The panicked look on his face dials down as I lean in, kissing one corner of his delectable mouth. "You wave that asshole flag around, wearing it with pride, but I'm onto you." I playfully tweak his nose, softly smiling. "You do it to keep people away. To stop yourself from feeling. I recognize the signs, so don't try to deny it. But it's not who you are. Underneath that façade hides a different man. One I really want to get to know."

His hand moves to my hip. "I've told you things today I haven't fully shared with anyone. You're already getting under my skin." His eyes drift to my mouth.

"You're getting under mine too," I whisper, pushing my body in closer to his. My eyes drop to his lips, and I want to know what it would've been like if Ash hadn't interrupted us in the orchard that Sunday. Drawing on inner reserves of strength, I pin him with a confident gaze. "Kiss me." I tighten my arms around his neck, moving our faces closer. "Kiss me like you'll die if you can't taste my lips."

A chuckle rumbles through his chest. "You English students." He shakes his head, his eyes turning a darker shade of green as his hands move to my hair. Slowly and methodically, he removes the tie from my hair, and glossy dark strands fall around my shoulders. "Are you sure this is what you want?" His gaze skims over my face as his fingers thread through my hair.

"Oh my God. Just kiss me already."

He moves us back a little from the edge, wearing his trademark smirk the entire time. His lips part in a glorious smile, revealing his twin dimples, and we move at the same time, our lips colliding in perfect synchronization. Angling his head, he kisses my lips in an unhurried fashion, like we have all the time in the world. I cling to his shoulders, pressing myself in flush to his chest as our kiss continues. Heat skates over my skin, seeping into my bones, warming every part of me. Butterflies are doing cart-wheels in my chest, and blood thrums in my ears. My hands dive into his silky-soft hair, and I moan into his mouth. Grasping the opportunity, he eases his tongue between my lips, groaning as he diligently explores my mouth. A throbbing ache pulses between my thighs, and when he pulls us down to the ground, lifting me over him so I'm straddling his thighs, I don't raise any objection.

His arms clamp tightly around my back, keeping me in place so we don't fall off the hill in the height of passion. Our kiss turns more heated, and we're devouring one another, and it's still not enough. He hardens underneath me, and black spots burst behind my closed eyelids as I grind against his erection, wishing we were skin to skin, yet knowing I'm not ready for that yet.

"Jesus, Viv." Dillon moves his mouth from my lips to my ear, sucking on the sensitive flesh there. "What the fuck are you doing to me?"

"Less talking. More kissing," I pant, and he chuckles, pressing a trail of hot kisses along my neck and across my collarbone before returning to worship my lips.

We kiss and kiss until we're forced to break apart or risk lockjaw. Scooting back even farther from the edge, he leans against a smooth rock, holding me in his arms with my back pressed to his chest.

I cling to his strong arms, trailing my fingers along his skin, marveling at how safe and secure I feel in his embrace. At how easy this is. I lean my head back against his warm, hard chest, and a blissful sigh slips from my lips. Angling my head, I look back at him, loving how swollen his lips are from my kisses. Our eyes remain glued together, and we stare at one another for an indeterminate period, not talking, just drinking our fill.

It's not awkward.

Not in the slightest.

If feels like the most natural thing.

It's like looking into the mirror of my soul and seeing all my emotions reflected at me. No words are spoken, but words are redundant. My chest heaves with a rush of emotions, and I close my eyes as he plants a soft kiss to my lips. "On a scale of one to ten, how would you rate my first attempt at a date?" he whispers over my mouth.

My eyes pop open. "Are you serious?"

"As a heart attack."

I blink profusely. "I'm seriously your first ever date?"

"Woman. Am I the kind of guy who would lie about such a thing?"

"Valid point." I grin, inwardly squealing as I lightly drag my nails through the bristle on his chin—just because I can. I get an inordinate thrill when my hands move to his hair because I have wanted to play with his hair so many times. "I love your hair." I rub the silky strands between my fingers before fisting it in my hands.

"Fuck," he hisses, his eyes glinting with unconcealed lust. "If you keep doing that, all gentlemanly thoughts will fly from my head and I won't be responsible for my actions."

Slowly, I extract my fingers from his hair, but it's a chore.

"Ten," I whisper, giggling when I spot his frown. "On a scale of one to ten, this date is a ten."

"Huh." He doesn't look pleased, and I arch a brow. "Only a ten?" He nips at my earlobe, and I squirm. "I'll have to try harder next time."

I shake my head, fighting a smile. "Spoken like a true overachiever," I tease. "It's a ten, and the date isn't even finished. I'm pretty sure you'll struggle to top this."

"Ha!" He barks out a laugh. "Challenge accepted, milady."

I laugh, rolling my eyes again. "You're such a dork."

"As long as I'm *your* dork," he says, and the moment turns heavier.

I smile, but I don't reply. I don't want to force labels on whatever this is. I just want to exist in this moment with him. He must agree because he lets it drop, and I face the front again, snuggling into his arms as I look out at the stunning view.

Dillon dots kisses in my hair, against my temple, my cheeks, and my neck, as we sit in silence, watching the gentle motion of the waves far below us, listening to the sound of excited children running around someplace behind us, and it's sheer heaven. I could sit here like this with him for eternity.

The sun lowers in the sky, and a faint gray hue replaces the previous bright blue canvas. Swirls of cool air waft over us, and I shiver. "Time to go," he whispers, planting an openmouthed kiss against my neck.

"Do we have to?" I grumble.

I can almost see his smile as he presses a kiss to my cheek. "Let's grab some fish and chips and eat it on the beach," he suggests, pulling us to an upright position.

"I think you've just elevated this date from a ten to a twenty." I circle my arms around his waist, grinning up at him.

"Hell yeah!" He fist pumps the air. "That's what I'm talking about!"

CHAPTER 45

"HEY, ARE YOU OKAY?" Ash sticks her head through the door of my bedroom the following morning. Concerned eyes meet my bloodshot ones. "I heard you crying."

"No," I admit, sobbing openly.

She strides across the room, bundling me into her arms. "If my dickhead brother has caused this, I'm going to fucking castrate him," she seethes.

I know how much Ash loves Dillon, so the fact she's willing to instantly go into battle for me means more than I can say. Ash was out last night when I got home, so we haven't had a chance to speak about my date. "It's not Dillon's fault. It couldn't have been a better date, and he couldn't have been more of a gentleman."

"Ah." She hugs me close, smoothing a hand along my back. "You're feeling confused and guilty."

I nod even though it's more than that.

"The first time I slept with someone after Cillian, I physically threw up. Then I crawled into my bed and cried for three days straight." She stares off into space while stroking my hair. "No one understood. They assumed I was over him because it'd been six months since things ended. They didn't understand that grief and heartache don't work to a specific timeline or understand how I could seem to be over him one day and be disconsolate the next."

I've suffered those whiplash mood swings too. The type that makes me feel like I'm an emotional headcase and I'm going insane. "Yes," I sniff, shucking out of her arms and sitting back against the headboard. "Yes to all that, but it's also the bitter-sweet feeling that I'm moving on, and why do I feel so fucking guilty? I was the one who was betrayed. Reeve and I have been broken up for almost four months, so why am I wracked with guilt? Why does it feel like I've cheated on *him*?"

"Because you meant forever when you promised him that." She sits beside me, tucking her petite legs into her chest. "If there's one thing I remember from that time, it's don't try to find logic or make sense of everything you feel. You feel it for a reason. You're justified in feeling it, and it's all part of the bigger picture. It's all part of healing."

"I really hope you're right because I'm done feeling like my emotions are playing ping-pong with my head and my heart."

She turns to face me. "You had a good time with Dillon though, right?" Expectation lights up her pretty face.

A genuine smile crests over my lips. "I had the best time. It was awesome. Dillon was awesome." I fill her in quickly on where we went and what we did, including the fact we kissed.

"Yes!" she exclaims, making a funny gesture with her arm. "Ro owes me twenty."

I quirk a brow. "Do I want to know?"

"He said there was no way you'd get on the bike with Dil, but I knew you would, so we bet on it." She nudges my shoulder, smiling. "Lunch is on me on Monday."

"You're lucky you won that bet." I swipe at the dampness coating my cheeks. "Because it was definitely touch and go at the start."

She repositions herself on my bed, sitting cross-legged. "I know you have a rebellious streak in you, Viv. It's not obvious, unless you dig deep, but it's there. You haven't had a chance to let loose because of how you grew up and *where* you grew up, but you can be anyone you want to be here." She touches my arm. "That's the other reason I knew you were better suited to Dil and not Ro. He'll help you embrace that inner part of yourself you've never explored."

"Are you high right now?" I peer into her clear blue eyes.

She laughs before swinging her legs off the side of the bed. "Deny it all you want, but I know what I see."

I roll my eyes because she's clearly delusional. I don't have a rebellious bone in my body.

"Ro will be here shortly to get the bus with me. Why don't you come with us? You know Mum would love to see you. She was just asking me this week when you're coming back for dinner."

"Your mom is one of the sweetest, kindest people I've met, and I hate saying no, but I'll just be a Debbie Downer if I come. I'd rather eat ice cream in my pajamas while watching back-to-back romantic movies."

Sympathy splays across her face, and I know I don't need to explain it. Ash understands in a way most girls our age wouldn't. "Don't be too charitable. I'm guessing she's hoping you'll call your mum again so she can talk to her one more time."

I grin despite my present heartache. "I have it on good authority that she's about to receive a special care package from L.A. this week."

"Get out!" Ash's eyes widen.

"Don't breathe a word. Mom wants it to be a surprise."

She bounces on the bed, jostling the mattress. "What is it?"

"A bunch of DVDs, some signed promo shit, and Mom included some local L.A. produce. Candles, candy, skincare stuff, and God knows what else. Knowing Mom, she went to town." Mom is delighted Ash's family have taken me under their wing. I think it helps to reassure her knowing there is a mother figure in my life when I'm so far away.

"Oh my God. Mum is going to go crazy when that arrives." She gives me another hug. "Thank you! And thank your mum from me."

"You can thank her in July. My parents are flying over for a week in between work commitments. We're planning on going to Cork and Kerry, and Mom said to ask you to come."

"I would love to, provided I can get the time off work. I usually work longer hours during summer break." She chews on the corner of her lip. "Do you think she'd have time to drop into my house? I think Mum would about die if she got to meet her in the flesh."

"Mom has a pretty hectic schedule planned, but why don't we get your mom over here for lunch the day they arrive?"

"That's a brilliant idea. Message me the date, and I'll make it happen. It's a pity they aren't coming in June. They could've come to Shane and Fiona's wedding with you." I was pleasantly surprised to receive a wedding invite last week. I can't wait to experience an Irish wedding; I've heard they can be pretty wild. Ash said the hotel they are getting married at is in County Wexford and it's gorgeous.

Ash glances at her cell, hopping up. "Shit. I need to get a move on, or I'll miss the bus. Are you sure you don't want to come?"

"Positive. Tell everyone I said hi." I grab my purse from my bedside table, rummaging through the contents. "Hang on a sec," I call out. Finding my keys, I throw them to her. "Take my rental. Mom's assistant got you added to the insurance. Just don't wreck it. I know Dil isn't the only O'Donoghue with a reckless streak."

She squeals, racing across the room and yanking me into a fierce hug.

"Can't breathe," I croak, only half-joking.

"You are the most thoughtful, generous person I know. How did you even manage this?" She takes pity on me, letting me go.

"I snuck a copy of your driver's license and sent it Moira. She did the rest."

"Seriously, thank you for organizing this. It sure beats the smelly bus."

After Ash leaves, I take a long soak in the tub, trying to quiet my hyperactive mind, but it's no use. I wish I was the kind of girl who took everything in stride. But I'm the kind to overthink everything, and I just want it to stop.

I like Dillon.

A lot.

Even more so after yesterday.

He opened up to me, and I saw a different side to him. A side I want to explore. Yet I'm freaking terrified too. Terrified of getting my heart trampled on again. He's a moody prick at times, and I have no experience dealing with that. I get the sense he's hiding something, and that concerns me. What if I place my trust in him and he lets me down too?

"Ugh." I scrub my hands down my face before dunking my head under the water. When I come up for air, I'm still stewing over everything. Are my fears founded? Or am I letting the past cloud my perspective? Is this what I'm going to be like with every new relationship going forward? Will I doubt every guy because Reeve betrayed my trust? Will I think every guy is hiding something from me if he doesn't immediately open his heart and spill every vulnerable secret? Is that in any way fair to the guy?

My brain churns these thoughts, over and over, round and round in circles, and I get out of the cold bath, shivering and annoyed at my inability to just go with the flow. As I dry myself, I decide it's not fair to hold Reeve's sins and my past over Dillon's head. I've got to give him the benefit of the doubt unless he does something, or says something, that justifies concern. It doesn't mean I have to trust him out of the gate. No one should be trusted until they've proven themselves, but that doesn't mean I should automatically distrust every guy I meet either.

Wearing fresh pajamas, with my damp hair in a messy topknot, I'm scrolling through the movie options on my TV when the doorbell chimes. I pad along the hallway in my bare feet, startled to see Dillon's gorgeous face staring back at me through the peephole. He sticks his tongue out, and I'm smiling as I open the door. "What are you doing here?"

"I'm hoping you're up for some company," he says, lifting the plastic bag in his hand. "I come bearing gifts. Ice cream, chocolate, and wine." He waggles his brows, piercing me with that infamous cocky grin.

My heart melts a little, and tears prick the backs of my eyes. Fuck, I'm a hot mess these days, and I've got to get a grip.

"Hey." The grin slides off his mouth as he steps closer. "Don't be upset."

Acting on instinct, I fling my arms around him, hugging him tight. "I'm happy you're here."

"Does that mean you're going to invite me in?" His flirtatious tone and cheeky grin papers over the fractures in my heart, and I grab his hand, pulling him into the apartment.

"Won't your mom be mad if you don't arrive for dinner?" I inquire, guiding him to the kitchen.

"Nah. She'll be grand. Especially when she discovers I'm keeping her new favorite person company."

I bend down to grab a couple of bowls from the cupboard, and when I straighten up, I catch Dillon staring at me with his mouth slightly open. Setting the bowls down on the counter, I cross my arms and fix him with a knowing look. "Were you just checking out my ass?"

"I was," he readily admits, slowly dragging his eyes up my body. "Don't blame me. You were wiggling it right in my face."

I snort out a laugh. "You're incorrigible." I reach overhead to grab some wine glasses, and my top lifts a little, exposing a sliver of skin.

"Damn, Hollywood. Those pajamas should be illegal."

I spin around, finding his eyes are now fixated on my bare legs. He rakes his gaze up the length of my legs, over my stomach, lingering a little on my chest, before meeting my face. Hunger radiates from his eyes, and I catch my breath.

"Those legs should be illegal, as well as other parts of your body," he says in a gruff, deep tone that sends shivers sweeping over my skin. My nipples harden to sharp points, poking against my cotton pajama top like a calling card. Of course, he notices, and the look he gives me makes my knees buckle and my core tremble with need.

"I can change," I croak, not trusting myself in the face of such intense chemistry.

I move to walk off, and he darts forward, planting his hands on the counter, caging me in.

"Don't," he whispers, leaning in to kiss my neck.

I grab the counter, tilting my head to one side as if on autopilot, granting him more access. He trails his lips seductively up and down my neck, and every part of my body is on fire. Without warning, he pulls back, adjusting himself in his jeans before running his hands through his wild blond hair. "Sorry." His voice is thick with the same need coursing through my veins. "I didn't come here for that."

"What did you come for?" I ask, straightening up.

"I came to watch movies, drink wine, eat ice cream, and cheer you up."

Tears well in my eyes again. "Sorry," I sniff, swiping at the moisture clinging to my lashes. "I'm a bit of a basket case today."

"It's okay." Without hesitation, he pulls me into his arms, enveloping me in a firm hug I desperately need. I cling to him, siphoning his warmth and his strength until I feel fully composed. "Thank you," I quietly say, looking up at him.

He brushes his mouth against mine in the sweetest kiss. "You don't have to thank me. I'm right where I want to be."

I stretch up and kiss him quickly. "We best eat this ice cream before it melts."

"I'll make you a deal." He removes the carton of chocolate ice cream from the bag. "I'll serve the ice cream while you change into tracksuit bottoms or a black sack or anything else as long as it's baggy and it conceals those tempting legs."

"I thought you said I wasn't to change." I pin him with a faux innocent expression.

"If you want me to keep my hands to myself, covering those gorgeous legs is your best bet."

I'm not sure I want him to keep his hands to himself, but the fact I'm indecisive means he probably should. "On it," I purr, smirking as I sashay to my bedroom to change.

"Oh, fuck, no!" Dillon vigorously shakes his head, glaring at the TV screen. "Are you trying to torture me, woman? Anything but *The Notebook*. I'm begging you." Closing his palms together, he begs me with his eyes, but it only makes me more determined. He doesn't wait for my reply before continuing to plead his case. "Why can't girls' go-to movie be *Deadpool* or *Jason Bourne*, huh? Fuck, I'd even sit through *A Star is Born* and be happy."

"Are you insane?" I raise my hand. "Actually, don't answer that." I smirk at his scowl. "That movie does *not* have a happy ending, and I can't watch a romance without a happy ending."

"*The Notebook* doesn't have a happy ending either!"

"The ending was my favorite part of the book. Although it's poignant, it still made me smile because they're together for eternity and their love will live on. *A Star is Born* made me ragey as hell. I wanted to cut a bitch after I watched that movie."

"That kind of turns me on." He smirks, and I roll my eyes.

Curling my bowl into my chest, I swing my covered legs up onto the leather couch, as I press pause on the remote. "I'm going to admit something very few people know." He flops onto the middle of the couch with a resigned sigh, lifting my feet and plonking them in his lap. He gives me his undivided attention as I scoop a big spoonful of ice cream. "I've never watched *The Notebook*. I was only four when it premiered in movie theaters, but I have read the book. I was *not* impressed."

His mouth hangs open and his eyes pop wide. "So, why the hell do you want to watch the movie?" Incredulity drips from his tone.

"We were discussing it recently in my American lit class, and everyone said the movie is ten times better. I want to see if it's true."

"It's not," he deadpans. "We should just watch *Deadpool*."

"Not happening, dude." I wave my spoon in his face.

"Now *I'm* going to admit something. Something lots of people unfortunately know," he wryly replies, shoveling a large mouthful of ice cream into his delectable mouth. I watch in fascination as he swallows it in seconds. "I've seen this movie way too many times to count."

"How does that even happen when you've never had a girlfriend?"

"I had a heartbroken sister who watched it nonstop for weeks. I was the only sucker in the family strong enough to endure that shit on a continuous loop." He makes a face before shoving the spoon into his mouth again. His aim is a bit off, and chocolate ice cream paints the corner of one side of his mouth.

Without pausing to think about it, I put my bowl down and crawl to him. "You are the best brother. Ash is so lucky to have you." Before he can respond, I lick the ice cream off his face and press my lips to his. He kisses me eagerly, and I plunge my tongue into his mouth, groaning as the taste of ice cream and Dillon explodes on my tongue. He puts his bowl down on the floor without breaking our lip-lock, and I'm impressed. Grabbing my hips, he repositions me until I'm straddling him, and our kissing grows more frantic.

Dillon is an amazing kisser, and I could do this all day.

"Wait." He rips his lips from mine a few minutes later, and I instantly miss his mouth. He scoops some ice cream onto his spoon and shovels it between his lips, winking.

Catching on, I grin as I lean down and kiss him. He slides some of the ice cream into my mouth, and I moan against his lips, grinding my hips against his when I feel his erection nudging me.

We finish the rest of our ice cream like this, and by the time we're done, I'm hotter than lava, and my body is aching to be filled by him. Dillon clearly feels similar things as he flips me over on my back, so I'm underneath him, and then he proceeds to kiss the shit out of me. Closing my eyes, I lose myself in his kisses, reveling in the blissful sensations flowing through my body. I don't think I've ever been so turned on just from kissing.

My back arches off the couch when he presses his long hard body down on top of me, careful not to crush me with his weight. My legs automatically wrap around his waist, and I thrust up against him, groaning at the hardness pushing against my soft center. We grind against one another as our kisses grow more demanding, and I'm seconds away from ripping my clothes off and jumping on his cock when he pulls back. "Fuck, Viv." Rocking back on his heels, he claws his hands through his hair as his chest heaves.

My pajama top is stuck to my back, and my panties are soaked, dripping with desire for this man. I have never wanted anyone as much as I want him in this moment, but I'm glad he stopped it. I don't want to move too fast. This morning proves my emotions are still out of whack, and I need to put the brakes on. I don't want to sleep with him and subsequently fall apart. That wouldn't be fair to either of us.

Dillon extends his hand, pulling me up into his arms. The steady rhythm of his heartbeat under my ear soothes me, and I close my eyes, savoring the feeling of being in his arms. "You make it so hard to resist you, but I'm determined to do this the right way," he whispers in my ear.

"At least one of us has self-control." My words are muffled against his chest.

"God fucking help us if we're relying on mine." Sarcasm is thick in his tone, and I giggle. "Come on." He repositions us on the couch until we're comfortable. He's sitting, and I'm lying down on my side with my head on a cushion on his lap. "Let's just watch this bloody movie. I might as well get it over and done with."

CHAPTER 46

"THEY ARE SO ADORABLE," Ash says, regaling Cat with details of my and Dillon's escapades this week. "Seeing Dil like this makes me so unbelievably happy. Who knew he was such a closet romantic?"

Ash came back Sunday night to discover us curled against one another on the couch while *Bohemian Rhapsody* played on the TV. Remnants of the chicken pasta dinner Dillon cooked were left in the kitchen, along with the empty ice cream carton and wine bottle.

"Your brother is very romantic," I agree with the biggest smile on my face.

We've been pretty much inseparable since Sunday except for during the day when I have school and Dillon is doing whatever aspiring rock-stars-slash-songwriters do. He showed up outside Trinity on Monday, holding a bunch of lilies and asking me to dinner. Tuesday, he took me to this little boutique movie theater to see *Breakfast at Tiffany's*. On Wednesday, we worked out together in the gym in my building before he and Ash cooked their mom's special chicken curry. Then last night, we took off on his motorcycle for Trim Castle, a historical three-storied keep that was featured in the *Braveheart* movie.

I'm learning Dillon is fascinated with the past, and he appears to have a huge knowledge of Irish history. He told me he'd considered studying history at Trinity, but he hates being cooped up indoors, and he doesn't think the structure would suit him, so he chose not to go to college and to focus on the band instead.

The more layers I'm uncovering, the more I'm intrigued. He is nothing like I first expected him to be and everything I never saw coming. While he is different from the prickly, rude guy I initially met, he still has little moments where that brash, obnoxious side of his personality rears its head.

I haven't had any other meltdowns since Sunday, but I know that's partly because I'm busy, and when I'm with Dillon, there is no room to think about Reeve or the confusing emotions still swirling around my brain when I'm not quick enough to shut them out.

"Aoife looks like she wants to gouge your eyeballs out with toothpicks," Cat murmurs, bringing me back to the present. I look in Aoife's direction, and sure enough, she's glaring at me with unconcealed venom. When Dillon was here earlier, she was all smiles and sweetness, but the second the guys moved to the main event room, she stabbed me with the full extent of her jealousy. During the guys' set, we stayed well clear of her, and I'll be grateful when Dillon reappears as her clear resentment has me on edge.

"Should I be worried? And does she go to Trinners, or does she just hang around Jamie there all the time?" I ask, needing to understand how big of a threat she poses.

"She isn't a student. She works full-time in Dunnes." Dunnes Stores is a leading Irish grocery chain. "I'd watch my back if I was you," Ash adds. "But she'll probably just switch her attention full-time to Jamie now."

"I'm sorry." I know Ash is staying away from Jamie, but that doesn't mean he's not occupying real estate in her head.

"Thank fuck." Ash sighs, glancing over my shoulder.

"What's wrong?" Dillon asks, and I whip my head around, grinning as our gazes connect.

"Your ex-fuck-buddy over there didn't get the memo you're off the market. She's been sending daggers at Viv all night."

Dillon lifts me out of my chair, frowning. "I didn't see anything, and I've been watching." Sinking down on the seat, he pulls me into his lap. His arms band around me, and he brushes my hair to one side, pressing a kiss to my neck. I lean back against him, my chest humming in satisfaction as I melt into his arms.

"She's only doing it when you're not around, dumbass." Ash rolls her eyes. "Honestly, men are so fucking thick. Of course, her claws aren't going to come out in front of you! She wants you to think she's all sweetness and light. I expect she's biding her time, waiting for you to return to her skanky ass."

"Ash." Dillon's tone contains censure. "You shouldn't call her that."

"Why not? If the cap fits," Ash retorts, gulping back a mouthful of beer. "Weren't you the one who lectured me about not labeling women who enjoy casual sex as sluts?"

"Groupies are different. It's not that I have an issue with her sleeping with multiple guys, or even multiple guys at the same time"—she drills him with a pointed look, referencing the threesome she saw him having with Jamie and Aoife—"it's the fact she has an agenda. Aoife has dollar signs behind her eyes. She sees you as her ticket out of here. That's why I called her a skank."

"Fair enough," Dillon concedes, nodding. "It's not like I don't know that, and I'm done with her now anyway, so it doesn't matter." He turns my face slightly, pressing his mouth to my ear. "I don't care about Aoife unless she's making you uncomfortable. Is she?"

"She is." I look him straight in the eye. "Her nasty looks are forcing me to relive my past. I know I'm probably more sensitive than most, but I agree with Ash. She has an agenda, and I don't want to be caught in the crossfire."

"I'll talk to her and make sure she cuts it out. Next time, you need to tell me. If anyone pulls any crap, you come straight to me, and I'll handle it, okay?" I nod. "I won't let anyone disrespect you." Resituating me on his lap so we're face to face, he drills me with a solemn look, and I get the unspoken message—He's not Reeve, and he won't let his groupies treat me like shit.

A layer of stress lifts from my shoulders. "Thank you."

He cups my cheek. "Show me how grateful you are?" His eyes shimmer suggestively, and I need no further encouragement.

All week, we've been kissing and making out like demons, and I'm on the verge of spontaneous sexual combustion. A few of our sessions have grown very heated, and there's been plenty of groping over clothes, but we haven't taken it further, and he hasn't put any pressure on me. Dillon is letting me set the pace, like he promised. I'm growing more and more relaxed with him and finding fewer and fewer reasons to hold back from taking our relationship to the next level.

Tired of waiting for me to show him, Dillon grabs my face and slams his lips to mine. My arms snake around his neck, and I angle my head, opening my lips to welcome his skillful tongue. The small circular ball of his ring gently scrapes against my tongue, and I can't help imagining what it would feel like if he went down on me. That thought heightens my arousal and elevates the anticipation every time we kiss, and this is no different.

He kisses me deeply and passionately, uncaring we have an audience, until all my worries have flittered away.

"Get a room!" Ro shouts, and we reluctantly break apart.

"*You* get a room!" Dillon retorts, gesturing to where Ronan's new girlfriend is presently draped all over him. Thankfully, everything is great between all of us, and Ash was right. Ronan has moved on, and he doesn't appear to harbor any grudges. I haven't seen much of him, as I've been spending a lot of time with Dillon alone, but any time he has been around, it's just like always. I'm hugely relieved.

"I won't be able to see you now before Wednesday," Dillon tells me later that night as he walks me home. "We've got to rehearse a lot before the ball." The guys managed to secure a twenty-minute slot at the Trinity Ball, which is a big deal for them.

"Will the groupies be there?" I ask.

"No fucking way. Even if it wasn't a closed rehearsal, we wouldn't bring them. I'd only want you there."

"Okay. Good."

"Don't worry about them. For as long as we're together, you're the only woman I'll be with. You're the only one I want." He lifts our conjoined hands to his lips, kissing my knuckles. "I talked to Aoife, and I set her straight. She won't give you any more grief." His eyes drill into mine. "If she does, you let me know, and she'll be cut off completely."

His words hint at our inevitable ending, but I refuse to linger on that now. I still have months left in Ireland, and I'm determined to have fun with Dillon for however long it lasts. We're both going into this with our eyes open, knowing this has a termination date. As long as my heart doesn't get invested, it'll work out fine.

"I won't share you," he adds, "and I hold myself to the same standards. I know I don't have much experience to go on, and I understand if you're reluctant to trust me, but I promise I won't cheat on you or mess around with other girls. I know what you've been through, and I could never hurt you like that. I've seen what it did to my sister. I never want to be that guy."

He says all the right things, and I want to accept his words at face value, not read into everything, but it's hard when your trust in the male race has been completely decimated. Still, I made a vow to myself that I wouldn't punish Dillon for Reeve's sins, and I meant it.

"Thank you." I peck his lips, hating how much reassurance I crave. He must think I'm so clingy and needy, and that's not who I am deep down inside. "I needed to hear that."

"I know." His eyes are all seeing as he tightens his arm around my shoulders, holding me closer to his side as we walk.

"I guess I'll just have to find a way to survive without you for a few days," I say, replying to his original statement. "I've tons of studying to keep me occupied, and I have to turn in my next article for the paper." The *Trinity News* student paper published an article I wrote on being an American student in Dublin last month to favorable feedback, so they asked me to write something else. "I've also got to finish an assignment for my scriptwriting class, so it should be enough to keep me from missing you too much."

He pushes me into the nearest wall and kisses me like he might never get to do it again.

"What was that for?" I pant, when we finally surface for air. "Not that I'm complaining." I grin.

"You said you'd miss me. I liked hearing that."

Sweet baby Jesus. This guy is going to ruin me. If he keeps this up, I'm going to have a hard time stopping my heart from becoming invested. Pressing my body against his, I wrap my arms around his neck. "Won't you miss me?"

His lower hand slides around my back, and he pulls me in tight to his body. His erection presses into my stomach, shooting darts of desire straight to my pussy. "I think that answers your question."

He smirks, and I nip at his earlobe. "So, you'll only miss my body?"

Holding my hand, he steers me in the direction of my apartment. "I will miss everything about you, Viv. I just love being with you, full stop." He glances at me, and sincerity radiates from his eyes. "I love how you constantly challenge me and you're never predictable. You always surprise me. I love your excitement for new things and how brave and strong you are."

His beautiful words wrap around my heart like a comfort blanket, and I can almost feel some of the fissures being repaired.

He squeezes my hand, drawing circles on my skin with his thumb. "It feels like I've known you forever, and I've never felt this happy with any girl. I've never met anyone who consumes my every waking thought like you do." He flashes me a boyish grin. "You're under my skin, Hollywood. In more ways than one."

CHAPTER 47

"DO YOU WANT TO COME UP?" I offer, when we reach my apartment building.

One side of his mouth lifts, and his eyes heat. "For a nightcap or..."

"I'm not fucking you. I'm not quite ready yet, but I—" I pause to summon my courage, dropping my tone a couple of octaves. "I thought you might like to stay the night. We can do other things, just not full sex."

His lips kick up at the corners as he winds his hands in my hair, pulling my head toward him. He rests his brow against mine. "You're adorable when you get all flustered." His lips brush against mine. "I'd love to spend the night." Still holding my head, he tips my chin back. "You set the pace. Always."

I practically drag him to my bedroom, and we're kissing and grinding against one another the entire time. We collapse on my bed in a tangle of limbs, and slowly our clothes come off until I'm only in my bra and panties, and he's in his black boxers, the outline of his long thick dick obvious against the thin cotton.

He crawls over me, holding himself upright by his elbows as he bends down to kiss me. "Can I touch you?" he purrs in my ear, and my core screams out a "hell yeah."

"Yes," I rasp, running my hands up and down his back.

In a lightning-fast move, he removes my bra, burying his head in my chest. "These are beautiful." He cups my breasts, grinning and licking his lips as he looks up at me.

"I'm glad you approve," I tease, my body tingling in anticipation.

He rakes his gaze up and down my body. "Oh, I definitely approve. Your body is to die for." Warmth spills into me from his complimentary words, helping to relax me. He lavishes my breasts with attention, sucking and biting my flesh as I moan and writhe underneath him. I hiss when he drags one of my nipples between his teeth, tugging on it as his fingers roughly tweak my other nipple, and a painful-pleasurable sensation courses through me with his forceful touch. Lifting his head, he pierces me with intense dark eyes. "If this is too much, tell me to stop and I will."

"Don't stop," I blurt, needing more.

The grin he sends me is nothing short of devilish. Lowering his mouth to my breast again, he sucks hard on my flesh, and I cry out when his tongue laves against my nipple, feeling the cool metal stroke against my taut peak. He sucks and fondles my breasts for a few minutes before sliding down my body.

Pushing my thighs apart, he runs his hands up and down my legs. "These legs have a starring role in my fantasies," he says, continuing to stroke my skin. "So beautiful." He trails his hands higher and higher until he reaches the apex of my thighs. Shoving his face in my pussy, he inhales deeply. "Fuck, Hollywood. You're fucking soaked." He rubs me through my lace panties before ripping them off with his bare hands. Strips of lace float around the bed as I stare at him in shock. He chuckles. "I'll replace them if that's what you're worried about."

"I'm not worried. I'm just—" I blush, and he inches up my naked body, putting his face in mine.

"Don't be embarrassed. Tell me."

"I've read about guys doing that in books, but it's never happened to me before," I sheepishly admit, grabbing clumps of his gorgeous hair. "It's fucking hot."

He grins before claiming my lips in a searing kiss that curls my toes. Rocking his boxer-covered cock against me, he works me into a frenzy in no time, and I'm wondering why I'm holding back on the fucking front. "I need to taste you," he says, biting my lip. "Can I fuck your cunt with my tongue and my fingers?"

He's so crude, but it cranks my arousal up a few notches. "Oh God." I yank his mouth to mine. "Yes, please."

His mouth trails a path from my lips to my neck, and he spends a couple of minutes sucking on my flesh, grazing his teeth along my collarbone and nipping my breasts before he returns to the apex of my thighs. I scream when he sucks on my inner thighs, softly biting and then soothing my sensitive skin with his tongue.

"Watch me," he grits out, flicking his eyes to mine as he settles in between my thighs, lying flat on his stomach. I prop up on my elbows, my body wound tight with anticipation and raw need. Butterflies race around my chest, and lust spools low in my belly.

When he thrusts my legs over his shoulders, his nostrils flare, and his eyes burn with desire as he spreads my pussy lips with his thumbs and stares at my most intimate parts. My chest heaves, and I swallow thickly as he drinks his fill before he leans in, licking a path up and down my slit. "So fucking gorgeous," he murmurs. "You taste like heaven on my tongue." He wiggles his tongue up and down my slit, lapping it against my clit, and when his ring hits my swollen bundle of nerves, I almost come off the bed.

"Holy fuck." I throw my head back and close my eyes as the most delicious tremors zip up and down my body. I can already feel my climax hovering, waiting to explode, and I don't think it's going to take much to reach orgasm.

He chuckles. "Like that, Hollywood?"

"Hell, yeah. Do it again."

"Eyes on me," he commands, and I open my eyes and lower my chin. "I'm going to fuck you now, and you're going to explode all over my face."

With a wicked grin, he plunges his tongue into my pussy and devours me. Keeping my eyes on him is hard because I want to throw my head back, close my eyes, and just savor the intense sensation as he slides his tongue in and out of my cunt. That silver ball in the middle of his tongue is doing amazing things to my insides, and my climax is building fast. My hips are moving, pushing against his mouth, as he works me over like a pro. Every nerve ending in my body is alive with static electricity, and I'm drowning in sensations, both familiar and new.

Dillon is setting the oral sex bar extremely high, and I have a feeling this man is going to ruin me for all others.

Yanking fistfuls of his hair, I pull his mouth in even closer to my pussy, tugging on strands of his hair in a way I'm sure is painful. His lustful growl tells me he approves, so I continue pulling his hair as he worships my cunt with his naughty tongue.

Rubbing two fingers against my clit, he pushes down on my nub, stroking it in a relentless, harsh pace that matches the thrusts of his tongue and I have no time to warn him before I come apart. I scream out his name as I buck and writhe on the bed, shoving my pussy in his face as I ride the waves of the most intense orgasm of my life.

"Yum," he murmurs, with his face still between my legs. "Hold still, I want to lick every last drop." With one hand, he pushes my ass back on the bed, holding me in place, as he laps all my juices, making appreciative noises that almost have me coming again. "Fuck, that was sexy." He slides his body against mine as he crawls back up to me. "I can't wait until my cock is filling every inch of your sweet tight cunt."

He's so dirty, but I love it.

His glossy lips are covered with my cum, and I like seeing my essence smeared across his mouth. A primal possessiveness sweeps over me, and I yank him down flush on top of me, scraping my nails up and down his back. "Taste yourself," he says, slamming his lips down on mine.

Teeth clash as we violently kiss, sucking and biting on each other's lips until mine feel swollen and bruised. I'm holding him flush to my body, my hands roaming his back, grabbing handfuls of his ass, and I need to see all of him, taste all of him. "Stop," I pant, shoving at his shoulders. "It's my turn to taste you."

A familiar smirk crosses his mouth as he jumps up, ripping his boxers down his legs and kicking them away. He stands over me, his feet on either side of my legs, stroking his impressive erection. His crown is glistening with beads of precum, and I bolt upright, swiping my tongue across his tip, moaning at the salty taste coating my tongue. "Sit up against the headboard, and prop pillows at your back and under your arse," he demands, fixing me with his hungry stare as he slowly pumps his straining dick.

I do as I'm told, excitement bubbling up my throat as he moves toward me. "Tilt your head back, as far as you can go, and open your mouth wide." His lips twitch. "How good is your gag reflex?"

"Uh…I'm not sure it's ever been tested." My cheeks flare up again. I don't know why I'm getting embarrassed. I've had sex. I've sucked cock. But I'm not used to being with someone so experienced. I'm used to a gentler touch, so this rougher version of sex is new to me, and I'm feeling a little out of my depth. Don't get me wrong—I'm fucking loving it; I'm just feeling a little inexperienced around a guy like Dillon.

He comes closer, and his gorgeous dick salutes me. "I'm going to fuck your mouth," he warns, dragging one hand through my hair. "If it's too much, grab my wrist, and I'll pull out." Bending down, he kisses me hard on the lips. "This is about your pleasure and enjoyment as much as mine. If you're not enjoying it, I need to know."

I love how attentive he is to my needs. "I'm loving everything so far. I'm sure I'll love this too."

Letting go of his dick, he cups both sides of my face. "You are so sweet, Vivien Grace. Sexy as sin but sweet as sugar at the same time."

"You say the nicest things."

"It's all true." He straightens up but keeps his knees slightly bent so the angle is right. "Now, open wide, Hollywood."

I follow his instructions, and he slaps his cock against my cheeks and my mouth, teasing me with his tip, brushing it lightly against my lips. My tongue darts out, licking him any chance I get, until he slowly eases into my mouth. I suck his tip, my tongue swirling around the two ends of his piercing, and he curses, jerking his hips as he pushes in deeper. Grabbing his ass, I widen my mouth as he continues inching in, almost choking when his crown hits the back of my throat.

"Good girl." He looks down at me before grabbing my hair and twisting it around his hand. Then he fucks my mouth without restraint, sliding in and out aggressively while tugging on my hair and stretching my neck back. I suck and lick him while he thrusts in and out, pivoting his hips and rolling his cock inside my mouth. Tears leak from my eyes, and I almost gag a couple times, but he eases back when it happens, stalling for a second to ensure I'm comfortable, before picking up his punishing pace.

I don't even consider stopping, even though my neck and jaw are stretched uncomfortably, because I'm enjoying it too much. The look of bliss on Dillon's face as he rocks into my mouth almost undoes me. I love that I've put that expression on his face. That I'm the one giving him pleasure. He doesn't hold back, thrusting, moaning, and cursing as he fucks my mouth with abandon. "I'm going to come," he groans, as his ass cheeks stiffen in my hands. I look up at him through wet eyes, urging him to keep going.

His entire body locks up, his powerful thighs strain, and he shouts my name as ropes of hot salty cum hit the back of my mouth, gliding down my throat. Releasing his hold on my hair, he pops out of my mouth and slumps to his knees beside me. His lips collide with mine, and he kisses me urgently, moaning into my mouth as his tongue slips inside me. He wraps his arms around me as he kisses me like I'm precious treasure.

My heart is full, my body sated, and I'm feeling even closer to him.

"Holy fuck, Viv," he rasps, eventually pulling back. "You never cease to amaze me." I beam with pride at his words. Holding me tight against his chest, he peers into my eyes. "Was that okay for you?"

"It was more than okay. I loved it, and I love your piercings."

"Wait till you feel my cock inside you. This will sound arrogant, but fuck it, I don't care if it's true. I will give you the best sex of your life, and that's a fucking guarantee."

"I don't doubt it." I thread my fingers through his hair. "And I'm working my way up to it."

He plants an adoring kiss on the corner of my mouth. "There's no rush. My blue balls can wait." He flashes me one of his signature grins before sliding off the bed, extending his arm to me. "C'mon. Let's clean up in the shower, and then we can go to bed."

I don't stop to think about it, leaving no space to second-guess myself, clasping his hand and letting him pull me up.

CHAPTER 48

"HAPPY BIRTHDAY, BIRTHDAY GIRL!" Ash screams, bouncing on my bed on Wednesday morning, dragging me from a deep sleep. "Oh my God, Viv. You're sleeping with it now." She shakes her head, grinning as she yanks the pillow out from under my head. "You've got it so bad for my brother."

"Give me that!" I snatch it back, pulling it into my chest. "This just happens to be one of the best presents I've ever received."

"It's certainly the cheesiest."

I reread the words on the pillow, as I have done countless times since Dillon had it delivered on Monday.

"When you're in need of a hug, give me a squeeze."

He'd added a note in his distinctive handwriting saying he knew this was a poor substitute for one of his hugs, but he hoped it would help if I was feeling sad. I honestly can't fathom how Dillon hasn't had a relationship before because he's either the world's greatest fake or the most genuinely romantic guy ever.

"Speaking of the sap," Ash adds. "He sent breakfast over for both of us, so get your lazy arse out of bed and join me in the kitchen." Her lips pull into a smile. "You also have presents. Lots of presents, so come on, get up!" Yanking on my foot, she tugs me down the bed, and I throw a cushion at her.

"I'm getting up. I need to pee and brush my teeth, and I'll be out then."

I watch her leave, smiling at Dillon's latest romantic gesture. I know he feels bad he couldn't be here this morning for my birthday. I reassured him a million times on FaceTime last night that it's fine. Toxic Gods has been rehearsing around the clock, ahead of tonight's Trinity Ball, and I don't hold it against him. We'll get to celebrate later, and I can't wait to see him. Excitement races through my veins as I sit up, a combination of birthday happiness, enthusiasm for the ball, and elation at the prospect of seeing Dillon tonight.

I've decided I want tonight to be *the night*.

I've thought about it these past few days, and I want to have sex with Dillon. I'm ready.

Waking up that Sunday morning, after he blew my mind with his skillful tongue, mouth, and fingers, was incredible, and it felt right. His strong arms had kept me safe all night, and I had the best sleep. Snuggling into his warm chest, and feeling his ripped masculine body against mine, was perfect and I want to take things to the next level. Coming to Ireland, I made a decision to be brave and strong, and this is me doing that.

I'm taking control of my life and my sexuality, and I'm not going to feel guilty for giving in to my desires.

A tiny kernel of guilt had attacked Sunday morning because waking up wrapped around Dillon had reminded me of similar mornings with Reeve. I didn't mention anything to Dillon because I never want to hurt him or have him compare himself to my ex, but I think he could tell anyway.

My therapist, Sheila, says it's normal to feel like this and completely natural. That little things will trigger memories of Reeve, especially because we share such an extensive history. She says a lot of women do it subconsciously when they move from one relationship to another. She also says, in time, I will find a way to make peace with it all, and I will be able to look back on my good memories with fondness.

I really hope she's right.

Grabbing my journal, I add another entry to my list of personal promises: Stop comparing Dillon to Reeve.

The journal was another one of Sheila's ideas, and I've been writing like crazy—recording my feelings, my thoughts, and my hopes for the future. I've also documented the past, both the good and the bad, and it's helping me to process my emotions.

After a quick bathroom stop, I head out to the kitchen, slamming to a halt at the sight that awaits me. Familiar spicy notes tickle my nostrils, and my jaw drops to the ground as I stare in shock at all the bouquets of lavender roses. There are enough to open a florist, and the smell is almost an assault on the senses.

"There are twenty-one bouquets, in case you're wondering," Ash says, pouring boiling water into a teapot. "That colorful bunch in the vase on the table are from your parents. The other twenty are from Reeve. One for every year you've been on the planet." Her scathing tone matches the mocking sneer on her face, making her feelings clear.

I stare at my Irish bestie, the unspoken question still lingering on my tongue.

"Don't be mad, but I opened the cards. Today is a big day for you. It's your birthday, and I know how excited you are about the ball. I just wanted to ensure nothing he had written would upset you. I apologize if I crossed a line."

I know her actions are coming from a good place, so I let it go even if it does feel like an invasion of my privacy. I'd have shared them with her anyway. "It's okay. I know you did it to protect me, but in the future, maybe check with me first?"

She nods, walking toward the table. "Come on. Let's eat before it gets cold."

After a gorgeous breakfast, I open the gifts from my parents, Ash, Cat, Ro, and Audrey. "Mum baked you this," Ash says, lifting the top off a cake tin to reveal a gorgeous chocolate cake with "Happy 20th Birthday Vivien" written in red icing on the top.

Happy tears pool in my eyes, as I haul my friend into a hug. "Your mom is the best. I want to call her to thank her."

Ash pulls out her phone, punching in numbers. "Dil wants to give you your present tonight," she supplies, thrusting her phone at me. "I'm really hoping that's not a euphemism for what I think it is."

I burst out laughing just as Mrs. O'Donoghue answers the call, and I have to hurriedly compose myself. We chat for a few minutes, and I pass her over to her daughter while I clear the table and load the plates and silverware in the dishwasher.

When I'm finished, I take the silver-foiled package into the living room, drumming my fingers on the arm of the couch, as I question the wisdom in opening Reeve's gift. He's been giving me my space, but he's still fighting for me too. Sending housewarming, Valentine's, and birthday gifts is chipping away at my resolve, and I'm so conflicted. My heart hurts again. One part of me loves he hasn't forgotten me and he's still fighting hard for our relationship. But another part of me wants him to stop because how can I truly move on if he keeps sending me reminders of the Reeve I love? He's making it more difficult to hold on to my anger, and I'm not okay with that.

And then there's Dillon.

God.

Tossing the package on the couch beside me, I cradle my head in my hands. This is not how I saw today panning out.

"I can open it, if you want," Ash says, plonking down beside me when she's finished her call.

I lift my head, staring at the package like it's a ticking time bomb. I suppose it is, of sorts. "I don't know if I want to open it at all." I flick my gaze to my friend. "Why is he doing this?"

"I think he's regretting his actions and he's worried he's lost you for good."

"You could be right, but I'm not sure I can deal with this today." Dillon's gorgeous smile surfaces in my mind's eye, and my heart jumps in elation. Whatever will happen or not happen with Reeve in the future doesn't change what's happening in the present. I swore I wasn't going to let my ex interfere in my life, and I meant it. Knots loosen in my shoulders as I reach a decision. "I need to contact him and tell him I have a new boyfriend." I wave my hands around the room, gesturing at the flowers. "This has to stop. It's not fair to Dillon."

"It's not fair on you either. It's making things harder."

I nod, exhaling deeply. "It is," I agree, "and it's going to end here. But first I need to see what he sent me." I rip the paper open before I change my mind.

I'm going to give myself to Dillon tonight, and I need to see what's in this gift to know I can leave Reeve in the past and move forward.

I remove the heavy bubble-wrapped interior package, unpacking it with slightly trembling fingers. Ash scoots in closer to me as I open the leatherbound album. Our names are printed within a love heart on the front, and inside, Reeve has filled the album with memories from our past, from the time we were little right up to now. I don't dwell on the photos, unwilling to revisit the past today, so I skim through the book until I come to an envelope about halfway through the album. The rest of the pages are blank, and I can guess why.

"Wow. He knows what he's doing sending you this. It's the sneakiest form of psychological torture."

"I know," I whisper, running my finger under the envelope. I suck in a gasp when I withdraw the card and the recent photo of Reeve. I raise trembling fingers to my lips as my gaze roams over the heart-shaped tattoo with my name inked over Reeve's chest. The message on the card is short and simple, but it drives his point home:

You're now imprinted on my skin the same way you're imprinted on my heart. You're in my blood, Viv, and that will never change. I miss you. I love you, always yours, Reeve.

At the back of the album is a larger envelope containing architect sketches of a vast property.

"What's that?" Ash inquires, curiosity overriding her derision.

"It's our dream home," I whisper. "We've been talking about the kind of house we wanted for years. I'd drawn rough sketches. He must have kept them and commissioned someone to draw these."

"That's super intense for being so young," she murmurs.

"Reeve grew up in an empty house with a father who abandoned him after his mom died. Yes, he spent tons of time at my house, and yes, my parents stepped in to help raise him, but he still spent a lot of time alone in a massive house with only paid staff for company. More than anything, he wanted a home to call his own and a loving family. It's why we had such grand plans. He always seemed so sure of what he wanted."

"Pity he didn't remember that before he threw away what you two had," Ash scoffs.

Sadness washes over me, and I'm regretting opening the package. I didn't want to feel this today. Reeve really has upped his game. Usually, he'd buy me diamond jewelry for my birthday, so this is not the norm. I get what he's trying to do. Remind me of the happy memories and the plans we made for the future. Inking my name on his body isn't just for me. It sends a clear message to the world. But I can't forget what he's done. I think I'm moving into a space where I can forgive him, but forgetting is that much harder.

Reminding me of the plans we made for our future only strengthens my resolve. He threw away everything the first time he was truly tested, and that speaks volumes.

I close the album, smiling sadly. I can't hold on to this. It will only keep me tethering on the edge of sanity, seesawing between the present and the past.

I need to move on.

I'm *ready* to move on.

Maybe things might be different in the future. Maybe we both need time apart to fully appreciate what we had. Maybe we need space to experience the world with other people. Maybe we'll eventually come full circle and find our way back to one another. Or maybe this is the end. All I know for sure is that I want to move forward with Dillon, and I can't do that while clinging to the past.

I know Reeve didn't mean for his gift to have this effect, but in a warped way, it's actually helped. "I'm going to return the gift, and I'll talk to Ciara downstairs and see if they can use the flowers around the building instead."

Relief floods Ash's face, and I realize she was worried on her brother's behalf. Those two are so close, and I'm slightly envious of their relationship. "That sounds like a plan." She squeezes my hand. "I'm so proud of you. You are much stronger than I was."

"You are one of the strongest people I know, and I'm sure that's not true."

"What doesn't kill us makes us stronger, right?"

"Damn straight."

Ash glances at the time on her cell. "We have a couple of hours before the makeup artist and hairdresser get here. We're low on food, so I was thinking we could run out and stock up now. Trust me when I say you'll be incapable of doing much of anything over the next two days. The Trinity Ball is hardcore."

Snagging our jackets and purses, we head out into the city to the nearest grocery store. We grab enough food for the next few days so we don't have to step foot out of the apartment if we're as hungover as Ash predicts we'll be. We've just paid for our purchases, when the headline on *OK!* grabs my attention from a nearby newsstand. My feet move of their own volition, and my heart is pounding erratically behind my chest as I walk toward the magazine stand.

Bile swims up my throat as I stare at the cover of the magazine in horror. The headline reads "Reeveron cozy up with PDA on Mexican beach!" Splashed across the front is a picture of Saffron and Reeve on a sun lounger by the sea. She's straddling his waist, wearing only a thong, leaning into him with her face angled to the side so her features are clearly visible. Reeve has his hands on her bare ass, and his face is buried in her naked chest. It's not as easy to discern it's Reeve from the pic as most of his face and torso are hidden, but I know it's him. I know his body, and he's wearing the board shorts I bought him when I was in Europe last summer.

"Fuck." Ash comes up behind me, sliding her arm around my waist. "What a fucking shithead."

I pick the magazine up, but Ash snatches it from my hand. "Do you really want to look at that?"

My chest tightens, and tears cling to my lashes.

This is just like Christmas all over again.

Reeve is trying to hide his betrayal behind a grand gesture. Sending me that birthday gift is another attempt at manipulation. But just like Christmas, it won't work.

"Don't do it, Viv," Ash pleads. "All it will do is hurt you even more. That bastard has claimed enough of your tears."

She is right. I don't need to see inside to read what's written or stare at more damning pictures. Swallowing thickly, I nod, placing it back on the stand, letting her drag me out of there before I change my mind.

I stumble out of the store and along the sidewalk with Ash's arm looped through mine. I clutch the grocery bags for dear life, and I'm in a dazed kind of fugue state as we head back to our apartment, but it doesn't last long. Initial hurt gives way to red-hot anger, and by the time we reach our place, I'm seething and hell-bent on destruction.

"Give me a second," I tell Ash, leaving her by the elevator as I seek out the manager on duty. Thankfully, it's Ciara. She's the nicer of the three property

271

managers. I tell her what I need, and she promises to send people up to our apartment ASAP.

"What's going on?" Ash asks, when I stomp back to her.

"I'm getting rid of the flowers and the gift."

"We could go up to the roof, destroy the flowers, and take a pic to send to him," she suggests, as we step foot in the elevator.

"The thought had crossed my mind, but the flowers haven't done anything. I can't justify wrecking something so beautiful. Let someone else get enjoyment from them because I sure as fuck can't."

After the flowers and the gift are gone, I open the champagne chilling in the refrigerator and hand a glass to Ash. We weren't planning on drinking until much later, as we need to pace ourselves, but this is an emergency, and I fucking need alcohol. "Let's toast," I say, grinding my teeth to the molars. "I'm finally free. Fuck Reeve Lancaster. And fuck Saffron Roberts. I hope she makes him miserable as sin." We clink glasses.

"I hope she gives him the clap and his dick falls off," Ash says, and I almost choke on my champagne.

"Amen to that!"

CHAPTER 49

MY ARM FLIES OUT, and I grab Ash's elbow before she takes a tumble. She snort-laughs, and I grin as I loop my arm through hers. "I told you, you should've drank more water at dinner." Ash and I finished the bottle of champagne before the hair and makeup people arrived at our place. Then we sipped vodka while they were dolling us up. We were giddy as fuck as we climbed into a taxi that took us to the campus where we traveled between a few different pre-ball parties. By the time dinner was served, my head was spinning a little and I felt a teeny bit nauseated, so I purposely switched to water and shoveled food in my mouth to line my stomach. It worked, and now I'm a hell of a lot more sober than my friend.

I want to be in full control and look my absolute best when I see Dillon and tell him I'm ready to fuck his brains out. We haven't seen the guys yet because they're busy getting things set up for their performance. Toxic Gods is one of the first acts on stage, so they'll be able to join us for the remainder of the night, and I'm already on a countdown.

"Water is for pussies," Cat says, giggling. "It's the Trinners ball! That means we need to get fucking wasted."

"Amen, sister." Ash raises her fist for a knuckle touch, and I think I'll have my work cut out with these two tonight.

Wandering into a tent, we grab some drinks before making our way back outside. Dillon and Jamie are a few feet in front of us, glancing anxiously around the packed space. "Dillon!" I holler, tugging Cat and Ash with me as I head in their direction. A few others in our group trail behind us.

Dillon spins around, and the look on his face is almost comical. His jaw drops to the floor, and heat scorches a blazing trail across my flesh as he drags his hungry gaze slowly up and down my body. I know I look good. The blue satin dress turned out exactly how I wanted it to, and I'm flashing plenty of leg, which I knew Dil would like. Soft bouncy curls cascade over my shoulders, complimenting my smoky eyes and nude lips.

Dillon stalks toward me, his nostrils flaring, desire evident in his dark eyes. Without saying a word, he reels me into his arms, claiming my lips in a possessive kiss that has my ovaries swooning and tripping over themselves. When he dips me down low, without breaking our lip-lock, I swear I hear a collective sigh from the women around me. "Damn, Hollywood. You look beautiful," he purrs in my ear, as he straightens us up. "Are you trying to get me arrested for indecency because right now I'm having a hard time not dragging you behind one of those tents to fuck." He bites my earlobe, before nuzzling his head into my shoulder.

I purposely let his comment slide. If I respond, there's a strong chance I'll let him drag us back there and have his wicked way with me. "You like my dress?" I ask, biting my lip and smiling coyly at him.

"Yes. It's stunning, like you," he growls, sliding his hand under the slit in the skirt and stroking my thigh. "Easy access." He winks. "Me likey a lot."

"You have sex on the brain," I tease, grasping his shoulders.

He arches a brow, smirking. "Haven't we had this conversation before?"

"We have." I stretch up on my heels, pressing my mouth to his ear. "I'm ready," I whisper in my most seductive tone. "Later, I say we ditch the after-parties, go back to my place, and fuck for the rest of the night."

His hands move to my hips, and he yanks me against him, grinding his pelvis into my stomach. "There's your answer." His expression softens and turns more serious. Twisting one hand in my hair, he tilts my face up. "Are you sure?" I bob my head. His eyes probe mine carefully. "I wasn't expecting this reaction. I thought you might be upset tonight."

"Ash told you."

"She did." He plants a feather-soft kiss on my brow, and I melt against him. "Are you okay?"

"I am now."

His eyes drill into mine. "I can't believe I'm going to say this," he murmurs, smiling a little. "We don't have to bang tonight. In fact, I'd rather we didn't if it's a knee-jerk reaction to your dickhead ex." He pecks my lips briefly. "And for the record, he *is* a dickhead, but it's lucky for me. His loss is definitely my gain."

"I'm glad you think so." Holding his arm, I peer deep into his eyes. I want Dillon to understand this is only about me and him. "I had already decided this morning that I want to take our relationship to the next level. What Reeve has done doesn't change how I feel about you. Reeve is my ex for a reason. He's in the past. I prefer to exist in the here and now. With you."

His kiss this time is unhurried, slow, and passionate, and I know I've made the right decision. I'm glad I worked all the anger and hurt out of my system earlier. That I used the time getting ready to wrangle those emotions into a lockbox. Reeve only has the power to hurt me and ruin my life if I give him that power, and I refuse to do that anymore. Tonight is proof I have wrested back control. I'm having a good time, and the night is only getting started.

We move closer to the stage right before Toxic Gods appears, screaming and whistling encouragement as they play a medley of five songs. The crowd is apprecia-tive, and it's so weird to see people in ball gowns and tuxedos rocking it out on the grass. I'm happy there are no groupies in sight, which eliminates any lingering stress. I thought for sure Jamie would've gotten tickets for Aoife and the others. But, if the looks he was throwing Ash's way earlier are any indication, he has ulterior motives. Ash swears she's not going near him, but I can see it happening. The attraction between them may not be as palpable as it is between Dillon and me, but it's there. I'm not going to judge; I just worry about Ash getting hurt, but she's a grown-ass woman, capable of making her own choices.

"Miss me?" Strong arms wrap around me from behind a while later, and the spicy scent of Dillon's cologne tickles my nose.

"So much," I say, turning in his arms. Opening my mouth to congratulate him on his performance, I let the words die on my tongue when I see him in a tuxedo. He was wearing his usual black jeans and T-shirt combo on stage. He didn't attend dinner, so there really was no need to rent a tux. I know he did this for me, and I fall a little harder in this second. "Wow," I choke out, "you look so fucking hot." He really does. He managed to wrangle his messy blond waves back off his face, and his jawline is smooth for a change. He's still got his piercings in, and the edges of his tattoos creep out from under the sleeves of his jacket, but he looks handsome and sophisticated.

And so very mine.

Producing a long-stem white rose from behind his back, he hands it to me. "For the most beautiful girl at the ball." My nose brushes against the soft petals, and I breathe in their delicate scent. "White roses represent new beginnings and rebirth," he explains, offering me his hand. "Will you be my new beginning? And can I be yours?"

Be still my beating heart. This man slays me in all the best ways.

Ash makes a gagging sound, but I ignore her, taking Dillon's hand and beaming up at him. Our gazes connect, and a zap of electricity shoots up my arm the second our skin touches. My chest heaves as I stare into his beautiful face, and butterflies swoop into my belly, turning somersaults. My heart swells, soaring to dizzy heights the longer we just stand there staring, lost in an intimate moment, despite the noise surrounding us.

A flash pops, and we both turn sideways. "You are sickeningly cute. Mum said I was to take pictures, so get in closer," Ash says with a happy smile on her face. We pose for several pictures, with our arms wrapped around one another, and I make her send them to me so I can forward them to Audrey and my parents.

Dillon leads me over to a quiet corner, handing me a badly wrapped pink pack-age. "Happy birthday, Viv." He kisses me sweetly, and my cheeks are flushed when we break apart.

"You didn't have to get me anything."

He narrows his eyes. "You're my girl. I'm pretty sure it goes against the boyfriend code to not buy your girlfriend a present on her birthday."

His words send an enormous thrill through me. "You already got me a gift. Thank you for breakfast," I add, having forgotten to tell him previously.

"Open it." He shuffles nervously on his feet, shoving his hands into the pockets of his black pants.

I tear the pink paper off with zero patience, and he grins. There are two gifts inside. The first is a photo album.

"To make new memories," Dillon explains, rubbing the back of his neck.

I'm momentarily frozen to the spot. How ironic that Dillon chose a similar gift to Reeve's. Shaking myself out of my temporary melancholy, I stop overthinking it. It's not that unusual. Dillon knows I'm documenting my trip through photos. It makes sense he'd give me something like this. "Thank you. I bet I have enough photos to fill half this album already."

"I look forward to filling the rest." He smiles, making me swoon again.

My heart is in my throat as I lift the lid on the small black box, and I gasp as I lift the silver necklace from the cushion. "Dillon, it's beautiful."

"It's a Claddagh necklace. The Swarovski crystal represents your birthstone. April is actually diamond, but until Toxic Gods makes it big, I rob a bank, or win the lotto, that's all I can afford," he half-jokes.

"It's perfect. I love it." I fling my arms around his neck. "Thank you so much." I dust kisses all over his stunning face, and my heart is fit to burst. "Help me to put it on," I say, easing out of his embrace. I remove the silver diamond choker around my neck, stowing it carefully in the inside zip pocket of my purse. Dillon looks at it, frowning, and I can guess where his mind has gone to. "It was a birthday present from my parents," I softly say, and his puckered brow smooths out.

I hold my hair up so he can fasten it around my neck. "All done." He presses a kiss to my temple as I finger the delicate chain.

"Take a picture of me wearing it. I need to show Audrey."

Wordlessly, he takes my phone and snaps a pic, and I send it to my bestie.

Grabbing more drinks, we join the rest of Toxic Gods and our friends, spending an enjoyable few hours dancing and listening to music. Dillon is attentive, and he never leaves my side. He even insists on coming with me to the bathroom, keeping me company as we stand in the long line. Back outside, I burst out laughing as he and Jamie search through some large bushes at the side of the field, emerging with twigs and leaves stuck to their suits. "Laugh all you want, but we have tequila," Jamie says, waggling his brows and raising the full bottle.

"They have tequila at the bar," I remind them.

"We have to pay through the nose for that," Jamie says.

"Not all of us are loaded Americans," Dillon says, and his words slice a layer off my happiness.

He makes the odd cryptic remark about money at times that irritates me. I mean, it's not like he grew up poor. Ash has explained the challenges that come with running a farm and supporting a large family. I know things haven't always been easy, but none of them ever went without, so I don't understand why Dillon has such a chip on his shoulder. It's unfair I should be punished for growing up in affluence. It's not like either one of us has gotten to choose our families.

"Sorry," he murmurs, pulling me into his arms. "I didn't mean to upset you. I guess we just have different outlooks on money."

"If it bugs you that much, maybe you should pursue the band's interests more thoroughly."

"It's not about being rich per se." He sways to the music with me in his arms. "And we get by. We're lucky we have a regular slot in Whelans, and we're starting to earn decent money from streaming our EP."

"Then what is it?"

He shrugs. "My own hang-ups, I suppose." He kisses the tip of my nose. "I know it's not fair to take it out on you. You didn't choose your upbringing, and you're not flashy with your money or mean either."

"I know I'm fortunate, and this is cliché, but money doesn't guarantee happiness. Look at my ex. He had every material possession, yet he would've given it all up to have his mom back, his dad present, and a loving family environment."

Dillon snorts, and a sneer pulls up the corners of his mouth. "Please don't use *him* to make a point. That dickhead had everything handed to him, you included, and he doesn't fucking appreciate it."

"Woah." I run my hands up his chest. "Where is all this coming from?"

His Adam's apple bobs in his throat, and air whooshes out of his mouth before he tightens his arms around me, burying his head in my shoulder. "Sorry, I'm just pissed on your behalf. He hurt you, and that's not okay with me."

I relax against him, running my fingers lightly through his hair. "I'm sorry. I shouldn't have brought him up."

He lifts his head. "It's okay. I know he was a big part of your life. I know you don't intentionally do it. I understand he's tied to a lot of your memories."

Dillon's mood swings give me a headache sometimes. He seems to veer from one emotion to the next and back again all within the same minute. I don't call him on it, though. I don't want anything to ruin this incredible night. "Thank you for under-standing." Stretching up on my heels, I kiss him. "But let's not talk about him anymore."

We drink shots of tequila and dirty dance in the crowd, kissing and groping one another, while drunken revelers party hard around us. By the end of the night, bodies litter the ground and groups of disheveled students sit on the grass outside tents, smoking, drinking, and laughing.

The night is still young though, by Trinity Ball standards, and many attendees start wandering off to parties while others stay put, content to wait a few hours for the pubs to open. According to Ronan's girlfriend, some students party hard from the day before the ball to the day after, and it's not unusual to spot students in ballgowns and tuxes in pubs across the city.

"What do you want to do?" Dillon asks, breathing tequila fumes across my face.

"Ride your cock like a porn star all night long," I reply without hesitation.

"And the prude has left the house!" Jamie pipes up, looking highly amused. I flip him the bird, and he cranks out a laugh.

Ash spits her beer all over the path. "TMI, Viv. Holy fuck. I did *not* need to hear that. Please, someone scrub my ears out." Jamie whispers something in her ear, and she levels him with a glare. Dillon watches the interaction with a muscle popping in his jaw.

"Dil." I tug on his sleeve, dragging his gaze away. "What are we doing?"

He clasps both sides of my face. "You're sure you want to do this with me tonight?"

"One hundred percent."

He stabs me with an intense look I feel all the way to my core. "C'mon, then. Let's get out of here."

CHAPTER 50

"HURRY, DILLON," I pant, holding up my hair so he can unbutton the back of my dress. A trickle of sweat rolls between my breasts, and my skin is a little clammy. We couldn't find a taxi, so we ran all the way back to my apartment, both of us anxious to be together.

"I'm trying. Could you have made these buttons any smaller?" He curses, and I giggle. "Done," he adds a few seconds later.

Wiggling out of the dress, I let it pool at my ankles before turning to face him in just my blue lace thong and my silver Louboutin sandals.

"Fuck. Look at you." His eyes rake up and down my body, and I can almost feel the sensual caress. "We need to capture this moment." Kneeling in front of his duffel bag, he pulls out his phone. "Can I take a photo?"

I chew on the inside of my mouth, not sure if this is a good idea.

"I promise I won't show it to anyone. This is just for me." He reassures me, flashing me one of his infamous panty-melting grins, and I'm a goner. "Ammo for the spank bank," he adds. Cupping his crotch, he strokes his hard-on over his pants.

Jeez. As if a girl could resist. "Okay, but from the neck down." I don't want my face shown in case it ever ends up in the wrong hands.

He snaps a pic, drops his cell on top of his bag, and closes the distance between us. Leaning down, he plants a row of drugging kisses along my jawline and my neck. He tweaks my nipples, hardening them instantly. "You looked like Hollywood royalty at the ball," he says, bending his head to suck my nipple into his mouth. "Tonight, you're my queen." I'm guessing his use of queen over princess is on purpose, and his thoughtfulness only makes me crave him more.

"You're wearing too many clothes," I complain, pushing his shoulders. "Strip for me, baby."

He levels me with a devilish glint in his eyes. "Undress me." Standing up straight, he stares at me, challenging me with a heated look, waiting for me to make the next move.

"Gladly," I purr, slipping the jacket off his shoulders and tossing it on the back of the chair. Next, his shirt and bow tie come off, and I take my time exploring the dips and curves of his abs, the broad expanse of his chest, and the defined muscles in his biceps and arms.

My fingers trail over the ink covering both his arms, skimming across Celtic symbols, skulls, crosses, roses, and knives. Musical notes and song lyrics are inked across his chest. Walking around him, I examine the scorpion on his back. He jumps when my fingers move along the intricate drawing. "This is gorgeous. Does it have any special significance?"

He shrugs, but his muscles seem tight until I start pressing kisses into his back, kneading the corded knots in his shoulders, easing the tension I find there.

"The scorpion represents a lot of things that have meaning to me," he says after a few beats.

"Like what?" I trail my fingers around to his front and slowly open his pants. His erection brushes against my hand as I work the zipper down.

"Determination, rebirth, resilience."

"I like it," I whisper, moving around to his front. "I love all your ink." Tugging his pants down along with his boxers, I kneel in front of his straining cock with saliva pooling in my mouth. "That's not all I love," I tease, grinning up at him.

"You look good on your knees." Grabbing my head, he guides me toward his dick.

I lick the precum crowning his tip as he fondles my breasts with his free hand. Slowly, I take him into my mouth, sliding my lips up and down his velvety-soft length.

"Touch yourself," he demands, thrusting into my mouth in slow, measured strokes.

My hand trails down my body, and I slip my fingers into my panties, circling my swollen clit and moaning around his cock.

"Push two fingers into yourself," he directs, and I do as he says. "Work them faster."

"Fuck, yeah." He thrusts more forcefully into my mouth as I finger myself, growing wetter by the second.

"Enough," he commands after a few minutes, withdrawing from my mouth. "I want to come in your pussy after I eat you out."

Throwing me back on my bed, he shreds my thong with his teeth, and it's so fucking hot I almost come instantly. Parting my thighs, he dives in, feasting on my pussy, using his magical tongue and fingers, until I'm shattering against his mouth and he's dry humping the comforter. Ripping the foil packet open, he slowly and carefully rolls a condom down his length. "Are you still okay with this?" He checks one final time.

"Yes. Hell yes. Fuck me, Dillon. Do it now."

"It would be my pleasure, Hollywood." He runs his hands up and down my legs as he situates himself between my thighs. Throwing my legs over his shoulders, he dips two digits inside me, coating his fingers in my juices, before bringing them to his mouth. "Tasty." He winks, and it shouldn't be sexy, but it is.

Guiding his cock to my entrance, he pushes inside me in one fluid thrust, shoving his dick in to the max. "Jesus, you're so tight." He holds himself still, letting us both adjust. Muscles bunch in his abs, and his shoulders are rigid with the exertion involved in restraining himself. After a few seconds, he leans down, claiming my lips in a hard demanding kiss, as he starts to rock inside me.

Stars explode behind my eyes as he fucks me, and the feel of his piercing is unlike anything I've felt. It drags across my insides in the most blissful manner, heightening my pleasure. When he slams inside me, pushing to the hilt, I scream as the most intense sensation whips through me. Every thrust is like a mini orgasm, and I'm clinging to him, writhing and moaning, spewing curses and begging him to go harder.

Dillon straightens, pulling my legs up a little, and this new angle is even better. Pivoting his hips, he pounds into me with almost animal savagery. Sweat glistens on his chest as he maintains a punishing pace, and his stamina is as impressive as his skill.

Screaming his name, I detonate like a firework on the Fourth of July, sparking across the universe in bursts of colorful light that seem never ending. Before I've come down from my high, he flips me over and yanks my butt up, nudging my thighs farther apart with his legs. I have no time to recover when he rams into me again, and I scream from the pit of my lungs as he slams into me like a madman. Digging his fingers into my hips, he thrusts powerfully inside me, hard and fast, before he yells out as his own release reaches its peak.

Dillon continues thrusting, holding my hips steady, until he's milked his climax. Then we collapse on the bed in a tangled sweaty heap, both of us struggling to get our breathing under control. His arms band around me from behind as we spoon. After a few minutes, he brushes my hair aside, nipping at my neck. "Well, Vivien Grace? Did I live up to my promise?"

I have never been fucked like that, and there's no contest—that was definitely the best sex of my life. Twisting around in his arms, I sweep my fingers across his cheek as I smile. "Yeah, baby. You definitely did."

I can barely walk the next day when I eventually surface from bed and stagger into my en suite bathroom to pee. We got home just after five, and we fucked relentlessly for hours, desperate to explore one another and all the ways we could induce pleasure from our bodies. So, I'm currently running on fumes and a few hours' sleep.

Staring in the mirror as I wash my hands, I survey the faint bruising on my breasts, my hips, and the inside of my thighs and the two hickeys on my neck with an amused smile. Perhaps I'm sick in the head, but I love seeing his marks on me. Love feeling the pulsing ache between my thighs, knowing he fucked me good last night.

Allowing my mind to wander to Reeve, I test my emotions, and, nope, I'm good. I have zero regrets. Dillon blew my mind last night and then some. There is no part of me that regrets sleeping with him. I brush my teeth before heading back into the bedroom, where Dillon is stirring.

"Ugh." Dillon pulls my special pillow down over his head. "Make it stop."

My cell is vibrating across the bedside table, so I grab it and crawl back into bed. Dillon's arm juts out, and he pulls me back into his chest, nudging my ass with his morning wood. My pussy pulses with need like the greedy cunt she is as I retrieve my messages.

I have several from Ash, asking me to call her when Dillon leaves to head home. That can only mean one thing—she spent the night with Jamie. Hoping she doesn't regret it, I read Audrey's message next. She wants me to call her the instant I wake, no matter what time it is. That doesn't sound good, and my spidey senses tell me it's something Reeve-related.

"Why the sigh?" Dillon asks, dotting kisses along my bare back.

"It's nothing," I lie, not wanting to talk about my ex.

"You sure?" He grazes his teeth along my neck, and I close my eyes as he jerks his hips against my ass.

"Yep."

His fingers slide around my waist and creep lower. "Are you sore?" he whispers against my ear, sending a flurry of tingles along my sensitive skin.

"Not that sore," I confirm, eagerly parting my legs for his hand.

He dips two fingers inside me. "Always so wet. I fucking love it." Slowly he pumps his fingers in and out of me while his other hand kneads my breast. Anticipation coils in my belly while he rolls a condom on, and I'm reveling in the newness of our intimacy. When he slips into me from behind a few minutes later, I let loose an appreciative moan, arching my back and pivoting my hips in sync with his thrusts. He's gentler today, and while I hate I can't see his face or kiss him, I love this angle and how it grants him access to touch me everywhere.

We both come within seconds of each other, and we lie there, silent and sated, pressed as close as two people can be. Dillon dusts kisses all over my neck, my shoulders, and my back, and I could happily stay like this all day. Until my tummy rumbles, reminding me it's been hours since we ate. "I think that's my cue to get us some breakfast."

"Brunch, you mean," he says over a yawn. "It's already one."

Kissing his strong arms, I slide out of the bed, perching on the edge of the mattress while I pull pajamas out of my drawer. The bed jolts behind me, and Dillon curses. I whip my head around to see what's wrong. Dillon is on his knees, with his back facing me, his fingers frantically searching the bed. I lean over, placing a hand on his back, and he jumps. "What'd you lose?"

"My, ah, mobile phone. I think it went down the back of the bed."

I frown, glancing around the room until I see his bag on the floor under wrinkled clothing. Getting up, I move to it, finding his phone under his crumpled pants. "I found it." He buries his face in the pillow as I approach, and I set his phone down on the table. "What's the matter?"

"My head is pounding," he says, his words muffled as he speaks into the pillow. "Could you get me some tablets."

"Of course." I press a kiss between his shoulder blades before heading out to the kitchen.

When I return a few minutes later, he's sitting up against the headboard, cradling his head in his hands. Slivers of buttery light filter through the blinds, casting him in a golden light.

I've never seen anything more beautiful.

The comforter is bunched at his waist, and his naked chest is a work of art. He's all smooth skin, defined curves, and ripped muscles. The ink on his body only adds to his hotness, and I wish I could capture this moment on film. His hair is sticking up all over the place, disheveled from my fingers, but he still looks sexy as fuck.

Dillon could easily be a model if the rock star thing doesn't work out for him.

"Here." I hand him a glass of water and two pain meds.

"Thanks, Viv." He knocks them back before pulling me down on top of him. "How about I cook us some eggs and bacon, and then we come back to bed?"

He kisses me, and from the minty freshness of his breath, I can tell he's made a trip to the bathroom too. "How about you stay right here, and I'll bring us omelets in bed?" I suggest.

"I want to look after you." He trails his hands up and down my sides.

"It's my turn to look after you." I massage his brow. "You're the one with a headache."

A funny look crosses his face before he smiles. "If you're sure."

"I am."

After stealing more kisses, I reluctantly leave him to make food.

CHAPTER 51

I CALL Audrey from the kitchen while I'm preparing our food, not wanting to have this conversation with Dillon in proximity. I didn't have time to call her yesterday, but I'd messaged her to say I had seen the *OK!* picture and I was fine. I am about to hang up when her sleepy voice finally answers. "Are you okay?"

"I'm fine. Better than fine." I smile to myself as I put her on speaker, chopping onions and tomatoes while I proceed to fill her in on the ball and spending last night with Dillon.

"Good for you, babe. How was it? The sex, I mean?"

"Out of this fucking world. I lost count of the orgasms he gave me, and I can barely walk today with the ache between my legs."

"I hope he's nowhere in the vicinity. Let's not give him an even bigger head."

There's a slight edge to her tone I don't much care for. "He knows he's good, and he deserves all the praise. Trust me on that score."

"Are you happy, Viv?" she asks, after a few tense beats, in a more somber tone.

"Yeah, yes, I think I am."

Another pregnant pause ensues. "I'm not going to lie. I've been worried sick since I saw that picture. I thought you might do something reckless."

"Does riding my new boyfriend's cock for hours pass as reckless?" I quip, needing to lighten the inexplicable tense atmosphere.

"I'm sure to Reeve it probably would."

"Good," I snap.

"I called him," she admits, and I nearly slice the tip of my finger off.

"Why would you do that?"

"I was worried this would undo all your progress, and I wanted to know if it was true."

Setting the knife down, I grab the counter, not sure if I want to hear this.

Audrey takes the decision out of my hands. "He says the picture was taken in

Mexico ten days ago, when they were nearing the end of the promo tour. They were all out by the pool drinking and doing drugs."

A bitter laugh escapes my lips. "Let me guess. It was a mistake. He wasn't in his right mind. He thought she was me."

"Yeah, it went something like that."

"He must think I'm such a fucking idiot! Sending me those gifts, thinking it would make everything okay." Bile floods my mouth as I dice chorizo.

"Here's the thing. Reeve has been working on that photo album for months, and he got that tattoo weeks ago. He sent it before Mexico happened, so I think the gesture was sincere."

"I don't fucking care, Audrey," I hiss, lowering my voice. I don't want Dillon to come out and investigate.

"Viv. I'm on your side. Always."

I've never had reason to doubt that before, but it doesn't sound reassuring right now. "So, what is this? It sounds to me like you're rooting for Reeve." I crack eggs into a bowl, trying to rein in my anger. I don't want to fight with my bestie, but she's pissing me off and ruining my good mood.

"It was hard to talk to him and not feel some compassion. He's messed up, Viv. Alex and I are worried about him. But it's not just the partying and the drugs. It's that *bitch*. She's still manipulating him, and he's struggling to shake her off. She's hell-bent on sticking her claws into him. At this point, he's convinced she's only doing it to get at you. He doesn't think she's really into him or ever has been. It's more the thrill of stealing him from you."

"She can have him. I'm done." I won't let Audrey or Reeve guilt me into changing my mind. I know she's just concerned about him, and in the past, I would've jumped to help him, but I've got to prioritize myself, or I'll undo all my good work.

Technically, Reeve hasn't done anything wrong this time. He's single now, so if he wants to cavort half-naked on a sun lounger on a Mexican beach with that whore, he's free to do so. It clearly doesn't matter that it's disrespectful to me to find out like that, on my freaking birthday, but whatever. I'm so done with this. My wrist works overtime as I vigorously whisk the eggs, hoping Audrey will just let this drop.

"He's hired a top-notch investigator. A guy who specializes in this kind of investigation. He knows she leaked the photo to *OK!*, and he suspects she is in cahoots with Cassidy and Bianca. He's going after them, Viv, and he's already issued an ultimatum to the studio."

"What ultimatum?" I hate that I ask the question before I've had time to engage my brain.

"He told them he won't do promotion for the final movie with Saffron. That they have to be split up, in different countries, or he's not promoting it at all."

"I'm glad to see he's finally growing a pair, but it's too late for us."

"He's talking about coming to see you," she adds. "He's due to resume filming *Sweet Retribution* in a few days, so it won't be anytime soon. But he has a week off, in the middle of June, before he starts filming that superhero movie over the summer. I think he'll turn up then."

Reeve has been continuously auditioning for other parts, and he's in high demand off the back of his *Rydeville Elite* success, but I don't know what other jobs he has booked. That Australian movie he made last summer is due to release in early August, and it's just another milestone I won't be around to share. Mad as I am, I'm still proud of him and glad his career is taking off in the way he'd always dreamed of.

"Thanks for the heads-up. I'll make sure it doesn't happen."

"What are you going to do?"

"Send him a message that tells him loud and clear to leave me alone."

After we've eaten, I ponder what to do about the Reeve situation. I know, for a fact, without checking, he's been blowing up my US cell. Thank fuck, Moira hadn't passed my Irish cell phone number on. I discovered Mom's assistant was the one who gave Reeve my Irish address before she knew we'd split. Mom explained in time to stop her divulging my new cell, and I've made it very clear to Audrey, on several occasions, that she's not to share my Irish number with Alex or Reeve.

But I know my ex inside and out. I know he's been trying to reach me, and I need to respond because he *cannot* come here. I refuse to allow it. I won't let him blow my cover and damage my new relationship. I'm happy, and Reeve showing up would ruin everything.

"Penny for them," Dillon says, rolling over and propping up on his elbows. He's lying on his stomach staring inquisitively at me.

"I need to deal with Reeve. I'm just trying to figure out how."

He purses his lips. "How about you give him a taste of his own medicine?" he suggests with a gleeful glint in his eye.

"What are you thinking?"

"Send him a pic of us together in bed, and I'm sure he'll get the message."

He waits patiently while I consider it. I know it would get my point across, and I know it would hurt him. A part of me wants him to know what it feels like. But is this stooping to his level? Shouldn't I rise above that?

"He deserves to know, and it's not like you'd be blasting our photo all over social media for the world to see," Dillon quietly says, as if he's reading my mind. Briefly, I contemplate doing just that, but I discard the idea as fast. I went off social media for a reason, and I'm not falling down that rabbit hole again. I also don't want to drag Dillon into my shit, even if the exposure might be good for Toxic Gods. Dillon has his own little following here already, and if I start sharing pics of us online, I risk the wrath of more groupies. I haven't forgotten how viciously I was attacked by Reeveron fans, and I still, occasionally, have nightmares about the assault.

But the most important reason why I can't go on social media is I don't want to expose my location. Someone would figure it out, and my safe haven would be gone. No revenge is worth that sacrifice.

"You're right," I tell Dillon. "Sending it privately is more respectful than how I found out about him and that whore." I switch on my US cell, and it pings successively with a ton of notifications. Dillon leans over my shoulder, tucking his arm around my waist. "Holy shit. You have hundreds of notifications from him."

"I haven't switched it on since I arrived here. Knowing him like I do, he's been messaging me daily, and he was obviously frantic to get ahold of me once the pic leaked," I add, scrolling through the long list of calls and messages from the last two days.

"He's certainly persistent." Dillon watches as I group delete everything. "I don't understand it. Why is he trying so desperately to win you back if he's fucking his costar?"

His words sting a little, but I try not to let it show because I understand the point he's making. "I have no idea what game he's playing, but I'm done playing it with him."

We strip out of our clothes and lie down in the bed. Dillon has his arms wrapped around me in a way that shields my breasts but makes it clear we're naked. "Bury your head in my neck," I say. "I don't want him to see your face."

"Why not?"

"Reeve seems a bit unhinged right now, and I don't want him coming after you."

A pang of sadness slaps me in the face. I can't believe it's come to this. But it has, because I don't know him at all anymore. Who knows what he's capable of now? I agree with Dil. I don't know why Reeve is trying so hard to get back with me if he's still messing around with Saffron. He's clearly still taking drugs, which makes me hurts for him. I'd never have thought Reeve would follow this path, and I hope he stops before he reaches the point of no return.

"I don't give a fuck if he comes after me. I can handle him, but it's your call." Dillon turns away from the camera, pressing his lips to my neck and shielding his face. It's actually way sexier like this. Resting my hand on Dillon's back, I stare at the camera and take the pic.

We straighten up against the headboard as I get ready to compose my message. "Can you send that to me too," Dillon asks, resting his chin on my shoulder. "That is one sexy ass photo."

"We look good together," I quietly say, forwarding the pic to my Irish cell. I want a copy of it too.

"We really do." He kisses my lips sweetly, watching silently as I type out a message I hope will stop Reeve from getting on a plane.

Don't you dare come here, Reeve. No one knows I'm in Ireland, and I want it to stay that way. I'm in a good place. Don't take that from me. Please stop messaging me, and stop sending gifts. It's over. I've moved on, just like you. Accept we are done, and you have no one to blame but yourself. Have a good life. All I've ever wanted is for you to be happy.

Before I can overthink it, I press send. Then I turn off my cell and shove it back in the drawer.

CHAPTER 52

"FREEDOM!" I yell, fist-pumping the air and bouncing around in the passenger seat of my SUV. "Exams are over. The sun is shining—shocker right there—and I have all summer to hang out with my friends. I'm so happy I could scream!" I exclaim, beaming like a complete loon. But it's the truth. I'm radiating happiness, and I don't care who knows it. I'm deliberately not thinking about the fact next week is the first week in June and I only have ten weeks left in Ireland. Going there would totally burst my bubble, and I refuse to acknowledge that yet.

"You are such a dork." Dillon shoots me an amused smile, chuckling, as he drives one-handed.

"I am, but I'm *your* dork." Unbuckling my belt, I stretch across the console and smack a loud kiss on his cheek. He's wearing a white, black, and red T-shirt I bought him over shredded dark jeans that hug his long powerful legs. Slowly, I'm trying to introduce color into his closet and his life. I even got him to trade the biker boots for sneakers, which is a feat. Dark designer shades hide his beautiful eyes, the usual layer of dark stubble coats his chin and cheeks, and his glorious face is tan from being outside these past couple of weeks in the warmer weather. Muscles flex and roll in his arm as he drives, looking cool and confident, and he couldn't look any hotter.

One look at him is all it takes to inflame my heart and stoke my libido.

These past six weeks have been amazing, even if our time together has been largely confined to Friday nights in Whelans and my apartment. Cramming for exams was no fun, but I got there in the end, and now I'm on the other side. We have the rest of the summer to be together, and I'm excited for some of our plans.

Dillon swats my ass. "Too fucking right." His sexy smirk has my ovaries doing a happy dance. "You're mine. *All mine*," he growls in that husky voice I love so much.

"Gross," Ro and Ash say in unison from the back seat.

"This is old news," I scoff.

Everyone is used to our PDAs by now, but it's more like PDLs—public displays of lust.

Reeve was very touchy-feely with me, but it was always appropriate affectionate gestures like sweet kisses, cuddling, and holding hands.

Dillon is like the modern-day equivalent of Neanderthal Man, groping me excessively any chance he gets, giving zero fucks to anyone who happens to be watching. He's always slapping my ass, grabbing my hips, ravishing my mouth or my neck, or biting my earlobe with the odd sneaky boob touch thrown in for good measure. I'm sure there are some girls who would hate that, but I freaking love it. I love how much he wants me and how hard it is for him to keep his hands off me. Dillon has proven he's capable of the sweeter PDAs too, but I like it when he's rough with me.

Slinking back into my seat, I fasten my seat belt and add, "Unless you're Aoife." I make a face, like I do anytime I'm around Dillon's ex-fuck-buddy. It's true she has quit giving me shit, but I don't miss the longing looks she sends Dillon's way every Friday night at Whelans. It's really grating on my nerves.

Like, fuck off and get your own man, bitch.

I guess she's pissed she no longer has the attention of any members of the band. Conor rarely touches the groupies. Ro is seeing a different girl now. Dillon is clearly taken. And Jamie has blown her off.

Something appears to have shifted between Jamie and Ash since the Trinity Ball, but he still won't officially claim her as his girl, much to Ash's frustration. Hence why she's presently not speaking to him. I haven't gotten the deets yet because Dillon has been with me all weekend. All I know is she returned to our apartment late last night with steam practically billowing from her ears.

"I think I drilled the point home on Friday." Dillon winks, showcasing a wicked smile. "Literally."

My thighs squeeze together when I remember the raw possession in his gaze as he fucked me mercilessly in the bathroom in Whelans. After we returned to our table, a chorus of whistles and cheering rang out—from everyone but the groupies. I guess my freshly fucked hair, swollen lips, disheveled clothing, and overall disorientation gave the game away. "You did that on purpose?"

"I don't need an excuse to fuck you, Hollywood. You know I can't keep my damn hands off you"—Dillon grabs my thigh, smirking—"but I felt like Aoife needed stronger reinforcement. I'm sick of the way she looks at me. It's disrespectful to you."

This is why he's so perfect for me. He understands without me having to say it, and he doesn't hesitate to jump in to defend me and our relationship. Dillon is making it incredibly difficult to stop my heart from becoming permanently invested. "Goddamn it. I really want to jump your bones right now."

"Double gross." Ash makes a gagging sound.

"I'll just message Ma and tell her we'll be late for Sunday dinner because Dillon's busy corrupting you again," Ro deadpans.

Dillon flips his brother off through the mirror. "Jealous much, bro?"

"Hardly. One woman isn't enough to satisfy me." Considering he's on to girl number three since I had my little chat with him, he is more than proving that point.

"Maybe *I'm* the one corrupting Dil." I swivel in my seat to look at Ro. "Have you ever considered that?"

"Nah. You're far too sweet, and everyone knows it."

"I say we ditch these two at the side of the road and bang in the car," Dillon suggests while simultaneously giving someone the finger through the window. The other driver blares his horn, speeding past us, and I level my boyfriend with a stern look, warning him not to give chase like he did the last time he got into it with someone on the road.

I recently had Dillon added to the insurance, and I usually let him drive because he's a terrible passenger, and it's not worth the hassle. He bugs me nonstop about my driving skills if I'm behind the wheel. I'll admit I'm not the world's greatest driver. I've been driven around a lot, either by my parents' driver or Reeve, but it's not like I'm the worst driver either. Mainly, I don't go fast enough for my impatient boyfriend, or I'm too polite. It incenses him if someone cuts me off or beeps their horn and I don't retaliate.

We always end up arguing if I drive, so now I just give in and let him drive instead. Lately, I've had a couple of near misses when I've turned off one street onto another and automatically gone to the American side of the road, almost causing an accident. So, Dillon driving is probably for the best. Saves me a headache and a ton of stress. Not that I'll ever admit that to my boyfriend!

"You two fuck like bunnies," Ash says. "I heard you going at it all night long—thanks for the sound effects, by the way—so I'm sure you can manage without banging each other till you get home."

Dillon chuckles. "If only they knew the truth. That you're insatiable and as far from pure and a prude as they come." He waggles his brows, and I know what he's referencing. I let him take my ass last night, and he rocked my world. I've also discovered I like being tied up and spanked, and I love when he bosses me around in the bedroom. Dillon is a very considerate lover, and I like how he takes control and always ensures I'm satisfied.

Lifting one shoulder, I smile sweetly. "I tried to tell you when I first arrived, but no one would listen. You were all too busy judging the book by its cover."

"I know the truth now," Dillon says with a suggestive gleam in his eyes.

"And you can keep that truth to yourself, thanks very much," Ash drawls. "I already know too much, and I've seen *way* too much." A full-body shudder works its way through her, and Dillon and I bust up laughing.

"What don't I know?" Ro asks, sitting up straighter with an inquisitive expression on his face.

"Dillon didn't realize I'd come back to the apartment last night, and he wandered out to the kitchen earlier in all his morning glory. I almost barfed up my breakfast," Ash explains.

"Hey, I'll have you know my cock is a work of art. Your best friend certainly seems to think so." Dillon winks, and I giggle.

"Sisters do *not* need to see their brother's dick piercing." She flops back on the seat, rubbing a hand over her chest as her lips pull into a grimace. "Honestly, I feel ill all over again."

Ro joins in the laughter this time, and I can't keep the grin off my face the rest of the way to Kilcoole.

"Pass the spuds," Ciarán says, looking across the table at Dillon. But my boyfriend doesn't hear him because he's too busy trying to jam his hands between my thighs under the table. This is only my third time at Sunday dinner, and I'm sweating buckets, thinking everyone can see the tug of war going on between us.

I don't know what's gotten into Dillon today.

Maybe he's friskier because he took my anal virginity last night, but he hasn't stopped groping me all day. However, even I have some hard and fast limits. I definitely draw the line at being fingered under the table in front of his entire family, so I've spent the last ten minutes swatting his hand away and warning him to behave.

"Earth to lover boy," Shane bellows, nudging Dillon from his other side. "Get your paws off your woman and pass your brother the spuds."

My cheeks inflame, and it feels like I might pass out from a combination of embarrassment and overheating.

"Sorry." Dillon smirks, squeezing my thigh one final time before releasing me, passing the potatoes to Ciarán. "I get hugely distracted whenever my girl is around."

"We've noticed." Shane smirks, and I can see where Dillon got his smirk from. "Oh, how the mighty have fallen. I am going to enjoy giving you all the crap you gave me when I fell for Fiona."

"Stop teasing your brother," Cath, Dillon's mom, says. "I think it's wonderful to finally see Dillon happy and in love." She beams at us, oblivious to the fact her son has just turned to stone beside me.

Shane subtly nods his head in his mother's direction, and her smile fades when Dillon abruptly stands, scraping his chair back. "I need a smoke." Bending down, he pecks my lips. "Finish your dinner. I'll be back." Without another glance in my direction, he stalks to the back door and leaves.

CHAPTER 53

DILLON DOESN'T COME BACK, and I don't know if I should go out and look for him or if it would be considered rude to get up from the dinner table when we're not finished. Everyone continues talking and eating as if nothing's wrong, and I wonder if Dillon storming off and everyone pretending it's fine is normal.

"Will you help me serve up dessert, Vivien?" Cath asks, breaking me out of my troubled inner monologue.

"Of course." I get up and follow her into the kitchen. The others remain seated at the table at the other end of the room, talking and laughing.

Cath stands in front of the window, sighing. I stand alongside her, seeing no sign of Dillon outside. Her smile is sad when she turns to me, patting me gently on the back before she walks to the refrigerator.

I whip the cream while Cath removes the apple and rhubarb crumble from the oven. "I'm sorry if I offended you," she says as we work amicably side by side, spooning servings of crumble and cream into bowls.

"You didn't offend me, and I don't think you really offended Dillon either. He struggles to talk about his feelings. I'm sure you know that better than me."

Dillon is gradually opening up to me, but anytime the conversation veers into heavy subject matter, he tends to clam up. He still hasn't told me what happened when he was seventeen, but he has alluded to it a few times. I'm torn between wanting to push him—because I want to know everything there is to know about him —and letting it drop. Our relationship has a termination date, and encouraging him to fully open himself up to me emotionally will only make that inevitable ending all the harder. Right now, we're having tons of fun, and we talk about all manner of things when we're not out in a pub or fucking like bunnies. I've decided not to push it. To just go with the flow and accept our relationship for what it is.

Cath clasps my hand, and her eyes are shining with tears when she looks at me. "You're breaking through those walls he has around his heart, and I love that. I see the way he looks at you. The way you look at him. But it isn't my place to put a label on your relationship, and I shouldn't have said what I said. I just want him to be happy." She bats tears away.

"I want that for him too. He's an amazing guy, and he deserves every happiness."

"I'm so glad you came into his life, Vivien. Sometimes, the right people have a way of showing up when we least expect them." She places her hand on my arm. "Just don't give up on him. I know he struggles to accept love and it's hard for him to reciprocate, but it seems to come so naturally when he's with you."

I don't know that Dillon's in love with me because that's another thorny topic I refuse to discuss—even with myself—but we are damn good together, and the connection we share is more than the initial intense attraction we both felt.

I am perplexed why he finds it so hard to receive love and be worthy of it.

Love practically seeps from the walls of this house, and I doubt you could find a more loving, supportive family anywhere in the world. "I'm trying to understand it but coming up empty," I admit. "You have the most loving family. You only have to look to see it. It's a joy to behold. And I know you and Eugene are amazing parents. I don't need your children to tell me that, so why does Dillon feel like this?"

"Dillon has been fighting different demons his entire life," she explains, scooping crumble into the last bowl. I add a dollop of cream as she continues. "We have tried to support him to the best of our abilities, to let him know how loved and cherished he is, that he's no different—"

"Ma!" Dillon snaps, appearing in the doorway. "Stop." Some silent communication passes between them, and the shroud of sadness etched on Cath's face hurts my heart. I don't know what has gone on in the past, but whatever it is still pains Dillon's mother.

"Are we eating dessert or what?" he asks, striding toward us and snatching two bowls up, like nothing is wrong.

Cath collects herself, pressing a kiss to her son's cheek. "Of course. Let's go."

"Come with me," Dillon demands, an hour later, looming over me and extending his arm.

"You need to chill out, Dil," Ash says, blowing smoky puffs into the air.

"Gimme that." I snatch the joint from between Ash's fingers, taking one last drag before I clasp Dillon's hand. If I wasn't mildly stoned, I might be concerned about the look of thunder on my boyfriend's face.

"You need to butt out." Dillon tells his sister, hauling me to my feet. His hand wraps around mine as he steers us away from the orchard, toward the front of the farm.

"Where are we going?" I ask, jogging to keep up with his long-legged strides.

"To deliver your punishment," he says, stopping abruptly and slamming his lips down hard on mine. He swats my ass. "You've been a naughty girl, Hollywood."

He continues walking toward a structure in the near distance.

"I didn't mean to be nosy," I protest, understanding exactly why he feels the need to punish me.

"Doesn't change the fact you were."

"Your mom worries about you, and I care about you. Neither of us were speaking out of turn behind your back."

"If you want to know something about me, Viv, you ask me." He swivels his head, piercing me with a pointed look. "Me. Not my ma. Not Ash or Ro or Jamie. *Me.*"

"You don't tell me anything," I grumble, almost tripping as we approach what looks like a barn.

"Ask me anything, and I'll tell you," he challenges, unlocking the steel doors to the barn. He opens them fully before stepping aside to let me enter.

"What happened when you were seventeen?" I blurt, letting my eyes roam our surroundings. I was expecting to find cows, a milking shed, or a room stacked with supplies, not a recreation area of sorts. There's a large pool table on the left and a bunch of beanbags and couches on the right. Three freestanding heaters are dotted around the space. A long, scratched pale wooden table is propped against one wall, housing a TV and stereo system. Some beers and a half-empty bottle of vodka are tucked into the corner.

"You know what happened." Dillon leads me to one of the couches, pushing me over one of the arms, on my belly. "I failed my sister. She tried to kill herself, and it almost killed me." He yanks my dress up. "Any more questions?" he asks in a clipped voice, and I'm instantly chastised. I don't know why I think there's more to it than what happened with Ash. Maybe it's a sixth sense, but I've got to let it go. It's clearly painful for him and everyone in the family.

"No. I'm sorry," I whisper, feeling a rush of cool air waft across my ass as he tugs my panties down my leg.

Whack! His hand comes down firm on my butt, and a whimper flies from my mouth. Red heat floods my body, blood pools in my core, and my arousal leaks from my pussy, trickling down my legs as Dillon delivers a swift punishment, slapping me in quick succession. "God, I love when you're a naughty girl, Viv. It makes the sex even hotter." The telltale ripping of a condom wrapper and the lowering of a zipper have me squirming on the arm of the leather couch. Dillon folds his body over my back, licking my ear, and I squeal. "This will be hard and fast because Fiona is arriving shortly with my niece, and it won't take Chloe long to find us."

"Hard and fast is my favorite," I pant, feeling his dick nudge my pussy from behind. "Do your worst, Dil."

He slams into me, and we both groan as he fills me to the brim. Wasting no time, he grabs my hips and fucks me into oblivion, thrusting deep with every stroke, making me see stars. Just before he comes, he rubs two fingers back and forth over my clit, and my orgasm hits the same time his does.

He helps me to stand when we're both done. "Hold your dress up," he instructs, kneeling in front of me. He removes a pack of wipes from his back pocket, cleaning between my thighs with tender care, and tears prick my eyes. This side of Dillon has the power to undo me in a major way.

I can't fathom how fast Dillon can switch from sweet to sour, but he certainly makes life interesting, that's for sure. I wish I understood what secrets he keeps under lock and key, and I wish I was around long enough to uncover them. For the first time in weeks, I crack open the cage around my heart, letting myself feel. Allowing the truth to shine.

My heart is already invested. My head too.

I'm falling for this complicated enigma of a man.

And I'm terrified what that will mean come August when it's time to leave.

Dillon locks the barn, tucking me into his body and slinging his arm over my shoulders. "Are you okay?" He peppers my cheek with warm kisses.

"I'm perfect." I snuggle into his side, glad he seems to have snapped out of whatever mood he was in.

He chuckles before stopping suddenly at the corner of the barn. Pressing my back against the wall, he places his hands on either side of me, lowering his brow against mine. Closing his eyes, he breathes deeply as I lightly hold his hips. "I know I'm not the easiest person to be with," he whispers. "I know I'm a moody prick, and I have anger issues, but they're never directed at you."

"I know."

His eyes pop open, and I'm shocked to see such naked emotion staring back at me. "You make everything better, Viv." He cups one side of my face. "I never knew it could be like this, and sometimes I'm terrified beyond words."

"I get that." I brush my mouth against his in a featherlight kiss. "And it's okay to feel what you're feeling, Dillon. Just sometimes, I'd like it if you could let me in."

"I'm letting you in more than most people." Frank honesty is etched across his face. "I want to let you in more. Just be patient with me."

"I can be patient." Time is our enemy, but I'm not voicing that. Neither of us ever mentions August for obvious reasons. Snaking my arms around him, I press my body flush to his, overwhelmed with a sudden burst of intense pain.

Letting this man go is going to hurt me.

Yet there is nothing I can do to protect myself from that pain.

Slowly, Dillon has weaseled his way into my heart, and I don't want to shove him out.

"You've come to mean everything to me, Viv," he whispers in my ear as we clutch one another tightly. "It's happened so fast. Like lightning. I didn't think it would be like this, and it confuses me as much as it makes me happy." He eases his head back, so he's looking into my face, while still clinging to me. "Does that make any sense?"

"It makes perfect sense." I kiss him, fighting a bout of emotion. "I feel the same way too." This is the closest we've come to admitting our feelings, and my heart is racing around my chest cavity like a car with broken brakes.

"I don't know where we go from here when—" I nod when he stops mid-sentence, understanding without him needing to say it. "I just know I don't want to stop. I want to keep doing this with you. I—"

A guttural moan carries on the wind, cutting Dillon off. My startled eyes meet his suspicious ones when another moan rips through the quiet country air. Dillon snags my hand and pulls me around the corner of the barn. I gasp out loud, clamping my hand over my mouth far too late.

"You fucking bastard!" Dillon seethes, slipping his hand from mine and racing toward the couple screwing against the side of the barn.

"Dil, no!" Ash cries, dropping her dress and quickly pulling her panties up her legs. "Go!" she yells at the unfamiliar man with the dirty-blond hair and panicked expression. She shoves his shoulders as he rebuttons his jeans with shaky fingers. His wedding ring glints in the late afternoon sun, and I instantly know who he is.

"Oh, Ash," I whisper, coming out of my comatose state and running toward my friend.

"I'm going to kill you, you motherfucking bastard," Dillon yells, charging Ash's married ex.

Dillon grabs him around the throat, throwing him up against the wall of the barn as Ash stands rooted to the ground, horrorstruck. I pull my friend into my arms, and she immediately comes apart, sobbing against my shoulder. "I'm a horrible person. What have I done?" she cries, clutching my dress and clinging to me.

I'm torn between comforting my friend and preventing my boyfriend from being hauled in on a murder charge. "Dillon, stop!" I shout, cradling Ash in my arms as he throws Cillian to the ground, jumps on top of him, and starts punching him with his fists.

Cillian is tall and stocky, and I'm sure he could take Dillon on and it'd be fairly evenly matched, but he's not fighting back. He's letting my boyfriend beat the living daylights out of him. I don't know the man, but I guess he's carrying at least some guilt over what happened. Whether that's now, or in the past, I'm unsure.

"Dillon. That's enough!" I call out as blood flies from Cillian's nose spraying Dillon's shirt. Dillon's fists keep flying, and Cillian is fighting back now. Panic is clear in his eyes. He's afraid Dillon is going to kill him, and so am I.

"Ash, babe. I'm going to put you down on the ground, but I'll be back." She nods, looking dazed as I place her on the ground. Tears stream down her face, and I ache for her. She will beat herself up for this when she sobers up.

Rushing to where Dillon and Cillian are, I drop down on the ground, putting my face all up in my boyfriend's. "Dillon." I cup his face, repeating his name, asking him to stop over and over, but he's in his own little world. Cillian groans, swinging his fists, trying to push Dillon off, but it's like Dillon is fueled with supernatural fighting ability. He just keeps striking him, and if he doesn't stop, he *will* cause serious damage. A few of Cillian's punches get through, hitting Dillon in the face and the stomach, but it's not enough to stop him.

The situation calls for drastic measures, and I spring into action, yanking fistfuls of Dillon's hair and pulling his head back. He has a cut lip, and one of his eyes is swollen. Acting on instinct, I smash my lips to his, pushing my tongue into his mouth as I kiss him hard.

I need to bring him back to me, and this is the only way I can think to get through to him. Gradually, I feel him loosening against me, kissing me back, and I breathe a sigh of relief.

Until I'm shoved from behind, and Dillon and I tumble to the side, away from Cillian.

Fresh rage builds behind Dillon's eyes as he helps me to my feet, pushing me behind him, using his body to shield me as he faces off against his former friend. Wrangling out of his hold, I move to his side, grabbing him to keep him from charging again. "You cheating cunt! You stay the hell away from my sister, and if you ever touch my girlfriend again, I'll fucking kill you!" Dillon roars.

"You're a crazy bastard, O'Donoghue." Cillian sways on his feet, spitting blood onto the ground. He lifts the hem of his shirt, using it to dab blood off his face. "I let you have the first few punches, because I deserved those, but you don't get to threaten me, asshole. Your sister wanted it. I've done nothing wrong."

"Except cheat on your wife," I hiss.

"This is nothing to do with you." He jabs his finger in my direction. "Butt out."

Dillon jerks forward, and I grab his shirt, yanking him back. "Let it go," I say, working hard to sound calm. "This ends now."

"Like fuck it does," Cillian yells. He points his finger at Dillon. "I'll have you arrested for assault, you prick." Clutching his middle, he grimaces.

"I'll have you arrested for trespassing," Ash shouts, climbing to her feet, as she appears to emerge from her fugue state.

I step forward, glaring at the degenerate in front of me, done with playing nice. "You will not press charges against Dillon. If you even breathe a word of what happened here today, we will go straight to your wife and your parents and tell them you've been stalking Ash for months and you forced yourself on her today when she was stoned and incapable of pushing you away."

"That's bullshit," he splutters. "No one will believe you."

I wave my cell in his face. "I recorded you," I lie. "Whatever the circumstances, it shows your wife you were cheating on her. And if ruining your marriage isn't enough, I'll ruin your fucking career too. I'll email this to your boss. I'll post it on social media. I'll destroy your reputation." I would never, in a million years, do any of those things. Even saying it feels like I'm sinking to new lows, but there is nothing I won't do to protect Dillon and Ash.

His eyes narrow suspiciously. "Who are you?"

"I'm your worst fucking nightmare." I glare at him, taking another step forward. "Don't fucking push me, Cillian. I can ruin your life like that." I snap my fingers.

"You're all fucking mad," he says, his gaze bouncing between the three of us. "And you two are a match made in hell." He jabs his finger between Dillon and me.

"Leave," I command. "Don't say a word about Dillon or Ash. Not if you value the life you've got."

"Crazy bitch," he mutters, and Ash and I pounce on Dillon to hold him back.

Cillian walks off, shaking his head and muttering to himself. Wow. Ash sure knows how to pick 'em.

Not that I can throw stones.

Cillian staggers down the driveway, almost falling a couple times. A car slows going past him, and I spot Fiona behind the wheel. Thankfully, she doesn't stop, heading toward the house.

"Well, that was fun." Sarcasm drips from my tone as I stare at brother and sister. "We should do that again some time."

"Bloody hell." Dillon reels me into his arms. "Is it wrong I'm turned on right now?"

"Yes," Ash and I say in unison.

"Let's get back to the house." I thread my fingers in his. "We need to clean you up, and you." I swing my gaze on Ash. "You, my friend, have a lot of explaining to do."

CHAPTER 54

"WHAT HAS GOTTEN INTO YOU TODAY?" I ask Dillon, ten minutes later, as I tend to his injuries in the main bathroom. My man is shirtless, sitting on the closed toilet seat, with me in between his legs attempting to clean him up. We left Ash downstairs to explain the mess she made to the family. I have no clue what she's going to tell her parents, but I doubt it'll be the full truth.

"I'm not sorry I beat that shithead's ass." He winces as I clean the cut on his lip. "Just sorry you had to see it." He grabs my wrist, stalling my movements. "I don't know why you're with me when we both know I'm not good enough for you."

"I know nothing of the sort."

He looks at me with such vulnerability I almost cry. "Hey." I wrap one arm around him, holding him gently to my chest. "I'm with you because you're an amazing person. You're talented, sweet, sexy, funny, caring, thoughtful, and you make me happy."

"Do you really mean that?" he asks, rubbing circles on the inside of my wrist with his thumb.

"I do, Dil." I press a kiss to his head.

Silence engulfs us for a few beats. "I'm also moody, short-tempered, and an angry bastard a lot of the time. I definitely curse too much. And I should probably go easier on the beer and the weed."

"You forget reckless and a rule-breaker," I tease, smoothing a hand up and down his back.

"Those too. And that's exactly it. You deserve so much better than me. I'm not worthy of you, Viv."

His self-deprecation is killing me. Why can't he see the things I see in him? Why doesn't he see himself the way his family does? Ash would tie herself to a stake for Dillon, and I'm pretty sure his mom would walk over hot coals for him. Ruffling his hair, I kneel in front of him. "Dillon. Please don't do this. I'm with you because I want to be with you. I like all the different sides of you, and no one is without flaws. Not even me," I joke, desperately wanting to lighten the moment.

"You're perfect," he murmurs, bending down to kiss me. "I know I made a joke of it outside, but you standing up for me to him meant everything." A familiar smirk appears on his face along with those cute dimples I love, and I silently rejoice. "It *did* also turn me on." Taking my hand, he places it on his crotch, waggling his brows.

"No more sex until we get home," I warn, standing and grabbing the washcloth.

"What now?" Dillon asks, sighing wearily as we step foot in the hallway. I have cleaned up his lip, put an ice pack on his eye, and applied arnica cream to the faint bruising on one cheek. Soft cries filter out from the living room, and we walk inside, hand in hand, wondering what drama is unfolding now. Surely Ash didn't tell them she was fucking Cillian outside? "What's wrong?" Dillon casts worried glances around the room.

"The bridesmaids' dresses have gone missing in the post, and the designer can't ship new ones in time," Cath explains.

The wedding is only a few weeks away, so I feel Fiona's pain, and maybe I can do something about it. "Does anyone have a picture of the dress?" I ask.

"I do." Ash pulls out her phone. Her eyes light up as she passes it to me, and I know she knows where I'm going with this.

I examine the pretty knee-length strapless silk and chiffon dress in jade green. It would be easy to make, and I can rustle them up in next to no time now I have zero commitments. I hand the cell back to Ash, trading a conspiratorial smile with my Irish bestie, before I face the bride. "I can make replicas of that dress, no problem. How many do you need?"

"What?" Fiona splutters, turning around in Shane's arms, pinning me with red-rimmed swollen eyes.

"Vivien has offered to make the dresses for you, love." Cath pats her back while beaming at me.

"You can do that?" Fiona asks in a shaky voice.

"Of course, she can. I showed you our dresses from the ball. Viv made both," Ash proudly explains. "These are simple in comparison."

"They are," I reassure her. "And now my exams are finished, I have plenty of time to make them before the wedding."

"Oh my God." Fiona rushes toward me, yanking me out of Dillon's arms and squeezing me to death.

"Eh, Fi. You might want to let Vivien breathe, or she won't live long enough to make your dresses." Shane appears behind his fiancée. "Thank you," he tells me.

"It's my pleasure."

Fiona gives me the measurements for her sister and Ash, who are the only brides-maids, and little Chloe's measurements. They try to give me money for supplies, but I won't hear of it. "Consider it my wedding gift to you."

Dillon hauls me back against his chest, almost smothering me like his soon-to-be sister-in-law. "That was unbelievably generous. Thank you so much. I'm in awe of you." Before I can respond, he kisses me passionately, holding me tight in his arms, surrounding me with his love. When we break our lip-lock, he doesn't let go, his protective arms keeping me close to his chest. Cath smiles at us, leaning her head on her husband's shoulder.

We leave a short while later. Ro isn't coming back to the city as he has to stay home to study. His Leaving Certificate exams are only eight days away, and his parents are refusing to let him play with the band until after the exams are over. The second we pull away from the house, Dillon levels Ash with a fierce look through the mirror. "Start talking."

I toss a sympathetic look over my shoulder at her. Her hands are knotted in her lap, and she looks like she's sweating bullets. "I told Ma and Da that Cillian showed up unannounced and he was trying it on. I said I stupidly kissed him, you found us and then went apeshit on his arse."

"What really happened, Ash?" Dillon growls, pulling out onto the road.

She gulps nervously. "Mostly that. He appeared in the orchard. I told him to go. He begged me to talk to him. I took him around the side of barn so no one would see us. He said he still loves me and he'd leave her for me."

"Jesus Christ, Ash." Dillon rubs his temple.

"I knew it was bullshit. I know he won't leave her even if he is as miserable as he says he is."

"Why the hell did you let him fuck you then?" he barks, and tears spill down Ash's cheeks. Running my hand along his thigh, I urge him to calm down with my eyes. He blows air out of his mouth, visibly pulling in the reins. "I shouldn't have shouted at you. I'm sorry. I'm just worried, Ash. He's bad news. Look what happened the last time." His voice cracks.

"Pull over," I say. His eyes lock on mine. "Pull over and let me drive. I only had three pulls on that joint, and one glass of wine at dinner, and it was hours ago. I'm not drunk or stoned. You get in the back and talk with your sister." He doesn't argue, pulling to the side of the road, and we swap around. When we take off again, the conversation resumes, and I listen as I drive us home, casting quick glances in the mirror at them every so often.

"I'm sorry, Dil. I'm so, so sorry." Ash cries into his shoulder.

"Shush." He hugs her tight. "You don't have to apologize. But I do need you to promise me you'll stay away from him. He's a selfish prick to keep preying on your emotions like this. He had his chance with you, and he blew it. Tough shit if he's not happy. That's all on him."

She sniffles, nodding.

"He's not good for you, Ash," Dillon continues. "You deserve so much better than Cillian." Our eyes lock through the mirror as he repeats the words he said to me, a little over an hour ago. "You deserve better than Jamie too," he adds, shocking both me and his sister.

Poor Ash. She looks like she's going to throw up. "You know?" she croaks. He nods. "How?"

"I've had my suspicions since last summer. I asked him once, and he denied it, so I let it go." Dillon looks briefly out the window as I pull out onto the highway. "I warned him off you, and I probably shouldn't have done that." He looks back at his sister. "I just wanted to protect you. You were vulnerable, and I didn't want anyone else to hurt you. Jamie is sound, but I'm not sure he has it in him to do the relationship thing."

"No one thought that about you either, and now look at you," Ash says, peering up at him.

Dillon smiles softly at me. "Valid point." I return his smile, wishing I could kiss him right now. Dillon looks at his sister again. "Which is why when he asked me this morning if he could go out with you, I said I wasn't the one he should be asking."

Ash jerks her head up. "Wait! He told you about us? This morning?"

Amusement lingers in Dillon's tone. "Yes, this morning when I went home to get changed."

"Oh God." Ash buries her head in her hands. "I'm such an idiot. I was feeling low and upset after our argument last night, and that dickhead Cillian played on my vulnerabilities. Jamie won't want anything to do with me when he finds out."

"Ahem." I clear my throat. I'm not having that. "Jamie's been fucking Aoife and God knows who else for months." I hate double standards.

"He hasn't been with her since April," Ash says. "We've only been with each other, and it was an unspoken rule that it stays like that." She has a point, and she shouldn't have fucked anyone else, especially not her cheating ex, but Jamie hasn't been a saint either. He's hurt her, and it's clear Ash's broken parts aren't mended—they're only glued together. I'm going to suggest she sees my therapist when we're alone. Sheila has really helped me to process my feelings and move on, and I think Ash could use her support too.

"You weren't officially going out," Dillon says. "And it's only an issue if you tell him. I don't see that he needs to know."

"You mean *you're* not going to tell him?" Her jaw slackens.

He shakes his head. "I'm not." His mouth curls into a lopsided grin. "Don't look so shocked, Ash. You're my sister."

"But he's your best friend."

"He is, but you're my *sister*. If it comes to sides, I'm always on yours."

"Well, what's the impression of your first Irish wedding?" Dillon asks, twirling me around the dance floor of the ballroom of the gorgeous hotel just outside Gorey, County Wexford.

"It's been magical. You can just feel the love in the air." I beam up at him, throwing my head back as he spins me around.

He chuckles, pulling me in close to his chest. "You're such a romantic." His arms encircle my waist.

I swat his chest. "Says the man who sang a song he wrote for me at his brother's wedding." My throat swells, and I choke up.

"Oh God. Don't cry again," he says, looking genuinely panicked.

My lower lip wobbles, and happy tears well in my eyes. "I still can't believe you did that."

Fiona and Shane hired a local band to play at their wedding because they wanted their brothers to enjoy the night, not to have to entertain their guests. However, the band was a good sport and let the guys play a few songs while they took a short break.

Ash barely held me together as Dillon told the whole wedding that "Terrify Me" was a song he'd written for me and about me. Thank God, Ash had the foresight to record it on her cell—and I'm sure the official videographer captured it too—because I was in such shock I didn't fully appreciate the lyrics or the fact it's a much softer, more romantic sound for Toxic Gods.

"You must know you're my muse," he says, breaking me out of my head.

My heart thuds proudly behind my chest. "I am?"

He nods, sweeping his fingers across my cheek. "I've been writing nonstop in that journal you made me. You're the inspiration behind all my lyrics."

I found a songwriting journal at a local store, and I crafted a Toxic Gods cover, incorporating their logo, out of crushed velvet. The other guys in the band were so envious I ended up making them similar notepads just to shut them up.

"Everything about you inspires me, Viv," he murmurs, kissing the tip of my nose as we dance to the music. "You have such a good heart. Helping others makes you happy, and that's how I know you're inherently good."

Fiona was delighted with the dresses, and Shane was profuse in his praise during his speech. "Seeing little Chloe looking so angelic in her dress has been one of the highlights of this day," I say.

He kisses me softly. "There. That's what I'm talking about." He looks deep into my eyes with so much emotion I'm choking up. They say weddings make you emotional, and this one most definitely has. I can't help being affected by the outpouring of love in the room, and I know we're not the only ones feeling it. *"You're an angel, and I'm so happy to have met you."*

"Thank you," I whisper, blushing a little.

A new song starts up, one I don't know. Dillon smiles down at me, emotion practically oozing from his pores, and I'm not sure my heart is going to withstand this day intact.

"Dance with me under the stars?" he asks, and my knees almost go out from under me. I nod as if in a trance, high on so many glittering emotions. As if I could ever turn such a request down.

Lacing his fingers in mine, he leads me out a side door to a small courtyard. Cath and Eugene watch us leave with matching giant smiles, and I get the sense they're hoping Dillon and I will give them a day like this in the future. Butterflies swoop into my belly, and a fluttering sensation spreads across my chest at the thought.

Dillon sweeps me into his arms in front of the impressive gardens, holding me close, as we move in time to the beat. He purposely left the glass doors open so the music filters outside.

"What song is this?" I ask, listening intently to the beautiful lyrics.

"It's an older song by a group called Savage Garden. The song is "I Knew I Loved You." It's always been a favorite of mine." He tilts his head back a little so he can look at me. "Especially now," he adds, in a whisper.

I stare into his gorgeous green eyes as he sings to me, and my heart pounds louder and louder in my chest, swelling with so much emotion it almost feels like I'm drowning. Tears prick my eyes as the words sink deep, their meaning registering on so many levels. Dillon pours everything he's feeling into his singing, swirling me softly around the courtyard under the backdrop of the twinkling stars, never taking his eyes off me.

Drops of rain fall from the sky without warning, but I barely feel them, hypnotized by this amazing, beautiful, complex man spinning me in his arms. Singing his truths because he can't form the words behind the sentiments.

The rain comes down heavier, plummeting in thick sheets as we continue dancing, plastering our hair to our faces and our clothes to our bodies like second skins. Another song starts, and Dillon twirls me around faster and faster, and I laugh, tipping my head up to the dark sky, letting the water cleanse me of all my fears and uncertainties.

When he pulls me in close, locking me in his protective arms, his laughter dies along with mine as our gazes connect with an intensity so powerful it seems bigger than both of us. His chest heaves in sync with mine as we stop dancing, staring at one another because there is nothing that can drag either one of us away from the other. I want to stay like this forever. Secure in his gaze. Trapped in his adoration. Surrounded with emotion that threatens to unravel everything I thought I knew about myself.

My heart is open, and I'm shielding nothing. From him. From myself.

I knew this was the risk.

But I barreled headfirst into this relationship anyway, and I'm not sorry I did.

How could I have any regrets when it's brought us here, to this place, to this realization?

I know neither one of us is going to put words to the emotion.

Yet we both know it exists.

Our truths are traded when we move as one, our lips meeting as if for the first time, and I know, for the rest of my life, I will never *ever* forget this moment.

The moment I realize I am utterly and unequivocally in love with Dillon O'Donoghue.

CHAPTER 55

THE WEEKS FLY by in a mad flurry of activity. Toxic God's EP is getting more notice, and one of their songs is getting decent airplay on some Irish radio stations. Things are definitely picking up for the band. They are playing three to four events a week now, and the crowd is getting bigger and their following is growing.

One of Glen Hansard's US contacts has reached out—an A&R scout who works for a major record label—and it sounds promising. Apparently, he loves the stuff he has listened to. He's due to arrive in Dublin in three weeks to see them perform live, and he wants to talk to them about their future. The guys are freaking out. Giddy with excitement. But I sense reticence within Dillon. Of course, when I ask, he deflects my questions, and eventually, I let it drop.

In between events, Dillon and I wander the Irish countryside on his motorcycle. I've kissed the Blarney Stone, explored the incredible *Titanic* museum in Belfast with my jaw trailing the floor, marveled at the Stone Age tombs and passageways at Newgrange, and given in to my inner sex goddess when I let Dillon fuck me against the cross on the top of Bray Head under the shadow of night.

It's just as well I'm not religious or I might have been struck down for that last one.

We've gone camping with our friends in the Wicklow Mountains, ridden bicycles around the Sally Gap, hiked the Sugarloaf Mountain, watched a few GAA matches, and attended a three-day music festival in Marlay Park, which was basically a three-day-long drink-and-weed-athon.

The highlight of my Ireland trip was definitely the Cliffs of Moher. Words don't exist in our vocabulary to describe the rugged beauty of the landscape because it was a truly magical, breathtaking, out-of-this-world experience. We spent a full day there, touring the visitor's center, walking the pathways on either side of the cliff, and I was even brave enough to lie down flat on my belly on the slab front, beside Dillon, while we stared over the ledge. Most visitors stayed back, and we were among the few crazies peering down the steep edge of the cliff side. It was an incredible rush, and an impressive lesson in the true wonder of Mother Nature. It was only later, back in our hotel room, I discovered some tourists have actually died there. It was a sobering moment, and I doubt I'd have been so brave if I'd known that at the time.

My parents' visit rolled around fast, and we had a fantastic week together exploring Cork and Kerry and driving along the Wild Atlantic Way. Audrey traveled with my parents, and it was amazing to see her. I have really missed her. Initially, she was planning on spending more time in Ireland with me, but I'm on borrowed time with Dillon, and now she's back together with Alex, we came to a mutual understanding it was best if we spent this summer apart. We still got to spend quality time together during the week, which was amazing, if a little strained.

Ash came to Cork and Kerry with us, and things were a teeny bit awkward between her and Audrey. Ash is naturally Team Dillon, and while Audrey has nothing against her brother, she is clearly rooting for Team Reeve. I really don't understand why. She's been pretty tight-lipped, and all she has said is he's missing me, working hard to make amends, and she has her reasons for suggesting I don't rule him out. Part of me is incredibly upset with her, even though she insists she is firmly on my side. Not wanting to fight with her over it, I suggested we agree to shelve all talk of men on our trip, and just enjoy ourselves.

That suited me fine as I was still annoyed with Dillon over his outright refusal to meet my parents. Apparently, he doesn't "do the parents thing." It stung. Especially after he'd been so romantic in the weeks leading up to my parents' arrival. It's not like I asked him to travel with us. I knew he couldn't take a full week off with his band commitments, but would it have killed him to come for lunch with his mom and Ash? Ash claims he's in love with me and that has him scared shitless, but it's no excuse for being rude.

Mom didn't say anything, but I could tell she wasn't impressed, even if she loved Cath and they hit it off from the get-go.

Honestly, Dillon gives me a severe case of emotional whiplash at times. He turns hot and cold as often as the Irish weather, and I still can't figure him out.

Nonetheless, I love him and his stupid stubborn ass.

Finally allowing myself to accept what I've known for some time was both liberating and crushing in equal measure. Reeve is still there, still claiming a piece of my heart, and I suspect he always will. It's not like I can just switch off feelings I've nurtured for years with the snap of my fingers. They are like my memories in that regard. An inherent part of me, and no amount of denial will force them away.

I have always been skeptical of love triangles in books and movies, struggling to understand how someone could love another man when they're already so much in love with someone. However, I know now I was naïve to believe it doesn't exist. Now I've had cause to seriously think about the subject, it makes perfect sense. I love my mom *and* my dad. I love both my besties. When I have children, I imagine I will love them all with the fullness of my heart. So, it stands to reason I can love two men at the same time. I just never looked at it like that before.

I want to hate Reeve for the things he's done that have hurt me, and for splitting us up, but how can I hate him when his actions have led me to this point?

Coming to Ireland has undoubtedly changed me. I feel like I have found myself and found my way. I have discovered aspects of my personality that have never had the time to flourish, and Dillon has helped to coax those parts of me to life. I am stronger and more confident to go after what I want—to demand things that will fulfill me and to not let anyone stand in my way or tell me my desires don't matter.

Dillon has awakened a side of me I never knew existed, and I wish I could continue this journey of self-discovery with him because he brings me immense joy. He pisses me the hell off at times too, but what we have is so very real. This is a no-holds-barred love, and while we haven't said those three words, we both feel it and live it every day.

Our love is an intense fiery passion, a soul-deep connection that kicked into place the instant we laid eyes on one another, and while similar in some regards, it is also vastly different to what I had with Reeve.

Dillon loves me with a fierceness that scares us both. His need is all-consuming, and all it takes is one look and we fall into one another, lost to everyone and everything that isn't us. Ours is a love that could raze kingdoms and burn worlds, and that realization is as terrifying as it is exhilarating.

Neither of us has said the words out loud, but as our inevitable separation looms in the near future, I'm struggling to not break down in tears. How will I ever leave this man? Yet, in ten days, it will happen. The very thought of it feels like a stake has been driven through my heart.

"Earth to Hollywood." Dillon grazes his teeth along my neck, pulling me out of my depressive thoughts. "You look like you've been in your own little world."

Hearty laughter and boisterous conversation surround us in the busy pub as the bartender calls out last orders. The guitarist entertaining us with her gorgeous voice and dry wit is packing up her stuff, but no one else is making any move to leave. Our friends are still huddled around the table, joking and drinking.

Resting my head on his shoulder, I snuggle into his side. "I was just thinking back over the past few weeks. We crammed a lot in."

His arm slides around my shoulders, holding me close. "I wanted to show you as much as possible." *Before you leave me* is missing from the end of his sentence.

A heavy silence rests between us like usual lately. We are both too chickenshit to say it, but we feel it crushing our souls.

"Do you know this pub was the scene of a famous murder almost twenty-five years ago?" Dillon says, in between mouthfuls of beer.

"Now he tells me," I deadpan. A shiver tiptoes down my spine. "If you tell me some ghost haunts this place, I'm out of here."

"Two ghosts," Jamie pipes up, clearly eavesdropping on our conversation. "If you count the Black Widow. She died a few years ago in prison."

"She actually died in a hospice," Dillon clarifies. "They had moved her there when her cancer progressed and they knew she was close to death."

"They should have let her rot in jail," Ash says, bumping my hip. "Drink up, it's almost closing time."

"What happened?" I lift my vodka cranberry to my lips.

"The owner's wife murdered him here back in ninety-six, but she didn't get away with it. She was sent down for life," Dillon explains.

"It put Jack White's Inn on the map. It's infamous," Ro says, waving his hand around the crowded pub. "Even now."

"Welp, that was a lovely way to end the night." Another shiver rocks through me. Dillon smirks. "Just keeping it real, Hollywood."

"And who says the night is ending?" Jamie drains the last of his beer, slamming his hands down on the wooden table, rattling glasses and spilling drinks.

"Arsehole," Ash mutters, rolling her eyes. Our gazes connect, and we smile. She says that, but I know the truth. She is head-over-heels, ass-over-tits, in love with him, and he is the same with her. I know she harbors guilt over what went down with Cillian, but they would not be here, looking all loved up if she'd told him what happened. It's best left in the past. No good would come from spilling that truth. Jamie grabs her face, smushing his lips to hers, and Dillon's mouth pulls into a grimace.

To be fair, he hasn't given them shit, but he watches like a hawk, and I feel a little bad for Jamie sometimes. If he even raises his voice to her, Dillon gets ready to knock him flat on his ass. It must feel like walking on eggshells sometimes. I know Dillon's protectiveness comes from a place of love, but he's got to accept he won't always be there to shelter his sister. Plus, she's a grown-ass woman capable of making her own decisions, and he needs to let her live her life and deal with the consequences of her actions.

The transformation in Jamie is astounding. Though I suppose it was the same with Dillon. Neither of them even glances at the groupies. They only have eyes for us.

Until you leave. My snarky inner devil whispers nastily in my ear.

"Come on, dickheads." Jamie slams his hands on the table again, knocking Conor's bottle of beer to the floor. He must have a death wish.

"You're such a jerk, Jay," Cat says, but there's no heat in her tone. Her boyfriend whispers in her ear, and Ash sends me a knowing look. She isn't Stephen's biggest fan because rumors of his infidelity have been circulating since just before our exams, and she doesn't trust he's being faithful to her friend. Ash and Cat had a big falling out when Ash told her what the gossipmongers were saying, and they've only just started talking again. I haven't heard from Cat in weeks. I guess she assumed I would take Ash's side, but I don't really care. She earned a place on the bottom of my shit list with the way she reacted to news of Reeve being my ex.

"I'll pay you back from my stash," Jamie tells Conor.

Conor just shrugs, in that affable laid-back manner of his. I swear, in the entire seven months I've been in Ireland, I have only heard that guy say a handful of sentences. The shy blonde tucked under his arm doesn't seem to care. I have no clue how they know each other, whether they are dating, or if he just brought her along to Brittas Bay this weekend.

"Let's get this show on the road," Jamie says, standing. "Time to head back to the house and finish the party there."

CHAPTER 56

"WHO'S UP FOR SKINNY-DIPPING?" Dillon suggests when we arrive at the beachside vacation house that belongs to Conor's grandparents a half hour later. The walk back here from the pub was dark and perilous, but we made it in one piece.

"Hell to the no." I shake my head, crossing my arms around my waist.

"Prudish much?" Jamie smirks, and I thump his shoulder.

"That's not the reason. If the water was that freaking cold earlier, I'm not willing to test the temperature at midnight." The beach at Brittas Bay is stunning. Grassy dunes surround miles of gorgeous sandy shores. Crystal-clear shallow water looks deceptively inviting until dipping a foot in and realizing it's cold enough to freeze body parts.

"Bawk, bawk." Ro and Jamie make chicken sounds, flapping their arms about.

"I'll keep you warm," Dillon purrs, wrapping his arms around me.

"You can't return to the US without skinny-dipping in the Irish Sea," Ash says, and I throw caution to the wind.

"If I die of hypothermia, it's your fault," I tell my bestie.

We grab towels from the house, heading out through the back garden that leads directly to the sand dunes. Racing one another to the beach helps to warm me up but not much. This will be a true test of endurance, but I'm up for the challenge.

It's pitch-black on the beach with only faint illumination glistening on the water from the moon overhead. Behind us, most of the properties closest to the beach are in darkness, which makes sense, as this is mainly a family destination and I expect most people are in bed.

Dillon undresses in front of me, shielding me with his body while I yank my jean shorts down my legs and tug my sweater and tank off over my head. "Bra and knickers too," Dillon says, shoving his boxers down his legs, standing proudly in all his naked glory.

Shrieks and squeals rip through the silent night air as our friends run toward the water, completely naked.

Unclipping my bra, I let it drop to the sandy floor, leveling my boyfriend with a pointed look, even if he can't properly see it. "I do understand the meaning of skinny-dipping, Dil." He strokes his hardening length as I clutch his arm to steady myself while I pull my panties down.

Predictably, he tweaks my nipple. "I love it when you get snarky with me. Keep it up. It just turns me the fuck on."

"Everything turns you on." I shriek when he yanks me in flush to his body, thrusting his hard length against me.

"Everything about *you* turns me on," he corrects, taking my hand. "Come on." We sprint toward the water, and I'm already shivering. "Don't think about it. Just run in and duck down under the water. It'll be a shock at first, but I know how to warm you up." His tone is suggestive in the extreme.

The others are already in the water, laughing and messing around, splashing water at one another.

"Eyes on your girl, Ro," Dillon snaps as we near the water's edge. I'm not sure what skinny-dipping etiquette exists, or if there even is such a thing, but I'm not surprised Dillon is getting possessive. Frankly, I'm amazed he suggested this. He doesn't like anyone looking at me, and he made his point about not sharing clear from the very start.

Gripping my hand harder, Dillon pulls me into the ocean. Shock blasts through me as a blanket of ice slams into my body, leaving no part immune to the chilly effects. I scream as if I'm being murdered, and the others all burst out laughing. Acting out of instinct, I try to wrench my hand from Dillon's and retreat, but he's having none of it. Throwing me over his shoulder, he wades through the cold water, whacking my ass as his arms band around my body before he dunks us under the water.

My organs go into instant shock, and I thrash about futilely. Every part of my body feels like I've been pelted with an ice gun. When we burst through the water's surface, my teeth are chattering, and I'm too cold to even scream. "Wrap your legs and arms around me," Dillon says, helping my frozen limbs to cooperate. He bobs us up and down as he treads through the water away from our friends. I'm facing them, and they're all coupling off, kissing and sliding hands under the water.

"Is skinny-dipping in Ireland code for fucking?" I ask, genuinely curious.

Dillon chuckles, keeping me upright as he wades a little farther away. "Not that I'm aware of, but I'm down with that plan."

"Don't pretend like this wasn't your entire motivation for suggesting skinny-dipping in the first place."

He nips the underside of my jaw. "Is it a problem I want you so badly all the time?"

"Never." I tighten my arms around his neck. "And it's definitely mutual."

He kisses me then, over and over, running one hand up and down my back, while holding me up with the other. I grind my pussy against his pubes, building friction as he lowers his mouth to my breasts and worships them. Gradually, I forget the cold water and the breeze wafting around our bodies.

"Hold on, and don't scream unless you want to scream my name. That's totally fine." I can hear the smile in his voice.

"You're crazy. You all are," I add, watching the moving shapes of our friends in the near distance.

"Crazy about you," he murmurs, claiming my lips as he slowly lowers me down a little more into the water, positioning me on his cock.

I forget about everything but him the instant he fills me. His piercing rubs along my inner walls, and when he presses against my cervix, I seriously see stars. Clamping my legs around his waist and suctioning my arms around his neck, I thrust up and down in sync with his movements, moaning and whimpering as he fucks me. Everything seems heightened tonight, and maybe it's the water or…

"Oh my God. No condom!" I shriek, stalling my movement.

"You're on the pill, and we're both clean," he grunts, continuing to rock into me. Veins throb in his neck and his arms with the exertion involved in holding me up and fucking me. "I'll pull out before I come if it makes you feel better," he offers.

"Okay." I relax, pivoting my hips and resume fucking him.

Dillon pulls out a few minutes later, groaning as his cum shoots all over my upper stomach. I didn't come, but I wasn't expecting to out here in these Arctic conditions. Dillon cleans his cum off my skin, and I flinch at the coldness of the water now I don't have his cock to distract me. He kisses me before hoisting me farther up his body. "Climb up, Hollywood, and drape your legs over my shoulders."

"What? No." The others aren't that far from us now, and they'll be able to see enough to figure out what's going down. "You can finish me off back at the house."

"Like fuck I can." He shoves me up his body by my butt. "Do as you're told, or I'll eat your arse out in front of everyone."

Well, that would be infinitely more embarrassing, so I climb up his body, eventually managing to slide my legs over his shoulders, gripping his forearms for dear life as he devours my pussy with his tongue. His arms hold me in place at my back, and I'm in awe of his strength and stamina. At least if he drops me, it won't be life-threatening, not unless I actually freeze to death. As his expert tongue plunders my pussy, I forget all my concerns, riding his face with no shame and screaming his name as I come loudly.

"Guess I can't call you a prude anymore, huh?" Jamie teases, a few minutes later when we reunite with the others.

I splash water in his face, fighting a grin as the others crack up laughing.

"Your neighbors are dickheads," Jamie tells Conor, as we're forced to move our party from the outside deck to the living room.

"Be fair, Jay," Ash says, looping her arm through his. "They have small kids, and we are pretty obnoxious and loud."

"You forgot drunk and stoned," I tease, sinking onto Dillon's lap while he sits in the recliner chair. Cat and Stephen went to bed when we got back from the pub, so it's only the eight of us now. I hate to be mean, but the atmosphere is more relaxed when Cat's asshole boyfriend isn't around. No one likes him, and I bet Ash is regretting inviting them this weekend.

"Too drunk and stoned to sing?" Jamie inquires, removing his guitar from his case.

"Definitely not." I'm actually not drunk in the slightest, having paced myself tonight, and I'm only mildly stoned. I purposely stayed relatively sober because I've been planning this surprise for a couple of weeks.

"What's going on?" Dillon asks as I get up to sit beside Jamie. He's perched on a little ledge in front of the elevated open stone fireplace.

"I'm going to sing for you," I explain while Jamie strums a few strings on his guitar.

"What song?" Curiosity rings in Dillon's tone.

"'She Moves Through the Fair.'"

A slow smile spreads across his mouth. "Yeah?"

"Yeah." I return his smile, my heart beating fast. "I know you wanted to hear me sing, and after watching *Michael Collins* the other week, I knew it had to be this song." This song speaks about love and loss, and it's heartachingly beautiful with sentiments we can relate to.

Dillon missed out on the rooftop singalong during the housewarming party we threw back in February—because he was being a dick—but the guys told him I have an amazing voice, and he's been begging me to sing with them for months. I absolutely refuse to get up on stage, even though a part of me feels an enormous thrill thinking about it. However, my abhorrence of the spotlight overrules any temporary adrenaline rush.

I considered singing at Shane and Fiona's wedding, but after Dillon serenaded me with his song, I was a pile of goo on the floor and incapable of anything but swooning.

Dillon singing to me that night made me determined to find an opportunity to sing to him, and after we watched the *Michael Collins* movie with Liam Neeson and Julia Roberts, I knew what I wanted to do.

I wanted to honor Dillon's Irish roots and his love of the Irish history by learning a traditional Irish song. In the movie, Sinead O'Connor sings a slightly altered version of "She Moves Through the Fair" where the pronouns are altered from female to male to suit the film. Man, she has such a stunning voice, and her rendition is hauntingly beautiful. I could watch the video of her singing it live on stage a million times and never grow bored. Yet, I chose to sing the original version, practicing when Dillon wasn't around, using a YouTube video performed by a talented singer named Caitlin Grey for guidance. After I had a pretty good grasp of it, I practiced with Jamie. He and Ash gave me some direction until we felt it was perfected.

"Ready?" Jamie asks, and I nod, stuffing my nerves back down my throat. Wiping my clammy hands down the sides of my jean shorts, I clear my throat.

Jamie strums the chords, and I start singing, staring at my boyfriend as the lyrics leave my tongue. My heart swells as my voice soars, and I have everyone's undivided attention. Passion flows from my mouth as I sing the devastatingly beautiful song, feeling so many emotions as the words embed deep in my soul.

Dillon's Adam's apple bobs in his throat as he watches me in raptured awe. Our connection vibrates across the room as we stare at one another, and I see the same overwhelming set of emotions flit across his eyes.

When the song ends, I'm greeted by initial silence, and then a communal round of applause breaks out. My cheeks flush, and my heart is jumping around my chest as Dillon stands, striding toward me with a determined look on his face. His arm extends as he reaches me, and I let him pull me to my feet. With fierce tenderness, he reels me into his embrace, locking his arms around me and burying his face in my hair. My arms automatically wind around his back, and I rest my head against his chest, closing my eyes and fighting tears.

I don't know how long we stand there, in the middle of the room, wrapped around one another while our friends probably don't know where to look. Eventually, Dillon tips my head back, and I'm startled to see such raw emotion in his glassy eyes. He stares at me, chest heaving, and I see his love written across his face as plain as day.

Pain presses down on my chest, but I won't give in to it. I can't. I don't want this last special weekend in Ireland to be marred by sadness. I'm not sorry I sang that song even if it has forced both of us to face our reality. Stretching up, I kiss him, and our lips rest against each others' as we silently speak our truths.

Hours pass, and we sit around the living room, drinking, eating chips and cookies, talking, and laughing, and I never want the night to end. Dillon is cocooned around me, like he's afraid to let go. I'm cuddled into his side on the reclining chair, unable to untangle my limbs.

Orangey-red streaks paint the sky outside, signaling the start of another day, and we finally depart to our bedrooms except for Ro and his girlfriend. They drew the short straw, so they're sleeping on the couch.

Dillon stumbles as I lead him up the stairs, and I realize he's far drunker than usual. Circling my arm around his back, I let him lean on me while I steer him to the room we're staying in. Dropping him on the bed, I bend down to kiss his brow. "I'm going to grab us some water. Be back in a sec."

"Stay," he murmurs, reaching his arm out.

I smile, lifting his palm to my face and pressing a kiss to his skin. "I'll be right back."

When I return a few minutes later, he hasn't moved a muscle. I prop pillows against the headboard and force him to sit up against it. "Drink." I shove the water in his hand. Kneeling in front of him, I remove his sneakers. Grains of sand fall on the hardwood floor, so I grab a towel from our weekend bag and gently clean his feet.

"You care about me," he says, but it's more of a statement than a question.

"I do." I toss the towel on the floor and pop the button on his jeans.

"I...I care about you too." He slurs the words a little.

"I know you do, babe." I brush his messy hair off his brow. "Drink," I order, tugging at his jeans.

"I need to tell you something," he croaks, and I stop pulling his jeans down his legs.

"Okay." I peer into his face, instantly seeing the turmoil there.

"I'm afraid to tell you."

I gulp over the ball of nerves in my throat, wondering what it is he has to say, instinctively knowing it's not something I'll want to hear. I pull his jeans off and tuck his legs under the covers.

"We promised each other honesty, Dillon. If it's something I need to know, just tell me." I whip my clothes off and crawl into bed beside him.

His eyes flutter closed before popping open again. "I never planned this. It wasn't supposed to happen," he slurs. "Now I'm going to be like the man in that song, driven mad by the loss of the woman he loves." His head drops back against the headboard, and his eyes close again.

My heart stutters in my chest, and tears well in my eyes. I don't know if they're happy or sad ones.

The bottle slips between his fingers, and I grab it in the nick of time.

"Why did he tell me? Why couldn't it have been like this." He points a shaky finger between us, as I place his bottle down on my bedside table. "The way it's meant to be."

"I don't understand." He's not making any sense.

Dillon slips down under the covers, and I lie on my side, gently wiping the quiet tears falling from his eyes with mounting concern.

"You're mine, Vivien." He pulls me into his warm naked chest. "You're mine. Not his. *Mine. Mine. Mine.*"

Now it's my turn to cry, and I'm working hard to hold my sobs inside. To keep shoving that pain back down inside. To not think about this because there is nothing I can do about it. It's not like I can stay even if I want to. Dillon is right about one thing; it wasn't supposed to be like this. My heart was not supposed to get involved. It was supposed to be fun, and I could walk away without looking back.

A loud snore rips through my desolate thoughts, and I look up at my boyfriend. He's out cold. Head back. Mouth slightly open. Oblivious to the emotional torment twisting my insides into knots.

I guess I fall asleep because the next thing I'm aware of is the bed shaking as Dillon gets up. I have no clue what time it is, but my eyelids are too heavy, and they refuse to open. I'm just drifting back to sleep when the bed dips and Dillon wraps himself around me from behind. I smile in my semi-sleep state, loving how safe and warm I always feel in his arms. His lips brush my ear. "I love you, Vivien Grace. You are the one. The only one. For now and eternity."

CHAPTER 57

THE BED IS empty when I wake next, and sunlight is streaming through a small gap in the curtains. Dragging my tired body out of bed, I pee, brush my teeth, and take a quick shower before changing into a purple, pink, and white full-length summer dress. Slipping my feet into my low-heeled silver sandals, I grab a light, white cardigan and head downstairs.

Ro, Conor, and their girlfriends are in the kitchen, and Ash is standing over the stove flipping bacon. "Where's everyone else?" I ask.

"Jay is sleeping off his hangover," Ash supplies, looking at me over her shoulder.

"Cat and the dick left, thank fuck." Ro's eyes roam quickly over my dress. "You look pretty today." Hurt flickers across his girlfriend's face, and I don't blame her. I don't think Ro meant it intentionally, but he should think before he speaks. If Dillon were here, he'd probably punch him for that comment.

"Um, thanks." I shuffle awkwardly on my feet. "Where's Dillon?"

"He's outside." Conor jerks his head at the sliding double doors.

"I just made a fresh pot of tea if you want some?" Ash says, as I move to the kettle to make some coffee.

"You know me, girl. I need my caffeine fix first." I make two mugs of coffee and wander outside to find my boyfriend.

Dillon is out on the deck sitting on one of the wicker lounge chairs, leaning forward with his shoulders stooped and head cradled in his hands.

"Hey." I take the seat alongside him, setting the mugs on the ground. Gently, I place my hand on his shoulder. "Are you okay?"

Slowly, he lifts his head. "I'm fine," he says without looking at me, staring straight ahead.

"Dillon. Please look at me."

He turns his head, and my heart aches at the tormented look on his face. His eyes are bloodshot, the layer of stubble on his face is thicker than normal, and he looks pale.

"What is it? What's troubling you?"

"I'd have thought that was obvious, Viv," he softly says.

I nod, wetting my dry lips. Handing him a coffee, I take a sip of mine. "Are we going to talk about it?"

"What's the point?" He cups his large hands around the mug, and I rest my head on his shoulder.

"I hate this."

"Me too." He threads his fingers in mine, and we drink our coffee in silence, staring out at the ocean in the distance.

"You said some stuff last night," I say, when we put our mugs down. Panic skips across his face, and his back stiffens. "You don't remember?"

He shakes his head. "What did I say?"

"That you had something to tell me but you were scared."

"That's all I said?" he asks, staring me straight in the eye.

"You mumbled some other stuff that didn't make sense." I want to tell him he told me he loved me twice, but I know he won't want to hear that, and I can't have that conversation. Yet I am curious as to what secret he was going to divulge.

"It's nothing." Pulling his hand from mine, he stands. "Don't take this the wrong way, but I just need a little space right now."

It's hard not to feel hurt by that, but I nod.

"I'm going for a walk. I'll talk to you later."

I watch him walk off until his form is just a speck in the distance. My heart throbs painfully the entire time.

"Have you spoken to your brother?" I ask Ash on Friday morning. It's been four days since we returned from Brittas Bay, and Dillon is officially ghosting me.

"Nope. Jay said he's been locked away in his bedroom all week writing and pining."

"I don't get it." I curl into a ball on the couch, grabbing a cushion and clutching it to my chest. "I might as well have left already. I thought he'd want to spend every last second with me." Tears fill my eyes, and I angrily swipe them away. I swore I wouldn't cry over any guy ever again, and look at me now. I've been a pathetic mess this past week. I have four days left in Ireland, and I did not plan to spend them crying into my pillow with a new broken heart.

"Aw, Viv. Don't cry." Ash bundles me into a hug. "It's like I said on Monday. Dillon telling you he loves you is huge. H.U.G.E."

"Don't make excuses for him. What he's doing is unacceptable after everything we've shared."

"You're right. He's hurting you, and he's a coward. It isn't okay, and I'm going to give him a piece of my mind when I next see him. I just want to explain why I think he's withdrawn. Dillon loves you, like *really* loves you, and you don't realize how big of a deal it is he said that. The only time he's ever told me he loves me is when I tried

316

to kill myself. He was holding me in his arms, crying and telling me he loved me. As far as I know, that's the only time he's told anyone he's loved them since he was a little kid."

"He doesn't even tell your mom?"

"Nope."

"That is really fucking sad." His family is big on the "I love yous." I have noticed Dillon never says it back, but I assumed he was just more private about it with his mom.

"I know." She rubs my back while I stare at the ceiling. "He's terrified." She snorts out a laugh, and I look at her, wondering how she finds any humor in this. "Sorry, I don't mean to laugh. I was just thinking how apt that song he wrote you is. He is literally running scared."

"He doesn't even remember he said it."

"Trust me, he remembers."

"What do I do?"

"You get your sexy Yankee arse into the shower, dress to impress, and then we're going to Whelans. You're going to get your man back."

I don't see Dillon before their set, but he sings every song for me, staring at my face as he belts out the lyrics. The crowd goes nuts when they debut "Terrify Me," and I'm glad he didn't mention me by name when he dedicated it to "his mot." I don't think my heart could take another direct hit. As soon as they finish, Dillon hands off his guitar, jumps off the stage, and stalks toward me. Without warning, he pulls me into his arms, hugging me tight. A sob escapes my mouth before I can stop it. "I'm sorry, Viv. I didn't mean to abandon you all week. It just hurts."

"How do you think I feel?"

"I can't bear the thought of you leaving. It's killing me inside."

"So, you thought you'd ghost me all week and start the breaking early?"

He moves us off to the side where it's quieter. "I don't know how to process this. It wasn't intentional. I was just all up in my feels, and I shut myself away, pouring my emotions onto the page." He sweeps his fingers across my face. "I thought it might be easier to go cold turkey, but I was wrong. I'm sorry. I'm no good at this stuff."

I cup his face, relieved to be back in his arms, even if it's only delaying the inevitable. "No one is, Dillon. There is no rule book for this kind of thing."

"I want to rewind time and do things differently," he blurts.

I jerk back. "Why would you say that? I wouldn't change a single thing about our time together except it'd be nice if you didn't give me emotional whiplash so much. But I know that's part of your charm. Part of who you are." Honestly? I'd even take his mood swings if it meant I was with him.

"I'm going to make it up to you. We're going to have the best few days. We still have time."

Dillon and I are inseparable over the following days, even more so than usual. We cling to one another, always finding ways to touch, and we largely stay confined to my apartment, spending hours tangled together in bed. Dillon's anger and frustration are most obvious when he's fucking me, venting his emotion through hard thrusts and rough touches that speak to my very soul. We are hangry for one another, punishing our bodies for the sins of our hearts and minds.

"Come with me," Dillon says on Sunday evening, dragging my lazy, melancholy butt off the couch and pulling me into the bathroom.

"What is this?" I stare at the tub with a physical pain in my chest. Scented steam rises from the water, tickling my nostrils. Rose petals float across the water, and soft music is playing in the background.

"I have plans for us tonight. I kicked Ash out. I'm commandeering the kitchen, and you're to get your beautiful self in the bath and relax."

"Jesus, Dillon. Are you truly trying to destroy me?"

He brushes a tear off my cheek. "Time is running out, Hollywood," he whispers. "I want our last night together to be memorable."

Toxic Gods has a booking tomorrow night which they tried to get out of, but couldn't, so this is it. I've been trying hard not to think about it all day, but my bad mood can attest to my failure.

"Take your time in the bath, and then get dolled up. But you're to stay in your room while I set things up. I'll come get you when I'm ready." He produces a glass of bubbly from behind his back, handing it to me.

I love you.

It's on the tip of my tongue. I want to say it so badly, but it's only going to make things worse. I can't stay in Ireland. I've got to return home. "Thank you." I kiss him softly. "You're the best."

I cry quietly in the bath, wishing things could be different, cursing my fragile heart for falling for someone I can't have. Even if there were a way for me to stay in Ireland, Dillon probably won't be here for much longer. Toxic Gods is going places. It's only a matter of time before his star explodes, and I can't go through that whole scene again.

I've got to let him go. For his sake and mine.

I just don't know how I'm going to do it.

"Don't peek," Dillon says a couple of hours later, leading me up the stairs to the roof with his hand over my eyes.

"I'm not," I lie, totally trying to squint through the gap in his fingers to see what he's done.

He brings us to a halt and removes his hand. "Surprise."

CHAPTER 58

"DILLON," I whisper, staring in amazement at the small marquee erected on the roof. Strings of colored lights decorate the interior, and the floor is covered in a myriad of vibrant patterned beanbags and large cushions. In the center is a low glossy black table set with candles and silverware. Incense wafts through the air from a few diffusers set up around the space. In the corner, a narrow rectangular table holds plates and covered silver platters.

"Do you like it?" he asks, and I realize I haven't said more than his name. He looks at me with so much vulnerability, and he seems so young in this moment, so unsure of himself.

I clutch his arm, smiling up at him. "I love it. This is amazing." I skim my eyes over his black button-up shirt and black pants, and my mouth waters. The sleeves of his shirt are rolled to the elbows, highlighting his gorgeous, strong muscular arms. He's tan from spending so much time outside with me this summer, and it looks good on him. "As are you." Grabbing his biceps, I press a long, lingering kiss on his lips. "You look so freaking hot."

Leading me inside, he kneels to remove my high heels so I can sit cross-legged on the large cushion in front of the table. "I cooked an Asian-themed meal so I thought we could eat like this," he says, looking nervous.

Leaning down, I kiss him. "This is fantastic. Thank you for going to so much trouble."

After an exquisite meal, all cooked by Dillon, I sip prosecco while he serenades me with his guitar and that husky voice I could listen to all day.

When it gets chilly, we head inside to my bedroom. Dillon clearly snuck in here when he said he was going to the bathroom because there are rose petals on the bed and the only light is from the various flickering candles strategically placed around the room. My half-packed luggage is propped against the wall, serving as a poignant reminder of my imminent departure. But I'm not thinking about that now. I want to enjoy every second of our last precious moments together.

Throwing my arms around him, I kiss him hard, devouring his mouth as my fingers pop the buttons on his shirt. I slide my hand under the band of his pants, finding him hard and warm, ready and waiting. Without speaking, I remove his pants, boxers, sneakers, and socks and crawl on my knees between his legs, taking him into my mouth.

His fingers weave in my hair as I suck and nibble on his straining length, wanting to savor every second. Dillon's gaze is brimming with emotion and burning with desire as I lavish attention on his dick.

Lifting me by the arms, he pulls me to standing, planting a firm kiss on my lips, sliding his tongue into my mouth while lowering the zipper on my dress. It falls to my feet, and I step out of it as Dillon scoops me into his arms, carrying me to the bed. He makes quick work of my bra and undies and begins licking and kissing a path along my skin, taking his time worshiping every part of my body.

There's a softness to his gaze, a tenderness to his touch, that is wholly new, and I'm enjoying this gradual sensual buildup until neither of us can take it anymore. Nudging my thighs apart, he holds himself still, his cock poised at my entrance. He leans down, brushing his nose against mine, planting a sweet kiss to one corner of my mouth, and then the other, before claiming my lips in the lightest kiss as he slowly and carefully inches inside me. He's not wearing a condom, but we stopped using them after Brittas Bay. Now I've felt him moving inside me without one I can't go back. I'm on the pill and he usually pulls out, as an added precaution, coming on my stomach or my breasts.

Every other time we've been together, it's been fucking. But not tonight. Tonight, Dillon makes slow sweet love to me, and if I wasn't completely in love with him before this, I certainly would be now. He is unhurried, teasing sensations from my body with rolling hips, sensual thrusts, and tender strokes. His lips skim across my face and my neck, while his hands roam my breasts, softly cupping their weight, before he gently sucks on my nipples as he moves inside me with utter devotion.

I don't even realize I'm crying until he kisses my tears. Then he's crying too.

How can my heart feel full of joy and pain at the same time? How is this happening when I have to leave and there is no promise of a future for us? What have I done to deserve such wicked suffering?

"Viv." He kisses me as he quickens his pace. "God, I don't ever want to stop feeling this."

"I know," I sob, throwing my arms around his neck and holding him close as my legs tighten around his waist. "This is the best feeling in the world."

We come together, bodies joined in every possible place, and we stay entangled in one another for a long time, both of us afraid to move, unwilling to break this connection.

Eventually, he pulls out of me, and we lie side by side, skin to skin, fingers laced together. He's wearing the saddest, most heartbreaking expression, and I feel something vital rupture inside me. Something inherent is imploding inside me in a way I've never felt.

"I love you," he blurts, and I simultaneously want to jump for joy and die.

No, Dillon. No. Please don't say it to my face. Don't make me say it back. It will destroy me to tell you I love you and then leave.

"Don't leave," he adds when I say nothing because I can't force my vocal cords to work. I'm in too much pain to speak. Tears cascade down my face. "Stay," he whispers. I cry again, my chest heaving as pain ravages my body, forcing every muscle to shudder and shake uncontrollably. His lips brush my ear. "Say I'm the one."

My heart cracks wide-open, and I want to scream yes! I want to tell him he *is* the one. That I long to stay with him. But I can't. It isn't possible. There are too many obstacles in the way. Lifting my tearstained face to his, I plead with him to understand. "I can't. I'm sorry."

I watch him shutting down. Bit by bit, the wall goes up, and he retreats behind it. Nodding tersely, he swings his legs out of bed. "Then I guess that's it."

I sit up, panicked and confused. "Please don't go. I thought you were going to stay tonight?"

He cracks out a bitter laugh as he pulls his clothes on. "Why delay the inevitable? We might as well do this now." Shoving his feet in his sneakers, he turns around with his pants on and his shirt unbuttoned. I cower at the aggression and rage painted across his face, pulling the covers up over me to shield my body, feeling suddenly vulnerable. "It's not like you really care. If you did, you'd want to stay."

"I do!" I stand, wrapping the sheet around myself. "I wish I could stay here with you. I swear I do. But it's not possible, Dillon."

"Anything is possible if you want it badly enough."

"That's not fair!"

"What's not fair is you making me love you and then leaving to go back to that prick!" he roars in my face, spittle flying in the air, and I take an automatic step back, plastering my back to the wall.

"That's not what I'm doing," I protest.

"Bull-fucking-shit." An ugly sneer slides across his mouth. It's one I haven't seen since the early days. "You're pathetic. Crawling back to him after he's probably spent months fucking his costar."

"Reeve has nothing to do with this. He won't even be in L.A." I actually have no clue what his schedule is like, but I'm pretty sure that's the truth. He's in hot demand, and his schedule is usually jam-packed.

He jabs his finger in my face. "You can't even admit it to yourself."

"Dillon, my entire life is back in L.A. My classes are starting in ten days. I've signed up for an evening costume design course. I have taken out a lease with Audrey on an apartment near UCLA. My parents are there."

"You could transfer to Trinity permanently, but you never even tried, did you?"

"The thought did cross my mind."

He harrumphs. "Yet you did nothing about it."

Anger simmers under my skin. "Hang on here a second. You never gave me any indication until right now that you wanted me to stay! Do you think I'm a mind reader?"

"Cop the fuck on, Hollywood. We both know what we're feeling. Or maybe I was the only one who fell." He purses his lips in disgust as he buttons his shirt.

"You know that's not true, and what difference would it make anyway, Dillon?

You're not going to be in Dublin for much longer. The band will take off, and you'll go with them. You'll be gone for years, and there'll be groupies and women coming out of the woodwork, and I'll be pushed aside. We'd try to make it work, but it wouldn't. I know. I've already been there."

His fists clench at his side, and a muscle pops in his jaw. I have never seen him so angry, and I'm a little bit scared. "Know one thing, Vivien. I am *not* Reeve Lancaster!" he yells, and I wrap my arms around myself. "I would *never* cheat on you. *Never.*"

He walks toward the door, and I stand rooted to the spot in so much pain I can barely breathe.

How did a perfect night become such a nightmare?

His shoulders slump as he turns around in the doorway. All the fight has left his face. "I would have stayed for you, Vivien. I would have fought for you. No matter what happens, know it was real." He shakes his head sadly. "Goodbye, Hollywood. I hope everything works out for you."

CHAPTER 59

MY TEAR DUCTS ARE BROKEN. Worse than they were when Reeve splintered my heart. I can't stop crying. I haven't been able to since Dillon walked out of my bedroom last night. Pain is an ever-present pressure on my chest and lump blocking my throat. Spindly fingers have a vise-grip on my heart, and they refuse to let go, squeezing and squeezing until I can barely breathe. Anxiety and heartache kept me awake most of last night. At least it might mean I can sleep on the plane. My flight leaves at four in the morning, but I have to be at the airport by one, so tonight is officially my last night on Irish soil.

Packing the last of my things in my suitcase, I glance at my cell, but Dillon still hasn't returned any of my calls or messages. Although he was cruel last night and he said a lot of hurtful things, I know he lashed out because I hurt him first. I froze when he told me he loved me, and I was wrong not to say it back. I was wrong to keep that truth locked up inside me for so long instead of letting it out. Maybe if I had opened that conversation earlier, he would have asked me to stay, and we might have found a way of making it work. I'm not really sure how, but we never gave us a chance to find out.

It's too late to do anything about that now, but I can rectify at least one thing.

Ash props her hip against the door. "Are you sure about this?" she asks, her eyes skimming over my empty room. She's moving in with Jamie at the end of the week when the rental agreement officially ends here. They have found their own one-bedroom place, and it's a big deal for them. I'm happy for my friend, and I hope Jay doesn't fuck things up. She's going to need him in the coming weeks because I know she will miss me as much as I'll miss her.

"Yes. I can't leave things how they were last night."

"I'm worried." She pushes off the door, entering my room. "He was so drunk and so angry last night. I've seen my brother press the self-destruct button before. It's not pretty, and he's liable to do or say anything."

"I appreciate the heads-up, but I've still got to do this."

"I don't want to see you hurt." She pulls me into a hug, and we cling to one another. "I am going to miss you so much. You better phone me every day."

"I will, and I sent my US number to your cell as I won't be using my Irish cell anymore."

"Are you sure you can't stay?" she asks, shucking out of our embrace.

"I don't see how it's possible." I push air out of my mouth. "I mean, I could probably arrange a permanent transfer to Trinity and come back, but what good is me being here if Dillon is off traveling with the band?"

"You know he's got concerns about going to the US, and that's even if this meeting with the A&R guy pans out. It might turn into nothing."

"I doubt that. The guys are way too fucking talented to be passed over forever. If it doesn't happen now, it will happen at some point."

"He'd drop out for you."

My eyes widen. "He said that?"

She shakes her head. "He doesn't have to say it for me to know it's the truth. I know he would choose you over the band in a heartbeat."

"I wouldn't want him to do that. I wouldn't want him to pass up such an amazing opportunity for me. It would come back to haunt us, and I couldn't live with that kind of guilt."

"You could go with them. Switch to online classes and travel the world with the band. That's what I'm going to do if it takes off for them."

"You have it all worked out." I smile sadly.

Her hands land on my shoulders. "I am the last person in the world who has her shit together, but it's not insurmountable. You can make this work if you want to. I just hate to see you both miserable and hurting. He loves you. You love him. That should be enough."

"It should be, but it often isn't." Of course, my mind instantly wanders to Reeve. I thought our love was enough to weather any storm, to climb any mountain, but it wasn't.

"Don't bite my head off for saying this, but is your past with Reeve clouding your judgment when it comes to Dil?"

"Undoubtedly," I agree without hesitation. "But I can't help how I feel. I took a risk once before, and it burned me in a bad way. Even if it was possible to travel with Dillon, there will still be the groupies and the media, and I don't think I can do that again."

"They'll be there when you return to L.A."

"They don't care about me anymore. I'm no longer newsworthy."

"You will be if you get back with Reeve." Her eyes narrow a little.

"I have no plans to do that." Truthfully, I don't know what will happen with Reeve and me when I return home, and I don't have the brain capacity to contemplate it now.

"All I've heard about Reeve, from you and Audrey, tells me he's not going to give up on you. You have history and a bucketload of shared memories. What chance does Dillon stand against that?"

"Ash, stop." I rub a tense spot between my brows. "Don't do this. I don't want to fight with you before I leave. This has never been a competition between them. I love them both. You know that. I really do love your brother." My heart cracks, and a sob bursts from my lips. "I love him so much, and that's why I'm stepping into the lion's den tonight. I'm going to tell him what I should have told him last night."

"I'm sorry." She hugs me again. "I don't want to hurt you, but I will always ship *Dillien*."

A laugh rips from my throat before I can stop it. "I can't believe you gave us a ship name."

"You deserve one, because the love you two share is *epic*. I'm a hopeless romantic now, in case you missed that memo." She loops her arm through mine, tugging me into the kitchen. "Let's do drinkies before we leave for Bruxelles."

"I feel sick," I admit, stopping outside the door to the pub a few hours later. My bags are all packed at the apartment, and I just need to be back there around midnight to get changed before Micheál picks me up.

"I'm here for you." Ash threads her arm through mine. "Just remember he loves you and he's hurting."

Fighting nerves, I push through the door and enter the pub.

"Don't forget the asshole gene is part of his DNA too," she shouts in my ear as we're immediately accosted with laughter and loud conversation.

Rock music blares out of the speakers, and the place is thronged. Then again, summer in Dublin City is usually like this. Bars and restaurants are teeming most every night. This is only the third time Toxic Gods has played here, but it's one of my favorite Dublin pubs.

"Fuck, shit, piss." Ash clings to my arm, and my eyes swivel in the same direction as hers.

My heart gives out the second I locate Dillon, spread-eagled on a chair at a table in the back, with Aoife perched on his lap. All the blood drains from my face, and my instinct is to run back out the door, but I won't give him or her the satisfaction. I am strong and brave, and I will hold my head up high as I do what I came to do.

Acid churns in my gut, and an anxious fluttering sensation creeps along my chest as I grip Ash's arm tighter and walk toward the band's table on wobbly legs. Pain stabs me in the heart, like a thousand fine pinpricks, as Aoife wraps her arms around Dillon's neck, bending down to dot kisses along his jaw and his neck. He isn't touching her. He isn't paying her any attention, sprawled in the chair, gripping the armrest in one hand and bottle of beer in another, shooting me that annoyingly smug grin as I step toward him.

"Well, well, look what the cat dragged in?" He lifts his beer to his lips.

Aoife fixes me with a gloating look, and I'd love nothing more than to yank her from his lap and slam her pretty face into the table.

Higher moral ground. The angel on one shoulder helps me to remain calm and remember what I came for. "Could I speak to you in private?"

He glares at me with naked hostility, and I'm reminded of our initial meeting. "Nah." His nose scrunches up. "I said all I needed to say last night."

"Well, I didn't." I wet my dry lips.

"Don't you have a plane to catch, Hollywood?"

"Dillon, please."

Aoife giggles, running her hand back and forth across his chest, and I want to break every one of her fingers.

"I don't know why you're laughing, bitch," Ash says. "You know he's only using you to piss Viv off. He doesn't give a shit about you. He loves Vivien, not you."

"Shut the fuck up, Ash," Dillon hisses, pointing his bottle at her.

"Don't talk to her like that," Jamie barks, standing and moving to Ash's side.

I let go of her, letting her boyfriend slide a protective arm around her.

"You are seriously out of line, Dil," Ro says, pinning his brother with a cutting look. "You need to apologize to Ash and Viv."

"Still trying to get in her knickers, eh, little bro?" Dillon glances at his phone. "She's got a few hours. Be my guest." He waves his hands in my direction. "Knock yourself out."

He hits the bull's-eye, smashing my heart into smithereens with his cruel, dismissive words. I need to do what I came here to do and leave. Ignoring Dillon and the tramp, I turn to the others. "I just wanted to say goodbye in person, and I hope everything works out with the band. It's been great meeting you all. Ireland more than exceeded my expectations, and a lot of that was down to you guys."

Dillon snorts, and Aoife giggles, but I ignore them. One by one, the guys get up and hug me. Ro's girlfriend gives me a little wave, but she's never been a big fan of me anyway. She probably can't wait to see the back of me. Catriona surprises me, apologizing for not being a better friend and wishing me well back home.

"I know this isn't the last I've seen of you," I tell Jamie as he hugs me. "Whether you're in L.A. with the band or visiting me with Ash, I expect I'll see your annoying face again."

"You betcha, Hollywood."

His use of Dillon's pet name sends a fresh wave of pain hurtling through my chest, but I put a brave face on it. "He's hurting bad," he whispers in my ear. "She's nothing but a tool to piss you off. Don't buy into it. He loves you big-time, Viv."

I squeeze his arm, grateful for his words. Maybe there is hope for Jamie Fleming after all. I sure hope so, for my friend's sake.

Turning around, I face Dillon again. I wanted to say this in private, but I'm not ashamed to say it in public either. When I walk out of this door, I need to know I am leaving with my head held high.

Aoife gloats like the cat that got the cream, eyeing me with smug haughtiness as she dusts kisses all over his face. I ignore her the best I can, staring Dillon straight in the eye. "I should have said this last night, but I froze. Actually, I should've said it when I first realized it." My heart jackhammers behind my rib cage, and butterflies swoop into my chest. "I love you, Dillon. I love you more than words could ever express. For as long as I live, I will never forget you."

CHAPTER 60

MY LOWER LIP WOBBLES, and tears threaten as I stare at his impassive face. I wasn't expecting a reply, not really, but I was expecting to see some kind of emotion on this face. This blank, emotionless reaction hurts more than anything. Spinning around, I give a little wave to the guys, pretending I don't notice their pitiful expressions. Ro and Ash look like they're ready to rip Dillon limb from limb. "Take care, everyone." Somehow, I force my legs to move, putting one foot in front of the other.

"Thanks for the sex, Hollywood! It was fun while it lasted. Say hi to Reeve for me," Dillon shouts after me, hammering the final nail in the coffin.

I barely make it out the front door before I throw up, emptying the contents of my stomach all over the cobblestone path. Tears stream down my face as I retch.

"He's not worth it," Ash says, crouching down beside me a few minutes later. She rubs her hand up and down my back. "He was a total prick in there to you, and I told him that. I want to kick his arse all over town. I have never been more disappointed in my brother than I am right now."

"It doesn't matter." I straighten up, wiping my mouth with the back of my sleeve. "I said what I came to say, and I'm ready to go home now."

For the first time, I really feel those words. I want to return to L.A. and put as much distance between me and Dillon as possible. I want my mom. I need her to hold me in her arms and tell me everything will be all right.

"I'm proud of you, Viv. That took huge guts. You're a true princess and my hero." Ash hands me a bottle of water, and I rinse my mouth out. "We can say goodbye here," I tell her. "I know you want to see the band."

She thumps me gently on the arm. "Don't be stupid. I'm coming with you. We'll say goodbye at the apartment, like we planned." Ash wanted to come to the airport, but I asked her not to. Saying goodbye to Audrey at LAX only added to my pain back in January, and I'm keen to avoid that this time. Plus, my flight is at an ungodly hour. No sense in Ash hanging around Dublin Airport until four a.m.

We grab a taxi, and I let my friend comfort me on the silent ride back to our apartment. When we get home, Ash gives me some space to call Audrey while she sets about making us something to eat. She's worried now I puked up my dinner. I don't have the heart to tell her I doubt I could eat and they'll be plying me with food and drink in first class. I know she needs to do this, so I let her.

Audrey picks up on the fourth ring. "You're not coming back, are you? You're staying with him," she blurts before I've gotten a word out.

I crank out a harsh laugh in between sobs. "You've got that all wrong. I can't get home quick enough."

"Oh no, Viv. What's happened?"

I tell her everything, sobbing and choking over the words as tears roll down my face, ruining my makeup.

"Fuck, Viv. I'm so sorry. You sound as bad as you did when Reeve and you broke up."

"I can't do this again," I cry. "I can't take this heartache again."

Silence descends on her end, and the only sound is the permanent tearing of my heart as I cry my eyes out to my bestie.

"You really love him," she says when I compose myself.

"I do," I whisper hoarsely.

"More than Reeve?"

I don't answer for a few minutes. I won't deny I've had similar thoughts these past couple of weeks as I've contemplated returning home and what that means. "I love them both in different ways. Both of them speak to my soul."

"I feel guilty. I had written Dillon off, believing it wasn't really that serious, but I was wrong. I see that it is. I still think you need to hear Reeve out, and the selfish part of me wants you two to fix things so it can be like old times with the four of us all together."

"It can never be like old times. That ship has sailed." We're in different places now. Logistically and metaphorically speaking. And we are different people.

"If you love Dillon, Vivien. If you really love him and he's the one, then fight for him."

"He doesn't want me to."

"Bullshit. He told you his truths last night. He's hurt and lashing out. You should still give him shit for that Aoife stunt, but fight for your man if he's the one you want."

"I did that before, and look where it got me."

"I can't believe I'm saying this, but Dillon isn't Reeve. If he meant what he said last night, he's prepared to put you first in a way Reeve didn't when he got his big opportunity." There's a pregnant pause while we both stop to process her words. "If he's not the one, if Reeve is, get on that plane and don't look back. But if Dillon is the one, you can't leave without making that clear to him. Otherwise, it will haunt you for the rest of your life."

After we hang up, I write a long letter to Dillon, telling him everything I should have said weeks ago. I'm going to drop the letter off at his place on the way to the airport. Pubs close early in Ireland on Monday, so I know the guys will be back at their place by midnight, giving Dillon enough time to come and get me. I've told him the ball is in his court now. I'm not chasing him. I told him I loved him in front of everyone, so he knows where my head is at. If he wants me to stay, he needs to come to the airport and stop me from getting on that plane.

I don't tell Ash my plans, because I know she won't be able to help interfering. If Dillon wants me, I need to know he's acting of his own free will and not because his sister is putting pressure on him.

I manage to swallow a few mouthfuls of the gorgeous chicken pasta Ash made before pushing it aside. "I have something for you, and I need a favor," I say, sipping my water.

"What is it?" Ash looks as glum as I feel, and I hope my gift will cheer her up.

I drop the keys to the rental in her palm. "The car is yours. I bought it and put it in your name."

"Get the fuck out!" Her mouth opens and closes like a fish out of water. "Why would you do that?"

"Because you're my bestie. I love you, and I'm going to miss you. Plus, I know how much you hate the smelly bus. This way, you'll be able to pop back home and see your folks whenever you want."

She bursts out crying, flinging herself at me. "You're the best friend I've ever had, Viv, and it's not because you bought me a car, you crazy bitch." Sniffling, she eases back, swiping her tears away. "You have helped me more than you realize. I see your strength and your humility and your amazing heart, and it inspires me to be a better person."

"You *are* a good person, Ash. One of the best I know."

"I don't think I've ever had a true friend before you. I don't have this bond with Cat. I can tell you anything, and I know you'll never judge. I will miss you more than words."

"This isn't goodbye, Ash. Only goodbye for now." Reeve's face appears in my mind's eye, and I hear him telling me that back in January. A pang of longing sweeps over me, and what I wouldn't give for one of Reeve's hugs now.

"I am seriously in shock." Ash tosses the keys in her palm. "I can't believe you bought me a car."

"You're welcome. I feel happier knowing you're not risking life and limb taking the bus," I joke, trying to bolster my mood. "I need one last favor."

"Anything. You know that."

Walking to my room, I retrieve the special edition Fender from my closet.

She gasps when I arrive back in the kitchen with it. "I got this for Dillon. I had hoped our last night would go differently, and I had planned on giving it to him myself. Will you see he gets it?"

"He doesn't fucking deserve it," she snaps, still mad at her brother.

Taking it out of the case, I run my fingers over his name etched into the wood.

"Jesus, Viv. It's beautiful. He's going to feel like such an ass when I give this to him." She folds her arms across her chest. "If it didn't have his name on it, I'd probably have given this to Jamie."

I burst out laughing. "At least you're honest."

"Then I'd take it back off him when he did something to piss me off and give it to my brother when he redeemed himself." She traces her fingers over the guitar strap where Toxic Gods is embedded in the leather.

"Look after him for me," I say in case he doesn't come through as I hope.

"I will if you promise to look after yourself."

"Always." If there's one thing I've learned on this journey of self-discovery, it's that I can't care for anyone if I don't care for myself first.

"This isn't goodbye, Viv." Ash hugs me close. "It *is* only goodbye for now. I feel that deep in my bones as if it's been ordained by God himself."

I don't know if she's right. I guess time will tell.

CHAPTER 61

DILLON DOESN'T SHOW. I dropped the letter in his mailbox, and I know there were people inside because music and laughter vibrated through the door. Someone would have found it and given it to him. I frantically pace the floor in the boarding area, glancing every few seconds at the clock on the wall, peering down the hallway, hoping to see his white-blond head racing toward me, but it never does. I wait to board until the very last second, only doing so when the flight attendant states the flight *will* leave without me if I don't go now. Momentarily, I consider skipping the flight and returning to Dillon's apartment, but I can't. I laid my heart on the line tonight. It was his turn to prove he meant what he said Sunday night, and he's failed me.

I manage to hold the tears at bay until the plane lifts in the air, leaving Ireland and my love behind, and I can't contain my heartache any longer. Clutching Dillon's pillow to my chest, I sob to my heart's content, uncaring I'm making a scene. Thumbing through the photo album he bought me only makes it worse. Dillon helped me choose every pic, and every photo holds a precious memory. Burying my face in the album, I cry louder, and it truly feels like my heart is broken beyond repair this time.

Hysterical laughter breaks through my snotty tears as a thought lands in my mind. How ironic I spent the plane ride to Ireland sobbing over Reeve, and now I'm just as heartbroken leaving the Emerald Isle, crying endless tears over another man.

Only I could do this to myself.

Is it possible to be both healed and wounded? To feel whole and broken at the same time? Because that's how I feel. Like the part of me that was broken and lost on the way over has been mended—Dillon's love played a big part in helping me to reach that point—but now other parts of me are damaged, and I'm feeling more lost than ever.

The flight attendant moves me to a private cabin, keeping a close eye on me the entire time. She told me she has a daughter, around my age, and I can tell she's worried about me. She looks at me—crying hysterically as I listen to Toxic Gods songs on my phone, clutching the pillow Dillon bought me, scribbling manically in my journal, and rubbing my fingers repeatedly over my Claddagh necklace—like I might need to be committed. Perhaps I do, because this time, it feels like there is no coming back from this loss.

I knock back the Valium Ash snuck me before I left, and eventually I fall asleep.

When we finally land at LAX, I'm all cried out and numb. The relief I should feel at being back on Californian soil is hidden behind a wall of grief and pain. I move as if on autopilot, shoving my oversized shades over my eyes to disguise the state I'm in, shuffling through customs and out into the terminal, moving toward the man holding a placard with my name.

I know my parents would greet me if they could, but even at this early hour, they'd be spotted by fans or the paparazzi who hang out at the airport, and I don't need that shit the second I arrive. It's strange Max, our full-time driver, isn't the one picking me up though. This man doesn't say much as he pushes my luggage cart outside to a sleek black Mercedes, setting it against the trunk, before opening the back passenger door for me.

I slip inside, gasping when I see who's waiting for me.

"Hey, beautiful." Reeve angles his body so he's facing me. "You are a sight for sore eyes."

I can only stare at him in shock. His hair is back to normal, the brown strands threaded with natural blond highlights, and his jawline is smooth, showcasing his tan skin and the beauty mark over his lip I love so much. He's wearing a blinding-white designer T-shirt over khaki shorts and his old Vans. The golf watch I bought him for his seventeenth birthday is strapped to his wrist. Familiar blue eyes stare at me with love and hope, and it's like looking at the Reeve of my past. The boy who was my everything before he became the man who took an axe to my heart. But none of that matters right now, because he's here, and I'm glad to see him.

I fling my arms around his neck, blinking back tears when his arms automatically lock around my back. "I'm happy to see you." It's the truth. His warmth and the familiar scent of his cologne reminds me of so many happy times. I ease out of his arms, my eyes skimming over his handsome face. "You look good."

"So do you." His smile is wide, his eyes happy and relieved as they drift briefly to my lips.

Butterflies flutter gently in my chest. "What are you doing here? Where are Mom and Dad?" I was expecting my parents to be waiting in the car for me, and I don't know what he has said or done to get them to agree to this.

"I've spoken with your parents a lot this summer, and we're building bridges. I asked them if I could pick you up, explaining my reasons, and they agreed." Reeve scoots closer, his knee brushing against mine through my jeans. "I missed you so fucking much."

I missed him too, but I was also busy with my new boyfriend, so reiterating his sentiment doesn't feel right. Especially when I spent a large early portion of my trip brokenhearted. I can't forget what Reeve did or how his actions made me feel.

Confusion swirls through my mind, clouding my brain. I hang my head, unable to do this now.

"Viv, look at me. I need to see your eyes, baby." He tilts my chin up with one finger, and I don't stop him when he removes my shades, revealing my red-rimmed bloodshot eyes and tearstained splotchy skin.

His Adam's apple jumps in his throat. Fear and pain are etched upon his face as he stares at me. My chest heaves with powerful emotion as I look at him, hating he can see through me so easily but loving that he does too. Reeve knows me better than anyone, as I know him. You can't spend virtually your whole life with someone and not know them inside and out.

The protective layer around my heart thaws a little as our connection crackles in the tiny gap between us. Loving Reeve has always been this all-consuming entity with no start and no end. All the same feelings are there, hidden behind a shit ton of complexity and confusion.

"Am I too late?" he whispers, tentatively reaching out and cupping one side of my face.

On instinct, I lean into the warmth of his soft palm, contemplating how to reply to that question.

"Viv?" His concerned gaze scrutinizes mine. "Have I lost you for good?"

I can't answer that when I'm so lost within myself. "I don't have the mental or emotional capacity for this conversation right now, Reeve." Tears fill my eyes. "I feel lost all over again." A tear leaks out of one eye, and he pulls me into his arms without hesitation. My head drops against his chest, and I let him comfort me even though I know I probably shouldn't.

"It's okay, baby." He strokes my hair as his other arm bands tight around my body, keeping me flush to his chest. "I'm here now, and I'm going to make everything better." He instructs the driver to leave, and the privacy screen goes up. "I know you're not in the mood for talking, but can you just listen?" I nod against his chest. "I need you to know I still love you. I've never stopped loving you. I wanted to hop on a plane to Ireland at least once a week, but I promised I'd give you space to work through things, and I wanted to keep my word."

A gnarly sort of sound escapes my mouth, and I jerk out of his hold. "This is all sounding far too familiar and not in a good way."

"You are right, but things are different now. I'm me again, Viv." Taking my hand, he threads our fingers together, and fiery tingles shoot up my arm. His touch still affects me, but I'm not surprised. It's not like I ever fell out of love with him. It would've been so much easier if I had, but I know I will love Reeve Lancaster all my life.

Doesn't mean we'll be together though.

"What does that mean?"

He tucks a piece of my hair behind my ear. "You were right about everything, and I should have believed you. You have always had my back, and instead of letting you in, I shut you out. I'm disgusted with myself." He shakes his head, sighing. "I made a lot of bad decisions. I chose to believe the wrong people and it cost me the most precious thing in the world—*you*. I'm not excusing my behavior. Not at all. I'm just trying to explain how I ended up in such a bad place. At the start, being away from you unsettled me more than I could have imagined. I was overwhelmed with everything expected of me on set and really feeling my age. The other actors were all older and more experienced in movies and life. I felt lost and young, and I was definitely out of my comfort zone. Bianca and Cassidy were pushing me to break up with you, and the stress of that combined with the movie responsibility and the long hours took its toll. Saffron—"

I growl at the mention of her name. It's an automatic reaction, one I can't control.

"I know you hate her with good reason. I hate her too, but I need to tell you everything. You need to know it all, and I can't not mention her name."

"Fine." I clip the word out because I want to hear what he has to say. I'm stronger and wiser now, and I won't give her the power she once held over me.

"She suggested I pop a few uppers. She said it was how everyone coped with long shifts on set. She said everyone was doing it. I'd seen the guys snorting coke, so I stupidly believed her." His tongue darts out, wetting his lips. "I hid the true extent of my drug use from you because I was embarrassed. I had always been anti-drugs, as you know. It was a slippery slope, and I was plunging headfirst down it. I know now that I should have confided everything to you, but I didn't want to see the disappointment in your eyes. I wanted you to be proud of me. I wanted Dad to be proud of me."

He briefly closes his eyes. "I should have gone to your mom and sought her advice before signing that new contract, but I was already fucked up from pills and coke and Saffron was mouthing in my ear, saying fake relationships were the norm and if you loved me you wouldn't have a problem with it."

I lean my head back against the headrest, wondering if my parents know any hitmen. I would really love to put a bullet between that conniving bitch's eyes.

"I'm doing all the things I should have done from the start," he continues before I can question him on what exactly has gone on between him and his costar. Or ex-costar now, I suppose. "I will explain everything I've discovered back at my place. For now, I need you to know I'm done with letting assholes manipulate me. I've cut ties with Bianca. I have a new supportive team around me who genuinely cares about me and my best interests. I've signed with Margaret, and Edwin Chambers is my publicist. I pulled out of the movie I was due to film this summer so I could get to the bottom of things and make amends," he cryptically adds.

"What about her? I need to know what happened, and I don't want you holding anything back. This is your only chance to fess up, Reeve. You're lucky I'm even giving you a chance to explain."

"I know that, Viv, and I'm grateful."

"Have you fucked her?"

Slowly, he nods, and I close my eyes as pain jumps up and slaps me across the face. "Have you fucked other women since we broke up?" I ask, forcing my eyes open. I need to look at him when he says this to know if he's telling me the truth.

He vehemently shakes his head. "Nope. I haven't so much as looked at another woman. The only woman I want is you." He rubs the back of his head. "With Saffron, it was only one time," he rushes to assure me. "In Mexico, when those pictures were taken. I was high and drunk, and I have no recollection of it. All I know is I woke up beside her, and it was obvious what we'd done."

Tears pool in his eyes. "I threw up the second I realized the truth and what it meant for us. That fucking bitch laughed. She stood over me while I puked my guts up in the toilet, laughing and smiling while snorting a line." Anger flares in his eyes. "She had the audacity to assume we would be together after that, but I made it abundantly clear I would never have fucked her if I'd been sober and I wanted her nowhere near me. I went to the studio and told them I would walk if they didn't keep her away from me when we weren't filming. I told them the only way I'd promote *Sweet Retribution* was if she was nowhere near me."

That matches what Audrey told me a few months ago, and I know he's telling me the truth. It's written all over his face. The knowledge he only fucked her once helps a lot. Given the circumstances, the fact we were broken up, and I was already with Dillon means I can't hold it over him. It wouldn't be fair to do that to him.

"They agreed, and that pissed her off," he continues. "I found out afterwards she had staged the whole thing. Had a photographer hiding close by to take the money shot. She timed it perfectly to ruin your birthday. I'm so sorry."

"What a pity you hadn't done that the first time it was obvious she was interfering." There is no heat behind my words, and though it still hurts, especially that public kiss shared around the world, I have learned to deal with it. Sheila, my therapist in Ireland, helped me to process all my feelings, and I've come to accept what has happened. I will never forget it or how it made me feel, but I can discuss it now and not want to scream in a fit of rage.

"I should have. Everything would've been different if I hadn't been so weak. So stupid. I failed myself as much as I failed you." He twirls a lock of my hair around his finger, and fierce determination washes over his face. "I won't ever fail you again, Viv. If you give me one more chance, I will prove to you I'm worthy of it."

CHAPTER 62

I CAN SEE he really means that, but I can't just accept his word for it. Reeve has a long way to go before he proves himself to me, and that's if I even want that. I am so confused right now. My head is a complete mess over two different guys, and I don't know whether I am coming or going. Jet lag isn't helping either. I deliberately don't respond to his statement. "You have changed," I murmur, seeing him in a slightly different light.

"I've worked hard these past few months to right my wrongs and focus on the things that matter. In case it's not clear, that means you first and then my career. I've spent so long trying to win my dad's affection I didn't realize I was taking yours for granted. Your parents too. Losing all of you was the wake-up call I needed to pull my head out of my ass. Fuck my dad. I'm done trying to please him. Ironically, he's actually made more of an effort, but it's too little, too late for me."

The car pulls into the underground parking lot of a low-rise apartment building, and I frown as I look out of the window. "Where are we?"

"My apartment in Pacific Palisades."

"You own an apartment?"

He nods. "It's only a stopgap. I found a couple of perfect sites to build our home, but I wouldn't dream of buying anything without your involvement."

I squirm on the seat. This is too much heavy. "Reeve…"

He flashes me a boyish smile and my heart thump-thumps behind my chest cavity. "I know I'm probably coming on too strong. I promised myself I wouldn't do that, but I'm going to win you back, Viv. I'm not giving up." His smile fades a little. "Not even if you tell me that Irish guy has a fighting chance."

Pain eviscerates my heart and punches me in the lungs, and I struggle to breathe. For a while there, I'd actually managed to forget about Dillon.

"Fuck." Reeve gently grips my arms. "I've got you, Viv. Breathe in and out. Nice and slow." He breathes with me until I've regained my composure. His eyes lower to my collarbone, and his face pales. "Did he buy you that?" he asks, and I glance down, only now realizing my fingers are stroking my Claddagh necklace. I nod, and he squeezes his eyes shut.

The car glides to a halt, and when his eyes pop open, they are full of pain. I should probably feel some modicum of pleasure to have inflicted even an ounce of the agony he inflicted on me, but I get no joy out of seeing him hurt. "Do you love him?" he whispers, piercing me with an anguished look.

I'm not going to hide anything, and I have done nothing wrong. "Yes."

He buries his head in his hands, and the urge to comfort him is riding me hard, but I don't move a muscle. After a couple minutes of awkward silence, he lifts his head, spearing me with fearful blue eyes. "Do you still love me?"

"Yes. I do. I love you."

Relief floods his face. "I can work with that."

"Reeve…"

"I know, Viv. You don't need to say it. I know you, remember?"

Taking my hand, he helps me out of the car, and I let him hold me as we take the elevator to the top of his apartment building.

"I got the penthouse, but it's not huge. At least, not compared to where we both grew up." Taking his keys out of his pocket, he opens the door.

"I lived in a penthouse in Dublin, and I actually loved that it was smaller. Much easier to clean."

"I can't wait to hear about your trip. What is Ireland like?" he asks, pulling me into a large bright open living space. On the right is a massive kitchen with white cabinets, stainless-steel appliances, and dappled white-and-gray-marble countertops. A matching island unit separates the kitchen from the dining table, and beyond that is the living room.

"It was amazing. I'll tell you all about it, but wow. This view is to die for." I march past the gray leather sectional toward the far window. All the windows in this space are floor-to-ceiling windows offering incredible views of the Pacific Ocean in the near distance.

"I bought this place for the view," he states, coming to stand alongside me. "I probably should've bought a place in Beverly Hills or West Hollywood to be closer to the studios, but I wanted to be near the ocean. Now that I'm clean and sober I've taken up running again, and I jog every morning at five a.m. down at Santa Monica Pier."

"Clean and sober?" I inquire, looking sideways at him.

"I attended an outpatient rehab clinic for a couple months to wean myself off all the shit I was doing. I saw a therapist there too."

"It was that bad? Why didn't I see it?"

"It was hella bad after that photo surfaced. I reached a real low point, but ultimately, it was a turning point. It was at that juncture I decided to turn my life around. As for why you didn't see it—I didn't want you to see it, Viv. And, before you ask, I didn't do much shit when I was with you. I didn't need to." He softens his voice, brushing his fingers across my cheek. "You're the only drug I need."

"No drug is healthy, Reeve. They're all addictive and damaging to your health."

"Except you. You were always good for me. I was a fucking fool to have vented my frustration at you instead of confiding in you and letting you help me make the right decisions. I've grown up a lot these past few months. I missed you like crazy." He traps my face in his palms. "You're so fucking beautiful, Vivien. I have missed your gorgeous face."

Staring into Reeve's handsome face, being back in L.A. with him, I realize I've really missed him too.

"Do you think you can ever forgive me?"

I circle my hands around his wrists. "I already have." He arches a brow, looking shocked. "I needed to forgive you to heal. I saw a therapist in Ireland, and she helped me to that realization. I know you didn't intentionally set out to hurt me, Reeve. I'm angry you made so many stupid decisions. I'm mad you turned to drugs and that bitch instead of me, but hearing your explanation helps me to understand it a little better."

He moves to kiss me, and I jerk back out of his hold, raising a hand. "That doesn't magically solve everything. You still betrayed me, and that's not something I can forget in a hurry. Earning my trust again will not be easy, and I can't promise you anything, Reeve. You don't own my full heart anymore, and I'm a bit of a hot mess now, in case you didn't notice."

"I know I have a lot to do to prove my intentions are true. I need to work hard to regain your trust, but I'm going to do it. I've already set things in motion, and I won't stop until I've got you back." He closes the gap between us again, gently pulling me into his arms. "I can't exist in this world without you, Vivien Grace Mills. I've tried, and it's not worth living if you aren't there by my side."

Romantic Reeve may yet be the death of me.

My tummy rumbles, saving my bacon.

"You must be tired, and you're clearly hungry. Sit. Let me make you something to eat."

"I got some sleep on the plane, but I didn't eat much." I couldn't stomach food, but I feel like I could eat now. "I need to stay awake to reset my body clock," I say, stifling a yawn. "That will be challenging."

I randomly scroll through the TV, flicking through channels, while Reeve putters around in the kitchen. Twenty minutes later, we are enjoying gorgeous spicy chicken wraps from the decent-sized balcony off to one side of his apartment. My nostrils twitch, and I soak up the sun and the hint of salty sea air. "California sun, oh, how I've missed you." I lean back in my chair, patting my full stomach.

"You *are* looking a little pasty," Reeve quips, and I flip him the bird. "I'm really glad you're home," he quietly adds, his adoring gaze raking over me. "You look good, Viv."

"I am good." It's not really a lie. Setting my newly rebroken heart aside, I am in a good place.

"I love seeing you here. I knew when I was buying this place you'd love it. And wait until you see the properties I've earmarked for our forever house. They will blow your mind. Did you even look at the architect plans before you returned your birthday gift?" The words fly from his mouth with urgency.

"Reeve, enough with the heavy. Please. I've had the most horrendous forty-eight hours. Can't we just chat and catch up?"

His crestfallen face confirms he's disappointed, but surely, he can't expect me to get off the plane and fall straight back into his arms?

"I know I'm getting carried away, but I've been waiting for a chance to start making it up to you for months, and I'm a little anxious."

It's hard to remain immune to those words. "I understand, and I like that you're trying to make amends. It reminds me you're still you, but I just got off a plane, Reeve, and I'm tired and emotional."

"Of course. I won't overburden you, but I do need to fill you in on the Bianca, Cassidy, Saffron situation, as well as what I've been doing this summer."

"So, fill me in." I drink some of my sparkling water.

"I know your parents hired a PI to find those girls who attacked you, but he was making no leeway. I found a guy who specializes in these kinds of investigations, and I worked closely with him until we had enough paperwork to tie most everything to Bianca and Cassidy."

I remember Audrey mentioning this guy too. "Not Saffron?"

"She was most definitely involved, but I can't go after her without hard evidence, and we don't have that yet. She's a sneaky bitch. She got others to do her dirty work, so there's no footprint. I've spoken to the assistant director she was dating, and he's pretty sure she sabotaged the footage the night before our prom, but he has no way of proving it. He actually dumped her after that though she pretended she was the one who ended things."

"They were behind all of it?"

He bobs his head. "According to Cassidy, it was Saffron who suggested you be shoved in a corner at my premiere." He rubs the back of his neck. "Something I wasn't aware of, by the way, until your father ripped me a new one the next day. Cassidy made it happen. You already know Bianca was the one who hired a hacker to hack your computer, but now she's insisting it was Cassidy's idea. They didn't just remove your post though. They connected to your cell via your laptop and planted tracking software on it."

"Those fucking bitches! I can't believe the nerve of them, or actually, I can. Nothing should surprise me anymore." I shake my head, shocked, angry, and relieved that Reeve is getting to the bottom of everything they did to me. To us. "That's how Bianca knew where I was the day she accosted me at the café." I sit up straighter. "So, it was Bianca who set those fans on me?"

He shakes his head. "I think that was Saffron too. Bianca said she provided details of your location, but she claims she had no idea what Saffron was planning."

A likely story.

"Did you find those girls? If one of them testifies against her, we can get Saffron that way, right?"

"They are still in hiding, but my guy will keep looking for them. Like I said, it's hard to prove Saffron's part, but we have indisputable evidence of Cassidy's and Bianca's wrongdoings. I went to the studio and showed them everything. Cassidy's been fired, and her name is dirt in the industry. I have filed a Class A lawsuit against Bianca. That's mainly the angle I've been working all summer. I figured I couldn't be the only client she has done this to. I visited some of her other clients, and we discovered proof of shit she'd done to them too." A satisfied smile slips over his mouth.

SAY I'M THE ONE

"She is done in this business. She has lost all of her clients and every shred of respect. By the time we are through with her, she will only have the clothes on her back."

"Wow. I knew she was a piece of shit, but that is truly disgusting. I'm glad those two got what they deserve, but I hate we can't pin anything on Saffron."

"Yet," he reiterates.

"It will really piss me off if she gets off scot-free."

"She hasn't escaped unscathed," he adds, topping up my glass of sparkling water. "She's officially finished with the production. She won't be at the premiere, and she won't be doing any promotion."

I remove my shades, staring at him. "How come?"

"She OD'd, and her sister has sent her to rehab." He reaches across the table, taking my hand. "She's gone from our lives now, Viv. She can't hurt us anymore, and in case she gets any ideas when she emerges from rehab, I have already instructed Carson Park to apply for a restraining order in both our names." Carson is the Lancasters' family attorney.

"Thank you."

"One final thing." He gets up, pulling me to my feet and reeling me into his arms.

"I did a thing."

"Oh God, Reeve. What now?" My heart lurches to my mouth.

"A good thing, I hope you'll agree. I did an exclusive interview with Oprah, and I told her everything. I needed to publicly clear your name and let everyone see how viciously you've been treated and how stupid I was not to believe you from the outset. I came clean about the drugs and the stress of carrying such a big movie and how I didn't respond well to the pressure. Obviously, I had to be careful what I said about Bianca with the impending court case and I can't accuse Saffron of shit when I have no proof to back up my claims. Bianca's and Cassidy's words don't count because they're both nasty backstabbing bitches, and their reputations are in the toilet."

"How the hell did you get the studio to agree to that?"

"When it airs next month, it will generate a huge amount of publicity for the franchise, ahead of the release of the last movie. All publicity is good publicity, so they're on board."

This is what my parents and Audrey were hinting at in July when they visited Ireland. They knew he was doing all this. It definitely goes a long way toward rectifying things with us, but it doesn't mean I'm ready to jump right back into a relationship with Reeve. I don't know my own heart right now, and I can't make any hard and fast decisions. But I am grateful he has done this, and I won't deny how much it means to me.

"Thank you, Reeve." I hug him briefly. "Thank you so much for doing that. It helps. It really does."

"Yeah?"

"Yeah."

"Come and watch the interview. If there is anything you don't like, I can have it edited out. Margaret helped me get a clause added to the contract that gives us editorial rights."

I sit on the couch with Reeve for the next hour, watching the interview with a constant lump in my throat. Gradually, we gravitate toward one another, sitting with our arms wrapped around each other, thighs pressed close together. Heat rolls off him in waves, thawing all the frozen parts of me. It's impossible to keep my hands to myself as I listen to him telling Oprah how much I mean to him. Sharing snippets of how we fell in love and opening his personal photo album, showing the world pictures of us from the time we were babies until we were teens. Every milestone is represented, and I'm a blubbering mess by the time he switches it off.

"Hey." He brushes tears from my cheeks as I attempt to get my emotions under control. "Happy or sad tears."

"More happy than sad," I truthfully admit. I sling my arms around his neck, and my entire body is trembling with emotion as he wraps me in his warm embrace. The citrusy scent of his cologne is like a balm to my aching heart, and if I thought I was confused earlier, it's nothing on how I feel now. Heartwarming memories resurface in my mind, and I'm reminded of all the reasons why I love this man. He has gone to so much effort to rectify his wrongs, slicing his chest open and showing the entire world how much he feels for me in that interview. As grand gestures go, it's at the tippy-top of the scale.

"I love you, Viv. I love you so much. I'm sorry you ever felt like that wasn't true. I am going to spend the rest of my life making it up to you, whether you'll let me or not."

I snort-laugh because it's so typically stubborn of Reeve. Easing back, I peer into his gorgeous blue eyes. "Always the charmer."

"Every word is true, Viv." His lips lower to my mouth, and my pulse throbs in my neck. "I lost my way for a while, and I hurt us both in the process. I will not make that mistake again." Before I can stop him, his lips are on mine, insistent and demanding, devouring me like he never thought he'd get to taste my mouth again.

Tingles cascade over my skin, reaching every part of me, and I'm arching toward him, clinging to him, with a need that is unflinching and indisputable. His fingers weave through my hair as his tongue slips into my mouth, and I'm drowning in Reeve, consumed with his touch, taste, and the feel of being back in his arms. I'm kissing him back without restraint or regret, drowning in the familiarity of being with him like this. It's as easy as breathing. As if we've spent no time apart. As if we haven't been to hell and back these past few years.

I don't stop him either when he removes my clothes and his own, lying me down flat on the couch, kissing and touching me everywhere, helping to remind me that what we share is a love that will never die. His lips blaze a trail from my mouth to my neck, and he sucks on that sensitive spot just under my ear. Blissful tremors shake me to my foundation, and there is no thinking, just feeling, as I immerse myself in the pleasurable sensations Reeve is awakening in me. My hands roam his body, reacquainting me with every inch of his skin.

When his mouth closes over one nipple, I arch my back, almost falling off the couch as I feel a pull deep in my core. My body reacts instantly to Reeve's touch as if my skin has memorized the sensory response when he caresses me in certain places. He worships every part of me with his lips and his fingers as I slide a hand between us, grabbing his hard length and pumping him in my hand. He moans into my mouth, whispering my name over and over as he molds my body to fit to his.

His fingers slip inside me, finding me ready and willing, and there's no hesitation.

Lifting my hands up over my head, Reeve presses his body down on mine, linking our fingers as he claims my mouth in a passionate kiss. "I love you, Viv. Over everything and everyone. The only thing that matters to me is you. You have my heart for now and eternity." My thighs open for him, and our eyes remain connected as he inches inside me with tender care. "God, Viv." Tears prick his eyes, and I dust kisses all over his face.

"Let me feel your love, Reeve. Show me you mean everything you've said today."

He kisses me senseless while he moves his cock in and out of me. My legs wrap around his back, and my hands roam his spine and his firm ass, holding him close as he pivots his hips, thrusting deeper inside me, until it feels like he's buried so deep he's a part of me. We kiss and kiss, both of us as greedy as the other, and I moan as his fingers fondle my breasts and sweep along my sides, eliciting a rake of fiery shivers every place he touches.

Lost to the incredible intimacy of being with Reeve like this, I feel a sense of inner calm, inner peace, that can only come when two people know each other as well as we do. Reeve is my home, as I am his. So much of who I am is entwined in Reeve, and he reminds me of the parts I haven't visited in months, connecting me to elements of myself I had locked away along with memories of us.

As he thrusts inside me, making slow passionate love to me, I realize what this means. I'm irrevocably in love with Reeve, and our connection is still very much alive. I don't know what this means for our future, but I know I need him back in my life, in some guise, because I miss him. I miss this.

We come together, and it breaks me apart and heals me at the same time. As we descend from our high, we curl against one another, skin to skin, with my head buried in his shoulder. My fingers trace over the heart-shaped tattoo on his chest with my name inside. I still can't believe he got this for me because he's always been adamant he didn't want any ink. Thinking of ink naturally leads me to thoughts of Dillon. Reality hits, and I'm crying before I realize it.

My heart and soul forever belong to two men.

It's an irrefutable truth that won't ever change.

Reeve is the air I breathe.

Dillon is the fire that consumes me.

How am I expected to live without a part of my heart?

I don't know what this means for my future or where I go from here, but I can't deny the truth any longer—I'm deeply in love with two men, and I'm a hot mess because I have no clue what to do.

Reeve kisses every tear, giving assurances, whispering how much he loves me, promising me it is going to be all right. I sob into his shoulder, clutching him to me, hating myself for what I've just done, because it feels like such a betrayal so soon after leaving Dillon, while another part of me desperately clings to the man I have loved my entire life, never wanting to be separated from him again.

My emotions veer back and forth, going round and round, until I literally make myself ill from trying to work out the complex machinations of my heart. Nausea swims up my throat, and I race to the bathroom, vomiting the entire contents of my stomach.

Reeve comforts me as I retch and cry until I'm physically and emotionally drained. He passes me a toothbrush to use while propping me up before he carries me back out to the living room and plies me with water. He cradles me protectively in his arms as I cling to him like a limpet. I'm all cried out and no closer to knowing what I'm going to do with my love life. Reeve doesn't pressure me to talk. He just holds me for an indeterminable amount of time.

After a while, he helps me into my underwear while he pulls on his boxers. He carries me outside to the balcony, placing my feet on the ground. Pulling me back against his chest, we hold one another as we stare at the placid ocean. His arm bands around my bare breasts, shielding me. He dots kisses along my neck, and I arch my head back, both loving and hating how much his arms feel like home. Like I belong here and this is exactly where I'm supposed to be.

"I know you're upset, and I can guess why. I'm not going to lie and say I'm happy you love this Irish guy, but it's my fault you were even there in the first place, so I've got to man up and accept the situation." He spins me around, hauling me in close as his lips brush softly against mine. "He's not here, Viv. I am. And I'm all yours in every sense of the word. I won't be making any decisions about my career without your involvement. Everything I do from here on out will be done placing your needs above mine. I know you need time, and I'll give you that, but please say you'll give us another chance. If we try and you say it's not working for you, it will kill me, but I'll walk away. I will do whatever it takes to make you happy, because that is the only thing that matters to me anymore. You are my entire world, Viv, and I won't stop until I have proven that to you."

CHAPTER 63

Five+ Years Later

STARING out the window of my home-office-slash-library, I smile as I watch Easton's brown head bob excitedly when his dad lifts him up onto the top of the slide. Pure exhilaration is etched upon his handsome little face as he shoots down the slide. He grows more and more like Reeve with every passing day. I can't believe he will be five in May.

Smoothing my hand over my small bump, I hum to my little princess, awash with happiness. Family life with Reeve is everything I had hoped it would be and more. Being married to the man who has been my significant other, in so many ways, from my earliest memory, is equally fulfilling.

Reeve and Easton are my world, and I know my daughter will be too. Okay, we don't know if it's a girl yet, but I have a sixth sense. I just feel it in my bones. We have our sixteen-week ultrasound in three weeks, and Reeve is more excited than a kid on Christmas morning.

I stare adoringly at my husband as he chases our son around the playground, more in love with Reeve now than I've ever been. As a dad, Reeve is everything his father isn't, and I know he never wants Easton to doubt he is wanted, loved, and cherished. Easton is the apple of his father's eye, and Reeve is the most amazing dad, showering Easton with love and being there for all the important moments, unlike his own absent father.

Watching them together is beautiful, and I'm so grateful for the love we share. I will never take it for granted.

My cell vibrates with an incoming call, and I rush around my desk, swiping the screen to accept Audrey's video call. I've been calling her all week since I discovered the news, needing my bestie's advice.

Alex and Audrey got married two years ago, and they live in Boston where Alex is the head football coach at a local high school. I'm hoping they might return to L.A. once Audrey graduates next year because I miss her a lot. She is in her last year of med school and snowed under with hospital rotations, classes, and assignments. With the time difference and our busy schedules, it is murder trying to find time to talk, let alone meet up.

"Squee. I see a bump! Look how cute you are," she says. Her gorgeous face looms large as she peers in close to the screen.

I run my hand along my slightly enlarged stomach. "It's only barely noticeable, but I'm definitely bigger than I was when I was pregnant with E."

Audrey snorts. "That wouldn't be hard. No one even knew you were pregnant until the very end. You were tiny carrying him."

It's true. I was able to remain at UCLA until March of my junior year, disguising my growing bump with baggy tops until I woke one morning and my belly seemed to have ballooned overnight. I moved in with my parents then and switched to online classes.

Easton Jonathon Lancaster was born at three thirty a.m. on May fifth weighing a teeny six pounds five ounces. You'd never know it looking at him now. He's tall and a healthy weight for his age.

"Earth to Viv. You're in la-la land again." Audrey grins, slouching in her chair in her hospital scrubs.

"I'm blaming my pregnancy hormones this time." I sit down on the chair behind my desk and get comfortable.

"You're glowing, babe. It's great to see. I hated how stressed you were when you were carrying E."

I rub my lips as I contemplate one of the most stressful periods of my life. "I love that I can embrace my pregnancy this time, but I feel guilty that I didn't with E."

"It wasn't your fault."

I burst out a laugh. "Eh, I'm pretty sure it was. I was the slut who slept with two men in two days on two different continents and then freaked the fuck out when I got pregnant and spent my entire pregnancy stressed over who my baby daddy was."

"It all worked out perfectly in the end."

"Thank fuck." Reeve was ecstatic when I finally announced I was pregnant. I'm ashamed to admit I had known for two months before I told him. It took me that long to work up the courage to say it. Well, that and I was waiting to see if Dillon would reach out to me, but he never did.

He never made any effort to talk to me after I left the pub in Dublin that day.

What a disappointment he turned out to be, but like my bestie just said, it all worked out perfectly in the end.

"I still feel guilty I lied to him," I admit. A few weeks after I confirmed I was pregnant, Reeve asked me if there was any chance the baby wasn't his.

I lied and said no.

God, I still feel such horrendous guilt over that.

"If you'd told him the truth, you would've taken away his enjoyment of your pregnancy, and maybe you wouldn't be married to the love of your life with the family and career you always dreamed of living in a house you designed as kids."

"It doesn't mean it was right, and what if the baby hadn't been his?" A full-body shudder works its way through me.

"Don't do this to yourself, Viv. There's no point looking back on the what-ifs. Fate brought you back to Reeve and you're happy, right, babe? You are happy?"

I bob my head. "I am. I love Reeve and Easton with my whole heart. I'm excited to meet the new addition to our family, and I'm excited for this new show I'm working on. The producer even approved me to work from home so I can be around for E. I just have to attend the weekly team meetings at the office. Reeve is shooting in Georgia for the next couple of months. He leaves five days after the Oscars."

Reeve's career has been full steam ahead since the *Rydeville Elite* series, and he's one of Hollywood's most in-demand and highest-paid stars. The beauty of that is he can pick and choose his roles, and he only commits to two or three projects a year so he can be at home as much as possible. He tries to pick films that pique his curiosity and satisfy his artistic passion and roles that aren't too far from home. Of course, it doesn't always pan out like that, but we make it work.

Reeve has never broken his promise to always put me first, and we decide everything as a team now, always prioritizing our love and our son. Rather than taking the job I was offered with a leading production company, I set myself up as a freelance writer as it gives me more flexibility. I have been working a lot with Netflix on original content and adaptations, and I've also been writing some books in my spare time. I'm not sure if I'll ever publish them, but they feed my creative soul.

"Speaking of." Audrey kicks her feet up on the table in front of her. "I read an interesting article about this year's Oscar ceremony. Is it true Collateral Damage is performing on that night?"

"Why do you think I've been blowing up your cell all week." Anxiety skates across my chest, like it does anytime I think about the impending shitshow. "They're nominated for best original song."

"What are you going to do?"

"Stay out of their way. The Dolby Theatre is large enough I should be able to avoid him and the other band members. There are tons of industry after-parties, so the chances of us being at the same ones are slim." Reeve has been nominated for best actor, so it's not like I can't be there, especially when he's the favorite to win.

"What if he comes looking for you?"

I pick at imaginary dirt under my nails. "He won't come looking for me. He never has. Why would he now?"

"Maybe you should tell Reeve Dillon is the Irish guy. Just in case you cross paths and Dillon says something."

Reeve knows what went down with Dillon. He asked me a few weeks after I got home, and I told him the important parts without going into intimate details. Reeve never asked his name, and I never volunteered it.

"I'm not going to just bring it up after all this time, Rey! Can you imagine that conversation? Oh, hey, darling. Remember I told you I was in love with the guy I met in Ireland? I neglected to tell you it's Dillon O'Donoghue, lead singer and songwriter of mega-bestselling Irish rock band Collateral Damage. "Terrify Me," the first of their songs to reach number one on the billboard Top 100, was actually written *for* me and *about* me, and I have a video on my cell of him serenading me with it at his brother's wedding. I'm also pretty sure "Hollywood Ho" and "Fuck Love" were about me too, but who the hell knows why Dillon wrote such vitriol when he's the one who rejected me."

Audrey is the only one who knows about the letter I sent and how I sat in Dublin Airport for hours crying and praying to every deity known to mankind that he would show up. My heart aches, and acid crawls up my throat. "Ugh." I rest my head on my desk. "I can't believe it still hurts so much after all this time."

"You still love him even now?" she softly asks.

"You know I do," I whisper. "I've tried to evict him so many times from my head and my heart, but it never works. I guess I'm destined to love him forever." I rub my temples. "Gawd, I'm a terrible person, Audrey. A terrible wife to still pine after another man."

"You can't help how you feel, and I know you love Reeve fiercely. You're not a terrible wife. You're a great wife, and he adores you. You two have been written in the stars since inception."

I'm not sure she'd say that if she knew I have all the band's songs on my phone and I listen to them repeatedly. I try to avoid watching them on TV because I'm not sure I could disguise the pain and longing on my face from my husband.

Sometimes, when I can't sleep, I go out to our sunroom, lie down on the couch, close my eyes, and cry as I listen to Dillon's husky voice roll over me like one of his possessive caresses. Other times, I go through the photos and videos I have hidden on my phone from my time in Ireland, just because I need to see his face.

It's not healthy.

I know that.

And I feel so disloyal to Reeve, but this soul-deep ache in my chest never goes away, no matter how happy Reeve makes me.

And Reeve does make me happy.

He's an incredibly attentive, supportive, and loyal husband. It took a while for him to earn back my trust, and I kept him at arm's length a lot that first year, out of necessity for my sanity. I couldn't be sure who the father of my baby was, and I wouldn't accept Reeve's marriage proposal or be seen with him in public until after Easton was born and the paternity test confirmed he was his dad.

Even then, I had to think long and hard about my motivations before finally agreeing to marry Reeve. I needed to ensure it was for the right reasons.

I spoke with a therapist at length, and she helped me to untangle my jumbled emotions. She helped me to understand the complexities of a woman's heart. To accept that it was okay to love Dillon from a distance while promising to share my life with Reeve. I don't regret that decision. Reeve loves me, and I love him, and we're good together, but Dillon will always own a piece of my heart.

"I knew this day would come. I knew I couldn't continue to avoid events where Collateral Damage was playing. It's a miracle I've gone this long without bumping into one of them."

"What if Ash seeks you out?" Audrey quietly inquires.

Positioning my cell against the stack of books on my desk, I sigh as I lean

348

forward. "If she does, it's probably to strangle me. I'm ashamed of lots of things I did that year, but ghosting my Irish bestie is the worst." It wasn't by choice. It was a necessity, but that doesn't make it any easier to live with. I hate I let her down. That she must be wondering what she did to deserve the cold shoulder.

"Don't beat yourself up, Viv. You know you couldn't stay in contact with her while there was a possibility the baby was her brother's kid. At least in cutting her off you weren't lying to her."

"A lie of omission is still a lie, and it must have hurt so bad. I know it hurt me."

I still miss Ash. So fucking much. She's the band's manager, and I'm sensing she might have been behind the change in name. She always thought Toxic Gods was a shit name for a band, but I felt it suited them.

Pictures of her are everywhere, and she travels with the band full-time, just like she told me she would. Her relationship with Jamie seems solid too. News of their engagement was splashed all over social media last year. Ronan had a baby with his Irish girlfriend a few months ago, and, apparently, they are getting married soon. Dillon and Conor are regularly pictured with different women on their arms, and rumors suggest Dillon has an alcohol problem. That pained me to hear, and I wonder who is looking after him. I know Ash must be trying, but she's got her own life to lead, and she can't babysit her brother forever.

I'm not on social media much, having learned that lesson the hard way years ago, but Audrey fills me in on shit she thinks I need to know.

"I wish I could be there with you."

"Me too. We need to plan a vacation soon before I get too big to fit into a plane." She rolls her eyes. "Always with the drama."

We chat about her job, Alex's desire to start a family as soon as she graduates, and her creep of a stepdad before she has to go. She wishes me luck at the ceremony tomorrow night, and before we hang up, I promise to message her if anything happens.

"Mommy!" Easton comes bursting into my room. "I found more worms." He holds up a jar of wriggly, writhing creatures, and I clamp my lips shut, rubbing my stomach to ward off my shivers. Ugh. Any kind of wriggly creepy-crawly makes me shudder.

Reeve chuckles, sauntering into the room, looking hotter than sin in his jeans and tight-fitting Henley. "Buddy, what have I told you about bursting into Mom's office without knocking?" He ruffles his hair before bending down to kiss me, grabbing a sneaky feel of my ass. "You look beautiful, my love. Pregnancy really suits you. I should knock you up more often."

"I'll take that under advice," I semi-joke.

"What does knock you up mean?" Easton asks. His big blue eyes bounce between me and Reeve.

"This one's on you, babe." I cross my arms and smirk at my husband, wondering how he's going to explain this to our inquisitive son.

CHAPTER 64

"YOU HAVE no reason to be nervous, babe. I know you hate the cameras, but you are stunning. Easily the most gorgeous woman in the room and on the planet," Reeve says, leaning in to kiss my cheek. I've been a basket case since arriving at the Dolby Theatre three hours ago, but it's not for the reasons my husband thinks.

My best friend guilt joins my other friend panic, and they take turns punching me in the face.

I know the members of Collateral Damage are about seven or eight rows behind us as I spotted the top of Dillon's bleach-blond head when we were walking to our seats in the front row. It's a miracle I didn't throw up on the spot. I about died when Reeve stopped at the row in front of them to say hello to a few actor friends. Prickles of awareness danced across the bare nape of my neck, and I just knew he was looking at me. The urge to turn around and lock eyes with him was almost insurmountable, but I managed to resist, and thankfully, Reeve didn't linger too long.

Nerves fire at me from every angle as Collateral Damage takes to the stage. I have no choice but to look at them because we're in the front row and the camera regularly sweeps our way. Trying to keep a fake smile plastered across my face while my heart feels like it's being ripped out of my chest is monumentally hard.

Dillon owns the stage like he always does, and it's hard not to get swept up in the song. They are so good live. Incredibly talented, and I'm very proud of them. I wish I could tell people I knew them when they were a talented local band in Ireland, but to do that would be risky when Reeve doesn't know. Volunteering that information now, after all this time, would hurt my husband, so I won't go there.

Dillon's laser-focused gaze slides to mine, and I stop breathing. He's got one leg elevated, resting on a speaker, as he makes love to the mic, belting out the lyrics in his unique style.

He hasn't changed much at all. His blond hair is a bit longer, tucked behind his ears, the length resting at his nape, and he has more ink, judging by the designs peeking out from the top of his T-shirt, but that's it. He's still wearing all black. Still wearing his piercings. Still ripped in all the best ways.

He looks hot as fuck and every bit the tormented soul I fell in love with.

I feel Reeve glance at me, as Dillon continues staring at me, but I pretend I don't notice anything strange, smiling and dancing in my seat along with the other guests. Inside, I'm screaming at Dillon to knock it off before he outs us to the entire freaking world. Ro glances my way from behind his drums, quickly averting his gaze when our eyes meet. Conor is in his own little world, as usual, and Jamie sends daggers my direction a couple of times.

I'm sweating bullets under my gorgeous red Christian Dior dress and squirming in my seat like I'm sitting on poison ivy.

"Are you okay?" Reeve whispers in my ear, noticing I'm hella distracted.

I whip my head around to my husband. "I need to go to the bathroom," I lie. "Do you think it would be okay to slip away now?" We're supposed to wait for breaks to leave our seats, but I'll play the pregnancy card if I need to.

"Go. If anyone gives you grief, you let me deal with it. Do you want me to come with?"

"You can't leave, and I'm a big girl. I can make it to the bathroom by myself."

I don't look at the band as I creep out of the auditorium, releasing the breath I was holding when I hit the hallway leading to the bathrooms.

I'm trembling as I sit on the toilet seat after I've attended to business. Seeing Dillon again has rattled me. It's dredging memories to the surface. Memories I've worked hard to bury, and my heart is splitting open again. I dab at the tears spilling silently down my cheeks, praying I can do a good enough repair job with my makeup to disguise my anguish from my husband.

Tonight is special for Reeve, and he deserves my full attention and devotion. I've got to pull myself together and get back out there to support him.

Why did I have to fall in love with two men, and why isn't it getting any easier? Hurt lances me on all sides and I grip the sides of the stall, begging someone to take the pain away. Needing help, I call Audrey, and she talks me off a ledge like only my bestie can.

Hurrying to the sink, I patch up my makeup, hiding all evidence of my heartache. I don't know how long I've been gone, but I'm sure Reeve is worrying, and I need to get back to him. Smoothing my hair back into its chignon, I admire my gorgeous red gown in the mirror, reminding myself I look composed on the outside even if I'm falling to pieces on the inside.

Stepping outside, I almost take a tumble when I find Dillon waiting for me. One part of me half-expected this. The pain I felt inside the theater watching him up on that stage is minuscule compared to the pain I feel looking at him up close and personal. He drills me with an intense look that takes me back in time. My skin prickles with awareness as he slowly rakes his eyes up and down my body. His gaze is as intimate as it's always been, and my heart pounds wildly behind my rib cage.

Memories flash through my mind.

Rough touches.

Demanding kisses.

Animalistic fucking that never quite sated my thirst for him.

His wicked smile as I screamed when he pulled a risky maneuver on his motorcycle.

His boyish grin as we lay on our bellies peering over the side of the Cliffs of Moher.

His adoring eyes as he serenaded me on my roof the last night we were together.

A sob travels up my throat before I can stop it. Clutching my purse to my chest, I will my hormones to simmer down, telling my wayward tears to fuck the hell off. Heartache plus pregnancy hormones is clearly not a good combination.

"Hey, Hollywood," he says, his raspy voice sounding as choked as I feel inside.

"Dillon," I whisper.

He pushes off the wall, sauntering toward me with that cocky swagger I've missed so much. I'm trapped in his magnetic gaze, rooted to the spot, as he cages me in with his arms. "Vivien Grace," he murmurs, staring down at me with a familiar hunger in his eyes. "Still so beautiful." Whiskey fumes fan across my face, and I realize he's drunk at the same time I realize I cannot be caught with him like this.

Ducking down, I slip out from under his arms. "I've got to go."

"Run away, Hollywood," he calls out after me, a discernible sneer creeping into his tone. "After all, it's what you do best."

I'm tempted to turn around and give him a piece of my mind, but arguing with a drunk Dillon never ended up well in the past.

"There you are," Reeve says when I reach the end of the hallway. He looks over my shoulder before his gaze dips to mine. "What's going on?" His brow puckers.

"Nothing. Let's go. I've already missed enough of the ceremony." I drag him back to our seats, grateful he doesn't protest or probe further.

Reeve wins best actor, for a low-budget indie film, and everyone in the place is up on their feet applauding him. Well, not everyone, if I had to guess. He gives the most beautiful acceptance speech, dedicating it to me and Easton, and his gushing praise produces more tears.

We drop by a couple of after-parties, but I can't relax because I'm terrified a drunk Dillon is going to turn up and say something. I'm sorely tempted to use the pregnancy card to get us out of here—knowing Reeve will leave with me—but I can't do that to him. This is his night, and he deserves to enjoy it. However, my thoughtful husband insists we leave at a reasonable hour, knowing I've got to be tired and unwilling to say it.

As my husband makes passionate love to me that night, pouring all his adoration into every touch, thrust, and caress, I feel incredibly unworthy of his love and devotion.

"He's a total prick," Reeve rages the next evening when he still hasn't heard a peep from his father.

"He is," I readily agree, massaging his tight shoulders. "I can't believe he hasn't called to congratulate you."

Reeve turns, wrapping his arms around me. "Why do I care, Viv? Why do I still let him get to me? It's not like he's ever shown me more than fleeting attention, so why do I still need his approval?" Reeve has spent time in therapy dissecting his relationship with his father, but he still struggles.

"He's your father. Your only living parent. It's natural to seek his approval even though he doesn't deserve you for a son. He never has." I run my fingers through his hair, feathering kisses on his cheeks. I hate to see him hurting, time and time again, over that ungrateful bastard who is little more than a sperm donor. "You are the most incredible father to our son. You are everything to Easton your father is not. You are a far better man than him, Reeve, and I hope someday you will be able to let it go because I hate seeing you tormented like this."

Reeve kisses me, sliding his tongue into my mouth and holding me close as I run soothing hands up and down his back. I moan into his mouth as he gradually kindles a slow-burning fire inside my body, clinging to him as desire surges through my veins. I wish I could drag my gorgeous husband to bed and ride him to distraction, but it's almost E's bath and bedtime, so sexy times with Reeve will have to wait until later.

When we break apart, he rests his forehead against mine, sighing wearily. Pain is etched across his handsome face, and I will strangle Simon Lancaster for putting a dampener on what should be a special time for Reeve. He lifts his head, and steely determination glints in his eyes. "I'm going over there. I'm confronting him. And then I'm cutting him out of our lives. It's not like he makes any effort with us or his grandson."

It's true. Simon Lancaster has little to no interest in Easton. I only invite him to birthdays and Christmases for Reeve's sake. Easton doesn't have much time for him, and he doesn't care. He adores my parents, and they spoil him rotten, lavishing him with attention, love, and far too many gifts. As far as Easton is concerned, his grandpa is Jonathon Mills. Simon Lancaster is an afterthought, as he deserves to be.

"Are you sure you want to do that?" I know it will hurt Reeve, and this should be a happy time for him after his win last night.

"I'm done making excuses for him."

"I'll come with you."

He shakes his head. "I appreciate the offer, but this is a conversation I need to have alone." He pecks my lips. "Besides, you have to stay with Easton. One of us should be here to put him to bed." Lust flares in his eyes. "When I get back, I'm so having my wicked way with you."

I press a demanding kiss to his lips, letting him know I'm down with that plan. "I'm holding you to that, lover."

Picking up my hand, he presses a kiss to the underside of my wrist. "You know I always deliver. Keeping you satisfied is always top of my wish list."

"Love you." I wrap my arms around him, channeling all my love into my hug. He will need it for this conversation with his father.

"Love you too." He eases out of our embrace, softly ruffling my hair. "I'll see you later, beautiful."

"Okay, but call me if you need me to come over." Our house isn't far from our parents, all of whom still live in North Beverley Park.

I'm bathing Easton forty minutes later when Reeve calls. Swiping my sudsy son up out of the tub, I wrap him in a large fluffy towel, settling him on my lap on top of the closed toilet seat as I answer my husband.

"Viv," he croaks, the second I answer, and my heart stops. "I need you."

"Are you okay? Are you hurt?" I ask, instantly panicked. Simon has never physically hurt his son. His abuse was more of the emotional, psychological kind, but I wouldn't put anything past that coldhearted bastard.

"He's dead," he blurts.

"What?" I pull Easton into my chest, covering his tiny ears with the towel so he doesn't pick up any of this conversation.

"I found him in his bed. The staff hadn't gone near him all day because they had strict instructions never to disturb him in his bedroom."

"God, Reeve." I don't say I'm sorry because the only emotion I'm feeling is concern for my husband. I know you shouldn't speak ill of the dead, but maybe this is for the best. Perhaps this is the release Reeve needs to finally put his father and his heartless neglect behind him. "I'll be right over. I'll ask Charlotte to put Easton to bed."

After arranging for our live-in housekeeper to take over with E, I rush out of the house, telling Leon, my bodyguard, that he's not needed.

Reeve is one of the most famous actors on the planet, so I didn't object when he hired a team of bodyguards to protect us. We tend to only bring them when we're going out somewhere in public, and Leon drives me to and from work so he can watch out for me. There are plenty of crazies out there—I know that from personal experience. Unfortunately, we never found the girls who assaulted me, and we never found evidence to charge Saffron Roberts.

But karma came through in the end.

She's a known junkie who has fallen off the wagon several times. There are videos of her losing it, ranting like the psycho bitch she is, and her career is in the toilet because no one will go near her. Her looks have been ravaged by drugs, and she looks like shit. All her so-called friends ditched her, and her sister—her only sibling—publicly exclaimed she has cut ties with her, that she's beyond help. Last I heard, she has resorted to starring in porn to feed her habit.

Maybe I should feel sorry for her, but I don't. Not one little fucking bit. If that makes me a bad person, then so be it. She caused me a world of pain when she tried to ruin my life, but in the end, she ruined her own future.

I have zero sympathy. She brought it all on herself.

The coroner and the cops are arriving at the house as I am, and I hurry up the steps, sliding my arms around Reeve and holding him tight. His arm sneaks around my shoulders, and he clings to me, his whole body trembling. He's as white as a ghost and clearly shocked.

I stay by his side, squeezing his hand, as he gives a statement to the police. I complete some paperwork for the coroner, and we watch from the hallway as his father is led out in a body bag.

Sitting Reeve down on the couch in the main living room, I place a glass of whiskey in his hand, urging him to drink, while I gather the household staff and talk to them about the future. They are shocked but also worried about their jobs, so I reassure them it's business as usual for now, until Reeve decides what he wants to do with the house, and not to be concerned as we will ensure they are all looked after.

Taking Reeve's hand in mine, I lead him outside, placing him in the passenger seat of my car and strapping him in. Tears prick my eyes as I press a kiss to his brow. I hate seeing him like this. He's in a daze, staring numbly into space, and my heart aches for him. Even though they had a dysfunctional relationship, he was still his father, and I know this is going to hit Reeve hard.

A few days later, the coroner's report confirms the time of death, and we learn that Simon died of a massive heart attack around the time Reeve was collecting his first Oscar award.

Even in death, Simon Lancaster is finding ways to fuck with his son.

Reeve flounders in the weeks after his father's death. Technically, Reeve is an orphan now, and his father's passing has raised an almost obsessive need to discover everything he can about his mother and his parents' relationship. Mom and Dad talk to him at length, sharing everything they were there to experience, passing on photos and trying to support him the best they can.

Reeve doesn't cry. He goes about his day, as normal, but he's not himself, and I'm worried. One night, a couple of weeks after the funeral, he finally cracks, sobbing like a little boy, and it hurts my heart. He clings to me with a desperation that pains me. Making love becomes a regular nightly occurrence, not that I'm complaining—hello, pregnancy hormones—but he struggles to sleep a lot, and I'm at a loss how best to help him.

I know losing a parent is hard, but Reeve didn't have a close relationship with his father, and I didn't think he'd struggle this much. When I ask him, he says he's realized he lost the chance to ever put things right, and that kills me because Reeve tried everything to get through to his dad. He seems to have forgotten he was going there that day to cut him off, but I don't remind him of that. I can't relate, and I don't fully understand what's going through his mind, only he's trying to process the loss of a wishful hope rather than the passing of the actual man.

I suggest therapy, and I'm glad when he agrees.

Reeve pulls out of the movie he was due to film, and I take time off to care full-time for my family. Easton is a source of enormous comfort to Reeve. Father and son grow even closer during this time. Holding his family tight is important to Reeve, and we're here for him. My pregnancy is another source of comfort, and Reeve is thrilled when our scan reveals we are expecting a little girl.

Gradually, he returns to himself, but I still encourage him to continue seeing his therapist. Reeve has a lot of unresolved emotions when it comes to his father, and I don't want to see him derailed.

"Carson Park wants to see us," Reeve announces the day after my twenty-sixth birthday. Reeve spoiled me with lavender roses and too many gifts including a beautiful, framed photo of him and Easton and another of our scan pic. We had a sumptuous meal at our favorite restaurant last night, and my husband spent hours at home worshiping every inch of my body as he made sweet, sweet love to me. It was the perfect way to celebrate, and I'm feeling all loved up today.

"How come?" I ask. "We already know the contents of the will."

Simon left everything to Reeve, including his shares in Studio 27.

Up until his death, Simon was CEO of the hugely successful production company. His second-in-command has already been promoted in his stead. The studio knows Reeve has zero interest right now in following in his father's footsteps, but they have a vested interest in knowing his intent with regards to his inherited investment. The new CEO and a couple of the directors are keen to take the shares off his hands, but I don't like it. I suggested Reeve hold off making any firm decision, as there's no rush. Down the line, he may want to take a more active role, and I don't think he should limit his options.

"I have no clue. He just said there is a matter he needs to discuss. I made an appointment for noon tomorrow."

"Okay. I'll let my boss know I'll be offline for a few hours."

"What's this about, Carson?" Reeve asks the next day after we have taken our seats in the attorney's office.

"Your father trusted me with a personal matter many years ago. He left instructions that after his death I was to tell you the circumstances. I had planned on talking to you the day the will was read, but I could tell you weren't in the right place to hear this news."

"What is it?" Reeve automatically laces his fingers in mine, and I rub reassuring circles with my thumb on the back of his hand.

"There is no easy way to disclose something like this, so please excuse me if I'm blunt."

Reeve nods curtly, and I'm starting to get a bad feeling about this.

"You are aware of the circumstances of your birth and your mother's tragic passing, but you aren't privy to the full facts."

Reeve and I share a perplexed expression. "What facts?" I ask.

"Your mother died during childbirth, but it wasn't giving birth to you."

Shock splays across Reeve's face, matching my own. "What do you mean?"

"You have a twin, Reeve. An identical twin brother."

What in the actual fuck? I'm not sure what I was expecting him to say, but it sure as hell wasn't that.

"What? No? I don't…" Reeve splutters, clutching my hand tight. All the blood has drained from his face. "How is that possible? My father said nothing to me about a brother." He looks into my eyes. "And your parents never said anything about my mother expecting twins."

"Your parents didn't know they were expecting twins, Reeve. One twin was hiding behind the other. It can happen with identical twins where the babies share the same amniotic sac. It's extremely rare, and usually, later scans detect the second fetus, but this was almost twenty-seven years ago, and ultrasounds were not as advanced as they are now. There are examples all over the world where the parents didn't find out it was twins until the delivery. That is what happened in this case."

"What happened to my…twin. Did he die?" Reeve asks. I have jumped to the same conclusion.

Carson links his hands together on the table, fixing Reeve with a sympathetic look. "You were born first, and everything was fine. Your mother held you in her arms and smiled for a picture."

"I know. I have it in a frame on the wall in our living room. It's the only photo I have of me with my mother."

I slide my arm around Reeve's back, instinctively knowing he's going to need it.

"Then they realized there was another baby, and that's when the complications arose. Your mother died on the table, and they had to deliver your twin brother by caesarean section."

"Oh God." I clasp a hand over my mouth, and I can only imagine how traumatizing that must've been for Reeve's father.

"What happened to my brother?" Reeve asks again, and I hear the impatience in his tone.

Carson clears your throat. "I have known your father my whole life, and I have never seen a man love a woman as much your father loved your mother." His eyes soften as he glances at us. "You two remind me of them."

"Carson," Reeve grits out, and a muscle clenches in his jaw.

Screw protocol and societal norms. Getting up, I climb into Reeve's lap, curling my arms around him, holding him close. His body is trembling with the shock of this revelation.

"Your father was holding you in his arms, crying over your mother's lifeless body, when his other son's cries rang out in the room."

"He blamed him," Reeve blurts in a daze. "He blamed my brother for my mother's death."

Carson nods sadly.

"He was only an innocent baby! It wasn't his fault," I cry, and any hint of sympathy I was just feeling for Simon flies out the window.

"He couldn't bear to look at his son knowing it had cost him his wife, so he wanted to get rid of the baby," Reeve surmises, staring off into space, and I fear this shock has plunged him back into a difficult place. Reeve lifts his head, and his pained eyes stare right through me. "He might as well have gotten rid of me too. This explains so much. Deep down, he must have blamed me too."

I'm horror-stricken because in a twisted way that makes sense. Why did Simon hold his sons accountable for something they were not responsible for? Why didn't he cling to them and shower them with love because they were the last gift from his wife? I will never understand.

"My understanding is the medical staff tried to make him see that," Carson continues explaining, "but he was inconsolable and absolutely determined he wanted nothing to do with your twin. He told me all this many years later, and I don't mind admitting I was in complete shock. It's not my place to judge anyone, and I never said it, but your father went downhill in my estimation when he confided that in me. I had thought things were different between you and your father, and it pains me to hear they were not."

"He didn't want me either," Reeve says, his voice dull and devoid of emotion.

"What happened to Reeve's twin?" I ask again because Carson still hasn't told us. I'm terrified he's going to say Simon arranged to have the baby killed because I think that will push my husband to his breaking point. I hold Reeve closer, pressing kisses into his hair, hoping he feels my love.

"Your father arranged for a quick hush-hush adoption."

Thank God. It's the lesser of two evils.

"Does he know?" Reeve asks, rubbing his eyes.

"That's something you'll have to ask him. If you would like, I can set up a meeting."

"You know where he is? You know who he is?" Reeve clutches me with a death grip.

"I do. I can get a message to him."

"What's his name? Does he look like me?"

"I have never met him in person, so I can't say. However, it's a common misconception that identical twins look identical. Even though they share the same DNA, they aren't necessarily exactly alike. They can be different in appearance, temperament, or personality, and environmental as well as chemical factors play a part. As for his name, I can't reveal that until I have spoken to him and gained his permission. Let me reach out to him and see if he would be agreeable to a meeting."

"Reeve might need a little time," I suggest because he's just been dealt some heavy blows.

"I understand and I won't arrange anything until we have spoken. I will just test the waters."

CHAPTER 65

"YOUR GUEST IS HERE," Charlotte says through the intercom system. "Leon escorted him to the living room."

It's surreal to think Reeve's twin is only one floor below us.

We don't know a thing about him other than he seems as keen as Reeve to meet up and he readily agreed to come here rather than meeting in public. I'd surmise it's because he knows who Reeve is except names haven't been exchanged yet, per his request.

"Thanks, Charlotte. Does Angela still have eyes on Easton?" I inquire. Angela is our part-time nanny, and she usually only minds E when I have to work. However, we asked her to come over today so we could talk with Reeve's brother without interruption.

"They are right here beside me, baking cookies for the party," Charlotte confirms as I massage the corded muscle along Reeve's shoulder blades. My husband is excited but cautious and more than a little tense.

"Hi, Mommy!" Easton's cute little voice trickles into the room.

"Hey, E. Bake some extra cookies for me and your little sister." Easton is super excited to meet his new sibling. He and Reeve sing to my bump every night before his bedtime, and it's the cutest thing ever.

"Be a good boy for Angela, and I'll take you out to the playground after," Reeve promises. Easton has his own personal playground, obstacle course, and treehouse in our backyard, just like we had as kids. It's easier organizing playdates at the house than going out in public and dealing with nosy assholes and vile paparazzi.

"Yay, Daddy!"

"See you in a while, buddy."

"Okay! Love you, Mommy! Love you, Daddy!"

"We love you too," we say in unison, smiling as they disconnect.

Reeve tucks his blue button-up shirt into his black pants. "If our daughter turns out anything like her big brother, we'll be extremely blessed."

"That we will." Easton is an amazing kid, and he's made parenting him much easier than I expected. "Right, ready?" I peer up at Reeve, smiling softly.

"I feel sick," he admits, running his hands repeatedly through his hair. "What if he doesn't like me or he doesn't want to form a relationship with me?"

I understand his nervousness. In the two weeks since we discovered the truth, Reeve has been knocked off-kilter. It's one thing entirely to discover the circumstances of your mother's death weren't exactly as you'd been told—like finding out your lying piece-of-shit father is an even bigger lying piece-of-shit father—and quite another to discover you have a brother. *A twin.* A part of you out there in the world you never knew existed. Reeve has so many questions and expectations, and I hope he finds some answers today.

Truth is, I'm almost as anxious as Reeve. I know he's hoping this meeting will go well and he'll get an opportunity to know his brother, to develop the relationship they should've always had. They say twins share a deep connection, and I wonder what it does to them when they are separated, as happened in this case. Will they form an instant bond the second they meet? Or will it no longer exist because it hasn't been nurtured since birth?

Having a brother in his life would be the icing on the cake for my husband, and I really hope they hit it off. We don't know the circumstances of his adoption. It's possible he has other siblings, and this might not be as big of a deal to him. But Reeve is his only flesh and blood, his only living connection to their parents. Surely that counts?

Right now, my husband needs reassurance, and I intend to give it to him. I cup his face, kissing him briefly. "He's your *twin.* It's probably been as big of a shock for him as it's been for you, but how could he not love you? You're an amazing person, Reeve. A wonderful husband, son-in-law, and father, and I know you'll be an excellent brother too. If he doesn't want to get to know you, that's all on him." I rest my hands on his toned hips. "It's a good sign he's here. That must mean he's open to it." I sincerely hope so because I'm not sure what it'll do to Reeve if his twin doesn't want to have anything to do with him. "Just don't expect miracles. It might take both of you some time to come to terms with everything, but I'm sure it'll work out. You're not just brothers. You're *twins.* That's an extra special connection."

"True." His lips come down on mine, and he kisses me softly and slowly until I melt in his arms. "I know I've been a basket case these past few months. Thank you for putting up with me."

I slide my hands up over his chest. "Reeve. I love you. I love you so much." I peck his lips, winding my arms around his neck. "Supporting you is never a chore. I've just been worried, but I think you're about to turn a corner." I offer him my most reassuring smile. "We should go. We don't want to leave the poor man waiting too long."

I am fascinated to see if Reeve's twin looks like him or if they share any of the same character traits. I've been reading up on identical twins since Carson broke the news, and he was correct. They aren't always identical. While they are born with the same features, they can develop in different ways as they grow. They can have different heights, different builds, different facial traits, and different facial expressions. They can be completely different in personality.

His Adam's apple bobs in his throat, as I grab his hand. "It's going to be fine. Breathe, and remember I'm here with you. This is an exciting moment," I add, wanting to reinforce the most important part of today. "You have a brother."

Anxiety is replaced with cautious elation on my husband's face. "It's surreal."

"It's wonderful."

Please, please, let this go well for him. I offer up silent prayers the entire way down to the living room.

My heart is racing when Reeve stops outside the closed doors, drawing another deep breath and squeezing my hand tight. I'm tingling with nervous adrenaline so I can only imagine how my husband is feeling.

Reeve opens the door, and we step into our plush living room. We usually only entertain guests in here, preferring our informal living room when it's just us.

A tall man stands in front of the window with his back to us and his arms folded in front of his chest. He's wearing a black T-shirt over fitted black jeans and boots. My heart does a funny little jump, and all the tiny hairs stand at attention on the back of my neck. I examine him more carefully, and I can't shake the sense of unease crawling over my skin. His brother has a couple of inches in height on Reeve, and he's broader in the shoulders. His hair is cut similarly to Reeve's. It appears to be the same shade of brown minus the natural blond highlights Reeve has acquired thanks to the Californian sun.

Reeve clears his throat, looking at me with one brow raised in question. He must have heard us come into the room, yet he has made no move to turn around, which is a little rude. Perhaps he's a bundle of nerves too. "Hello," Reeve says so there can be no doubt we are here.

The man turns around and walks toward us. Everything blurs, and it happens as if in slow motion. My heart speeds up, and I hope Reeve doesn't notice how clammy my hand is in his grasp or hear how loud my heart is banging against my rib cage. I am rooted to the spot, staring at his brother in confusion, wondering what kind of mind fuckery this is.

The guy looks like Reeve. He's not exactly identical, but there is more than a strong enough resemblance to easily identify them as brothers. However, that's not why my legs are threatening to go out from under me and my heart is galloping like a racehorse just let out of a gate.

The guy looks like Dillon.

If Dillon had blue eyes instead of green and brown hair instead of blond. He has the same scar over his eyebrow, the same ridge in his nose—from when he got in a fight in school—and identical piercings, and when my gaze lowers and I see the familiar ink on his arms, I know who I'm looking at, but I can't make sense of it.

"I'm Reeve Lancaster," Reeve says. "And this is my wife, Vivien."

"It's nice to meet you both." His husky Irish voice confirms any last flicker of doubt. "I'm Dillon O'Donoghue."

CHAPTER 66

MY KNEES BUCKLE, and I sway on my feet. Nausea swims up my throat, and I think I'm going to be sick. Reeve reacts fast, slinging his arm around my back and holding me upright. "Darling, what's wrong?"

A hysterical giggle lies trapped at the base of my throat. Where do I even start?

Gripping Reeve's arm tight, I cling to his body as shock races through my veins like lightning. My brain is fried. A multitude of questions dances around my head, and it feels like I'm losing my mind. This cannot be happening. What is happening?

Lifting my gaze, I lock eyes on Dillon, and it's disconcerting seeing Reeve's eyes on Dillon's face. How is this possible? Have my eyes been deceiving me? I don't understand. There were occasions when I thought I saw hints of blue in Dillon's eyes under certain lighting, but I never gave it more than a passing thought. Now I know it's because he must have been wearing contacts. But why? This makes no sense.

Dillon's eyes drop to my swollen stomach, and a muscle clenches in his jaw. He didn't look surprised to see me, so either he knew whose house he was visiting or he's pretending. Neither scenario provides any reassurance.

"Viv. Baby. Talk to me." Reeve's alarmed voice breaks through to me, and I snap out of it.

"I'm okay," I croak. "I just got a little dizzy."

"Come and sit down." Reeve guides me over to the couch, and I'm working hard to contain a full-body shiver. I'm super cold, inside and out, and I can't stop the trembling that emanates from pure unadulterated terror as old fears quickly resurface.

Blood rushes to my head and thrums in my ears, and the voice screaming questions in my head is all I can hear, but I need to get a grip. I need to do damage control until I figure out what the actual fuck is going on. I avoid looking at Dillon because I'm not sure I can look at him without having a complete meltdown.

Reeve helps me sit on the couch, gently pushing my head between my legs. "Deep breaths, babe, and keep your head down. It will get rid of the dizzy spells. I'll grab you some water." Training my eyes on the ground, I inhale and exhale, trying to calm down. I see Reeve's feet moving away. "It's been a particularly stressful time for both of us recently," Reeve tells Dillon. "Stress isn't good for the baby, and I've been trying to get Viv to take it easy, but she's been worrying too much about me."

"Congratulations. This is your second child, right?" Dillon says, and I almost choke on air, emitting a strange gargled sound.

"Shit." Reeve rushes back to my side, setting a bottle of water and a glass down on the coffee table. "Maybe you should lie down upstairs."

"No!" I blurt. "I'll be okay in a minute." There is no way in hell I am leaving Reeve in a room alone with Dillon. God knows what he might say!

"Take a seat," Reeve tells Dillon, pouring water into the glass for me.

Dillon sits directly across from me, and like the coward I am, I keep my head between my legs, pretending I'm still dizzy. I'm sweating bullets, and my brain is rapid-firing questions at me from all angles.

"Drink this, babe." Reeve holds the glass out to me, rubbing his other hand up and down my back.

Wiping my sweaty palms down the front of my summer dress, I lift my head, ignoring Dillon, and focus on my husband. My hand visibly shakes as I take the glass from Reeve, and I almost drop it. Reeve's brow creases with fresh concern. "Perhaps we should call the doctor." He wraps his hand around mine, helping me to drink. Then he places his other hand against my brow. "You don't feel too hot, but you're a little clammy."

"I'm feeling better now. Stop worrying." Shucking his hand off, I grip my glass more firmly, taking sips of water and purposely avoiding looking at my ex.

"Are you sure?"

"Yes." Grabbing Reeve's arm, I place it around my shoulder, snuggling into his side, hoping his body warmth will heat up my ice-cold limbs. "I'm sorry I derailed your meeting. Talk to your brother."

Let me freak out in silence while I try to figure out why Dillon is here. I just need to survive this ordeal and then call Audrey. I'm deliberately not thinking about the most pressing question, because if I go there now, I'm liable to pass out stone-cold.

Charlotte enters, depositing a tray with tea, coffee, and cookies on the coffee table. I spot the curiosity on her face as she looks at both brothers, but she remains discreet, leaving as quickly as she arrived.

"Would you like something to drink?" Reeve asks Dillon, gesturing with his hand to the tray and the bottles of water sitting on the side table. "I can get something stronger, if you like?" If I wasn't pregnant and it wasn't only eleven a.m., I would be demanding vodka.

"Coffee is fine."

"Why do I get the feeling I know you from somewhere?" Reeve asks Dillon, as he pours coffee into a mug.

I clamp my lips shut, saying nothing. Reeve doesn't know I listen to the band's music or I saw them perform tons of times on stage while I was in Ireland, so I can't be the one to tell him without rousing some suspicion.

"I'm the lead singer for Collateral Damage," Dillon confirms, taking the mug from his brother.

His twin.

Oh my God. How did I never realize it? I knew Dillon's birthday was in January, but he never said the date. There were occasions when I felt a familiarity around him that was odd, but I never stopped to analyze it. Then again, who would? I was on a different continent, Dillon is Irish, I had no idea he was adopted because no one told me, and we had no idea Reeve had a brother back then. Why would I have gone looking for meaning behind that familiarity?

Dillon looked totally different with his bleach-blond hair and green eyes, and he wasn't as tan back then. With his ink and piercings, his bulkier frame, additional height, and the little facial differences like his dimples, he didn't look identical on the surface. But I slept beside him. I knew every inch of his body. Surely, I should have noticed something? Now that I reflect on it, the way he used to tilt his head to one side and rub the back of his neck is so like Reeve.

The clues were there, and I never picked up on them.

I feel like such an idiot until I remember Audrey met him too and she didn't notice any resemblance either.

"Yes! That's it," Reeve exclaims, pulling me out of my inner monologue. "We saw you perform at the Oscars in February, didn't we, Viv?"

"We did." I force a smile on my face.

"Congrats on your win, by the way," Dillon smoothly says. "I loved your acceptance speech."

I sink a little lower in the couch. To anyone else, it would appear Dillon is sincere in his compliment. But I know it's bullshit. I want to throw him out of my house, rewind to two weeks ago, and tell Carson Park not to tell us anything. That secrets are best left to die with their owners. Because there is no scenario where this ends well.

"Thanks. I'm sorry things didn't go the band's way that night," Reeve says. "Collateral Damage walked away empty-handed, but it's still an enormous honor to be nominated for such a prestigious award."

Dillon shrugs, but I notice a muscle clenching in his jaw, and it's clear Reeve inadvertently hit some kind of nerve.

Reeve drums his fingers on his knee, a telltale sign he's nervous. "So, you grew up in Ireland? Viv spent some time there, and she loved it." He smiles at me while my pulse throbs in my neck as liquid adrenaline courses through my veins. If Dillon is going to say anything, it will be now.

Dillon eyeballs me, and he has a pleasant smile on his face, but it's as fake as mine. Reeve glances between us, his brow puckering in confusion.

"I did. Ireland is great," I say, snuggling in closer to Reeve, wishing I could bury my face in his shoulder and cry my eyes out.

"Did you like growing up in Ireland?" Reeve asks him, his shoulders relaxing a little.

"It was good. I grew up on a farm with my adopted parents, three brothers, and my sister."

Reeve's eyes pop wide. "Wow, so you have brothers and a sister. That must've been nice."

Dillon smiles, and it's the first genuine smile I've seen on his face. "Yeah, it was cool. Things were fairly wild growing up as teenagers in Ireland."

"Are you close to them?" Reeve asks, and I know he's internally gauging where he'll fit in Dillon's life while I'm trying to figure out how to extract Reeve from this mess before he gets hurt.

"We're a close family." Dillon smiles as he looks pointedly at me, but this one doesn't meet his eyes. "I'm especially close to my sister, Ash. She manages the band. And my younger brother Ro is our drummer."

Ground, gobble me up now.

I swallow thickly over the messy ball of emotion clogging my throat, squeezing my eyes shut.

"Are you okay?" Reeve asks, tightening his arm around my shoulders.

"I'm fine." I fake the biggest smile while it feels like my heart is breaking anew. Sitting here is excruciating on a variety of levels, but sitting across from the other love of my life and pretending like I don't know him, like we don't share tons of incredible memories, is tearing strips off my heart.

I don't know why Dillon hasn't said anything or what his motives are for being here, but the longer I sit here with the knowledge I have, the more painful it becomes. I'm close to cracking.

How can I keep who Dillon is to me from Reeve? If he is to form any relationship with his brother, I need to tell him about Dillon and me. How do I do that? And if I tell him, what will it mean for their relationship? What will it mean for ours? And what about Easton?

Oh God. The smile drops off my face, and I almost suffocate on the pain crawling up my throat.

Reeve opens his mouth, to ask me if I'm okay, I assume, and I need to redirect this conversation ASAP. "Did you know?" I blurt, looking at Dillon. "Did you know you were adopted?" *Why didn't you tell me?* "Did you know who your bio parents were?"

"My parents told me I was adopted when I was six, so I've always known. I toyed with the idea of finding my birth parents as a teenager, but I didn't pursue it." He quirks a brow, and his brow ring lifts with the motion. "Why would I? I have the most amazing family. I didn't need to find the parents who abandoned me."

"Our mother didn't abandon you," Reeve says. A host of different emotions is splayed on his face, and I know this is a lot to process for him. "She died giving birth to us."

"So I've just discovered." Dillon scrubs his hands down his face.

"You just found out too?" Reeve asks, sitting up straighter.

"It's been such a shock."

I regard Dillon warily, trying to figure out if he's being honest or lying.

"I know." Reeve nods, biting on his lip. "Simon was wrong to do what he did to you. To us." His voice breaks, and I reach out, threading my fingers in his. Dillon's eyes track every touch, making me feel self-conscious. "It's just another reason in a long list of reasons why he was a shit dad."

Dillon leans forward on his elbows. "You didn't get along?"

Reeve shakes his head. "No. He might have kept me, but it was in name only. He could hardly bear to look at me sometimes."

Dillon looks to the ground, and his knee jerks up and down. When he lifts his head, after a few beats, he looks calm and composed, and I'm immediately on guard. He smiles at Reeve. "Well, he's not here now, and there's nothing to stop us from getting to know one another. Brother to brother." His eyes dart briefly to mine. "Twin to twin."

"I would really like that," Reeve says, oblivious to my mini meltdown.

What the fuck is Dillon playing at? Is he serious about getting to know his brother? Did I genuinely mean so little to Dillon that our history doesn't matter at all and that's why he's not mentioning we know one another? I shouldn't care about that. Not if it means Reeve has a chance of getting to know his twin, but what kind of relationship will they have if it starts on a lie? Like I said to Audrey recently, a lie of omission is still a lie. The bigger issue is, I know something Dillon clearly doesn't, and that knowledge could change everything. I need to keep my son away from him, at least until I investigate the situation and what it might mean.

I chew on the inside of my mouth, thoroughly confused and scared. My head is such a mess right now, and I don't know what to do. Where to go from here. This is so bad.

"I would also really like it if you'd accept half of my inheritance," Reeve says, and I'm a little surprised he brought that up already. We have talked about it, but I didn't think he would mention it today. "It rightfully belongs to you."

"I don't want anything from that man," Dillon hisses, digging his nails into his thighs. "And I don't need his money anymore."

Reeve gulps. "It's not just money. There's some property and shares in Studio 27. You don't have to decide now. We can talk about it again."

"I need to go," Dillon says, standing abruptly.

He's pissed; that much is clear. Relief threads through me as I just want him out of my house. At some point, I'm going to have to speak to him, but not now. Not when I can't think straight. I can't leave it for too long though, in case he decides to tell Reeve, but I need at least twenty-four hours to try to wrap my head around the implications of today's monstrous reveal.

"You can't stay a little longer?" Reeve's disappointment is clear on his face, and I want to cry.

Fuck you, fate.

Fuck you. Fuck you. Fuck you.

"We have time booked in the studio, and the guys are already waiting on me. But let's meet up at the weekend, yeah?" Dillon steps in front of Reeve, his anger now firmly hidden behind a wall I'm accustomed with. "It was good meeting you."

"I wish we hadn't lost so many years." Reeve stands, and the strained look of anguish on his face almost undoes me.

In a super surprising move, Dillon pulls Reeve into a hug. "We have plenty of time to catch up," Dillon says, fixing me with an ugly sneer I haven't seen in years.

All the blood in my body turns to ice as I stare at the man who still owns part of my heart. He—

"Daddy!" Easton bursts into the room, dashing toward Reeve. My heart stutters in my chest, and I can scarcely breathe over the knot of anxiety blocking my airwaves. "I made extra cookies for my sister. Look!" He holds out a napkin with two cookies as Reeve scoops him up into his arms.

"Yum." Reeve chuckles as cookie crumbs sprinkle over his shirt when Easton waves his hand around.

"Who are you?" Easton asks, fixing his wide-eyed blue gaze on Dillon.

I clamp a trembling hand over my mouth as Dillon stares at Easton. His intense penetrative gaze is one I'm familiar with, and I don't like how it's fixed on my son. I want to move, to take Easton out of the room, but shock has rendered me immobile. I can't speak over the horror of this moment. Where the fuck is Angela? I'm going to string her up for letting E out of her sight.

"This is your Uncle Dillon," Reeve says when Dillon doesn't reply.

"Cool! Is he coming to my birthday party tomorrow?" Easton innocently asks, and I feel the ground opening underneath me.

"Tomorrow?" Dillon says, finally finding his voice. It sounds off, and goose bumps sprout along my arms. "I thought your birthday was in June?"

CHAPTER 67

OH FUCK! He already suspects, and now he knows. Panic whirls through my veins, and it's a miracle I don't puke on the spot.

Reeve chuckles. "The media thinks it's June because we manipulated them into believing that, but he was actually born five weeks earlier."

I can almost see the cogs churning in Dillon's brain as he calculates the dates. "Why would you do that?" he asks, sounding and looking dazed.

Intense pressure sits on my chest, and I can't breathe. I can't move. I can only sit and watch it unfold in complete and utter shock.

"We've had issues with the paparazzi in the past," Reeve says. "The last thing we want is them hounding us every year on Easton's birthday. This way, we get to cele- brate without them breathing down our necks. Win-win."

Dillon stares at me, genuine shock splayed across his face, and I can't take this a second longer. I stumble to my feet. "I don't feel so hot," I tell Reeve. "I need the bathroom." I don't wait for him to reply, rushing out of the room.

I barely make it to the nearest bathroom in time. Crouching over the toilet bowl, I vomit repeatedly while tears stream down my face. I retch until there is nothing left in my stomach, and it mirrors the pained hollowness I feel everywhere. I flush the toilet and slump against the wall, running my hands back and forth across my swollen belly, struggling to understand how my life could be so perfect one second and then everything falls to shit the next.

None of the heartbreak I've endured in the past comes close to how I'm feeling right now. I stand to lose everything, and I'm beyond terrified. Fresh panic slaps me in the face, and I clamber to my feet. I shouldn't have left the room! What if Dillon has said something to Reeve?

I rinse out my mouth and wash my hands. I'm drying them on the towel when the door opens, and Dillon slips silently into the room.

My heart thrashes frantically around my chest. "You can't be in here!" I shriek.

"We need to talk," he says in a clipped tone. His lips pull into a half-sneer as he flips the lock on the door. "Don't worry about your *precious husband*. He's upstairs getting cleaned up. Easton threw up over both of them, and I said I'd come to check on you."

"Oh my God. Is Easton okay?"

"He probably ate too many cookies though Reeve thinks he might have the same tummy bug you have." He barks out a harsh laugh. "Except we both know why *you're* feeling sick."

"Why are you here?" I cross my arms over my chest, as if that will ward off the trembling stealing over my body.

"I came to meet *my twin*."

"Why? And quit with the bullshit, Dil." His scathing tone tells me all I need to know. Whatever that was in the living room was all an act.

"Ah, there she is." He walks toward me, and I back away. "My fiery little ball-buster. I was beginning to wonder if Reeve had knocked all the life out of you."

I thrust out my hand. "Stay away from me."

He laughs, twirling his finger around a lock of my hair as he crowds me against the wall. Or he tries to. It's a little difficult to do with my pregnant belly in the way. Dillon looks down, and tension bleeds into the air. I rub a protective hand over my stomach, feeling a need to shield my unborn daughter from whatever vitriol this man is about to spill. Slowly, he raises his head, pinning me with ocean-blue eyes I still can't get over. "Is this one Reeve's, or is there a possibility it's another man's too?"

"Fuck you!" I slap him across the face. "I'm faithful to my husband."

He smirks that annoying smirk I used to love to hate. Leaning in, he presses his mouth to my ear. "But is he faithful to you? That's the million-dollar question."

"What?" I blurt, momentarily blindsided until I realize he's just fucking with my head. "Reeve loves me, and he loves our family. He wouldn't do that."

"But he did before, Hollywood, or do you have a selective memory?" He winds his hand around the nape of my neck, putting his face all up in mine. "You know what they say, once a cheater always a cheater."

I shake my head, glaring at him. "Not Reeve. He made mistakes, but he made up for it, and we got past it. He's loyal to me, and I know you're just messing with my head." I shove at his shoulders. "Take your hands off me."

"No." He twists my hair, yanking it around his fist and tilting my head up. "Did you conceal Easton's real birthday to hide him from me?" he demands.

"No," I truthfully reply. "I gave birth to him at home, and I didn't venture outside for the first few weeks, because I wanted to shield him from the media. Reeve and I weren't officially together, and I'd hidden my pregnancy, so——"

"So I wouldn't find out," he says, cutting across me.

I could lie, but what's the point? I know where this is leading. A shuddering breath flees my lips. "Yes. I wasn't sure who the father was, and I wanted to wait until I had the paternity results before saying anything to Reeve or you."

"Would you have told me if he was mine?"

I nod. "Yes. That was my plan."

His nostrils flare as he glares at me. "Liar!"

"I'm telling the truth! You can ask Audrey."

He rubs his thumb along my mouth, and I jolt as a rush of sensations skates over my skin. I have been trying to deny the hum of electricity crackling in the air, because I'm trying to deny the existence of our connection, but one little touch from him ignites a flame inside me I can't extinguish. "That's why you cut Ash off."

"I didn't want to, but I didn't want to lie to her either. I knew if she found out I was pregnant she'd ask me if it was yours. If I told her, she would tell you." I hang my head, unable to look at the disgust on his face. "I'm ashamed I did that to Ash. I love her like a sister, but I didn't see I had any other option. I contacted her after Easton was born, after the paternity test confirmed Reeve was the father"—I whisper that last part because we both know that is no longer proven—"but she didn't take my calls, and then they started bouncing back, and I knew she'd blocked me."

"I'm pretty sure that was the day we discovered you'd gotten married and had a baby without telling her or me," he grits out. "Look at me," he snaps, and I swing my eyes back around to his. "I couldn't give two shits about your lying ass, but I do care to know if that little boy is mine."

"Why?"

"Because he could be my son!" he yells.

"Keep your fucking voice down!" I hiss. "He could still be Reeve's."

"Or he could be *mine*. That test you got proves nothing because our DNA is the same. We need a specialized test with samples from both of us to prove paternity conclusively, and I want that test taken ASAP."

My chest heaves. "How do I explain this to Reeve?" I cry.

"Not my fucking problem," he snaps.

"This isn't just my problem. It's yours too! He's your *brother!*"

"He's not my brother," he growls. "Shane, Ciarán, and Ronan are my brothers. Reeve is just the selfish prick I shared a womb with."

I gasp at the venom in his tone and the hatred on his face. Tears leak out of my eyes, and my heart hurts for my husband. Obviously, everything Dillon said back there was bullshit. "How can you say that?" I thump his chest. "It's not Reeve's fault Simon Lancaster was a twisted fuck who blamed *both* his sons for what happened to their mother! Reeve didn't know about you until two weeks ago! He grew up with a father who couldn't give a shit about him, and if it wasn't for my family, he'd have been all alone."

"Save your bleeding-heart crap for someone who gives a shit. FYI. That's not me." He grips my chin, and I flinch at the look of loathing in his eyes. "That prick has taken everything from me, and I think I'm owed a little payback, don't you?"

Certain things slot into place in my head. "You knew! You've known the truth for years." My stomach lurches wildly, and I dry heave as the reality of the situation dawns on me in full technicolor horror.

"I was seventeen when Simon Lancaster found me and told me the truth." Dillon releases me, stepping back, dragging a hand through his hair. "He said I murdered my mother and I was lucky he'd given me up for adoption because he couldn't bear to look at me and he'd most likely have killed me if he'd taken me home."

I raise a shaky hand to my mouth. How could any man say that to his son? Simon Lancaster was a monster, and I'm fucking glad he's dead. I know this must have gone down around the same time Ash tried to kill herself, and I can only imagine the pain

373

Dillon was in. Irrespective of our present situation, I would never wish that on him. My heart aches for him, and my body longs to comfort him, like I would have done in the past.

But this isn't the past.

And it's obvious Dillon isn't the same Dillon.

He's twisted with anger and rage, his judgment is clouded by the things he mistakenly believes, and that makes him wildly unpredictable. Especially when he seems to be channeling most of that rage unfairly in Reeve's direction.

I can't let him destroy my husband. Whatever agenda he has, I know he's focused on hurting Reeve and I'm not letting him do that. Right now, my priorities lie with my husband and my son. Protecting them from pain is my focus. "Why did Simon contact you?" I ask.

Dillon rubs the back of his neck as pain flares in his eyes. "He offered me one million dollars to sign an NDA so the world would never find out I was Reeve Lancaster's secret twin."

I stare numbly at him, sure my ears must be deceiving me. "Why?"

"He was protecting the son he loved!" he spits, and I'm dumbfounded again. "He said Reeve was going to be a massive star and he couldn't have skeletons in his closet. He wanted to make sure I would never come forward. That I would never seek out Reeve. That I would slink away in the shadows and pretend like I was invisible."

"Jesus, Dillon. That is heartbreaking. But I'm telling you now, Simon wasn't protecting Reeve. He was protecting himself. He knew he would've been outed as a monster if the truth was revealed. I hated Simon when he was alive for what he did to Reeve, but I absolutely despise him in death."

"For what he did to *Reeve?*!" Dillon shoves his angry face in mine, and I protectively cradle my stomach, reeling from the poison spewing from Dillon's mouth.

It's as if I never knew him at all.

What happened to the troubled broken boy who opened his heart and showed me the sexy sweet soul hidden underneath? I see none of that boy in the man who stands before me now, radiating anger like it's an entitlement. "Reeve had everything! He grew up wealthy in L.A. with every opportunity handed to him on a silver platter."

"No, Dillon. You've got it backward." My eyes plead with him to see reason. To see the truth that is so blatantly obvious to me. "You are the one who was truly wealthy. You have a loving family who adores you. You cannot place a value on that."

"I refused to sign the NDA at first," he says, staring absently at the wall, as if I haven't spoken at all. "Instead, I changed my appearance because I wanted to look nothing like that arrogant selfish wanker, and then I thought of different ways I could make both of them pay. I raged for years, plotting how I could make it happen, and then you landed in my lap." His lips curl up at the corners as he stares me in the face with cold, cruel eyes.

All the blood leeches from my body. He laughs as I stare at him with a fresh wave of horror. Pain slices across my chest, cutting soul-deep.

"It was the perfect plan of revenge. Reeve had taken everything from me. Now it was time to take something from him. Something so precious he would never recover." He brushes his fingers across my cheeks as silent tears pour down my face. "Yes,

374

Hollywood. I purposely set out to steal your heart, and you fell for it hook, line, and sinker. It was almost too easy to make you fall in love with me. My greatest triumph was when you told me you loved me in front of everyone. I guess acting must run in my blood." His dry chuckle is like a dagger straight through the heart.

"Aw, don't cry, Vivien Grace." He smooths my tears with his thumb, smirking, and I slap his hands away. "It didn't quite go according to my plan. You were supposed to return to him broken and used up. You weren't supposed to get a happy ever after, but this is even better."

"Don't do it," I croak. "Whatever it is you're planning, don't do it. It won't make you feel better."

"I beg to differ." Leaning into me, he nips at my earlobe. "You've done me a massive favor, Hollywood. Thank you for being a stupid slut and running straight back into his arms. This time, I will take everything from him—his son, his wife, his reputation, his sanity. By the time I'm done with both of you, you'll wish you were dead."

GLOSSARY OF IRISH TERMS/SAYINGS

The explanation given is in the context of this book. Also includes pronunciations.

Aisling – female Irish name. Pronounced Ash-ling.

Aoife – female Irish name. Pronounced Efa.

Birds – women

Black stuff – Guinness

Blow-in – outsider/new kid on the block

Catriona – female Irish name. Pronounced Cat-ree-na.

Ciarán – male Irish name. Pronounced Kirawn.

Deadly – cool

Dragged up – brought up/raised

Fake knockers – implants/fake boobs

Fecking – freaking

Full stop – period/end of

Hound – player/manslut/manwhore

Howya – hello

Is not on – not accepted/not cool

Leaving Cert/Certificate – state exams you sit in 6th year of secondary school (senior year of high school)

Lift - elevator

Looker – good-looking

Micheál – male Irish name pronounced Mee-haul

Missus – wife but can also mean girlfriend/female partner

Mot – slang for girlfriend

Motorway – highway

On tenterhooks – waiting nervously for something to happen

Plastic tits – implants/fake boobs

Sláinte – Irish for cheers (when having a drink)

Slow coaches – slow poke

Swanning around – going around/walking around

The jacks – toilet/bathroom

The Liffey – River Liffey in Dublin

Tracksuit bottoms – sweats/sweatpants

Trinners – Trinity College Dublin/TCD

Trousers – pants

Trying it on – making a pass

Wanker – prick/asshole/jerk

LET
ME
LOVE
YOU

USA TODAY & WSJ BESTSELLING AUTHOR
SIOBHAN DAVIS

NOTE FROM THE AUTHOR

This book contains scenes which may upset some readers. If you have specific triggers you are concerned about, please email siobhan@siobhandavis.com

All of Me Duet playlist: https://bit.ly/3eu9gdo

There is a **glossary** at the back of this book you can refer to, which includes some explanations of Irish words/phrases and Irish/Gaelic pronunciations. We phrase some things differently, so if some of the Irish characters' dialogue seems a little odd, that is why!

PROLOGUE

DILLON – THE NIGHT VIVIEN LEAVES IRELAND

"YOU DISGUST ME." My sister's pretty face contorts into a scowl as she glares at me before shooting daggers at the gold digger situated in my lap. Aoife paws at my chest, her fingers creeping upward to my neck. Before Viv, Aoife's touch used to turn me on. Now, she makes my skin crawl because the touch is all wrong. Too desperate. Too harsh. Not the soft loving caresses from the only woman who matters. A woman who has just poured her heart out to me in front of everyone. A woman who just bled her truths at my feet.

But it's not enough.

She's still leaving.

To go back to *him*.

Anger glides up my throat, and a muscle clenches in my jaw, the same way it always does whenever I think of Reeve Lancaster.

"More than that, you disappoint me," Ash continues, shaking her head sadly. "I know you love her, Dil. You can deny it until you're blue in the face, and I won't believe you. You love *her*. She loves *you*." Leaning down, she puts her face all up in mine. "Fight for her, for fuck's sake."

I tried, and it didn't work. Even if I were to run outside and chase her, it won't change a damn thing. Viv is still getting on that plane to return to L.A.

To return to my *twin*.

I asked her to choose me, and she rejected me.

It's over, and the sooner my sister understands that, the better.

"It was a summer fling, and we both knew it had an end date." I shrug, bringing my beer to my lips. "The only one who doesn't seem to get that is you." I swallow a healthy mouthful of beer, hoping the alcohol will calm the violent emotional storm brewing inside me.

"I never took you for a coward, Dil, but that's exactly what you are."

Aoife drops a line of kisses on my neck, and my skin itches like I've stumbled

383

upon a bed of nettles. I need my sister to fuck off so I can get rid of the parasite on my lap. My gaze lifts to my best friend in silent communication.

"Ash." Jamie reaches for my sister, but she swats his arm away.

"I'm going after Viv," she tells him, "because someone has to make sure she's okay." She sends one last scathing look in my direction before storming off.

Aoife giggles at Ash's retreating back. "You're well rid of that stuck-up American bitch," she says, pressing her ass down on my flaccid cock.

I shove her off my lap, needing her the fuck away from me. Ro rides to the rescue, grabbing Aoife around the waist before she hits the deck.

"What the hell, Dil?" Aoife plants her hands on her hips, pinning me with an angry stare.

"Fuck off." I don't look at her as I spit the words out, bringing the bottle to my lips and draining the rest of my beer.

"I can tell you're in one of your moods, so I'll forgive you." She plonks down on my lap again.

"Are you fucking deaf as well as stupid?" I hiss, shoving her harder. This time, she lands unceremoniously on the ground, whimpering while fixing me with hurt eyes. "I don't want you. I've *never* wanted you. You were nothing more than a hole to fuck when I needed a release."

Ro helps Aoife to her feet, glaring at me. "Don't be an even bigger asshole. It's not fair to take this out on Aoife. You fucked this up. *You.* Not anyone else."

Jamie whispers in Aoife's ear, and she leaves, taking her three friends with her. "Ro." Jamie shakes his head. "Drop it."

"No, Jay. I won't drop it. He needs to get his head out of his ass and remember where his priorities lie."

Conor leans back in his chair, nodding in silent agreement.

"We have a real opportunity this time," Ro continues, "and he's not going to fuck it up for all of us."

An opportunity we wouldn't have if it wasn't for Viv. My brother seems to have forgotten that. "Don't hold back, bro. Say what you really think."

"You knew what you had with her was temporary, so stop acting like someone ran over your dog. You should apologize and end things amicably. Ash is right in that respect, but you have no right to be pissed at Viv for returning home when it was the plan all along."

He has no idea how close I came to giving it all up. How I was prepared to quit the band and stay by her side if she had told me she'd stay.

I love music. I love performing. I'm happy doing what we're doing, and it's enough for me because I don't want the nasty side of fame. I don't want my private life under a microscope, and not because the truth about my twin brother would most likely come out. Why can't the music be enough? We could make a comfortable living producing and streaming our own stuff. Playing local events. Building a loyal fanbase locally. But it won't be enough for Jamie and Ronan. Even Conor is champing at the bit at the prospect this A&R scout might want to sign us.

Going to America and making it big has never been my dream, but I'll do it for the guys, for my brother, because there is nothing holding me here now anyway.

"What is she doing here?" I slur a few hours later, spotting Aoife standing a few feet away, scowling in my direction.

"Ro invited her." Jamie flops down beside me on the sofa. He hands me a beer, and I drain the last dregs of the one in my hand before tossing it on the carpeted floor. "You know your brother is a bleeding heart. Apparently, she was crying in the toilets at Bruxelles, so he took pity on her."

"I hope he's planning to fuck her because I'm not ever going there again." I pop the cap on my beer, glugging a few mouthfuls.

"You should go after Viv. It's not too late," he says, glancing at the time on his mobile phone.

"Nah." I scrunch up my nose. "Ro is right. It was always leading to this point."

"I'm calling bullshit." Jamie scrubs a hand along his stubbly jawline. "There is no shame in admitting you're hurting. I know you love her. We all saw it happening."

It wasn't supposed to go down like this.

I was going to steal *her* heart.

She wasn't supposed to steal mine.

But steal it she did. The plan was to make her fall in love with me and then break her heart so badly he got a shell of the woman he loved back. My heart was never meant to get involved, but she reeled me in before I even realized what was happening. She made me feel things I have never felt before. Love. Hope. Possibility. She made me believe I was worthy. That things could be different, and for a little while there, I believed in a future where we were together.

Yet it wasn't real. She was always preparing to return to him.

Now, I'm the one left nursing a broken heart while she swans back to that selfish prick.

How does he do this? How does he always come out on top? I have never hated anyone as much as I hate Reeve Lancaster and his father. I hate them with a burning intensity that grows hotter and stronger with every passing day.

"What is that slut doing here?" Ash snaps, materializing in front of us an hour later. The party is in full swing now, and our small living room is bursting at the seams. Music thumps through the loudspeakers, almost drowning out the sound of conversation and laughter.

"Hello to you too, sister," I slur, swiping the joint out of Conor's fingers before he can lift it to his lips.

"I'm not talking to you," she hisses, pinning me with red-rimmed eyes as she crawls into Jamie's lap. Ash curls into a ball against her boyfriend, sniffling into his neck.

She has the saddest expression on her face, and pain presses down on my chest as the realization dawns. "She's gone."

"No thanks to you." Ash swipes at the dampness on her cheeks.

"It's nothing to do with me." I blow smoke circles into the air. "This was always the way it was meant to be."

She opens her mouth, and Jamie whispers something into her ear. A hushed conversation ensues, and they both glance at me as they debate something. Jamie kisses her, and a pang of longing for my girl hits me square in the face.

I force beer down my dry throat, needing to numb myself to all thoughts and emotions. Ash stares at me as she cuddles with her boyfriend, letting him comfort her, but her angry expression has been exchanged for something worse—pity. I pretend I don't notice, sitting there stewing in a mess of my own making, drinking and smoking to drown out my pain.

The rest of the night is a blur, and I don't budge from my position on the sofa, observing the party raging around me like an objective bystander. I'm vaguely conscious of Jamie and my brother carrying me up to my room at some point, and everything is a blank after that.

Muffled voices tickle my eardrums, attempting to lure me from sleep, but I ignore them. Drums are pounding a new beat in my skull, and my tongue feels like it's superglued to the roof of my mouth. Someone prods me in the leg, but I play comatose, knowing they'll go away if I continue playing dead.

"Aarghhh!" I bolt upright as ice-cold water drenches my upper torso, waking up every single cell and nerve ending in my body. "What the fuck?" I shout, shaking droplets of water all over my duvet as I push wet hair back off my face.

"Get up!" Ash says. "We need to talk, and I'm done waiting."

"Fuck off, Ash." I glare at her through blurry vision.

"You can't speak to Ash like that," Jamie says. "She's only trying to help."

I rub at my eyes, and my vision focuses. Jamie and Ash are standing in my bedroom, leaning against the wall, eyeballing me with an intensity that scares me. "I don't need any help," I mumble, pulling myself up against the headboard.

"Said the blind man as he was standing on the edge of the cliff," Ash deadpans, pushing off the wall and perching on the dry side of my bed. "I love you, Dillon, but you're a stupid fucker at the best of times."

I open my mouth to protest, but she clamps her hand over my lips. "Nope. You're going to sit there and shut up. I've got shit to say, and I'm saying it. Besides, your breath reeks, and I'm about to pass out from the fumes." She passes me a glass of water and two paracetamol. "Take those." She twists around, looking at Jamie. "Babe, can you make coffee? Lots and lots of strong black coffee. We need to sober him up fast."

Jamie nods, walking out of my room. His feet thud on the stairs as he heads down to the kitchen.

I knock back the painkillers because my head is pounding and pain rattles around my skull, reminding me I completely overdid it last night. "Spit it out," I tell my sister, needing to get this over and done with.

"I won't pretend to know the exact inner workings of your mind, nor am I asking you to tell me, but you're my brother, and I know you well enough to know part of what is going through that thick skull of yours." She grabs a towel from behind her, gently mopping the wetness on my face. "You love her. I know you do. Like I know it terrifies you to trust your heart to someone. I understand she hurt you, but she's hurting too. I should've knocked your heads together weeks ago and forced you to have a conversation about the future. You've both been skating around it instead of just talking."

"We did talk. I told her how I felt. I asked her to stay, and she said no."

"You sprung it on her at the last minute, Dil! You didn't even give her time to consider it before you stormed off all butthurt."

"She rejected me, Ash." I rub at the tightness spreading across my chest. "She was never going to choose me over him. She's been in love with him most of her life. A few months with me isn't going to change that fact."

"Dillon. Jesus." She crawls up beside me, wrapping her arms around my wet chest. "She broke up with him because he betrayed her. He let her down, and she might never be able to forget that. She came here to heal. She didn't plan to meet anyone let alone fall in love. But she did. She fell in love with *you*." She taps my chest, directly where my heart beats sluggishly. "You caught her off guard when you asked her," she continues. "She's confused, and her past is compounding the situation, but it doesn't mean she doesn't love you like crazy because I know she does." Ash grabs my face between her small, soft palms. "She told you she loves you in front of everyone last night. Didn't that mean anything?"

Of course, it did. That took huge guts, something Viv has in spades. I know I should have chased after her last night, but I was already drunk and hurting too much to think logically. All I wanted to do was hurt her, so she'd know what it feels like.

"It did, but it's too late now," I say, spotting the time on my mobile. It's already seven in the morning and her flight left at four. "She's already in the air. And I'm not sure her saying that changes anything."

"You won't know unless you fight for her." Ash scrambles off the bed as Jamie reappears, carrying a steaming mug of coffee. "Stay here. I've got something to show you." She disappears as my best friend hands me a coffee.

"What are you going to do?" he asks, lighting up a cigarette.

I shrug. "What can I do? She's gone now."

Ash returns, carrying a brand-spanking-new guitar case into the room.

"What's that?" Jamie inquires, walking around the bed.

"It's for Dil. From Viv."

I set my mug down on the bedside locker, taking the case from my sister's hands.

"Holy fuck." Jamie kneels on the floor as I remove the expensive Fender from the case. "Is that what I think it is?"

My fingers run along the curved edges of the guitar with reverence. "It's a sixtieth anniversary American vintage 1954 Stratocaster."

"That's good, right?" Ash asks.

I can barely nod over the lump in my throat. "Just under two thousand of these were manufactured back in 2014."

"They're collector's items," Jamie says, his eyes still out on stalks.

"I thought it was new." Ash shrugs, not understanding the significance of this gift.

"It basically is," I admit, knowing from looking at it that whoever she bought this off hasn't used the guitar.

"She engraved your initials," Jamie says, rubbing his thumb along the DOD etched into the glossy wood.

"Look at the strap," Ash prompts, and I hold it out, examining the custom-made Toxic Gods strap. My heart, swollen with so many emotions, slams against my rib cage. I can't believe Viv did this for me. We spoke about it one time. She knows my goal was to buy one of these at auction someday.

"Bro. She must really love you to leave you this after how you treated her last night." Jamie pulls a drag on his cigarette before Ash swipes it from his hand, stubbing it out.

Shame washes over me for the first time, and I'm embarrassed at how poorly I treated Viv at Bruxelles. I let my pain take control, hurting the girl who means everything to me.

"I wasn't with Aoife," I blurt, eyeballing my sister. "I just did that to hurt Viv."

"I know, dumbass. It was a shitty move, and you hurt my best friend." Her eyes turn glacial. "I don't know if I'll ever forgive you for that, even if you do make things right with her."

I set the guitar aside, too guilt-ridden to test it out right now. "I don't see how. She's gone, and I missed my chance to fix things."

Jamie and Ash trade conspiratorial looks. My sister grabs my mug, thrusting it into my hands. "Drink."

"What are you up to?"

"Do you love Vivien, Dillon? No bullshit. It's just us three here."

"I do. I love her so much."

"Then get on a fucking plane, and tell her that. Talk to her. Make her see she has options. That this doesn't have to be the end for you two." Ash's eyes blaze with determination. "I think she just needs to hear the words from your lips and she'll change her mind."

Ash isn't aware of everything. I wonder if she knew the truth if she would still want me to chase after her best friend. Going after Viv is risky as fuck, and there are no guarantees. This could all end badly and cause a shitstorm of epic proportions. She could take his side when she discovers the truth. "What if she doesn't?"

"You won't know if you don't try, but you've got to hurry. Reeve is going to try to win her back, and she's vulnerable now." Ash extracts her phone from her jeans pocket. "There's a flight leaving for LAX in four hours. Say the word, and I'll book the ticket."

Of course, he's going to try to get her back. I've known that all along.

Reeve Lancaster always gets what he wants.

Except this time.

Fuck it.

I'm not a coward.

I'm not a quitter.

And Vivien is worth fighting for.

It's time to man up and claim my woman.

He is *not* taking her from me.

I will fight him to the bitter end because I love her. I love her more than life, and she's worth risking everything.

With my mind made up, I wish I could click my fingers and be in L.A. already. I don't know how much a plane ticket costs, but I have some measly savings, so I can probably just about afford it.

"Don't worry about the cost," Ash says, as if she's a mind reader. "I'll get it, and you can pay me back when you make it big. I haven't paid rent all year, so I've managed to save a lot. I'll book you a plane ticket and a hotel room. Just say the word." Her finger hovers over a button on her phone.

"How will I find her?"

Ash flashes me a triumphant grin. "I have her US mobile number. You can call her when you get there and arrange to meet."

Ripping the duvet off, I swing my legs out of the bed. "Book it. I'm grabbing a shower."

Ash squeals, and I hope I'm doing the right thing.

"Pack my shit," I tell Jamie, knowing time is of the essence. "Enough for a week."

"A week?" He lifts an eyebrow. "Don't forget the scout is coming to see us perform in ten days."

"I need some time to work through things with Viv, but I promise I'll be back in time for the event."

Navigating my way out of LAX and finding the shuttle bus to my hotel is challenging because the place is ginormous, but eventually I find myself on the right bus, nabbing a window seat at the back. Thank fuck, I managed to sleep off my hangover on the plane, so I'm not feeling too bad, despite the change in time zone, climate, and culture. My nose is pressed to the glass as we leave the airport, heading for downtown L.A.

Viv wasn't joking about the traffic, and it takes forever to reach my hotel. After checking in, I grab a quick shower, order some room service, and map out what I want to say to her.

I've got to lay it all on the line. That means coming clean about everything—Reeve, Simon, my initial plan, and how I ended up falling completely and utterly in love with her to the point I know she's the only woman who will ever own my heart. I know it might mean losing her for good, because she's going to be pissed, but I can't beg her to come back to Dublin with me if she isn't privy to all the facts.

It's a huge risk, because she'll want to run straight to Reeve with the truth, but she deserves to know he's been lying to her too. She deserves to know what kind of man she's been in love with all these years. I hope the fact I've come all this way will help. That she'll see how important she is to me and how sincere I am about never keeping secrets from her again. I'm even willing to set aside my vengeance for her. If she agrees to be with me, I will drop all plans for revenge. Viv means more to me than getting even with my twin and my father. If she loves me as much as I love her and she agrees to spend her life with me, that is all I will ever need.

I know it's not black-and-white.

There's a lot of gray matter to trudge through, but she is all I want.

Nothing else matters except having her by my side, now and always.

Nerves fire at me and my palms are sweaty as I press dial on her number. Her voice mail automatically kicks in, confirming her phone is off. Maybe she's sleeping or it's out of charge.

Or she's already with him.

I rage at the devil on my shoulder, not needing his pessimistic comments right now. Viv wouldn't do that. Even though I was a total prick to her before she left, I know she loves me. She wouldn't run straight back into his arms because what we shared meant something to both of us.

I try a couple more times, but it's the same. Always sent to voice mail. Frustrated, I toss my phone on the bed, pacing the room as I contemplate leaving her a message. I decide against it. I'd rather speak to her in person so she can't duck out of meeting me.

I turn on the TV for something to do, instantly wishing I hadn't. All the color leaches from my face as I turn up the volume. Pain slices across my chest as the image of Reeve with Viv fills the screen. They are on an apartment balcony, and he's holding her in an intimate embrace, his chest to her back. The photo only shows from the waist up, but it's obvious they are naked. Reeve's arm is wrapped around Viv's bare breasts, and he's nuzzling into her neck, kissing her.

She's clinging to his arms, smiling like she hasn't a care in the world. Like she wasn't in my arms mere hours ago. Like she didn't just leave me behind in Ireland. She shows none of the emotion I saw in her eyes yesterday when she was telling me she loved me. I don't even look like a distant memory. I'm like a speck of dust that's there one minute and gone the next.

Pain eviscerates me on all sides, and I drop to my knees clutching my aching heart as tears sting the backs of my eyes.

The image changes to a live feed, and a reporter thrusts a mic into Reeve's face as he emerges from a high-rise building. "Reeve! Is it true you are back together with Vivien Mills?" a pretty blonde reporter asks, claiming his attention. "Is the photo from earlier today proof you are in love with your childhood sweetheart again?"

"I've always been in love with Viv," Reeve says, stopping to talk to her. He pins her with a wide disarming smile, and he's practically glowing. A swarm of reporters crowds around him, and camera flashes go off in his face. "I never stopped loving her, and I never will. She's the only woman for me." He stares pointedly at the camera, and I want to wipe the superior look off his smug face. "Nothing or no one will ever come between us again." He might as well be saying it directly to my face because I know this message is directed at me. "She's back in my arms, exactly where she belongs. Where she's going to stay."

I throw the remote at the screen, cracking the glass, as rage infiltrates my veins, replacing the blood flow. Anger unlike anything I've ever felt before races through me, and I tear through the room, ripping pictures off the walls, tossing the furniture around, destroying the curtains and bedding, and throwing anything that isn't pinned down at the walls and the windows. I can't see anything over the red layer tainting my vision and the angry tsunami sweeping through my insides, obliterating everything in its path.

I'm still in a monstrous rage when security enters my room and I'm hauled outside the hotel in handcuffs. I lose my shit in the back of the police car as they take me to the headquarters of the Los Angeles Police Department and throw me into a cell. Fury continues to pummel my insides even as the mad adrenaline rush leaves, and my exhausted body slumps against the bench. Vengeance returns, a million times stronger than before, and I know what needs to be done.

I am such a fool, and Viv has played me for a right idiot.

She never had any intention of staying with me. She waltzed straight back into his arms—into his bed—only hours after being with me. How could she do that? Did I mean so little to her that she could fuck me and then fuck him without any remorse or guilt? Because I saw zero regrets on her face in that picture. She was basking in his possessive adoration, like I no longer existed.

The walls around my heart harden along with my resolve.

Simon and Reeve are no longer the isolated entries on my shit list. I've now added Hollywood to the mix.

She will pay. They will all pay for treating me like I don't matter.

The seriousness of my situation hits home when I let my mind wander, and I realize how badly I've fucked up. It's quite likely I will be kicked out of the US and forbidden from ever returning. We can kiss our music dreams goodbye if that happens. I wouldn't care except it will devastate the guys. They are banking on things working out with this A&R guy, and I won't be the reason things fall apart. I need someone with clout in this town to make this go away, and I know just who to call. My mind churns ideas as I align both goals. It will take longer to achieve if I do this, but it's the only way.

Standing, I grip the cell bars, shaking them to get the attention of the woman behind the counter outside. "I want my phone call." I've watched enough US police dramas to know my rights.

Ten minutes later, I'm sitting in a small interview room while the surly cop rummages through my duffel bag. "This?" he asks, holding the wrinkled brown envelope in his hand.

"Yeah. See that number written on the top? That's the number I need." Thank fuck, I thought to stuff the old NDA into my bag before I left home. I've held on to it all these years because I knew there might come a day when I'd have to sign it. Some sixth sense told me to bring it with me, and now I know why. It's the leverage I need to get myself out of this mess and begin to put a new plan of revenge in place.

The cop picks up the handset and gives it to me. I punch in the private number, holding the phone to my ear as I wait for him to answer.

"Simon Lancaster," he drawls, arrogance dripping from his tone.

"I'll sign it on two conditions," I say, knowing he already knows who I am. "I want five million dollars, and I need your help to extract me from a situation."

CHAPTER 1

VIVIEN

A few days after the end of SITO

ROLLING UP MY YOGA MAT, I head into the changing room to get showered, hating how quickly I lose my inner Zen. Panic jumps up and slaps me in the face, and my mind races with so many scary thoughts. It's been the same since Dillon resurfaced in my life, turning my world upside down.

Thankfully, he didn't show up for Easton's birthday party, but it didn't stop me from fretting on the day, terrified he was going to make an appearance. I have barely managed to grab more than a few hours of sleep each night because I'm too stressed to switch off. My brain spins thoughts on a continuous loop until it feels like I'm going crazy.

I shower and dress as if on autopilot, my mind preoccupied to the point I don't see anything around me and I'm not aware of my movements. I'm exhausted in every possible way.

Standing in front of the mirror, I rest my hands on the edge of the sink as I examine my lackluster complexion. Whatever pregnancy glow I was sporting has evaporated in the days since the news broke that Dillon is my husband's twin. The thought he could be Easton's father is beyond anything I can comprehend.

How can I tell Reeve?

I know this will break his heart, but I can't hide it from him for much longer. Dillon warned me not to mention anything to my husband, making veiled threats to force me into toeing the line, but he can eat shit. He doesn't get to show up and start dictating what I do and what I say.

Audrey was as shocked as me when I told her everything. She can't believe Dillon seduced me in Ireland as part of some sick revenge pact, but I believe it because I saw the hatred in his eyes a few days ago. Dillon hates me, and he hates Reeve, and he's not going to stop until he's sucked all the joy from our lives.

How could I be so gullible to fall for his ruse? No wonder he didn't come to Dublin Airport. He must have been reading my letter and laughing his head off at how easily I fell under his spell. I feel like such an idiot. Especially considering Dillon owns part of my heart to this day. I desperately want to reclaim it because he doesn't deserve any part of me.

Including my son.

God.

Tears prick my eyes, and I hang my head, clutching the countertop as I barely hold it together. A sob escapes my mouth, and I'm grateful the other ladies have already left and I'm here alone. I wouldn't want anyone to witness this. I break down; letting days' worth of pent-up emotion leak from my eyes.

I've been walking on eggshells around Reeve, plastering fake smiles on my face in the hope he doesn't notice anything amiss, but I can't do it for much longer.

I'm trying to decide if I should fess up now or wait until I have the paternity test results. I know Reeve's first concern when I tell him the truth will be Easton. It would be nice to reassure him with the test results—assuming Reeve is revealed as his father. If it turns out Dillon is his biological father, waiting will be in vain. I'm also worried about the impact this will have on my marriage. Concealing this from Reeve is a massive abuse of his trust. I'm not sure he'll forgive me if I continue to keep this a secret from him.

My cell pings in my purse, forcing me to get a grip. I'm going to be late if I don't hurry. Drying my eyes, I apply some makeup to disguise my blotchy cheeks before running a comb through my hair. My quick blow-dry means my long brown hair falls in unstructured waves over my shoulders, but I have zero fucks to give right now. My pretty summer dress highlights my blossoming bump, and I run my hands over my swollen belly, drawing comfort from my unborn child.

I owe it to my daughter to pull myself together. All this stress can't be good for my baby, and Dillon only has the power to destroy me if I let him—which I won't.

Sliding my sunglasses over my eyes, I grab my purse and head out of the yoga studio to my car. I managed to ditch my bodyguard, but I could tell he was suspicious. Thank fuck, Reeve is at production meetings all day, or he would never have let me leave the house without Leon.

The hour-long drive to the medical laboratory just outside of Santa Clarita is anything but soothing. My nerves are shot to pieces by the time I pull into the parking lot of the small gray brick building. Dillon arranged the testing, but I insisted on being here because I don't trust him and I want to ask the doctor some questions.

Climbing out of my car on shaky legs, I draw a brave breath as I walk toward the entrance doors. As I make my approach, I spot Dillon waiting outside for me. He's leaning against the wall, looking at something on his cell, appearing at ease, as if he hasn't a care in the world.

He's got a ball cap and sunglasses on, shading his recognizable face. His usual black T-shirt stretches tight across his ripped upper torso, pulling taut along his toned biceps. Ripped navy jeans and black and white Nikes complete his understated look.

Leather bands wrap around one wrist, and he's sporting a bunch of silver rings on his right hand.

Dillon was always effortlessly hot, and today is no exception. I hate how good he looks almost as much as I hate myself for noticing.

He looks up, as I step onto the sidewalk, coolly sliding his cell into the back pocket of his jeans. Although he's wearing shades, I feel the intensity of his gaze crawling over every inch of my skin, heating me from the inside out.

I come to a standstill in front of him, and we stare at one another in silence. A multitude of emotions blankets the air between us. I have so many muddled feelings when it comes to this man. Tightness spreads across my chest as we stare wordlessly at one another with all the what-ifs going unanswered.

"You have the samples?" he asks, in a gruff tone, after a few beats of tense silence.

A retort lies idle on my tongue as I nod. "Let's just do this." I want to get in and out as fast as possible.

Dillon holds the door open for me, and I enter the building first. I take a seat in the small waiting area while he talks to the receptionist. A tall thin man in a white lab coat comes to collect us, and we follow him in strained silence to his office.

My heart pounds behind my rib cage as I take a seat alongside Dillon in front of the doctor's desk. Removing my sunglasses, I knot my clammy hands on my lap, willing my frantically beating heart to slow down. The man's eyes widen as he looks at me before he hurriedly composes himself.

Clearing his throat, he hands an envelope to Dillon. "The NDA has been signed by me and all the laboratory staff though there really was no need. We are always discreet. The nature of our work commands it, and our stellar reputation rests upon it."

"I'm sure you can understand the need for extra precaution," Dillon smoothly replies, in that husky Irish tone I used to love so much, jerking his head in my direction.

"I can assure you both you have nothing to worry about. I am personally handling your case, instead of one of our geneticists, to ensure your confidentiality is protected." He shoots me a reassuring smile that does little to reassure me.

If Reeve were to discover the truth via the media, he would never forgive me.

It's just another reason why I need to talk to him sooner rather than later.

"As agreed, I will enter the samples under false names as an added safeguard," the doctor continues, his gaze bouncing between Dillon and me.

"Thank you." I remove the two sealed plastic bags from my purse, placing them on his desk. "The blue toothbrush is my husband's, and the smaller red one is my son's," I explain, almost choking on the words. "Are you sure these will be enough to extract a DNA sample?"

"The DNA in a person's blood, saliva, hair, or skin cells is exactly the same. Toothbrush samples are commonly used for forensic testing, and it's no better or more less accurate than a cheek swab or providing a blood sample, provided there is enough DNA on the sample," he says, helping to alleviate some of my concerns.

Pulling on surgical gloves, he rounds the desk, standing in front of Dillon with a swab in his hand. Dillon opens his mouth without hesitation, and I watch with mounting trepidation as the doctor swabs the inside of his cheek. He then secures the swab in a sealed bag and writes labels that he attaches to the three samples.

"How long will it take to get the results?" Dillon asks, beating me to the punch.

"Approximately ten days to two weeks."

That is way too long. "Can't you expedite it? We can pay more," I offer.

"That is as fast as we can deliver the results. This is not a routine paternity test. In order to determine paternity in cases of identical twins, we need to examine more than just the standard markers. There is no way it can be rushed."

"And you're sure you can conclusively determine paternity with these samples?" I ask.

He nods. "We will examine the entire genome sequence which will isolate at least a single mutation in one of the twin's genetics that has been passed on from father to son. The test will confirm which twin fathered your son."

Warmth spreads to my cheeks at his words. What must he think of me? Not that that's even high on my list of worries at this point.

"We'll await your call." Dillon stands. "Thank you."

The doctor shakes both our hands before showing us back out to the reception area.

"I need to speak to you," I tell Dillon, not looking at him as we make our way outside. "We can talk in my car," I add, not waiting for him to reply, striding across the half-empty parking lot toward my SUV.

CHAPTER 2
VIVIEN

I SLIDE behind the wheel as Dillon climbs into the passenger seat. My SUV has tinted windows, so we're shielded from potential nosy bystanders. Cranking the AC to the max, I moisten my dry lips with my tongue before I turn to face him.

It's still such a shock seeing him with darker hair and blue eyes, so much like Reeve. I don't know if I'll ever get used to it. Yet he's uniquely Dillon too with that slight bump in his nose, the small scar over his eyebrow, his dimples, and the defining piercings and ink. He looks like my husband *and* like himself, and I can't wrap my head around it.

A familiar smirk curves the corners of his lips. "Did you want to talk or just ogle me?"

Snapping out of my trance, I scowl at him. His arrogance clearly hasn't faded with the passing of time. I'm trying to be mature about our situation. To not let my feelings toward him distract or derail me, but he makes it difficult. I'm so angry with him, and there's a whole lot of hurt and pain mixed in with fear and anxiety and the sheer helplessness of the circumstances.

My priority is Reeve and Easton, and doing right by them is my sole focus. I can't lose sight of that. "I need to tell Reeve, and it can't wait ten days. I'm telling him everything tonight." I cannot keep this from my husband any longer. Not without causing irreparable damage to our marriage. As much as I might want to wait for the results—in the hope they'll confirm Reeve is Easton's bio dad—I can't lie to him for that long. Every day that passes tears another fragment off my heart.

All humor drains from Dillon's face, and a muscle pops in his jaw. "No."

"You don't get to decide this." I grip the wheel tighter, as tension bleeds into the air.

He barks out a harsh laugh. "Yeah, I'm pretty sure I do."

"No, you don't!" I hiss, letting anger get the best of me. "My husband deserves to know the truth, no matter how painful that might be for all of us."

"Oh, Reeve *will* hear the truth." He puts his face all up in mine. "But he'll hear it from both of us when we have the results."

"You're crazy if you think I'll agree to that. I don't know why I even bother trying to reason with you. You don't care about anyone but yourself." I glare at him, while he swipes his finger along the screen on his phone. "Just go, Dillon. I have nothing more to say to you." That's not exactly true. There is something else playing on my mind I wanted to ask him about, but screw it. I don't have the mental capacity to deal with him right now.

"You will say nothing to Reeve, or I'll post these photos online." He shoves his cell in my face.

I gulp over the sudden lump in my throat as I scan the old photo. It's from the first night we slept together. Just after the Trinity Ball. I'm topless, wearing only a flimsy lace thong and silver stilettos. I remember that night as vividly as if it was yesterday. That he's attempting to use one of the most special nights of my life against me hurts so much. Anger comingles with sadness as I lift my head and stare at him. "Why are you doing this? Why are you twisting all the good memories I have of us? Of you?"

"Those memories are as fake as the man you call your husband."

"You're wrong. On both counts."

He barks out a bitter laugh. "How can you be so gullible?!" He snaps his fingers in my face. "Wake the fuck up, Hollywood. Your husband has been lying to you for years, but you don't give a damn."

He made the same accusation a few days ago, and it's the other thing I wanted to ask him. "What is it you think you know about my husband? Hmm? Last I checked, I was the one who grew up with Reeve. I'm the one who knows him inside and out. Not you!"

"He's known the truth for years!" he roars, his nostrils flaring. "That charade he put on the other day was all an act. How can you not see him for who he truly is?"

"I know who Reeve is! I was there when he found out about you, and he's not acting!"

"Why do you think Simon Lancaster looked me up at seventeen?"

My brow puckers in confusion. "We already discussed this. Simon was protecting his own ass."

"Wrong." Dillon removes his ball cap, dragging a hand through his hair as he sighs. "Reeve knew about me, Viv. He's the one who sent Simon to buy my silence."

I shake my head. "That is ridiculous! I would know if Reeve knew about you, and he didn't! He was overjoyed when he discovered he had a twin, and he couldn't wait to meet you. Those are not the actions of a man who knew." I slap a hand over my chest. "Reeve would have traded a limb for a sibling growing up. He had such a lonely existence. If he knew you were out there somewhere, he would have looked for you." I turn pleading eyes on him. "You don't know him like I do. He would've moved heaven and earth to find you if he'd known."

Dillon's jaw flexes. "He knew, Viv. Reeve was the one who shunned me. He's the one who believed I murdered our mother."

"Oh my God." I throw my hands in the air. "Can you just stop and listen to yourself right now? That makes no sense. Reeve was only a baby when his father made the decision to give you up for adoption. How the fuck was Reeve the one who shunned you?"

"I'm not denying Simon put those notions in Reeve's head, but he went along with it! Simon told Reeve when he was twelve. He told him he would find me if Reeve wanted to reunite with his brother, and Reeve told him no."

I rub my pounding temples. "That never happened. Simon lied. He said whatever he needed to say to keep you away, and boy, did he do a number on you." I shake my head again as a veil of sadness shrouds me. "C'mon, Dil. You've got to hear how this sounds."

"Your blind faith in him beggars belief."

"If you won't believe me, then tell Reeve. Look him directly in the eye and tell him what happened when you were seventeen. We all just need to sit down and work this out."

He shoots me a scathing look. "You'd like to package this into a pretty box so your perfect life isn't disturbed, but that's not how this is going down." Determination splays across his face. "I've paid the price for long enough. Now it's Reeve's turn."

I wonder if Dillon requires psychiatric care, because he genuinely sounds insane. Maybe I should reach out to Ash. This behavior is not normal.

I make one last attempt at getting through to him. Tentatively, I reach out, touching his arm. Delicious tremors dance across my skin, reminding me what we once shared is still lying dormant, waiting to be woken from slumber. "Please, Dil. Let's just go to my house and talk to Reeve. Let's get everything out on the table and sort through all the lies."

He wrenches his arm back, glaring at me. "No. I told you we're doing this my way. You won't breathe a word to him. You'll do as you're told, or I'll release the photo."

"Go ahead. Post it and see if I care. You can't even see my face. No one will know it's me." I'm not bluffing. It will take more than that to force me into doing his bidding.

"Reeve will." He swipes his finger across the screen, moving to the next pic, showing me the photo of us I sent to Reeve all those years ago. While Dillon's face isn't visible in this one—he's hiding against my shoulder—you can see the ink on his back and his arms, and my features are unmistakable. "I'm guessing this image is imprinted in his brain the same way the image of you and him on that balcony is imprinted on mine."

Wait? What? "Why would—"

"If you need more convincing, I think these photos will seal the deal." He thrusts his cell at me, swiping in quick succession, revealing a host of photos I didn't know existed. They are all of me, taken without my knowledge or consent. Some are of me in bed asleep, and others are pictures of me laughing or goofing around, either by myself or with Ash. There are even a few where I'm reading or sketching designs on the couch in my old apartment, so lost in a book I didn't realize my boyfriend was stealing sneaky pics.

Why the hell did he hang on to these photos? Did they serve as a way to reconnect with me when the pain and loss got too much, like my photos were for me? Or has he been plotting to use them as part of his revenge plan for years?

"Say one word to him now, without me, and I'll share all of these online along with the truth of our relationship and who Reeve is to me." He shrugs, repocketing his cell as I stare at him in shock. "I'm sure everyone will be able to join the dots from there."

"You unimaginable bastard." I rub my hands over my bump as I contemplate various ways to murder Dillon O'Donoghue. "You had no right to take those pictures without my permission!"

"You were my girlfriend. I had every right, and we both know it."

"Why, Dillon? Why are you doing this?" I know he has issues, and I get that, to a point. What I don't understand is why he's hell-bent on taking it out on Reeve and me.

"We will tell Reeve together because I want to see his face the moment he realizes he's lost everything to me."

He is delusional if he truly believes that. "Even if Easton is your biological child, Reeve is still his father." I work hard to keep my voice controlled and calm, running my hands back and forth across my bump. "Reeve is his father in all the ways that matter, and that will never change. And he will never lose me. I would never leave him for your selfish, manipulative ass!"

"You won't be the one to make that call. Do you think he'll still trust you when he finds out the truth?"

"I know my husband, and I've done nothing wrong. I didn't know he was a twin when I got pregnant. I did the right thing and waited to prove paternity." I *did* lie to him about that, and Reeve will be pissed when he finds out, but I did it to protect him. Once he gets over the initial shock, he'll come around. I'm more concerned about concealing the truth of what I know now from him. "And he knew about you. I just didn't tell him your name or that you were in Collateral Damage. Reeve never asked because you were a part of my past he didn't want to know about."

"I will sue you for joint custody," he adds, drilling me with a dark look. "He'll have to watch me develop a bond with *my son*. He'll have to live with me there for every birthday, every Christmas, every family occasion. I might not be an expert on relationships, but even I know that kind of situation isn't conducive to a happy marriage. I will make it my life's mission to inject myself into every aspect of your lives. To make you as miserable as sin. It's nothing less than you both deserve."

CHAPTER 3

VIVIEN

"THAT'S NOT how it works! You would never get joint custody! You don't even live here full-time, and your reputation would work against you."

Why is he so vindictive?

So determined to ruin Reeve and me?

I just can't wrap my head around this. It's blatantly obvious Simon manipulated both his sons. They should be working together to undo everything he did; instead Dillon is planning to destroy his brother. His *twin*! As angry as I am with him, I'm also hurting for him too because he clearly still struggles to accept and embrace love. He's choosing to hate Reeve, instead of trying to forge a relationship with his brother, and I won't forgive him if he continues on this path.

He smirks that annoying smirk I used to hate to love, and I want to slap him. "When I'm not touring, I spend more time at my L.A. house than my Dublin one. I've hardly drank since February, and I've already begun the naturalization application. My US citizenship is a given. I was born here to US parents. It's only a matter of cutting through some red tape." His eyes drill into mine. "My lawyers are every bit as experienced as yours and Reeve's. If I go for joint custody, I'll get it."

I know he will, but it will most likely take time. Years maybe. Even then, any access he is granted to Easton will be gradual and supervised by the courts. It's not as black-and-white as he seems to think it is. "That doesn't mean you'll be entitled to encroach on our family time. If you are Easton's dad, we won't stop you from developing a relationship with him or from seeing him, but that doesn't automatically give you a free pass to participate in family occasions and events. Your relationship with him will be separate from ours."

I won't let Dillon come between me and Reeve or my family. I can't stop him from getting to know Easton if it turns out he is his father—nor would I want to—but he doesn't get to inject himself into our lives purely to fulfill his vengeance agenda. "This is all hypothetical anyway until we get the test results and way too premature."

"I'm not going to argue with you over this. You say nothing to Reeve until I say the time is right."

His arrogant tone pisses me off, and I'm not letting him boss me around. "Fuck you, Dillon. You don't dictate what I tell my husband."

"I'll post right now," he threatens, extracting his cell again, his finger hovering over the keypad. "You won't even have time to call him before he discovers the whole sordid truth online. And how do you think his fans will react to this news? Hmm. How do you think *my* fans will react? They will come after you with the full extent of their disgust, and the hatred you endured in the past will pale in comparison to this." He waggles his brows, and I want to punch him in his handsome face.

I know exactly how this would play out in the media. I'll be the villain in this tale, while Reeve and Dillon will come out smelling like roses. I'll be branded a cheater and a whore, and it'll give further ammunition to that element of Reeve's fanbase who have never thought I'm good enough for him. Dillon's fans will think I've done wrong by him and lash me for it.

There is no scenario where I come out of this well.

However, I don't care about that. The fans and trolls can throw shade at *me* all they want, but I can't tolerate the idea of anything or anyone hurting Easton. While he is young, he's not immune to the impact of social media on our lives. If Dillon is his father, we will need to work out how and when to tell him. I don't want this getting out in the media and forcing our hand before any of us are ready.

Easton is the reason I need to keep this private. He is the only way Dillon can force my hand now. "If you do this, you will hurt Easton. He's either your son or your nephew. Would you really do that to him?"

He schools his features into a neutral line, and he looks so cold and clinical when he says, "Easton is a child. He won't be privy to what's being said online and in the media. I can make it disappear fast, after I've achieved my goal."

My stomach sours, and I wonder if I ever knew Dillon at all. "You're a despicable person and not worthy of being a father to my child."

Dillon reaches across the console, gripping my chin in a tight hold. "You know nothing about me or what I'm capable of as a father."

"I know any man who would try so hard to destroy a child's mother's happiness is not a good father. Trying to ruin Reeve, the only man Easton has ever called Daddy, is not the actions of a good person."

Dillon releases my face, his hands dropping to his lap. "You continue to act like you're both blameless. I'm not the only villain here. Reeve is as fucking manipulative as his father, and that doesn't make him a very good role model either."

"You're so wrong."

He harrumphs, shaking his head. "He manipulated you the second you got off the plane that day."

"You're delusional." I'm genuinely contemplating calling Ash because Dillon has serious issues.

"You're fucking naïve." He jabs his finger in the air. "Who do you think arranged that photo of you two on the balcony?" His brows lift as he pins me with a challenging look.

I burst out laughing. "You cannot seriously be suggesting Reeve was behind that? After everything we'd endured at the hands of the media at that time? Come on, Dillon. Don't be ridiculous."

"God. He really has pulled the wool over your eyes, hasn't he?" Dillon tugs on his eyebrow ring before leaning into my face. "I saw the little statement he gave to reporters later that day. His message was clearly directed at me."

"His message was for Saffron! He was warning her to stay away from us. Besides, you didn't give a shit about me. Sending me home in tears was all part of your plan, so why the fuck do you even care?"

"I never said I did." A mask of indifference cloaks his face again. "I'm merely pointing out Reeve isn't so squeaky-clean himself. Be careful before you throw stones at me."

I deliberately ignore that comment, because we're starting to go around in circles. "Believe whatever you want, Dillon." I huff out a sigh. "It doesn't change the fact I'm not keeping this from Reeve."

"You don't have a choice." He eases back in his seat. "I tell you what. I'll sweeten the deal. I'll cancel lunch with my *beloved twin* on Saturday, and I'll stay away from him until we have the results."

That would help because I'm petrified of Reeve spending time alone with Dillon. For two reasons. One, I'm scared what Dillon will say, but it seems like he won't blab anything until he knows if he's Easton's father or not. Two, I hate the thought of Reeve growing close to a guy who's pretending to like him while plotting to destroy his life behind his back.

Letting Dillon reveal the truth to the world, in such a cruel way, would devastate my husband and hurt my son. The last thing we need is the entire world speculating over Easton's paternity before it's confirmed.

I hate I'm letting my ex blackmail me, but I don't see how I have any option. Dillon is determined to keep this from Reeve until it suits him to deliver the worst possible blow.

Maybe he is calling my bluff and I should challenge him on it, but I'm not sure that's a risk I want to take. Would he really do this knowing he could be hurting his own flesh and blood? Is he saying this to force me into toeing the line, or is he callous enough to do it without losing sleep? The Dillon I once knew could be deliberately cruel with his words and his actions, lashing out in anger, yet deep down, I always knew he didn't mean it. It was a defense mechanism to protect himself. But he's no longer the same man I knew, so I can't rely on my past experience to guide me now.

I could lie. I could tell Dillon I agree and still come clean to Reeve, but I know if I fess up Reeve won't be able to resist going after Dillon and Dillon will then release everything to the press and our lives will become a media circus. We would have no choice but to tell Easton, and he's too young to have this thrust upon him, without building up to it.

If Dillon *is* Easton's bio dad, I will need time to introduce that information to my son in a way that doesn't upset him too much. He will have to get to know Dillon as an uncle first, and when the time is right, he can be told the truth that he has two dads.

I can't let Dillon force my hand with Easton, so I have no option but to agree to his evil plan.

Even if I know it means Reeve may never forgive me for keeping all of this from him.

CHAPTER 4

VIVIEN

"YOU MISSED DINNER," Reeve says, entering my home office, carrying a tray.

"Sorry." I lift my head from my laptop, offering him a guilt-ridden half-smile. "I know I've been working a lot, but I really need to finish this script before I can consider going on maternity leave," I semi-lie.

"I'm worried about you." Setting the tray on my desk, he moves behind me. His hands land on my shoulders, and he slowly massages my tense muscles. "You're working too much, and you've been so quiet this past week. Are you sure something isn't troubling you?"

"I'm just trying to get organized so I can stop working in a couple of weeks."

"You're only twenty-nine weeks. You can space your workload out more evenly and still finish up in plenty of time before Lainey arrives."

"I want to spend ample quality time with Easton and you before our daughter makes her grand entrance." That's not exactly a lie. I just have added motivation for finishing work early now. Even if the test confirms Reeve is Easton's father, I still have to tell my husband about Dillon and everything that has gone on since he showed up here twelve days ago. Reeve is going to be upset with either outcome, and I want to focus my sole attention on my family.

Plus, working around the clock helps to keep me distracted from the impending paternity results.

And it helps me to avoid Reeve.

A pang of guilt and remorse wallops me in the face. I hate I've been avoiding my husband, but I'm terrified he'll see the fear on my face and coax the truth from me. Dillon texts me a picture every day, and it's all I need to be reminded of what's at stake. He doesn't need threatening words. Sending those photos of me from the past works like a charm. I can't bear the thought of Reeve discovering the truth from the internet. He deserves to hear it from my lips.

Every night, I have been praying the results confirm Reeve is Easton's father.

Dillon loses all power with that outcome, and I can tell my husband everything without his twin's gloating face in the room. So what if Dillon releases the pictures of me after the fact? All it confirms is I was in a relationship with him while Reeve and I were broken up. It was before I knew they were twins. Yes, some of the photos are intimate and show me semi-naked. That isn't something I want out there in the world, but it's a small price to pay to protect Reeve and Easton now.

"You're so tense, babe." Reeve digs his fingers into the corded knots in my upper back. "Please call it a night. You can eat that while I run you a bath. Then maybe we could watch a movie together in bed." Leaning down, he presses a kiss to my cheek. "Let me take care of you. I need it as much as you do."

A fresh wave of guilt washes over me. Reeve is upset Dillon seems to be withdrawing. He canceled their planned lunch meeting, and he has been reluctant to set a new date, citing crazy work schedules, but Reeve is no idiot, and he senses there is more to it. My husband is bitterly disappointed by his twin's apparent apathy toward him, and I'm partly responsible. "Okay." I clasp his hand, bringing it to my lips. "That sounds nice." I kiss his fingers. "I love you, Reeve," I whisper with tears clouding my eyes. "I love you so much."

"Hey." Reeve drops to his knees in front of me, taking my hands in his. "I love you too." He tilts his head to one side, examining my face. "I wish you'd tell me what's wrong." Concern is etched upon his gorgeous face, and I feel like the worst wife on the planet. I'm clearly not a good actress either if Reeve suspects I'm hiding something from him.

Panic claws its way up my throat, and I stuff my tears back down inside, forcing a smile. "Don't mind me. It's just pregnancy hormones."

Reeve leans in, dotting kisses all over my bump through my dress. "Hey, little Lainey. How's Daddy's girl? Give Mommy a big cuddle, and no kicking tonight. She needs to relax."

As if on cue, our daughter delivers a mighty kick, causing my stomach to visibly move. Reeve runs his fingers over the protruding lump, his eyes lighting up at the sight of it. "Lainey is going to be a troublemaker, I think." His gaze jumps to mine as he rubs my bump. "I can't wait to meet her."

Placing my hands over his, I lean down and kiss him. "Only eleven more weeks."

"We should bring E with us to the ultrasound on Wednesday. Let him see his baby sister." I nod because it's a great idea. "Maybe we could take him to the zoo after and then grab a bite to eat?" His hopeful eyes lock on mine, and I can't say no.

"That sounds like a perfect plan."

Reeve straightens up, kissing me softly before placing a fork in my hand. "You eat, and I'll go run your bath."

"Mommy, Mommy!" Easton tries to jump out of Reeve's arms. "I see her leg! I see my sister's leg!" He points at the screen where Lainey is wiggling her legs.

"That's right, buddy." Reeve hugs Easton closer, his eyes turning glassy. "That's your baby sister."

"I love her." Easton's lopsided smile melts my heart. "I can't wait for her to come out of Mom's tummy so I can hug her. I'll even let her play with my Hot Wheels and my monster truck."

My heart swells to bursting point. This kid slays me every day. "That's really sweet, E. Your sister is so lucky to have you as her big brother." Reeve and I exchange a look loaded with emotion. I reach out for his hand, needing to touch him, needing to believe we are going to get through this, even if Easton turns out to be Dillon's.

Reeve sets Easton down in the chair, taking my hand and pecking my lips, uncaring the doctor and nurse are in the room. "I love you," he whispers against my mouth. "You are amazing." He slides his arm around my back as the nurse wipes the goop from my exposed stomach.

The doctor smiles at us as she switches off the machine. "I bet she'll be every bit as adorable as her big brother." She pats my hand. "Everything looks great, Vivien. You're on track for a healthy, normal delivery."

"You might tell her to stop working so hard," Reeve says, arching a brow in my direction.

"I'm sure Vivien has it all under control," the doctor replies with a smile. "Try not to worry, and whatever you can do to alleviate her workload will be appreciated, I'm sure."

"Reeve takes good care of me," I assure her. "He just worries too much."

"Why can't my sister come out now?" Easton huffs as Reeve straps him into his booster seat in the back of my SUV.

"She's still growing and developing," Reeve calmly explains. "Lainey will come out when she's good and ready."

"Brody says his sister was all covered in green slime when she came out of his mommy's belly. Will my sister be covered in green slime too?" His cute button nose scrunches up, and I suppress a giggle.

"Nope." Reeve ruffles his hair, fighting laughter as well. "Your sister will be perfect when you meet her. Just like you were when you were born."

Seeming satisfied with that answer, Easton turns on his iPad, losing himself in cartoons.

"Green slime." Reeve chuckles as he gets behind the wheel. "What the hell are kids talking about these days?"

We spend a wonderful few hours at the Los Angeles Zoo despite the irritating paparazzi following us around at the start. Reeve sent Leon to complain to security, and the paps were told to leave. Some people stop to ask Reeve for autographs, while other families shoot curious looks our way, but most leave us to enjoy our family outing in peace.

This isn't our first time here, but Easton is as excited as every other trip. The Rainforest of the Americas is still his favorite exhibit, and he races across the wooden bridge toward the two-story Amazonian stilt house, hollering and screaming with sheer excitement. From the upper level, we see the eagles' habitat and the otters messing around in the lake below. From the lower level, we get up close and personal with piranhas, stingray, and other aquatic species. The monkeys and jaguars are Easton's favorites, and I snap plenty of pics of Reeve posing with our son beside the enclosures.

"That was awesome," E proclaims, holding my hand and Reeve's as we leave the zoo. "Next time, can we bring my sister?"

"We sure can, buddy." Reeve crouches down. "Want to climb onto my shoulders?"

Easton doesn't need any further invitation, scrambling onto his dad's shoulders without hesitation. My heart aches behind my chest cavity as I watch E perched on top of Reeve with his legs dangling over his dad's shoulders. Reeve loops my arm through his, and we walk toward the parking lot, flanked by Leon and a second body-guard. The paparazzi snap photos of us as we head toward our car, but I do my best to ignore them and the painful ache spreading across my chest. This is probably the last time we will enjoy an outing as a family before the truth is revealed.

I know my husband. I know he'll be devastated if Easton isn't his, but it won't change who he is to Easton or how much our son means to him. Reeve will still be my husband, and Easton's father, even if Dillon is thrust upon our lives.

"Penny for your thoughts?" Reeve whispers, tucking strands of hair behind my ears as we wait for the waitress to bring our drinks.

"Did you imagine this?" I blurt, turning my head to face him. "All those years ago when we were kids. Did you think we'd end up here?"

"Yes," he admits with zero hesitation. "I often dreamed of this. Marrying you. Having a family and a successful career. It's all I've ever wanted." He kisses me, and I'm glad we're tucked into a private booth, away from prying eyes, in our favorite Italian restaurant. "I'm glad we're giving Easton a sibling." He flashes me a cheeky grin, waggling his brows. "The first of many."

"Define many," I say, watching Easton out of the corner of my eye. The waitress gave him crayons and some paper, and he's coloring to his heart's content. Our body-guards are seated at a table next to us, keeping an eye on everything.

"Three. Four. Five. An entire football team." Reeve shrugs, and my jaw trails the ground. His arm slides around my shoulders as he chuckles. "Don't look so alarmed. You know you're in the driver's seat."

I thread my fingers through his brown hair. "It's a joint decision, but I'm not sure this body is up for another four or five pregnancies." Though, in this moment, I would give Reeve anything his heart desired if it helped to lessen the blow of what's coming.

"You can withstand more than you realize. We both can. I think we've already proven that." It's not like Reeve to directly, or indirectly, refer to our past, so I'm surprised he's gone there. "Viv." He clasps my face in his palms. "You know I love you completely and utterly with no limitations or boundaries. You know there is nothing you could say or do that would ever change that. Right?"

My heart jackhammers against my rib cage, and my pulse vibrates in my neck. Are his words coincidental, or does he know something? "I know that. And I love you the same way. You have given me everything, Reeve, and I have never regretted my decision to marry you. I love what we've created together, this wonderful life we share, and I would do anything to protect our family. I hope you know that." It's slightly risky saying this, but I need to get those words out.

"I know." He kisses me, and I'm surprised at the intensity of his kiss as his mouth works against mine. When he breaks our lip-lock, he rests his forehead against mine. "You're my world, Vivien. Nothing matters more to me than you, Easton, and Lainey."

Unspoken words hover in the air between us, and I'm grateful when the waitress arrives with our food. If Reeve had asked me again what was wrong, I think this time I would've told him.

I hope I get the results in a couple of days so I can finally talk to my husband and tell him what's been going on.

Reeve's cell rings in the car on our way home, but he quickly silences the incoming call, switching off his phone so as not to disturb our sleeping son.

When we get home, Reeve carries Easton to his bedroom, leaving me to undress him and tuck him into bed.

After settling E, I pad into our master suite carrying my shoes and stifling a yawn. "Do you want me to run you a bath?" Reeve asks, buttoning up a new shirt.

I shake my head. "Going someplace?" I inquire, dropping my shoes on the floor.

"I need to head out to meet Edwin. He wants to discuss potential options for announcing the new baby."

"And he needs to do that at eight on a Wednesday night?" My brows climb to my hairline. "We have weeks until our daughter is born."

"You know my publicist. He's organized in the extreme. He has a few potential magazine offers."

I reach around my back, my fingers struggling to touch the zipper. "I hate that we have to do this." And I'm not sure we'll want to commit to anything with the impending bomb I could be dropping.

"Here, let me." Reeve tucks his shirt into his pants, striding toward me. Brushing my hair aside, he presses a kiss to my shoulder before lowering my zipper. "I know it's a pain, but it's better if we control the situation. Giving official interviews and exclusive photos keeps the fans happy and ensures we're not giving the paps the ultimate scoop. I feel safer knowing we're managing them instead of the other way around."

I know if we feed the media regularly, we can manage them, to an extent, so what Reeve is saying makes sense. If we share exclusive news, in a manner that's controlled by us, it leaves less of a window of opportunity for the gossipmongers to make up shit too. It's hard to create bullshit when you're confronted with the evidence of the love we share and our joy at expanding our family.

Except this time is different. For reasons my husband isn't aware of yet.

More guilt darkens my soul.

"What time will you be home?" I ask, stepping out of my dress.

Reeve's hands gravitate toward my bare belly. "I won't be too late." Bending down, he kisses my stomach before straightening up and lifting his lips to my mouth. His kiss is as urgent as earlier, and when he slides his tongue into my mouth, devouring me with possessive need, I don't protest, meeting him thrust for thrust.

Reeve unclasps my bra, tugging it away before cupping my fuller breasts as he continues to worship my lips. I groan into his mouth, and heat pools in my core. "Fuck it." He trails a line of kisses along my jawline, down my neck, and onto my chest. "He can wait a while longer." His mouth closes over my nipple, and I arch into him, whimpering as a jolt of desire ripples through my body. Reeve backs me up to the bed, and I fall flat on the mattress, automatically spreading my legs.

Reeve rips my panties down my legs before shucking out of his clothes. When his hot mouth lands on my pussy, I almost explode on the spot. He fucks me with his tongue and his fingers, and it doesn't take long for me to reach a sensual peak. Reeve knows my pregnant body, inside and out, so it's no surprise.

We crawl up the bed, and I press a reverential kiss against the ink on his chest. My fingers trace gently over the heart with my name. Just underneath it, to the left, is a smaller heart with the initials EL. Reeve has already stated he'll be adding LL as soon as our daughter makes her arrival. If we end up having as many kids as he wants, he's going to run out of space to ink their initials. "I love you," I whisper, kissing his lips quickly as he helps reposition me on my side.

"Right back at ya, Mrs. Lancaster," he whispers, as he carefully eases into me from behind. "I love you more than words can say." He dots soft kisses along my back as he moves his cock in and out of my pussy, while cradling my belly, and it feels so damn good. Warm breath tickles my skin as he presses his mouth to my ear. "Can you come again?"

I giggle, angling my head back as he picks up his pace, thrusting into me more urgently. I peck his lips. "Don't you know your wife?" I quirk a brow, offering him a teasing grin.

Reeve stares deeply into my eyes, tenderly kissing my lips as his hand moves to my clit. "Ready?" He rubs two fingers against my sensitive bundle of nerves as he slams in and out of me with greater need.

So many emotions swirl inside me as I nod, clinging to my husband, drinking everything in. The feel of him flush against my hot skin. The comfort of his body wrapped around mine. The pleasurable sensations he invokes in my body as he pivots his hips, driving deeper and deeper inside me. The almost pained expression on his gorgeous face as he stares at me while stroking my clit, bringing me to new heights. I shatter around his cock, my inner walls tightening and pulsing, and he throws back his head, grunting my name as he deposits his seed inside me.

Sighing in contentment, I melt into the bed, holding my husband to me in the aftermath of our lovemaking, never wanting to let him go. I nap in his arms, blinking my eyes open when he tucks me carefully under the covers. "Love you," I murmur, reaching for him. I cup his face, and he plants a kiss on my palm.

"Rest, my love."

I drift in and out of sleep while Reeve gets dressed. "Sleep, sweetheart. I'll be back later." He kisses me sweetly, and I smile at him before my heavy eyelids shutter. I'm descending into heavenly darkness when his mouth brushes my ear. "It's all been for you, Viv," he whispers. "Everything I've done was for you. Please let it not have been in vain."

CHAPTER 5
VIVIEN

STRETCHING my arm across the bed, I frown when my hand finds nothing but cold sheets. Rubbing the sleep from my eyes, I haul myself upright, glancing at the time on my cell. It's four a.m., and Reeve isn't in bed. Trying not to panic, I swipe through my call log, but there are no messages or missed calls from my husband. He has never not come home before, and he said he wouldn't be late. If something popped up, he would have contacted me, knowing I'd worry. Acid crawls up my throat as panic twists my stomach into knots.

What if something has happened to him?

I press his number on my cell, biting the inside of my mouth as I listen to it ring. *Pick up, Reeve! Goddamn it!* I try a few more times, before climbing awkwardly out of bed, working hard to stop my growing hysteria from reaching coronary-inducing proportions.

Grabbing my silk robe, I tie it around my balloon-sized belly as I slip my feet into my slippers. I keep dialing his number as I head out of our bedroom, wondering what to do. Fear raises goose bumps on my arms and lifts all the tiny hairs on the back of my neck. *Please let nothing have happened to my husband.*

I'm just about to end the call and call Reeve's publicist when I hear the sound of a phone ringing coming from one of our guest bedrooms. Another familiar sound tickles my eardrums as I approach the room, and a layer of stress instantly flitters off my shoulders.

The door is ajar, and I push it open, almost collapsing in relief when I discover Reeve, fully clothed, facedown, sprawled across the top of the bed, snoring like a freight train.

Whisky fumes tickle my nostrils as I softly step into the room. Edwin and Reeve obviously indulged in a few drinks after their meeting, and it's just like my husband to sleep it off in one of our spare bedrooms rather than risk disturbing me.

He knows my sleep has been erratic lately. He's always so thoughtful, and as I stand staring at his sleeping form, I'm almost overwhelmed with the love I feel for this man. Powerful emotion sweeps over me as I contemplate losing him. I pray he'll be able to forgive me for all my sins and we emerge on the other side stronger and more united. I've got to believe that, or I'd be an even bigger basket case.

He looks much younger in sleep, but his features aren't at peace. An almost pained look contorts his handsome face, even in slumber. Seeing him vulnerable like this hurts because I know the next few weeks are going to be hard for him. Reeve already senses something is wrong, but it's still going to come as a big shock.

Kneeling on the carpet beside the bed, I carefully brush strands of hair back off his face, pressing a gentle kiss to his brow. Tears prick my eyes as I peer at him with a heavy heart. He's in a deep sleep. Not even budging when I set another kiss on his cheek. Breathing softly, I stand and walk out of the room, quietly closing the door behind me.

Easton wakes me a few hours later, jumping on our bed, full of boundless energy. "Mommy! Wake up! Can we go swimming? Puh-lease." I pry my eyes open, smiling when I see he is wearing his swim shorts back to front.

"Sure, sweetie. Just give me a few minutes to get ready." I ruffle his hair before pointing at my face. "And I need kisses. Lots of kisses to help me get out of bed."

Easton peppers my face with a slew of sloppy kisses, and I wrap my arms around him, holding him close. "I'm gonna kiss my little sister too. Just like Daddy does," he adds, pulling the comforter back and gently kissing my tummy through my silk night-dress. I thread my fingers through his hair, offering up silent thanks for my precious son. Even on dark days, he always brightens my world.

Ten minutes later, we are walking hand in hand along the hallway, ready for swimming. I check on Reeve, making Easton promise not to make a sound. It's early, and he needs more sleep. If the alcohol fumes still wafting around the room are any indication, he'll have one hell of a hangover today.

Easton and I take a swim in our indoor pool, and we have fun messing around until hunger attacks us both, and we get out to grab breakfast. We are both wearing bathrobes and flip-flops when we land in our large kitchen where Charlotte—our live-in housekeeper—is busy making pancakes. "A little bird told me someone was swimming," she says, leaning down to kiss Easton on the cheek. "I hope you're hungry."

"I'm always hungry for pancakes," E says, climbing onto a chair beside me at the kitchen table. "Especially if you have strawberries and chocolate." He rubs his tummy, his eyes popping wide as Charlotte slides a plate with two pancakes, choco-late, and strawberries in front of him. "Yummy. Thanks, Lotty." He blows her a kiss, making my heart melt.

Charlotte smiles affectionately at E before turning to me. "I can make you an omelet, or would you like some fresh fruit and yogurt this morning?"

I pour fresh orange juice into a glass for Easton. "Fruit and yogurt would be perfect though I expect Reeve will need something more substantial." My lips twitch.

"Oh. Mr. Lancaster has already eaten and left for the day. He said to tell you he'd be home in time to pick you up for the charity event."

I frown. "Reeve's already gone?" Prickles of apprehension tickle the back of my neck. Reeve never leaves without kissing me and Easton goodbye. He would only do this if he was deliberately avoiding me.

Something has happened, and I need to find out what.

I spend most of the day pacing the floor in my office, panicking as all my calls go straight to Reeve's voice mail. After lunch, I finally hear from him, but his text is brief, telling me he's in meetings with Margaret and Edwin all day and he'll talk to me later. His words do little to reassure me.

Later that evening, Carole and her hairdresser wife are just leaving, after helping me to get ready for tonight's event, when I receive another text from my husband, informing me he's running late and Leon will drive me to the hotel. Now I know for sure Reeve is avoiding me, and I almost empty the contents of my stomach all over my bedroom floor.

Does he know?

Has he somehow found out?

Wrapping my arms around myself, I fight tears as there's a knock on the door.

"Vivien?" Leon's deep voice booms through the door. "There was a delivery for you."

"I'm coming." I force myself to my feet and walk across my bedroom, opening the door. "Thank you." I slap a fake smile on my face as I take the envelope from him, hoping he doesn't notice how badly my hands are shaking.

"You don't look so hot. Are you feeling okay?" he asks, tilting his head to the side as he examines my face.

"I'm fine," I lie. "Just trying to psych myself up for tonight. It's hard to wear heels and a constant smile for hours when I'm carrying a giant watermelon in my tummy." I run my hands over my swollen stomach, and where it's normally soothing, right now, nothing could quell the storm rising to catastrophic proportions inside me.

"I'll have Charlotte send up some water and a snack. Why don't you rest up until we have to go?" He glances at the watch strapped to his wrist. "It's still early. We don't need to leave for an hour."

An hour to compose myself—when this envelope might contain news that will upend my world—is nowhere near long enough, but Leon is being sweet, and I don't want to worry him. "Thanks, Leon. I'll do that."

I close my door and pad in my bare feet to my dresser, sitting down in front of my mirror, staring at my reflection with mounting horror. I hold the envelope in my trembling hands, terrified to open it. This will either help soften the blow or make it ten million times worse. I'm tempted to shove it in a drawer to deal with tomorrow, but the knowledge Dillon has received a similar envelope means I need to look at it now. I know Dillon will, and I won't remain in the dark and give him additional power over me.

But I can't do this alone, so I grab my cell and call my bestie, praying she answers. Audrey is the only person who knows exactly what's going down because I needed someone to help keep me sane.

"Hey, babe." Audrey sounds breathless when she picks up.

"Where are you?"

"At the train station," she pants. "I'm out of breath because I just jogged up several flights of stairs and still missed the damn train."

"I got the results," I blurt.

"Shit. Give me a sec to find somewhere more private to talk."

I nibble on my lips and my foot taps on the floor as I wait for her to move to a quieter spot.

"Okay. I'm good now. Talk to me."

"I haven't opened the envelope. I've just been staring at it, feeling like I'm going to throw up."

"Rip the Band-Aid off, Viv. At least this way, you will know what you're dealing with."

"I'm so scared, Rey," I whisper, as I cut the top of the envelope with my silver letter opener. "I don't want anything to change. I don't want Reeve to leave me. I don't want to ruin Easton's life."

"Breathe, Viv. Please just breathe. God, I wish I was there with you."

"Me too," I admit, pulling the report out of the envelope with trembling fingers.

"It's going to be okay. Reeve won't leave you. He will be upset and angry for a while, but he loves you and Easton too much to walk away. And look at it this way; if Dillon is Easton's father, he gets two dads. That won't ruin his life. He might be confused for a while after he finds out, but you will love him and reassure him, and he'll be okay. He's an awesome little boy. He'll be fine."

"Thank you." I swallow over the thick lump in my throat. "I needed to hear that."

"I know you did, babe. You've got to remember this isn't your fault. You didn't know they were twins."

I place my phone on speaker, setting it down on my dresser as I unfold the letter. Tears blur my vision as I read, plopping onto the page with finality. Sobs burst from my chest as the floodgates open.

"Viv? What does it say?" Audrey asks as I cry.

"I...it's...I," I splutter, unable to form words over the messy ball of emotion clogging the back of my throat. Audrey waits me out, reminding me she's here for me. I stare at my tearstained face in the mirror. My makeup is ruined, but that's the least of my concerns. Grabbing a tissue, I dab at the dampness on my cheeks and try to rein in my emotions. "Oh God, Audrey," I rasp as a fresh layer of pain presses down on my chest.

"You're going to be okay, Viv. Take deep breaths. In and out. You need to calm down."

I do as she suggests, and gradually, I am composed enough to confirm what I've suspected since the twin truth was revealed. "Reeve isn't Easton's father. Dillon is."

CHAPTER 6
VIVIEN

MY HAND SHAKES as I lift my glass of sparkling water to my lips, keeping the false smile plastered on my face like I've done all night, from the moment I set foot in the hotel. The paternity results are only one of my concerns though. Reeve has barely spoken to me since I arrived. While it's been difficult to get alone time—because Reeve is the guest speaker this year, and he's in high demand—there have been a few moments at the table during dinner when we had time to ourselves, and my husband ignored me, eating his dinner instead of talking to me.

I've suspected all day that something happened last night, but I'm one hundred percent confident now Reeve is avoiding me because he's discovered at least part of the truth. It's the only explanation for the cold-shoulder treatment I'm receiving.

I wish I could drink alcohol because I could really use some vodka right now.

Reeve avoids eye contact with me as he delivers an emotional speech, from the podium at the top of the room, discussing the many ways the charity supports disadvantaged children and those removed from their homes due to neglect and abuse. Genuine tears pool in his eyes as he flicks through slides showing the various facilities the charity is building to offer an alternative home to some of these kids. Strong Together is a cause we are both passionate about, and we always attend the annual fundraising gala to throw our weight behind such a worthy cause.

Tonight is the first time I'm wishing we were anywhere but here.

I need to talk to Reeve.

Especially as Dillon is blowing up my cell, only adding to my stress. The sooner we get home, the better. I've decided I'm telling my husband everything tonight. I can't hold off for Dillon's showdown because it's clear Reeve already knows something.

It's time to come clean.

Now Dillon has the proof he is Easton's father, I very much doubt he will broadcast the news over social media. It's still a risk, but it's one I have no choice but to

415

take. My husband can hardly look at me, and the only thing worse than the truth is fragments of the truth. In this moment, I have no clue what he believes, and that's a truly scary prospect.

After posing with Reeve and the charity directors for photos, I manage to grab him to one side for a few seconds. "Can we make our excuses and leave?" I whisper.

"Eager to get home or eager to get away from me?" he asks in a sneering tone I don't much care for.

"We need to talk, and this can't wait."

"You're right," he snaps. "It can't."

I rub my hands over my belly, fighting tears as Reeve levels me with an angry look I haven't seen in a long, long time. His eyes bore into mine, and he drops the invisible mask he's wearing for a second, showcasing his devastation for the entire room to see. Thank fuck, no one is paying us any attention right now.

A half hour later, we finally make our goodbyes and leave the room, hand in hand. The instant we are out in the hallway, Reeve drops my hand like it's on fire. Pain stabs holes in my heart as I hurry after my husband, half running to keep up with his long-legged strides.

Rain is plummeting from the sky in a heavy downpour that is most unusual for May. Reeve bristles with anger as we stand under the shelter of the awning while the valet retrieves our car. The porter opens an umbrella as our sleek black and gold Maserati draws up to the curb. Reeve slides his arm around my back, holding me in close as we walk carefully on slippery steps toward our car. At this proximity, I feel his entire body trembling, and my mouth turns dry.

This is bad. Really fucking bad, and I'm terrified I'm going to lose him.

Reeve directs me to the passenger side, and I turn to him as he opens the door. "You've been drinking. I'll drive."

He shakes his head, his jaw pulling taut. "I only had a few, and I'm not drunk."

"But it's raining and—"

"You really don't want to push me right now, Vivien." His eyes burn with conflicting emotions as he stares at me. "Do you honestly think I would drive if I wasn't fit to drive? Do you think I'd put your life and our unborn child's life at risk by driving if I wasn't in full control of my faculties?"

Swallowing thickly, I shake my head.

"Then get in the damn car, Viv."

I'm a quivering mess as I climb into my seat, buckling my seat belt with trembling fingers while I attempt to control my errant tear ducts.

Reeve tips the valet before sliding behind the wheel. Beads of rain cling to his hair and the shoulders of his black tuxedo jacket as he straps himself in. He doesn't speak or look at me as he starts the engine and glides out onto the semi-busy street.

Reeve avoids the highway, choosing to travel home on less busy roads. I stare out the window, wrapping my arms around myself as I cry invisible tears. Turmoil has been my constant companion since I got the results, and the pain in my heart is so intense I wonder if this is what it feels like when you are on the verge of a heart attack.

Reeve says nothing, quietly seething, until we're on a quieter stretch of open road, and then he rounds on me. "Is there nothing you want to say to me?"

Slowly, I turn to face him, flinching at the angry look on his face. "I think we should wait until we get home to talk."

His grip tightens on the wheel, and his nostrils flare. Rain pelts against the windscreen, and the wipers are working overtime to keep it clear. "Are you fucking him?" He takes his eyes off the road for a second to stare at me. "Are you fucking my *twin*?" he hisses, his tone elevating a few notches.

Oh God. He knows who Dillon is, which means he must know what we once meant to one another. "What? No! Of course, I'm not! Why would you say that?"

"Where did you disappear to when you gave Leon the slip last week?"

Shit. I bite down hard on my lower lip. "I can explain, but not like this, and you should slow down. The rain isn't showing any signs of stopping."

"Just answer the goddamn question, Vivien!" He slams his hands down on the wheel, and I jump.

"I was with Dillon, but it's not what you're thinking. I haven't been with him. I would never cheat on you, Reeve. Never. You've got to believe me!"

"I waited for you to tell me. It's been almost two weeks, and you said nothing!" he shouts as all his pent-up anger flies free.

"You've known all along? Why the hell didn't *you* say something?"

"Because I needed to hear it from my wife! I needed to know the trust I've placed in you all these years wasn't for nothing. I needed to know we are a solid team."

"We are, Reeve." I reach for his arm, but he shucks me off, sending splintering pain ricocheting throughout me. "How did you find out?" I ask, hastily swiping at the tears rolling down my face. This is all going to shit, and it's my fault for making the wrong call. I should've risked it and spoken to Reeve the instant I returned home from the laboratory.

"Your reaction the day he showed up at our house tipped me off, and I saw the way he was looking at you. His reaction to Easton's birthday was a major trigger."

My brows knit together in confusion.

"He said he thought E's birthday was in June," Reeve clarifies.

Maybe my brain is foggy because I'm so stressed, but I'm still not getting the point.

"We hadn't exchanged names in advance. Our identities were supposed to be hidden. I can understand how he might have recognized me, but knowing our son's birthday was reported as being in June, not May, was a major flag. I knew for sure something was amiss. Then I remembered that photo you sent me when you were in Ireland, and I recalled seeing a guy with the same kind of hair behind you in the hallway at the Oscars. Things started slotting into place. I was praying I was wrong. That it was just a coincidence your ex had bright blond hair and my twin used to." Our tires squelch as we race along wet back roads. "Until last night when I met with the owner of the private security firm I'd hired to watch you in Ireland."

"What the what?" I shout, my eyes popping wide. "What do you mean?" I splutter. The fact he went to a stranger instead of asking me—his wife—speaks volumes. But that's secondary to the main issue.

Reeve pins me with sharp blue eyes. "Did you really think I'd let the love of my life wander around Ireland without someone protecting her from harm? In case

SIOBHAN DAVIS

you've forgotten, you'd been viciously assaulted a couple of months previously, and I wasn't taking any chances."

"You had someone spying on me the entire time?" Disbelief lies heavy on my tongue, even as I recall the guy Dillon spotted hanging around outside my apartment one time. Dillon was sure he'd seen him outside Whelans too. Back then, I'd assumed it was paparazzi, but when nothing appeared in the media about me and the guy never reappeared, I forgot all about it.

"Not spying. *Protecting*. I hired a guy in L.A., and he found a reputable local firm in Dublin. They had guys watching you twenty-four-seven to ensure you were safe."

"That is… I can't believe you did that." Shock splays across my face. "What did they tell you? Have you known who Dillon is all along?"

"If I knew who he was, I would've thrown the motherfucking asshole out of my house the second I laid eyes on him!" Reeve yells, his voice cracking. When he looks at me, tears fill his eyes. "Back then, I knew there was a guy before you told me because the security firm sent me weekly reports."

I clamp a hand over my chest, rubbing at the sudden tightness. "That is such a massive invasion of my privacy. I can't believe you did that, Reeve. I asked you for space!"

"And I fucking gave it to you!" he shouts. "Every week when I got the reports, I wanted to hop on a plane and bring you back home. It took colossal willpower to stay away, but I did it because you asked me to. It almost killed me, Viv. I legit felt like my heart was breaking on a daily basis. I knew you were with him, and I risked losing you permanently. The only thing I could do was try to make amends and hope to fuck you were still mine when you came back. *If* you came back."

His chest heaves, and the car swerves a little when he places his head down on the wheel.

"You need to slow down," I caution again. "Please, Reeve." Tentatively, I touch his arm. "Why don't you pull over and I'll drive?"

"That day in Mexico was the day I found out about him," he continues, ignoring my pleas. "There were photos, but I refused to look at them. I knew my heart couldn't bear to see that, so I never saw any photographic proof." A tear leaks from the corner of his eye as he glances at me. "They were left out of my reports because I couldn't tolerate seeing you with him. I got trashed that day to numb my pain." A bitter laugh bursts from his mouth. "My twin was fucking shit up for me even then. This is all his fault. I found out about him, got drunk and high, and ended up screwing that psycho bitch."

CHAPTER 7
VIVIEN

VITRIOL SPILLS from Reeve's lips and pours from his eyes, and it's so unlike him. He's starting to sound as twisted up and angry as his brother. And just like Dillon, he's blaming his twin when it was others who were responsible. Simon set everything in motion. And Saffron manipulated Reeve in Mexico to aid her agenda.

Will this cycle of blame and hostility ever end?

"I saw the photos last night. They confirmed my suspicions about everything." He shakes his head, and the look of disappointment etched across his face is crystal clear. "You let him fuck you against a cross at the top of a hill in the middle of the night? And in the sea when others were around?"

Disgust replaces disappointment on his handsome face, and it makes me mad. It's not like Reeve is a prude or the type of guy fixated on vanilla sex. We're adventurous in our own way. Yes, we have never fucked in a public place, but that's only because it's too damn risky given his celebrity status. I don't like his judgy, hypocritical attitude one little bit. "You don't get to judge me, Reeve. I was with my boyfriend, and everything was consensual. At least my photos didn't end up splashed all over the tabloids and social media. You were spared that humiliation." That's a low blow for me, but I'm riled up now and seething at the sickening invasion of my privacy.

"Do I even know you?" he continues, narrowing his eyes, and I see red. He has no right to look down his nose at me. Certainly not after all this time. "Do you have any idea what it did to me seeing that?"

It's just like Reeve to try to turn this back around on me when he's the one in the wrong. "Well, maybe you shouldn't have invaded my privacy in such a revolting manner! Do *you* have any idea how it feels to know someone was watching me with *my boyfriend*? Capturing our most intimate moments on film?" Anger mushrooms inside me until it explodes. "Those photos should never have been taken! And they sure as fuck shouldn't be sitting in some pervy PI's office like a ticking time bomb." I'm enraged and horrified and feeling a ton of other emotions.

"I didn't know they'd done that because I didn't ask for it, and I never looked at the photos. After I got you back, I didn't give them a second thought." He pulls a thick white envelope from the glove compartment, tossing it into my lap. "There you go. That's all of them. Carson already got signed declarations from the US and Irish security firms confirming no other copies are in existence in physical or digital format."

I swivel on my seat, the leather squelching with the motion. "Did you arrange that photo of us on the balcony the day I came home?"

A muscle pops in his jaw, but he says nothing.

"Answer me, Reeve. We might as well bring all the skeletons out of the closet."

He looks at me with pleading eyes. "I was so scared I'd lost you. You were really upset. I knew you were in love with him. Possibly more than with me, and I wasn't risking losing you forever." Fierce determination glistens in his eyes. "I'd gotten friendly with a photographer. He'd suggested we could have a mutually beneficial arrangement. I called him that day and set it up."

Oh God. Dillon was right. My head drops back against the headrest, and I close my eyes as if that will ward off the incoming fresh wave of pain. Tears fall from my eyes, almost in sync with the drip-drip of the rain as it pelts our car. "You seduced me on purpose so the photographer would get the money shot and you'd use it to drive Dillon away."

"Don't rewrite history, Viv." I open my eyes, noticing his fingers digging into the wheel. "I seduced you because I fucking love you and I missed you. I wanted to feel close to you again. Staking my claim, and warning that prick off, was secondary." He casts a quick glance at me as he rounds the next bend. "You're mine, Viv, and that's never going to change."

I'm dumbstruck, and my brain is clouded with so many emotions. Did Reeve want me back for the right reasons, or am I a possession he was determined to win from his competition? Has Dillon been right about everything? I don't even know what is real anymore. All I do know is Reeve has been lying to me. And I've been lying to him. Which is worse? Are they even comparable? Can I call him out on his shit when I've been concealing big things from him these past two weeks? Are we both as bad as each other?

I can't make sense of the warring thoughts churning through my jumbled brain. "I always thought you stopped to talk to the reporters that day to send a message to Saffron. To let her know we were back together and to not try anything. I never stopped to consider you were sending Dillon a message too. I was so fucking naïve."

"Two birds. One stone." He shrugs, like it's no biggie, and I lose the tenuous hold on my emotions.

"Don't act so freaking flippant! You lied to me! Manipulated me! How often have you done that in our marriage, Reeve? What else don't I know?"

"Oh no, Viv. You don't get to throw that shit at me." The car accelerates as an angry red flush creeps up his neck and onto his face. "You've done exactly the same! You should've confessed the second we stepped foot in our living room that day. You should've told me immediately who Dillon was. Instead, you sat there and let him try to make a fool out of me."

"I wanted to tell you," I cry. "I was planning to, but he blackmailed me into keeping quiet."

"He what?" Reeve roars, and I cover my ears at the bellowing sound.

"He took photos of me, when we were together, without my permission. He threatened to post them online along with the truth that he was your twin and that E…" I break down, sobbing into my hands.

"He has no intention of developing a relationship with me. He's here for you. You and…my son," he croaks.

I lift my face, staring at Reeve through blurry eyes. "We are yours, Reeve. He can't take us from you."

"If you didn't meet with him to fuck him, there is only one other reason you would." His chest heaves, and silent tears stream down his face. "You did a paternity test. Didn't you?"

I nod, swiping at the hot tears coursing over my cheeks. "He insisted on it. I wanted to tell you, but he blackmailed me into keeping silent. Then I thought maybe it was for the best to wait until we had the test results, but…" I sob into my hands, unable to keep my emotions in check.

"No, Viv. Please, God, no. Don't say what I think you're going to say."

His choked tone is killing me, along with the intense pain pressing down on my chest, making it difficult to breathe. "I'm sorry, Reeve. I'm so sorry. I didn't know you were twins! I kept my distance when I first returned from Ireland because I wasn't sure you were the father. I'm sorry I lied about that, but I was trying to protect you. I was so happy when Easton was born and the test confirmed he was yours." My cries bounce off the insides of the car.

"I knew you lied," he says, and I jerk my head up, my tears faltering.

"What?"

"You told me you'd been sleeping with him. I'm not an idiot. Of course, I knew there was a chance the baby wasn't mine. I knew you were refusing to commit to me, to accept my proposal, because you wanted to make sure. I don't hold that against you, Viv. I respect you for trying to do the right thing by me and your baby. It's why I never said anything, and if you're beating yourself up over that, don't."

"Oh, Reeve," I choke out, in between sobs, placing my hand on his.

He clears his throat and looks at me. Pain is written all over his face, and my heart is breaking. "Please tell me Easton is my flesh and blood? Please tell me he's *my son*. I love that little boy with everything I am. Please don't say he's his. I can't lose him."

I can scarcely speak over the lump in my throat. "Pull over, please," I croak. We're not that far from home now, but I can't tell him this while we're driving.

"No, Viv. Just say it. I can't bear it a minute longer!"

Tears leak from my eyes of their own volition. "You are still Easton's dad, Reeve. In all the ways that matter, he is still your son."

"Vivien," he rasps in a strangled voice. "Is he my biological child or Dillon's?"

Strained tension bleeds in the air, and the only sound is the whoosh-whoosh of the wipers and the pitter-patter of rain as it continues tumbling from the dark night sky. "He's Dillon's," I whisper, my lower lip wobbling.

"No!" Reeve's anguished cries fill the small space, almost smothering me. "No. He can't be. He's *my* son! He's mine. *You're* mine. He can't have you!" Tears cling to his lashes and his cheeks as he stares at me with the same lost, vulnerable expression I used to see on his face as a kid when his dad did something hurtful.

"I'm sorry, Reeve. I'm so sorry." I scrub at my eyes, smoothing a hand across the tight pain in my chest. "But he's still your son. You're still his father, and I'm still your wife. That won't change."

"You can't tell me this doesn't change things, Viv, because it does," he yells.

The car jerks forward as he accidentally presses down on the accelerator. Slamming his palms down on the horn, he pushes it repeatedly in a scary display of frustrated anger and anguished hopelessness. The horn blares along the dark, desolate stretch of road. Plush homes shielded behind high walls and gates are too far back to complain about the ruckus. Tall, old oak trees line the other side of the road behind flimsy fencing. Some are leaning at precarious angles; their branches battered by the brutal rain dumping from the heavens.

"Calm down, Reeve. Please. You're going too fast."

"Don't fucking tell me to calm down!" His eyes look wild as he fixes them on me. "I have sacrificed so much for you! For our family. And he's going to try and take it all from me!" Scrunching his fist, he slams it into the dashboard over and over.

Sacrifice? What sacrifice? "What the hell does that mean?"

"My heart is breaking, Viv." He stares at me with tears pouring down his face. "I don't want him near my son. I don't want to have to explain this to Easton. I can't lose him. I can't lose you. I won't. I—"

"Watch out!" I scream as a car pulls out onto the road from a small side road. Visibility is poor, and they haven't seen us.

Reeve reacts fast, swerving and accelerating to outrun the car, but it clips the rear end of our Maserati, sending us into a tailspin on the slippery road. I scream as Reeve struggles to regain control of the car, both of us bouncing up and down in our seats.

It all happens so fast.

Reeve yanks on the wheel, and my head whips forward and then back with the motion as the car jerks violently to the left. A distressed sound rips from my husband's lips as our car darts forward, breaking through the rickety fence bordering the left-hand side of the road. Pieces of wood fly all over our car as we bounce forward. Reeve wrestles with the wheel, trying to regain control. I'm screaming, but it's as if someone else is making these high-pitched screeching noises.

The next few seconds happen as if in slow motion. Reeve curses before unlocking his seat belt and throwing his body across me. His arms band firmly around my upper torso as he clings to me. I want to shout at him to strap himself back in. To not be a martyr. But I can't get the words out of my mouth. I can't stop screaming. Adrenaline shoots through my veins as liquid terror plays havoc with my insides.

Metal scrapes loudly, piercing my ear drums, and I'm jostled forward with force as we plow into a tree. My terrified eyes startle in extreme shock and gut-wrenching panic as a looming darkness descends over our car. The tree lands horizontally on top of us with an earth-shattering thud. The roof buckles, pressing down on us, flattening the space in the car and crushing Reeve. Fear for my husband is my last conscious thought as my head slams into the side of the window and my world is plunged into pitch-black darkness.

CHAPTER 8
VIVIEN

"MISS? CAN YOU HEAR ME?" an unfamiliar voice asks as I slowly come to. Pain rattles around my skull, pounding, like someone is hammering on my head from the inside. I'm hot. Too hot. And there's a dead weight pressing me into the seat, gluing my ballgown to my back. Slowly, I blink my eyes open, wishing instantly I could close them again.

It all comes back to me in horrifying technicolor, and I cry out. The air is cloying and thick as it wraps around me. My eyes scan the confined space with mounting trepidation. "Reeve," I croak, lifting my hand, tentatively touching the back of my husband's head. I scream as thick blood coats my fingers. "Honey," I sob, shaking Reeve's frozen shoulder. "Wake up! Please, Reeve, I need you." Tears stream down my face as I stare at my husband's prone body. He's trapped between the dented roof and me, and the fallen tree ensures he can't move even if he was presently conscious. I don't have the strength to lift his head, to see his face, and I'm terrified to attempt to dislodge either one of us.

"Miss?" The voice speaks close to my ear, and I startle as the sound of blaring sirens echoes in the near distance. "Are you okay?"

I wince as I angle my head back, peering at the gray-haired stranger poking his head through the windowless back door. "Help," I croak. "My husband needs help." My eyes pop wide with shock as warmth pools under my butt, and I know what's happening. "My baby." I pin panicked eyes on the man. "Something is wrong. Please help us." All the lights are out in the car, so I can't see the blood spreading under my ass, but I feel it.

"Help is on the way. They should be here soon. I'm so sorry." I stare at him blankly with tears pouring down my face. "I was driving the other car. I didn't see you. It was dark and—"

He hangs his head, but I don't have time to concern myself with him. I'm too busy worrying about my baby and Reeve. Placing one hand on my bump and the other on top of Reeve's head, I pray like I've never prayed before.

Sobs rip through the eerily still night air as I barely cling to my sanity. "Reeve, please wake up. Please, baby. Don't leave me!" I cry. "You can't leave me. Not like this. Not when we were so angry with one another. Please, God," I scream, tilting my head up, brushing my forehead against the battered roof of our car. "Please don't take my husband and my daughter! Haven't you done enough already?"

The sirens draw closer, and I will them to hurry up.

I watch in a numbed haze as the firemen work to remove the fallen tree and lift the roof so they can reach us. Large lights shine down on the car as they work, illuminating the carnage. Physical and emotional pain ravages my body as I survey the wreckage I'm trapped in. There is blood everywhere, and Reeve still hasn't moved. I'm terrified and barely clinging to sanity. I whisper apologies to my husband as I run my bloody fingers through his hair. I beg him to wake up. I plead with him to hold on. I silently beg my little Lainey to fight. My head pounds, and my vision blurs in and out, but I refuse to close my eyes. I fight to remain conscious for my husband and my unborn child.

A paramedic asks me questions through my open window, but I can't answer her. I only have enough energy to focus on my family. Fear has a vise grip on my heart, squeezing and tightening until it feels like I can't breathe. My breath oozes out in wheezy, panicked spurts, and I'm struggling to get enough air into my lungs. An oxygen mask is carefully placed around my nose and chin just as the roof is finally lifted off.

A fireman wrenches the driver side door away, leaning in to press his fingers against Reeve's neck. He avoids eye contact with me while holding his fingers against Reeve's pulse point. Looking over his shoulder, he shakes his head at the male paramedic waiting behind him. He turns back around, and his sympathetic eyes lock on mine. An anguished sob escapes my mouth. "No!" I scream. "No! Don't say it! Don't you dare tell me that!" Hysteria bubbles up my throat, and I tighten my fingers in Reeve's hair, crying as I silently plead with the universe.

It's a mistake.

It's got to be.

Reeve would never leave me.

He's promised me so many times.

"Mrs. Lancaster," the kind paramedic lady says. She told me her name, but I can't remember it. "I'm so very sorry for your loss. There is nothing we can do for your husband now. We need to focus on you and your baby."

"Reeve." I hold on to him, clinging to his shoulders, crying with the worst, most unimaginable pain sitting on my chest. "You can't leave me. I love you too much! I can't go on without you. Please, wake up. Baby, please." It physically feels like my heart is rupturing behind my rib cage. Wracking sobs heave from my chest, and I want to die too.

"It's time, Mrs. Lancaster," the paramedic says, squeezing my arm in a show of support. "You need to let my colleagues remove your husband from the car."

"No," I sob. "Don't take him from me." Tears coat my face in a steady stream, and fluid leaks out of my nose.

"You need to let go, sweetheart." A male paramedic gently pries my hands from Reeve as they pull him from the car and lay him on a stretcher. A blue sheet is placed over him, covering him from head to foot. My tears crawl to a stop, and I'm in a daze as I'm lifted out of the car and placed on a stretcher on the ground while the paramedics check me out.

"Mrs. Lancaster?" Kara—that's her name—says. "Can you feel the baby moving?"

I shake my head, running my hands over my bump. Warm liquid gushes down my legs. "She's not kicking," I whisper, closing my eyes. If I lose my daughter too, I won't survive this.

"We're going to airlift you to the hospital," she explains, pointing to a chopper in the middle of the field behind us. I hadn't even heard it land. I look up, spotting other helicopters in the sky. "Your baby is in fetal distress, and you're hemorrhaging badly. We need to get you to the delivery room."

Nausea swims up my throat, and I feel disoriented. My eyelids grow heavy. "Stay with me, Vivien," Kara says, her voice sounding distant. "We're losing her!" she shouts as I'm lifted off the ground, and that's the last thing I'm conscious of before I pass out.

CHAPTER 9
DILLON

"TURN ON THE TV," Ash shouts, barging into the recording studio on the grounds of my L.A. pad, with tears streaming down her face. "Hurry the fuck up, Jay!" she yells at her fiancé, impatient with his slow reaction. "Stick CNN on now!"

"What's going on?" I ask, immediately alarmed.

"Dillon," she sobs, throwing herself at me.

Goose bumps sprout on my arms, and my mouth is suddenly dry. Keeping one arm around my sobbing sister, I remove my guitar, setting the Fender aside. Ro shoots me a quizzical look, as Jamie flicks through the channels. Conor is sprawled across the leather couch, smoking a joint, oblivious to the tension in the air.

"This is bad, Dil," Ash whispers, wrapping both her arms around my body as the screen loads. "So, so, bad."

All the blood drains from my face as I read the headline flashing across the screen.

REEVE LANCASTER AND PREGNANT WIFE IN LATE-NIGHT CAR ACCIDENT

My heart throbs painfully behind my chest cavity, and I hold my sister tight as the reporter speaks from the scene of the crash. Yellow police tape cordons off the road, and I watch with mounting horror as the shattered remains of a black and gold Maserati are hauled onto the back of a tow truck. Crowds of reporters, photographers, and innocent bystanders surround the cordoned-off area, holding up umbrellas to ward off the heavy rain that continues to fall.

"What can you tell us, Claudine?" the anchor in the studio asks the reporter.

"All we know at this time is that Reeve Lancaster and his pregnant wife, Vivien, were returning from a charity event when their car was hit by another vehicle.

According to a local resident, who witnessed it from his bedroom window, Reeve lost control of the car and they crashed into a tree. The couple was trapped in their vehicle until firemen from a nearby station cut them free. Unofficial reports say Reeve was confirmed dead at the scene while a severely injured Vivien was airlifted to the hospital."

I tune out after that, shucking out of my sister's hold as I grab my jacket and keys. Panic slaps me in the face, and bile churns in my gut. "I need to go to her." I toss a look at Ash over my shoulder as my fingers curl around the door handle. "Find out which hospital they're at, and call me on the way."

"Like fucking hell I will." Ash stomps forward. "I'm coming with you."

"Will they even let you near her?" Ro asks, standing from his seat at his drum kit. "It's not like any of us have had any contact with her since she left Dublin."

Guilt swirls in my veins. I've been keeping so much from everyone, and it's all about to come out in the worst possible way. But I can't think about that now. All I can think about is getting to the hospital to see Vivien. "They'll let me in." I have no clue if they will, but I'll use the brother-in-law card if I have to.

"We're coming with you." Jamie slides his arms in his brown leather jacket.

"Conor can stay here and lock up," Ro says, stalking toward me. Conor grunts, barely aware of this conversation. Jamie grabs my car keys from my hand. "I'll drive. You sit in the back with Ash."

We race outside, climbing into my Land Rover. "I need to tell you something," I say after Ash has made a few calls and confirmed which hospital they have taken Viv to. Ro eyes me through the mirror as Jamie takes the next exit onto the highway. "I've seen Viv recently."

"What the fuck, Dil?" Ash fixes me with an incredulous expression. She jerks her head back suddenly, her eyes narrowing in suspicion. "Please don't tell me you're having an affair with her behind Reeve's back?"

"Jesus. Of course not." Vivien would be the last person to cheat on her husband, and my sister knows how I feel about the subject. I shake my head. "It's nothing like that."

"Then what is it like? And why are we only hearing this now?"

I wet my dry lips and exhale heavily before admitting the truth. "Reeve Lancaster is my twin brother."

Ash gawks at me. Jamie's mouth hangs open, and Ro's expression conveys shock. Silence descends for about three point five seconds before my brother, my sister, and my best friend all explode, talking over one another, as they fight to get the first word in.

"I fucking knew it!" Ash thumps me repeatedly in the arm. "You fucking laughed when I said you looked uncannily like Reeve after you removed the contacts and returned to your natural roots."

"Jesus Christ." Ro glares at me from the front passenger seat. "You knew all along, didn't you? I remember your reaction to Viv that night we first met her. You knew who she was, and you said nothing!"

I nod, and Ash thumps me again. "Stop fucking hitting me. I know you've got a shit ton of questions, and I promise I'll answer them, but not now." My throat clogs with emotion. I take a shuddering breath, clamping my hand over my mouth as the seriousness of the situation hits me full force. "If anything happens to her—" I croak, horrified when tears stab my eyes. "She's got to make it. She's got to pull through." I cannot imagine a world without Vivien in it. It doesn't matter that we've been separated for so long. She still means everything to me.

Ash's pretty features soften. "Oh, Dil. It's still her, isn't it? Even after everything."

I nod, locking eyes with Jamie as he indicates to turn right. My best friend is the only one who knows I've been pining for her all these years. He knows she's the love of my life and how badly I wish I could change the events of our last few days together.

But Jamie doesn't know the rest of it. I purposely didn't tell anyone so they weren't accomplices. Shame crashes over me as I think of the stress I've put Vivien under these past couple of weeks. If my actions have caused this, in any way, I will never forgive myself.

"Does he know?" Ro asks. "Does Reeve know you're twins?"

"Yes," I say through gritted teeth. My feelings toward my twin are a clusterfuck of epic proportions. I hate him. He represents everything that was denied to me, and he has everything I want, but I have never wished him dead. I wouldn't wish that on anyone, no matter how much I despised them.

"The reporter said he died," Ash whispers, clutching my arm. "If it's true, it will devastate Viv."

"Let's not second-guess anything until we get to the hospital and find out what's going on," Jamie supplies.

"I have a son," I blurt, my gaze bouncing between my siblings and my best mate. "Easton. Vivien's son. He's mine. I only found out earlier tonight."

"What. The. Actual. Fuck?" My brother's shell-shocked expression drills a hole in my skull. His face pales. "I can't believe you've kept all this from us." Hurt and some indecipherable emotion glimmer in his eyes, and I feel like a total shithead.

Jamie glances back at me, his eyes showcasing his disbelief.

"Keep your eyes on the bleeding road, Jay." Ro glares at our bandmate and soon-to-be brother-in-law. "We don't want a second accident tonight."

The weather is still shite, but the rain isn't as heavy as it was earlier, showing signs it might be stopping soon.

"That's why Viv blanked me after she returned to L.A.," Ash muses, staring off into space. "She got pregnant and didn't know if the baby was yours or Reeve's." My sister is as sharp as ever.

I nod again, rubbing the back of my neck. None of it seems to matter now. What good was me loving her and her loving him if they both end up dead? Pain pierces me through the heart at that thought, and I bury my head in my hands, struggling to keep my composure. Viv can't die believing I hate her when the truth is the complete opposite.

Ash stares at me, as if she's looking through me, and there is nothing as scary as a quiet Aisling O'Donoghue. "I'm so fucking mad at you, Dillon," she says, a few beats later, as Jamie turns off the road toward the entrance to the hospital. "How could you keep all of this a secret?"

"I had my reasons, and I was planning on telling you. I was waiting for the paternity results."

"When did you find out Reeve was your twin, and did you deliberately target Viv?" she asks, working hard to keep anger from her tone.

"Our bio dad found me when I was seventeen. He offered me a million bucks to sign an NDA so I wouldn't come forward and ruin Reeve's movie career." Ash sucks in a sharp gasp, and I know she'll make the connection with the timing. "As for Viv, it was a pure coincidence she showed up in Dublin. I did go after her with an agenda, at first, but she got to me, and by the end, I was crazy in love with her." I peer deep into my sister's eyes. "You know that. You've seen what losing her has done to me."

Ash quietly nods, reaching out to squeeze my hand.

"You didn't win that money in the US lottery, did you?" Jamie inquires.

Shit. I really don't want to get into this now, so I give them an abbreviated version. "I renegotiated with that asshole Simon Lancaster when I found myself in a tricky situation after I chased Viv to America. I signed his damn NDA and pocketed the five mil, using it to fund our relocation to L.A."

"Fucking hell." Ro drags his hands through his messy brown hair. "I feel like I don't know you at all." He shakes his head. "I'm your brother. We're your family, and you didn't say a fucking word to any of us!"

"I'm sorry." It's pretty pathetic, but it's all I've got right now.

"Do Ma and Da know?" Ash asks.

"No. I didn't say anything to them either," I admit as we turn left into the hospital entrance. I poke my head through the gap between the front seats, watching the commotion up ahead. Thank God, my car has dark tinted windows and no one can see in.

Hordes of photographers swarm the front of the hospital, and several policemen are herding them behind a barricade. "I hate those fucking bloodsucking leeches." I crack my knuckles, wishing I could be let loose on them. With the amount of turmoil swirling in my veins, I reckon I could easily take a bunch of those dickheads out.

"Take that turn to the left up ahead," Ash instructs Jamie. "My contact said there's a side door we can enter. He has arranged for someone to meet us there."

Thank fuck for my sister and her connections. She's a kickass manager, and I know we wouldn't have achieved half of our success without her stellar management skills.

Jamie drops the three of us off before leaving to park my car.

As arranged, some PR jerk in a charcoal suit is waiting for us inside the door. He asks some loaded questions, and it's pretty clear we won't be getting near Vivien unless we have a justifiable reason. Reluctantly, I confess I'm her brother-in-law. The dude looks suspicious until Ash pulls up a picture of Reeve on her mobile phone, shoving it in his face. He looks between me and the photo, scrubbing his smooth jawline. After a few beats, he nods, mumbling a feeble apology, spouting shit about procedure and policy as we follow behind him.

Ash keeps him occupied with mindless chatter as we make our way through the hospital, doing our best to avoid drawing attention by keeping our heads down and our mouths shut. The last thing Vivien needs is the press sniffing around and uncovering the full extent of our sordid tale.

Mr. PR Prick Face takes us up in the elevator, escorting us to a private waiting room. Confirming someone will be along to talk to us in due course, he leaves. I'm grateful no one else is here so I can pace the floor, like a crazy person, without judgment.

"Sit the fuck down, Dil. You're making me even more nervous," Ash says, tapping away on her phone as Jamie slips into the room a few minutes later.

"It's a total shitshow outside and even more news vans are arriving," he explains as he slides onto the seat beside my sister, slinging his arm around her shoulders.

"Reeve's a big deal in Hollywood. What did you expect?" Ro says, arching a brow.

"Can't they ever show some respect?" Jamie shakes his head.

"We've lived here long enough to know they respect fuck all." I lean my head back against the wall, exhaling heavily. "When the fuck is someone coming to talk to us?" I snap, rubbing a tense spot between my brows.

"I'll see if I can find anything out." Ash stands. She drags her lower lip between her teeth as she contemplates me.

"Spit it out," I say, knowing she's got something on her mind.

"I regret it," she softly says. "I regret rejecting her when she reached out to me. I shouldn't have blocked her number. I let it go on for too long."

"Don't tell me. Tell her."

"I will." Fierce determination swims in her eyes as she stalks toward me. My sister is still the same pint-sized terror she's always been. "She's going to be okay. Vivien is tough as nails, and she's a fighter." She wraps her petite frame around me, and my arms automatically encircle her small body. I squeeze my eyes shut to contain the tears I long to spill. "If Reeve is gone, she's going to need you and me. Easton will too."

I know she'll have her parents and Audrey. I've seen photos of them online, so I know they are still friends. But Ash isn't wrong. She will need me, and I'm Easton's father. I want to be there for my son and his mother. Whether Vivien will let me help is another matter entirely, and I can't say I'd blame her. I've been a prick to her since I reappeared in her life, filling her head with the idea that I don't care about her anymore. God knows I have tried to forget about her over the years. But she has burrowed her way into my heart and my head, and I've never been able to get her out.

I can hardly breathe over the lump wedged in my throat. I've scarcely had time to let the news about Easton sink in.

I was elated earlier when I got the results. I assumed if I got confirmation he was mine that I'd be thrilled knowing how much the news would hurt Reeve and harm their marriage. But as I stared at that piece of paper, I didn't feel any of those things. All I was feeling was overwhelming joy I had made a precious little human with the only woman who has ever owned my heart. His adorable little face swam before my eyes, and my heart was overflowing with instant love and an almost insurmountable need to get to know him.

My son.

A little part of me, and a little part of Viv.

Now, everything has been turned upside down. I have no idea how things will pan out. I don't know if Vivien has survived or what's happened to her unborn baby or my...twin.

As Ash slips out of the room with Jamie, I sit down and pray for the first time in years.

CHAPTER 10

DILLON

"ALL WE COULD FIND out is that Viv is in surgery. They won't tell us anything else until her parents arrive," Ash says as she and Jamie reenter the waiting room. "They are en route from Texas and should be here within the hour." Ash clears her throat. "I spoke to Audrey."

"How did you get in contact with her?"

"We swapped numbers in Dublin. She's still using the same one. She's at the airport in Boston with her husband. Alex is Reeve's best friend." Ash flops down on the chair beside her fiancé, resting her head on his shoulder. "It seems Viv told her about you. She knows Easton is your son, but she's pretty sure Mr. and Mrs. Mills have no idea. She suggests you keep your gob shut for now."

"I'm not a fucking imbecile." I drag my hands through my hair, and I could kill for a beer or a smoke. "Viv is the priority right now." I have wondered who is taking care of Easton, but I'm guessing one of the staff they have at the house looks after him when they go out.

"You don't seem concerned about your twin," Ro says. "Why is that?"

"I can't get into all that now."

"I've often wondered if Viv and I would ever find a way to reconnect. I never imagined it would be under these circumstances," Ash says. "I should've spoken to her at the Oscars."

"Hon. Don't beat yourself up. There's no point wondering about all the what-ifs. You're here now. *We're* here now. That's what matters." Jamie kisses her on the lips, and she clings to him.

I turn around and face the window. Sometimes, it's hard to be around my best mate and my sister. They are so into one another, and it reminds me of everything I've lost. I rest my forehead on the glass, looking down at the chaos outside. The rain has petered out now, unlike the crowds, which appear to have trebled in size.

Time ticks by so slowly, and every minute feels like an hour. I can't sit still. I can't stop my mind from churning. Rehashing all the mistakes I've made, wondering if I'll ever get the opportunity to put them right. I'm thinking of everything and anything but the possibility Viv might not survive this because I cannot contemplate that scenario.

If I don't think it, it won't be true.

I jerk my head up when the door opens an hour later, and Vivien's parents enter the room. Lauren looks distraught. Her eyes are bloodshot, and her skin is puffy from crying. Jonathon holds her in his arms, and he's trying to put a brave face on it, but I can see the pain swimming in his eyes. Lauren frowns, her eyes creasing in confusion as she looks around the room. "Aisling?" She fixes her gaze on my sister as Ash stands. "What are you doing here?" she blurts.

"We came as soon as we saw the news. We couldn't not be here for Viv." Tears pool in my sister's eyes as Lauren pulls her in for a hug, sobbing. Jonathon's chest heaves, and he looks down at his feet.

Ronan and Jamie shoot me anxious looks.

"I'm glad you're here," Lauren says in a raspy voice that tells of copious shed tears. "Viv will be happy to see you. She misses you, you know."

"I miss her too." Ash glances up at Viv's mum. "Did they tell you what's going on? They won't tell us anything other than Viv is in surgery."

"They are sending someone in shortly," Jonathon says. "If they don't, I'll be screaming bloody murder."

Lauren eases out of Ash's embrace, approaching Jamie and Ro. "I'm Lauren, Vivien's mom. And this is my husband, Jonathon." She glances back at her husband, and he tips his head at my brother and friend.

"I'm Jamie, and this is Ronan."

"I wish we were meeting under better circumstances, but thank you for being here. I know it will mean a lot to my daughter."

Lauren moves back to the comfort of her husband's arms, and her eyes connect with mine. Her brow creases. "Who are you?" she asks, exchanging a puzzled look with her husband.

I clear my throat, shoving my hands in the pockets of my jeans. "I'm Dillon O'Donoghue. I'm Ash and Ronan's brother."

"You're Viv's ex-boyfriend!" Lauren steps away from her husband, walking toward me. "I saw pictures of you," she adds, scrutinizing my face. "But you didn't look like this." Jonathon steps up behind her, circling his arms around her waist as he regards me with suspicion. "You look like——" She clamps a hand over her mouth, sucking in a sharp gasp.

"He looks like Reeve," her husband says, rubbing his hand up and down her arm. "What is going on here?"

Lauren's hand drops to her side. "Oh my God. It's you! You're Reeve's twin!"

I nod. "I am. Viv didn't tell you we met two weeks ago?" I remember she was close to her parents. Her mum especially, and I know Reeve is like their prodigal son. I assumed they would've told them.

"What the hell is going on?" Lauren glares at me. "We knew you existed because we spoke to Reeve after he discovered he had a twin, but we left for location then." Lauren glances briefly at her husband before her eyes drill into mine. "Neither of them said a word on the phone, but I sensed something was troubling my daughter. She seemed distracted. Stressed."

She fixes me with a scary look, and her hands clench into fists at her sides. Honestly, she looks like she's seconds away from punching me. "I'm beginning to understand why. I don't believe in coincidence. You didn't want to meet us in Dublin on purpose. You were afraid we would recognize you." She hits the nail on the head, not that I'm confirming anything right now. I have zero desire to leave this hospital in a body bag, and with the way Viv's parents are glaring at me, it's a distinct possibility. "You knew who she was. You knew about Reeve. What sort of sick game were you playing?"

Viv's dad straightens up, regarding me with blatant hostility. "I'd like to know the answer to that question too," he says as the door opens and a man in blue scrubs enters the room.

"Mr. and Mrs. Mills. I'm Dr. Dwyer, and this is Officer Lawson. He's investigating the accident," he adds, stepping aside to let a tall man into the room. He has a head of thick black hair and a slight paunch, and he's wearing a wrinkled black suit. The cop's eyes widen when he gets a load of Jamie, Ro, and me, but he quickly composes himself. The doctor shuts the door, and tense anticipation bleeds into the air.

At least Viv's parents have forgotten about me.

For now.

My heart is ping-ponging around my chest, and I think I might throw up. Ash walks to me, looping her arm through mine. Her lower lip wobbles, and she's as white as a sheet. I know she's every bit as terrified as me.

"Is our daughter out of surgery? Is she okay?" Lauren asks in a shaky voice.

"Vivien is in recovery, and she'll be moved to a private room shortly. You can see her then. She lost a lot of blood, and we also discovered some internal bleeding. We found the source, repaired the damaged blood vessel, and cleaned out the pooled blood. She has a few bruised ribs, a concussion, and a sprained wrist, but she will make a full recovery. She needs rest and time to heal."

Relief floods my system, and I wrap my arms around my sister, squeezing my eyes shut as I press a kiss to her head.

"Thank God," Jonathon sobs, losing control of his emotions.

"What about the baby?" Ash asks.

The doctor's features soften, and Jamie is up on his feet, striding toward us with purpose.

"We delivered the baby by C-section, but she was stillborn. She was deprived of oxygen for too long, and we didn't get to her fast enough. I'm so sorry for your loss."

Ash bursts into tears, and I release her into Jamie's care. This will bring back traumatic memories for them.

"Oh no, Jon." Lauren buries her face in her husband's shirt, sobbing her heart out.

Pain slices across my chest. If Viv has lost Reeve too, I don't know if she'll be able to come back from this. "What about my brother?" I ask. "Where is Reeve?"

The cop clears his throat, clasping his hands in front of his body. "Mr. Lancaster was pronounced dead at the scene," he confirms, his features solemn.

I blink profusely, unable to process what he's just said or understand how I'm feeling.

"Oh my God. No!" Lauren wails, and her legs almost go out from under her. Her husband keeps her upright, even though I can tell he's struggling with the news too. "Not Reeve too! Not our son! She'll never get over this, Jon."

Lauren's tearstained face almost undoes me. Ro gets up, walking to my side, offering me quiet comfort.

"Why is this happening?" she cries. "Why is God doing this to us?"

Ash is full-on crying too, and Jamie is doing his best to console her.

"What happened?" Jonathon asks the officer while holding his devastated wife. "How did our son-in-law die?"

"It appears Reeve unbuckled his belt and threw himself across Vivien to shield her and the baby before the tree toppled on their car. He took the brunt of the injury. The paramedics at the scene said your daughter would most likely have died if he hadn't protected her."

Every ugly thought I've ever had about my twin, and every ugly word I've ever spoken about him, comes back to haunt me. I know his actions tonight don't exonerate his sins, but it's possible Viv was right.

That I didn't know the real Reeve.

And now I never will.

He sacrificed his life to save her and his unborn child, and that speaks volumes about the kind of man he was.

I hang my head as shame and a myriad of different emotions clouds my brain.

"I can't process this," Lauren says, clinging to her husband's tear-soaked shirt. "Please tell me this is a nightmare and I'm going to wake up and Reeve will still be alive and Vivien will still be carrying little Lainey."

Jonathon's shoulders heave as he wraps his arms around his wife, and it's clear he can't form words.

"I know you need time to grieve," the cop says, "but I just wanted to let you know we have taken the other driver in for questioning, and we're conducting a full investigation. He has openly confessed to not seeing their car and clipping the back of their vehicle, which ultimately caused the accident."

"Can we discuss this another time?" I say through gritted teeth. "I know you're only doing your job, but they are in no state to hear this."

"Of course." He hands me his card and gives one to Jonathon too. "I'll be in touch, but if you need anything else, feel free to call me." He retrieves a bloodstained large white envelope from inside his jacket, handing it to me. "These were found in the car. They are not evidence, but I didn't want to leave them where they might fall into the wrong hands." His dark brown eyes drill into mine. "I believe they are safest left in your care."

I nod, too numb to say anything. The officer leaves the room, nodding respectfully at Mr. and Mrs. Mills as they speak in hushed tones with the doctor.

"What is it?" Ro asks, staring at the envelope in my hands, ever the nosy bastard.

I open the top and pull out a bunch of photos, skimming through them with an aching heart. They are all of me and Vivien from Ireland, and they bring back so many happy memories. I peek into the envelope, spotting tons more. There must be hundreds of photos.

I wish the officer hadn't left yet so I could thank him for being a decent fucking human. This gives me faith there are at least a few good people left in the world. He would have made a fortune selling these, and it would've ruined Viv's reputation and clued the world's media in to our story. I shudder even thinking about it.

I slam my hand over the next photo before Ro can see, grinding my teeth to the molars as rage crawls up my throat. What the actual fuck? This photo was taken the night I took Viv up Bray Head and fucked her against the cross. Was someone spying on us? Automatically, my mind pivots to Reeve. Without proof, I just know he's behind this, and my wrath returns with a vengeance.

Forcibly dialing my anger down, I return the photos to the envelope and wrap it inside my jacket on the chair beside Jamie. Whatever this means, it will have to wait. There are more pressing matters like getting in to see Viv.

Ro and I sit down as Jamie comforts Ash, and Lauren and Jonathon cling to one another. Eerie silence fills the room, only interrupted by anguished cries. I'm on the verge of losing it when a nurse walks into the room, explaining Vivien is awake and ready to see her parents.

"I'm coming too," I say, standing.

"No, you're not." Lauren gives me a serious case of evil eye. "You are probably the last person my daughter wants to see."

"Please." I walk toward them, shielding nothing from my face. "Please let me go with you. I need to see her."

"We will ask her if she wants to see you," Jonathon offers, leading his wife to the door. "It will be Viv's choice."

CHAPTER 11

DILLON

I WAIT until they have left before rushing after them. "Dillon!" Ash hisses. "I know you're anxious, but they are right. Just wait for them to come back."

"They don't want me anywhere near her, Ash, and I need to see her. I need to see with my own eyes that she's okay."

"Let him go," Ro says. "He needs this."

I slip out of the room, spotting the nurse and Viv's parents up ahead. Keeping a few steps back, I trail them to the ICU, cursing when the door shuts after them and I can't get in without a nurse or the security code. I spend ten minutes arguing with the nurse behind the ICU reception desk, but she won't let me in. Nothing works as a bribe, and I'm forced to give up when she threatens to call security and have me thrown out.

Slumping, I make my way back to the waiting room, with my tail tucked between my legs. I pace the floor like a lunatic while my siblings throw question after question at me. I get it. There is lots they don't know. We have hours to kill, and they want answers. But I can't get into it all now. They are going to hate me for what I've done and call me a selfish prick, but I can't handle that now. Ro falls asleep, lying on his side across a few chairs, his soft snores rippling through the room. But Ash doesn't sleep, and she continues asking me shit I can't even think about, let alone answer.

"Enough, Ash!" I roar when I can't take it anymore.

"Watch your fucking tone," Jamie snaps, instantly defending his woman.

"I know you need answers, and I will give them to you. But not now." I grab fistfuls of my hair, hating I cut it, vowing to let it grow out again. "I'm hanging on by a thread here, Ash." I fix her with pleading eyes. "Viv means everything to me. She's everything." I thump my closed fist over my heart. "I love her," I croak. "And I've made such a mess of things. I need to speak to her. To tell her I lied. To see she's okay with my own two eyes. I need to fix the mess I've made. I—" Air whooshes out of my mouth as my legs give out, and I sink to the floor, cradling my head in my hands.

"It's okay." Ash sits on the floor beside me. "I'm sorry for pushing. I know you'll tell us when you're ready." She rubs her hand up and down my back. Strained silence fills the space between us. "You shouldn't expect much from her, Dil. She's bound to be in shock, and pain, and you can't lay anything heavy on her. You don't want to make things worse."

It's good advice. Advice I know I should take. But I'm itching to take all my cruel words back. "I said some horrible shit to her recently. I need her to know I didn't mean it," I explain.

"She won't hear it now," Ash softly supplies. "She's too consumed in grief. I know I was when we lost our baby," she adds, looking at Jamie with glassy eyes. She presses a kiss to my head, breathing deeply. "Viv has been dealt a double blow. I get you needing to see her, to know she's okay, but that is all you should do. Let her grieve, Dillon, and when things have settled, you can talk to her."

The hours roll by, and early sunlight bathes the room in hazy yellow hues. Ash is asleep with her head in Jamie's lap, and Ro is still out for the count, but Jamie and I haven't slept a wink. We don't talk though. He's too hung up worrying about Ash. Concerned this situation is dredging up their own loss, and worrying what it will do to her, no less. I'm too busy beating myself up for mistakes I've made that go back years. If only I had chased after her that night in Bruxelles. I should have gone after her when she told me she loved me and asked her one final time to stay. I didn't fight hard enough for her, and by the time I'd pulled my head out of my ass, it was too late.

The door creaks as it opens, and a tired Mr. and Mrs. Mills enter the room. Ash is instantly awake, rubbing sleep from her eyes as she sits up. "How is she?"

"She's in a lot of pain. Physical and emotional. She slept mostly," Lauren explains, ignoring me and focusing on my sister. "When she was awake, she was groggy and not very lucid." Lauren leans her head against her husband's shoulder, and he cradles her to his side. "I don't think she has fully grasped what has happened."

"You shouldn't be here," Jonathon Mills says, eyeballing me like he wishes he could slice my head off my shoulders. "I don't know what has happened between you, but my daughter doesn't need any additional stress."

"Leave or we'll arrange to have you escorted off the premises," Lauren adds.

"I just want to make sure she's okay. I'm not going to cause any trouble. The last thing I want to do is hurt her or add to her stress," I say, rising to my feet. I hold my shoulders back. "I love your daughter, and I have always regretted letting her go. She means everything to me."

"I don't trust a word that comes out of your mouth," Lauren replies. "And Vivien is in no fit state to make any decisions. If you care for her, like you say you do, you will leave. When Vivien is strong enough, she can decide if she wants to see you or not."

I want to tell them it's not that cut-and-dried. I want to tell them I'm Easton's father. But I won't add to their grief. Now isn't the time and my needs are bottom of the list of priorities. I don't want to leave without seeing Vivien, but I don't want to fall out with her parents either. I can always come back later, when they are not here, and sneak in to see her. "Okay. I'll go."

"I would like to see her," Ash says. "Is it okay if I stay?"

Lauren looks undecided.

"Stay," Jonathon says. "Audrey and Alex will be here shortly. Talk to Audrey. See what she thinks. If she says it's okay, it's fine by us." Lauren closes her eyes, and she looks like she can barely stand any longer. "I'm going to take Lauren to the house to freshen up. We want to be there when our grandson wakes."

"Maybe we should swap numbers," Ash says. "That way we can keep each other informed if there are any developments."

They exchange numbers as I rouse Ro. "Come on," I tell him. "We're leaving." I hug my sister. "Keep me posted too, please."

"I will. I promise."

I jerk my head at Jamie, dragging my brother to his feet. Wetting my lips, I eyeball Viv's parents. "I'm very sorry for any distress I may have caused you or your daughter. I just wanted to be here for her. I know I have made mistakes in the past, and I can only imagine what you must be thinking, but Viv is the love of my life. There has never been anyone but her. I know she's devastated and traumatized right now, and I would never add to that. I will give her space, but you should know I'm going nowhere. I let her walk away from me once, and I've regretted it every day since. Being apart from her all these years has killed me, and it's a mistake I won't be making again."

After a trip to the bathroom and the hospital cafeteria, Ro and I make our way outside, using the side entrance, keeping our heads down. There's a big ruckus out the front of the hospital, where the fans and reporters are, and I'm guessing the Millses have stepped outside. At least it means no one is focused on us, and we make a quick dash across the parking lot, finding my Land Rover exactly where Jamie said it would be.

I'm behind the wheel, ready to pull out of the space, when Ash calls me. "Have you left yet?" she asks.

"I'm still in the parking lot."

"Come back inside. Lauren and Jon have gone. Audrey and Alex are with Viv now. She's been moved to a private room, and I know where. You can take a glimpse at her, but that's all, Dillon. No talking to her, and you can't let her see you. That's the dealio. Take it or leave it."

"I'll take it. Thanks, Ash." I couldn't love my sister more in this moment. I know she's mad at me, and she's going to be even madder when I tell her everything, but she's still going to bat for me.

"Stay here," I tell Ro, handing him the keys. "I won't be long." He lowers his seat, to take another nap, while I grab a hoodie from the back seat. Yanking the hood up, I climb out of my car and head back inside the hospital.

Ash is waiting for me as soon as I step out of the lift. "Good call with the hoodie," she murmurs, dragging me down the corridor. "Security just found a reporter on this floor, snooping around."

"We need to get protection up here for Viv," I say.

"I've already messaged her parents asking if they want me to organize that. It

441

seems Reeve has his own team of bodyguards. They are sending a couple over, which means you have to do this fast. Audrey will be pissed when she sees you, Dil, so just take a quick look at Viv and then go."

Jamie nods at his fiancée as we pass by. He's crouched over the nurses' desk, distracting the burly-looking blonde behind the counter, so we can sneak past.

Ash slams to a halt at a closed white door. "This one," she whispers, pointing.

Without stopping to second-guess myself, I open the door and step inside Viv's darkened room. She is semi-propped up in the elevated bed, her tangled hair resting on a bunch of pillows. A large purple bruise on her cheekbone matches one on her right temple. A white bandage is strapped around her wrist, and she's hooked up to a drip and another machine. Lighting is low, and the blinds are closed, to help with her concussion, I'm guessing. She looks battered and bruised and lost, but at least she's alive.

"What the hell, Ash?" Audrey says from her place beside the bed. She is stroking Viv's hand, and exhaustion is clearly evident on her face.

A tall guy with sandy-blond hair and red-rimmed brown eyes growls at me from the other side of Viv's bed. This must be Alex. Audrey's husband and Reeve's best friend. Hostility rolls off him in waves as he stands. "Get the fuck out of here before I make you."

Viv winces, slowly turning her head in my direction.

"Alex," Audrey murmurs, shaking her head.

A cry bursts from Vivien's lips, and her tortured hazel eyes fill with tears. She tries to sit more upright in the bed, clutching her stomach, in obvious pain, at the sudden movement.

"You need to stay still, babe," Audrey says. "You'll rip your stitches."

"Reeve!" Viv cries, staring at me with bloodshot eyes. "Tell them to bring Lainey back. They took our baby!" Her hands move to her deflated stomach. "I can't feel her, Reeve. She's not kicking." Her eyes stretch wide as she looks up at me.

Horrified shock splays across Audrey's face as she stares between us. "Come sing to her, like you usually do," Viv adds, shoving the covers down and running her hands over her much smaller bump. "C'mon, Reeve. She'll wake up when she hears you singing. You have such a gorgeous voice."

I am rooted to the spot in horror. I shouldn't have come here. This is only making things worse. I want to leave, but I'm afraid to leave now. I don't know what I should do. I look at Audrey, beseeching her to tell me what to do. Silent tears are streaming down her face. She turns to face her husband, pleading with her eyes for him to do something. But he's as shell-shocked as we are.

This is tearing strips off my heart. I don't know how to handle it. I don't want to do or say anything to set her off. She's clearly traumatized and probably still drugged up and disoriented.

"Reeve, please." She stretches her arms out. "I need you," she wails, as tears trek down her face.

I move toward her as if on autopilot, hoping my instincts will guide me. Alex has moved over beside his wife, cradling her in his arms as she cries her eyes out. They watch me, and it only adds to the responsibility I'm feeling. Cautiously, I sit on the edge of Viv's bed, struggling to hold my own emotion inside. All I want to do is hold her and tell her I still love her. That I never stopped.

But I know I can't.

She grabs my left hand. The one I don't wear rings on. "Where's your wedding ring?" she asks, her voice rising. "Where is your ring, Reeve?" She stares into my face, and her eyes pop wide. She drops my hand as if it's poisonous. "You're not Reeve!" she croaks in a hoarse voice. "You're not him. You're not my husband." She pummels her fists against my chest, but there is no strength in her motion. "Go away! I don't want you! I want Reeve! Reeve!" she rasps, her fragile voice bouncing off the walls. "Reeve! Where are you? I need you."

I don't even realize I'm crying until tears drip off my chin, sloping down my neck and onto my chest. My heart is breaking in a combination of pain for her and for me. I know she's having a breakdown, but she will never want me. It will always be him.

"Vivien. It's Audrey." Audrey has pulled herself together. Bending over her best friend, she brushes hair back off her face as Alex glares at me like he wants to murder me with his bare hands. "You need to calm down. Please, babe. Just take deep breaths."

"I want Reeve! I want my husband. God can't take him too!" She swings tormented eyes on me. "This is all your fault! He knew! Reeve knew I was lying to him! He knew about Easton. He was so mad. So upset. He wouldn't slow down! I told him to slow down! He wouldn't listen. He didn't listen." The words spill from her mouth in a torrent of anguish and pain while her eyes dart wildly around the room. More words gush from her mouth, in a stream of nonsensical statements, and I'm seriously worried about her mental state. Viv's sobs echo through the clinical room, and each one strips another layer off my heart.

Her eyes connect with mine again, and there is no warmth in her gaze. "My husband died thinking I betrayed him because you blackmailed me into keeping quiet! He thought I was fucking you!" she croaks, rubbing a hand over her chest. "I hate you!" She beats me with her fists again, but she's so weak they hardly register. A part of me wishes she was strong enough to inflict real physical pain because it's the least I deserve.

"I hate you so much, Dillon!" She slaps my face, but I barely feel it. I let her attempt to hit and punch me as Alex presses the button to call the nurse. Audrey has her hand over her mouth, sobbing as she watches her friend self-destruct. "You ruined my life," Viv sobs, collapsing against her pillow as all the fight leaves her. A line of red stains her blue hospital gown across the middle. "You have taken everything from me, but you can't have E." She fixes me with dark eyes. "You don't deserve him. Reeve is his dad. Reeve will always be his dad. You'll have to cut my heart out of my chest before I let you take him."

"Dil." Ash quietly tugs on my sleeve, pulling me away from the bed. I had forgotten she was even here. "Let's go."

"Keep him away from me, Ash!" Viv shouts. "He did this! He did this to me!"

A nurse rushes into the room, and I watch helplessly as Viv is sedated while Ash tries to drag me away. My sister is a feisty, determined little thing, but she's no match for my height and my weight. Silent tears leak from my eyes as I watch Viv's eyelids close.

"Get him out of here," Audrey says, ignoring me and looking at Ash. "Get him out of this hospital. I don't want him anywhere near Vivien or my godson."

Jamie enters the room, and together, he and Ash drag me away. I stumble along the hallway, heartbroken and full of self-loathing. Shucking my sister and my best friend off me, I slump to the ground in the hallway, bringing my knees to my chest as I let it all out. I don't care that others are a witness to this. My chest heaves and my shoulders shake as I cry. Pain pummels me from every angle, and I wish I'd been driving. I wish I was the one lying on a cold table in a morgue. I wish I could rewind the years and do so many things differently.

Ash kneels, bundling me in her arms. "It will be okay, Dil. She didn't mean it. She's traumatized and grieving."

"I fucked up, Ash." I lift my eyes to her, hardly able to see her through my tears. "I fucked up real bad. Viv is right. This *is* my fault, and she's never going to forgive me. She will never get over losing her husband and her baby, and she will always blame me."

CHAPTER 12
VIVIEN

"ARE you sure you want to do this now?" Mom asks, stalling at the door to my bedroom.

"I can't keep putting it off. He's confused. Every time he asks for his daddy, I fall apart."

My parents have been keeping Easton sheltered at the house since the accident. They told him Mommy and Daddy were away for a few days, purposely keeping the details vague. Mom knew I would want to tell E myself, but I was so out of it when I returned home, and I've been unable to do much more than sleep and cry. My parents deflected his questions, and I know how hard that has been on them. They don't want to lie to their grandson, and I can't continue to keep him in the dark. Easton needs to know, and that responsibility falls to me. I've been trying to pluck up the courage to tell him for the last twenty-four hours.

How do you tell a five-year-old that his daddy is dead and the little sister he was so excited to meet died in my womb the same night?

How am I expected to go on when it feels like I died that night too?

Thank God for my parents. They have been caring for Easton, and it brought me comfort to know he was well looked after when I wasn't here to do it and after I came home when I was incapable of doing much of anything.

It's been four days since I was discharged from the hospital and six days since I lost Reeve and Lainey, but it already feels like an eternity. Tears pump out of my eyes as that thought lands in my mind, and Mom rushes across the floor to hold me in her arms. "Darling, I wish I could take your pain away."

"The pain helps me to remember, and I never want to forget."

"Sweetheart." Mom strokes my hair. "You will never forget them. Don't cling to the pain because you won't heal unless you try to let it go."

"I'll never heal, Mom. I'll never get over losing them. I miss Reeve so much already." Heaving sobs wrack my chest, and I'm crying into her shoulder, clinging to her, wishing I could wake up and discover it's all been a bad dream. Pain races across my chest, infiltrating my bloodstream, invading every part of my body.

Physically, I'm still suffering after the accident, but that's the kind of pain I can tolerate. The strong pain meds the hospital prescribed help a lot. I wish there was a pill I could pop to numb the ever-present emotional pain.

"I know, honey. I know how much you will miss him. He's been such a huge part of your life, but he wouldn't want this for you. He wouldn't want to see you like this. He died saving you."

Mom's tears mix with my own as they have done so often in the past few days. Reeve was more than just a son-in-law to my parents. He was a son to them, from the instant he was born, except in name. "I know it's too soon. You need to process these emotions. We all do," she adds, sniffling. "But you need to find the strength to live because that is the best way you can honor Reeve. And that little boy needs his mommy, now more than ever."

I want to be there for Easton, but I've been so distraught these last few days that I haven't been able to support him. That ends now. My son needs me, and I need him. He is all I have left. I dry my tears with the sleeves of my silk robe. "I won't fail Easton. I will fight to go on. For him."

She kisses my temple. "That's my girl. But make sure you do it for you too, Vivien. You deserve to continue to live your life to the fullest. It won't happen yet, or anytime soon, but you are not alone. We are all here for you, and we will be with you every step of the way."

That's not exactly true. My parents will have to return to the movie set soon. Oh, I know them. I know they are both trying to extricate themselves from the production. But there is no way that can happen. They can't lose the director and the leading lady. They can't reshoot a movie that's halfway through filming, and every day the movie is on hold costs hundreds of thousands of dollars. They will have to return after the funeral, and I'll just have to learn to cope by myself.

It's a scary proposition. One I'm not sure I can manage, but my son needs me to be strong, and I'm determined to at least try. "Can you get Easton now? I'm okay." As long as I try to keep thoughts of Reeve and Lainey from my mind for the few minutes it takes to break my little son's heart.

It feels like I've lied to him and betrayed him. E was there every day with Reeve, singing and talking to my belly, and I am letting him down in the worst way imaginable. He was so excited to meet his sister, and he's going to be so upset. My lower lip wobbles, and tears threaten, but I manage to hold it together.

"Mommy." Easton races across my bedroom, flinging himself into my arms.

"Careful, sweetheart," my mom says. "Remember we told you Mommy wasn't feeling well? Well, she has some pains in her tummy, and we need to be gentle with her."

"What about my little sister?" Easton asks, looking worried. "Does she have pains too?"

Gulping over the messy ball of emotion in my throat, I breathe deeply as I pat the space beside me on the bed. "Come sit here. I need a cuddle."

Easton snuggles into my side, and I wrap my arms around him, closing my eyes as I brush my nose against his hair. The sweet strawberry smell from his shampoo provides comfort as does the feel of him in my arms. I hold him a little tighter, careful not to crush him. I wish I could put him on my lap, but I already ripped my stitches out once, and I've been warned not to do any lifting or holding for another few weeks. "Honey, I need to tell you some sad news," I start, working hard to keep the tremble from my voice. "You remember when we talked about Holy God and the angels and heaven?"

I'm not overly religious. Neither was Reeve.

His handsome face swims in front of my eyes, and I long to return to three weeks ago and do everything differently. If I had, we wouldn't be here now. Reeve wouldn't have been angry at me that night. He wouldn't have been drinking so much because he thought I was having an affair behind his back with his long-lost twin. We would have made it home in one piece, and I wouldn't be sitting here now about to crush my son's heart into itty-bitty pieces. Pain stabs me through the heart, and I briefly squeeze my eyes shut.

"Yes," Easton says, sounding confused and scared.

That snaps me out of my head. I open my eyes and place a kiss on his cheek. "Daddy and I were in a car accident. I was in the hospital getting better, but Daddy and Lainey have gone to heaven to be with God and the angels."

Inwardly, I'm screaming as the words leave my mouth. Right now, I hate God as much as I hate Dillon O'Donoghue.

Easton blinks, staring at me in confusion. "Why would Daddy go to heaven instead of coming home? Why didn't he get better in the hospital like you?"

Pain crawls up my throat, and I can barely force the words out this time. "If Daddy could've made the decision, he would have come home with me." I pause, emitting a few sobs. Mom makes a move, but I shake my head, needing to do this myself, even if I am making a mess of it.

"I don't understand," E says as tears roll down his cheeks.

I hold him closer, dotting kisses on the top of his head. "Neither do I, baby. But sometimes things happen, and we don't ever know why. This is one of those times. God needed Daddy and Lainey, and at least they are together. I bet they're up in heaven cuddling right now, just like we are."

"I don't want my daddy to go to heaven!" Easton bursts out crying. "I want him to come home and play with me on the slide!" he wails, burying his little face in my chest. I can scarcely see through my blurry vision, but I see enough to know Mom is crying too.

Will this ever get any better?

Will this pain ever go away?

"I know, honey. I wish for that too, but it's not going to happen." I hate to do this to him, but I can't leave him with false hope either. "Daddy is your guardian angel now. He's going to be watching over both of us from heaven."

"I want him watching over me from here," Easton sobs into my chest, and I don't know what else to say to make him understand. As I hold my heartbroken boy in my arms, I vow to do everything to help him get through this, even if it means papering over the cracks in my own heart to do it.

CHAPTER 13
VIVIEN

"YOU NEED TO EAT," Audrey says, zipping up my black dress from behind. "You look so thin."

"I know," I deadpan. I know a body needs food to sustain it. That I'll perish if I don't fuel my body, but I can't eat. Even the thought of food makes me ill. You can't tell I was ever pregnant now, and that only adds to my sadness. I'm barely surviving despite my silent promises to myself to do better for Easton's sake.

My son is struggling. He doesn't understand why his daddy hasn't come home. He's convinced himself Reeve is away on a movie set, and the only way I know to get through to him is to bring him to the funeral with me today.

Alex and Audrey have been a lifeline for me in the same way my parents have. They too have put their lives on hold to be here for us. I've wanted to keep Easton at home, away from prying eyes, and our best friends have been helping to keep him occupied while Mom tries to glue me back together. Dad is dealing with practical matters, like arranging the funeral, sorting out legal shit, and dealing with the police.

I told Officer Lawson I didn't want to press charges against the man driving the other car. It was a horrible night. Visibility was terrible, and it was an accident. Faulty airbags didn't help, and toxicology reports taken during Reeve's postmortem confirmed he was over the legal limit. He should never have been driving. I should have forced him into the passenger seat and insisted I drive. I should have refused to get in the car until he agreed.

Round and round my mind churns, going over all the what-ifs.

"Are you sure you want Easton to attend the funeral?" Audrey asks as she runs some serum through my wavy hair. I've been like a zombie as my bestie got me in the shower, dried and styled my hair, and applied makeup to my pale face. She even helped me to bind my breasts, which are engorged and rock hard thanks to my milk coming in. Every time I touch them and they hurt, I'm reminded of my loss all over again.

"I asked him, and he said he wants to go."

She looks at me like I've truly lost my mind, and I get it. I know I said some mad shit in the aftermath of the accident when I woke in the hospital. Mistaking *him* for my husband being the worst of it. I turn around to face my friend. "I know he is young. Probably too young to make that decision, but I don't want him to turn around to me in the future and blame me for not letting him attend his father's and his little sister's funeral." I'm expecting tears to form, like usual, but my eyes are suspiciously dry.

Perhaps I have worn out my tear ducts.

"I know this will be horrible. I'm dreading it so I can only imagine how Easton is feeling, but it might help in a warped way. Maybe if he sees the coffin and he has a chance to say goodbye, it might sink in." I know I'm hoping it will for me because most days I still wake up believing it's just a bad dream. Until reality sets in, and I'm devastated as if I'm hearing the news for the first time.

Audrey reels me into her arms. "I can't believe we are here. I still can't believe this has happened." She holds me tighter, sobbing. "It's not fair."

"I know." I sound devoid of life as I smooth a hand up and down her back. This past week has taken everything from me. Especially the last few days; hosting visitors who came to pay their respects. It almost felt like a test. Like God is continuing to push and push, to stretch me to my limits, to see how far he can go before I completely break. It's left me emotionally drained, and feeling completely unprepared for today.

"Ash called me," she says, easing back. "I don't want there to be any surprises, so you should know she'll be there with her family. With him."

I gulp painfully. "I don't know why he insists on being there. He made no secret of the fact he hated Reeve. It's too late now to care."

"I get the impression he's there for you and Easton."

Anger boils in my blood, and I grind my teeth to the molars. "He better stay the hell away from my son!" A red haze coats my retinas. "You tell Ash to keep him away from me and my son."

"That message has already been relayed. She assures me he won't approach you. That he just wants to pay his respects."

I snort. "A likely story."

"I can talk to your dad and Leon. We can refuse him entry to the church."

I shake my head. "I don't want to make a scene. Especially not in front of the media." Reporters and paparazzi are stalking us since the accident. They are all desperate to get photos of me and Easton. Desperate to hear what happened that night.

I hate them as much as I ever have.

Reeve's publicist, Edwin, dropped by the house to pay his respects. He suggested I talk to him when I'm feeling up to it. He says it's better to talk to the press in an arranged interview and he can make them go away, but I doubt I will ever be strong enough to do that.

"What are you going to do about him? From what Ash has said, he's not going to drop it."

"I don't expect him to, but I can't think about that right now. I just need to get through today." I know I need to tell my parents. They deserve to know the truth. Easton does too, and I won't lie to him about his parentage. But there is no way I'm mentioning anything to him yet. He needs time to grieve for Reeve. Only then will I even contemplate how to tell him who Dillon is to him. I know I won't be able to hold Dillon off that long. That we need to talk. But I can't talk to him yet.

Ash and I spoke when she came to visit me in the hospital. It was a brief conversation, and I was in and out of consciousness a lot of the time. I'm touched she came and that she wants to meet up. I think I'd like that too, but I need to survive today first. Easton is my sole priority and the focus of all my energy. I don't have room or the strength for anything else.

Easton clings to my side as we sit in the front pew of the church staring at the coffin. I asked for our daughter to be buried in her daddy's arms. While my faith in God is seriously tested right now, I take comfort in knowing wherever they are they are together. I know my husband is caring for our little girl in the same loving, adoring way he cared for me and E.

The church is packed as are the roads outside. Thousands upon thousands of mourners line the streets of L.A., coming out to pay their respects to Reeve.

The outpouring of love for my husband has been incredible. Fan posts occupy most every social media platform, and Margaret Andre and the woman who runs Reeve's fan club have had to hire additional temporary staff to cope with the influx of cards and gifts. A lot of it is for me. Some is for Easton too. Mom is handling all of that, sorting through it and boxing it up in case I want to look at it sometime in the future.

The minister says nice things about Reeve, but neither of us were practicing Catholics, so he's talking through his ass. It's only when Mom gets up to speak that we're hearing about the real Reeve from someone who knew him.

"Thank you all for coming," Mom says, her voice projecting to the back of the church.

She looks beautiful with her hair pulled off her face in an elegant chignon. She's wearing a black hat with a short black lace veil. I hold a confused Easton tighter, ignoring the sharp pain in my ribs from the motion. "I know my daughter would be up here, saying these words, if she could, but it's been an extremely difficult time for her. For Easton and for all of us." Mom's eyes fill up, and I wonder if she'll be able to do this. My dad gets out of his seat, walking to stand beside her. She leans against him, drawing strength from his presence.

"Reeve is beloved by many people the world over. People who have loved his movies and followed his career from those early days. But those of us who are here today knew the man, not just the actor. Jon and I were privileged to watch Reeve grow up. He was an integral part of our lives from the moment he was born. In all the ways that matter, he was our son, and we will miss him dearly." Her sobs echo through the microphone, bouncing off the walls of the eerily quiet church. A few cries and sobs surround me, but still, I don't cry. I press kisses into Easton's hair, clinging to him for dear life.

"Reeve loved Vivien from the time he was a little boy," Mom continues in a wobbly voice. "Jon and I would watch them playing together, and we always knew they were destined to be together. Reeve worshiped Vivien with an intensity that is rare for someone so young. No matter what he chose to pursue, whether it was acting or our daughter, Reeve did it to the fullest of his ability because he had the biggest heart and so much love to give. Watching him grow from a young boy into a man and later into a father was one of the most rewarding experiences of my life. Reeve adored our grandson, and he was the most amazing father to Easton."

"Mommy." Easton tugs on my sleeve. "Why is Grandma talking about me?"

I lower my head. "She's telling everyone how much Daddy loved you."

"He was so happy to welcome the new baby, singing every night to Lainey and making plans as only an excited father could do," Mom continues.

"Mommy." Easton pulls my head down to his face. "Is Daddy in there?" he asks, pointing at the coffin.

"He is. And Lainey is there with him so they can be together." I kiss his cheek as I see realization dawn on his handsome face.

"Reeve's last selfless act on this Earth said everything about who he was as a man, a husband, and a father. He didn't hesitate to protect Vivien and their unborn child, sacrificing his life so our daughter could live. We can never thank him for that." Her cries ring out around the church, and a chorus of tears surround us. "Or for all the joy he brought to our lives. His legacy will live on through Easton," she adds, and a lump forms in my throat.

I should've told my parents before the funeral there is no piece of Reeve left living on this planet. That hurts so much because my husband wanted tons of kids and the kind of family he was deprived of as a child. That he should die without that destroys me. All that remains are my memories and our cherished mementos and his legacy on the screen. He didn't leave any flesh and blood behind except for a twin brother who hated him and never wanted him in his life.

I hate that for Reeve and for myself. If God had to be cruel to take my husband, couldn't he have given me his daughter so I could love her for the both of us?

"I want my daddy!" Easton screams, breaking me out of my inner monologue. I watch in horror, like I'm floating overhead, as he wrestles out of my arms and races toward the coffin. He places his hands on the side of the coffin as heartbreaking cries trickle through the congregation. "Wake up, Daddy! Please!" he sobs, and I know I should go to him, but I'm frozen in place.

Running footsteps echo along the tile floor behind me. Alex stands, striding toward Easton and gently pulling him into his arms. Easton wraps his arms and legs around his Uncle Alex, crying into his shoulder. "I've got this," Alex says, in a clipped tone, looking over Easton's shoulder.

I glance around, spotting Dillon standing just behind me, staring at Alex with Easton. Pain ravages his face as he looks at his son, and I'm guessing he wishes he was the one comforting him. But Dillon is a stranger to Easton. They only met one time, and he is not who Easton needs right now.

I rise, walking to Dillon's side. "Please don't make a scene. Not here," I whisper in his ear.

"That's not—" Dillon drags a hand through his hair. "I just want to help."

"Then leave." I eyeball him, even though it almost kills me. Seeing Reeve's eyes on Dillon's face upsets me even more now. "If you want to help, that's the best way."

Tormented eyes peer deep into mine as rumblings from the crowd remind me that we have an audience. "I'm so sorry for your loss," he says in a choked voice. "More than you could ever know."

CHAPTER 14

VIVIEN

THE GRAVEYARD PROVES to be my breaking point, and I fall apart, collapsing against Dad as the casket is lowered into the ground. The finality breaks my heart all over again, and my tortured cries almost drown out the minister's words.

Reeve is gone, and he's never coming back. I will never again see his handsome face or melt into a puddle of goo when he fixes that flirtatious smile on me. The taste of his lips is lost to me forever, as is the protective strength of his arms. Waking up tangled between his legs with the comforting sound of his heartbeat against my ear will exist now only in my memories. Never again will I feel him moving inside me, coaxing pleasure from my body.

Sharp pain pierces my chest walls, embedding deep, and I want to die. I want to crawl into that casket with my husband and my daughter and never wake.

How could God take my husband and my baby? How much pain can one person endure in their life? Our daughter was the purest, most innocent treasure. A precious gift, cruelly snatched from us before she ever got to live. Our little girl never got to take her first breath. I will never get to hold her in my arms or to smell that gorgeous newborn smell. I won't get to feel her tiny fingers curling around mine or hear her desperate cries when she's hungry or unsettled or just craving a hug.

All of that has been denied to me.

Dad carries me back to the car when it's clear my legs are malfunctioning, and I sob into his shoulder, clinging to him as Mom rocks a sobbing Easton in her arms.

I manage to compose myself, just before we get back to the house, enough to hold Easton. He is hurting too, and I feel guilty for my thoughts back at the graveside. I need to be here for my son. He needs me, now more than ever, and I can't be selfish. Not even in my thoughts. We cling to one another, and I hold him close, telling him how much I love him and dotting kisses into his hair. I know my son is the only way I will survive this pain. I need to find the strength to go on for this little boy.

I take Easton to his room to get changed while Mom talks to Charlotte about last-minute arrangements. We're expecting guests to arrive any minute. "How are you feeling?" I ask E as I help him out of his little black suit.

"Sad. I'm really sad, Mommy."

I wrap my arms around him, hugging him tight. I understand exactly what he means. Before, sad was just a word, but now it's a state of being. It consumes every cell, overtakes every other emotion, and my bones feel weighted down with the feeling. It's as if this is the only way I know how to exist. Covered in this blanket of sadness until there is nothing else.

"Me too, honey. But we won't always be sad," I add, forcing a soft smile on my face as I ease back, brushing my fingers along his cheeks. I hope I'm not lying to him. I want to—no, *need* to—believe in this truth. "Daddy wouldn't want that for us. He would want us to try to be happy again."

"I miss him so much." Tears stab his eyes, and I hug him again.

"We will always miss him, but I have something that might help. Put your shorts and T-shirt on while I get it."

I return to Easton's bedroom a few minutes later, carrying a few items. E is wearing his clothes, and he's slipping into his sneakers. "Sit up here beside me," I say, resting on the edge of his bed. I prop the framed photo of Reeve on his nightstand, ignoring the piercing pain in my heart. "Daddy is always going to be watching over you, and I thought you might like to say goodnight to him every night." Easton sniffles, snuggling into my side. "Anytime you want to talk to him, to tell him about something exciting that happened in school or maybe finding more bugs, you can talk to his picture, and he'll hear it in heaven."

"He will?" He lifts his head, his wide eyes staring at me with so much trust and hope.

I nod, hoping I won't be struck down. I hand him one of Reeve's watches. "This one was your daddy's favorite. It's a golf watch. I bought it for him when he turned seventeen. I think he would want you to have it." Easton slides it on over his wrist, trying to tie it. "It's too big for you to wear now, but maybe you could keep it in your drawer for when you're older."

"Yeah. For when I play golf too."

"Exactly." I smile as he opens his drawer, very carefully placing the watch inside.

"And this was one of Daddy's favorite T-shirts. I bought it for him when I was in Greece one summer. Maybe you might like to sleep in it or keep it for when you fit into it. The choice is yours."

Easton brings it to his nose. "It smells like my daddy."

Tears pool in my eyes. "Yeah, buddy. It does." I threw a hissy fit when Mom permitted Charlotte to change my bedsheets. I hadn't planned on ever changing them. Not as long as Reeve's smell was still embedded in the fibers. Now, I've resorted to sleeping in his shirts so I can still smell him.

I haven't sorted any of his things yet, and it's on my long list of things I'm dreading.

I hand Easton the last item. Going into the nursery to retrieve it had almost undone me again. "I think your little sister would like you to have this," I whisper, giving him the fluffy pink stuffed rabbit. "You will always be Lainey's big brother, and when you feel sad about her, maybe you can cuddle her bunny rabbit or sleep with it," I suggest.

"I'm glad Daddy is looking after my sister. I don't feel as sad knowing Daddy is with Lainey."

I gulp painfully, fighting more tears. "Me too, buddy."

"Is the funeral over now, Mommy?" he inquires, scrunching his cute nose as he hugs the stuffed animal close to his chest.

I thread my fingers through his hair. "Lots of people are going to be here in a little while. But I figured you'd much rather play outside, so Nash is coming over with his mom, and you can play in the playground with him. Angela will be there too." I think today has been taxing enough for my child. "Grandpa organized pizza for later, and you can eat it in the treehouse, if you like."

"Yay!" Easton puts Reeve's shirt under his pillow before throwing himself at me. My breasts, my ribs, and my stomach protest the enthusiastic hug, but I will never complain. "Thanks, Mommy. I love you."

"I love you too, little munchkin. So, so much." I pepper his face with kisses as Angela appears in the doorway.

"Hey, pipsqueak! Guess who just arrived downstairs?"

"Nash!" Easton bounces off the bed, almost tumbling in his impatience to get to his friend.

Angela laughs, ruffling his hair. I stand, and her expression softens as I approach. "It was a beautiful service, and your mom's eulogy was perfect." She squeezes my arm.

"It was."

"I'll take good care of Easton. Don't worry about him."

"Thank you." I blow E a kiss. "Have fun and be good for Angela."

"I will, Mom. Bye." He races off toward the stairs with Angela hot on his heels.

I find Mom and Dad downstairs in the formal living room, greeting the first guests. They offer condolences, and I thank them for coming as I eye the bar with longing.

Charlotte hired a catering company today, along with waitresses and bartenders.

"I need to talk to you both," I tell my parents, jerking my head toward the door. If I don't grab them now, we won't get to speak, and I know Dillon's family will be here because Mom mentioned she spoke to Cath outside the church and invited them. I'm sure she didn't want to invite Dillon but she was too polite to upset his mother.

Funerals are a lot like weddings in that regard. You're forced to put up with guests you wouldn't ordinarily invite, except it's the done thing.

My parents follow me into my office, and Dad closes the door. I'm sorry I didn't grab a vodka cranberry for this conversation. "I have something you both need to know. Something I should've told you sooner, but, honestly, I've been trying to forget it." I sit on one of the leather couches, knotting my hands in my lap.

"Whatever it is," Mom says, dropping onto the couch beside me. "We'll deal with it together."

Dad squeezes my shoulder, before sitting on the couch across from us. "We've got you. Now and always, princess."

Tears prick my eyes. "I know you do. I can't thank you enough for everything you've done." I look at my father, and he seems to have aged so much in the past week. "I know you think you haven't helped much, Dad, but taking care of the funeral arrangements, and pushing the reading of the will back with Carson, and handling stuff with Margaret and Edwin means so much to me. I could not have coped with any of that."

"We hate to see you in so much pain," Dad says. "Whatever we can do to help make it better, we will."

"Love you, Daddy."

Dad gets up, leaning down to give me a gentle hug. "You're our whole world, Vivien. You and Easton will always be our priority."

"Love you too, Mom," I say when Dad has moved back to his seat. "I could not have gotten through this week without you, and I know how hard it's been on you as well. I know how much you both loved Reeve. How much you were both looking forward to meeting Lainey." A lone tear treks down my face.

Mom cradles me in her arms. "It's going to be okay, sweetheart. We will all get through this together."

"I need to talk to you about Dillon."

Mom nods. "I didn't want to push you, but we need to know what's going on."

I tell them. I tell them everything. Giving them a summary of how it went down since Dillon showed up here that fateful day, explaining the things he told me and ending with the confirmation Dillon is Easton's father.

"Oh my God. Vivien." Mom clamps a hand over her mouth as tears stream down her face. "And Reeve knew this before he died?"

Tears leak out of my eyes. "Yes. My husband died angry with me for lying to him and with the knowledge the son he worshiped wasn't his flesh and blood," I croak. "I hate myself so much."

"Don't," Alex says, entering the room with his wife. Audrey is carrying a tray of drinks.

"We thought you might need these, and we wanted to let you know the O'Donoghues just arrived," Audrey says. I had told my bestie I was telling my parents everything right now.

"Don't hate yourself, Viv." Alex perches on the arm of the couch. "It's not your fault."

"It is no one's fault," Audrey says, shooting her husband a warning look. "It was a tragic accident, and pointing the finger of blame *anywhere* won't help." She sets the tray with drinks down on the coffee table.

Alex scrubs a hand along his stubbly jawline. "I can't believe we're here. I can't believe he's gone. I'm going to miss Reeve so fucking much." His eyes turn glassy, and I squeeze his hand.

"He loved you like a brother. I hope you know that."

Alex nods, rubbing at his eyes, before grabbing a bottle of beer. "I heard what you said in the hospital that morning and just now, and you're wrong, Viv. Reeve loved the shit out of you. You were always it for him. Yes, I'm sure he was angry and hurt at the things he discovered, but he didn't die believing those things of you. His love for you drove his actions that night. He died protecting you and Lainey. Trust me

458

when I say Reeve would not have wanted it any other way and he would not want you blaming yourself."

Mom clenches her hands into fists. "As much as I'd like to point the finger of blame in Dillon's direction, Audrey is right. It was a tragic accident, compounded by several things. That doesn't mean Dillon is off the hook though. He has a lot to answer for. His scheming contributed."

"I always believed Easton was conceived in love, but Dillon never loved me. I was a means of exacting revenge. That was all. I was such a fool." I loved him for years, feeling horrible guilt for harboring longing for my ex when I was blissfully happy with my husband. Discovering that Dillon played me the whole time makes me sick to my stomach.

"I wouldn't be too sure about that," Dad says, and I arch a brow. "Dillon was at the hospital with Ash and Jamie and Ronan, for hours, in the waiting room. You probably don't remember this, darling," he adds, facing Mom, "but he gave quite a heartfelt speech before we asked him to leave." Earnest hazel eyes meet mine. "He said he loved you. That he regretted letting you go and you were his everything."

Alex harrumphs. "Yeah, his actions these past few weeks really showed that," he sneers.

"I'm not defending the man," Dad continues, "but I think he should be given an opportunity to explain himself before everyone throws shade. I believe he was sincere at the hospital, and let's not forget the part Simon played in all of this."

"I have never wanted to dig up a body to whale on it more in my life," Mom says, and it helps to ease some of the tension.

Giggles bubble up my throat, and I don't fight them, setting them free. It's too funny hearing Mom say such things. "I say we dig him up, piss on his bones, then pour acid over him, and watch him disintegrate into nothing but ash that flitters away in the wind," I add, accepting a vodka cranberry from my bestie.

"Creative." Audrey kisses my cheek. "And a little bloodthirsty. I approve." She leans into Alex, and he slides his arm around her.

I look away, unable to bear witness to their love, which makes me feel like a bitter bitch. It's funny. I remember feeling a lot like this when I first fled to Ireland after Reeve had broken my heart. I thought every loving couple, every PDA, was going to kill me until Dillon helped me to heal. It might not have been real on his end, but at least he gave me that much.

"How could Simon keep so much from us? From me?" Dad shakes his head. "I thought we were friends, but I never knew the man. Not really."

"Come on, Jon. The friendship was tentative, at best, after Felicia died. He pulled away from us, and all the respect I'd had for him evaporated with his neglectful treatment of his son. Then to find out he'd given Reeve's twin away." Sadness ghosts over her face. "Look at what he set in motion. All the pain his actions have caused. Dillon was wrong to direct that anger at Reeve, but I can fully understand his feelings toward Simon. What Simon did to him was unforgivable."

Silence descends for a few minutes. "It doesn't change anything though," I say in between sips of my vodka. "And I'm the one left to pick up the pieces." I glance out the window, spotting Easton and his best friend Nash playing in the playground.

"The wrong twin died," Alex says, a muscle popping in his jaw. "Reeve was innocent in all of this, but Dillon knew what he was doing. If anyone had to die, it should've been him."

"Thanks for that," a familiar husky voice says, and I whip my head around, spotting Dillon and Ash standing in the doorway with the rest of their family in the hallway outside. "Don't hold back on my account," he adds, striding into the room.

CHAPTER 15
VIVIEN

"ALEX!" Audrey hisses, elbowing him in the ribs. "You should apologize."

"I'm not apologizing for speaking my mind," her husband says, glaring at Dillon as the O'Donoghues file into the room. They aren't all here. It's just Ash, Jamie, Ro, Cath, and Eugene. I know the rest of the family is here somewhere, because Mom confirmed they were at the funeral. Ciarán, Shane, their wives, and kids, too. The only people missing are Ronan's girlfriend and their baby daughter. I don't know if they purposely stayed away, for my benefit, or some other reason. I'm touched everyone else came, but I'm sure it was more to support their brother than me. No doubt, they all know about Easton and they are keen to meet him.

"It's fine, Audrey," Dillon says. "He's loyal to Reeve. I get it."

Dillon is wearing a black suit with a black shirt and tie to match his black soul. The usual rings and piercings adorn his hands and face. His hair flops in brown waves over his brow, and I'm grateful he didn't style it like Reeve usually did. I know I mistook him for Reeve at the hospital, but I'm chalking that up to stress and a drugged-up hallucination. Now when I look at him, I see glimpses of Reeve, but he's wholly Dillon.

"It's not fine," Ash says, working hard to rein her anger in. She walks right up to Alex. "I understand if you hate my brother, even if you don't know him and you're not privy to all the facts. We're all pretty pissed off with him right now too. But to say you wish he had died instead is horrible. Nobody should have to hear what you just said."

Two red spots appear on Alex's cheeks. "You're right," he grits out, lifting his head and eyeballing Dillon. "I don't like you. For a lot of reasons, but that was harsh and uncalled for. I apologize."

Dillon shrugs, eyeballing Alex in return. Cath glares at her son, and Dillon purses his lips before running a hand through his hair. "Apology accepted," he begrudgingly says.

461

It's fair to say there will never be any love lost between those two men.

Mom stands, ushering Mr. and Mrs. O'Donoghue over to the couches, making them sit down. She calls Charlotte via the intercom, asking her to bring some food and drinks to my office.

"We're sorry for barging in here like this," Cath says, narrowing her eyes at Dillon. "We know this is a very harrowing time, and we're so sorry for your loss, Vivien. So incredibly sorry." Tears well in her eyes as she leans across Mom to hug me. "We've missed you, and I hate we are meeting under these tragic circumstances, but we felt it best to speak when we are all in the one place. There are things we should discuss."

Dillon and Ronan move the chairs from the front of my desk over beside us for Audrey and Ash to sit down. Dillon, Alex, Ronan, and Jamie all stand to one side. Dillon's eyes drift to the window, instantly locking on Easton. Pain splinters through my chest, along with other indecipherable emotions.

"I'm not sure Vivien is up to discussing this right now." Mom drags me back into the conversation.

"It's fine," I say, my voice devoid of emotion again. "Might as well get all the breaking done in one day."

Dillon jerks his head around at my words, staring intensely at me, in the way he always does. I avert my eyes, knocking back a few mouthfuls of vodka, needing the liquid courage.

"We had no idea Reeve had a brother," Mom says, addressing Cath. "Felicia was my best friend, but she didn't know she was expecting twins, and Simon said nothing to us afterwards." Anger flares in her eyes. "I am curious though. How did Dillon end up being adopted by you?" Mom slides her arm around my back for support.

Charlotte enters the room, depositing sandwiches, cookies, cake, and tea and coffee on the table, along with plates and napkins. I thank her, and we wait for her to leave before the conversation resumes.

"My Eugene is adopted," Cath begins explaining, patting her husband's thigh. "And when we got married, we decided we would like to adopt too. But Shane and Ciarán came along quickly, and we shelved the idea while they were young. My sister Eileen was working with an international adoption agency based in London. She let us know they were looking for a family for an American baby and asked if we wanted to apply. We almost declined. Aisling was only a year old, but we both felt a calling in our hearts." She looks over at Dillon, smiling. "We just knew this was the child for us, so we processed the paperwork, met with representatives of the agency in Dublin, and a month later, we were waiting at the ferry in Dun Laoghaire to collect our beautiful baby boy."

Dillon rubs a hand along the back of his neck in a familiar gesture so much like Reeve it hurts. I close my eyes briefly, exhaling heavily. Mom gently squeezes my side, and I force my eyelids to open. Audrey exits the room discreetly as I set my empty glass down on the table. Dad hands me a plate with some sandwiches, and I accept it to be polite, even though I can't stomach the thought of food right now.

"Did you know he was a twin?" I ask Cath.

She shakes her head. "That was not disclosed to us, and Eileen died eleven years ago of cancer. God rest her soul." She blesses herself. "So I don't know if she was aware. The first we knew Dillon was a twin was when he phoned the other night to tell us."

"You didn't even tell your family?" Disbelief drips from my tone as I stare at him. "No. He didn't." Ash thumps him in his stomach. "And he's getting hell for it."

"Love." Cath tilts her head to one side, peering into my face. "You remember our little chat in my kitchen that Sunday?" I nod because I haven't forgotten a single second of my time in Ireland. "Dillon kept all those demons locked up inside. He was always so guarded, no matter how hard we tried to break down his walls. You were the only one who got through to him."

"Ma." Dillon shakes his head.

"No, Dillon. You will not silence me. There have been too many secrets and lies. It ends now."

"Amen to that," Mom agrees.

"What Dillon has done has disappointed us as a family, but we love him, and we'll forgive him because we know the kind of man he is inside. I wouldn't blame you for thinking the worst of him, Lauren, and I'm not making excuses for my son, but he has struggled with abandonment issues his whole life. It has broken my heart." Her voice cracks, and Dillon looks down at his feet. Mr. O'Donoghue presses a kiss to Cath's temple, holding her close.

"Ma. Stop." Dillon lifts his head. "I'm fully responsible for my actions. It's not your place to apologize or make excuses for me."

"I couldn't agree more," Alex grits out.

"Could I talk to you alone?" Dillon asks, drilling me with piercing blue eyes I'm so accustomed to.

"No. Anything you want to say to me you can say here." If we go somewhere alone, I'm liable to murder him in cold blood.

A muscle clenches in his jaw. "Fine. I know you hate me. With good reason. And I know I've fucked up. I—"

"Good speech. Mirrors my sentiments exactly," I say, glaring at him as I cut him off. "Was there anything else?"

"I lied, okay?" He claws a hand through his hair.

"About what?"

"Pretty much everything."

"So, you didn't really hate your twin and you didn't spend years plotting ways to take Reeve down? You must be thrilled you got your wish after all."

A strangled sound escapes Cath's mouth, and I instantly feel chastised. "I'm sorry you had to hear that," I quietly admit. "But Dillon has hated Reeve when there was no justification, and he used me to try to get back at my husband. Reeve was so happy when he discovered he had a twin, and he didn't deserve the way Dillon treated him." Just thinking about it enrages me all over again. I lift my eyes to Dillon's. "You never gave him a chance or an opportunity to speak to you. If you'd only talked to him, you would've realized Simon manipulated him too."

"You think I don't know that now, Viv? You think I don't know I fucked everything up with my twin? Simon spouted all that shit, and it made sense at the time. I was hurting, and confused, and there was other stuff going down. It was easier, in a way, to channel all that emotion into hating Reeve and Simon. Then I saw what he did to you, and I felt justified. He treated you like shit back then, proving he was a selfish prick so obsessed with his career he betrayed the one person he claimed to love more than anything."

"He was young and thrown into a world he was not prepared for!" I retort. "He trusted the wrong people, and he was manipulated and outmaneuvered. I don't need you to tell me how much he hurt me. I haven't forgotten how he made me feel. How heartbroken I was at that time."

"Until I pieced you back together, and then you ran straight back into his fucking arms."

I stand, glaring at Dillon. "You didn't piece me back together! I did that myself." He helped. Ash did too. The whole Irish experience helped me to heal and to grow. But I'm not admitting that now. "And I didn't get back with him until after Easton was born. Until he'd proven himself. And he did. He made up for his mistakes, which is more than can be said about you!"

"I'd like a chance to make up for mine, but you won't let me!" Frustration is evident on his face, and I'm glad to see it.

"Damn fucking straight, I won't!" I plant my hands on my hips. "The difference is Reeve was just a kid back then, but you're a grown man who should know better."

CHAPTER 16

VIVIEN

"YOU DON'T HAVE to explain yourself to him," Alex snarls as Audrey slips back into the room carrying a fresh vodka cranberry. "You owe him nothing." Alex rounds on Dillon, putting his face all up in his. "You don't get to come in here today, of all days, after the shit you've pulled, and the stress you put a pregnant woman under, and demand a second chance like you deserve one. Reeve was worth a million of you, and he loved Viv with his whole heart." Alex shoves Dillon in the chest, and I'm terrified things are about to go south.

Audrey places the vodka in my hand, fixing me with apologetic eyes. "Alex and I are going to look after your guests until you're done here." She levels her husband with a look. "Aren't we, honey?" She yanks on his arm, pulling him away from Dillon before he can retaliate with his words or his fists.

Alex mumbles under his breath but doesn't protest as she drags him out of the room. Air whooshes out of my mouth in grateful relief. As much as I'm thankful to Alex for standing up for me, I don't want a fight breaking out.

"Good riddance," Dillon mutters, and I level an evil eye in his direction.

"Immature much?" Sarcasm drips off my tone.

"Jesus Christ, Dil." Ash yanks him down, forcing him into Audrey's vacant seat. "You are your own worst enemy."

He sighs heavily, loosening his tie and unbuttoning the top button of his shirt. "For the record, I might have hated Reeve, but I never wished him dead. I'm willing to admit I was wrong. If you say Reeve didn't know and Simon was the one who manipulated me, then I believe you."

"Oh, *now* you believe me." I throw my hands in the air, almost dislodging the plate of uneaten sandwiches on my lap. Mom lunges for them, setting the plate down on the table. "Now he's dead, you're willing to accept the truth. I was blue in the face telling you it was all lies, and you refused to believe me!" I yell.

"Because I was upset and shocked and I'd believed what that asshole Simon said," he yells back.

"Don't you dare shout at my daughter. Act civilly or you can leave this house." Mom jabs her finger in the air at Dillon.

"Dillon. Please." Cath's teary eyes plead with her son.

Ignoring both moms, Dillon looks me straight in the eye. "I've spent years nurturing this hatred, Viv. How stupid do you think I feel knowing I was played completely? I believed Reeve knew about me. I thought he was a selfish prick who didn't give a shit about me. What I read about him on social media seemed to confirm it. Look at what he did to you! You were a mess when you first landed in Dublin."

"I know how I felt, thank you very much. I don't need a history lesson from you, and we've already covered this."

"He hurt you, but you forgave him. I'm just looking for the same opportunity. Please let me make amends. Please give me one more chance. I won't let you down. I promise." Desperation bleeds into the air, seeping from his words and the pleading expression on his face. "I know what I did was wrong. I see that now. I wish I could turn back the clock and do so many things differently." He thumps his chest. "I will have to live with that guilt for the rest of my life. I didn't know my brother, and now I never will. I know that's partly on me. If I could trade places with him, I would."

"Dillon, no!" Cath cries. "Don't say that."

Dillon's Adam's apple jumps in his throat, and I feel Cath's pain. "Sorry, Ma. I don't mean to upset you, but I've made a mess of things. Sometimes I think it would've been easier if Simon had just murdered me when I was born."

Fucking hell.

Cath's cries are louder, and Ash, Ro, and Jamie stare at Dillon in shock. I don't know what to think. Whether he's being sincere or if this is still a game he's playing. Mom and Dad look troubled, and I'm just so over this day and ready to draw a line under it.

"Don't say that, Dil." Ash shakes her head. "Yes, you're a dickhead. Yes, you've fucked up and hurt my best friend. But you've hurt yourself too." Her worried gaze meets mine. "We shouldn't have come here today. It wasn't fair on you. Emotions are still too raw. I know you distrust Dillon now, and I don't blame you. I really don't, Viv. I'm putting myself in your shoes, and I would feel the same way, but what you had in Ireland was real. Deep down, you know that too. One day, when you're not mourning your beloved husband and beautiful little girl, maybe you might be able to look at it differently. That day isn't today, and I think we should go." She looks at her parents, and Cath nods, swiping at the tears flowing down her face.

Ash slings her arms around her brother, squeezing him tight. Her apologetic gaze locks on mine, and there are so many unspoken words between us. I know I need to fix things with her. Especially now she will be in my life. She's Easton's auntie, and I can't continue to deny that fact, even if I'll be keeping contact with the O'Donoghues to a minimum until Easton has properly grieved Reeve and Lainey.

"Ash is right, and we will go, but I need to get this out first," Dillon says. "I know you're traumatized and heartbroken and you don't need any more of the heavy. But you need to know my biggest lie was what I told you about my feelings for you. I led you to believe I didn't care, but that's not the truth. *I care.* So fucking much." His eyes bore into my face. "I know you're not ready to hear this, but I need to say it. I still love you, Vivien Grace. I never stopped."

What a crock of shit, and I'm not buying it. Actions speak louder than words, and that is most definitely true in Dillon's case. I school my features into a neutral line, as he continues.

"I can see you don't believe it, and I can't force you to. But we need to try to find a way to get along, because Easton is my son, and—"

I interrupt his desperate word vomit because I refuse to listen to one more word of his bullshit. I see it now. I see what new game he's playing. Spewing all this shit, trying to win me over to his side, just so he can slide in and steal Easton away from me. Over my dead body will that happen!

"He's not yours!" I shout, rising abruptly. "He's Reeve's son! Reeve will *always* be his daddy, not you! You're just a sperm donor in the same way Simon Lancaster was."

Mom sucks in a breath, standing. "Vivien." I can tell I've shocked even her, and I know I'm being callous, but how dare Dillon show up here, thinking he can mouth some pretty words at me and all will be forgiven.

"We shouldn't have come," Dillon says, unfurling to his full height. Pain radiates from his eyes. "I'm sorry."

"Ya think?" I shout, shucking out of Mom's grasp. "My husband and my baby were only buried today, and you're over here already staking your claim on *my* son!" I stalk toward him, shoving his chest. "He's *my* son. He will never be yours! Never! Fuck you, Dillon! Fuck you! Fuck you! Fuck you!"

Ro's brows climb to his hairline, and concern is splayed across his face. Jamie's too. Neither of them has contributed to the conversation, and Ash has been quieter than normal.

"Princess." Dad wraps his arms around me from behind. "It's okay, sweetheart. Let it all out."

"He can't have Easton, Dad," I sob, curling into his warm chest. "He's not taking my son from me! E is all I've got left."

"Viv," Dillon's voice is deliberately soft. "I would never take him from you, and I would never do anything to hurt him or add to his pain. I was never going to share anything online. I just said that to make you do things my way, but I wouldn't have told the world about him or posted any of your pictures. I know you don't trust me, but you will see the truth in time." Hurt and longing shimmer in his blue eyes. "I just want to get to know my son. I understand it'll take time, but I'm begging you to let me develop a relationship with him as his uncle."

I sob into my Dad's shirt, unable to deal anymore. I'm physically and emotionally spent. The well is dry, and I just want them to leave.

"I know there are things to discuss, but this isn't the time or the place. You need to leave." Mom's stern tone leaves no confusion.

"I'm very sorry, Lauren," Cath says. "We shouldn't have come here today. I can see we've only added to Vivien's stress, and that wasn't our intent." She turns to me. "Honey, please forgive us for intruding on your grief in such a selfish way. My heart breaks for you and for Easton. Take care of yourselves."

"I'll give you my number," Mom says, compassion flaring behind her steely determination. "Call me, and we'll try to arrange something before you return home."

"I'm sorry, Viv. I'm sorry for everything," Dillon says, and I twist my head, staring at him through blurry eyes.

Ash approaches with tears streaming down her face. "I hate seeing you in so much pain, and I hate that our friendship was a casualty of all this. We always said we wouldn't let my brother come between us."

On instinct, I reach out, hugging her. "That one's on me. Not you," I sob, clinging to her. "I never wanted to cut you off. It hurt me to do it."

"I understand." She eases back. "And I understand some of what you're going through now. When you're ready, please call me. Let me be here for you now. If there is anything I can do to help, anything at all, just pick up the phone, and I'll do it." She presses a business card into my hand.

"Thanks, Ash. I've missed you."

"Missed you too. So fucking much."

Cath pulls me in for a hug. "We love you." She kisses both my cheeks.

"I love you too." It's true. I've always loved their family. They cared for me as if I was one of their own. I have no beef with Dillon's family, and I'm not surprised they turned up en masse today. It's who they are, and I haven't forgotten how they opened their house and their arms to me in Ireland.

It's not their fault their son is a lying, scheming bastard.

She kisses my brow. "You mind yourself, and hopefully, we'll see you soon."

"I'll give you space," Dillon says as his family walks toward the door. "But we do need to talk soon. I won't pressure you into anything. I just want a small window to get to know Easton."

And I just want to pound my fists into your self-centered face until you bleed. "Goodbye, Dillon," I snarl.

He glances out the window, his expression a mix of pain and longing, before casting one final look at me. "I meant what I said. I know you don't believe me, but I still love you. I always will. Even if you can never forgive me."

CHAPTER 17
VIVIEN

"ARE your parents flying in for the reading of the will?" Audrey asks, handing me some of Charlotte's delicious homemade lemonade.

"They can't take any more time off, so they're going to join us via video." My parents only returned to the set last week, and it took massive amounts of persuasion to get them to leave. The studio had run out of patience, and they were threatening to sue for breach of contract. I won't have my parents bankrupted or their reputations sullied because of me.

Easton threw a hissy fit when they left, and he had nightmares the first few nights. He's terrified they're not coming back, and I can relate. I'm clinging to my son, gluing him to my side, because I'm petrified something is going to happen to him.

"Reeve was so organized." Audrey drops down onto the lounger beside me. "We don't have a will. I guess it's something we should get around to."

"That's probably the only good bit of advice Simon Lancaster ever gave his son. When we got married and built this place, he told Reeve to ensure his affairs were in order."

I never imagined it would turn out to be prudent. Pain licks at my insides, and I'm tempted to make some vodka cocktails, but that's a slippery slope I don't want to fall down. If it wasn't for my son, I think I'd be numbing my pain in a vat full of Grey Goose or a box of Valium.

Easton is splashing in the pool with Nash, and I'm glad he's presently happy. His moods are as fickle as mine lately. One minute, he's laughing, and the next, he's lashing out at something or someone. I know he's struggling to process his feelings, hence why I've hired a grief counselor to come to the house. She's going to do a session with Easton—with me present—and then do a one-on-one with me.

Mom forced me into it. It was the only way she would agree to return to the movie set. If it was up to me, I'd wallow in misery and grief because the thought of talking through everything with a shrink makes me want to puke.

"Did you speak to Easton's camp instructor today?" she asks, lathering sunscreen on her legs.

Easton has been attending summer camp since he was three years old. It's the same one Reeve and I attended as kids, and it's where his love of acting developed into his passion. There is a huge focus on the arts, and Easton loves the singing and drama classes, but they also do sports and outdoor activities too. I really didn't want to let him go this summer, as I panic any time he is away from me. But he wanted to go, and I know it's important to keep up his routine.

To help to give him some sense of normalcy, so I've been driving him there and back each day. I still can't get in a car with anyone else driving. I need to be in control. To know if anything happens, I control the outcome.

"Yes. She was sympathetic," I explain. "She understands he's grieving, but, at the same time, he can't go around hitting other kids." There was a situation yesterday where Easton got into a fight with another boy when they were outside playing football. I was terribly upset last night, because it's not like E at all. He's always been sensitive to other kids' distress, and he's usually the first kid to reach out a helping hand if anyone is hurt at Little League.

"Did Easton say anything else?"

I tried talking to Easton last night, but he was angry and sulking and he wouldn't talk about it. I didn't push, waiting until this morning to ask him again when he had calmed down. "The other boy told him his daddy was a drunk and he deserved to die," I say, through gritted teeth.

Unfortunately, the toxicology reports from the accident were made public and it's been reported in the media. I haven't watched any of the TV reports or read anything online, because I don't want to know how they are tearing my husband's reputation to shreds. Of course, Reeve's fans are defending him to the hilt, according to Edwin Chambers, Reeve's publicist. I have retained his services for the moment, as we deal with the aftermath of the accident and his death.

Audrey gasps. "What a little shit."

I nod my agreement. "It's no wonder Easton got angry and lashed out though I had to explain that he can't do that again. I told him he can defend his daddy with his words, but he can't use his fists. I said if anyone says anything nasty or mean it's best if he tells one of the instructors and lets them handle it."

It's hard to tell your kid not to retaliate when someone says something so horrible. I can't let violent behavior go, but I'm not punishing my child for protecting his daddy's memory either. I'm hoping by the time Easton returns to school in August things will have settled down and the press will have moved their focus to someone else. "I feel like I'm failing as a parent," I add. "Maybe I should remove him and just keep him home."

We haven't ventured outside our property, except for camp, because the paparazzi follow us every time we leave, hounding me for a quote and shouting shit at my son. I almost punched a photographer in the face last week when he asked Easton if he talks to his daddy's ghost. Some of these people are scum of the earth and they have no empathy or respect for our privacy.

"I know it's hard, Viv, but I think routine is important for Easton, and being around other kids is too."

"I just want to swaddle him in cotton wool and keep him safe here." I sip my lemonade through the straw while I share the truth with my bestie. "I've been having these nightmares." I swallow painfully. "I'm trapped in the car, but this time, Easton is there too. He's looking in the window, crying, and I can't reach him. He runs away, continuing to cry, and I watch as he races out onto the road and—" A sob bursts from my chest, and I set my drink down on the small glass table, turning to the side so Easton can't see me upset. "I can't even say it, but I'm scared, Rey. I'm scared of something happening to E too. He's all I have left."

A fluttering sensation builds momentum in my chest, spreading across my upper torso, and my heart feels like it's beating too fast, like it's trying to find a gap to erupt from my rib cage and escape. My breath oozes out in sputtered starts, and I'm struggling to pull enough oxygen into my lungs.

"Put your head between your legs and draw deep breaths, Viv. In and out, nice and slow. I'll do it with you."

I'm so busy concentrating on calming down I don't hear the little pitter-patter of feet. "Mommy!" Easton cries, and I whip my head up. "What's wrong?" he shrieks, racing toward me and flinging himself at me. Water droplets cover my skin as he clings to me, sobbing.

"It's okay, honey. I'm okay." I hold him close as tears stab my eyes. I meet Audrey's compassionate gaze over his shoulder. "I was just doing some exercises," I lie.

"You sure?" he asks, lifting his head to stare at me. His gorgeous blue eyes drill into mine, and I hate to see so much worry there. I need to do better. "I'm sure." I stand, taking his hand. "Who would like ice cream?" I ask as Nash hangs back nervously at the edge of the pool.

"Me!" they scream, and I take them inside, fixing a bowl with vanilla and chocolate ice cream and strawberry sauce with sprinkles for each of them. The boys take their ice cream back outside, sitting side by side on one of the loungers, whispering and laughing as they devour their treat.

"You're not failing, Viv," Audrey says, continuing our previous conversation when I lie back down alongside her. "You are doing the best you can, and it's not easy. You're both trying to deal with this enormous loss. It's okay to admit you need more help."

I twist my head to the side. "I can't ask any more of you, Audrey, and I know you keep deflecting this conversation, but you need to return to Boston. I'm not letting you throw years of studying away because of me."

Alex had to leave, to return to Boston, a few days after the funeral because he got a huge opportunity to help coach at the New England Patriots summer youth camp. It's a once-in-a-lifetime opportunity to be around top coaches and players. It might open the door to a college job or an entry-level job in the pros. He was going to pull out so he could stay here with his wife and support me, but I can't expect my friends to give up their careers for me. I told him I'd never speak to him again if he passed on the chance, so he left a few weeks ago.

"I'm good for another week or two." She shrugs casually, as if it's not a big deal. I have no idea how she made it work, but she got extended leave on compassionate grounds. However, she can't stay here indefinitely, and I need to learn to cope on my own. She wets her lips and sits up a little straighter. "I will feel better about going once you talk to the therapist, and I think you should talk to your doctor about anti-anxiety and depression meds. They will help."

"It's not that bad," I lie. "I just need time."

"What the fuck is he doing here?" Audrey hisses the next morning as we get out of the car in the underground parking garage attached to the attorneys' offices.

"Who?" I spin around, and my mouth hangs open as Dillon and Ash walk toward us. He's wearing his signature black tee and ripped jeans with sneakers, and I wonder if he just buys the same clothing in multiple quantities.

"Hey." Ash steps forward, yanking me into a hug. "How are you holding up?"

"I rejoice when I can get out of bed in the morning," I truthfully admit, and she squeezes my hand. She looks very sophisticated in a gorgeous cream pants suit, looking like she's ready for a professional meeting. Unlike her rock star brother. "What's he doing here?" I ask, jerking my head in Dillon's direction.

"I'm right here, Hollywood. You don't have to keep pretending like I don't exist." I ignore that little dig and avoid looking at him, crossing my arms over my chest.

"Carson Park told us to be here," Ash explains after a few beats of awkward silence. "He said Dil is named in the will."

My eyes almost fly out of my eye sockets in shock. "What?" I splutter. Audrey and I exchange startled expressions.

"That's all we know." Ash tentatively smiles at Audrey. "Hey, Rey. Sorry I didn't get to speak to you at the funeral."

Tension lingers in the air. Ash and Audrey have a checkered history. They were bosom buddies at the start until they both took sides in the Dillon versus Reeve situation. I know Ash reached out to Audrey after I returned to L.A. from Dublin, when I was ghosting her, and Audrey ghosted her too, so I'm not surprised things are a little strained, even if Ash must know why by now.

Audrey surprises me, leaning in to hug my other bestie. "It's good to see you. The three of us need to catch up."

"I would really like that," Ash says, looking relieved.

"We should head inside," I say before Audrey sets a date and Dillon decides to invite himself. He's been calling and texting, and I've been ignoring him. I know I can't continue to do it forever, but I cannot deal with him right now. I'm doing my best to put one foot in front of the other, and I'm trying to help Easton process his feelings. I don't have time to worry about Dillon's hurt ones.

"We need to talk," Dillon says when we're all trapped within the close confines of the elevator taking us up to Carson Park's office.

"Not now," I snap, staring straight ahead.

He repositions himself so he's directly in front of me, and I have no choice but to look at his face. "When then? You're ignoring my calls and texts."

"Because you're harassing me," I hiss, and Audrey and Ash turn around.

"I'm not harassing her," Dillon says, eyeballing both women. "I've messaged her and phoned her a handful of times in the past week because we need to talk about Easton."

"Not now we don't," Ash says, drilling her brother with a warning look. "You never learn," she adds, shaking her head.

The doors ping open, and I push past Dillon, walking into the reception area.

Carson's secretary escorts us to a small conference room where the Lancasters' attorney is already waiting for us. My parents' comforting faces greet me from the wall-mounted screen. Introductions are made, and then Carson gets down to business. "As I mentioned on the phone last week, Vivien, we had a small reading of a part of the will a couple of weeks ago. Reeve made several donations to charities, and I met with representatives of those bodies to explain the terms."

I nod because this isn't news or surprising. Reeve left a sizeable sum to Strong Together, as well as a number of other charities he had affiliations with.

"Today, I'd like to discuss the terms of the personal aspects of the will."

I listen dejectedly as Carson confirms Reeve left the bulk of his estate to me. I have my first meltdown when he mentions Reeve has set up trust funds for the kids. Of course, I knew there was one for Easton, but I didn't know he'd created one for Lainey too. He also left them personal items. Lainey's will revert to me. I wish I had known before the funeral because I would have had them buried with her.

Carson stops talking while I sob against Audrey's shoulder, and Mom swipes at the tears streaming down her face. After a few minutes, I manage to compose myself, and the attorney continues. I purposely avoid looking at Dillon across the table, staring at the glossy walnut tabletop, wishing I could press the fast-forward button because I don't know if I can survive this.

Reeve left a few personal items to Easton too. The golf watch I've already gifted him is one of them, and I burst into tears again as another wave of grief washes over me. We knew each other inside and out, and our thoughts were often in sync. Our connection is so intimate it even transcends life and death, and I'm missing him so acutely right now. What I wouldn't give to feel his comforting arms around me or to hear his quietly uttered assurances.

I feel so lost without him. Like I'm wandering aimlessly through life, with no one to guide me along the right path. Reeve isn't here to hold my hand when I veer in the wrong direction, to help me to get back on track. Unlike the last time, there is no overcoming it because Reeve isn't merely on a different continent. He exists in a different realm. He's gone, and he's not coming back. He won't be waiting for me like last time. He can't ever be there for me again, and I want to die every time I remember that. It feels like I'm missing half my soul, half my heart, without him, and that's before I contemplate the gut-wrenching loss of the baby I had nurtured so lovingly in my womb.

The pain is never-ending, and I'm like a shell of the person I used to be.

Carson asks if I want to reschedule the meeting, but I struggle through my pain, shaking my head as I blot my tears with the tissues Audrey hands me from my purse. I've stashed tissues in all my purses and bags because I never know when grief will attack. Sometimes, the smallest things set me off. Something almost insignificant will happen to remind me of Reeve or the daughter I lost, and I'll fall apart, crying until my throat aches and my eyes sting. I tell Carson to continue, and he moves along to the next item.

Reeve bequeathed some personal belongings to my parents, along with the vacation house on the Italian Riviera. We hardly got to vacation there, with our busy schedules, while Mom and Dad spent several summers relaxing at the small Mediterranean-style villa. It makes sense Reeve would leave that to them, but it's odd in another way. It's almost as if my husband had a sixth sense about his passing. Why else would he leave my parents a house when they should have been gone before he was? My heart swells painfully as these thoughts flip-flop around my brain.

To Alex, he leaves a couple of his prized sports cars, a few of his expensive watches, and some mementos and framed photos from high school.

Audrey gasps when she discovers Reeve purchased a unit in a new modern office building being built in downtown L.A. in her name. Carson explains it is for her future medical practice and Reeve had initially planned on surprising her with it upon graduation.

Now it's Audrey's turn to dissolve into heartbreaking tears while I comfort her. She holds my shoulders, crying into my neck, and her pain speaks to mine. Reeve was her friend, and she's tried to be so strong for me, but she's entitled to her tears. She's allowed to mourn him too, and I feel selfish in this moment for not even considering her grief as I've been drowning in mine.

"Did you know?" she croaks, swiping at tears.

I smile softly, nodding at my best friend. "We were out for lunch one day, and we came across the development. The guy building it happened to be there, and he and Reeve got talking. He told me a week later he had purchased one of the larger units, thinking you might want to do something with it in the future. He made me promise not to tell you." Probably because he knew Audrey would not accept it easily. "You don't have to do it though," I add, not wanting my bestie to feel like she's forced into coming back to L.A. after she has graduated or that she even has to set up her planned practice here. "It's yours to do with as you please. Use it, or sell it, or whatever." I shrug casually as if I wouldn't be devastated if my bestie never returned home.

"Viv." Audrey kisses my cheek. "We were always coming back to L.A. after my graduation. Alex even has a potential job offer on the table."

Shock splays across my face—even if I'm thrilled—because this is the first I'm hearing of it. "Why didn't you say anything?"

"We were going to tell you on our Mexican vacation."

We had planned a trip to Mexico for September. It was going to be our first family vacation with our new daughter. I squeeze my eyes shut as brutal pain slaps me in the face. It is always like this. I might find a few minutes where I've forgotten the shitshow my life has turned into, and then something happens to remind me of everything I have lost.

"I'm sorry."

I blink my eyes open, brushing tears away. "It's fine," I whisper, deliberately not looking at Dillon or Ash. I'm clinging to my sanity by my fingernails at this point.

"I think it's wonderful you'll be permanently returning to L.A.," Mom says from the screen. "And now, thanks to Reeve, you have a location for your new practice."

"Yes, I do." Audrey hugs me quickly, and we manage to compose ourselves so Carson can finish the meeting.

"That brings us to the last item." Carson shuffles some papers on the table, pushing his glasses up the bridge of his nose as his gaze moves between me and Dillon. "Reeve came to see me one week before he died to make an alteration to his will." He wets his lips before reading from the papers in front of him. "In the event of my death, the inheritance I received from Simon Lancaster's Last Will and Testament, excluding the shares in Studio 27, will be split equally with one share going to my children, to be divided between them, and the remaining share will transfer to my twin brother, Dillon Thomas O'Donoghue."

CHAPTER 18
DILLON

"WHAT?" I almost fall off my chair in shock. Why the hell would Reeve add me to his will at the eleventh hour?

"It's a substantial inheritance," Carson Park continues as if he hasn't noticed the startled expressions on everyone's faces. "As well as the bank accounts, there are investment portfolios and several properties. The forty percent stake in Studio 27 now transfers to Vivien, as a caretaker, until her eldest child comes of age, and then it will pass to Easton."

"I don't want it," I blurt, gripping the edge of the table. "I don't want anything that once belonged to my asshole sperm donor."

Carson blinks at me through his glasses.

"What my brother means is, he needs time to digest this," Ash says, slipping into a practiced diplomatic role. She smiles that bullshit polite smile she usually rolls out at these rodeos. "You have my number. Please send me all the paperwork, and I'll handle it."

"Why would Reeve do that?" Viv asks, looking as confused and shocked as I feel. Her gaze bounces between the solicitor and me. "He suspected who you were. Yet he changed his will? I don't understand." She chews on the corner of her mouth, and the familiar gesture is like a punch in the gut.

Being around her hurts so much.

More so because I see how much pain she is in and I want to help glue back the broken pieces of her heart, but she won't let me. She won't let me in at all. She's still the same stubborn feisty girl I met in Dublin, buried under a bigger mountain of pain and grief.

And I'm still the same impatient determined fucker.

Viv can push me away until the cows come home. She can hurt me with her words and her anger and her indifference, but I'm going nowhere.

We're both still the same people we were, yet we're not. She's a mother now, and her protective instincts are strong. Her sense of self-preservation might be rocked in the aftermath of her loss, and she might feel like she's drowning, but she knows who she is and what she wants in a way she didn't understand when we first met. It's unlucky for me what she wants is my body transported to Mars where she never has to see me or deal with me ever again.

I know what I want too. I have clarity in a way I've never had it before. I want Vivien and Easton. I want a chance to prove I can be there for them. I don't know if Viv can ever love me again, but I will take her any way I can get her. Even if we are never more than friends and coparents.

I know I can never replace Reeve.

Nor would I want to.

My feelings for my twin are still a clusterfuck of epic proportions. I have accepted I got some of it wrong, but Reeve wasn't the perfect angel Viv seems to think he was. Those photos are still burning a hole in my pocket, and I'm fucking dying to know how they ended up in their car that night. I'm guessing Reeve hired a PI to spy on Viv when she was in Dublin. It's the only explanation that makes sense. I remember that guy I spotted creeping around a couple of times, and I'm convinced he was paid to watch us. My blood boils thinking about it. Every memory I have of our time together is singed around the edges now, knowing some fucking asshole was taking pictures of us and sending them back to Reeve.

No wonder he was lying in wait for her the instant she stepped off the plane that day. He knew we were in love, and he was determined to get her back and willing to play dirty to do it. Begrudging admiration wars with seething rage as I think of how he manipulated things. And, yes, I know I'm a fucking hypocrite.

The truth is, we both manipulated Vivien in different ways. Neither one of us was ever worthy of her.

"I don't know, Vivien," Carson says, dragging me out of my head. "Reeve didn't explain his decision. He just asked me to make the amendment to his will."

"You can have it all," I offer, locking eyes with her for the first time since we entered the room. "I'll reassign it back to you."

"I don't want it or need it," Vivien says. "I'm just shocked Reeve would do that. I know he spoke about giving you your share that day you were at the house, but that was before he suspected who you were."

"We won't ever know his motivations for sure," Ash says. "But I for one think this shows the kind of man your husband was. He was ensuring Dillon got the inheritance that was rightfully his. No matter what he thought of him, he didn't let it interfere with doing what he felt was right."

Vivien nods, and I glance at the blank screen on the wall, wondering when Viv's parents exited this conversation. I must have been lost in my thoughts when they said their goodbyes. "Perhaps your brother should dwell on that in light of his actions." Viv speaks to Ash as if I'm not even in the room, and it fucking infuriates me to no end.

"If I wanted to transfer the inheritance to Easton, is that possible?" I ask the solicitor.

He nods. "Of course. It's yours to do with as you please."

I expect Viv to object, but she says nothing, looking like she's checked out again.

Carson draws the meeting to a close, and I tune out his nasally voice, studying the woman who owns my heart. She stares at the wall, as if she's staring through it, while nibbling on her lower lip. I've noticed Viv zoning out, every so often, staring off into space with the most forlorn look on her face.

I never doubted she loved Reeve. She never tried to hide that from me, and I respected her for her integrity. But it's painfully obvious now how much he meant to her. He was her everything, in a way I've never been, and that's a bitter pill to swallow.

I know I shouldn't be envious of my dead brother. It's a pointless emotion. But I can't help how I feel. I have always been in his shadow, and I will continue to remain there, even though he is no longer here.

"Earth to dumbass," Ash says, tugging on my arm. "The meeting is over. Everyone is gone. I thought you wanted to talk to Viv."

"Shit." I jump up. "Yes. Come on. You need to hear this too." I drag my poor sister out of the room, telling her to take off her shoes so she can chase me down the stairs. The lift is already gone, taking Viv with it, and I need to stop her before she leaves.

Short of turning up on her doorstep—which I'm reluctant to do because a confrontation is the last thing Easton needs to witness—this is the only chance I may have to speak to her. Viv needs to know, so we can get ahead of this.

I burst through the doors of the car park just as Viv and Audrey reach their SUV. "Wait!" I holler, racing toward them. Viv, predictably, ignores me, climbing behind the wheel. I grab the door before she can close it. "Don't. Fucking. Ignore. Me."

"What do you want, Dillon?" Audrey asks, leaning across the console to stare at me.

"To get to know my son and the opportunity to make things up to the woman I love, but"—I raise one palm, keeping my other hand firmly on the car door, as I don't trust Viv not to slam it in my face—"I know what the reply would be, so that's not why we currently need to talk."

"Jesus Christ, Dillon," Ash says, materializing behind me. She's panting and a little red in the face. "I think I just ripped the seam of my trousers. If I did, you're buying me a new suit."

"I have nothing to say to you," Viv says, looking straight ahead.

"Look at me," I snap, getting sick of this crap. I know she's in mourning. I know I'm a piece-of-shit dumbass fuckface. But she can still look at me when she's talking to me.

"What, Dillon?" she hisses, turning to face me. "What do you want?"

"We have a mutual problem we need to discuss."

"What problem?" Ash straightens up, putting her serious face on.

"Don't freak," I tell my sister, knowing it's pointless. "I only found out about it this morning."

"Found out about what?" Audrey asks, looking troubled.

I blow air out of my mouth, hating I have to blurt it out like this, but if I don't, Viv will run off and she'll find out in the worst possible way. "The press know about me. They've found out I'm Reeve's twin brother."

"How?" Ash asks when it's clear Viv is in a state of numbed shock.

"A reporter noticed the resemblance as I was leaving the funeral, and she started digging. She got her hands on a copy of my naturalization application. It lists Reeve as my brother. She wants an exclusive interview with me. She's given me forty-eight hours to agree or she's running the story."

"Fuckity-fuck." Ash expels a breath heavily. Throwing a concerned look at a shell-shocked Viv, she addresses Audrey. "We need to strategize. We need to discuss our options and decide how best to minimize the impact so it doesn't bring any more heat down on Viv."

CHAPTER 19
DILLON

"I DON'T LIKE THIS," Viv says, traipsing moodily behind me as I enter the hallway of my L.A. pad.

"Don't worry, Hollywood. I won't kidnap you and tie you to my bed." I flash her a cheeky grin. "Unless you want me to."

She slaps me across the face, and it fucking stings. "I'm leaving." She turns on her heel but not before I see the tears glistening in her eyes. Shit. The last thing I want to do is hurt Viv, but I seem to have foot-in-mouth disease whenever I'm around her.

Ash levels me with a dark look that scares me. Outwardly, things might look perfect between us, but that couldn't be further from the truth.

After what transpired at Viv's house the day of the funeral, I had to come clean to my family about how I'd threatened her into keeping silent. Seeing the disappointed looks on my parents' faces made me feel horribly ashamed of my actions. My entire family are reeling from the revelations and feeling hurt I excluded them. Ma can't believe I've been harboring all this resentment and dealing with it alone. She doesn't understand why I didn't tell her and Da when Simon accosted me at seventeen. Why I chose to handle it myself.

It's going to take me some time to make it up to everyone.

As for Ash, to say my sister wants to murder me for the cruel way I treated her best friend is an understatement. She has blanked me for weeks, only speaking to me when it was official band business. Today is the first time since the funeral she has spoken directly to me, like we used to, and the first time I've felt we might be able to get through this without causing irreparable damage to our relationship.

I love all my siblings, but I'm closest to Ash. If I have permanently damaged our relationship, I won't come back from that. She is more than my sister. She's become my closest confidante and the person I trust most. I can't lose her without losing a part of myself.

It's the same for the broken woman standing before me, too lost to even steer her rightful anger in my direction. Instead, she's planning to flee, and I can't let her leave. "I'm sorry, Viv. Please don't go." I drag a hand through my hair. "You know this is my default setting, especially when I'm nervous. I'm not trying to be an ass on purpose."

"It just comes so naturally to you," Audrey drawls, scowling at me as she makes her feelings clear. She's never been a big fan of mine anyway.

"My husband—*your brother*—died a month ago, Dillon." Viv whirls around to face me with sad eyes and a trembling lower lip. "You cannot say those things to me. I didn't want to come here, and you're not making me want to stay."

I risk a step closer, gulping over my fear. "I'm sorry for upsetting you. That wasn't my intention. I know you don't want to be here, but we have little choice. To go out in public together right now is a disaster waiting to happen. I'm willing to go back to your place, but I didn't think you'd want me there with Easton."

I would happily chop off a limb for the chance to go to her house and see my son. Not being able to see him is killing me. I'm trying to be sensitive to the situation, because I know how difficult this is for Viv, but I have already missed out on so much of his life, and I want to be there for him now. I know he's hurting. I know he's missing Reeve. I know I can't replace who he was to him, but I want an opportunity to form my own relationship with my son.

"We need to deal with this, Viv," Ash says. "If you don't feel up to talking about it, I can reach out to Edwin Chambers, and we can discuss a strategy for handling it together."

I glare at my sister, even though she's only trying to help. But I'm starved for Viv's company, and she's offering her a "get out of jail free" card.

"I want to know what's going on and how this will impact me and Easton." Viv straightens her shoulders, and a determined glint flashes in her eyes, reminding me of the woman I love. I know she's still in there, and I'm making it my mission in life to help her to rediscover herself. My shoulders relax a smidgeon now I know she's not going to leave. "We will definitely need to involve the PR people, but let's talk it through first now."

I lead them through the lobby, past the vast open-plan kitchen on one side and the games room on the other, and out to the patio. It's a glorious day. Sun shines brightly, illuminating my spacious back garden. Buttery beams glint off the inviting water of my large outdoor pool. Thanks to my expert gardener, the lawns and flowerbeds are pristine, colorful, and plentiful.

I show my guests to the seated area, pulling out one of the comfy wicker chairs for Viv. Ash opens the matching umbrella, providing much-needed shade. "Let me organize some drinks," I say when the ladies are seated. "I'll be back in a few."

I stride into my kitchen where Nancy, my full-time housekeeper, is busy at the cooker. I tell her what I need, and she rushes me back outside, assuring me she's on it.

The girls are talking when I return, their gazes fixed on the large wooden structure in the near distance.

"It's the band's main recording studio," Ash is explaining as I plop down on the chair across from Vivien.

"When we're not booked into Capitol Studios by the label," I add.

482

"Should we get the others?" Ash asks, her gaze darting to the soundproofed building where Conor, Jamie, and Ro are busy working on tracks for our next album.

"Nah." I scratch the stubble on my chin. "This isn't band related. We can fill them in later." After my revelations, things were a bit strained for a couple of weeks with the band. Conor exists in his own little bubble, so he said jack shit to me. Ro was quietly seething although he didn't bitch me out like Jamie did. Jamie was pissed because I'd upset and angered his fiancée.

"You'll have to grant that bitch of a reporter an exclusive interview," Ash says. "It's the only way to control the narrative."

"I agree," Viv says, drumming her fingers on the glass tabletop. "But what exactly are you going to say?" She stares at me across the table, but I can't see her eyes, thanks to the ginormous shades she's wearing. "No one else, apart from your family and us, knows you discovered the truth when you were seventeen, right?"

I nod. "Carson knows too, obviously, but he's not going to say anything." He's loyal to the Lancaster family.

"You can say you only found out after Simon Lancaster died," Ash says.

"Both of you only found out after he died," Viv corrects. "And you can say you had only just met Reeve and you hadn't had a chance to form a relationship with your twin. No one needs to know that was intentional. You can garner the sympathy vote by lying, and it's not like that will be a stretch for you."

Fuck. She really despises me.

"I'm going to land the blame squarely at that fucker sperm donor's door," I say through gritted teeth. "It will help to deflect the attention. Let them make it about the revered Studio 27 boss who loved his wife so much he banished the child he believed caused her death during childbirth and lied to his other son about being a twin. The world's media will lap that shit up."

Audrey looks at me with a glimmer of sympathy I fucking hate. I know in doing this I will be opening myself up to more of it, but I'll cope if it means they will focus on me and not Vivien and Easton.

"Are you comfortable with that?" Ash asks Viv. "We might attract some heat from Studio 27 if we paint Simon as the villain."

"Simon is the villain," Viv replies as Nancy appears carrying a tray with drinks. "I have no issue in tarnishing his reputation."

Nancy sets the tray down, and I distribute drinks, handing Viv a pink gin cocktail. "We don't have 7UP, but Sprite tastes almost the same." Her chin tilts up as she stares at me, and I wish I could see her beautiful hazel eyes. She audibly gulps, and I wonder if her mind has thrown her back to nostalgia lane like mine has. After a few beats of awkward silence, I set the drink down in front of her. "I can get iced tea or lemonade or a coffee if you prefer?" I offer as Nancy appears in my peripheral vision.

"This is fine," she croaks, wrapping her fingers around the stem of the glass. "I haven't drank one of these since Ireland."

I walk to meet Nancy, taking the second tray from her. "Thanks a mil."

"Will your guests be staying for lunch?" she inquires, tipping her head in Audrey's and Vivien's direction.

"Probably not, but make extra just in case."

"No problem, Dillon." When Nancy first came to work for me, she tried to call me Mr. O'Donoghue, which made me sound like an old fart. I told her Mr. O'Donoghue was my father and if she wanted to keep her job to call me Dillon. She hasn't messed up once since that day.

I carry the tray with crisps, biscuits, and fruit over to the table, depositing it in the middle before reclaiming my seat.

"What about your hair and your eyes," Viv says. "She is going to ask about that. How will you explain it?"

Kicking my sneakers off, I stretch my legs out under the table. "I'll tell her I experimented with my looks a lot when I was a teen. That I went through a rebellious phase and wanted to alter my appearance as a fuck you to the parents I never knew who had abandoned me. I'll say when I found out the truth and reconnected with my twin, I chose to change my look. I wanted to see how close the resemblance was and what our individual differences were." I'm sure the reporter will think it was a sweet gesture. A way of feeling closer to my long-lost twin, the brother she believes I hadn't known about my entire life.

There is no way she will know it was a premeditated attempt to mess with my twin's wife. Another way of driving the knife home to the love of my life, reminding Viv she picked the wrong brother.

No one needs to be privy to those disgusting truths.

Truths that make me want to lobotomize myself so I can never think of them again.

Awkward silence descends as the reality of my unspoken words resides in the space between us. We all know why I changed my look and why I changed it back. I'm only fooling myself if I think otherwise. There is no getting away from the full horror of my sins, and that is something I will have to live with for the rest of my life.

CHAPTER 20
DILLON

GRABBING A BEER, I guzzle it back as the usual blanket of guilt and remorse washes over me. So many times, I have wished I could go back to that last night together and do everything differently. If I had, everything might have turned out differently. Viv might be sitting here as my wife, and I might have been the only father Easton has ever known. Reeve would most likely be alive.

Or maybe nothing would've changed even if I had thrown myself at her feet a second time and begged her to stay. Offered to drop out of the band just to be with her. To this day, no one knows those were the thoughts floating through my mind back then. Even if I had told her what I was willing to sacrifice, it most likely wouldn't have been enough. The only way it would have worked is if I'd come clean and told her everything. I'm pretty sure she would still have walked.

I try not to look back at the what-ifs, but it's hard not to when I have so many regrets. If I had known at seventeen what I know now—how every action and reaction had a consequence with the most tragic fallout—I would have chosen differently. If my punishment is to have permanently lost the love of the only woman I will ever give my heart to, then so be it. I will have to accept that fate and try to find some way to make peace with it. But I refuse to lose my son in some form of twisted penance.

One thing I know for sure is I am going to fight for them to the bitter end. I won't stop trying to make amends for all the ways I have wronged Vivien, even if I haven't the foggiest notion where to start.

Viv drinks her cocktail like it's water, and I'm shocked to see it's almost half empty. She was never a big drinker. Even on special occasions, where everyone was knocking back drinks like they were going out of fashion, she always paced herself.

She stiffens, sitting up straighter and putting her drink down. "Wait. We're forgetting something." Air whooshes out of her mouth. "There are people in Ireland who knew about us. People like Cat and *Aoife*." Her mouth pulls into a hard line as she basically spits out Aoife's name. "That bitch won't hesitate to sell her story." She rubs at her temples. "Fuck. I can't have that coming out. They'll twist it and say I was cheating on Reeve with his twin brother and make it this whole sordid thing. It will all start up again. I'll be hated, and how can I protect Easton from that? It's already bad enough." The words tumble from her lush mouth in streams of liquid panic.

"Deep breaths, Viv." Audrey says, smoothing a hand up and down her back. Viv's chest heaves painfully as she draws exaggerated breaths, white-knuckling the table as she rides out her panic attack.

Ash and I trade concerned looks as we watch Audrey talk Viv off a ledge.

"You don't need to worry about anyone back in Ireland," I tell Viv when she's okay. "They won't say a word."

She barks out a harsh laugh. "I'm pretty sure your whore will have plenty to say on the subject. She's vindictive enough to cause trouble. Her gloating face that last day is something I've never forgotten." Hurt glides across her face, and I feel like a worthless piece of shit.

It's time to fess up.

"I'm sorry about that. What I did that night was shitty, but you should know I wasn't with her. Not that night and never again. It's like Ash said. I used her to hurt you because I was hurting so badly and I wanted you to feel what I felt."

Viv yanks her glasses off, almost crushing them in her hand as she leans forward, glaring at me. "You think I wasn't hurting?" she shouts. "I was hurting a whole lot before you did that and a whole lot more after. I cried nonstop the entire plane ride home. And don't make out like you cared. Everyone here knows it was a setup, and I was the gullible fool who fell for it."

"No." I vigorously shake my head. "It started out as a setup, but what I felt for you was real. I told you that. I told you, no matter what happened, to believe it was real."

"And then you told me a few weeks ago that you lied! You can't turn around now and say you meant it all along!"

"I was devastated, Viv." I hop up, grab my beer, and throw it at the side of the house as frustration does a number on me. I'm so pissed at myself for fucking everything up. It hits with a sharp thud, smashing into pieces, spraying beer over my cream-colored stone patio. "I loved you, and you left me for him." She might as well have taken an ax to my heart, because she left me a broken, shattered mess and I still haven't recovered.

Her hands are trembling as she puts her sunglasses back on. "There is no point rehashing old shit. I can't do this now. I won't do it." Ignoring me, she turns to face Ash. "How do we silence Aoife?"

And just like that, I've been relegated to the sidelines again.

"Dillon took care of it years ago," Ash explains, squeezing Viv's hand. "We thought he was stupid at the time, but it seems he was smarter than any of us gave him credit for."

I'm too angry and strung out to appreciate my sister's half-assed compliment.

"Took care of it how?" Viv asks, still ignoring me.

Grabbing another beer from the tray, I sit back down, staring neutrally at Audrey as she glares at me. "I gave her a hundred grand in exchange for signing an NDA," I explain, eyeballing Viv, even if she's not looking directly at me. "If she speaks out, she's breaking the terms, risking prosecution and a large financial penalty. No matter how vindictive she might be, she won't say anything. None of them will. I got everyone to sign it. All the groupies. Cat. That dickhead she was going out with and your other friends from Trin-ners." I smirk as I bring my beer to my lips. "At least that asshole's money came in handy."

"Why would you do that?" Audrey asks, staring at me like I'm a puzzle she needs to figure out.

"I didn't want anyone spouting shit about me to the press."

"You mean you didn't want anyone ruining your little revenge plan," Viv says. "If Aoife or any of the others had mentioned anything about me, you would've tipped Reeve off, but you wanted to wait to time that revelation when it would cause maximum exposure."

She's not entirely wrong, but that wasn't the main reason. "Simon's NDA was watertight. I was not to mention anything about Reeve or you or any children you may have. That's why I did it."

"Yet you had no qualms about coming forward after Simon's death," Audrey says.

I laugh. "It's not like he's going to arise from the dead and slap me with a lawsuit for breaching the terms, is it?"

"His estate could still come after you," she retorts, irritating me with her smug superiority.

"You think *my son* is going to sue me?" I snap.

"*I* could," Vivien says, slamming her empty glass down, almost shattering it. "But you knew I wouldn't. You knew Reeve wouldn't. You waited until the villain was dead before assuming his mantle."

I say nothing because I can't defend myself. While Simon was alive, my hands were tied. I knew the only way I could exact revenge was to manipulate the media into breaking the news, in a way that couldn't be linked back to me, or to wait for the bastard to kick the bucket. I had been working on Plan A when Plan B happened, but I will take that secret to my grave.

"Have your PR person draw up a press release and a contract," Vivien says, speaking to Ash. "Send it to me and copy Edwin on it. I want the details of what's to be said at the interview listed in bullet points and a commitment from Dillon that he will not deviate from the agenda."

"I won't say anything that will hurt you or Easton." I offer her what I hope is a sincere expression. "I will deflect the attention off you. I promise. I'll make it about Simon and the poor little abandoned Irish boy he gave away. I'll ensure the focus is all on me."

"Make sure you do." She grabs her bag, ready to leave.

"When can I see him?" I blurt.

Ash rolls her eyes and shakes her head. Audrey glares at me again, and Viv stares at me as if she's looking through me. "When he's ready."

"Can you give me a ballpark idea of when? I'm going out of my mind here, and we're leaving on a US tour in seven months. I—"

"Don't pressure me, Dillon," she snaps, cutting me off midsentence. "And there is no timeline for this situation. God, it's like you've never been around children. Like you don't have nieces and nephews."

Shit. She's right, and I know I'm being unfair. I'm just so desperate to spend time with my child, and believe it or not, I know I can help. I can help them if she'll just let me in. Even a little bit.

"Easton is going through a rough time, and I won't do anything to upset him. He's not ready to meet you yet. I will contact you when the time is right. Until then, stop fucking harassing me." She stalks off with Audrey, and Ash races after them.

I'm too heartsore to follow so I sit back down, sulking as I drink my beer.

"Dillon. What the hell?" Ash says, storming toward me a few minutes later. "How can someone so talented and so smart be so fucking dumb at the same time?"

"You'll have to enlighten me because I've no idea what you're talking about," I truthfully reply.

She sighs, kicking off her heels and rolling up the legs of her trousers. Carefully, she maneuvers down at the edge of the pool, dipping her feet and lower legs in the water. "Come over here, dumbass, and let me explain it to you."

I push the legs of my jeans up to my knees and join her, welcoming the tepid water as it laps at my bare flesh. I hand her a beer, and she readily accepts. We have no other appointments today, and I plan to vent my frustrations in the studio as soon as this little chinwag is done.

"I know you're dying to meet Easton. We all are, Dillon, but you've got to stop making this about you. This is about Easton and Vivien, and they've just been through hell."

"I know that, and I want to help. How is wanting to be there for them so wrong?"

She rubs my arm. "She's not ready to hear it or accept it, and, Dillon, you've got to at least consider the fact she may never want you like that again. You have hurt her, time and time again, and a lot of years have passed since you were together. People change. Feelings change."

"I love her, Ash." Pain bleeds into every corner of my being. "I love her so fucking much it kills me to see her in pain and not be able to do anything about it."

"You can't force your love on her, Dil. You can't force anything on her. Especially not when she's grieving."

"What do I do? I'm not walking away from her, and I'm sure as fuck not walking away from my son. I have missed out on so much of his life already, and he needs me now."

"You need to be patient." I scowl, and she chuckles. "I know it's about as natural as a colonoscopy, but you can't fuck this up, Dillon. You have one chance to make this right." She drills me with a warning look. "One last chance, Dil." She jabs me in the arm. "Don't blow it."

CHAPTER 21

VIVIEN

LAINEY'S pitiful cries wake me from sleep, and I crawl out of bed, careful not to disturb Easton as I head on autopilot toward the nursery. As I stumble from my bedroom, her cries grow louder and more insistent, and I'm overwhelmed with the need to erase my daughter's suffering.

The nursery door crashes against the wall, waking me from whatever quasi sleep-slash-comatose-slash-illusionary state I was trapped in. Pain slams into me like a freight train, knocking all the air from my lungs and taking my legs out from under me. I collapse on the floor in the doorway of the nursery, hacking up gut-wrenching sobs birthed straight from my splintered soul.

I don't know how long I cry for, but then Audrey is there, cradling me from behind, her cries mixing with mine. In between sobs, I tell her what happened. "Am I going crazy, Rey? Am I losing my mind?" I stare at the pretty pink and white nursery with the Tinkerbell mural on the wall with a new layer of horror. I can't lose my grasp on my sanity. I am all Easton has, and he needs me to get a grip. It's been six weeks since I lost Lainey and Reeve, and it doesn't feel like it's getting any better. Maybe I should try the meds Audrey and my therapist are suggesting.

"The brain is a complex organ." Audrey cradles me in her arms with my back to her chest. "One we will never fully understand. And you're not going crazy. You're traumatized, and grief manifests in different ways." I sniffle, nodding. "What are you going to do about the nursery?" she asks me, after a few beats of silence.

"I don't know. I can't even look at it without immense pain. It's why I never go in there. Reeve, Easton, and I picked every item for her nursery together. We even helped the artist paint parts of the mural. Everything is so personal I can't bear to throw it away, but I can't look at it either. It's the most painful reminder of my loss."

"I can't even imagine how difficult it must be for you, Viv. But I've seen enough grief and trauma in my medical journey to know it's not healthy to cling to the past.

If looking at it prolongs your agony, I think you should consider clearing it out. There are plenty of charities you can donate the less personal items to. Maybe you can remodel the room for a different purpose?"

"Maybe," I murmur, knowing she's right but unable to contemplate even stepping foot in the room, let alone clearing it out.

"You should do the same with Reeve's things," she quietly adds. "I can help you pack up his stuff before I go." Audrey is leaving to return to Boston in two days, and I'm trying not to think about how broken I will be without her.

"I don't want to give his things away," I say, climbing to my feet. Audrey stands, and I close the nursery door, heading toward my bedroom. "I'm not ready."

"Okay." She tugs on my arm as I open my door. "But promise me you won't put it off indefinitely. It's not healthy to cling to him, Viv. I know it will hurt." Tears fill her eyes. "But it's got to be done." She glances over my head where my little boy is sleeping soundly in bed, occupying Reeve's vacant space. "And E needs to return to his own room. I know he comforts you and vice versa, but he can't replace Reeve, and you can't become his crutch. He needs to process his feelings, even if he can't put a name to them. You can't shield him from that."

"He's doing much better," I say, my tone more than a little defensive.

"All the more reason to get him to sleep in his own bed. Kids deal with things differently, and he takes a lot of his cues from you. I know you needed one another at the start, but it's time, Viv."

"Goodnight, Audrey." It takes mammoth willpower not to slam the door in my bestie's face. As I climb under the comforter and curl my body around my son's sleeping frame, I know she is right. Like I know she only has both of our best interests at heart, but having Easton sleep beside me helps to lessen the pain. Is it wrong to draw comfort from that?

"Can we talk when you get back?" Audrey asks the next morning as I'm getting ready to drive Easton to camp.

"Sure." My tone is a little cold, and I want to slap myself upside the head for being like this with my bestie, but my emotions appear to be ruling me, not the other way around.

"I don't want to fight with you, and the things I said last night weren't said to hurt you." Her sad eyes drill through my frosty outer layer, and I thaw instantly.

I pull her into a gentle hug. "I know, and I'm sorry. I don't want to be reacting like this, but it's so hard to think about moving on even though I want to and I need to." I ease back. "You're my best friend, Audrey. I could not have gotten through these last few weeks without you. Thank you for everything, and I'm going to try."

"You're strong, Viv. You know you can do this. As much as I hate leaving you, I think it's time. You need to fight to push through to the next level. You need to learn to start living again." Easton comes bounding into the room with his little backpack on his back. "For both your sakes."

She crouches down, doing a high-five with Easton before hugging him. "Have a great day, little man. I want to hear all about it when you come back."

"We're going hiking today," Easton confirms with an excited gleam in his eyes. "Mommy bought me hiking boots. Look." He lifts his leg, almost kicking her in the face.

Audrey chuckles, straightening up. "They are awesome boots. Have fun."

"Bye, Auntie Audrey." E waves as he clutches my hand with his other hand, dragging me out of the kitchen.

"Can Megan come over to my house after camp today?" Easton asks as I pull into the parking lot. He hasn't stopped talking the whole journey, and it's good to see him so excited. The familiar black SUV rolls into the space beside me. Leon and Bobby climb out of the car, wearing jeans and T-shirts, looking awkward as fuck. Turning up every day with our bodyguards looking like something from *Men in Black* was drawing way too much attention, so I asked the guys to dress casually so we can attempt to fit in. "Mommy? Can she?" he asks when I haven't replied.

"I don't know Megan's mommy, so I'll have to check. She can't come over today, but maybe one day next week."

"Mom!" My son fixes me with puppy-dog eyes through the mirror, and it's so hard to deny him, but I won't let anyone near my house until they've been carefully vetted. I don't trust any strangers who come into our lives. I hate I have to be like this, but I won't take chances with my son's safety. While there haven't been any other incidents of kids taunting Easton, I'm not naïve enough to believe it's gone away. I know people are gossiping and whispering behind my back. A couple of the moms say hello to me in the mornings, but most just stare, saying God knows what when I'm gone. I don't give a flying fuck as long as E is protected.

I overheard Audrey talking to Mom on the phone this week, and I know I've received some hate mail from that crazy element of Reeve's fanbase. They blame me for letting Reeve get behind the wheel when he'd been drinking, and they're mad he risked his life to save mine. Yet they are hailing him as a hero at the same time. Apparently, it's all my fault he's dead and I should have been the one to die with my baby daughter.

Stupid whores.

"When can she come over? I'm bored at home." E's pouty face pulls me away from the dark thoughts in my head.

"I said I'll talk to her mother. I can ask Nash's mom if he wants to come over for a playdate today?"

"He's got his cousin's party," he grumpily replies.

"Well, how about I call up some of your other friends from school and ask them to come over? I can get a bounce house and McDonald's, and you can have a spontaneous summer party?"

"Yay!" He jumps up, crawling through the gap in the front seat to hug me. "You're the best mommy ever. Thank you."

Crisis averted. For now. "Come on, buster. Let's get you into the hall before you're late for rollcall." I open my door, and Leon grabs Easton, while Bobby retrieves his backpack from the backseat.

Leon leads the way through the parking lot, heading toward the front entrance to the large redbrick building, as Bobby guards us from the rear. We have just reached the bottom of the steps when I'm jostled from behind. Screams ring out, and I almost take a tumble when Bobby staggers into me from behind. It all happens so fast, but I react immediately, thrusting Easton at Leon, aware there's some threat.

Blood rushes to my head, and adrenaline floods my veins as I spot someone tall in a hoodie racing toward me out of the corner of my eye. The next thing I know, I'm sprawled on top of Bobby on the ground with another body covering me. Piercing screams and shouts surround me, and whoever is on top of me jerks, grunting as if in pain.

"Are you okay?" Bobby asks, frowning as he eyes the stranger on top of me.

"I'm unhurt but struggling to breathe," I admit as the weight of the man covering me crushes me on top of my bodyguard. "Are you okay? Are you hurt?" I rasp.

"I might have a few bruises, but I'm fine. I'm sorry, Vivien. They caught me off guard, shoving me from behind."

Whoever is on top of me shifts a little, but they are making no move to get off me, which means the threat must still be present. I'm conscious of being pressed between two men, and there are various camera flashes going off.

There are always a few paps waiting at camp each day, hoping for something like this. Honestly, I wouldn't altogether rule out them setting this up just to get a story. Interest had grown in the initial aftermath of the interview Dillon gave confirming he was Reeve's long-lost twin. Reporters chased me for quotes, but I remained tight-lipped and the interest leveled off pretty quick. According to the text I received from Ash, the media is hounding Dillon for more information, so he has deflected some of the heat away from us.

"Shit, man," Leon says from above me. "Did that crazy bitch hurt you?"

The weight is lifted off me, and air whooshes out of my mouth as the sounds of a scuffle ring out in proximity.

"Let me go, asshole!" a woman with a high-pitched voice says. "I'm not the one you should be holding! Arrest *her*!"

Leon helps me to my feet while my mysterious rescuer bows his head, bending over at the waist and breathing heavily. I whip my head around, relieved to find Easton safe, with one of his instructors, at the top of the steps. He's crying, and I want to go to him, but I need to find out what's going on first. I need to ensure the threat has been neutralized. I blow him a kiss before turning around, hoping to reassure him with a smile.

Two camp security officers are restraining a skinny blonde with long stringy hair. She's thrashing about, trying to get free while snarling at me. "You fucking murdering bitch!" she shrieks. "Reeve should never have married you. You got him killed! He should've married Saffron, but you stole him away from her." Spittle lands on the asphalt beside me, and I fold my arms around my body, schooling my features into a neutral line, even though I want to take out her jugular.

Three photographers draw closer, taking pics, and I refuse to give them anything juicy to report.

"Fuck off," a man with a familiar Irish accent says from beside me, and I jerk my head around to Dillon, attempting to disguise my shock. The photographers are trigger-happy, snapping more pics as Dillon takes a step toward them. "I said fuck off," he snarls, yanking the camera from one of the men. He throws it to the ground and stomps on it.

Well, shit. I guess that's one way of dealing with it.

"I'll sue your ass!" the photographer yells, grabbing Dillon by the scruff of the neck. He must be a rookie because no experienced pap would lay hands on a celeb in this situation. He's just ruined any opportunity he might have had to take legal action against Dillon.

Good. We don't need any more freaking drama.

The hood of Dillon's gray hoodie falls, and I barely manage to stifle my shocked gasp. I didn't realize he had dyed his hair again, and it takes me back in time. Messy white-blond strands fall over Dillon's brow as he shoves the guy away.

"Dillon, look here!" the second photographer says as sirens blare in the background. These idiots clearly have no sense of self-preservation. Dillon stalks toward him, leaning a little awkwardly on his left side and I spot the tiny trail of blood he leaves in his wake.

Oh my God. He's injured.

Panic bites me in the face. "Get Easton," I tell Bobby. "We're leaving." I face Leon. "We need to get out of here before more paparazzi arrive. Can you handle the police? Tell them we want to press charges against her. Send them to the house, and we can give statements there. And can you talk to the camp coordinator too?"

He nods once. "I've got this. Don't worry," Leon adds before following Bobby back up the steps.

The woman is still hurling obscenities at me, but I tune her out as I advance on Dillon before he does something that will land us in even more hot water.

"You lot are fucking scumbags," he says to the second photographer. Dillon is in his face, pushing him back, but the photographer is still snapping away while retreating. His camera is on a strap around his neck that is fixed to the top of his shirt so Dillon can't rip it away as easily as the last one. "Can't you leave them alone? Give them some fucking privacy."

"Dil." I reach for his shoulder, and he winces, cursing out loud. My fingers are coated in blood, and I freeze, instantly taken back to the scene of our accident. I'm shaking all over as I stand rooted to the spot, the sounds of approaching sirens doing nothing to drown out the screaming in my head.

Dillon is saying something to me, but I can't hear him. I'm locked in my head, fighting an intense bout of panic as I'm trapped between the present and the past. Reeve's lifeless form resurfaces in my mind's eye, except this time it's Dillon's face staring at me.

Dillon is hurt.

He's bleeding.

He could be dying.

That crazy bitch did something to him.

I don't remember hearing any gunshots, but it all happened so fast.

Blood trickles from my fingers down my arm, and I stare in a horrified daze at it.

No! Oh my God, no! My heart pounds painfully behind my rib cage at the thought of something happening to Dillon as well. I offer up silent prayers to a God I no longer believe in, begging him to let Dillon be okay.

The overriding thought ping-ponging around my frantic brain is I can't lose him too.

CHAPTER 22

VIVIEN

DILLON CARRIES me to my SUV, ignoring his pain, to get me away from the vultures. We arrive at my car as Bobby is strapping a sobbing Easton into his seat. "No!" I protest when Dillon places me in the back seat. "I need to drive."

"You are in no condition to drive, Mrs. Lancaster," Bobby says, sliding behind the wheel. "Climb in the back with Mr. O'Donoghue. You need to check his injury to see how bad it is. I can drop you and Easton at home before taking him to the hospital."

"I don't need a hospital," Dillon says, helping me into the car beside E. He climbs in after me and shuts the door, gritting his teeth as a glimmer of pain races across his face. "She stabbed me, but I don't think it's deep," he adds in a lower voice so Easton doesn't hear.

I want to run back and gut the bitch.

"Are you sure?" I ask, swallowing painfully.

He nods. "It's not serious." His eyes skate past me, to Easton, and his features soften as he drinks him in.

Bobby reverses the car out of the space and heads out of the parking lot.

"Are you okay, sweetie?" I ask my son, examining his face and his body to reassure myself he is unharmed.

He nods. "Are you?" His brow scrunches up as his worried eyes meet mine.

"I'm totally fine." Thanks to Dillon's quick thinking. Gratitude wraps around me, even if I would like to know what the hell he was doing here.

"Can I go back to camp?" he asks after giving me a quick once-over.

"Not today." My heart could not take that. "But if everything is okay, you can return tomorrow." I want reassurances from our security team and the camp officials before I'm letting Easton step anywhere near that place.

"But what about my hike?!" His lower lip wobbles as he pouts. He thrusts his leg out. "I want to try my new hiking boots."

"I'm sorry, sweetie." I rub my throbbing temples. "I know you're disappointed, but I'm sure there will be more hikes."

"It's not fair," he wails, balling his hands into fists. "I want to go back!" Tears well in his eyes, and I hate upsetting him, but this is nonnegotiable.

"It's not safe, and I'm not arguing with you about this. I'm the grown-up, and it's my decision."

Easton opens his mouth to protest some more, but Dillon cuts in, stopping whatever he was about to say. "Hey, Easton." Dillon leans forward, smiling at his son. "Do you like yo-yos?"

Easton's tears dry as Dillon produces a red, black, and gold yo-yo from his pocket. It has the Collateral Damage logo on the side, so it must be official band merch. Dillon's hopeful expression does something to me, and guilt mixes with panic, swooping down and pummeling me from all sides. After cleaning my hands with a tissue, I smooth the front of my summer dress as a familiar fluttery feeling invades my chest. E's brow puckers as he looks between me and Dillon, and I try to focus on my son and not the blossoming panic attack I'm fighting to keep under control. Easton gets real upset when I have an anxiety attack, and I try to avoid him seeing me like this.

"This is your Uncle Dillon," I say, almost choking on the words. "Remember you met him once before?"

"You look different," Easton says, still frowning.

"I like to change up my look." Dillon's Adam's apple bobs in his throat as he stares in amazement at his son. Tiny pinpricks stab me all over my chest. It's a bittersweet moment—watching Dillon engage with his son and feeling immense pain for all Reeve has lost.

Easton looks deep in thought as he reaches out, taking the yo-yo from Dillon's hand, effectively distracted. He traces the logo on the side with his finger. "What does this say?" he asks, the words too difficult for him to read.

"It says Collateral Damage," I explain.

"It's the name of my band," Dillon adds, leaning against the side of the door, while maintaining eye contact with E.

Bile swirls in my stomach as I spot the growing bloodstain on the upper left-hand side of his gray hoodie.

"You're in a band?! That's so cool." Easton's eyes are the size of saucers as he attempts to roll the yo-yo while staring at Dillon with newfound respect. "Do you play guitar or the drums?"

"Guitar," Dillon says, beaming at his son. "My brother Ronan is in the band too. He plays the drums."

I shoot daggers at Dillon. Opening this line of questioning will only lead to trouble. He needs to tread carefully.

"Is Ronan my daddy's brother too?" Easton asks, looking confused, and this is exactly what I hoped to avoid. Reeve had explained who Dillon is to Easton, telling him he grew up in Ireland with his adopted family, but I'm not sure he fully understands the implications.

Dillon shoots me an apologetic look that seems sincere. "No. Ronan is my adopted brother, and he's an awesome drummer. I bet he'd let you play his drum kit some time."

Easton drops the yo-yo in his excitement, bouncing in his booster seat. "Can I Mom? Puh-lease."

Wow, Dillon is pretty much a master of distraction techniques. Not that it should surprise me. This is what he does best. My lingering guilt poofs into thin air. "Sure thing, buddy. We can arrange something later in the summer, when camp is finished." That seems to appease him. I pull out my cell as I reach for the yo-yo, handing it back to Easton.

"I can show you how to roll it," Dillon says, watching Easton struggle with the toy. "It's all in the wrist action." I tap out a message to Audrey so she knows we are on the way and that Dillon needs medical attention.

"Cool." Easton eyes Dillon curiously as the yo-yo lands on the floor again. "What songs do you sing?" he asks, seemingly more interested in the band than the yo-yo.

"Mainly rock songs. You want to hear one?"

Acid crawls up my gut, and I draw a deep breath in preparation.

"Yes! Yes!"

Dillon's smile is so wide it threatens to split his face in two, and I hate how endearingly sweet it is. Then I feel like a bitch because I should be pleased they are bonding so naturally. Dillon hooks his cell up to Easton's iPad on the back of the seat, and a few seconds later, the opening notes of a familiar song start up. My eyes meet Dillon's green gaze as my heart dances wildly in my chest.

Of course, he'd pick this song—the very first one he wrote for me.

I suppose "Terrify Me" is a better choice than "Hollywood Ho" or "Fuck Love." I should probably be grateful for small mercies, but it's hard when it's resurrecting so many perfect moments. Moments I've refused to remember since Dillon reappeared in our lives because they all seemed so tarnished.

As we stare at one another, I'm transported back in time to Shane and Fiona's wedding, where Dillon serenaded me from the stage with so much love and longing on his face there was no mistaking the genuine emotion.

I'm so confused. So conflicted. I don't want to feel the things I'm feeling right now. I prefer to hold on to my hate and my anger because it's far easier than admitting the truth.

Dillon brushes an errant tear from my eye as his soulful voice floods the car. "It's still my favorite song to sing," he whispers in my ear, sending delicious shivers racing up and down my spine. "Every time I sing it, no matter what part of the world I'm in, I'm always singing it for you. I'm always remembering how you looked at the wedding when I sang it for the first time."

Tears clog the back of my throat as his husky voice wraps around me, offering comfort if I want to reach for it. Thankfully, my son comes to the rescue before I'm tempted.

"I know this song!" He jumps around in his seat. "My mommy has this song on her phone!"

My eyes swivel to my son's. How on earth does he know that? I was always careful to hide my semi-obsession with Collateral Damage from my husband and my son.

"She does, huh?" Dillon asks, and I hear the smile in his tone.

"I should check your wound!" I blurt, desperately needing to divert this conversation. "Audrey says she can tend to it provided it's not too deep."

"It's a flesh wound at most," he says, smirking that annoying smirk I've always loved to hate. Of course, he knows I'm deflecting.

"It seems to be bleeding a lot," I murmur, not wanting to alarm E.

"A knife in the back tends to do that."

"Don't make light of it. It freaked me out seeing it."

His humorous expression alters in a heartbeat. "I know." He tucks a piece of my hair behind my ear, brushing my cheekbone in the process, and I hate how my body yearns to lean into him. I can't forget all the ways Dillon has hurt me and Reeve. I don't know if I'll ever be able to forgive him for it. "Are you okay?"

"I should be asking you that." My eyes latch on to his familiar green gaze. I wonder why he's reverted to his previous look. Is it to divert attention from his resemblance to Reeve, or is there some part of him that hopes I might remember what we once shared if he looks the same? Or is he merely returning to what's more comfortable? The look his fans fell in love with?

"I'm fine. Nothing some stitches and a few painkillers won't cure, I'm sure."

"Thank you," I say as Easton sings along with the song, guessing the words. "Thank you for saving me back there."

"I would jump in front of a crazy bitch every day to save you if you'd give me the chance."

"Do I want to know why you were there?"

He shrugs, moving his mouth to my ear again. His warm breath wafts over my flesh, sending a fresh wave of shivers cascading over my skin. "You won't let me see him, so I've been showing up every morning at camp just to catch a glimpse."

That's borderline stalking, but I don't blame him. I have left him no choice. In this moment, I feel like I've been very unfair to Dillon. In my defense, I did it to protect Easton, but he's turned a corner these past two weeks, and I can't continue to refuse Dillon. Look how they've already bonded, and I can't deny my son the opportunity to get to know his father. That doesn't mean I'm going to let Dillon off the hook that easy. "You really don't understand the word no."

"That surprises you?" he asks, keeping his face close to mine.

"Not really." I sigh in relief as we turn into our driveway. I managed to survive a journey with someone else behind the wheel, and I successfully fought an anxiety attack. Perhaps there is hope for me after all.

"I'm the same irritating impatient asshole you hated to love in Ireland." His eyes sparkle as he teases me, and it would be as easy as breathing to fall back into his arms. Except there are too many secrets and lies between us, too much hurt and pain, and I don't know if I'll ever be able to overcome them.

Besides, starting anything with Dillon again would be the ultimate betrayal to Reeve. Dillon needs to be back in my life, but his place in it is clearly defined. He is Easton's father, and we will be coparents.

That is all he will be to me.

"Things are different now," I say as Bobby pulls the car to a stop outside our front door. "I'm different, and no matter how much we both might want to turn back the clock, we don't have a time machine. You'd do well to remember that."

CHAPTER 23
VIVIEN

"FUCK, THAT STINGS," Dillon hisses as he lies on his stomach on the couch in our formal living room while Audrey tends to his injury.

"Stop being such a baby. I'm only cleaning the wound."

I've watched silently as Audrey helped him to remove his hoodie and shirt and lie down, saying nothing as my heart ached at the sight of the scorpion tattoo on his back. Dillon told me once it signified determination, rebirth, and resilience. Now I know the missing pieces of the puzzle, it makes so much sense.

Without thinking, my fingers trail over the edge of the design while Audrey threads the needle, ready to stitch him up. She doesn't have any local anesthetic and Dillon refused alcohol, so this will hurt like a bitch. Perhaps I can distract him. "Did you know if you are born under the totem of a scorpion in Native American spirituality, it means you are defensive? That you should be wary of threats and protect yourself from them with speed and stealth and always strike first. After I learned that about scorpions, I thought it interesting you would choose to ink yourself with one."

"You googled my tattoo?" he asks, in between clenching his jaw. "That sounds very stalkerish."

I roll my eyes as Audrey concentrates on his back, holding his skin together with one hand while she stitches with the other. "Don't get a big head. You know your tattoos intrigued me. Did you know what it represented when you chose it?"

"Of course, I did. Why else would I pick a scorpion? Ah, fuck." He squeezes his eyes closed and bites down on his lip.

"I'm almost done, and you're doing great," Audrey says.

"Yay! Do I get a lollipop when you're finished?"

"It's not advisable to tease the doctor when she's currently got a sharp needle pressed against your skin," I warn. "And stop deflecting. That ink is the physical manifestation of your vengeance plan. Isn't it?"

"Every time I'd look at it in the mirror," he pants, grinding his teeth to the molars. "It would remind me I needed to strike back. That no one else would protect me if I didn't protect myself."

Audrey and I exchange sad expressions as she sets the needle down. Dillon has been cruel and heartless and done a lot to hurt me. There is no excusing that. But there is no denying how he was grievously wronged and how much his life has been shaped by Simon's abandonment of him. No child deserves that. So much of the enigma that is Dillon makes more sense to me now I have all the facts.

"I just need to give you a tetanus shot, and then we're done," Audrey explains.

Outside in the hallway, I hear Easton arguing with Angela. I told his nanny to keep him out of here, because I don't want him seeing Dillon's injury. Thankfully, he didn't see him getting stabbed back at camp. That reminds me I promised him he could have some school friends over this afternoon. It will help to ease the disappointment of missing his hike. I make a call to the guy who usually supplies us with bounce houses, offering him double if he'll come over ASAP and set one up.

"You're throwing a party?" Dillon asks, wincing as he sits up straighter. Audrey is packing her supplies away in her medical bag.

I avoid looking at his broad chest and ripped abs because he hasn't lost an inch of his hotness and I don't need to be reminded of it right now. Audrey has no such qualms, staring at his body like he was chiseled from marble by Michelangelo.

"I promised Easton he could have some friends over this afternoon."

"Can I stay?" he asks, and I lift my eyes to his pleading ones. My chest inflates and deflates as I contemplate what to do. "Please," he whispers, and I can't deny him after he threw himself in front of a crazy Reeveron fan for me.

"Okay, but you're here as his uncle, and that's the way it's got to be for now."

"That's not a problem." He darts in, planting a kiss on my cheek. "Thank you. I promise you won't regret it." He flashes me a giddy smile, and my heart jumps.

"Famous last words, Dil. *Don't* make me regret it."

"So, have you decided to let him in?" Audrey asks a while later as we prepare snacks in the kitchen for Easton's incoming guests. The police have come and gone, confirming they have the crazy bitch in custody. I will sleep easier tonight knowing that. I glance out the window, needing eyes on Easton to reassure myself he's okay. I can see Dillon and E in the near distance from here. Dillon is showing him how to spin the yo-yo, demonstrating more patience than I thought he possessed, and Easton is hanging off his every word. It's fair to say my son has been enthralled by him from the second he climbed into our car.

"Yes, but it will be baby steps. I need to ensure Dillon understands that."

"I think you're making the right decision." She dumps chips into a bowl as I finish slicing the apples.

"You do? I thought you were anti-Dillon."

"I'm anti anything that hurts you or my godson." She pops a chip in her mouth while tossing the empty bags in the trash. I wash my hands in the sink while we both stare out the window at father and son. It brings a massive lump to my throat to see them together. "I'm not saying I've forgiven him, because he has pulled some terrible shit, but I believe he deserves a chance. If not for him, for Easton."

I pour two glasses of wine because I have a feeling I will need some alcoholic courage today. "I've been trying not to think about him," I admit, watching him race Easton toward the playground. Dillon is wearing one of Reeve's shirts because his own clothing is covered in blood. Giving it to him was awkward in the extreme, for both of us, but it's not like any of my shirts or E's would fit him. "Seeing him in Reeve's shirt even feels like a betrayal."

"Don't do that." She takes one of the wineglasses from me. "You aren't betraying Reeve's memory by having him here. It's a messy situation, but it was something none of you knew. Don't feel guilty for letting him into Easton's life. It's the right thing to do."

"There have been so many secrets and lies, and I'm tired of letting them dictate my life, but how do I forgive him, Rey? How can I ever trust him or believe a word that comes out of his mouth?"

She tilts her head to the side, sipping her wine as she surveys me. "There is no doubt he needs to earn back your trust, and you're right to be guarded, but answer me one thing. How much was keeping him away to do with Easton, and how much was it because you were terrified to be around him again?"

"Honestly, it was all Easton up until that meeting at his house two weeks ago. Before then, I was too consumed in grief and anger to even remember the other feelings I had for him."

"And now?" she prompts.

I glance out the window. His blond hair is blowing in the subtle breeze as he pushes Easton on one of the swings, and it makes me nostalgic. One of my favorite things to do was run my fingers through his hair. Seeing him like this reminds me of the Dillon I fell head over heels in love with. I stare out the window, hugely conflicted. They are both laughing, and pain spreads across my chest for a multitude of reasons. "I am terrified."

"You still love him." She says it as a statement, not a question.

"How can I after what he did?" I'm speaking to myself as much as to my friend.

"He loves you. You only have to see the way he looks at you to know what's in his heart, and you have loved him in silence for years."

"It was so wrong," I whisper, turning away, unable to look at Dillon any longer.

"You can't help how you feel. You loved Reeve, and you made each other happy. But he's not here, and Dillon is. It's okay to love him, Viv."

"Jesus, Rey." I swing angry eyes on my best friend. "Reeve is barely cold in his grave, and you're already pushing me at his twin?"

"You know I'm not saying that." She places her wine down and fixes me with a serious look. "I know you. I know what you're going to do. You're going to bury the feelings you have for that man"—she jabs her finger toward Dillon—"out of guilt and fear, and I don't want you to do that. It's a different matter entirely if you don't love him anymore, but the kind of feelings you had for him don't disappear overnight, no matter how much he might have wronged you."

I gulp my wine, wishing we had never started this conversation.

Audrey's shoulders relax a smidgeon. "Look, babe, I'm not arguing with you, and

I'm not saying you should throw yourself back into something with Dillon. I know you're not ready to move on yet. I'm just saying don't close your mind to it and it's okay if that's where you end up. You have nothing to feel guilty or ashamed about. Reeve would want you happy."

I snort out a laugh. "I doubt he'd want me falling into his twin's arms."

"I wouldn't be so sure. Reeve knew you loved him. Yes, he didn't know it was Dillon or that Dillon was his twin, until more recently, but he knew you deeply loved your Irish boyfriend." She takes a sip of her drink. "I know Simon Lancaster was a bastard, and I hope he's rotting in hell, but you can't deny his twin sons share similar characteristics."

"In what way?" I prop my hip against the edge of the sink, waving through the window at Dave as he arrives to set up the bounce house.

"For starters, they share a manipulative streak." She drills me with a look. "You can't deny Reeve had his moments."

I nod because she's right. Reeve manipulated my feelings and used my fear and guilt against me during the time he filmed the *Rydeville Elite* movies and during our breakup. Now I know about the PI in Ireland and the photographer he spent years working with to stage photos, I can't help wondering how he might have manipulated me during our marriage in a bid to keep me sheltered from that side of his personality. I guess I'll never know because all his secrets have been taken to the grave with him.

"And all the Lancaster men are hardwired to only love once. It's an intense soul mate kind of love. Like swans. You're it for Dillon in the same way you were it for Reeve."

"You are assuming Dillon loves me because he loved me once, but we've been apart six years. A lot can happen in that time. You don't know he hasn't fallen in love with someone else."

She waves her hands in the air. "He's told you he still loves you on more than one occasion. He told your parents he loves you and regrets not fighting for you. He's not hiding his feelings. As for the other women he's been pictured with over the years? Come on. We both know they were nothing more than fuck buddies. He's never been pictured with the same woman more than once. If he was in love with anyone else, you'd know about it." Her tongue darts out, wetting her lips in an obvious tell. "You can always ask Ash. You know she'll give it to you straight."

"What did you do?"

"I invited her over. She's on her way. Don't be mad."

"I'm not. I want to repair my relationship with her, but I couldn't do that while I was keeping Dillon at arm's length because it would always be the elephant in the room."

"Good. I'm glad. I have spoken with her a few times. She wants to be here for you, and I would feel so much better knowing you have her back in your life. It will help me to not worry so much about you."

"I want Ash back in my life, but I'm scared too because it's going to dredge so many old memories and feelings to the surface, and I'm not sure I can handle it." Ash and I go way beyond her brother, and we have our memories separate from Dillon, but there's a lot of memories that are tangled too. It's hard to completely separate them, but I'm going to try because I need to make things right with my Irish bestie.

"Better out than in, babe, and Ash won't push you. She'll help to rein Dillon in."

"I'm not sure anyone is capable of reining that man in," I say, looking out the window again.

Easton is tugging on Dillon's hand as he talks to Dave while a couple of younger guys work on inflating the bounce house. Dillon swoops Easton up into his arms, which has got to hurt with his sore upper back, but the obvious joy on his face makes it clear any pain is worth it. Easton is animated in a way I haven't seen for weeks. I can't tell what he's saying, but his cute little mouth is working overtime as he tells Dillon something.

Memories resurface in my mind, and I remember how Dillon coaxed me back to life at one time. Dillon is a lot of things, but there's no denying he has this way of embracing life that is magical, and it's this part of his personality that really draws people in. "I'm not sure we should even try," I murmur.

Everything is about to change again, and I hope I'm making the right decision.

CHAPTER 24
DILLON

"MOMMY! Uncle Dillon has a surprise for me!" Easton yells the second we step foot into Viv's house on Friday afternoon. This past month has been heaven and hell. Heaven because I get to collect Easton from camp every Friday and spend the rest of the day with him and Viv. Hell because the six other days when I don't see them feels like six years.

East has instantly burrowed his way into my heart, earning a permanent place there. He is a breath of fresh air, and he has brightened up my world immensely. He takes so much joy in things, and I love that he loves the outdoors like me.

Not that he gets much of a chance to do stuff.

Viv is uberprotective, to the point I'm starting to worry. Apart from camp, she won't let East out of her sight, and they spend all their time cooped up at the house. I know it's not a chore. The place is frigging huge, and East doesn't want for a single thing. He has a pool, a treehouse, a massive playground and obstacle course, and an indoor playroom with every toy, activity, and game imaginable.

Viv fills his afternoons with playdates and activities so he's never bored, but I can tell he's feeling caged, and I'm wondering how to tackle it with his mum. I've considered calling Audrey to ask her if Viv is always this protective, but those two are thick as thieves, and I can't risk Audrey telling Viv. I'm treading on eggshells here, terrified if I do or say the wrong thing that Viv will change her mind and freeze me out again.

"He does, huh?" Viv says, appearing at the end of the hallway. Relief floods her features as her gaze roams her son, checking to ensure he's okay. Easton races toward her as she crouches down, opening her arms. He throws himself at her, hugging her close, and my heart does this twisty thing it always does every time I see them together.

She is such a good mother, always putting his needs before her own, spending hours playing with him or reading to him, and she ensures he eats well and he sticks to a daily routine that gives him comfort and structure. In a lot of ways, she reminds me of my ma, but in others, she is totally different.

Ma had a bunch of kids at home and a farm to run, so our routine was a lot less rigid, our house a lot more chaotic. I have always loved my parents, especially because they took me in and treated me as one of their own from the very start. But as I've grown older, I've developed a greater appreciation for them, especially Mum.

"Can I see it now?" East asks as I approach, bouncing from foot to foot. I chuckle, ruffling his hair. Intermittent blond strands lighten his brown hair, thanks to hours spent outdoors this summer. I can't believe it's the beginning of August already, and there is only five months left before we head out on tour. I have no clue how I am going to leave them behind. Even if Viv is still keeping me at a distance and there is no evidence of her thawing toward me at all.

Viv straightens up, smiling softly. "Everything was okay?" she asks, like usual.

"Everything was fine." I understand her concern, to a certain extent. After that crazy bitch came at her with a knife, the camp organizers asked Viv not to escort Easton anymore. They can't risk another incident, as it places all the kids in danger, so Viv had no choice but to reluctantly agree. Now, she drives Easton there and waits in the car while Leon or Bobby takes him inside.

Of course, the press went to town after the attack, and it dredged everything up again just as it had started settling down. Hate mail has doubled at the fan club, but Margaret Andre keeps it well away from Vivien. I have spoken to her and asked her to let me know if there are any serious threats made.

It seems crazy attracts crazy and that portion of Reeve's fanbase who never approved of Viv are more vocal online. It's ridiculous they are blaming her for the accident, and if I see one more post calling Vivien a murderer, I will lose my shit.

Ash changed the password on all my social media accounts after I started retaliating because fuck that crap. Does she really expect me to not say something when assholes are spewing poison at the woman I love? And don't even get me started on those lingering Saffhards.

Saffron Roberts is a junkie nobody these days, but she appears to have a core following who still think she's the bomb. They are loving a new opportunity to throw shit at Viv, and I couldn't not respond.

Until Ash put a stop to it, and now I'm banned from all my accounts. She has the band PA responding *appropriately*—her words, not mine—and I've just had to suck it up.

East tugs on my leg. "Uncle Dillon. Puh-leassssee can I have my surprise now?"

I bend down, tweaking his nose. "I wonder where you got your impatience from, hmm?" I flash him a smile, pretending I don't see the troubled expression on Viv's face. I know this is hard for her, but it still upsets me to know she's conflicted over my growing relationship with our son.

Ignoring the painful ache in my chest, I tell East to wait for me in the playroom while I run back out to my Land Rover to grab the small guitar case from the boot. I pull my weathered case out too and head back inside.

Easton is coloring at his desk in the playroom when I arrive. Viv is seated in the large high-backed velvet chair by the window, scribbling away in her journal. I have noticed her doing that a lot recently, and it brings a lump to my throat. She used to journal a lot in Ireland, at the outset of our relationship, and I know it was a suggestion from her therapist. I'm wondering if her current therapist suggested the same thing. If this is her way of coping. Of remembering Reeve and her little baby.

East swivels on his chair, and his eyes almost bug out of their sockets when he sees what I'm carrying. "Mommy!" he shouts, his chair screeching as he shoves it back. "Uncle Dillon got me a guitar!"

Vivien sets her journal down, lifting her head up. "I can see that." My shoulders relax at her genuine smile. I was a little worried how she might respond to this, but I didn't ask her in advance because I didn't want to give her an opportunity to say no.

"I thought you might like to learn how to play. I was five when I first started. I thought I could teach you."

"Yay!" He rushes me, clinging to my leg, and I stumble a little. "You're the best uncle in the whole wide world."

Fuck. This little fella kills me in the best possible way. He loves so freely and openly, and my heart is overjoyed at being included in his inner circle. I can't wait for the day when he will, hopefully, call me Dad.

Tears swim in Viv's eyes as she watches us, and I'm guessing it's as emotional for her but for different reasons.

"Come sit on the sofa," I say, handing him his case. "Careful with that little beauty."

We sit side by side on the leather couch, and I show Easton how to unpack his guitar and how to hold it. Viv watches silently, and her gaze is like a warm blanket spreading over every inch of my body.

"You still have it." Her gaze rakes over the Fender she gave me as a leaving present.

"It's my most prized possession," I say, peering deep into her beautiful hazel eyes. Today they look more green than brown, and I can see the little gold flecks in her irises that always mesmerized me.

Viv is still the most beautiful woman I've ever seen. And so effortlessly stunning. Her hair hangs in thick glossy sheets down her back, and there isn't a scrap of makeup on her tan skin. She is even more exquisite as she grows older, and my fingers twitch with a craving to touch her. Being around her again and not being able to touch her is one of the greatest challenges I've ever faced.

Snapping out of my melancholy, I run my fingers over the DOD engraving. "I purposely don't use this on stage, keeping it for recording and personal use. I even kept the Toxic Gods strap until it snapped and had to be replaced. Ash had a Collateral Damage strap made for me then."

"What's Toxic Gods?" East asks.

"It was the first name of our band. We changed it when we came to America."

"Why?" he asks, strumming his fingers along the guitar strings.

"Because our record label didn't like the name and they asked us to pick something else."

"I always assumed Ash was responsible for your name change," Viv says. "I know she didn't like Toxic Gods."

My lips pull into a smirk. "My sister is full of shit. Despite her very vocal protests, she loved that name and fought harder than anyone to keep it."

"Uh-oh. That's another dollar in the cuss jar." Easton waggles his finger in my face before thrusting his palm out for the money.

"I'll be bankrupt before the year is out," I deadpan, removing a ten-dollar note from my wallet and slapping it into my son's little hand.

"It's one dollar per curse," Viv reminds me as Easton hops up to run to the shelf.

"I'm planning ahead. I'm sure my tally will be up to ten by the end of the day." I fight another smirk, and Viv rolls her eyes.

"The idea is to stop cursing, not to just hand over cash willy-nilly."

I snort. "Willy-nilly? Really."

"It's no joking matter, Dillon. E said fucking hell in front of my parents the other day. They were *not* impressed."

Well, shit. I don't need to give Viv's parents any more reasons to hate my guts. They returned home last week for a couple of months. Then they are off to Canada together to film another movie. To say Lauren Mills was cold towards me last Friday is an understatement. I'd receive warmer vibes from Jack Frost. Jonathon Mills was friendlier, but he's understandably still wary. "I'll try harder, but I really don't get why cursing is such a big deal. It's still part of the English language."

"It's uncouth," she says as I watch my son climb up on a chair to reach the shelf. He removes the lid from the jar, carefully placing my money inside.

"Wow, you're really throwing out some beauties today. You eat a dictionary for breakfast or something?"

She glances over my shoulder, to ensure East isn't looking, before flipping me the bird.

Laughter rumbles from my chest. "I think rude gestures should be counted as cursing too. I demand you place a dollar in the jar."

"Mommy." East reappears at my side, placing his hands on his hips. "Did you say a bad word?"

"I did nothing of the sort. Uncle Dillon is just stirring shit." She clamps a hand over her mouth, and her eyes pop wide as I chuckle.

East stomps over to his mum, thrusting his hand out. "Hand it over, Mom." He shakes his head, but his lips twitch at the corners. "Shocking behavior."

I burst out laughing. This kid. He's the fucking best.

"You are such a bad influence," Viv murmurs, giving me the evil eye as she hands her son a dollar from her purse.

I sit back on the couch, stretching my legs out as I place my Fender beside me. "Never pretended I wasn't, and there was a time you didn't mind being corrupted." Our last weekend together in Brittas Bay resurfaces in my mind, and I remember coaxing her into the freezing cold sea where I fucked her hard and fast before she climbed up my body and I ate her out with her legs hanging over my shoulders.

My dick *loves* that memory, hardening in record time. I adjust myself in my jeans before Easton returns and notices. Though it might be fun to see what kind of question he'd ask. He's an inquisitive little boy, curious about the world around him, and he's always asking questions.

Viv notices my boner, but she looks away, pretending she doesn't.

I spend an hour teaching East the basics of guitar playing while Viv writes in her journal. Every so often, she peers over at us with an emotional look on her face. After,

I take him out to the playground for a couple of hours before dinner. We eat and then I give him a bath. It's one of my favorite things to do. I'm drying him with a fluffy towel that's about three times his size when he asks if I'll tuck him into bed and read him a story. "Sure, buddy." I kiss the top of his head as I help him into his pajamas. "Let's just okay it with your mom first."

"Mommy!" Easton races into the living room in his oversized slippers with semi-dry hair. He's so excited he barely let me blow-dry it. "I want Uncle Dillon to read me a story and put me to bed."

Viv's eyes fill up, but she composes herself fast, tentatively smiling at her son. "Okay. If that's what you want."

Easton jumps into my arms, and I hold him close as he wraps his little arms and legs around me.

A tear slips out of the corner of Viv's eye, and I hate she's upset. I can guess why, and I wish I could comfort her, but she'd never let me.

I wonder if she ever will.

CHAPTER 25
DILLON

"ARE YOU COMFY?" I ask, sliding under the covers beside my son in his bed.

"Yep." He grins up at me, and his obvious happiness at my presence does wonders for my self-esteem.

"Do you have a book you're reading, or you want me to tell you a story?" I wrap my arm around his shoulders as he snuggles into me.

"Mommy is reading me *The Enormous Crocodile* by Roald Dahl. You can read me that." He sits up against the headrest. "But first I need to tell my daddy about my day." Easton takes the framed photo of Reeve off his bedside locker, propping it on his lap. "Mommy says Daddy and Lainey are together in heaven and they hear me when I speak to them, so I talk to them every night before bed," he explains. Then he proceeds to mention everything that happened at camp and how we spent our afternoon.

I listen with a tight pain stretched across my chest, keeping my arm around my son as he tells Reeve all about his day. Staring at my brother's photo as Easton talks is a sobering experience. Ash says I need to process my feelings instead of burying them deep inside, and I know she's right. But I'm a chickenshit because I keep putting it off. Listening to Easton telling his daddy about his day opens the wound in my heart that little bit wider, and I know I'm going to have to face up to it, sooner rather than later.

"Night, Daddy." Easton leans in, kissing Reeve's picture. "I miss you." The saddest expression appears on his face as he reverently places the frame back on his locker. Grabbing a pink teddy, shaped like a bunny, he cuddles it, whispering, "Night, Lainey."

Aw, hell. A messy ball of emotion clogs the back of my throat, and I wish I could take my son's pain away. Wiping the moisture from my cheeks, I hug him closer. "Ready for your story, buddy?"

"I'm ready." His voice is smaller, quieter, and I wonder exactly what is going through his mind. He snuggles into my side, and I could quite happily never get out of this bed.

"Let's lie back down," I suggest, grabbing the book from the top of his locker, and we both snuggle under the covers. He turns a little in my arms so he's facing me. His big blue eyes are so innocent and trusting as he looks at me. My heart swells with love for him. I may have only known the truth for eleven weeks and I have only been involved in his life this past month, but my feelings kicked in immediately. I loved Easton from the instant I met him. It's hard not to. He's the most adorable little boy. Sweet, smart, caring with a fun sense of humor and a good heart, just like his mum.

He is everything I could ever wish for in a son, and there is still so much to discover.

I read some of the book, and it doesn't take him long to fall asleep against my shoulder. I stare at him for ages, noting every inch of his beautiful face, committing it to memory. He looks so young and innocent, and I silently rage at a world that would hurt him so much. Losing his father this young will always be a shadow on his soul. He might not understand until he is older, but it *will* leave its mark. He lost his sister too, but it isn't the same. Losing Reeve will always hurt him, even if he has me in his life.

As conflicted as I am about my twin, I can't deny the role he played in my son's life or how grateful I am to Reeve for the way he loved him. Easton adores his daddy, and I would never take that away from him.

With military precision, I inch out of the bed slowly so I don't wake him. My heart is both heavy and light, my head swimming with thoughts as I step out of his bedroom, slowly easing the door over. I don't know if Viv shuts it all the way over or not, so I leave it open a little.

Turning around, I find Viv sitting on the carpeted floor, with her back to the wall, silently crying. Tears cascade down her cheeks as she stares up at me. She looks so small, so lost, so broken, and there's a desperate pleading in her eyes that pains me to see. It's as if she's silently begging me to take her pain away even while another part of her is determined to push me away and never let me back in. I can tell from her blotchy skin that she's been out here for a while.

Without speaking, I bend down and scoop her up, cradling her against my chest. Her arms wind around my neck without hesitation, and she leans into me, quietly sobbing as I head downstairs.

She doesn't say anything as I step into her comfortable living room, and I don't push her. It's pretty obvious why she's upset. I scan the room as I walk toward the plush sofas positioned in front of the open fireplace.

I much prefer this space to the more formal living room they use for guests. There are family photos in both rooms, but the framed pictures on the mantelpiece and covering one entire wall in this room are the true history of their time as a family. Unlike the more formal portraits in the other room.

It hurts seeing them, but I'm glad Vivien and Easton had love in their lives. There is no way anyone looking at these pictures could ignore how much Reeve Lancaster loved his family.

When I was with Viv in Ireland, she would tell me some things about him, and he sounded like a possessive control freak. It made me wonder whether he truly loved her or if it was what she represented. Being around this house this past month has made me realize, once and for all, I was wrong. He did love her. Maybe in the same way I do. It's clear she was anything but a trophy wife.

The instant I sit down on the sofa, Viv crawls off my lap, scurrying to the corner and tucking herself in, as far away from me as possible. Hurt crawls up my throat, but I push it aside, focusing on her, like Ash suggested. "Are you okay?"

She shrugs, rubbing at her eyes. "Depends on your definition of okay."

"I'm not trying to replace him," I reassure her because I know I'm the trigger. "And I don't like upsetting you. I hate seeing you crying."

"It's not your fault, and you haven't done anything wrong. Easton already adores you, and I'm happy about that. I am." It sounds like she's trying to convince herself as much as me. "It's just hard seeing you doing things Reeve did."

I nod, understanding what she means. I wonder if it will always be this hard. Will I always feel like I'm in his shadow? Will my presence in their lives always remind Viv of Reeve?

"Can I get you something to drink?" I ask, handing her the box of tissues from the small end table.

"White wine," she rasps.

"Do you mind if I grab a beer?"

She frowns. "I thought you didn't drink anymore?"

I run a hand through my hair, loving that it's getting longer again. I feel more like myself. "Contrary to popular belief, I'm not an alcoholic. My stint in rehab was more about clearing my head and processing some shit than drying out." I stand. "Why don't I get the drinks, and we can talk?"

I'm half expecting her to kick me out, like she usually does after Easton goes to bed on Friday nights. But she nods, and I don't stop to question it, hightailing it out of there before she changes her mind.

The kitchen is empty, because Friday night is Charlotte's night off, so I rummage around, grabbing crisps and chocolate from the overhead press because I'm feeling peckish and Viv can easily handle the calorific treats. She's thinner than ever from a combination of stress and a lack of appetite. I pour her a chilled glass of wine and grab a bottle of beer before heading back to the living room with our drinks and treats.

Viv is staring off into space, looking deep in thought, and I wish I could read minds because I would give anything to know what she's thinking. I dump the goodies on the coffee table and hand her the glass of wine. Although I want to cozy up to her, I stay down my end of the sofa, giving her space.

"I used to drink far too much," I start telling her as I pop the cap on my beer. "But it was a conscious decision to blot out all the crap in my head. I wasn't addicted in the sense I physically couldn't stop myself from drinking although I know using it as a crutch is almost as bad. It's why I purposely don't drink as much now. That and I'm trying to be healthier." I have a son who needs me now. A son who has already lost one father, and I am determined to be there for him in every sense of the word.

"What crap is in your head?" She tucks her knees into her chest while sipping her wine.

"I wasn't in a good place after you left. Things happened pretty fast when the

513

A&R scout came to see us in Dublin. I used the money I got from the NDA to relocate us to L.A. After we signed with the label, they booked us into Capitol Studios to work on our first album. I'd been writing furiously all year, and we had enough songs for two or three albums."

"Were they about me?" she blurts, and my heart melts when a familiar red stain blooms on both her cheeks. "'Hollywood Ho' and 'Fuck Love,'" she clarifies.

I nod. "I went through a lot of stages after I lost you. The first year I was heartbroken and drowning in pain and guilt and remorse, and that's when I wrote 'You are my Only Reason,' 'Queen of my Heart,' 'Broken Love,' and a whole load of other songs which went on to become bestsellers. By year two, I entered the next stage, and I was fucking pissed." I knock back a large mouthful of beer. "It started when I discovered you had gotten married and had a kid."

"Did you suspect he might be yours?"

"I was suspicious enough to google Easton's date of birth. I read a bunch of articles which all said his birthday was in June, so that was that." I stare off into space, remembering one of the hardest times of my life. "You and Reeve were plastered all over social media, and it seemed like he was in every fucking bestselling movie that year. I couldn't get away from either of you and it was killing me. I wrote 'Hollywood Ho' and 'Fuck Love' at the height of my rage and my depression when I hated you for what you did to me."

"I cried the first time I heard 'Hollywood Ho.' I knew it was about me, and I couldn't understand how you could hate me that much."

"There's a fine line between love and hate, Viv. I've heard that bandied about a lot, but it wasn't until I was in that situation that I could truly understand what it means." She opens her mouth to speak, but I shake my head to stall her. I'm not finished, and I need to get this all out. I lean forward, straining toward her. She drinks her wine, giving me her undivided attention, and while this stuff is tough to wade through, I wouldn't swap this moment for anything.

I have always loved just existing with her.

Vivien brings a sense of inner peace to my soul whenever I am around her, in a way no one else does.

CHAPTER 26
DILLON

"I NEED you to understand everything is about you," I explain. "Every lyric I have written from the moment I met you is all you. And there are far more love songs than hate songs, because even when I wanted to hate you, I couldn't. Writing songs was a way of bleeding my emotions, of venting my anger, but I never hated you. Not in the true sense of the word." I take another swig of my beer before I stare her straight in the eyes. "It was impossible when I was so completely in love with you. I didn't want to be, because you were with him, but my heart refused to be swayed."

"Why didn't you fight for me?" She pins me with glassy eyes. "I paced the terminal at Dublin Airport for hours, silently begging you to come and claim me. I waited until the very last minute to get on the plane, and you didn't come. You just let me go."

I shake my head, moving closer despite my earlier self-promise. I need to be closer to her when I admit this truth. "But I didn't, Viv. I came after you. I flew to L.A. to beg you to come back to Dublin with me."

Shock splays across her face, and her eyes pop wide. "What?" she splutters.

"I was going to get on my hands and knees and beg for forgiveness. I was going to lay it all out on the line. I was prepared to quit the band and stay with you in Dublin. I would have agreed to anything as long as you agreed to be mine."

Her brow creases in confusion. "I don't understand. How didn't I know this?"

I drink more beer, briefly squeezing my eyes shut. Even now, it hurts to relive this memory. "I arrived at my hotel in L.A. around two. You'd gotten in a few hours earlier. Ash gave me your US mobile number, and I tried it repeatedly, but it was either switched off or it had powered off."

"I'd forgotten to charge it," she explains. "I was too heartbroken on the plane to remember to do it. It died sometime after Reeve picked me up."

"I didn't want to leave a voice mail which might be misconstrued."

Confusion crosses her face. "It's so weird I never saw any missed calls."

I don't think it takes much to figure out what happened. "I'm guessing Reeve deleted them from the call log." He was determined to keep me away from her and obviously willing to do whatever it took to ensure she didn't come back to me.

"I can't believe he'd do that, but it's the only explanation that makes sense." She rubs at her temples. "If I had seen those calls, it might've changed everything."

I nod because there are so many things that could've ended up differently if we had all reacted differently. But there's no point dwelling on it now.

"What happened after that?" she asks.

"When I couldn't reach you, I turned on the TV to waste some time, and that's when I saw the coverage of you with him. I saw you together on the balcony. I knew you were naked. I knew what that meant. And I knew he was sending a message to me. It wasn't just the statement he gave to reporters. It was the way he used his arm to cover your tits, just like I'd done in the photo we sent him the day of your birthday. I know he was shielding you too, and maybe I'm reading too much into it, but I got the message loud and clear anyway."

Setting my bottle on the table, I bury my head in my hands. Pain slices across my chest, like it does every time I recall that image. It's forever imprinted on my brain, and I have wished so many times I could scrub it out. "How could you run straight back to him?" I lift my head, staring at her through stinging eyes. "You told me you didn't know where he was. Was that a lie?"

She vehemently shakes her head. "It was the truth. I had no idea he would show up to collect me from the airport. I'd had no contact with him since my birthday. All I knew, from Audrey and my parents, was he was working on stuff to make up for his mistakes. But no one told me what he was doing because Reeve wanted to explain it to me himself."

"But you slept with him." I scrub a hand over my prickly jawline as an invisible weight sits on my chest. "That fucking killed me. Especially when it was over a year before I could even kiss anyone else." I didn't understand how she could do it. That realization drove a lot of my anger. That had me believing she had outplayed me. That made me question every fucking moment we shared.

She worries her lower lip between her teeth and tucks her hair behind her ears. "It wasn't planned, but I was so heartbroken, and he was there. Reeve has always felt like my home. He was always the one comforting me when I was upset." A shuddering breath escapes her lips, and she's on the verge of tears again. "I didn't want to hurt you back then, and I don't want to hurt you now, Dillon."

"You don't?"

"I think we've hurt each other enough." That sentiment lingers in the air, and it carries so much weight. "But you've got to understand something about me," she continues. "It was never a competition between you and Reeve. I loved both of you in different ways. You shattered my heart into a million pieces, Dillon, and I was even more heartbroken flying home than I'd been fleeing L.A. When Reeve showed up, I was happy to see him because he's always been the air I breathe. He explained everything he'd done to rectify his mistakes. He said all the right things, and when he kissed me, I didn't fight him because his love meant I forgot the pain of losing you for a few moments in time, and I clung to that. I needed it because I was more broken and lost than ever before."

She takes a big gulp of her wine, averting her eyes. "I wasn't proud of myself after. I broke down in tears because it felt like the biggest betrayal." She rubs at her chest. "I felt so bad for doing that to you, but then I remembered how cruel you'd been and how you'd let me leave like I meant nothing to you. I believed you were thousands of miles away in bed with Aoife, and that helped to lessen my guilt."

"We really fucked up, didn't we?"

She exhales heavily. "I don't see it like that. I can't. That would be like admitting the life I shared with my husband and my son should never have happened. There are things I regret, but I won't regret that."

"I would never ask you to. And I don't begrudge you that time even though I was miserable as fucking sin without you for all of those years."

"Is that the truth?" She cocks her head to the side.

"It is. I didn't want to love you, but I did. I do."

"What about other women? I know you weren't celibate. Nor would I expect you to be," she rushes to add. "But I've seen pictures of you with tons of beautiful women. You never had feelings for any of them?"

I shake my head. "Nope. I couldn't be with anyone at first. Then, in the height of my anger, I set out to bang as many women as I could, hoping I could fuck you out of my system, but it didn't work. It made things worse because none of them were you. After, I'd feel even lonelier and the pain seemed sharper. It only served to make me angrier and miss you more. It was a vicious cycle I couldn't break out of. And I was a prick, venting all my frustration at these random women because I couldn't bear to look at them, knowing they weren't you. No one ever came close, and I got sick of it. I turned to booze then."

"Are you saying I've been your only relationship?" Disbelief is clear in her tone.

"Yeah, Hollywood." I shoot her a lopsided grin. "It's only ever been you."

She nibbles on her lip as she stares at me with an assessing gaze. "You're different."

"I'm trying to work through my issues. Trying to be more open, more patient, and less angry. It's a work in progress." I rub the back of my neck. "I, ah, started seeing a therapist. I'd spoken with one in rehab, but Ash convinced me to see someone new to help me deal with everything that's happened recently."

"I've got a shrink too."

"Is that why you're journaling again?"

"Yes and no. I mentioned it was what Sheila had suggested when I was in therapy in Dublin, and Meryl said if it helped that I should try it again."

"Is it helping?" I grab a handful of crisps, stuffing them in my mouth.

"Yes," she quietly admits. "I'm documenting everything, and while it's sad, it's helping me to remember how fortunate I was to have known him. To have been loved like that." Tears brim in her eyes. "I miss him so much."

"I know you do."

Silence descends, but it's not awkward. It's the most comfortable silence I've shared with her since we have been back in contact.

"I missed you too," she whispers, pinning me with glassy eyes. "I thought about you a lot." She sniffles, gulping a mouthful of wine. "I harbored a lot of guilt during my marriage for still thinking about you."

"I went out of my way to avoid both of you at events, yet a part of me yearned to bump into you too. Even though I knew it would kill me to see you on his arm, I just wanted to see you again. To remind myself it had been real. That I hadn't imagined it all."

"You loved me?"

"Yes, Viv." I hate she still doubts it. I hate I was a prick to her and I've made her disbelieve everything I say. "I know you don't trust me, and I don't blame you for that. I did you wrong, and I hate myself for it, but I never stopped loving you. I've been stumbling through my life since you left, and it's been so lonely." I draw an exaggerated breath, gulping over the lump wedged in my throat. "I know I can't expect anything of you, but could we try to be friends?" We need to start somewhere, and I'm hoping she'll agree.

"I can't offer you anything more than that, Dillon," she warns.

"I know, and I'm cool with that." It's fucking bullshit. I'll be devastated if I'm permanently relegated to the friend zone, but I don't want to put her under pressure. I'm trying to prioritize her needs, and this is what she needs now.

"Okay. I'll try."

I flash her a blinding smile, and she looks momentarily dazed.

"Why did you dye your hair and start wearing the contacts again?" Her inquisitive eyes probe mine.

"Honestly?"

Her scowl is instant. "No, I want you to keep lying to me." Her eyes narrow.

Fuck. "I deserved that."

"You are going to be in our lives, Dillon. You'll be in Easton's life. We just agreed to be friends. The only way this will work is with complete honesty. Aren't you tired of all the secrets and lies?"

"I am, and it was all so pointless."

She nods. "We can continue to beat ourselves up for the mistakes of the past or choose to move forward. To try to put it behind us." Air whistles out of her mouth. "I can't keep doing this. I want to wipe the slate clean and try to move on."

"Will you ever be able to forgive me?" I hold my breath as I wait for her to reply.

"I want to, but I don't know if I can. All I can promise is I will try."

"I can't ask for more than that." I clear my throat. "I thought it might be easier for you to be around me if I didn't look so much like Reeve," I admit though it's only half of the truth. I was stupidly hoping if I looked the way I used to look that she might fall back in love with me.

Viv nods like she was expecting this answer.

We were so good together, and we had so many good times. I don't want our relationship to be defined by those awful last moments. Especially not when we created someone so precious in Easton. In the future, I want our son to know his parents loved each other. That last night, I made love to Viv with my whole heart and soul. It felt magical at the time. Now I know it was because we were creating this incredible new life.

Her eyes lock on mine, and I wonder if my gaze is as emotional as hers. There is still so much that needs to be said, but I think both of us are done for the night. We stare at one another, and I want to kiss her so badly, but she is giving me no indication she wants the same thing. She's still mourning her husband, and the very last thing I should be doing is pushing her into doing something she would regret. It hasn't been long, and I have to respect that.

We just agreed to be friends, and it's a huge step forward.

So, I will learn to be patient.

I will become so patient they'll have to canonize me when I die.

If Ash was privy to my inner thoughts, she'd be so fucking proud of me.

Viv looks away first, and I sit back in the couch, bringing my beer to my lips. I want to enjoy this. Just being with her. I hope someday my presence offers her comfort in the way being around her does for me.

We drink in silence, both lost in thought, though I notice the sneaky glances she sends my way when she thinks I'm not noticing. After a bit, she shifts on the sofa, swinging her legs around and planting her feet on the ground. "Could I ask you to do one thing?" she says, placing her empty glass on the coffee table.

"Anything." I pin her with earnest eyes.

She wipes her hands down the front of her dress in an obvious nervous tell. "Ditch the contacts, Dil. I want to see your gorgeous blue eyes."

CHAPTER 27
VIVIEN

"UNCLE DILLON'S HOUSE IS NICE," Easton remarks as I lift him out of his booster seat. His eyes scan the sprawling modern two-story property with enthusiasm. He was so excited for today I could hardly get him to sleep last night. I took Audrey's advice, and he's been sleeping in his own bedroom again, ever since the night Dillon put him to bed. I hate sleeping alone, but I know it's the right thing to do even if both of us are having issues adjusting.

The door opens, revealing Dillon and Ash, and I pretend I don't feel the quickening of my heart at the sight of him. Easton drops my hand like a hot potato and races toward his dad. My heart slams against my rib cage, like it does anytime they are together. I hang back, unsure if I can do this today. The urge to turn around, head home, and crawl into bed with a bottle of vodka is strong.

"Hey, you." Ash bounds over to me, hugging me without hesitation. "I'm so glad you agreed to come."

"I'm not sure about this." I watch Dillon throw Easton over his shoulder with a massive smile on his face. E shrieks in delight, and I'm glad he's not aware of the significance of today. "Maybe I should go home." I know it's bad if I'm considering leaving Easton here without me.

Ash loops her arm in mine as Dillon tosses Easton up into the air. Easton squeals and giggles, thoroughly enjoying himself. "You shouldn't be alone today. That would be a very bad idea."

I swing my eyes to hers. "You know what day it is?"

She nods, dragging me forward. "Audrey and I talk weekly. She told me."

I knew they were in touch, but I didn't realize it was a regular thing. However, I'm not angry. I know they are worried about me, and I like they are repairing their friendship. It's important to me that both my besties get along.

Ash has been coming over to my house weekly for lunch, and it's as if we were never apart. We still have plenty to catch up on, but I'm enjoying listening to her

521

stories of life on the road with the band and hearing about all the amazing places she's traveled to. I'm glad she's back in my life and grateful she's forgiven me for the horrible way I treated her. "I'm sorry I didn't say anything," I admit. "It's just so hard to say it out loud. Every time I think I might be turning a corner, something happens and it feels like I'm back to square one again."

"It's barely been three months. I think you're doing amazing. Losing a baby is one of the most heartbreaking things you can endure. I can't imagine what it must be like to lose your husband as well." Tears prick her eyes. "I get upset just thinking about your pain."

We stop walking, stalling a few feet from the front door. "Last night, when I was lying in bed, all I could think about was how different today should have been. I hardly got any sleep, which would have been the case if my pregnancy had gone full term, but I had no little angel squirming and kicking inside my belly." I place a hand over my flat stomach. "I've never felt more hollow."

A sob erupts from Ash's mouth, causing Dillon to look over and frown.

"I don't mean to upset you."

"It's okay," she croaks, squeezing my hand. "I know today is going to be hard for you, and it's why I didn't want you to be alone. I think we should get shitfaced and toast to your little angel in heaven."

"Now that's a plan I can get behind." It sure beats crying my eyes out alone in bed.

"Hey, Hollywood." Dillon stops throwing our son in the air long enough to greet me. He flashes me that devilish grin I used to swoon over, and his entire face lights up when he smiles. Easton is good for Dillon. It's blatantly obvious how happy he is whenever he's around our son, and I don't remember ever seeing him so carefree. I'm glad he's in therapy, because he has a lot of deep-seated issues to work through. That's something else I have Ash to thank for.

"Hi, Dillon." I force a smile on my face.

Things have been better between us since we talked last week and came to an understanding of sorts. Meryl has helped me realize holding on to my anger, and clinging to the wrongs of the past, is holding me back from healing. I can't change what happened. I can only control what happens from now on. Fooling myself into believing I hate Dillon is exhausting, and I'm done pretending. He is going to be in our lives, and it will be much easier for everyone if things are amicable, so I'm determined to start anew. He came over for dinner on Tuesday night and he's been on FaceTime with E most every night before bed.

"Mommy." Easton sounds winded. "I'm trying to reach the clouds," he shrieks as Dillon throws him up into the air again.

Trying to give me heart failure, more like. "How about you come back down to earth for a while before you get a tummy ache?"

"How about you give your Auntie Ash a big sloppy kiss?" Ash reaches her hands out for her nephew. E practically jumps from Dillon's arms into Ash's, dropping a slew of sloppy kisses on her cheek. Ash lets him climb onto her back, and they race off down the hallway.

I trail after Ash and Easton while Dillon closes the door. He runs to catch up to me. "For you," he says, handing me a long-stemmed white rose. Our fingers graze as

I take it from him, and little tingles spread up my arm, reminding me I am still very much alive. "I told you once white roses symbolize rebirth and new beginnings, but they also symbolize peace, innocence, and love. I thought we could plant some white rose bushes in honor of Lainey. I have everything outside, but if it's too much, we don't have to do it."

I stop walking, and my lower lip wobbles as emotion washes over me. I fight to regain control, smiling softly at him as I bury my nose in the silky petals, inhaling the familiar lemony scent. "That's a lovely idea and very thoughtful," I choke out. "Thank you."

"I also wanted to run an idea by you," he says, dragging a hand through his hair.

Blond strands tumble across his brow, and nostalgia slaps me in the face. Today is really doing a number on me. "What is it?"

"I want to build a memorial for Reeve and Lainey in your back garden. I thought Easton could help me with it. We can plant shrubs and roses and maybe erect a plaque against one of the trees and install a little stone bench. That way, East would have someplace he could go when he feels sad or he wants to talk to them."

"Dillon," I whisper as tears stream down my face. I clutch a hand to my chest. "That would be perfect," I sob.

Without hesitation, he pulls me into his arms, and I let him console me. I shut my eyes, letting his spicy scent wrap around me as he holds me close. I rest my head against his chest, and we stand there for an indeterminable time, just hugging one another.

Hugs are so underrated.

It feels so incredibly good to be held again.

To be held by *him*.

I jerk away from Dillon the second that thought lands in my mind, swiping the remaining moisture from my cheeks. "We should find the others."

He nods, looking sad as he shoves his hands in the pockets of his jean shorts. "I thought we could start the garden next week, if that's okay with you? I'd like to have it finished before East returns to school."

Easton starts kindergarten in ten days, but I'm having huge reservations. However, I don't want to think about that today. "Next week is good." I snap my gaze to his, instantly snared in his gorgeous blue eyes. I asked him not to wear the green contacts because I love him with blond hair and blue eyes. He's a beautiful man, and he shouldn't have to hide his eyes because he's afraid of upsetting me.

The truth is, I want to see his blue peepers. His eyes are the mirror image of my son's. Those eyes are familiar because I've looked into them most every day of my life, but looking at Dillon isn't like looking at Reeve. That would be wrong on so many levels. No, seeing Dillon with blue eyes helps me to see him in a different light, and it offers me comfort. "Thank you. It's a really nice gesture."

"I see how much he misses him. I want to help."

I nod, releasing a large breath as we resume walking.

"Before we get into the pool, I want to give you and East a tour of my studio."

"I'd like to see it."

"Cool. Come on." He lifts one shoulder. "We'll grab the little guy before he makes a beeline for the water."

Ash comes with us, but we leave Ro and Jamie lounging around Dillon's large outdoor pool. Dillon has a stone path that leads around the side of his house and all the way to the studio.

The studio is much larger on the inside than it appears from the outside and very stylish with high ceilings, asymmetric walls, and wooden floors. "This is the control room," Dillon explains to East as we step into a small rectangular room. A long console with tons of buttons rests under a glass window that looks into the studio beyond. A bunch of high-tech laptops and other gadgets fill the rest of the space in this room.

"What are these for?" East asks, gravitating toward the mixing console like a moth to a flame.

"That's for our sound engineers. They listen to the music and the songs as we record them, and they route the sound so it's balanced and adjusted."

"Awesome," East says, nodding as if he understands what that means. He sits in one of the large chairs, pushing buttons while Dillon gazes adoringly at him.

"He's an incredible little boy," Ash whispers, as we lean back against the wall, watching father and son. "Dillon never stops talking about him. The only other time I've seen him this happy was—"

"Yeah." I cut her off, unable to hear her vocalize it.

"It's okay to admit it, Viv. He's a part of your past, your present, and your future. I know your relationship isn't the same, but it's okay to admit you made each other happy."

"I can't think about that, Ash. Especially not today. It feels like too big of a betrayal to Reeve."

"I'll shut up, in a sec, because the last thing I want to do is upset you today." She steps in front of me as Dillon and East climb out of the chairs and exit the room. "I'm just going to say this, and there is no intent behind it. I know there is a lot of love between you and my brother. I know there are a lot of unresolved feelings. There is no pressure or expectation on you to feel a certain way, but I want you to know if you still have feelings for him, and if you ever want to act on them, that it's fine."

"Ash. It's three months next week since Reeve died. Only three months. It's too soon to even think about anyone else."

"There is no timeline for this kind of situation, and no one should tell you what's in your heart. I would never push you in Dillon's direction. I would never force you to do anything you didn't want to do. I'm just saying it's okay to love him. Whether that's now, next week, next month, or next year, it's no one's business but your own. Don't close your heart out of guilt or fear."

She makes it sound so simple. But it's not. Can you just imagine what the world would think if I started something back up with Dillon? I can visualize the horrid headlines already.

"Mommy!" Easton's high-pitched shriek almost bursts my eardrums. "You gotta see this," he screams.

"Such impeccable timing," Ash murmurs, grinning as she loops her arm in mine. "I think that's enough of the heavy for today. Come on. I think I know why the little munchkin is so excited."

Ash leads me past the door to the recording studio, but I sneak a quick peek as we walk by. Various mic stands are dotted around the room, and a bunch of different guitars is propped against the walls. A few guitar cases lie flat on the floor. Ro's drum kit is situated at the back of the space. Framed pictures cover the wall, celebrating their various gold and platinum albums and the numerous accolades and awards the band has won.

"I think we have a budding rock star in the making," Ash says, dragging me past the room to the next door where East and Dillon are.

My jaw slackens as I take in the mini recording studio with child-sized guitars, a mounted keyboard, microphone on an adjustable stand, and a drum kit. Colorful bean bags are littered around the space. There's even a miniature refrigerator, loaded with drinks, and a small desk and chair. My eyes lift to Dillon's. "You did this for E?"

He nods as East strums a few chords on one of the guitars. Dillon has only begun teaching him, so he's still a complete novice. "I thought he might be able to come over on occasion, and I can give him lessons here. Maybe, sometime, he could come and watch us record or come over and hang out with some of his buddies. I had the desk installed so he could do his homework or color if he gets bored."

He has put so much thought into this, and my heart is a swollen mess behind my chest cavity.

Easton puts the guitar down and races to the drum kit. He plops down, grabs the drumsticks, and starts bashing away to his heart's content. His face is animated in a way I haven't seen in a long time. "Look at me, Uncle Dil. I'm a drummer like Uncle Ro!" Something loosens inside me, and I burst out crying. My emotions are all over the place today, and this is too much. I rush out of the room before E notices, not wanting to upset him when he's so happy.

CHAPTER 28
VIVIEN

I FLEE THE STUDIO, gasping for air as I struggle to breathe. Ash dashes out after me, pulling me into her arms as I break down. "It's okay, Viv. I've got you." She leads me away from the main house, over to the other side of the garden, to a stunning little seated area set amid copious colorful flowerbeds and shrubs. Lights are strung up over the open-fronted wooden gazebo as she leads me over to the homey wicker couch.

Ash wraps her arm around my shoulders, comforting me as I cry. "I'm so sick of crying," I rasp, sniffling and swatting my tears away with the hem of my summer dress. "I'm sick of being sad all the time." And I'm so freaking lonely. But I keep that thought to myself.

"It gets better."

I lift my head, fixing her with blurry eyes. "What happened?" This isn't the first time she's alluded to something.

She shakes her head and smiles, but it's off. "Not today. Today is about Lainey."

"Ash." I take her hands in mine. "It can still be about Lainey even if you tell me your story. I know there is one. Please tell me."

Tears instantly fill her eyes, and now it's my turn to comfort her. "Jamie and I... We lost a baby last year."

"Oh, Ash. I'm so sorry." I hug her tight.

"It was an ectopic pregnancy. We lost our baby at twelve weeks. I nearly died too. One of my fallopian tubes ruptured, and Jamie had to rush me to the hospital. We were at home in Ireland, so we managed to keep it out of the press."

I was wondering why I hadn't heard anything.

"We found out I was pregnant at six weeks, and we were overjoyed." Tears roll down her cheeks. "We told Dillon and Ronan straightaway. Ro's girlfriend Clodagh was pregnant with Emer at the time. I was so excited our baby would have an automatic best friend in his cousin. We had only just flown home to tell our parents when I collapsed."

"I'm so sorry, Ash." It's no wonder she's been so understanding. She knows exactly what I'm going through.

"I was in bits for months." She shucks out of my embrace, and we sit back on the couch. "I couldn't stop crying. Jamie was great, but he didn't know how to make it better."

"There is nothing anyone can say or do that takes away the pain. It's a process of surviving each day, and gradually you learn to live with it."

She nods. "But it never goes away, and you never forget."

"Never." I agree, placing a hand over my heart.

"They had to remove one of my fallopian tubes, but we should still be able to have kids. It might just be a little bit harder. We've decided to wait until after we are married before we attempt it. I need to build up the courage."

"I can relate. Even if Reeve were here, there is no way I could consider trying for another baby yet even if a part of me believes it's the very thing that will heal me."

"I didn't want to pry in case I upset you, but is everything okay after the accident? You'll be able to have more children in the future?"

I nod. "Yes. Thankfully, there was no permanent damage. There should be no reason why I can't have more babies. Though that's the last thing on my mind right now."

She takes my hand, squeezing it. "No matter how long you mourn Lainey and Reeve, assholes are going to criticize you as soon as you move on. The timing really doesn't make any difference. So fuck what anyone else thinks. Life goes on, Viv. You have every right to look to the future and to think of having more kids. It doesn't dishonor them if you start living again. I'm sure it's what Reeve would want."

"I know he would, but I doubt he'd want me to move on with his twin."

"Wouldn't he?" Ash quirks a brow. "He knew there was love between you. A very special, rare kind of love, and Dillon is Easton's biological father. I didn't know Reeve, but the fact he included Dillon in his will speaks volumes. I think Reeve would be happy if you end up with Dillon. At least he knows his twin will love you as completely as he did."

I blow air out of my mouth. "Woah. This is a lot of heavy for a day like today."

"We're just talking." She smiles. "No one is pressuring you. Maybe Dillon and you will fall back into love, or maybe you won't. I'm just saying do things for you. Fuck what anyone else thinks."

I chew on the corner of my mouth, wondering if I should say this. But it's Ash, and I know I can tell her anything. "I have never stopped loving him, Ash. He has always owned a piece of my heart."

"I'm so happy to hear that."

"It doesn't mean anything will happen," I blurt because I can't even think of that without feeling enormous guilt.

"I know, but just promise me you won't dismiss your feelings because you are worrying about what others will think. If Dillon and you are meant to be together, it should happen naturally. Without any interference."

"How did me talking about being able to have kids in the future end up a conversation about Dillon and me?"

"There's a natural correlation with both those things."

I open my mouth to tell her that's the very definition of interference when she continues talking.

"You and I are always in sync in our lives. Back in Ireland, it was men. Now, it's this." She squeezes my hand again. "We have both endured the heartbreaking loss of our babies, but we will go on because we are strong and we can overcome the worst experiences to emerge even stronger."

"We *are* in sync, and I'm so glad you found it in your heart to forgive me."

"There was nothing to forgive, Viv." Her clear blue eyes stare earnestly at me. "I was so fucking pissed off at the time it happened, but after I discovered everything, I instantly forgave you. It wasn't your fault, and you did what you believed was the best for both Reeve and Dillon and for you and your baby. I would never, could never, hold that against you."

"I love you." I pull her into my arms. "You and Audrey are the sisters I never had."

"Right back at ya, Viv."

A crunching sound has us whipping our heads around. Dillon strides toward us, concern evident on his handsome face as he takes in our blotchy skin and our embrace.

"He worries about you," Ash whispers.

"Hey." Dillon steps inside the gazebo, his gaze immediately finding mine. "Are you okay?"

"I'm fine." I stand, pulling my Irish bestie with me. "I just got overwhelmed. Seeing you with E and seeing what you built for him...it was a lot. I'm extra emotional today."

"That's understandable." Dillon stares at me in that intense way of his, like he's drilling a hole into my chest in a bid to get to the heart of the matter.

"I'm fine too," Ash says, planting her hands on her hips and narrowing her eyes at her brother. "In case you were wondering why I was crying."

Dillon pulls his gaze from me, frowning as he takes note of his sister. "What's wrong? Why were you crying?"

"Why do you think, dumbass?" She rolls her eyes, and Dillon scratches the back of his head.

"I wouldn't ask if I knew."

Ash grabs my elbow, pulling me out past her brother. "Men are such idiots."

"I heard that," Dillon says from behind us.

"You were supposed to."

I giggle, and this is exactly what I need to get through the rest of this day.

That and pink gin cocktails, which are in plentiful supply throughout the afternoon. After we plant the white rose bushes in Lainey's memory, we all congregate by the pool. Dillon, Jamie, and Ro get in with Easton while Ash and I sunbathe around the pool, sipping our drinks. There isn't a cloud in the sky. The sun is beating down on us, and the sounds of my son laughing help to repair some of the cracks in my heart.

I will always remember Lainey, and I will always be sad I never got to meet her when she was alive. I got to hold her in the hospital for a few minutes, and she looked so peaceful, like a beautiful sleeping doll, bundled in her soft pink blanket with the white knit hat. Her eyes were closed, and she was unaware of her momma's pain as I sobbed and sobbed holding her.

I will never forget it, and my daughter will always be in my heart, but I've got to live in the present because my other child needs me.

I make a silent vow to only remember Lainey with happiness, not sadness, from now on. I owe it to myself and my son to try harder, and I will.

A subtle breeze gently lifts strands of my hair, and a serene sort of peace flows through me. Warmth infuses my insides, and the tightness in my chest is gone, as if a switch has been flipped. I stare up at the sky in silent awe, wondering what just happened.

"Is that you, my love? Are you watching over me today and helping to ease my pain?"

Tears prick my eyes, behind my sunglasses, but for once, they are happy tears. I am not a religious person, but something profound just happened, and I find enormous comfort and strength in the thought that Reeve is up there somewhere, still looking after me. Still loving and protecting me even after he's gone.

CHAPTER 29
VIVIEN

HOURS PASS PEACEFULLY, and I can't explain what happened. All I know is I feel more at peace within myself than I have felt in months. "Mommy! Come and swim with me," Easton pleads from his position on top of Dillon's shoulders. He's been taking turns diving off all his uncles' shoulders, and I'm sure his skin is wrinkled by this point—he's been in the water so long.

"I'm coming." I stand, removing my glasses and placing them on the lounger. I feel Dillon's eyes on me as I pull my hair into a messy bun on the top of my head. I'm wearing a one-piece black and gold bathing suit that is the most modest suit I own. Usually, I wear bikinis, but I didn't want to see my scar today and be reminded even more of my loss. By the way Dillon stares at me as I enter the pool, you'd swear I was naked. I'm uncomfortable with the intensity of his attention today, and I don't want to feel the way he makes me feel.

Desirable.

Horny.

Alive.

Like my skin is on fire in every spot where his gaze lands.

Like I might die if I don't feel his hands on me right now.

It feels wrong to feel like this, today of all days, and I wish he'd cut it out.

Water laps at my legs and thighs as I move farther into the pool, and the cool sensation is a welcome balm to my hot skin. "Yay, Mommy's here." Easton launches himself off Dillon's shoulders, plunging into the pool, drenching me all over. Dillon chuckles. Jamie grins, and Ro is rather expressionless as they wade by, exiting the pool to leave us alone.

I really wish they wouldn't.

"He's a little nutter," Dillon says as E bursts through the surface, splashing water droplets everywhere.

He throws himself at me, winding his little legs around my waist and his arms around my neck, as he plasters kisses to my face. "This is so fun." He fixes me with a toothy grin, and my heart melts. I live for these moments. I love seeing him happy and carefree without any lingering grief. Then he's gone again, diving under the water like a fish. We had an instructor come to the house when Easton was a baby, and by the time he was one, he was a bona fide expert in the pool.

"Yes. I wonder where he got that from?" I respond to Dillon's comment in a teasing tone, and it's good to be able to acknowledge the traits I see in E that belong to Dillon without feeling guilty or sad. "He's always been a little wild, but he's disciplined too, and he never gave Reeve or I any trouble."

"I have it on good faith that a certain Hollywood princess was a little wild when she was younger." Dillon waggles his brows.

"Lies. All lies," I protest, ducking down so my shoulders are fully submerged under the water.

Dillon mirrors my position as we watch Easton resurfacing. "I remember a story about someone climbing a tree and falling off and breaking her arm."

I smile at the memories. The original one, where Reeve caught me and injured himself. And the more recent one when I was sitting at the busy table in the O'Donoghues' house telling them who I was. "I guess I was a little wild," I say, treading water. "It's a miracle Easton isn't completely reckless."

"I think that must've been Reeve's calming influence."

I stare at him as if he's sprouted another head.

"You told me enough about him to know he wasn't a rule breaker," Dillon explains.

"If you had asked me in school, I would've agreed completely. But later, not so much." I'm still shocked Reeve turned to cocaine and other uppers during that awful period of our history.

"Do you have photo albums I could see?" he asks as we move around the water. East is swimming a few laps, babbling away to himself, seemingly content to be by himself while Dillon and I talk.

"You've already seen everything I have, and that reminds me. The prints I ordered for you are due to arrive next week." Dillon wanted to see every picture we had of Easton from the time he was born. We have hundreds of digital photos, which I gave him on a USB stick, but I always print out family photos and put them in albums. My parents did that for me, and I like to think I'm starting a tradition. One of my favorite things to do as a little girl was sit down with Mom and go through them.

"I meant albums of Reeve," Dillon clarifies.

I twist my head to look at him, frowning. "Why would you want those?"

"I want to get to know the real Reeve." He runs his tongue over his teeth. "My therapist thinks it will help."

"I have albums I can show you." I'm not sure I'll be able to look at them, but who knows, maybe they will help me too.

"Great."

"Mommy." Easton swims up to us. "Can I get on your back and you pretend you're a sea dragon?"

LET ME LOVE YOU

Dillon chuckles while Easton crawls onto my back. "Hold on tight," I say before swimming away with my son clinging to my back.

"I'm exhausted," Dillon says, an hour later, when we're seated around the table enjoying a few drinks. Easton is sprawled out on a blanket on the grass behind us, doing a jigsaw. "I don't know where he gets all his energy from."

"He's a livewire for sure. Wait until he's bouncing on your bed at six a.m. full of the joys of spring. It's especially awesome when you have a hangover."

"I can't wait," Dillon says, yearning clear on his face, and it's a strong reminder of how much he's missed out on and how badly he wants to experience everything with his son.

I know he's eager, but I'm not ready to let Easton have sleepovers with Dillon by himself yet.

Awkward silence descends until Ash breaks it as only she can.

"Aw, fuck it. Let's not do this. There have been enough secrets and lies. There is no point ignoring the elephant in the room. Shit happened." She eyeballs her brother. "You missed out on the first few years of his life, but you'll get to experience so much more going forward. And you, my friend"—she turns to me, squeezing my hand—"you have nothing to feel guilty about. It is what it is, and you both need to stop pussyfooting around it."

"I love the fuck out of you," Jamie says, leaning in to plant a hard kiss on her mouth.

"You owe one dollar to the jar, Uncle Jamie," East calls out without lifting his head from his jigsaw.

"Damn. He's one shrewd little hustler," Jamie says after dragging his lips from his fiancée.

"Make it two!" Easton adds, and Dillon's lips pull into a proud smile.

"We should be careful what we say," I murmur, not wanting E to overhear something he shouldn't.

"When are you going to tell him?" Jamie asks.

"Mate. Don't." Dillon shakes his head.

"It's too soon, but I won't leave it indefinitely." I look at Dillon through my sunglasses. "I know you must be dying to tell him, and I'm glad you're not pressuring me."

"I am, but I would never do that. It's about what's best for him." Dillon is trying so hard. I cannot deny that, and it gives me hope we can make things work.

"Aw, this is too much." Ash hops up, rounding the table and hugging Dillon. "I'm proud of you, dumbass."

"Do you have any photos of your daughter?" I ask Ronan, needing to switch the direction of our group conversation. He's been extremely quiet with me, and I wonder if I've done something to offend him.

"I do." He squirms in his seat, looking uncomfortable.

"Have I done something to upset you?" I ask, my honesty spurred on by the liquid gin sloshing through my veins.

"Why would you ask that?" His piercing blue eyes lock on mine briefly before flitting away.

"Because you can hardly look at me."

533

"I'm just not sure what to say. I don't want to upset you."

My brow puckers. "You and I never had an issue talking to one another. I thought we were friends."

"We were. We are." He drags a hand through his messy brown curls. His hair is much longer now, curling around his ears and the nape of his neck, but it suits him. Ronan has grown up in the years we were apart, and he's lost that boyish look from his face. "I was trying to be sensitive. You've just lost a baby. I didn't want to be parading pictures of my daughter in your face."

The O'Donoghue men are really wowing me with their thoughtfulness today.

Ash crawls into Jamie's lap, wrapping her arms around him. "That's my fault." Her gaze bounces between Ro and me. "It was hard for me after we lost our baby. Clodagh was pregnant, and I had to avoid her because it hurt so much I usually ended up in tears." Jamie runs a hand up and down her back. "That made me feel so guilty because it wasn't poor Clodagh's fault."

"It wasn't your fault either," Jamie says, kissing her temple. "You couldn't help how you felt."

"Clo never held that against you, Ash." Ro lights a cigarette. "She was upset for you."

"I know." Ash reaches out, brushing Ro's arm. "Are you sure you two can't make a go of it?"

Ash had explained Ro was sullen because his fiancée—the mother of his daughter— broke their engagement off two months ago. She has been in Ireland for the past five months while Ro has largely been stuck here.

He shakes his head. "She doesn't want me anymore."

Visceral pain underscores his tone, and I feel for him. "I'm sorry to hear that. It must be so difficult being away from your daughter."

"It's killing me." He takes a long drag of his cigarette, blowing smoke circles into the air.

"Fuck, this conversation is depressing," Dillon says. "We all need cheering up. Jay, put on the music. Ro, come with me to get the meat for the barbecue."

Ro unlocks his cell, pulls up some photos, and hands his phone to me. "Those are the most recent ones Clo sent me."

Emer is sitting on a blanket on the ground, giggling at the camera, looking happy and content. She has a shock of thick dark curls and the biggest blue eyes. "She's beautiful, Ro."

His smile is sad, and my heart hurts for him.

Dillon slides his arm around his brother's shoulder, squeezing him. "We'll knock the rest of the album out in the next couple of weeks, and then you can go home to see her."

Ro nods, shoving Dillon's arm off before wandering into the house to get the meat for the grill.

"Can I help?"

"Nah. We've got this. Keep your pretty arse on that chair and have another cocktail." Dillon puts his fingers in his mouth and whistles. "East! You're on barbecue duty with me."

Easton hops up, wrecking the jigsaw he so painstakingly made. "Fiddlesticks."

Jamie snorts out a laugh. "Let me guess, that one's all you?"

I flip him the bird when I'm sure E isn't watching. "Damn straight it is, and I'm not apologizing. I'm not having my son go around cussing like a sailor."

"Girl, good luck with that plan," Ash says, swiping my empty glass. "You have zero chance of protecting those sensitive little ears around us lot."

CHAPTER 30
DILLON

"MY BELLY'S FAT," Easton proclaims, rubbing his hands over his slightly extended stomach.

"That's what happens when you eat *two* burgers and a mountain of chips," Jamie says, grinning.

"Chips?" Easton frowns.

"He means fries," Ash supplies. "In Ireland, we call them chips."

"Huh." His nose scrunches. "What's Ireland like?" he asks, climbing into my lap. He snuggles against me, and when his little warm hand lands on my bare chest, I practically melt into the chair. Today has been amazing, and I want a million more days like this.

"Very green," I tell him.

He pins me with wide trusting eyes. "Like the sky is green and all the roads and everything?"

I chuckle, tweaking his nose. "No, silly. The sky is still blue and the roads are the same color as here. It means that there is lots of green grass and lots of mountains and trees and bushes. There aren't as many cities or as many tall buildings as in America."

He curls his legs up, snuggling closer, and I could die from contentment right now. My fingers weave through his dark hair as he looks up at me. "Can I go to Ireland with you, and can we climb mountains?"

"Hopefully, someday." I glance over at Viv. "If it's okay with your mommy."

Viv has her shades on so I can't tell her reaction. After a bit of a shaky start earlier, she seems to be processing everything okay. I swear that woman has immeasurable strength. She never ceases to amaze me.

"We can visit Ireland. Maybe next year after the band has finished their tour."

She let me tell Easton about our impending tour because neither of us wants it to be a huge shock when I have to up and leave. I know it will be hard for my son. It'll be excruciating for me, and I honestly don't know how I'm going to do it. I don't want to leave him or Viv. I never want to be without either of them again.

"Yay." East fights a yawn.

"We should get going," Viv says.

"Not a snowball's chance in hell." Ash pushes the jug with the pink gin mix toward Viv. "It's not even seven. There's no way you're going home yet. East is fine here."

Ash has been amazing with Viv, and I'm happy to see them renew their friendship. Ash struggles to make friends with other women, especially within the industry we work in. Most of the women she has met are trying to use her as a way to get to the band, and she doesn't trust easily. She rarely talks to Cat anymore. It's been too difficult with them living on different continents. Besides, Cat was never the friend Viv was.

I expect Viv to protest because I know she's a stickler for routine with Easton, which I respect and admire. She always puts him first, and I only love her more for it. But I guess her desire to not return to her empty lonely home is stronger today because she doesn't mount any further arguments, happily accepting the gin Ash pours into her glass.

Twenty minutes later, East is sound asleep against my chest. I press my lips to his hair, closing my eyes and inhaling the familiar scent of my son.

Nothing compares to this.

Not even standing in front of thousands of screaming fans.

This little boy is already my entire world, and I would do anything to ensure his happiness. Lifting my head, I find Viv watching me. She's removed her glasses, and I see the emotion swimming in her eyes. "I can put him to bed," I whisper, "and just carry him out to the car when you're ready to leave." If I have my way, neither of them will be leaving tonight, but I don't want to admit that and freak the fuck out of Hollywood.

She thinks about it for a few beats before nodding.

I get up slowly and carefully, repositioning my sleeping son in my arms. He stirs a little, murmuring in his sleep as I walk off. Viv comes with me, and we don't talk as I carry Easton inside, walking the length of the hallway until I reach the stairs to the next level.

Emotion is heavy in the air as I push open the door to Easton's nature-themed bedroom. Viv sucks in a gasp as I stride across the wooden floor of the large room, toward the custom pine bed. I'm glad I decided against putting his bed in the little treehouse fixed against the right-hand side of the wall. While the ladder is large and sturdy, there is no way I would've been able to climb up to it without waking East.

Viv brushes past me, pulling back the green and blue duvet. Very gently, I place our son down, grateful Viv made him change out of his swimming trunks before we ate dinner. He's wearing light Nike training shorts that are comfortable to sleep in. Viv tucks the covers up over him, leaning down briefly to kiss his cheek. When it's my turn, I press a lingering kiss to his brow, attempting to calm my errant emotions.

We tiptoe to the door, both of us turning around at the same time to look at him. I have pictured Easton in this room many times since I designed it for him in the weeks after I discovered he was my child. Throwing myself into remodeling the bedrooms and adding the room for him in the studio helped to distract me from all the shit that was going down.

"Dillon, this is just…wow," Viv whispers, her face lighting up.

Pride swells my chest as I scan the room. It turned out better than I expected. "I know he loves nature and animals and the outdoors, so I wanted to incorporate that in the design. I had a guy come in to build the tree and the treehouse, and Ash found this super talented artist who drew the murals, but I did the rest myself. Jamie helped me to make the bed."

Her mouth hangs open. "You made that bed?"

A genuine smile ghosts over my lips. "Jamie and I did woodwork for our Leaving Cert. It was the only subject I enjoyed in school. I got a kick out of making it for him."

Her chest heaves, and she blinks back tears. "You did an amazing job. It's stunning, and he's going to love it."

Warmth spreads across my chest at her words. I was afraid she might go nuts at me for being so presumptuous. Truth is, I can't wait for Easton to have sleepovers.

Viv pulls the door over, not fully closing it. The dim glow from the lightning-bug lamp by East's bed ensures he's not in complete darkness should he wake up and be scared. I purposely put Viv's room beside his so she's close by if he stirs during the night.

"Thank you for today," she quietly says.

"It's been my pleasure. I've loved having both of you here." Before I can stop myself, I'm twirling a strand of her hair around my finger. "You know I'd do anything for you. If I could absorb your pain and take it away from you, I would."

"I'm at war with myself so much recently," she admits, staring deep into my eyes.

I'm immediately hypnotized in a way only Vivien has ever been able to do. Her face just calls to me. Everything about her does. I drown in her gorgeous hazel eyes, swimming in the goodness I always find there. It's like being sucker punched in the heart and the dick at the same time. God, I love her. I love her so much, and I want her so badly. "Why?" I croak, finally managing to find words.

"Because you make me feel things, Dillon. You always have."

I lean closer, winding my hands in her hair as I tilt her face up. "There is nothing wrong with that, Viv, and you know how I feel about you. How I've always felt about you."

"How can something feel so right yet so wrong too?" She almost chokes on the words, and I see the torment ravishing her beautiful face.

"There is no rule book for the things you've endured and no one-size-fits-all model for dealing with grief and moving forward." I rest my forehead against hers. "Just be true to yourself. Do what feels right for you."

"I'm scared, Dil," she whispers, staring into my eyes. "I'm scared if I move on I'll forget him."

"I won't let you." The irony of that promise isn't lost on me, but I mean it sincerely. I know how much she loved Reeve, and I would never ask her to forget the past she's shared with him. I realize how far I've come. How much Dr. Howard is helping me to process my feelings.

"Do you really mean that?" she asks, clutching my waist.

"I do." As much as I don't want to pull away from her, I need her to see my face, to believe this truth. I lift my head, putting a little distance between us as I cradle her cheek in my palm. "Reeve has been an enormous part of your life. You loved him, and no one can take that away from you. Least of all me. I'm just hoping there's room left for me. That you can get to a place where we can move forward, together. I want your future, Viv, but I will never let you forget your past. I will help you to remember him because him loving you has helped to shape the woman you are today. I happen to love that woman very much."

"So much for friends." She narrows her eyes, but the gesture is lighthearted.

"I'm still your friend, Viv, but let's be honest. Our connection is too explosive to ever let us be just friends."

"You have matured so much, Dillon."

"You aren't the only one impacted by his death. It has forced me to face things I've been ignoring for years."

"I want to move on, but it's too soon. If we ever get on the same page, I want it to be a fresh start, where there is no guilt or feelings of betrayal coming between us." She slides out from underneath me. "That day hasn't arrived yet."

"It's okay," I semi-lie, shoving my hands in the pockets of my shorts. "I understand. Take whatever time you need. I'm going nowhere."

We return to the others, staying outside chatting and drinking until it turns dark. When we move inside, Jamie and I get our guitars while the girls go to check on East. Ro leaves to go back to his house despite us asking him to stay. My brother isn't in a good place. He really loves Clo, and the breakup came completely out of the blue. He's devastated, and I know what that feels like, so I don't push him to stay.

We play a few songs, and I even coax Viv into singing.

"You should officially sing with the band someday," Ash tells her. "Not like permanently, but you should record a song with them. That voice is way too beautiful to deny the world."

"Yeah...no." Viv kicks off her sandals, pulling her legs up onto the sofa beside me. "I hate the spotlight." She shivers. "Even thinking about it gives me goose bumps."

"We could always record something that's just for us," I say, taking a swig of beer as I set my guitar aside. "It could be fun. Think about it."

She lies back, and I lift her feet onto my lap, massaging them without thinking about it. She used to love my foot rubs, and I was fond of bartering for sexual favors in return. Fun times. Slotting back into a regular pattern with Viv would be as easy as breathing for me.

Jamie and Ash watch with bated breath to see how she reacts.

She closes her eyes, settling down into the sofa, getting comfortable. "Hmmm. That feels good."

My gaze meets Jamie's as I knead Viv's feet, and I know he's rooting for us. He's been a rock for me these past couple of months. Honestly, I don't know what I'd do without Jamie and Ash. Jamie smiles, quietly pulling Ash to her feet. They leave the room, and silence descends, but it's not uncomfortable.

Viv sinks farther into the sofa as I move my fingers from her feet to her silky-smooth calves, kneading her supple flesh as I move higher. I have always loved her gorgeous long slim legs.

Especially when they were wrapped around my neck.

My cock surges to life as I remember all the times I ate her out while she was dangling off my shoulders. Her taste fills my mouth as if it hasn't been over six years since I last had my lips on any part of her.

"Dillon!" Her urgent tone yanks me out of my head. One of her hands is wrapped around one of my wrists, stalling my upward trajectory. I didn't realize my hands had moved so far up her thighs. My dick thickens to the point of pain, and if she looks down, there'll be no disguising my monster boner. I was oh so close to the promised land, but now the gates are being thrown up, shutting me out.

"You don't want this?" I ask, my gaze lowering to her mouth. "Let me make you feel good."

"We can't," she whispers.

"Why not?" I inch my free hand higher, brushing the tips of my fingers against her lace knickers.

"It's not right." She pushes me away, tumbling off the sofa onto the floor. I reach down to help her, but she swats my hands away. "Don't touch me. Please."

I raise my palms and back off. "I won't do anything you don't want, but I see the lust in your eyes, Viv. I know you want it. Need it." It's been three months since anyone has touched her. I know sex isn't the answer to our situation, but a few orgasms will do wonders for her state of mind.

"It's not about me not wanting you, Dillon." She stands, wobbling a little, but she's not drunk. She stopped the cocktails a few hours ago, switching to sparkling water. "It's about dishonoring Reeve's memory on the day our daughter was due to be born."

I instantly sober up. "You would never dishonor his memory, and taking something for yourself on a difficult day isn't wrong. But I understand why you feel that way, and I would never pressure you."

"Thanks." She looks around. "Where did Ash and Jamie go?"

"They've gone to bed."

She glances at the clock on the wall. "It's almost midnight. I lost track of time. I'd no idea it was so late."

"You should just stay here. I have tons of spare bedrooms. You can take the one beside Easton's room." I don't want to admit it's been remodeled specifically for her because that will probably send her running for the hills.

"I don't think that's a good idea." She chews anxiously on her lip.

"I'm not going to touch you, Viv. Not unless you ask me to." I stand, walking to her. "Stay. Easton is comfortable. It's late, and you're tired."

"Okay," she relents, and I nod, fighting a smile. Getting to wake up knowing East and Viv are in my house brings me enormous joy.

We head upstairs, and I show her to her room. "I thought you'd like to be beside Easton. That way, if he wakes, you will hear him."

"Thank you." She flips the light switch on the wall, and her eyes pop wide as she spins around to face me. "Did you do this for me?"

I nod. "I wanted you to have your own room here."

Tears prick her eyes as she drinks in the four-poster bed with wispy white curtains. I had an interior designer come in to create this room because I wanted it perfect for Vivien. The walls are a purple-gray color. The furniture is dark wood, contrasting perfectly with the ash-gray wooden floors. A large patterned pink rug is soft underfoot, and the rest of the room is decorated in various shades of white, gray, pink, and purple. It's luxurious and comfortable, yet it has a cozy vibe too. Exactly what I wanted to achieve.

"God, Dillon." She clasps a hand to her chest. "I don't know what to say." Tears brim in her eyes as she stares up at me. "I appreciate your thoughtfulness so much and how you're not pressuring me or Easton. Thank you for understanding and for being so supportive."

"It's not a chore, Viv. I want to be here for you. If I can help to make things easier, I'll do it."

She sniffles, casting her gaze around the room again.

I don't want to leave, and physically pulling myself away from her is a wrench, but she needs her space. "I'm just down the hall." I point out through the door to the left where my master suite is. "If you need anything during the night, come get me."

She bobs her head. "I'm sure I'll be fine."

"There are towels and supplies in the en suite bathroom," I add, still reluctant to leave.

Her smile is shy. "I'll be fine, Dillon. Go to bed."

I lean in closer, pressing my mouth to her ear. I know I shouldn't say this, but hello, I'm me. "If you want me to make you feel good, my offer still stands. If you need to forget, I know just how to distract you."

She pushes my shoulders, forcing me back. "Goodnight, Dillon."

Her tone brooks no argument, but I don't give up that easily. I fix her with a cheeky grin, before blowing her a kiss. "Goodnight, Hollywood. You know where to find me if you can't sleep."

CHAPTER 31
DILLON

I CAN'T SLEEP KNOWING Vivien is down the hall, most likely tossing and turning in bed like I am. Today was a difficult day for her, but she surprised me, like she has a habit of doing. She handled it far better than I expected. I'd like to take some of the credit, but this is all on Viv. She is so strong. So brave. And I'm craving her worse than ever. For the first time since the accident, I feel a kernel of genuine hope kindling inside me.

She still has feelings for me.

Feelings she's fighting, but I can handle that.

Not feeling anything for me, or hating me, would be so much worse.

I slide my hand down over my stomach, wrapping it around my still-hard dick, deciding I might as well jerk off, right as the door opens, admitting a sliver of light from the hallway. My hand stalls on my cock, and I lift my head, spotting the shadowy figure in the doorway. "Viv?" She doesn't move, standing rooted to the spot, and I pull my boxers up and climb out of bed.

I walk toward her carefully, afraid to spook her. I stop a few feet from her. "Are you okay?" She shakes her head, stepping a little closer. "Can't sleep, sweetheart?" I brush my fingers across her cheek. She takes a step closer, and her chest brushes against mine. She's wearing the Collateral Damage T-Shirt I left on the bed for her earlier tonight, when I harbored hopes she'd stay, and she looks so fucking good in it.

"Dillon." My name is a whisper on her tongue, but it's enough. I hear the pleading in her tone. Planting one hand on my bare chest, she peers up at me, and I see it all in her eyes. She won't say it. That would be like admitting it to herself, and she's unable to do that right now. So I'll have to make the decision for her.

Taking her hand, I pull her into my semi-darkened room and close the door. "Are you sure?" I run my thumb along her lower lip, urging my cock to calm the fuck down because he's excited and presently trying to poke a hole through my Calvins.

She nods, and I back her up to the wall, caging her in on both sides with my arms. Her eyes dilate as we stare at one another, and electricity crackles in the tiny space between us. Tucking her hair behind her ears, I inspect every inch of her gorgeous face. She has no idea how stunning she is or how badly I want her. This is the culmination of every fantasy I've had since we broke up. I lean down, dying to kiss her, but she pushes my shoulders and shakes her head. "No kissing."

Disappointment crashes into me, and I could legit cry, but I force my frustration back down. This is about her. Not me. I don't turn the overhead light on, figuring it's easier for her like this with only a faint light illuminating us from the lamp on my bedside locker.

My eyes are glued to hers as I grip the hem of her shirt, slowly tugging it up her body. She lifts her arms without me asking, and I pull the shirt up, tossing it on the floor. Slowly, I drag my eyes down her gorgeous naked body, marveling at how truly exquisite she is, while precum leaks from my cock. It's quite possible I might come in my boxers like a horny teenager. It's been a while for me, and I've spent night upon night jerking off to thoughts of Viv, so it's no joke.

My hands are trembling as I sweep my fingers along her velvety-soft flesh. Rubbing my thumb and forefinger across her nipples, I feel like fist pumping the air when the rosy-pink buds harden under my touch. Bending my head, I lave my tongue along each nipple, gently drawing her tit into my mouth.

"Not gentle, Dil."

The unspoken end of that sentence is crystal clear. Viv likes it hard and rough. I was rarely gentle with her. Not until that last night when I made love to her with my very soul. But I know what she needs now, and I'll give it to her. Dragging her nipple between my teeth, I softly bite down, and she moans, throwing her head back to the wall and her gaze to the ceiling. "So beautiful," I whisper as I move my attention to her other breast. I spend a few minutes sucking, nipping, and kneading before I drop to my knees on the carpeted floor before her.

Pushing her legs apart, I take a few seconds to savor this moment. I never thought I'd get to taste her again, and my heart is beating so fast in my chest it feels like it might beat a path out of there. I rub my nose against her pussy, inhaling deeply, before I part her lips with my thumbs and trace my tongue along her slit from top to bottom.

A strangled sound escapes her lips as I lick her with a fervor that may well be the undoing of me. More precum leaks from my cock as I dive in, plunging my tongue inside her. I lift one of her legs over my shoulder so I can get better access as I feast on her tempting cunt.

She is magnificent, and I want this for the rest of my life.

She pivots her hips, grabbing fistfuls of my hair as she rides my face, needing more. I haven't forgotten how her body works, and I have no intention of dragging this out. Not tonight. She needs this release, and I will give it to her. I push two fingers inside her as my tongue swirls around her clit, and she rocks her hips against me, making all the sounds I love to hear as I devour her.

I add another digit, curling all three of my fingers in the right place just as I flatten my tongue against her clit, and she goes off, detonating like a firework on Halloween night. I pump my fingers harder while I suck her clit, keeping up my pace until I've milked every last drop of her sweet climax.

When I feel her sagging against me, I lift her up and place her on my bed, crawling over her. I want to kiss her mouth so badly, but I know it's too much for her, so I settle for worshiping every inch of her skin, kissing my way down her body, as I grind my hips against her.

Her legs part to accommodate me, and I'm losing control of myself as I lick and suck her hot skin, thrusting my boxer-covered dick against her pussy, wishing there was no barrier between us and I was slipping inside her. Fingers thread through my hair as I adore her body with my hands and my lips. I stop for a second when my lips touch the edge of the scar on her lower stomach. Planting a slew of soft kisses along her puckered skin, I feel her flinch under me, and that's all it takes to lose her from the moment.

"No!" she cries, scrambling off the bed.

"It's okay." I reach for her, but she crawls away, clambering awkwardly to her feet. "What have I done?" she sobs, ignoring me as she makes a grab for the door. I watch with a massive lump in my throat as she flies out the door, away from me, not knowing if I should chase after her or give her space.

Sitting on the edge of my bed, I bury my head in my hands. The urge to cry is strong, but I can't fall apart. Viv needs me, and I'm never failing her again. Decision made, I get up, swiping the shirt off the floor, and follow her to her room.

She's curled on top of the messy bed, in the fetal position, sobbing into her pillow in an attempt not to wake Easton. Pain stabs me all over, and remorse fills all the gaps. This was too much. I should have told her no. This is my fault, and I need to fix it.

I pad quietly across the floor, climbing onto the bed behind her. She continues to cry as I sit her up, sliding my shirt down over her body. She lies back down, still crying, and my arms go around her as I spoon her from behind, pulling her body into mine.

I hold her close as she tries to wriggle free, but I'm not letting her. I'm not leaving her to deal with this alone. "Don't fight this. I can't go back to my room and leave you here crying." I cover her upper leg with mine. "Don't feel guilty for accepting support when you need it."

"How can I not?" she wails, grabbing my arms.

"There is nothing wrong with seeking pleasure. You needed the release."

She twists in my arms, pinning me with the saddest eyes. "I'm so selfish. I was lying here in bed, thinking about you. Thinking about how you always made me feel so fucking good, and I went to you looking for that. How could I do that?"

"Shush, honey." I clasp her against my chest, running one hand over her hair and the other up and down her back. "Stop being so hard on yourself. You've been through hell, and it's okay to take this for yourself. Especially today."

"But that's it!" Tears stream down her face. "How could I let you do that to me today of all days? I should be in the delivery room right now with Reeve, holding Lainey. If the accident hadn't happened, that is where I would be."

I brush wispy strands of hair off her face. "I'm sorry you're not there, Viv. I know how much you wish you were. You're hurting, and there is nothing wrong with letting me comfort you."

She cries into my chest, and silent tears leak out of my eyes. I hate this. For her.

For me. For us. "I'm so sad, Dillon," she mumbles against my skin. "So sad and lonely, and I feel like this pain will never end."

I hold her tighter. "It will get better, and I'm here for you. Whatever you need. You've got it."

I wake the following morning to an empty bed with only the scent of Viv lingering on the sheets beside me. "Uncle Dillon!" East charges into the room, wearing a T-shirt and shorts and the widest smile on his face. He jumps on top of me, hugging me to death. "Thank you for my room! It's awesome!"

Discreetly, I adjust my morning wood before sitting up with him draped all over me. "I'm happy you like it."

"I love my treehouse. Do you think my friend Nash could come over and see it?"

"Sure. But we'll have to check with your mom and his. Maybe we could arrange it one afternoon after you go back to school." That gives me a couple of weeks to work on Viv.

"Easton. Come on. We've got to go," Viv says, and I look up.

She's leaning against the door frame, wearing a blue summer dress I know belongs to my sister. It's way shorter on Viv's taller frame, and the hem hits mid-thigh, offering me a tantalizing glimpse of smooth toned skin I've been recently reacquainted with. From the strained look on Viv's face, I'm betting that's the last time I'll be getting close to any part of her body.

"Why don't you stay for breakfast? There's no need to rush off." I really want to talk to her about this in the cold light of day. I know Viv, and she's going to beat herself up for last night if I can't get through to her.

"I have things to do," she lies, avoiding eye contact with me.

East crawls off my lap, pouting as he says, "I want to stay."

"It's not possible." She jerks her chin up. "Now, come on. I have everything packed in the trunk. It's time to go home."

"I'm not going." Easton stands, folding his arms across his chest. "It's boring at home. I like it here."

"I'm your mother, and you don't get to make these decisions. Don't disobey me, Easton. Thank Dillon for having a nice time and let's go."

He shakes his head before turning pleading eyes on me. "Can I stay with you? Mommy can go home, and we can play."

I would love nothing more, but I know Viv wouldn't be okay with that, and I won't usurp her authority. "Come here." I call him over to me, looking into his eyes. "I will come to see you in a few days, but you've got to go home with your mommy now. She's the boss, buddy."

"She's mean. I don't want to go home to my boring house and my boring mommy. I want to stay here with you and Auntie Ash and Uncle Jamie."

I know he's sulking, and he doesn't mean it, but he can't speak to Vivien like that. "That's enough, Easton. You won't speak to or about your mother like that. Do you hear me?" I stand, hoping he doesn't notice my semi, and take his hand. "You need to do what your mommy says." I look down at him. "Always respect your mother. She loves you, and she knows what's best."

"You're mean too." He yanks his hand from mine, stomping past Vivien and out to the hallway.

"Do you want me to talk to him?"

She shakes her head. "I'll have a chat with him when we get home."

"We should talk before you go." I hold Viv's arm as she moves to go after him.

"There isn't anything left to say."

"C'mon, Viv. You know we need to hash this out."

She wrestles out of my hold, stabbing me with those beautiful hazel eyes. "Last night never happened. It was a mistake. A mistake I won't be making again."

Her words hurt, but I'm guessing that's the intent. My natural inclination is to argue, but I'm trying to put her needs above my own. It takes considerable effort to speak calmly, but I do it. For her. "Pretend it didn't happen if that helps, but I'll be here whenever you're ready to face up to it."

CHAPTER 32
DILLON

"PENNY FOR THEM," Ash says, walking into the kitchen with Jamie in tow, like the good little lapdog he is.

I grip the counter harder, warring with my emotions. It's been two weeks since the night Easton and Vivien stayed here, and she's barely giving me the time of day. I can't stand it, and I don't know how much longer I can do this without cracking. Slowly, I turn around, sighing. "Vivien is freezing me out again. It's like we take one step forward and then ten steps back."

"She's running scared since she let you go down on her." Ash casually throws it out there, like it's normal to just blurt that shit.

"What the fuck, babe?" Jamie stares at her.

"What?" Ash looks between us, jabbing her finger in the air. "It's not like you two don't talk about us."

"Hell no." I push off the counter. I won't be having that. "I get zero details of what you two get up to in the bedroom. Even knowing you have a sex life freaks me out."

Ash rolls her eyes. "You're being ridiculous. We're all adults. We all have sex."

"Except Dillon isn't getting any, and I think that's the problem." Jamie smirks, and I'm tempted to punch him in the face.

I flip him the bird. "My hand is getting plenty of action."

Ash makes a face but refrains from commenting because that would make her a hypocrite.

I can't resist pushing her buttons. "I subscribed to a new porn channel. Damn, that shit is cheesy, but it does the job." I rub my hand up and down my crotch while I lie.

As if I need porn to get me off.

Just thinking about Viv gets me hard in seconds.

"Okay, enough." She holds up one palm. "You made your point, and *my point* is

Viv moved too fast. I'm surprised she even confided in me, but she feels disloyal to Reeve, and she's too stuck in her head over what people would think if she starts anything with you."

"I don't give a flying fuck what anyone thinks."

"You don't, but she does. There is a lot of bad history there, as we all know, so I get why she's concerned."

"It's not just about us. She's regressing with Easton too. He got into a little trouble yesterday in kindergarten. Some fuckface said horrible shit about Reeve, and Easton shoved him. He fell over and hit his head off the side of a desk, and now his parents are threatening to sue the school and sue Vivien. She's talking about pulling him out and getting him a home tutor, which would not be good. The only time she lets him out of her sight is to go to school. She won't even let him go to Nash's house. Nash always has to go to them. It's not normal, and it's not helping Easton."

"Have you told her that?" Ash pulls a carton of orange juice out of the fridge.

"I've tried broaching the subject, but I'm largely still biting my tongue around her."

Ash frowns as Jamie pulls a glass out of the overhead cupboard for her. "Why are you doing that?"

"More to the point, how?" Jamie asks, watching Ash pour herself a large glass of orange juice. "It's not like you are known for holding back."

"I'm doing what you told me to do," I tell Ash. "I'm putting her needs above my own."

"Oh my God." Ash dribbles juice down her chin. "Why are men so fucking dumb?" she mutters to herself as she swipes a blueberry muffin and heads outside to the patio table and chairs.

I'm not a massive fan of the warm California weather, but I've got to admit it's nice to spend so much time outdoors and not need a rain jacket. "Spit it out." I flop onto one of the chairs.

"I said put her needs above your own. That doesn't mean biting your tongue if things need to be said."

"If I tell her what I feel, it'll cause an argument, and that'll upset her. How is that being considerate of her needs?"

Ash rubs her temples. "I swear it's like dealing with children."

"Fuck you, Ash." Fire blazes from my eyes. "You are the one who told me to do this. Don't fucking turn around now and call me an imbecile and make out like this is all my fault. I'm doing the best I can." My voice cracks, and I feel like a pussy, but everyone seems to forget this has been hard on me too. Yes, I know some of it was my own doing, but I'm trying to make amends, and I'm only human.

Despite what people might think of me, I have feelings.

"This isn't easy on me," I admit. "You think I like holding back when I see the woman I love torturing herself because she believes she doesn't deserve to be happy? I know she has feelings for me, but she's going to bury them until she forgets they exist. And I have to hold back from telling my son he's my son because the timing needs to be right. Do you have any fucking idea how hard it is to be around that little boy and not tell him?" I lean my elbows on the table. "Do you know how badly I want him to call me daddy? And how badly I want to take care of both of them?

How I lie in bed every night thinking of them over in that big sad lonely house wishing I could be there to help ease their pain?"

Pressure sits on my chest. "We built that memorial garden for Reeve. The three of us. And I thought it would help her to see that we can do this together. That she doesn't need to handle everything alone, but she's more withdrawn than ever." I rub at my stinging eyes. "I don't know what to do anymore. I constantly second-guess myself, and I don't know if I'm even helping."

"I'm sorry, Dil." Ash reaches across the table, taking my hand. "No one is dismissing your feelings, and we know it's difficult for you."

"You're doing amazing with both of them," Jamie supplies. "And Vivien may not want to see it or accept it, but she needs you, and you can't give up on her."

"I'm never giving up on her, Jay. Never again. No matter how tough it gets, I'm going nowhere." I exhale heavily, kicking my feet up on the table. "Fuck, I'd kill for a smoke." I gave the ciggies up last February, but I still crave them.

Ash squeezes my hand. "I love you, brother. And I truly believe Viv does too. I'm sorry for making fun of you. That wasn't fair." She wets her lips as Jamie sneakily grabs her drink, finishing off her juice. "I didn't mean for you to deny who you are or to bite your tongue around her. You can be cognizant of her needs and still be you. In fact, I think you need to be more you. That's what she needs now."

"What exactly are you saying, Ash, because you're confusing the hell outta me."

"You need to be your normal dickhead self. Viv needs Dickhead Dillon. You holding back from speaking your mind is the worst idea. Stop overthinking it, and just be you."

I look at my mate. "Women are batshit crazy. They say one thing but mean another. You deserve a fucking gold medal for putting up with that shite for all these years."

"*Fact.*" Jamie mouths behind Ash's back, but he doesn't say a word out loud, because he's so fucking pussy-whipped he's terrified to admit I speak the truth.

Ash pinches my cheek. "Way to piss me off when I was starting to feel sympathy for you."

"Aw, whatever." I stand. "I'm out of here."

She eyes me suspiciously. "Where are you going?"

"I'm going to talk to Viv about Easton."

"What are you doing back here?" Vivien asks when she opens her front door to me.

"I need to speak to you, and it can't wait until Friday." Viv lets me collect East from school every Monday, Wednesday, and Friday. I dropped him off earlier, but I didn't stay because I was in a foul mood. Ash's words have given me the permission I felt I needed, and I'm feeling invigorated. I don't want to argue with Viv, but she needs someone to talk sense into her, and that job has got my name written all over it.

I push past her, not waiting for an invite.

"Dillon, wait." Her sandals clack against the tiled floor as she chases after me. I duck into the formal dining room because the playground can't be seen from this room. I don't want Easton to see me. At least not until I have spoken to his mum.

Viv races into the room, scowling at me.

"Shut the door."

"This is my house." She folds her arms over her chest.

I glance at the large family portrait that hangs on the far wall. "I'm well aware. Now shut the fucking door, Vivien Grace. We don't want Easton to hear this conversation."

"I'm not telling him yet!" she shrieks, slamming the door shut. "It's too soon."

"Stop panicking, Viv. I'm not here about that. We need to talk about this crazy idea you have about taking East out of school."

She crosses her arms over her chest again. "It's not a crazy idea. It makes perfect sense, and I've already got tutor interviews lined up."

"He needs to be around other kids, Viv, and he loves school."

"I know he does, but this is in his best interest. You know what happened yesterday and we had a similar incident at camp. It's not going to stop, and I need to protect him."

"Mollycoddling him isn't the same as protecting him. You need to let him fight these battles himself. Trying to shield him from them will only do more harm than good. This is the world we live in. There will be more assholes to contend with. He needs to understand that and learn how to handle it himself."

"He's only five years old, Dillon! How the fuck is he expected to handle it himself?" She throws her hands in the air, pacing the room.

"The same way you did. You can't tell me you didn't get shit thrown at you over your parents growing up."

"Of course, I did, but—"

"Well, there you go." I pin her with a knowing look.

"Don't interrupt me before I am finished speaking." She glares at me, and I'm kicking myself that I didn't do this weeks ago. Viv needs to be challenged. I almost laugh at the irony. I've been mollycoddling her for months instead of forcing her to face the truth. I think it was right to do that at the start when her grief was so heavy there was no other way to manage it. But not now. Now, the gloves come off, and it's time to push her to face her new reality.

I smirk, and she growls. I laugh before reining it in when I see the murderous look on her face. This isn't a game. I came here with a purpose in mind. "Continue."

She bites on her lower lip, and my cock jumps in my jeans. "I've had my fair share of shit thrown at me over the years, but—"

"But what?"

She looks at her feet. "Reeve was there. He always defended me."

"That may be the case, but I'm betting he wasn't always there because you know how to defend yourself. I've seen you in action."

"It's not about me anyway. We're talking about Easton."

"Easton needs to learn to fight his own battles, and he's a smart little kid. I understand you want to protect him. I do too. But this isn't the way. He'll only come to resent you for it, and it'll make things harder. Hiding him away from the world doesn't make it go away. You need to let him be a child, Viv. You need to let him go to his friends' houses. You need to bring him bowling, or let me take him on a hike, or go to the movies. You need to let him resume his life. It's the best way of helping him to move on."

Her nostrils flare, and she bares her teeth at me. "Are you done telling me how to raise my child?"

"He's my child too."

She harrumphs. "Aw, here we go. I was waiting for this to happen."

"I'm not trying to question your authority or replace Reeve, but he is my flesh and blood, and I won't stand by and watch you make a mistake which you will live to regret and our son will pay the price for. This isn't the way to protect him, Vivien."

"Get out." She points at the door. "Get the fuck out of my house, Dillon, and stay out. You don't get to come in here and dictate to me. I make the choices for my child. I've been the one doing it for years when you weren't here."

"That's not fair, Viv, and you know it."

"Fairness doesn't come into this. The fact is, I have been the one raising my child. Not you. If anyone is qualified to make these decisions, it's me. Not you."

"Can you at least reconsider?"

"No." She opens the door. "You've outstayed your welcome, Dillon. Leave."

"This isn't the end of this conversation," I say as I move past her.

"Yes, it is."

We'll see about that.

I rock back on my heels, staring up at the impressive house with a healthy dose of trepidation as I wait for the door to open. I hope I'm not making a mistake coming here, but if anyone can get through to Viv, it's her parents. They arrived back in L.A. nine days ago, but I know they only have a few weeks at home before they are on the move again.

The door swings open, and I'm greeted by a tall thin woman in an austere white and gray uniform. Her cold gray eyes and the grim set of her mouth are as unattractive as the outfit she's wearing. "Can I help you?"

"It's okay, Renata. We've been expecting Mr. O'Donoghue. I'll take it from here," Jonathon Mills says, appearing beside the unfriendly woman.

She nods before walking off.

I quirk a brow. "Was being scary and unwelcoming a trait you sought when you were interviewing for her position or a surprise addition to her skill set?"

Jonathon chuckles. "Renata is an acquired taste. A bit like beer." He shudders, and now it's my turn to laugh.

"I like beer."

"I guess there's no accounting for taste." He is smiling as he stands aside. "Come in, Dillon."

I step into Vivien's childhood home, feeling like a trespasser. She is going to be so pissed when she finds out I did this. But it's a small price to pay if it means she changes her mind and lets East stay in school.

"When the gate security called and said you were here to see us, I'll admit I was intrigued," he says, jerking his head and urging me to follow him.

I was half expecting to be turned away. I think if Lauren Mills was home alone that's exactly what would've happened. "I wouldn't have come if it wasn't a serious matter."

A frown mars his tanned forehead, and he looks deep in thought as we walk. "How are things going with Easton?" he asks after a few silent beats.

"Great. He's a fantastic kid, and I'm mad about him."

"That's good, Dillon." He squeezes my shoulder. "I'm glad to hear it." I can tell he means that. He comes to a halt at the end of the hallway, opening double doors which lead to a large sunroom, where Lauren awaits.

She stands as I enter the room, offering me a tight smile. "Hello, Dillon."

"Mrs. Mills." I nod respectfully.

She rolls her eyes. "Please. You know better than to call me that. Sit down, and let's hear what this is about."

She doesn't beat around the bush, and I like that about her.

I sit across from her and her husband. "I'm here about Vivien. I'm a little worried."

"In what way?" Lauren asks.

I clear my throat. "She is talking about pulling Easton from school and hiring a tutor for him."

Lauren knots her hands in her lap. "I was afraid of that. She called me yesterday, and she had worked herself into a tizzy over the incident at school."

"I'm going to deal with that," I say. "It will be a non-issue in a few days." I have already spoken with the school and reached out to the parents of the other little boy. I'm just waiting for them to return my call, but I'm confident I can make it go away.

"There will likely be more incidents," Jonathon says.

"I know, but I believe Easton can handle them once we provide the right support. I don't think taking him out of school sends the right message, but it's more than just this. Are you aware Vivien hasn't taken him anywhere besides camp all summer long?"

Lauren frowns. "What do you mean?"

"I mean, he goes nowhere. She drives him to and from school because she doesn't trust anyone else to drive him. Nash comes over for playdates, and occasionally some other kids, but that's it." I feel so disloyal telling Viv's parents this behind her back, but they need to know how bad the situation has gotten. "She is terrified of something happening to him. She can hardly bear to let him out of her sight."

"Oh, princess." Jonathon shares a concerned look with Lauren.

"Why didn't Audrey tell us this?"

"I'm not sure how much Audrey is aware of. She's been gone for weeks."

"Does Vivien know you're here?" Lauren asks.

"No, and she's going to kick my ass for it, but I just tried talking to her, and she won't listen to me. I thought she might be more inclined to talk to you about it." I wet my dry lips. "I love her and Easton so much, but she's still keeping me at arm's length, which I understand. I've given her space, but this is something I believe she'll end up regretting. I'm going to work on getting both of them out of the house more, if you could talk to her about the tutor thing."

"We'll talk to her." Lauren bobs her head. "I understand why she wants to do this, but you are right; it's not a good idea for Easton. He's an extrovert, and he loves being around others."

"Thank you for bringing this to our attention," Jonathon says.

"I hate going behind her back, but I didn't feel like there was any other option. She's moving full steam ahead already, so there was no time to waste."

"We will try to make her understand that you had her best interests at heart," Lauren says, fighting a smile. "But you know our daughter."

"I do." I stand. "Thanks for listening. I can see myself out."

"Don't go just yet, Dillon." Lauren lifts her brows, pointing at the seat I've just vacated. "I have something I'd like to say."

"*We* have," Jonathon corrects her, as I sit back down.

She pats his hand, and they share an intimate look that only comes from years of loving and understanding one another. Her expression is more somber when she turns it on me again. "I'm not happy about certain things you have done, and it will take a lot more convincing for me to fully trust you, but I've had a lot of time to think in recent months. We both have, and the only way to truly let the past go is to wipe the slate clean. We believe you are sincere when you say you love our daughter and grandson, and everything Vivien has told us about how you have behaved these past couple of months confirms that."

"We also know you were responsible for her happiness in Ireland," Jonathon adds. "She was glowing when we visited her, and we know she was deeply in love with you. Vivien is a good judge of character, and you are Easton's father, so we are giving you the benefit of the doubt."

"We loved Reeve. He was our son, and we miss him a lot," Lauren says, her eyes growing glassy. Jonathon slides his arm around her shoulders. "For him to include you in his will tells us a lot about his intentions. Reeve wasn't perfect. None of us are, but he loved Vivien, and he loved Easton with his whole heart. I know, without a shadow of doubt, that he would want them to be happy. If their happiness lies with you, we want you to know we won't stand in your way."

"Provided you always put them first," Jonathan supplies, drilling me with a look that his wife usually reserves for me.

"That's a given." I run my hands through my hair. "Even if Vivien and I never reunite as a couple, I will always be there for both of them. I give you my solemn promise. There is nothing or no one who could tear me away from them now."

CHAPTER 33
VIVIEN

"SO, is Dillon still in the doghouse?" Audrey asks, smothering a grin as she peers at me through the screen of my laptop.

"You'd better believe it." It's been two weeks since Dillon went behind my back and spoke to my parents, and I'm still livid. "I can't believe he went to Mom and Dad or that they actually sided with him."

"Is that what you really think?" Audrey arches a brow while leaning back in her chair.

I sigh. "No." I drum my fingers on the top of my desk. "I know they were right, and I know Dillon acted out of concern for E." It's why I canceled all the tutor interviews and Easton is still in kindergarten. I can't let my insecurities mess up my son's life.

"And concern for you," she reminds me.

"I'm working through my fears with Meryl, but it's hard. East is all I have left and I'm terrified of anything happening to him."

"Easton isn't all you have left, babe." Audrey looks up, lifting one finger. Her head lowers again, and she moves in closer to the screen. "You have Alex and me. You have your parents. You have Ash and Jamie and Ro." She pauses for dramatic effect. "And you have Dillon."

"He's irritating the fuck out of me. He's always on my ass about something, and he's being…all flirty and shit. When I say stuff to annoy him, it only seems to amuse him." She grins, and I narrow my eyes at her. "Don't tell me you've moved to the dark side."

She barks out a laugh. "He's being typical Dillon. I wondered how long he could keep the nice guy routine up."

"Hey, he's still one of the good guys," I blurt, instantly feeling the need to defend him, even if I'm still seething at his interference.

Her grin expands, and I flip her the bird. "I know he's a good guy, Viv. He has far

exceeded my expectations. From what you've said, he's great with Easton and pretty skilled with his tongue."

I roll my eyes. "I should never have told you or Ash about that."

"Aren't you tempted to go back for round two?" She waggles her brows.

"No," I lie. Truth is, I can't stop thinking about it or the way it felt to have Dillon's hands and mouth on me again. Now that he's on a mission to piss me the hell off, he's seriously getting under my skin and raising old memories to the surface.

"Liar." Rey calls me out on my bullshit.

I sigh again. "I can't stop thinking about him, but then I feel guilty. It's only been four months since Reeve died. How can I be thinking about another man already?"

"Babe, we've been over this. You've really got to stop doing this to yourself," she says as there's a knock on my office door. "And it's not like Dillon is just any other man. There is history there and a shit ton of love."

"It's the way I'm programmed," I tell my bestie, getting up to answer the door.

It's Charlotte. "Dillon is here to see you. He's waiting in the sunroom."

I glance at my watch, frowning. School hasn't let out yet, so I have no idea why he is here already. "Okay. I'll be there in a sec." I return to my desk. "Speak of the devil. Dillon is here early. He's probably come to torture me some more."

"I've got to go anyway. Tell Dillon I said hi, and call me this weekend, yeah?"

"I will. Love you."

"Right back at ya."

We disconnect, and I go out to see what he wants.

"Is something wrong?" I ask the second I step foot in my sunroom.

Dillon is standing, with his back to me, looking out at the garden. You can see the memorial we built from here. "Nothing is wrong," he says, turning around to face me.

Fuck me. How does he make a plain white T-shirt and normal jeans look so freaking hot? His hungry gaze roams the length of my body, making me feel self-conscious. I cross my arms over my chest in an instinctive protective gesture.

"Don't do that," he says.

"Well, don't look at me like that."

"Like what?" His lips curve up at the corners.

I drill him with a warning look. "You know what." I'm not playing this game with him.

He takes a step toward me, and I fight myself not to take a step back. He strides toward me like a hunter stalking his prey, and my heart slams against my rib cage in nervous anticipation. Dillon stops directly in front of me, leaving only a tiny gap between our bodies. Heat rolls off him in waves, crashing into me and almost taking my knees from under me. "Like I want to strip that pretty dress off your gorgeous body and worship every inch of your skin with my lips and my tongue?"

My cheeks sizzle as I stumble away from him. "Stop it. You can't say that to me."

Slowly, he drags one hand through his hair, grinning as he maintains eye contact with me. "We both know you'd love me to do it, but we can keep pretending. You know how determined I am when I want something, and I want you. I can keep this shit up for months." He leans in close again, still grinning. "Years, if it comes down to it."

I'm calling bullshit on that. Dillon is not known for his patience even if he has surprised me a lot these past few months. Saliva pools in my mouth as liquid lust rushes to my core.

I like sex, and I miss it.

I know I could ask Dillon to fuck me, and he'd happily do it, but I just can't do that to Reeve. Which I know is ridiculous, because Reeve is gone and I'm going to have sex with someone else at some time, but I just can't go there yet.

"Why are you here, or did you just make a house call to annoy the shit out of me?"

He chuckles, rubbing a piece of my hair between his fingers. "I came to tell you I'm taking East for ice cream after school."

"Like hell you are," I hiss, swatting his hand away.

He narrows his eyes at me. "We talked about this, Vivien Grace. I've been telling you for two weeks, and I'm not listening to any more of your bullshit excuses." He lowers his face to mine. "Just so I'm clear, I'm not asking permission. I called here as a courtesy because I know you will freak the fuck out. I am taking our son out for ice cream. I will bring Leon with me. I will message you when we get to the ice cream parlor and message you when we are on the way home."

Acid crawls up my throat, and bile swims in my stomach.

"Or you could come too?" he asks, a hopeful tone to his voice.

I immediately shake my head. Being seen out with Dillon in public is a recipe for disaster.

"I thought as much," he says as he walks toward the corner of the room, bending down to retrieve a bag I hadn't noticed before. "You are not going to sit around this house, pacing and panicking while East and I do something perfectly fucking normal." Walking back over, he hands the bag to me. "I want you to work your magic. Create something amazing. Make a new dress so you have something to wear when I finally convince you to come out to dinner with me."

I open the bag, gasping at the pretty silk material. It's a gorgeous rich blue with purple and white floral prints all over it. "Where did you get this?"

"In a sewing shop," he deadpans. "Where else do you think I got it? I hardly magicked it out of my arse."

"There is no need to be rude or crude."

He smirks, opening his mouth to say something dirty, no doubt, but I clamp a hand over his lips to silence him. "Do not say whatever it is you're about to say. Thank you for the material, but Easton isn't going."

He nips at the skin on my palm, and I yank my hand back. Before I know what's happening, he's backing me up against the wall. "Sweetheart, I already told you this isn't a negotiation."

"But—"

Now it's his turn to silence me with his hand. I glare at him, and he chuckles. "Be grateful it's not my mouth." He winks, and I squeeze my thighs together. "Listen up, Hollywood. I love Easton. He's my son, and I know he's the most precious thing in the world to you because he's all that for me too. I will guard him with my life. Nothing is going to happen to him. I promise." He removes his hand, darting in to press a kiss to the corner of my mouth. "Trust me. Please."

I stare into his stunning blue eyes and nod. "Bring my baby home to me safely."

"Always." Without warning, he bundles me into his arms. "I know you're scared, but it's going to be fine. This needs to happen. You know it."

After Dillon leaves, I head into my sewing room for the first time since Reeve and Lainey passed.

I try.

I really do.

I work on some dress designs, but I can't concentrate. I can't stop thinking about Easton and Dillon out there in the big bad world. Surrounded by paparazzi and assholes who think it's okay to stick their noses into our business. Briefly, I contemplate hitting the vodka, but it's only four o'clock in the day, and it's a habit I don't want to start. Instead, I pace the floor and panic, exactly what Dillon suspected I would do.

I'm standing outside by the front door when they pull up an hour later, and I almost trip over my feet in my hurry to get to Easton. Opening his car door, I lean in and hug him, almost suffocating the poor child. "Mommy. You're squeezing me to death!" he says, and Dillon chuckles.

"Hollywood, let the little guy get out of his seat." Dillon tugs me back, wrapping an arm around my waist as Easton unbuckles his seat belt and jumps out of the car.

"I had the best time, Mommy, and Uncle Dillon got you some chocolate ice cream. He knew it was your favorite." Easton holds a small paper bag out to me as Dillon presses his warm mouth to my ear. "Remember that time we ate ice cream off one another? I even licked it out of your—"

"Dillon!" I shriek, twisting out of his hold. "Not in front of little ears." I don't care that he was whispering in my ear. Easton has razor-sharp hearing and an uncanny ability to hear things I don't want him to hear.

"Were you being naughty again, Uncle Dillon?" East asks, grinning up at his dad.

"I was just reminding Mommy of a game we used to play and asking her if she wanted to play it with me again." He flashes me a devilish grin I long to wipe off his face.

"I love games!" Easton jumps up and down. "Let's play the game!"

I glare at Dillon, and he discreetly swats my ass. "It's an adult game, buddy," he says, crouching down to E. "How about we play cops and robbers?"

That basically means they get to chase each other all over the house, screaming and shouting like lunatics. Dillon is the biggest kid, but I can't ever be mad about it. Easton loves his special brand of crazy.

"I wanna be the robber this time!" Easton screams.

"Well, what are you waiting for?" Dillon lifts a brow. "I'll give you ten seconds before I come looking for you." Easton races into the house, almost knocking Leon over in his haste to get away from Dillon. "Apologies, sweetheart." Dillon kisses my cheek, grinning. "We'll have to take a rain check on the naked ice cream party."

CHAPTER 34
VIVIEN

"WHY DOES my daddy look like a scaredy-cat in this picture?" E asks, pointing to a photo of Reeve I took when we were thirteen.

The three of us are seated on one of the couches in the living room, looking through another one of my childhood albums. Dillon said he wanted to know the real Reeve, and we usually spend an hour after dinner on the nights Dillon is here looking into my past. I thought it would hurt, but it's actually helping.

"Did you know your daddy was scared of spiders?" Reeve had a serious case of arachnophobia, something he managed to conceal from his son and his fanbase.

Easton's eyes pop wide. "What? How could he be scared of spiders? Spiders are awesome." I'm not scared of them like Reeve was, but there's no way I'm as enthusiastic as Easton.

Dillon chuckles. "He wouldn't have lasted pissing time on the farm. Our house was full of spiders."

"Hand it over," East says, thrusting out his palm, without even looking up.

"You must be loaded by now," Dillon retorts, handing over a dollar bill.

"I am. Mom said she's going to take me to the bank to 'posit it."

"I'm impressed, and I approve." He looks proudly at me like I've agreed to climb Mount Everest, not just go to the bank.

"It's only the bank," I murmur, feeling a mixture of embarrassment and shame.

"It's a step back into the real world. This is good, Hollywood."

My finger twitches with the desire to flip him off.

"Why do you call my mommy Hollywood?" East looks at Dillon with a perplexed expression.

"I first met your mom when she came to Dublin to study. We were *real* good friends," he says, shooting me a flirty look, and I swear I'm going to kill him if he doesn't quit it with the innuendos. "And I liked to tease her by calling her Hollywood because Hollywood is in L.A. where she was from."

"Oh." He looks satisfied with that explanation. Turning to me, he tugs on my arm. "Tell me the story, Mommy. Why was Daddy scared?"

"We were thirteen, and your grandpa and grandma had taken us up to a cabin at Big Sur. They had gone out to get food while Reeve and I were unpacking. I heard your daddy shout, and I rushed into his room. There was this massive spider on top of the pillow on his bed, and he was freaking out. The look on his face was priceless, and I couldn't resist taking a pic."

"What happened to the spider?" E asks.

"I got a cup, scooped him up, and put him outside." I don't tell him Reeve stood there like a statue, pale, sweating, and shaking, because Easton thinks his daddy is a superhero, and I never want to change that.

"Do you like spiders, Mommy?" East asks, moving the page to the next set of photos.

"I'm not sure *like* is the right word, but I'm not scared of them."

"I love spiders," Easton says. "When I'm older, I'm gonna let all the spiders live in my house." A shiver rolls over my spine, and I could almost swear Reeve is listening to this conversation and freaking out.

"That sounds fun," Dillon says, winking at me. "But I think it's time for some-one's bath."

"Okay." Easton is always way more agreeable when Dillon is around. I think my little chat after his hurtful comments at Dillon's house has helped to settle him too. "Love you, Daddy." Easton kisses Reeve's picture before carefully closing the album.

A dart of pain glimmers in Dillon's eyes, and I know this is hard for him.

"Honey, why don't you go and get your pajamas and a towel ready. Uncle Dillon will be with you in a minute."

"Sure thing, Mom." Easton races out of the room, because that's the speed at which he lives his life, leaving me alone with Dillon.

Without second-guessing it, I reach out, linking my fingers in his. "He loves you too. He is always talking about you, and he misses you on the days he doesn't see you."

"I know Reeve will always be his daddy, but I want to be his daddy too."

"You are, Dillon. In all the ways that count, you are. And some day, we will explain it to him, and he'll realize how lucky he is to have two daddies."

Dillon folds his arms around me, holding me close. "I love him so much." When he eases back to look at me, I'm not surprised to see moisture in his eyes. "You too."

Reaching out, I brush strands of hair off his brow. "I know you do, and we're grateful to have you in our lives."

"Does that mean I'm forgiven?"

There's a double meaning there, and we both know it. I pause to consider my feelings, but it doesn't take long to confirm it. "It does."

"I want to kiss you so fucking badly right now." His eyes drop to my lips, and my heart starts running a marathon.

Blood rushes to my head, and I'm tingly all over as I place my hand on his chest and tip my chin up. We move closer, maintaining eye contact, and my heart is pounding like crazy as our mouths line up.

"I'm ready!" Easton shrieks, and we instantly jerk back from one another.

"Awesome timing, buddy," Dillon says, standing, and I lick my lips as I watch him discreetly adjust himself in his jeans.

"He's fast asleep," Dillon says, appearing in my kitchen forty minutes later.

"You're a miracle worker. Some nights he takes forever to fall asleep for me."

"I sing to him." He places his hands on the island unit. "My voice literally puts him to sleep."

I giggle, and it feels like forever since I've laughed. "Thank goodness it doesn't have the same effect on your fans!"

"Fuck, I've missed that sound. You need to laugh more, Viv. I'm making that my new mission."

I roll my eyes as I head to the refrigerator. "Do you want a beer?"

"I wish I could stay, but I can't. We're putting the finishing touches to the album tonight. Ro is desperate to get home to Ireland to see Emer."

Disappointment washes over me, but I disguise it behind a smile. "No problem." I remove the chilled bottle of white wine from the refrigerator, and Dillon strides to the cupboard, removing a glass for me. His fingers graze mine as he hands it over, shooting fiery tremors up my arm.

"I have something for you," he admits as I pour myself some wine. "I've had these for a while, but I wasn't sure if you wanted them back or when the right time was to hand them over." He pushes a plain, unmarked brown envelope toward me.

Opening it, I pull out a mountain of photos, and a rush of emotions slams into me. I grip the edge of the counter to steady myself.

"Shit." He's by my side in a second, wrapping his arms around me from behind. "I can take them back."

"No." I gather myself, staring down at the picture of Dillon and me. It's from one of our weekends away in Ireland. We were in Sligo in this old-fashioned restaurant that served the best fish. The picture is a little blurry, and you can tell it was taken through the window because of the angle, but it's clear enough to remind me of the memory.

Our arms are wrapped around one another, and we're both sporting the cheesiest grins as we stare at the stocky man with a protruding belly and shock of thick black hair holding Dillon's phone. We look so young and so in love. It practically radiates from the photo. "I remember the restaurant owner. He had this really loud booming voice and a bellowing laugh."

"I remember him too," Dillon supplies. "He insisted on taking that photo because he said we personified young love."

"We did," I quietly admit because there's no point denying the truth when it's staring us in the face. "How did you end up with these?"

"The cop investigating the accident gave them to me at the hospital. He found them in the car."

Pain glides up my throat, and I cling to Dillon's arms. "Reeve had only given them to me that night. That's how he confirmed who you were to me."

"I can't believe someone was following us the whole time you were in Ireland. I even spotted the fucker." Dillon's arms tighten around me. "I know he's not here to defend himself, but that was a total asshole move on Reeve's part."

"It was," I agree without hesitation. "And I told him that. I was disgusted someone was capturing our intimate moments on film. It makes me sick to think of someone watching us like that, but Reeve didn't know they had taken it that far. He told them not to send him the photos. He just wanted to know I was protected." Dillon is uncharacteristically quiet behind me, and I arch my head back, staring into his face. "You don't believe that?"

"Actually, I do." His eyes lock on mine. "Reeve was obsessive in the way he loved you. It stands to reason he'd have someone watching over you to ensure you were safe. Doesn't mean I approve or I'm pleased about it." Reaching down, he flicks through the photos, pulling up one that has me blushing furiously. "At least we got some incredible photos out of it."

I feel him hardening against my back as we stare at the photo of us in the sea at Brittas Bay. My legs are wrapped around Dillon's neck, and he's holding me up by my butt. My head is thrown back in the throes of passion as Dillon feasts on me. Intense heat creeps up my neck and onto my cheeks.

"I'm thinking of getting that one blown up and hanging it on the ceiling over my bed."

"No, you're not!" I twirl around in his arms, staring at him incredulously.

"Watch me." He flashes me his trademark smirk before kissing the tip of my nose and releasing me from his embrace.

I'm still staring in shock after him as he saunters out of my kitchen, whistling under his breath like he hasn't a care in the world.

He wasn't serious.

Right?

CHAPTER 35
DILLON

"YOU WANT A BEER?" Ro asks when we are settled in our booth in the VIP section of the bar. A waitress hovers at the edge of our table, trying to pretend she's not ogling me like I'm her meal ticket out of here. Ignoring her, I nod at my brother, and he places our order. Ro is returning to Ireland tomorrow, and I'm not going to see him now until Christmas.

"Thank fuck, we got the album wrapped in time." Jamie stretches his arms along the other side of the booth. "I am so ready for some sexy times with my woman under the hot Mexican sun."

"Do you want to kick him in the nuts or shall I?" Ro asks, leaning his elbows on the table.

"The honor is all yours. Go for it, little bro."

"You two need to get laid. Stat."

"I'm working on it," I say as the waitress returns with an ice bucket filled with cold beers. Her fingers brush mine as she hands me a bottle, batting her eyelashes and pretending to be demure. "You're wasting your time," I tell her. "I'm not interested." The only woman I have eyes for these days is a certain Hollywood princess who is determined to keep my current blue-balls status intact.

"I am." Ro leans back, leaving the ball in her court.

"Awesome. I'm on my break in thirty minutes."

"Looking forward to it, darling." Ro winks, but the instant she's gone, the smug smirk drops off his face.

"Getting back in the saddle?" Jamie asks, bringing his beer to his lips.

"More like forcing myself back in the saddle."

"Why force it if you're not feeling it?" I ask, instinctively knowing there's more to it.

Ro's Adam's apple bobs in his throat. "Clodagh is back with her ex." He drains half his beer in one go.

SIOBHAN DAVIS

"Fuck. Are you sure?" I swallow a mouthful of beer, and the cold liquid is soothing going down my throat.

"She told me herself." He rests his face in his hands, looking glummer than the Grinch on Christmas morning. "I'm such an idiot. You all told me we were moving too fast. Now I've sent her running straight back into that dickhead's arms."

"You haven't done anything wrong, Ro."

"Except fall for the wrong girl," Jamie unhelpfully adds.

"If you hadn't met her, you wouldn't have Emer," I remind him because he adores his little girl.

"I know. It just hurts that she'd leave and go back to Colin so fast." A muscle clenches in his jaw. "I don't want that prick anywhere near my daughter."

My phone vibrates on the table, and I swipe it up, answering when I see it's my sister. "You all done?" I ask, wondering if she wrapped her meetings up quicker than planned so she could get here earlier.

"Not yet. I've still got two more meetings."

We have decided to hire a new publicist because we need someone who is completely on the ball to manage our publicity going forward. Dixie is competent enough, but things will get real when the news finally comes out about Easton, and I want the best person on our side. Which is why Ash spoke with Viv's mum and then lined up preliminary meetings with a few top publicists she put her in contact with. She'll pick someone suitable, and then we'll meet with him or her to ensure we can work with the person before we make an official hire.

"So, what's up?"

"I got a call from Charlotte."

I instantly straighten in my chair. "What's wrong?"

"She said someone needs to come over to be with Viv. She's worried about her state of mind."

"Did something happen?" I was over there yesterday, and everything was normal. As in, she's trying to pretend the sexual tension between us isn't close to combusting and still clinging to Easton like superglue.

"All she said was Vivien was upset and someone should be there for her. Easton is on a sleepover with Lauren and Jon, and my guess is she's lonely and getting lost in her head."

"Okay. I'll go to her."

"Ring or text me when you get there. I'm concerned."

"I'll take care of her."

We hang up, and I sheepishly face my brother.

"It's fine," Ro says before I can say a word. "If Vivien needs you, you should go to her. At least you still have a chance at salvaging your relationship. Mine is dead in the water, and I would give anything to have another chance."

"I'm not sure if I'll be able to come back. It sounds like she's not in a good place."

Ro stands to let me out of the booth. He pulls me into a hug. "Go take care of your woman, and I'll see you at Christmas."

"Give Emer a big hug and kiss from me," I tell him, slapping him on the back. "I know what it's like to lose the woman you love, so if you think Clodagh is the one and

566

there's any chance of getting her back, fight for her. Don't do what I did." I'm not sure if I should be encouraging him because I happen to believe Clodagh *isn't* the right woman for my brother. He needs someone steadfast, not someone flighty. But I'm not going to be the one to tell him what he should or shouldn't feel.

Some indecipherable emotion flits briefly across his face. "I'm rooting for you guys," he chokes out. "I really hope it works out for you."

"Thanks, bro." I grab him into another hug. "Take care of yourself."

I salute Jamie. "Later, fucker."

"Dillon. Thanks for coming," Charlotte says, ushering me into the house.

"It's not a problem. Before I go home, let me give you my number so you can call me directly if you ever need to." I know Angela has my digits, but Charlotte really should have them too.

"That sounds like a good idea."

"Where is she?"

Sympathy splays across her face. "She's been in the nursery for hours."

Shit. She never goes in there, usually keeping the door locked. "Okay. I know my way."

I head upstairs with a heavy heart, wondering what I'm going to find. I slow my pace as I approach the door, not wanting to startle her. The door is ajar, and Viv is in the middle of the empty room, flat on her back, staring up at the ceiling as she sings. Two empty wine bottles litter the floor, along with a bunch of used tissues, and she's clutching a pink blanket to her chest.

She's singing "She Moved Through the Fair," and I'm instantly transported back in time. The haunting quality of her voice matches the sadness dripping from the lyrics as the words leave her lips. Listening to her sing this song is painful on several levels, but her grief adds an extra harrowing dimension. I prop my hip against the door frame, listening to the love of my life sing from her soul, wishing I could absorb her pain and erase the silent tears spilling down her cheeks.

Her chest heaves when she finishes, and she hiccups in between sobs. I rap softly on the door so as not to startle her. Sad bloodshot hazel eyes lock on my face as I step into the room. I don't speak as I walk over to her, dropping onto the floor and sitting cross-legged by her side. "Hey, beautiful." I brush the moisture off her cheeks as she stares at me with eyes drowning in deep emotion.

"Swans only have one partner for their entire life. Did you know that?" I shake my head, wondering if mention of the swan in the evening in the song has prompted her to share this. "They mate with the same partner until the bond is broken by death or they are preyed upon. They are the purest symbol of true love." She sits up, still clutching the pink blanket to her chest. "I think we're swans, Dillon." She hiccups, and the hint of a smile graces her lips. "Reeve, me, and you." Her lower lip wobbles, and tears pool in her eyes again. "And Lainey is an angel. They're both angels now."

"Was this hers?" I ask, gesturing toward the blanket.

She nods. "I kept it and the little hat she was wearing at the hospital. She was like a doll, Dillon. When I held her, she was like a beautiful sleeping doll. So tiny but so perfect." Her tortured cries bounce off the walls and stab me straight through the heart. "I don't want to give her things away. I know it's selfish. I know there are other babies out there who need her things, but I can't do it, Dillon. I can't."

I move a little closer, terrified to do anything that will spook her. "You don't have to do anything you don't want to."

"Audrey cleared out the room because I couldn't do it. Everything is in storage, and I'm gonna keep it. Lainey's little sister will wear her things and sleep in her crib. I think Lainey would like that, don't you?"

"I think that's a lovely idea."

"I have to have hope. Keeping her things gives me hope." She glances around the room, and her eyes dart to the far wall. "We helped paint that. Me, Reeve, and Easton."

I spin around on my butt, marveling at the amazing mural on the wall.

"It's Tinkerbell," she explains. "This was going to be a room for my fairy princess, but God decided he needed an angel instead."

I want to say fuck God, but that won't offer her any comfort, so I clamp my mouth shut.

"I'm going to turn it into a reading room, because I can't bear to paint over that mural. Not when it's one of the last things Easton and Reeve did together."

"You should totally keep it, and I think this room would make a great reading room. It has a nice window, perfect for a window seat, and you could fill that back wall with floor-to-ceiling bookshelves. Jamie and I could build them if you want? Easton could help."

She bursts out crying, and I pull her into my arms, hoping it's the right move. She collapses against me, and I dot kisses in her hair as she cries against my chest, clutching my shirt. "I love you," she says, and hope swells inside me. "I shouldn't, but I do." She lifts her head, piercing me with tear-soaked eyes. "I have loved you all this time, Dillon. I never stopped. I was a terrible wife."

"That isn't even remotely possible. You were an amazing wife."

"But was I?" she whispers before hiccupping again. "I mean, I really loved Reeve. Truly, madly, deeply. He made me happy, but I loved you too. And I never compared you because you both held an equal share of my heart. It didn't stop me from feeling guilty though. It's hard loving two men at the same time. Some nights, when I couldn't sleep, I would sneak to the sunroom and listen to your songs. I have all your albums on my cell, in a hidden folder, so Reeve wouldn't find them. I love your music." A scowl mars her pretty face. "When you're not singing about hating me."

I open my mouth to remind her of our previous conversation on the topic, but she continues, and I shove the comment back down my throat, letting her get whatever she needs to off her chest. Her thoughts are veering all over the place, and I'm guessing her emotions are too.

"You're super talented. And I love listening to your voice. It lulled me to sleep on difficult nights. When I really wanted to torture myself, I would watch the wedding video clip of you singing 'Terrify Me.' That always made me cry." She bursts into floods of tears again, and I wonder if I should try to get her to her bedroom or let her continue purging her thoughts.

The egotistical part of my personality keeps my butt planted right where it is. I want to know what else she's going to say. They say the truth comes out when you're drunk, and I've been starved of Viv's truths for years, so sue me if I'm being selfish.

She cries into my shirt, plastering it to my skin, and I rock her gently in my arms, holding her close. "I spent years thinking you hated me and that I was the biggest fool for still loving you even though I loved Reeve too. But I couldn't stop it, Dil. I couldn't make it stop."

"I can relate to that. Not a single day went by where you weren't on my mind."

"We were good together. I didn't imagine that, right?"

"We're epic, sweetheart, and everything was real. Everything *is* real."

"I think I was always destined to love you, Dillon. Have you thought about how things might've been if that dickhead Simon hadn't given you away?"

"I've wondered what my life would've been like if he'd given Reeve away instead of me," I truthfully reply.

"Would we have loved each other from the time we were kids?"

"Of course, we would have. There is no measure of time or distance where I wouldn't be in love with you, Vivien. I was in love with you before I even met you. I know things got fucked up, but I truly believe I was waiting for you to walk into my life and make sense of the chaos in my head. It was always you. It will always be you. There will never be any other love for me. We *are* like swans." An idea pops into my head. "We should totally build a lake and get swans."

She bursts out laughing, and my chest swells with pride that I can make her laugh when she's so upset.

"You're crazy."

"Crazy about you."

"I like romantic Dillon," she murmurs, and I press a fierce kiss to her brow.

"You bring out the best in me, Viv. You always have. My family saw it way before I did."

"I love your family." A whimsical look materializes on her face. "They are awesome."

"They are pretty great." Even after everything I put them through and how much I disappointed them, they don't bear any grudges.

I've made more of an effort to speak to my parents and Shane and Ciarán, on a regular basis, letting them know how grateful I am for their forgiveness. Ma can't wait to meet Easton. I was going to fly them over for a visit, but I don't want to confuse my son by bringing more people into his life or invite questions I can't answer yet.

"You were the lucky one, Dil." She slurs her words a little and her vision looks unfocused. "Trust me, you were. You have an amazing family. I love them. Did I ever tell you that? I love your family like they're my own."

"That's because they are." Or they officially will be, if I have my way.

"I love them, and they love you sooooo much. Reeve constantly fought for Simon's affection, but he had none to give."

"He was a cold fucker." I grit my teeth, unwilling to go down that road right now. I have let go of the resentment I had toward my twin, but I will never forgive Simon Lancaster or forget what he did.

"If you'd come home with Reeve, we would all have been friends." She peers deep into my eyes. "Don't you see? I was always destined to love both of you."

I think I was always destined to battle my twin for Vivien's heart.

"My heart was always going to be torn in two," she continues, confirming she's given this much thought. "It's why fate led me to you in Dublin because how else do you explain it? Out of all the cities I could have escaped to, I chose the one you lived in. And out of all the people who live there, I befriended Ash and we met. I mean, it's crazy, right?" A little spark flickers in her eyes.

"It is, and I think you're right. I don't believe in coincidence, so it's got to be fate." I have thought about what might've happened if Reeve hadn't died. Would she still be with him, or would she have left him for me? We'll never know, and I don't mention it because what's the point? He's not here, and I am. Trying to second-guess what would happen if he was still alive will only hurt both of us. Instead, I choose to believe in fate. Fate brought us together, tore us apart, and then reunited us. I choose to believe that would have happened even if Reeve was still walking the planet.

"Yes, yes." She nods before resting her head on my chest and grasping my shirt. "Can I ask you something?"

I nod as she peers up at me.

"You said 'once a cheater always a cheater' about Reeve. Do you know something I don't?"

Shit. I really was a fucking prick when I first showed up. I shake my head. "I threw it out there to annoy you. I have no proof he cheated on you, and from what I know of him now, I think it's fair to say he didn't. I'm sorry if I made you doubt him."

"You didn't. Not really. I knew he would never cheat on me again. He was always so quiet and melancholy on Christmas Day. I know he was remembering our breakup and how much it killed him to be separated from me. He loved our family and the life we shared. He wouldn't do anything to jeopardize that. I was sure of it, but I just needed to ask you about it."

"I was such an asshole to you. I'm sorry."

She waves her hand in the air. "It's water under the bridge now, Dillon, and I don't want to think about all that again."

Silence engulfs us for a few minutes, but it's the kind of comfortable silence I live for with Viv. There is such peace in sitting here holding her in my arms.

"I'm tired of feeling guilty, Dil," she admits, snuggling closer. "I'm tired of missing Reeve and Lainey, but most of all, I'm tired of not living. I want to be happy again. I just want to be happy." Her voice trails off, and she sounds dejected and sad.

"I want you to be happy too, sweetheart. Let me make you happy. Let me love you."

CHAPTER 36
VIVIEN

MY TONGUE IS STUCK to the roof of my mouth when I wake up in one of our spare bedrooms with Dillon draped around me from behind. Flashbacks of last night float across my mind, and I softly groan. I know I said a lot of stuff to him. As I examine my recollection and remember the things I said, I can't find it within me to regret any of it.

I forced myself to go into the nursery last night because it is time to remodel it. However, I wasn't prepared enough for the onslaught of emotions that hit me the instant I set foot in the room, and I came apart at the seams.

I think I needed to expel those emotions I was denying in order to turn a corner. Today, it feels like I have. As if a layer of pain has lifted from my body. I'm not saying I won't continue to grieve, because I know it's not as simple as that, but it's going to be different from now on.

Turning slowly around, I stare at the man sleeping beside me. When I fell asleep on him, he must have carried me in here. I'm glad he didn't take me to my bedroom because I couldn't sleep in my marital bed with Dillon without surrendering to enormous guilt. And I'm done feeling guilty for loving this man. Dillon is such an enigma, but he's really come through for me these past few months, and I can't deny my feelings for him any longer.

I love him.

I have loved him for years.

I don't know where we go from here, because I'm not ready to go full speed into a relationship, but he deserves honesty from me. I've kept him dangling from his fingertips, and it's not fair.

Reluctantly, I extract myself from his loving embrace, my heart melting when I find the pain meds and a bottle of water by the bed. He takes such good care of me. Just like Reeve did. I chug them down and get up, dragging my hungover ass into the shower.

After I'm dressed and feeling slightly more alive, I pad back to the bedroom to discover Dillon sitting up in bed. He's on his phone and he hasn't noticed me yet, so I take a moment to admire the fine sight of his semi-naked physique.

Broad tan shoulders give way to a toned chest and ripped abs. Ink covers both arms and one shoulder, and he truly is a work of art. With his messy white-blond hair and the stylish layer of stubble on his chin and cheeks, he could grace the cover of any magazine, and it would sell out in seconds.

"Done drooling yet?" he asks, not lifting his head from his phone, and I hear the smile in his tone.

"What has you so engrossed you can't even look at me?"

His head jerks up, and he pins me with that panty-melting smile of his. I have a hard time keeping upright. "I'm researching how to buy swans."

My mouth hangs open. "I thought you were joking!"

"Nah. I'm deadly serious. I'm getting us a lake and swans."

He's just stubborn enough to do it too. Dillon flashes me his famous grin again, the one that has his female fans fanning themselves, and his dimples come out to play.

That's it.

I'm a goner.

The dimples get me every time.

As if on autopilot, I walk across the room to the bed, climbing up beside him. "Hi." I smile shyly at him as a sudden bout of nerves attacks me.

"You're too cute for words." His fingers sweep across my cheeks. "I have missed this blush."

"Don't tease me right now. I have things I need to say."

His smile explodes across his face, and I lose all semblance of coherence. I stare at him in a daze. "You are too beautiful for words," I admit.

"If that's true, my beauty pales in comparison to yours. The instant you step into a room, I'm enchanted, Viv. You do the most amazing things to my heart." He fights a smirk. "My cock too." He winks, and I roll my eyes.

"You just can't help yourself, can you?"

"Not around you." He opens his arms. "Come here. I need to hold you."

I don't argue, snuggling against him and sighing contentedly. We fit perfectly, like we were crafted to seamlessly mold together as one.

"How much of last night do you remember?" he asks, tracing his fingers up and down my arm.

"All of it, I think."

"You said you loved me."

I tilt my head up, so I'm staring into his eyes. "I meant it. I love you, Dillon." I cup his cheek. "And I want to let you love me, but you'll have to continue to be patient."

"I can do that, but you have to set boundaries because my need for you is at an all-time high."

"Last night was a catharsis of sorts for me. My own 'come to Jesus' moment. I don't feel sad today. I feel more at peace than any other time since they died, and I want to move forward." My eyes penetrate his. "I want to move forward with you."

"Thank fuck." He bundles me in his arms, hugging me tight. Warmth from his skin rolls over me, heating all the frozen parts.

"I can't promise I won't have bad days. Days where I miss Reeve are a given because I can't just forget about him or not remember how much we meant to each other."

"I get that, and it's fine. All I ask is that you don't shut me out. Tell me you're missing him. I would rather hear it from your lips than guess why you're upset or noncommunicative or distant."

"I'll be honest; even if I don't want to hurt you, I promise I'll always tell you the truth."

He lifts my hand to his mouth, kissing my fingers. "I promise you the same. We will never keep secrets from one another again."

"Agreed."

"What else?"

"We need to be discreet around Easton. It's not that I want to hide us from him, but it will confuse him. We can't tell him yet." I hate the thought of sneaking around behind my son's back, but it's only been four months since his daddy died. I don't know how he'll react if he sees me kissing another man. Especially his uncle. It could lead to other questions we can't answer yet.

"I hate having to agree, but it's the way it's got to be. For now."

"We can't go public for the same reasons."

He sighs. "I know you're right, but this is beginning to feel like a dirty secret, and I'm not loving that much."

"Nor me, but this is the way it has to be. It won't be forever." I need time to work up the courage to tell Easton and to go public, and I have no clue how long that will take me, but I'm hoping this more patient version of Dillon will last and he won't pressure me into doing something before I'm ready.

"I'll try not to be my usual needy, greedy self. To remember that having you back in my life, even if it's not quite the way I'd hoped, is enough."

I run my fingers through his hair, holding his head. "I love you, and you love me. That won't change, and that's what matters the most. The rest is stuff we can work through in time."

He rests his forehead against mine. "I have waited years to hear those words again. I love you, Vivien Grace Lancaster. I love you so much, and I would wait until the end of time for you."

My heart beats with a zest that is new, all because of this man. I am truly lucky to have found such amazing love in my life. Not once, but twice. And to be given a second chance with Dillon, after everything we have been through, is more than I dared to hope for. "Just be patient with me, Dil. Like you were the last time."

"You set the pace, Viv. You call the shots."

"Look at me."

He lifts his head, peering into my eyes as my fingers weave in and out of his hair. "I still love your hair." My hands move lower, touching his eyes, his nose, and his lips, brushing against his cheeks, and rubbing the bristles on his chiseled jawline. "I love every part of you but especially your heart." I place one hand over his bare chest, and his heart drums steadily against my palm. "Thank you for being here for me. Thank you for caring for me and Easton."

"There is nowhere else I would rather be."

I lean in, keeping my eyes on his as I brush my lips against his mouth. "Kiss me, Dillon. Kiss me like you'll die if you can't taste my lips." We both smile, remembering another first kiss that started with those words, and a serene sense of calm settles over me. All the tiny hairs on the back of my neck lift, and a very subtle breeze sweeps fleetingly across my face. It might freak others out, but I think Reeve is here, and it comforts me. I think that is his way of telling me it is okay.

Dillon's mouth descends, and I sink into his arms and the feel of his warm lips moving against mine. He angles his head to deepen the kiss, and I open my mouth, letting him push his tongue in. I sigh into his mouth, our minty breaths comingling, as he strokes my tongue in long leisurely strokes. Winding my arms around his neck, I climb onto his lap, pressing my chest against his.

His hands rest respectfully on my lower back, and he makes no move to push this to the next level, content to kiss me while holding me tight.

I get lost in him.

Drowning in the taste of his kisses that are both familiar and excitingly new.

Flames lick at my skin as he ignites a burning desire that covers me from head to toe. Every part of my body feels the effects of his kiss. There is no part that is immune, and I never want to stop feeling like this.

Dillon always lit a fire inside me, and now he's nurturing the flames, coaxing them to jump higher, enabling them to burn bright so they never die out.

So *we* never die out.

I feel that truth deep in my bones, and as I cling to him, I know there will be challenging times ahead, but I believe we can overcome anything together. We will emerge from the flames a single entity, ready to burn anyone who dares step in our way.

My heart beats to a new rhythm, and my soul dances to a new hope, as we kiss and kiss like we can't get enough of one another.

I don't know how I ever thought I could deny this man.

How I could ever live without him.

Because he is embedded in my heart and imprinted on my soul, and from this day forward, I know he is the only man I will ever want by my side.

CHAPTER 37
VIVIEN

SEPTEMBER TURNS INTO OCTOBER, and we settle into a new routine. I drop Easton at school each morning, and Dillon collects him every day. On Tuesdays and Thursdays, he drops East at his Krav Maga class, staying to watch because he gets a kick out of it. Other afternoons, they go out for ice cream or burgers or go hang out at his house, and we've even managed a few family outings without being spotted. We've gone bowling, to the movies, and on several hikes so Easton finally got to wear his new hiking boots.

I've been writing a lot, documenting my story in a more cohesive fashion, drawing from all my journals. I suppose it's a book, but it won't ever see the light of day. I'm doing this for me and for Easton so that, one day, when he's old enough, he might read it and understand how I came to love both his daddies.

I'm also sewing again, and Ash has given me a list of requirements of things she'd like to take on tour with her next year. Mom loved the gown I made her for her next premiere. They left a couple of weeks ago to go on location, in Canada, but not before they both pulled me aside to tell me they approve of Dillon and me being together. I was so nervous telling them, and hugely relieved when they didn't judge. Not that I ever thought they would. I know they worry about me, and they've been watching Dillon like a hawk to ensure he doesn't step out of line.

We eat dinner together every night, as a family, and slowly Dillon is finding little ways of injecting narrative into our conversations that hints at our friendship and how Reeve would be happy we are such good friends again.

He's easing Easton into the idea of us as a couple with small gestures like placing his hand on my lower back as we walk in the garden, tucking my hair behind my ears, or brushing his fingers against my cheek, and our son hasn't balked when he's occasionally wrapped his arm around my waist.

But I won't let him take it further than that, and we haven't progressed beyond kissing and heavy groping. On nights when Dillon stays over, I usually crawl into his bed, ensuring I set my alarm so I can sneak back to my room before Easton wakes up.

Dillon hasn't pressured me at all, seemingly happy with the pace, and it helps. Gradually, my grief is becoming less of a tangible thing. I still miss Reeve, and I still think of him every day, but it is getting easier. I'm laughing more, having fewer bad dreams, and waking up more regularly with a smile on my face.

Which is progress indeed.

"Mommy, you look awesome!" East says as I step into the transformed room in Dillon's house as Wonder Woman. The noise levels are through the roof, and my ears protest loudly.

The lady Dillon hired to create a Halloween-themed room did an awesome job. Fake cobwebs hang from the ceiling, and there are a few token spiders residing in larger webs, in an ode to Easton's obsession with all creepy-crawlies. The ceiling has been covered in an eerie nighttime sky, and sheets of red chiffon cover all the lights, bathing the room in a reddish glow. Entertainers dressed as skeletons and ghosts roam the room, while a man dressed as a magician performs tricks from a temporary stage mounted at the very back of the space.

Round tables and small chairs occupy the center of the room, and the kids from Easton's class are due to congregate there in a while for burgers and fries. After, we're doing a trunk-or-treat out in the driveway so the kids get the trick or treat experience without any danger. Staff from the catering company Dillon hired are presently filling our trunks, and the trunks of the class parents who are here, with tons of candy and chocolate treats. Easton is going to be beside himself with excitement when he discovers it.

"Thanks, buddy. You look pretty awesome yourself." Easton high-fives me before shoving the mask of his Iron Man costume down over his face and rushing off to play with his friends.

"Jesus, woman, are you trying to kill me?" Dillon asks, his hungry eyes taking in every inch of my exposed skin. We chose a superhero theme as a family, and I stupidly agreed to let the boys pick the costumes. "There's not exactly a lot of room in this costume." He points at his tight Captain America costume, and it's hard not to drool. He sure gives Chris Evans a run for his money, and I don't say that lightly because Chris is fucking hot with a capital H.

But he's got nothing on Dillon O'Donoghue.

"If you don't want our son or his friends to spot me with a giant boner, I suggest you go and get changed. What was wrong with the Black Widow costume I got you anyway?" He pouts, looking completely ridiculous.

"God, he's insufferable," Ash says, coming up beside me. She's Bonnie to Jamie's Clyde. "I should shoot him for suggesting you wear that boring all-in-one yoke he gave you." She jabs Captain America in the chest with her toy gun.

"It wasn't boring. I know Viv will look hot in it but hot in a way that won't have me showcasing my hard-on to a bunch of kindergarteners. You hear me." Dillon quirks a brow at his sister.

Ash pulls the shield off his back, thrusting it at him. "Use that, dumbass. If you had a brain, you'd be the full package." She barks out a laugh. "Ha, see what I did there." I giggle while Dillon rolls his eyes. Ash shoves the shield down over his privates. "There, problem solved, and now my sexy bestie doesn't need to get changed."

We got ready together in Dillon's master suite, and Ash went all out on my hair and makeup. I feel like a million dollars, and I'm looking forward to after the kids' party when the adults get to play.

"You have really outdone yourself," I say, checking to ensure no one is looking before I plant a quick kiss on his cheek. "Easton is going to be talking about this party for years." He was so excited this afternoon as he sat at the kitchen table carving pumpkins with his dad while Ash and I made pumpkin pie and chocolate apples.

"That was the intention." He smiles as he looks over to where Easton, Nash, and a couple of other little boys are intently watching the magician juggle a bunch of balls in the air. "I want to make lots of special memories with him."

I loop my arm through his, wishing I could kiss the shit out of him, but it's too risky. Parents of the kids in Easton's class are in the room as well as staff from the catering company. "Does that go for me too?" I ask, deliberately batting my eyelashes at him.

He swats my ass. "You know it does, and if you keep torturing me, you know I'll get you back."

I waggle my brows as I grin up at him. "Oh, I'm counting on it."

"Dillon," I scream, as he lifts me from behind, throwing me over his shoulder.

"We'll be back," he tells Ash and Jamie. "I just need to teach this little vixen a lesson or two."

Ash howls with laughter as Dillon swats my ass and races out of the room. It's just as well Easton is out cold—and tucked up snugly in his bed upstairs, exhausted after his crazy party—because my screams are enough to wake all the neighbors.

"Dillon, put me down!" I demand, but his answer is another stinging slap. "My ass is hanging out," I protest. This costume is tiny, and from the cool air trickling across my butt cheeks, I know I'm flashing plenty of flesh.

"So what?"

"It's not very ladylike."

His chest rumbles with laughter. "Oh, Hollywood, you really crack me up. Do I have to remind you of all the non-ladylike things you let me do to you in Ireland? Or outline the things you're going to let me do to you again?"

My core pulses with need at his words and the images they conjure in my horny mind.

"I thought so," he says, sounding pleased when I don't mount any protest.

He ducks in through a door, taking me into the laundry room, closing it behind him before putting my feet on the ground.

His mouth is on mine in a nanosecond, and I forget everything but the fruity taste of his tongue as it pushes past my lips. Grabbing a fistful of his costume, I pull him to me, kissing him with urgency, needing him closer. His arms band around my body, and he crushes me to him. Our costumes are flimsy, and the evidence of his arousal pushes against my stomach, trying to poke a hole in both our clothing. Liquid lust rushes through me, dampening my panties, and I moan into his mouth, thrusting my chest against his, needing more. If I could climb inside him right now, I would.

"Damn, Hollywood. If you keep kissing me like that, I'm going to come in my costume."

"Take it off," I demand, rubbing my palm up and down his hard length. "I want to taste you."

"Yeah?"

I could cry at the look of hopeful anticipation on his face. I know he's dying for me as much as I'm dying for him, and I've kept him waiting months, but advancing things sexually is a big deal for me, and I only want to make love to him when I'm fully ready to commit to him. I am almost there, and this will take us one step closer.

Dillon rips at the costume, tearing it in half in his eagerness to free himself.

I'm crying with laughter as I drop to my knees before him, but my laughter dies when he shoves his compression shorts down and his erect cock springs free, bobbing in front of my face like the most heavenly temptation. He still has his piercing, and my pussy throbs with need. I remember how good his cock felt stroking my insides with the little silver balls taking my pleasure to new dizzy heights. Sex with Dillon was always out of this world, and we had a very active sex life.

I want to have that with him again.

Gliding my hands up his legs, I run my fingers along the inside of his thighs before I cup his balls. Lifting my chin, I stare up at him, keeping my eyes locked on his as my tongue darts out, licking his crown, both sides of his piercing, and the bead of precum glistening there.

Dillon cusses, jerking his hips as his eyes burn with desire. "I've got to warn you. I won't last long. It's been more than a while."

His words comfort me. "Give me every drop. I want it all." Gripping the base of his cock, I stretch his velvety-soft skin before I kiss, suck, and nibble along his length, enjoying every stroke of my tongue against his hot flesh. He groans, thrusting his hips, and I take pity on him, drawing him slowly into my mouth. I pump his cock at the base while I suck and lick, stretching my mouth wide to take as much of him in as I can. Dillon is big, and I almost choke when his tip hits the back of my throat, but the look of lust on his face spurs me on.

He grabs my hair, holding my face steady while he fucks my mouth, and I love it. I love that he doesn't treat me like I'm a porcelain doll. That he pushes me to my limits, always ensuring I'm enjoying it. Tears leak out of my eyes and saliva drips down my chin as I go to town, loving the taste of him on my tongue and the feel of him in my mouth.

"Viv," he grits out, a muscle clenching in his jaw. "I'm going to come."

With my eyes, I urge him to keep going, pumping and sucking him harder as he pivots his hips, thrusting into my mouth. I fondle his balls, moving one finger behind to rub his taint because I remember he liked that. A primal growl rips from his lips as he lets go, and ropes of hot salty cum splash my mouth, shooting down my throat. I stay with him, milking every last drop of his climax, until he pulls out.

Dropping to his knees, he reels me into his arms, plunging his tongue into my mouth and kissing me like I'm the air he needs to breathe. "Vivien, Vivien, Vivien." He dots kisses all over my face. "I must have done something right in this life to deserve you because you are a fucking goddess among women. I could live a hundred lifetimes and never be worthy of you." He presses his sticky brow to mine. "I fucking love you, Hollywood. I love you so much."

"That must have been some blowjob," I tease, but I'm secretly pleased. What woman doesn't want to bring her man to his knees? *Literally.*

"It was the fucking Oscar of blowjobs, sweetheart, and now it's my turn."

I shriek as he scoops me up, planting me on top of the washing machine. He flashes me a wicked smile, showcasing dimples and blinding-white teeth, as he turns the machine on.

"What the hell are you doing?"

"Giving you an Oscar-worthy experience." He winks while parting my thighs and shoving my skirt up to my waist. I'm not surprised when he rips my panties, tossing scraps of lace to the floor, because it's his signature. "Hello, pussy," he croons, leaning down so he's eye level with my vagina. "Miss me as much as I missed you?"

I snort. "Oh. My. God. You are seriously deranged," I say as laughter bubbles up my throat.

The second his hot tongue lands on my cunt, all laughter fades. He swipes his tongue up and down my slit while eye fucking me, and I'm already squirming when the machine picks up speed and the whole thing starts vibrating. "Oh!" I exclaim as sensation rockets through me. "Oh my."

"Hold on tight, Hollywood. I'm about to give you the best damn orgasm of your life."

I grip the edges of the machine, holding on for dear life as Dillon ravishes me with his fingers and his tongue while the vibrations from the machine send me into another realm. My booted legs wrap around his neck, and the sight of his blond head bobbing up and down wrecks me. It's been so long since I was touched it doesn't take much to have me shooting for the stars. When Dillon hooks his fingers inside me and gently bites my clit, I explode, screaming his name as I come apart on his face.

I melt against him as he lifts me off the machine. "Holy hell, Dil," I rasp. "That was definitely Oscar worthy."

"We're so fucking good together," he reminds me, kissing me hard as he plants my feet on the ground. "Here, put these on. Ash will throw a hissy fit if I don't get you back to her ASAP." He hands me a pair of my lace panties, and I narrow my eyes suspiciously.

"Where did you get these?"

Fake innocence drenches his handsome features. "From your bedroom. Where else?"

"You were rooting through my underwear drawer?" I shriek.

He holds up his hands. "What else was a guy to do? I've had the worst case of blueballitis this side of the Pacific. Sniffing your knickers never fails to get me off in record time," he admits, smirking, as he grabs a pair of sweats from the laundry basket and pulls them on.

I gawk at him. "You are a very disturbed individual." I grab the machine to steady myself as I pull on my stolen panties.

He shrugs. "Desperate times call for desperate measures."

"How many did you steal?" I inquire as he takes my hand, hauling me into his warm bare chest.

"A handful."

I shake my head, but I'm smiling. "What am I going to do with you?"

"I can think of lots of things." He bends down to kiss me. "All of them X-rated." He thrusts against me, demonstrating he's hard again. "See what you do to me? I'm so hot for you, sweetheart. I'm hard all the damn time."

My hands creep up his chest. "I know you are, and I promise I'll be ready soon."

His features soften, and he gazes adoringly at me as he brushes hair over my shoulder. "You set the pace, Viv, and I'm happy. So fucking happy. Never feel under pressure to have sex with me. I can wait. This is more than enough. More than I ever thought I'd have again. I just love existing with you."

Tears prick my eyes. "I didn't think I'd ever feel content again. You have given me so much, Dillon," I croak.

"You have given me everything, Viv." He circles his arms around me, holding me close. "You have given me Easton, and I have you. I don't need anything else. I'm the happiest man on the planet."

CHAPTER 38
DILLON

"REMEMBER, YOU CAN'T SAY ANYTHING," I tell Ma as I hold my mobile phone out in front of me. "Keep it casual."

"I just want to say hello to the little guy, Dillon. Not give him the Spanish Inquisition." She rolls her eyes, and I really miss the fuck out of her. "When do you think you'll tell him?"

"Soon, I hope." I have a plan, which I hope Viv will agree to. Finding the right time to raise it with her is the issue. I don't want to spring it on her at the last minute because that fucked everything up the last time in Ireland. But the timing has to be spot-on so she won't overreact and tell me to take a hike. Things are perfect right now, and I don't want to mess anything up.

"Will you be bringing him home for Christmas?"

I rub the back of my neck, hating to do this to her. "About that."

Her face falls, and I feel like shit.

"Lauren and Jon didn't make it back for Thanksgiving today, but they'll be back for Christmas, and they want us to go there for dinner. It's tradition for all of them to go to the Millses' house, and it will be hard enough for East as it is. I don't want to do anything to upset him."

"It's okay, love. I understand. We'll miss you, but there'll be other Christmases."

"I'm sorry, Ma. I hate to be missing it, but I can't leave Vivien alone at Christmas. It's going to be tough on her." I know Reeve's loss will hit her hard then, and I need to be with her to help her get through it.

"I'm very proud of you, Dillon."

I arch a brow because I've done a lot of bad shit in the past. Things they only discovered when Reeve died, so I think saying she's proud is a bit of a stretch.

"You made mistakes, but you're atoning for them," she adds, seeing the incredulous expression on my face.

I've finally realized what Viv has been saying is true. Instead of focusing on revenge, I'm grateful for the life I've had. For the life I'm living. I know how fortunate I am to have my family and to have grown up surrounded by love. I took that for granted before. I only thought about the life that had been taken from me, not the one I was gifted. I didn't believe I was the lucky one, but I was wrong all along. It took letting go of my anger for me to see the truth.

"Every night, I say a prayer for you and Vivien and Easton," Ma continues, dragging me out of my head. "I knew the instant I met that girl that she was the one for you. I knew she was the girl you'd end up marrying, and I'm glad I wasn't wrong."

"Steady on, Ma, and don't go saying that shit to Viv."

She sighs. "Dillon, do you think I was born yesterday? I know better than to put my foot in it." She rolls her eyes. "Now go and put my cute little grandson on the line so I can wish him a Happy Thanksgiving."

"How did she take the news?" Viv asks as Easton says hello to my parents and extended family in Ireland via FaceTime. It helps that Ro is there as he knows him, but I'm sure he's wondering who the hell the rest of the freaks are. Ash is beside East, introducing him to everyone, and he's delighted with all the attention.

"She was a little disappointed, but she understands."

Viv chews on the corner of her lip, and I sneak my hand under the table, squeezing her fingers. "Stop worrying."

"I feel bad that you'll be away from your family at Christmas."

"But I won't be." I peer into her eyes. "I'll be with you and Easton. You're my family now."

She gives me a wobbly smile, and I'm guessing today is as hard for her as Christmas will be. This time last year, she was pregnant and celebrating with her husband.

"I'm sorry. I didn't mean to—"

"Don't be sorry, Dillon. You've got nothing to be sorry for." She glances at Easton to ensure he's not looking before planting a quick kiss on my lips. "And you're right. We are your family, and I'm lucky to get to do this with you. It's just hard today. I'm feeling a little sad."

I slide my arm around her shoulders, holding her tight. "I know, sweetheart, and I'm here for you."

Thanksgiving was harder than I thought it would be. Easton threw a few temper tantrums, and Vivien wore a sad smile on her face half the time, but we got through it. I yanked them out of bed this morning to go hiking at Pelican Cove Park because I want to do something fun today to put a smile back on both their faces.

The weather is cooler at this time of year, and Viv and Easton wrap up warm. My Irish bones don't need as much insulation, so I take a light jacket, and we head out up the coastal road.

We hike one of the shorter trails before heading down to the park and along the cliffs. Leon and Bobby trail us from a distance, giving us some privacy. Waves crash against the jagged rocks, and the sounds of the ocean are relaxing as we walk hand in hand. I keep Easton tucked in on the inside because he's got the same reckless streak

I have, and I don't want him running away and skydiving off the cliff. "How about some hot chocolate?" I ask him, spotting a silver van selling hot drinks and pastries.

"Oh, yay!" He tugs on my hand, hauling me forward.

"Do you want anything?" I call out to Viv.

She's smiling as she shakes her head, hanging back to admire the view as our son drags me along for the ride. There's a bit of a queue, so we get in line. Easton glances up at me before dropping his eyes to his feet. His brow puckers, and his nose scrunches up, the way it always does when he's thinking about something. "Spit it out, little dude. What's on your mind?"

He nibbles on his lips. "My daddy used to hold my mommy's hand like you did back there."

I gulp over the messy ball of emotion in my throat, sensing where this is going.

"Does that mean you're going to be my new daddy?"

Holy fuck. I look around for Vivien because I am so out of my depth here, but she's still staring out at the ocean, oblivious to my current panicked state. I run my hands through my hair, trying to think of the best thing to say.

"Does it, Uncle Dillon?" He looks up at me with so much hope and trust and innocence, and I would do anything for this kid. He means the world to me.

Taking his hand, I pull him out of the queue, off to the side where it's private. I bend down so I'm at his height. "Reeve will always be your daddy, buddy, but I'd like to be a permanent part of your life. If that's okay with you?"

He bobs his head, but he looks a little unsure. "I saw my mommy kissing you yesterday. Does that mean you're going to get married?"

Jesus, fuck. Where the hell is Vivien when I need her? I send juju vibes out to the universe, along with a silent plea, for her to come and rescue me. And someone must be listening because she appears beside me, and I release the breath I'd been holding.

"What's going on?" Her gaze bounces between East and me.

I scoop Easton up into my arms, grateful when he goes willingly. "I think we need to go back to the car and have a talk with East."

"I want my hot chocolate first."

"Okay. Come on. The line is gone now. Let's grab you a cookie and some hot chocolate."

After Easton gets his stuff, we walk back toward the parking lot in silence. I hand Vivien a coconut water, mouthing "He saw us kissing and holding hands. He has questions."

She nods, placing her hand on his shoulder and guiding him toward the car. The three of us climb in the back, and we keep Easton in the middle. I look to Viv, more than happy to let her take the lead on this.

She clears her throat. "I believe you have questions. What would you like to know?"

"Are you going to marry Uncle Dillon?" he asks, dribbling some hot chocolate down his chin. I dab the liquid with a napkin, cleaning it up before it can drop on his clothes.

"I don't know," she says, and it's as if she's thrust her hand into my chest and squeezed the life from my heart. "Maybe someday I will," she adds, and that helps a little. "Would that upset you?"

SIOBHAN DAVIS

He thinks about it for a few seconds as he sips his drink. "Would it mean he'd come to live with us and I could play guitar every day?"

Vivien smiles adorably at him. "Yes, except for times when Dillon is working."

He considers this for another few beats, and the suspense is killing me. "I suppose that would be okay."

Vivien and I exchange looks over his head.

"That's good because Dillon makes me happy."

"He makes me happy too," he says, and two red spots appear on his cheeks.

"Me three," I quip, sidling up closer to him. "You and your mommy make me very, very happy."

"So, you're like my mommy's boyfriend now?" he asks, eyeballing me.

I look to Vivien, and she nods. "Yes. Is that okay?"

He shrugs, and concern spreads across Vivien's face. "You can tell me what you're feeling. Whatever you have to say, you won't upset me or Uncle Dillon."

His hands wrap around his cup as he stares at his mum. "You used to kiss my daddy, and now you kiss Uncle Dillon. Does that mean you don't love my daddy anymore?"

Fuck. The poor little kid. I wonder if this is why he was acting out yesterday, and I wish I knew what thoughts were troubling his mind so I could put him at ease.

"I will always love your daddy, Easton." Tears cling to her lashes, and her voice sounds choked up. "Always. I loved Reeve my whole life, and just because he's in heaven now, it doesn't mean I don't love him anymore. You still love him, right?"

He nods.

"And you love Uncle Dillon too," she prompts.

He nods again, and my heart soars.

"So, it's like that for me. I love your daddy, and I love Uncle Dillon. Does that make sense?"

"Yes." He's nodding again as he turns to me. Tears glisten in his eyes, and his lower lip wobbles. "Are you going to leave me too?"

Pain sits on my chest, making breathing difficult. Taking his half-empty cup, I hand it to Viv, pulling him up onto my lap. "You know I work in the band and that I have to go on tour in January, but I will come back. I will never willingly leave you or your mommy." East needs to be reassured, but I don't want to lie to him either. No one can give him a rock-solid guarantee. What happened to Reeve was tragic, and tragedies can't be predicted.

"Promise?" he whispers.

"I promise," I say, telling him straight from my heart, hoping I never have to break that promise.

"Pinky swear." He holds out his little finger, and I don't know if my heart can withstand this.

But his expectant little face tells me everything. He needs this, and I won't deny him this reassurance. I curl my little finger around his, almost choking on the words as I say them. "Pinky promise."

A sob cuts through the air, and when I look at Viv, she's crying. "Come here." Keeping Easton on my lap, I stretch my arm out for her, pulling her into my side. Viv's arms go around Easton and me, and I kiss both their brows, holding them close

584

and silently vowing to do everything in my power to ensure I am always there for them. Even if it means severing ties with the band because right now there is no way in hell I can step on that plane in January and leave them behind.

"I want pizza!" Easton yells. "Pepperoni pizza and lots and lots of cheese!" We are on our way back after a fun-filled day, and we are all starving, so I suggested we head out for dinner. The three hours Easton spent racing around the indoor jungle gym, after our hike, hasn't dented his energy much, and he's bouncing in his seat, salivating at the prospect of pizza.

"Pizza it is," I say, knowing the perfect place. It's en route to my house and a little off the beaten track so we shouldn't be spotted. Viv is still paranoid about the media finding out about us, but we won't be able to evade them for long. Especially now she's going out and about again. Anyway, the band and I have eaten here a bunch of times, and nothing has ever appeared in the press, so it's a safe place.

I pull up to the curb in front of the family-run Italian restaurant and kill the car. Leon pulls up behind us, and I salute him through the mirror. They will wait outside and keep a lookout for paparazzi. After opening Vivien's door, I get Easton out of his seat and lift him onto the path. I grab both their hands, and we head inside.

Marco gives us my usual table at the back, and we have a lovely meal, filled with good food, good wine, and lots of laughter, and I wish every day could be like this.

"You look happy," Viv murmurs while we watch Easton shoveling ice cream into his mouth with one hand and coloring with the other.

"I am deliriously happy." I tuck her into my side and kiss her softly. "I love spending time with both of you, and Easton took the news better than I expected."

"He did. I'm pleased." She rubs her nose against mine, and her eyes are full of love as she props her chin on my shoulder. "Will you stay over tonight?" Her gaze glitters with unspoken promise, and my cock instantly hardens at the thought of what might be on the agenda.

I nip at her earlobe. "I will if you make it worth my while." I waggle my brows, and she shoves at me.

"Asshole," she mouths.

I reel her back into my side. "You know I'm joking." I press a lingering kiss to her temple. "Kind of."

Easton falls asleep in the car on the way back to Vivien's house. He's knackered after an action-packed day. We put him to bed together, carefully removing his clothes so as not to wake him. We stand silently by his bed, our fingers threaded together, both of us staring at this amazing little boy who is a piece of me and a piece of Vivien. My heart is so full it feels like it could burst.

Vivien leads me out of the room, softly closing the door. I expect her to turn right, to head downstairs, but she turns left, toward the guest bedroom I've commandeered as my own. Viv even had it redecorated in more manly shades of gray and blue. "What's going on, Hollywood?" I ask as she pulls me into the room and closes the door.

Her eyes flare with need as she pushes me back against the wall. "I can't wait any longer. I need you."

Hallelujah starts playing in my head and ringing in my ears. "Are you sure, because once we make this move, I'll be all over you. I won't be able to keep my hands to myself if I'm inside you again. So, choose your next words very carefully, Hollywood." I'm like a starving man who's been wasting away on a diet and the second he drops the discipline he goes wild, eating everything in sight.

If Vivien gives me the green light, I'll devour her and make no apologies for it.

She leans in, grazing her teeth along the column of my neck. "I'm all in, Dillon. I want you so fucking bad it feels like I might explode." Her fingers trail through the stubble on my cheeks, and she pushes her thumb into my mouth. Rabid hunger blazes from her eyes as she stares at me. "Fuck me, Dillon. Make me yours forever."

CHAPTER 39
VIVIEN

DILLON PULLS my mouth to his, kissing me with months', no, years' worth of pent-up longing, and I'm drowning in him. In a skillful move, he repositions us, without breaking our kiss, so I'm against the wall and he's crushing his hard toned body against me. His tongue plunders my mouth as he pops the button on my jeans, and I moan when his tongue piercing strokes along the roof of my mouth. My hands slide up his shirt, finding warm skin, and I scrape my nails up and down his back as he lowers the zipper on my jeans and shoves his hand into my panties.

Two fingers slide into my slippery pussy, and I press against his hand as I bite down on his lower lip. "Fuck," he hisses against my mouth, pumping his fingers fast inside me. "I need in you right now. I can't wait."

We stumble around the room in our hurry to get undressed, only breaking our lip-lock when it's necessary to remove our clothing.

We fall back against the bed in only our underwear, and I climb on top of him, grinding down on his dick as he yanks my bra down, sitting up and burying his face in my breasts. He shoves them together with his hands as he sucks and bites my nipples and my tender flesh, and I think I could come just from this. "Love your tits," he murmurs, taking as much of one breast into his mouth as he can.

"Dillon, please," I beg, grinding my pelvis against his, my pussy pulsing with intense need.

"Please what?" He rips my panties at the side, and the material floats around us. "Tell me what you need, sweetheart. Tell me what you want."

I shove him back by his shoulders, remove my bra, and fling it aside as I slide down his body, tugging his boxers down his legs. "You." My tongue darts out, licking the top of his pierced crown. "I want all of you filling every part of me." Without giving him time to answer, I lower my mouth over his straining cock, moaning as I run my lips up and down his hot flesh.

"Fuck, Viv. I won't last long if you do that." He grabs my hips, yanking me off him and throwing me flat on my back on the bed. Dillon pounces on me, running his hands all over my body as his lips ravish my mouth. I spread my legs, rubbing my pussy against his cock, and he hisses between his teeth. "Goddamn it. The things you do to me. Don't move," he commands, straightening up and bending over to pull out the top drawer of his bedside table.

My chest heaves, and my body trembles in anticipation as I watch him remove a condom and carefully roll it down over his length. Electricity crackles in the air, and I'm dying for him, impatient to feel him moving inside me. I fondle my breasts, spreading my legs wider as I wait for him to hurry the fuck up.

"Look at you." A devilish glint appears in his eye as he moves his face in between my legs. "All spread out for me like the most decadent feast." He licks his lips before he launches himself at me, shoving his tongue into my cunt while his fingers furiously rub my clit. "Pinch your nipples," he growls, looking up at me as he pushes three fingers into my heat. "And keep your eyes on me." His tongue darts out, and he licks my clit as his fingers pump faster inside me. Every time his piercing hits the sensitive bundle of nerves, a jolt of intense desire shoots through my core, and I'm a writhing mess under his expert ministrations.

My climax is rising, and I'm getting close. Impatient to experience the ultimate high, I grind my pussy against his face. "That's it, sweetheart, fuck my face."

Grabbing handfuls of his gorgeous hair, I keep him pressed against my most private parts as I thrust against him and he works me with his fingers and tongue.

Sparks transform to flames inside me as I self-destruct in the most glorious fashion. I can't stifle my cries as the most earth-shattering orgasm rips through me, turning my limbs to mush, rendering me a pliable pile of limbs on the bed. "Fuck, Dillon. I want to do that every single day for the rest of my life."

Pulling up to his knees, he pins me with the sexiest evil grin. "That can definitely be arranged." Flinging my legs over his shoulders, he pulls me forward, lifting my ass off the bed a few inches as he lines his cock up at my entrance. "Hold on tight, Hollywood. This is going to be hard and fast."

"My favorite kind of ride," I quip, shivering in delicious anticipation.

Dillon thrusts into me in one powerful movement, and I slap a hand over my mouth to stifle my cries. "Fuck, yeah, Viv. God, how I've missed you." He pounds into me while leaning down to kiss me. "I love doing this with you."

Grabbing his head, I pull him closer as I cross my ankles behind his neck, lifting my hips, so the angle is deeper. "I love sex with you. I just love you," I pant before claiming his lips in a searing-hot kiss.

Dillon drives into me like a man on a mission, pushing his dick as far as it will go, and I see stars. Our kissing is as frantic as our fucking because we can't get enough. I drag my nails up his abs, and he hisses. Removing my legs from around his neck and shoulders, he situates me on his lap without breaking our connection. "Ride me, sweetheart. Fuck me until I come." His arms go around me as he plants a line of drugging kisses along my collarbone.

Keeping my hands on his shoulders to control my movements, I bounce up and down on his erection, throwing my head back and thrusting my chest in his face. Dillon sucks on my breasts, tugging on my nipples with his teeth, while his fingers slip down to my ass, tracing a teasing line along my ass crack. His mouth suctions on my neck, right in the place where I'm most sensitive, and I groan as I slam up and down on his dick, feeling my orgasm building again.

Dillon shoves his cock up inside me, his movements alternating with mine, and I cry out when he pushes one finger into my ass, falling over the ledge instantly. Pushing me flat on my back, he rocks into me with a new intensity as I come down from my high. A muscle clenches in his jaw, the veins in his neck pulse, and his entire body locks up as he roars out his release.

It's a miracle we didn't wake Easton with how loud we were. He really must be exhausted after such a busy day.

The blissful look on Dillon's face brings tears to my eyes, and I pull him to me as he collapses on the bed beside me.

His arms wind around me automatically, and he draws me in close, tipping my chin up. "Are you okay?" Concern is splayed across his face.

"These are happy tears," I rasp, cupping his gorgeous face. "I love you, Dillon. I love you with everything I am, and everything I have to offer is yours."

"You're mine. You're truly mine." His eyes fill up.

"I'm yours, Dillon." I kiss him softly, and he tightens his arms around me.

"This is right where you belong, Vivien Grace, and I am going to love you with everything I have every single day for the rest of our lives."

"You took your rings off," Dillon says the following morning as we are finishing breakfast. Easton is in the playroom watching cartoons on the TV. Dillon stares at my empty ring finger, as my hand gravitates to my neck.

"I did. It was time." I cried removing my wedding and engagement rings after I got out of the shower earlier, but it was the final cleansing I needed to do. "I've given you my commitment, Dillon. I've told you I'm yours. I can't continue to wear Reeve's rings on my finger when I've promised to give myself to you fully."

My hand curls around the two necklaces I'm wearing. "I'm hoping you don't mind if I wear them around my neck." I put the rings on a silver chain I had ordered for this day, and I took the claddagh necklace Dillon gave me for my birthday in Ireland out of the memento box I'd kept hidden from my husband.

Now I'm wearing both.

Side by side.

Existing in tandem like my love for both twins.

Dillon stares at the necklaces, looking a little dazed.

"If it bothers you, I can take it off."

Slowly, he lifts his gaze to mine, shaking his head. "I told you I'm fine with you remembering Reeve. I don't want you to erase him. Wear his rings around your neck. Keep your photos up. Whatever it is you need to do, I'm good. I've made my peace with everything."

"Thank you." I reach across the table, threading my fingers through his. "You don't know how much it means to me to hear you say that."

"You kept it," he whispers, his eyes lowering to my neck once again.

"Did you think I wouldn't?"

He shrugs. "I didn't really think about it, but I'm glad you did."

"I must be a glutton for punishment because I kept all the stuff I have of yours, and all the things that reminded me of Ireland, in a box, hidden in my closet. I couldn't bear to part with any of it." I have photos, some of Dillon's T-shirts, some Toxic Gods merch, and tons of souvenirs from our many trips.

"Come here. You're too far away over there." He pushes back his chair, the legs squealing across the tile floor.

I get up and drop onto his lap, wrapping my arms around his neck. Our mouths move as one, meeting in a passionate kiss I feel all the way to the tips of my toes. Dillon hardens underneath my ass, and I break our kiss, quirking a brow. "I thought I exhausted you last night," I tease, squirming on his lap.

"Don't you know me? I'm insatiable." He nips at my earlobe. "Insatiable for you."

"Uncle Dillon!" Easton shouts, bounding into the room a few seconds later.

Dillon groans, burying his head in my shoulder. "He has the worst timing."

"Or impeccable timing."

"What's up, buddy?" Dillon says, keeping his arms around me.

"Will you play in the treehouse with me?"

"Absolutely." Dillon never refuses him anything.

"Awesome. I'll meet you outside!" he says, racing out of the room like a tornado.

"I see someone got laid," Ash says, grinning, a few hours later when she arrives for our lunch-slash-yoga date.

"Jesus, Ash. Tone it down, would ya?" Dillon points to where Easton is sitting at the kitchen table drawing pictures of Reeve and Lainey with the angels in heaven.

"Shit, sorry. I didn't see the little munchkin. All I saw was Viv's radiant glow." She waggles her brows.

"You know what you need to do, Auntie Ash," Easton says in a singsong voice, sliding off his chair and walking toward us. He slaps out his palm. "Hand the goods over."

Dillon chuckles, beaming at his son as his sister removes a dollar bill from her wallet and hands it to E. "I'll be coming to you instead of the bank for a loan soon."

Easton grins before turning to his father. "Uncle Dil? What does got laid mean?"

I snort laugh, grabbing my gym bag and my purse, wiggling my fingers at my man. "And that's my cue to leave. Good luck handling that one."

"You're mean," he mouths. "And I'll make you pay."

"I look forward to it." Bending down, I kiss my son on the lips. "Be good for Uncle Dillon. I'll see you later."

Easton throws his arms around me. "We're going to practice with my guitar. Love you, Mommy."

I pull him up into my arms and hug him tight. "I love you too."

"Where's my loving?" Ash asks, fake pouting.

"You don't deserve one after the shit you've landed me in." Dillon sulks, and it's priceless.

Easton projects himself from my arms to Ash's, giving her a quick hug. "Love you too, Auntie Ash."

"Right back at ya, cutie." Pretending to whisper, she says, "Give Uncle Dil hell, and don't forget he hasn't answered your question yet."

Oh my God. Dillon is going to kill her if the thunderous look on his face is any indication.

We're still laughing when we step outside, climbing into Ash's car.

Leon gets behind the wheel of the security SUV, trailing us down the driveway.

"Don't you ever get sick of having bodyguards following you everywhere? We need security when the guys are on tour, and I hate it even if I know it's for our protection."

"It's all I've ever known, and I've gotten used to it. Besides, Leon and Bobby are like family now they've been with us so long, and they are discreet. Most times, I forget they're even there."

"Have you given much thought to going public with Dil?" she asks, pulling out of my driveway onto the road.

"It's been on my mind," I truthfully reply. "I know it's best to get in front of these things, and I know that means we'll need to put out a statement or give an interview."

"You will, and I know you're worried about what people will say, but fuck them. Seriously, it's none of their business."

"I'll talk to Dillon about it tonight, but I'm thinking maybe we could do it after Christmas." That gives us a month and a bit to plan it and enough time for me to recover my lady balls.

"So, you two finally bumped uglies," she says, taking the exit for the highway.

"We did." I can't contain my grin. "It was incredible. Even better than I remembered. We barely got any sleep, and I can't wait until tonight so I can jump his bones again."

"Blech." She makes a face. "TMI, sister."

I laugh, buoyed up by great sex and Dillon's love. "Your brother is a fucking beast in the bedroom. The things he does to me."

"Yeah, Viv. I know you're all loved up and sexed up, but you've got to quit that shit, or I'm seriously going to puke."

I giggle, and her expression softens as she reaches across the console to squeeze my hand. "All joking aside, I am made up for you. Seeing both of you so happy after everything makes me incredibly happy."

"I'm happy too. It's like it used to be, but better, if that makes sense."

She nods. "I get what you're saying."

"I still get moments where I feel the odd bout of guilt, and I still miss Reeve, but I'm done with being sad all the time. It's been almost seven months. It's time to live again."

CHAPTER 40
VIVIEN

"WE'VE GOT A BIT OF A SITUATION," Leon says as Ash and I emerge from the locker room, showered and changed after our yoga class.

"What situation?" Ash asks, thrusting her shoulders back and adopting her serious business face.

Sympathy splays across Leon's face as he looks at me. "The media knows about you and Dillon. There are a ton of paparazzi out front."

My face pales, and bile swims up my throat. Ash grips my hand. This is what I was afraid of.

Leon gestures behind him to where Bobby and another two bodyguards are waiting. "You were in the middle of your class when the news broke. I didn't want to interrupt you, so I called in reinforcements. There's no back door in this place, so we've got no choice but to go out the main entrance."

"How bad is it?" I ask.

"Bad."

"Right, fuck those assholes." Ash straightens up, eyeballing me. "Ignore them, and don't look at them. We'll figure out what to do when we get back to the house." She looks at Leon. "I assume my brother is aware?"

He nods. "It was Dillon who called to warn me. He wanted to come and get you himself, but I didn't think that was a good idea."

No shit, Sherlock. It would have been a complete clusterfuck if Dillon had shown up here, and I'm glad he listened to sense for once.

"Okay, let's do this." Ash grips my hand tighter. "You ready?"

I nod even though I'm never ready for this shit.

Leon and Bobby cover us from both sides while the other two bodyguards cover us front and rear as we make our way outside.

The second Leon opens the door, a ton of reporters and photographers rush toward us, shouting questions and sticking cameras in our faces. I keep my head down, ignoring them as we're jostled and pushed from all angles. The bodyguards are taking the brunt of the shoving, doing their best to protect us, but it's a total shitshow as we battle it to our car.

"Vivien, is it true you're having an affair with Reeve's twin brother?"

"Vivien, were you sleeping with Dillon when Reeve was still alive? Is that why you were arguing in the car the night of the accident?"

"Vivien, can you confirm reports you eloped with Dillon and got married?"

"Vivien, did you get married because you're expecting Dillon's child?"

"Vivien, were you planning to leave Reeve for his brother before the accident happened?"

On and on it goes until it feels like my head will explode. Eventually, we make it to the security car, and I bury my head in my hands as soon as the door is shut behind us.

"Motherfucking bloodsucking assholes!" Ash fumes, circling her arm around me from behind. "Don't let them get to you. I know it's easier said than done, but we'll put out a statement, and if they choose to believe that bullshit, they're idiots."

I lift my head, sighing. "I fucking jinxed myself earlier. How the hell did they find out?"

"Let's call Dillon." Ash is already dialing his number as Leon tries to pull out onto the road. Swarms of reporters and paparazzi surround our car, trapping us. "Mow them fucking down for all I care," Ash says as Leon keeps his hand on the horn, slowly inching away from the curb.

"Call the cops if you need to," I add. These assholes know they're not allowed to do this.

"I'm putting you on speaker," Ash says into the phone.

"Are you okay?" Dillon asks, worry evident in his tone.

"We're surrounded, but Leon is doing his best to get us away," I explain.

"Who reported it, and what's been said?" Ash asks.

"I'm so sorry, Viv," Dillon says. "One of the waitresses at the Italian restaurant gave an interview to *ET Live*. She must have been watching us the entire time, and she shared a video of us kissing and hugging. I've already talked to Marco, and she's been fired. She was new and on a trial. He's extremely upset and very apologetic."

"That makes little difference now," I say glumly. I rub a tense spot between my brows. "We need to call Edwin and your new publicist."

"Already done. Both will be here by the time you arrive home, and I've spoken to your mum too. Your parents phoned me when they couldn't reach you."

My parents are pros at handling this stuff, and I'm sure Mom will have suggestions we can consider. They are still on location, but I can call her back when we're discussing options if I need to. "Okay. We'll see you at the house soon."

"It's going to be okay," he says, and I wish I could believe him.

Ash ends the call as Leon finally makes it out onto the road, picking up speed. Removing my cell from my purse, I log on to the internet.

"Are you sure you want to do that?" Ash asks. "It's all going to be bullshit."

"I need to know what I'm dealing with. Not just so we can respond appropriately but to understand what I need to tell Easton." There are a couple of nasty little shits in his class who seem to love rubbing Easton's nose in stuff that's said online. Thankfully, Dillon made that last incident disappear, but I hate he had to write a check to do it.

I pull up *ET Live*, and we watch the report and video. It's not too damning, but there is no doubting it's us in the recording even if it is a little blurry. The comments, however, are another matter entirely. Reeve's fans are out in full force, and I'm being called everything from a cheating slut to a murdering bitch.

Ash reads over my shoulder, and I can almost feel the anger rolling off her. "That is such horseshit," she snaps. "What kind of low-life scumbag would accuse you of fixing the accident and killing Reeve on purpose just so you could have your wicked way with his brother? These people are sick and twisted." She grabs the phone from me. "You've seen enough."

I have, and I'm sick to my stomach the rest of the ride home.

Dillon is waiting for me outside the house when we pull up, and I fall apart the second he pulls me into his arms. "Shush, sweetheart. It's going to be okay. I'm here, and I'm not letting anyone hurt you."

I cling to him as I cry, hating I'm back in this space again. It feels like all the progress I've made has just been undone. "They're accusing me of never loving Reeve. Of tainting his memory. Some are even saying I made the accident happen on purpose," I sob, looking up at him through clouded vision. "How could anyone accuse me of deliberately killing my husband and my daughter?" Pain punches me in the gut, and I cling to Dillon as the sounds of a chopper resound over our heads.

"You have got to be fucking kidding me." Dillon bristles with rage as we look up, spotting the news helicopter in the sky. "Let's get inside. Ash, call the cops. This is a massive invasion of privacy and they can't do that. I already reported a drone earlier."

Drones are becoming a serious issue for celebrities. They are trying to introduce laws, but it's a tricky subject.

"I'm already on it," she says, handing me a tissue.

I dry my eyes and pull myself together. I can't let Easton see me upset. Taking Dillon's hand, we step inside the house after Ash. I fix my makeup in the mirror in the hall, making myself presentable, as Ash hurries off to meet with the publicists. Dillon confirms Easton is over at his house with Jamie. He felt it best to distract him while we figure out what to do.

Dillon slides his arm around my shoulders as we walk toward my office. I lean into him, siphoning some of his warmth and his support. He stops outside the door, turning me around in his arms. He kisses me softly. "I love you, and you love me. The three of us are a family now, and we haven't done anything wrong. Not back then, and not now. Keep remembering that. You are a good person, Vivien, and those idiots deserve to rot in hell for the horrible things they are saying. But that's on them. Not you." He tilts my chin with one finger. "Hold your head high, Hollywood, and never forget you are a goddess among women."

A small smile curls the corners of my lips. I fling my arms around him. "Thank you for reminding me of what's important."

We step into the room hand in hand, greeted by matching grim expressions.

Edwin rushes toward me, pulling me into a hug. "We'll get on top of this, Vivien. Don't worry."

Ash introduces me to Farrah Lewis, the band's new publicist. I'm glad Ash also mentioned she was openly gay because the tall thin redhead is absolutely stunning and I might have worried otherwise. Not about Dillon. I trust him completely, but I know the way some women throw themselves at rock stars. It's no different than actors, in that regard. She shakes my hand. "I wish we were meeting under better circumstances."

"Likewise."

"Don't worry. Between all of us, we'll get a handle on this and put our own spin on it."

We all know it's not as easy as that, but I appreciate her attempts to reassure me. "Please take a seat," I say, urging everyone to move over to the two couches as Charlotte steps into the room with a tray.

"Thank you, Charlotte." This woman is worth her weight in gold.

"Let me know if you need anything else." She leaves the room, discreetly closing the door.

I pour coffees for everyone as we settle down on the couches. Dillon leans back, with one leg crossed over the other, looking calm and unruffled. At least one of us is. He slides his arm behind my back. "How do you suggest we respond to this? Issue a statement or do an interview?"

"I think we need to issue a statement asap to stop some of the vitriol online," Edwin says.

"We can issue a joint statement from both camps along with a request for privacy," Farrah adds. "But I think a scheduled interview with Oprah would really put all the nasty rumors to rest."

"How quickly can you get that set up?" Ash asks, sipping her coffee.

"I'm confident if we pool our efforts we can have a contract on the table within forty-eight hours. Everyone will be clambering for this story, and it's right up Oprah's alley," Edwin says.

"What about Easton?" I ask because right now he's my most pressing concern. I don't want our relationship to impact negatively on our son.

"I don't see any cause for concern." Edwin looks a little puzzled, and I know why. I turn to Dillon, and he nods.

"Easton is Dillon's biological child," I explain, and Edwin almost falls off his chair. To give Farrah her due, she looks completely unflappable, as if I haven't just dropped a bomb. I give them a quick summary of the background, and they both listen intently while I explain. Dillon holds my hand the entire time, offering me silent support.

"That changes things," Edwin says, when I've finished speaking, as Farrah's phone pings. "I know you don't want to be forced into telling him, but it's going to come out, Vivien. It's better that it's revealed from your mouth. I suggest you give that exclusive to Oprah, and we say nothing about Easton in the statement we'll issue today."

"Can you turn on *ET Live*," Farrah says, looking up from her phone with concerning frown lines. "And we will have to reconsider the entire strategy."

"Why?" Dillon asks, sitting up straighter as I turn the channel on.

My heart is in my mouth as the screen loads and I see the familiar face. Blood rushes to my head, and acid swirls in my gut. I think I might throw up. "That's why," I croak, pointing at Aoife's face on the TV.

CHAPTER 41
DILLON

I JUMP UP, glaring at the screen, wishing I could project myself into the TV and throttle the living daylights out of that conniving bitch. Everyone else stands, crowding around the TV. I tuck Viv into my side, hating how badly she's trembling and wishing I could make this go away, but I'm too late. The damage is done.

I'm seething as I watch Aoife talk to a Virgin One reporter in their Dublin studios. The news about Viv and me only broke three hours ago, so this must be live, which is crazy because it's after midnight there. I have no clue how she managed to set this up so fast, unless she was already in discussions with someone.

Despite reassuring Viv many months ago, I was worried Aoife might say something when the news came out about Reeve and me being twins. So, I contacted my Dublin solicitor and requested he send a reminder to all of those who had signed the NDA, reminding them of the considerable financial penalties if anyone spoke out.

Trying to ruin Viv and me must mean more to Aoife than money because she knows me well enough to know I'm going to go after her for this.

"Are you saying Vivien Lancaster and Dillon O'Donoghue had a relationship six years ago when Vivien studied at Trinity College Dublin?" the reporter asks her, in what is obviously a contrived interview.

"Yes. They were definitely a couple," the traitorous bitch says as old pictures of Vivien and me are shared on the screen. All the shots were taken in Whelans, which means the bitch was taking pictures of us on the sly.

"They look pretty infatuated with one another in these photos. Would you say their relationship continued after Vivien left Ireland and returned to America?"

"Most definitely," she lies. "I mean, why else would Dillon make me sign an NDA if not to protect his relationship with her?"

"That fucking whore." Ash clenches her hands into fists, seething as much as I am, when her phone rings. "Jay, I can't talk," she says, pausing for a few seconds. "We're watching it now. I'll call you back."

"Can you elaborate for the viewers? Are you saying you broke the terms of an NDA to talk to us today?"

Aoife nods, attempting, and failing, to look superior. "Censorship isn't right. Freedom of speech is a constitutional right, and I won't be bullied into keeping my mouth shut."

"What a dumbass," Ash says.

"Shut up. We're missing it," I say.

"Why did you speak out now? Why not when it was revealed earlier this year that Reeve and Dillon were twins?" the reporter asks.

"I wanted to, but Dillon's solicitor sent me a threatening letter, and I was afraid."

"Oh, please. You stupid bitch. You were waiting for the best moment to come forward." Ash grinds her teeth while Vivien is worryingly mute beside me. I hold her tighter, pressing a kiss to the top of her head.

"But it's not right, what they did, and someone needs to say something. That poor man died not knowing his wife was sleeping with his twin. For all we know, that little boy wasn't even his. I bet he's Dillon's. The timing is really suspect."

"You stupid fucking whore!" Vivien explodes, shucking out of my arms. She grabs a mug from the table, throwing it at the TV. Before I can stop her, she's grabbed another, throwing that one too. "That stupid fucking bitch!" She whirls around, fire dancing in her eyes, nostrils flaring, looking slightly scary. "I will kill her! I'm getting on a plane, and I'm going to strangle her with my bare hands." Viv grabs fistfuls of her hair and paces the floor. I stride toward her, attempting to pull her into my arms, but she swats me away.

"This is all your fault! You brought her into our lives. How could you have ever slept with that bitch?" Vivien asks, glaring at me. "I always knew she was poison."

"I tried to fix it. I—"

"I don't want to hear excuses, Dillon." She shoves my chest. "You were so confident you had it handled, but I've always known better when it comes to her. She always wanted to hurt me, and now she's found the perfect ammunition. I'm betting the next person who comes forward is that guy from the lab or one of his staff. This is going to be all over the news."

She breaks down, sobbing as she drops to her knees, all the fight fading. "We have to tell him now. It's only three weeks until Christmas, Dillon. His first Christmas without Reeve is already going to be hard enough. I didn't want to tell him until after."

We haven't actually discussed a timeline at all, so that's news to me. But I understand, and I share her concerns. The timing sucks, but we have no choice now. I sink to my knees too, wrapping my arms around her, but she pushes me away. Pain slices across my chest. "Don't touch me, Dillon. I don't want you to touch me." She climbs awkwardly to her feet. "I need some space," she adds before fleeing the room.

Ash extends her hand, helping me to stand. My shoulders slump with the weight of failure.

"She doesn't mean it," my sister says, giving me a hug.

"I promised I'd protect her. That I wouldn't let anything, or anyone, hurt her again, and I've failed already."

Ash grips my face hard. "Cut that shit out now, Dil. You haven't failed her. This isn't on you. It's on that stupid manipulative bitch."

Fury returns full throttle, and a muscle clenches in my jaw. "She's going to pay."

The two publicists hang back, afraid to intervene, I'm sure. Extracting my cell from my pocket, I punch the number for my Dublin solicitor. I don't care that he's probably sleeping. I pay the fucker enough he can take my call no matter how late it is. "Agree a statement with Edwin and Farrah," I tell Ash. "We need to get something out now. Viv's in no state to review it, so send it to Lauren and ensure she's okay with it before you issue it."

I look over at the two publicists as my call goes to voice mail. "Say nothing about Easton for now. We can't make that public until we have spoken to our son." I press redial as Farrah starts jotting notes on her phone. "Confirm we were in a relationship years ago before we knew Reeve and I were twins. Our relationship ended, and we didn't see one another again until just before Reeve died, when we discovered we were siblings. I've been helping Vivien during the grieving process, and we grew close again. We are now in a relationship. At no time did Vivien ever cheat on Reeve."

I growl as my call goes unanswered again. "You can add that Reeve was aware of my relationship with Vivien in Ireland." Everything I have said is true except for me not knowing about Reeve at the time. No one knows about that, so I'm comfortable telling that porky. I would gladly own up to the truth if I believed it would deflect the heat off Vivien, but I think revealing that will only make the whole story more salacious and ignite even more interest.

"Pick up the phone, you lazy fucker!" I shout as my call goes to voice mail again. I call him again, and I'm seriously considering chartering a private jet to fly me to Dublin when the prick answers. "About bleeding time!"

"Dillon, it's almost one a.m."

"Do I sound like I give a fucking shit what time it is?" I fill him in quickly, guessing he isn't aware of what's happened because he was in the land of Nod. "I want you to sue that fucking cunt. Take her to the cleaners! I want every fucking penny she got for that interview, and I'm sure that won't be enough to meet the financial obligations of the NDA, so take everything. When we're through, I want her left with nothing. I want her penniless and homeless with only the clothes on her back."

"That's the likely outcome," the solicitor says. "Are you sure you want to follow through? We could threaten to do it, lodge proceedings with the court, and scare her into shutting her mouth."

"Are you fucking deaf?" I roar down the phone. "She already opened her stupid gob. The damage is done, and she will pay the price. Start proceedings, and I want to see them carried through." I hang up before he can say anything else, tossing my phone on the couch as I drag my hands through my hair.

"I approve, and it will send a clear message to the others to keep their mouths shut," Ash says.

Not that they can do any more harm, so it really doesn't matter, but I get the point.

"She did this maliciously to hurt Vivien. She's always hated her, believing she stole you from her."

"Ha." I bark out a laugh. "Vivien couldn't steal something that never belonged to her. Aoife was nothing to me. She's even less now, and she's fucking lucky I live thousands of miles away because right now I actually believe I could commit murder. I want to fucking kill her for doing this to my family."

"Go and get Easton. It's getting late, and you should stick to his routine. I'll check on Vivien after we've finalized the statement."

"Thanks, sis. Love you." I bundle her into a hug, kissing the top of her head.

"I've got your back. Now go get your son."

I'm lying in bed, in Viv's house, unable to sleep, worried about her and Easton, obsessing over how he will take the news. Today has ruined everything. I just feel it in my bones. Vivien only emerged from her room to bathe Easton and put him to bed, but she was giving me the cold shoulder. She wouldn't even speak to Ash though she did talk to her mum on the phone, and Lauren called me after. She told me to give her some space to process it but not to let it go on too long.

I turn onto my side, pulling up photos on my phone, skimming through them with a heavy heart. I knew everything was too perfect. That something was going to happen to burst my happy bubble because that's the pattern of my life. Fuck it. I know I sound like a depressed head, but I can't help it.

Aoife is going to rue the day she crossed me. I fully expect some kind of pleading public message when she discovers I'm suing her, but there is nothing she can say or do that will get me to change my mind. She's a vindictive bitch, and it's time she learned there are consequences for her actions. Why couldn't she just be happy with the money I gave her? I know she used it to buy a house. Has she been stewing all these years, waiting for an opportunity to get back at Viv? All because I didn't fall in love with her?

I spoke to Ro earlier. He offered to go and torch her house. I was tempted to tell him to do it and to ensure she was inside when he set fire to it, but I won't have murder on my conscience. I'd much rather take everything from her—her house, her car, her money, her reputation, poor and all as it is. I've already emailed our label in Dublin and asked them to ensure she is banned from Whelans and other venues around Dublin we still sometimes play at.

I made my feelings known earlier when I posted on social media, and our fans are coming out in support. Aoife had to shut her accounts down after they attacked her in their thousands, and I hope she's gone into hiding, terrified for her life, because it's the least she deserves for what she's tried to do.

If she causes Viv to pull away from me, I don't know what I'll do. Time is running out. We leave in five weeks to go on tour, and I had finally plucked up the courage to ask Viv to come with me. East too. I was planning on asking her this weekend, but that's all shot to hell now.

The door creaks, and I lift my head, expecting to see Easton, but it's Vivien. I sit up, eyeing her carefully as she pads quietly across the room. I watch as she climbs onto the bed and wraps her arms around me.

"I'm sorry, Dillon." Tears pool in her eyes. "I'm so sorry for saying it was your fault. That was a terrible thing to say, and it's not true. It's not your fault. That's all on Aoife. I was just upset and scared and freaking out, but I shouldn't have taken it out on you."

Air whooshes out of my mouth in grateful relief as I pull her onto my lap, circling my arms around her. "I'm sorry I failed you and East, Viv, but I'm going to do my utmost to make it right."

She shakes her head, cupping my face. "You haven't failed us, Dillon. Not at all. And we'll get through this together."

I am so relieved to hear this. She was hysterical earlier, and I was really worried she was going to regress. "Stay with me." I plant a kiss on the top of her head.

"Yes," she says, "but not here. Come with me. I have something to show you."

I'm curious as she leads me out of my bedroom and along the hallway, opening the door to another one of her guest rooms. My eyes widen as I take in the large room with a giant four-poster bed, walk-in closet, seating area with a fire and wall-mounted TV, and an en suite bathroom.

"This is our new room," she explains. "I had renovators in a month ago to work on it. I got them to come on days when you weren't here because I wanted it to be a surprise." She spins around, holding my hands and peering up at me. "I know you're worried this has made me have doubts. I won't deny I'm really upset over everything and very worried about Easton, but it hasn't changed how I feel about you. I meant it when I told you I was yours." She leans her head on my chest, snaking her arms around my waist. "I love you, and I need you, now more than ever."

"You have me. I'm going nowhere." I scoop her up, cradling her against my chest. After closing the door, I walk to the bed, gently placing her under the covers. I slide in beside her, pulling her back against my chest. My arms go around her automatically because it's as natural as breathing to me. "We have endured considerable challenges to get to this point, and it hasn't broken us or destroyed what we have. Today was a shitshow, and I know you're worried. I'm worried about telling Easton too. I'd rather the timing had been of our choosing, but he'll be okay. He's not losing anything. He's gaining, and if he struggles to understand it, we will be there to comfort him and answer his questions." •

CHAPTER 42
DILLON

"I THINK I'm going to be sick." Vivien rubs her stomach, looking pale enough I believe it.

"I'm not feeling so great myself," I truthfully admit, rubbing a hand up and down her back. "But we've got to do this. We can't let him discover the truth any other way."

It hasn't even been twenty-four hours since that bitch of a waitress released her story, and things have escalated to scary levels. I've instructed my US attorney to slap her with a lawsuit too. California's privacy laws are pretty clear, and you can't record someone without their permission. I'll enjoy taking whatever payment she received for selling us out and teaching her a valuable lesson.

A horde of paparazzi, reporters, and TV crews has camped on the road outside the house, making us feel like virtual prisoners. They can't see anything from the road, so we're protected once we stay here. The second we have to leave, it's going to be crazy town. Our publicists are being inundated with requests for interviews. The only positive to come from that is we got agreement already from Oprah's team, and our interview is being lined up for next week.

Social media is exploding with all kinds of wild theories and #Dillien is trending. Ash is gloating, *a lot*, over that, because she coined our ship name years ago in Dublin.

Reporters have even been bugging my parents, and I'm glad Ro is at home to handle it. He hired a couple of bodyguards to guard their house after a reporter drove right up to their front door, asking for a statement. These people have no morals and no shame.

I confiscated Vivien's phone earlier because she was looking at some of the more lurid headlines and I could see she was twisting herself into even greater knots. She's working hard to keep it together, but the strain is obvious. She had a FaceTime session with her therapist this morning, and I'm seeing that as a positive sign. Lauren and Jon are due home next week from Canada, and I know their presence will help too.

"We can do this." I bring her hand to my lips, kissing her soft skin. "And you said you were planning on telling him after Christmas."

"I was going to talk to you about that last night, before everything went down."

"He's as ready as he will ever be. I know you didn't want it to upset him before Christmas, but it might help him get through it."

"You're right. I just hate being forced to do it today because of that bitch." Her mouth pulls into a grimace, and her eyes burn with anger, like they do every time Aoife's name is mentioned.

"She will regret it. I will make damn sure of that."

"Good." She throws her arms around me, kissing me hard on the lips. "I thought about it after you told me your plans. Briefly, I wondered if we should take the moral high ground and not go after her."

I arch a brow, hoping she didn't decide that because I really want to make Aoife suffer. Her actions have hurt the woman who will one day be my wife, and she has hurt my son.

Neither of us ever wanted to air our private lives in public. We knew there would come a time when we'd have to admit Easton's parentage, but that should have been at a time of our choosing and a narrative of our choosing. She took those options away from us, and I will never forgive her. I want to make her pay. Maybe I'm a bastard for wanting to go after her, guns blazing, but I don't care what anyone thinks of me.

You come after what's mine, and I'll fucking annihilate you.

"But I guess I'm not as magnanimous as I like to think I am because I want you to throw the book at her, Dillon. Make her pay."

I grab her ass, crushing her to me. "This is why we're so good together, and you can count on it, sweetheart."

We kiss for ages, and it soothes something in both of us. "I love kissing you," she says when we finally break apart.

"I love seeing your lips swollen with my kisses."

She takes my hand, pushing her shoulders back. "Come on. Let's go talk to our son. It's time he knows the truth."

We head out to the memorial garden with Easton because we thought this was the best way to keep Reeve's memory alive while we break the news to him. East is holding each of our hands, and we're swinging him between us. It's a nice day, warmer than usual at this time of year.

"Are we going to talk to Daddy?" Easton asks when we enter the little garden.

"We need to talk to you, and we wanted Daddy close by," Vivien says, looking like she's close to passing out.

I lean in, kissing her brow. "Breathe, Hollywood. We've got this."

I position Easton in between us on the bench, wrapping my arm around them.

"What's up, guys?" East says, and his sass helps to lighten the tension a little.

"We have something important to tell you," I say, "and it concerns your daddy and me."

"Okay." His nose scrunches.

"You remember I told you how babies were made," Vivien says, taking his hand in hers.

"Mommies and daddies kiss and hug, and they make the baby grow in mommy's tummy."

I cough to disguise my chuckle. I know he's only five, and it's the best way of explaining it, but it's fucking funny. Imagine how much the world would be overrun with babies if all it took was some kissing and hugging?

Viv nods. "And you remember how we told you Dillon and I were friends in Dublin?"

"Yup. I know all this." He shakes his head like we're wasting his time, and I ruffle his hair. This little kid slays me in the best ways.

"Your mommy wasn't married to your daddy then. They were just friends while Mommy was my girlfriend."

His brow creases, and he looks confused as his gaze bounces between us.

"Dillon was my boyfriend, and we only found out recently that it was Dillon who put the baby in my tummy."

Easton looks downright confused, and I don't blame him. This is virtually impossible to explain to a five-year-old. I try a different angle. "Reeve was the best daddy, right, buddy?"

"The best in the whole wide world." He stretches his arms out to prove his point, hitting both of us in the stomach.

"And he's still your daddy now even though he's in heaven," Vivien says, taking over when she sees I'm sweating bullets. "Reeve will always be your daddy, Easton." She takes his hands again. "But he didn't put you in my tummy. Dillon did." His brow creases, and the most heartbreaking, vulnerable look appears on his face. "Dillon is your daddy too, Easton."

He looks so lost when he looks up at me, and I tighten my arm around him, moving in closer the same time Vivien does. "You're my daddy?" he whispers, his eyes filling up, and my heart is rupturing behind my rib cage.

Tears pool in my eyes, and I don't try to hold them back like I usually would. "Yes, buddy. I'm your daddy, and I love you very, very much."

"You are really lucky," Vivien adds, rubbing circles on the back of his hand with her thumb. "You have two amazing daddies. Daddy Reeve is watching over you from heaven, and Daddy Dillon is here to always look after you."

Tears spill down his cheeks, and he leans into Vivien, sobbing against her chest. "I miss my daddy," he says, in between sobs, and pain has a vise grip on my heart. Vivien warned me not to expect too much, and I know he's confused, but I can't help how I feel. Rejection has always been hard for me, and though I know that's not what Easton is doing, the feelings are the same.

Until I snap out of it.

I'm being a selfish prick.

The instant the thought lands in my mind, I wipe my eyes and focus on my son.

This isn't about me.

It's about him.

"It's okay to miss him," Viv says, reaching out to cup my face as our son clings to her. "I miss him too, but Daddy Reeve would want us to be happy, and Daddy Dillon makes us happy, right?"

Easton lifts his head, turning to look at me. Seeing his tearstained blotchy face kills me. He sniffles, staring at me, and it feels like my heart is about to disintegrate. "Uncle Dillon," he says.

"Yeah, buddy." My voice is hoarse, emotion clogging my words as well as my thoughts.

"Do I call you Daddy Dillon now?"

Viv sobs, holding on to me and Easton.

Tears prick the backs of my eyes, and I can scarcely speak over the messy ball of emotion in my throat. "You can call me whatever you want, East."

He thinks about it for a second, and then his hand reaches out, and he curls his fingers around mine. "Daddy Dillon?" The trusting expression on his face knocks me for six, and I nod because I can't actually form words. This is the culmination of every fantasy I have had since I discovered he was mine. "Can we play on the slides now?"

Easton took it way better than any of us expected, and I'm delighted. There are still moments where I catch him looking a little lost, and I know he's still grappling to understand it all, but he seems to have accepted he has two daddies. I even heard him bragging to one of his little mates when I collected him from school on his last day before his Christmas break.

His mother is a different matter though. Although Vivien sleeps in my arms every night and we're together, in all the ways we can be together, she's emotionally distanced herself from me. From everyone.

The Oprah interview was a bit of a mixed bag. We gave a watered-down version of our story, not going into all the details but giving enough to try to explain the situation in a way that protects Viv. It fostered enormous online debate with camps split evenly down the middle. There are those who are sympathetic to the situation, who understand Viv's position, and wish us well. Most of my fans have been supportive, but there is an element who are jealous and lash out at Viv.

And don't get me started on Reeve's fanbase. They have all turned on Vivien, and the vitriol online is disgusting. I made Ash give me access to my accounts again so I could monitor things. But I had to shut them down before they banned me, because I was not holding back in my replies to the assholes calling my woman a slut, a cheat, and a murderer.

Someone started a petition to have Viv arrested for murdering Reeve, and it had over one hundred thousand signatures. Some of these people are legit lunatics who should be locked up in the nuthouse. How the fuck can anyone accuse a woman of deliberately killing her husband and baby in such a horrific way? They seem to forget she nearly died too.

Fucking assholes. I swear I want to punch the lot of them.

I have my US attorney working overtime, firing off threatening letters to publications and online sites and issuing legal proceedings. My Irish solicitor has begun the process with Aoife, and he's issued more reminders to the other NDA signatories.

The publicists are trying to put a positive spin on our official communications, and Lauren has her IT contact removing shit from the internet on a continuous basis. We have stepped up security and spoken to Easton's school and his friends' parents. There really isn't anything else we can do.

Understandably, it's gotten to Viv, and she's hibernating again. Refusing to leave the house. Going about her day on autopilot, and I can't get through to her. We're all worried, and I'm seriously contemplating quitting the band and pulling out of the tour. I can't leave her like this, and I haven't asked her to come with us either because I know she'll only say no.

Time is running out, and that calls for drastic measures.

On Christmas Eve morning, I decide it's time Dickhead Dillon came out to play. "Get dressed," I tell her when she emerges from our en suite bathroom surrounded by a steamy cloud. I'm fully dressed, sitting on the edge of the bed, waiting to battle her on this. "We're meeting Ash and Jamie and Audrey and Alex, downtown for lunch. Then we're taking Easton ice-skating at the outdoor rink at Santa Monica."

"No, Dillon." She shakes her head, beads of water dancing across her shoulders. "It will be crazy downtown, and I'm sure to get harassed."

"I'm not taking no for an answer, sweetheart." I pull her between my legs, ignoring the almost insurmountable urge to rip her towel off and fuck her until she agrees. "Today is no different than any other day in that regard." I pull her onto my lap and kiss her. "I know you're scared. I know some of the shit that's being said about you is awful. I hate how fucking sexist it is and how they're blaming you for everything. But it's not your fault. You didn't cause the accident. You didn't cheat on Reeve. And you couldn't help falling in love with me because I'm a fucking irresistible sexy bastard."

I flash her one of my trademark grins, encouraged when I see the hint of a smile on her beautiful mouth. "Remember what Meryl has told you. You can't control the media or jerks who post shit online. You can only control how you deal with it." I brush my fingers across her cheek. "I'm not being flippant when I say this. I know it's difficult to just shut it off, but they only have power over you if you let them. The people that matter know the truth. Fuck the rest of them."

I know this is difficult for her. She's been dealing with this kind of scrutiny since she was seventeen. I hate the attention that comes from being in a successful band, but what we endure pales in comparison to what Viv has to handle.

"You're right," she says, surprising the shit out of me. "I don't want this to be like the situation with Reeve. I don't want to end up broken or risk losing what we share." She snakes her hands around my neck. "But it is hard to forget it exists. People have been sending me death threats, Dillon. People actually wish I was dead." Her lower lip wobbles. "It's hard knowing that many people hate me."

"But they don't, sweetheart. They don't know you to hate you. They are projecting all their feelings of low self-worth on to you because it makes them feel better about themselves. This isn't about you. Everyone that knows you loves you. Easton loves you, and I fucking love you more than I ever thought it was possible to love another human being. Can't my love be enough?"

She inhales deeply. "You are so romantic, Dillon. You say the sweetest things."

"I write love songs for a living, Hollywood, and I'm damn fucking good at it. I live and breathe romance." I waggle my brows, grinning.

She rolls her eyes, and I count that as a victory. "I forgot about your ego," she says, standing. "God knows how when it's ever present."

I grab the hem of her towel, whipping it away. "Careful what you say when you're naked, sweetheart." I glance at the clock by the bed. "We have just enough time for me to punish you for daring to mock me." I wink at her, unbuttoning the top button of my jeans as she throws herself at me, wrapping her gorgeous legs around my waist.

Her eyes dilate, and she licks her lips. "Lock the door, and let the punishment begin."

CHAPTER 43
VIVIEN

WE ENJOY a casual lunch with our friends in a contemporary bar and grill in downtown L.A. Ash knows the owner, and he gave us a gorgeous circular table tucked away in a corner of the large stylish room. I'm surprised Alex agreed to come with Audrey, as he's made his feelings clear about Dillon, but he's been civil, and Dillon is behaving himself. Easton is in good spirits, chatting excitedly about Santa coming tonight, and he's looking forward to going ice-skating.

Easton is delighted Jamie and Ash chose to stay in L.A. for Christmas, and he's thrilled everyone is going to my parents' house for dinner tomorrow. I know they are all making the effort because they understand how tough it will be for both of us.

"Thank you for organizing this," I tell Dillon, wrapping my arms around him as he hands the waiter his platinum card to cover the check. "It's exactly what I needed." Yes, people have been gawking at us, but I'm feeling more confident surrounded by my closest friends, and I feel my bravado returning.

"That's my girl," he says, planting a passionate kiss on my lips. "How many fucks do we give, sweetheart?"

"Zero, babe." I rest my head on his shoulder, smiling at Ash across the way. "Zero fucks given."

Alex slides over to me when Dillon takes Easton to the bathroom. "You look happy," he says. "Are you?"

I nod. "I know you don't approve, but he makes me happy, Alex."

"It's not that I don't approve, Viv. I want you to be happy. Both of you. I'm just cautious."

"I get that, Alex, and you're a good friend, but you need to trust that I know what I'm doing. Dillon has been so patient and supportive, and I could not have gotten through this without him. We've chosen to leave the past in the past and concentrate on the present." I place my hands on my lap. "I can't force you to like him, but I hope in time you can learn to at least forgive and forget."

"As long as he does right by you and Easton, I'm sure I will."

I look into his eyes. "This might sound crazy, but I've sensed Reeve around." His eyes widen. "There have been a few occasions where I have felt his presence, and I chose to believe it's his way of approving and encouraging me to live my life. I will always love him, Alex. I will never forget him, and Dillon supports me. He's insisting we keep Reeve's memory alive for Easton, and he has gone out of his way to ensure we never forget what he meant to us."

"That's good to hear, Viv. And I know Reeve would want you to be happy."

Silence engulfs us for a few moments, and I see Dillon and Easton approaching from the corner of my eye.

"Easton loves him. That much is clear."

"They bonded instantly," I admit.

"Then I'm happy for you. Truly, I am." His smile is genuine. "Perhaps when we move back next year, we can try a regular couples' night out—get to know one another and try to let sleeping dogs lie."

"I would really like that." I lean in and kiss his cheek as my boys return to the table.

"Are we ready to go?" Dillon asks, quirking a brow at the sight of Alex sitting beside me. "Someone is super excited to get to the ice rink."

"Me! Me! Me!" Easton jumps up and down before hugging Dillon's legs. "Can we go now, puh-lease, Daddy Dillon."

Dillon chuckles, taking his hand. "Come on, Hollywood, before this little guy explodes."

I slide out of the booth, and Alex follows, high-fiving Easton. "Are you coming too, Uncle Alex?" he asks as Dillon threads his fingers in mine.

"I sure am."

"Awesome." Easton's smile is so wide it threatens to split his face.

"Hey, man. Thanks for inviting us today." Alex jerks his chin in acknowledgement at Dillon, and Audrey and I share a look.

"No problem. Easton wanted all his favorite people here, and Vivien needs to be surrounded by good friends right now."

I squeeze Dillon's arm, beaming up at him. I'm thrilled they are making an effort. I was a little worried things might be strained tomorrow at dinner, but those concerns have flittered away.

We head outside, and I do my best to ignore the finger-pointing, whispering, and the stares. We are walking up the sidewalk, heading toward where our cars are parked, when a woman steps out in front of me, appearing almost out of nowhere. "If it isn't the slut who murdered her husband so she could fuck his brother." Her eyes rake over me in a derisory fashion.

Dillon reacts fast, handing Easton to Jamie before turning around to glare at the woman. He puts his face all up in hers, and I would not like to be on the receiving end of that murderous expression. Camera flashes go off, and I spot a couple of paparazzi on the other side of the road, waiting to cross it. "Want to say that again to my face?" Dillon growls.

"I have no beef with you, and I can see the attraction." She blatantly eye fucks him with a smirk, and a red haze coats my retinas.

I pull Dillon back. "I've got this." I walk right up to the woman, loving the fact I tower over her by at least three or four inches. I enjoy looking down my nose at her. "How dare you approach me when I'm out with my family and hurl your hurtful accusations at me. You don't know me. You think you do, because you've seen comments online and reports on TV, but you know nothing about me. I loved my husband, and I miss him every single day."

She snorts, and I'm tempted to slap her stupid ignorant ass, but a crowd has formed now, and several people have their phones out, recording this. I won't lower myself to her standards, so I keep my shoulders back and my chin up as I ignore her derision and say what I need to say. "I honestly don't care whether you believe me or not, but you should take a long hard look at yourself." I glance over her shoulder to the young boy and girl, hanging back, clearly upset and scared. "What kind of a role model are you as a mother to accost an innocent woman in the street and level unfounded accusations at her? You don't care that your children are trembling with fright. You'd rather have your five seconds of fame. Well, shame on you."

She folds her arms and purses her lips, not paying her children any attention, and I feel for them.

"You're not fit to be a mother, and you have the nerve to throw shade at me? Get a life, you sad bitch. I'm done wasting my time on you." I grab Dillon's hand, pulling him in close. "And if you ever look at my boyfriend like that again, I will punch you in your self-righteous face. Go crawl back under that judgmental rock you came out of." I turn around, lifting one shoulder. "Come on, guys. We've got some ice-skating to do."

"Darling. Come in, come in," Mom says, almost blinding us with her dazzling smile as she steps aside, ushering us into the house. Dad is there too, and we exchange hugs.

"Merry Christmas, Easton." Mom bends down, pulling him into a hug. "Did Santa come?"

"He did, Grandma! And he even brought me a present from my daddy in heaven."

"Wow. That's amazing. I can't wait to hear about all your gifts."

Dad holds out his hand, smiling at his grandson. "I think I saw some under the tree with your name on them."

Easton rushes Dad, almost knocking him over. "Yay! More presents!" He starts tugging Dad down the hallway. "Let's go, Grandpa."

"Don't open them without me," Mom calls after him before reeling me in for another hug. "How are you holding up?"

"I'm okay." Dillon squeezes my hand, and I lean into his side. Truth is, I'm not sure exactly how I feel. I'm missing Reeve and sad he isn't here, but Dillon has gone out of his way to make this day so special already. He showered me with gifts that made me swoon, cry, and blush. I'm wearing some of the lingerie he bought me, having kept the racier stuff, as well as the sex toys, for our private time.

"Is this new?" Mom asks, fingering the pretty diamond bracelet on my wrist.

"It was one of my gifts from Dillon."

Mom smiles at him. "You have good taste. It's exquisite."

"I know." He wears a signature cocky grin, and Mom laughs.

"He also recorded an album of new songs, just for me, and he gave me this gorgeous printed leather album with the lyrics to his sweetest songs." I smile up at him. "He has spoiled me rotten all morning."

Mom leans in, hugging him, and it brings a tear to my eye. "I have come to expect no less." Her smile is warm as she squeezes his hand, and I almost burst into tears. Knowing my parents have accepted him is honestly the best Christmas present I could receive.

"Merry Christmas, Lauren." Dillon hugs her.

"How is E?"

"He's good. It was Dillon's idea to leave a gift for him from Reeve, and we took him out to the memorial garden to open it after breakfast. He wished his daddy and Lainey a Merry Christmas, and he's been fine since." I was so worried he'd be upset today, but he's taking it in stride.

"Dillon and Jamie were up until four this morning setting up his train set, and we had to practically drag him out of the house to come here." Dillon had his old train set shipped here from Ireland, and he found a guy to spruce it up and another guy to build a wooden base for it. "Dillon designed the set himself, and it's a miniature replica of Ireland with cliffs, mountains, woods, quaint Irish shops, traditional house-fronts, surrounded by the sea. There are even a few miniature people scattered around. The guys had to clear out the playroom to assemble it."

"That's wonderful. I can't wait to see it." She loops her arm in mine. "Come in and have a drink before the others get here."

I help Mom in the kitchen while Dillon joins Dad and Easton in the living room after he's opened his gifts from my parents. "I'll need to build an extension to the playroom at this rate," I joke as I sip my mimosa. "Easton has so many new toys."

"As long as he is happy."

"He is."

Mom leans back against the counter, facing me. "I can see that. I'm glad it's working out for you, Vivien. God knows you deserve every happiness after the year you've endured."

"I'll be glad to ring in the new year," I admit. "And I'm looking forward to the future, but I miss him today."

"You'll miss him every Christmas, darling." She walks to me, giving me a hug. "But this one will be especially hard because it's the very first one you have spent without him. Don't be too hard on yourself, and from what I've seen, Dillon understands."

"He does. He's been amazing. He really has."

"I'm happy to have been proven wrong about him. I saw the video last night, and I'm so proud of you, Vivien. I know it's not easy putting yourself out there, but you can't let these people destroy your happiness. Watching you defend yourself and your family yesterday brought tears to my eyes. You were so dignified."

"Dillon encourages me to be brave, and I didn't hesitate to defend myself."

"He's good for you, and you're different with him. I see you coming to life again and that's all I want for you. It's what Reeve would want too."

Dinner is a lively affair, and Easton is the center of attention. We FaceTime the O'Donoghues, and it's an experience. It's nighttime there, and they have a houseful of family and friends over. Drink is flowing, and they are all in good spirits. Easton is already begging me to take him to Ireland, and if Dillon wasn't leaving to go on tour in ten days, I would suggest we book a trip.

But he is, and I don't want him to go.

"You look like you could use this," Dillon says, coming up alongside me as I stare out the window of my parents' sunroom, looking at the old oak tree that holds so many memories. The others are playing board games with Easton in the living room, and I broke away, needing a few minutes alone. I should have known it wouldn't take Dillon long to find me.

I take the champagne flute from his hand. "Thank you."

He circles his arms around me from behind, and I lean back against his solid chest. "You can talk to me. I know you're missing him."

"This is the very first Christmas I've spent without him. I have lived twenty-five Christmases with him by my side. I feel disconnected without him here." Tears spill down my cheeks because I don't have the energy to hide them anymore. "These last few years, Reeve was actually very quiet at Christmas, and I longed to remove the sad look I always saw on his face."

Dillon brushes my tears away with his thumb. "You mentioned that before. The night in the nursery."

I nod, remembering. "We broke up on Christmas Day, and I know it played on his mind every year." A sob rips from my throat as I think back to that horrible Christmas. No wonder Reeve got upset. "I'm sorry," I whisper, hating to do this to him.

"Don't be sorry, Viv. I always want to hear what you're feeling and thinking." He tightens his arms around me.

I lean back, angling my head to press a soft kiss to his lips. "You love me so well, Dillon, and I feel like you get nothing in return." He must be so sick of my mood swings and my tears. I know I am.

"Are you kidding me? You give me everything just by breathing, Viv." He kisses the tip of my nose. "You made today so special for me. The photo album of Easton with all of your memories and written notes will help me to feel close to both of you on the tour. I can't wait to hang the framed family photo of us over my mantelpiece, and don't get me started on that Bob Dylan Martin D-28. I can't believe you got that for me."

It cost me a small fortune at the charity auction, but it was worth it to see the look of shock and sheer awe on Dillon's face when he realized who it used to belong to.

"But best of all is the gift of my son and this second chance with you."

I spin around in his arms, drying my tears. "I feel so lucky to have you in my life. Thank you for loving me, Dillon."

"Thank you for letting me."

We return to the others, hand in hand, and like always, Dillon has managed to clear the cobwebs from my head and add a smile to my face.

Mention of the tour has my mind churning with ideas. I meant what I said back there. Dillon has given so much of himself, going out of his way to prove his love for me and Easton, and I feel I need to make some grand gesture to let him know how much I appreciate and love him. The perfect idea pops into my head, and a bubble of excitement bursts in my chest. I wish I'd thought of it before, because I'm not sure if I can pull it off on such short notice. I don't want to get Dillon's hopes up if I can't make it happen.

I need to talk to my Irish bestie. If anyone can help me to turn it into reality, it's Aisling O'Donoghue.

CHAPTER 44
VIVIEN

"SEX with you just gets better and better every time," I pant, later that night when we're home in bed, after a second round of fucking. "I'm going to go crazy when you have to leave." I turn on my side, facing him.

He pushes damp strands of hair off my brow. "Why do you think I bought all those sex toys?"

"I'm insisting on nightly video sex."

He cups my cheek. "I'd like to promise I can do that, but things will be fairly hectic on the road, and it might not always be possible."

Unspoken words linger in the space between us as tension bleeds into the air. We have both known this day was coming, but I had purposely put it out of my mind because I was dealing with so much other stuff. But now it's looming, it's all I can think of.

Ash is excited about my plan, and while the deadline is tight, she has agreed to help pull out all the stops to try to make it happen. She agrees we should keep it between us so I can hopefully surprise him with the mother of all surprises.

"You could come you know?" He twirls a strand of my hair around his finger.

"I can't," I blurt, panicked. "You know how important routine is for Easton. He has school, and I think I'm going to return to work in the new year."

"We could hire a tutor, and you're freelance, so you can work anywhere."

"I must be available to attend weekly team meetings in person, and I really don't think the rock and roll lifestyle is one Easton should be around." I avert my eyes because I know I'm a shit liar, and he can probably see right through me.

"I'll quit the band."

"What?" I shriek, sitting up and staring at him like he's just sprouted wings. "You can't quit the band. Especially not at the last minute like this."

He sits up, leaning against the headboard. "I don't want to leave the guys in the lurch, but you and Easton are more important." He threads his fingers through my

617

hair. "I don't want to leave you. The thought of being apart from you makes me feel physically ill."

"You think I want to be separated from you either?"

He shrugs, and that pisses me off. "That was a fucking rhetorical question, Reeve."

He sucks in a sharp gasp, and pained eyes stare back at me. I don't understand what I've said until… "Oh my God." I crawl over to him. "I'm so sorry, Dillon. It was just a slip of the tongue. I didn't mean to upset you." I hope he's not remembering the hospital when I was confused and I thought he was Reeve.

"It's fine," he clips out, looking down at his lap.

"It's not fine. I'm really sorry, baby. Please forgive me." I squeeze his hands, willing him to look at me. I can't believe I slipped up like that. It's unforgivable, and I want to cry because I know I've just wounded him deeply, but he's not blameless either. "It wasn't intentional, Dillon. I was angry because you're discounting my commitment to you. You're acting like you're going to miss me more, but that's bullshit and totally unfair. I will miss you every bit as much as you'll miss me."

"I know. I'm sorry for insinuating you wouldn't. I just don't want to go without you. Please come with me, Viv. We'll find a way to make it work."

"Dillon, I want to, but I think it's best if we stay here," I lie. "Easton will have to get used to you being away for work. He needs to see you go and come back."

"Right." He removes his hand, and a muscle clenches in his jaw.

"We can come visit you on holidays and for weekends. I still have Ree—the private jet."

"Sounds great." He turns on his side, letting me know it's anything but great.

I chew on the inside of my mouth, wondering if I should just tell him. However, if I can't pull it off, he'll only be disappointed, so I decide to say nothing for now.

The next week is strained, and there's a distance between us caused by the elephant in the room. Dillon spends every spare minute when he's not rehearsing with Easton. He still sleeps here, in our bed, by my side, but he might as well be in outer space for all the attention he gives me. He's hurting, and I hate he is, but it will be worth it in the end to see the joy on his face when he realizes what I've done.

Dillon stays at his own house the night before the band is due to leave, and I don't protest as it gives me time to pack up our stuff without him noticing. Ash came through for me in the end, with some support from Mom, and it's happening. I'm so excited, and keeping this from Dillon now is virtually impossible, so it's just as well he hasn't been here much the last twenty-four hours. I haven't told Easton either because he'd never have been able to keep it a secret.

If I had known I could pull it off in time, I would've told Dillon last week and avoided hurting him. But it will all be forgotten in a few hours when Easton and I walk up the steps of the band's private jet and announce we are coming with them.

I bring Easton into my confidence just before Dillon arrives to say goodbye. He's bouncing off the walls with excitement, and I hope he doesn't let the cat out of the bag. At this late stage, I want to keep the surprise until the last moment. However, it backfires spectacularly when Easton says goodbye with a big smiley face and then runs off like it's no big deal that his daddy is leaving for seven months.

Dillon was already in a foul mood, but now he looks like he wants to burn the world down and then do it all over again.

"It seems like no one will miss me," he fumes, shoving his hands in his pockets. "And to think I considered quitting." He shakes his head.

"Dillon, that's not true. You know we're going to miss you."

He barks out a laugh. "Honestly, Vivien? This past week has me questioning everything I thought I knew."

Butterflies swoop into my stomach, but they're not the pleasant kind. "What do you mean?"

"Was I just the Band-Aid, Hollywood? You needed me to help you get over the true love of your life and now you're patched up, you don't need me anymore? Is that it?"

"Please tell me you are not serious right now." He cannot honestly believe that after everything we have been through. All because I said I wouldn't come with him, providing very valid reasons. It doesn't matter that it's not true because the fact he's even saying this shit to me now has me infuriated. How could he even suggest I used him as a temporary fix? He might as well have slapped me in the face. That's how much it stings.

He shrugs. "How else do you expect me to react when you are fucking rejecting me again?!"

"How else do you expect *me* to react when you spring it on me at the last second again?!"

"I was waiting for the right time to ask you, but it doesn't matter. You'll do what you always do. Run to Reeve, except he's not here anymore. He's dead, and I'm still living in his fucking shadow. I'm still second best, and that's all I'll ever be." His vitriol spews from his mouth like the worst sickness, and I stumble back, holding a hand over my mouth, disbelieving what I'm hearing.

"I'll call every night to speak to Easton, and we can make arrangements for the holidays," he says, opening the door of his Land Rover. "As for us, you're off the hook, Hollywood." Hurt is etched all over his face as he looks at me. "I guess I'll see you around."

I'm momentarily frozen in place. What the hell is happening right now? I snap out of it as Dillon fires up the engine, and I force my legs to move, racing toward his car as he takes off. To hell with the surprise. I need to tell him now. But I'm too late. He must see me in the rearview mirror, but he doesn't stop, and I give up chasing after him, standing in utter shock as I watch him leave.

Shock gives way to anger, pretty quickly, and I'm tempted to cancel our plans and tell him to take a hike.

But this is Dillon.

The man who has gone out on a limb for me, time and time again.

I know that was anger and pain talking, and a part of me understands even if I can't fathom how he could throw away what we've painstakingly rebuilt so easily. I know this is the past fucking with his head. How he's equating me telling him no to my rejection in Dublin. But it doesn't make sense because he has never been second best, and I told him that.

"I made a mistake," I tell Ash as Leon drives us to the airport. Easton has his

AirPods in, listening to Collateral Damage's new album, because he wants to know all the songs so he can sing along at the side of the stage. I haven't had the heart to tell him yet he'll be wearing soundproof headphones to protect his little ears from damage.

The album released last night, and it shot straight to the top of the charts. Something Dillon never even mentioned when he showed up.

"Please don't tell me you've changed your mind."

"I haven't. I meant I made a mistake not telling him what I was planning. We agreed there would be no secrets."

"This is different. You wanted to surprise him."

"Well, he's gonna be surprised all right. Especially when he just broke up with me."

"What?" she screeches in my ear.

I tell her how it all went down.

"He is such a dumbass. I'm going to kick him in the nuts when we get to the airport." I hear muffled talking in the background, and I'm assuming it's Jamie. Ro, Conor, and Dillon were making their own way to the private airfield where the band's private jet is waiting to take them to Texas to board their tour bus.

"I wanted to make a grand gesture, to show him how much he means to me, and I've ended up achieving the opposite result. And now I'm fucking pissed that he could say those things to me and dismiss what we have just like that, even if I know he's lashing out because he's hurt."

"I thought you guys had moved beyond this."

"So did I, but it appears your brother is still harboring doubts and comparing himself to Reeve. I didn't help the situation when I accidentally called him Reeve on Christmas night."

"You're only human, babe, and he knows you didn't mean it." There is more muffled conversation, and then she says, "We just arrived. I'll try not to punch the idiot before you get here."

"Traffic is shit, but we should still make it in time. I'll see you soon."

"But I wanna get on the plane now," East whines as we pull up alongside the band's jet.

"I need to talk to Daddy Dillon first, but I will come and get you as soon as we're ready. Watch a movie, or listen to your daddy's album again, or you could color," I add, pulling the box of coloring pencils and thick coloring book from the back of the seat where I keep an emergency supply.

He pouts but sits back in his booster seat, and I'm glad he's decided not to argue further. I'm in no mood to deal with *two* grumpy boys. "I shouldn't be too long," I tell Leon.

"I'll keep an eye on Easton. Go fix things with your man." He smothers a grin, and I narrow my eyes at him. Of course, Leon would have to be outside earlier when we had our fight.

I climb out, wiping my hands down the front of my skinny jeans, thrusting my shoulders back as I walk on high heels toward the plane. I'm wearing a white silk blouse under a formfitting black jacket, and a polka-dot chiffon scarf is artfully wrapped around my neck. My hair is pulled back off my face in a sleek ponytail, and I paid extra attention to my makeup.

I'm feeling confident and only slightly murderous when I walk up the steps and enter the plane.

The interior is luxurious, as I was expecting, with twelve leather seats, six on either side. Jamie and Ash are sitting side by side, facing Conor, while Ro and Dillon are sitting on the other side of the plane, facing each other. All eyes are on me. Ash and Jamie grin. Conor looks stoned already, and Ro looks confused.

Dillon smirks, leaning back in his chair with one leg crossed over his knee. "You're an asshole," I hiss, realizing this was all part of *his* plan. "I really want to slap you, but I don't condone violence." I walk closer to where he's sitting.

"Unless it's Aoife." Jamie throws it out there. "I bet you'd give her a few slaps."

I eyeball Jamie. "Truth," Ash and I say together.

"Put the dickhead out of his misery," she adds. "He's unbearable."

I don't doubt it because I know Dillon's hurt was real even if this was part of his game plan. His truths were mixed in with the bullshit, but he wanted me to chase him. "What if I hadn't come?"

"I would have quit the tour," he says, without hesitation, sitting upright and losing the grin.

Shocked faces and angry words litter the air.

I turn to his bandmates. "He's being an ass. Ignore him. I would not have let him quit." I face Dillon, crossing my arms over my chest. I'm still pissed at him. "You are the hardest person in the world to surprise."

Crease lines appear on his brow. "What do you mean?"

"I was planning to come all along, although the idea only came to me on Christmas Day. I didn't say anything because I didn't know if I could buy another tour bus and get it to Texas on time or if I could hire a tutor for Easton on such short notice."

I was less concerned about the latter. As long as the school was okay with me pulling Easton out, I knew I'd find a suitable tutor even if it was while we were on the road. And I can always homeschool him if I have to. "I wanted to surprise you. This was going to be my grand gesture of love, but you fucking ruined it all, and now, frankly, I'm pretty pissed."

"Sweetheart." He stands, moving over to me.

"Don't think your sweet talking will get you out of this hole you've dug."

"I was thinking my cock would do the trick." He waggles his brows as Ash makes a gagging sound behind us.

"Always lowering the tone." I shake my head, softening as his arms go around my waist. I let my arms drop to my sides.

"You bought us a bus?"

"Yes. There wasn't enough room on one bus for all of us, and I wanted us to be a family."

I also didn't want Easton around Conor and Ronan. They are both single, and I know they'll be entertaining groupies on the bus. Easton does not need to see that, and I'm sure they don't want Dillon's girlfriend and son raining on their parade. Separate buses are the only way this will work.

"Leon is coming with us too." Ash assured me they have plenty of security on tour, but Easton is familiar with Leon, and I want to make this transition as easy as possible for our son. I know he's excited, but this is a big adjustment for both of us.

"You're really coming on tour?" His eyes are bursting with happiness. "The whole tour?"

"Yes, dumbass," Ash says.

"We are, even though you might not deserve it after the shit you said to me earlier."

"I didn't mean to say all of that. I got carried away in the moment." He grips my waist harder, pulling me in to his body. "I'm sorry."

"I'm not letting you off the hook that easily, and I have something I need to say." I cup his face in my hands. "How can you think you are second best? I have told you time and time again it wasn't a competition, but the truth is, I chose you, Dillon. I chose *you*." I let that truth settle for a second before continuing. "But you didn't choose me. All you had to do was come to the airport and stop me from getting on that plane. I told you that in my letter, but still you didn't come." Movement in my peripheral vision distracts me a little, but I stay focused on Dillon, watching the frown appear on his brow.

"What are you talking about? What letter?"

"The letter I wrote you the night I left Ireland. I put it through your mailbox."

He frowns. "I didn't see any letter. I didn't get it."

My eyes startle wide. "Oh my God. This explains so much. I couldn't understand how you could write those hateful lyrics about me when the ball had been in your court. I waited till the very last second to board the plane, praying you would show up, but you didn't." And of course, now I know he tried to come after me, but Reeve deleted his calls, leading me to believe Dillon never truly cared for me.

"That fucking bitch!" Ash jumps up, eyes burning. "Aoife was there that night. That bitch must have taken it."

"She didn't," Ronan says, and I swing my gaze on him as Dillon turns around. Ro wets his lips, looking nervous as he looks us straight in the eyes. "Aoife didn't take the letter. I did. I threw it in the bin before Dillon had a chance to see it."

CHAPTER 45
VIVIEN

SHOCKED SILENCE FILTERS through the cabin. Ronan drags his hands through his hair as he stands. "I'm really sorry I did it. I have felt enormous guilt for years, but it was worse when we found out about Easton. Especially now I'm a father."

"Why did you do it?" I ask, circling my arms around Dillon's waist because I can tell he's on the verge of doing something he'll regret.

Ro lifts his eyes to his brother's. "I knew you were in love with her, and I could see it on your face. I knew you were ready to quit the band for her."

Dillon sneers. "Pull the other one, brother. You always had the hots for her. Admit you were jealous."

He vigorously shakes his head. "I'll admit I was jealous when you first hooked up, but I got over it. That wasn't the reason." His Adam's apple jumps in his throat. "We were so close to making it, and the band would never have gotten signed without you. You're the star, Dillon. You always have been. I couldn't let you throw it all away."

"That wasn't your decision to make, Ro," Dillon grits out. His body is visibly shaking with rage.

"I was young and dumb. I knew you loved her, but I didn't know it was forever love. I thought you'd get over her, especially once we made it big and there were women throwing themselves at you. But I was wrong. I've had to watch you suffer and press the self-destruct button, knowing it was all my fault."

"Why didn't you fess up?" Ash asks.

Ronan rolls his neck from side to side. "I wanted to, but the longer it went on, the harder it got. Then Vivien married Reeve, and I knew there was no undoing the damage."

"You're a fucking asshole," Dillon snaps. "You should've told me when I told you Easton was my son. That was the time to come clean."

"I wanted to, but I couldn't. I was going through my own shit, and—"

"You're a fucking selfish prick!" Dillon lunges for Ronan, grabbing him by the shirt and shoving him against the side of the plane. "I lost five years with my son!" he yells. "Years I could've been around for if I had gotten Vivien's letter and stopped her from getting on that plane. I will never forgive you for this." He shoves him. "Never."

"Stop." I step in between them, pushing them apart. "What you did was selfish and manipulative," I tell Ronan, "but I understand your motivations, and you *were* young."

"That doesn't excuse him," Dillon snaps.

I turn to face my boyfriend. "No, it doesn't, but Ronan is the one who will have to live with that for the rest of his life." My features soften, and I let Ro go, sliding both hands up Dillon's chest. "I could just as easily say this is my fault for not giving the letter to Ash to deliver to you or handing it to you myself."

"Why didn't you?" Ash asks.

I glance between her and Dillon. "I mean no offense, Ash, but I wanted Dillon to make the decision free of interference and influence. If he came to stop me from getting on that plane, I needed to know it was solely his choice because I was prepared to completely change my life for him, and I needed to know he was all in."

She nods slowly. "That makes sense."

"Why did you put it through the letter box?" Dillon says. "Why not hand it to me personally?"

I arch a brow. "You honestly have to ask me that?" He looks confused. Typical man. "I thought Aoife was in there with you, and I couldn't handle another rejection. I told you I loved you in the bar, and you acted like it meant nothing. I was broken-hearted, Dillon, and I couldn't face seeing you with her again."

He bobs his head. "It was natural to assume that, except she wasn't with me."

"I know that now, but I didn't back then."

"God, it's all so tragic." Ash shakes her head. "All these little things conspired to keep you apart."

"I know, but what's the point in looking back? We can't change the past." I cup one side of Dillon's face. "The truth is, we don't know what would've happened if you'd gotten that letter. Maybe you would have come after me, or maybe you were too drunk and you still would've gotten on that plane the next day and everything would have played out as it did."

"Or maybe I would have fought harder for you, knowing you had chosen me."

"But would you?" I peer deep into his eyes. "I hurt you by running straight back to Reeve. That hurt would still have been there."

A muscle pops in his jaw. "I would've come after you and stopped you getting on the plane. That would have stopped everything from happening."

"I'm not so sure, Dil." Ash gets up, crossing to us. "You were stoned, drunk and incoherent, and so full of anger and bitterness. I would have encouraged you to go after her, but honestly, I think you're too stubborn to have made that call until you had sobered up."

"The point is, it doesn't matter now." I can't think like that because it would be like saying if things had happened differently then Reeve would still be alive and maybe Lainey would never have existed, and I can't think of alternative realities when I have battled so hard for this current one.

"How can you say that?" Dillon cries, pinning me with bloodshot eyes. "I lost years with East. Years I might not have lost if I'd been given your letter."

My heart aches for him, and I feel his pain. "We can't turn back the clock, and dwelling on all the what-ifs has gotten us nowhere in the past. We have all made mistakes, which contributed to the situation, but we are here now, in the right place, united as a family. That's what matters most. That's what we should focus on." I kiss him softly. "I know you're angry and you're hurt. I can't tell you how to react to it. I can't tell you to forgive your brother. I *can* tell you what I think, which is we've suffered enough from the mistakes of the past. We're dangerously close to undoing all the progress we've both made."

"What are you saying, Viv?"

"I'm asking you to look inside yourself and find it in your heart to forgive your brother. We need to look to the future, not the past. You're going on tour. You need to be united. Your family forgave you for the secrets you hid and the lies you told. It should end here." The situation is not the same. I know that. But we have to draw a line somewhere.

"I can't even look at him right now."

I hug him. "You need time to process and time to calm down."

"How are you so calm? So reasonable?"

"It's actually given me closure. I always thought you'd received that letter and didn't care. Plus, I'm tired of hating and hurting and feeling sad. This is a new year, and I want it to be a fresh start."

The pilot pops his head out then. "We'll be taking off in fifteen minutes."

"We need to get E." I turn to walk toward the exit, but Dillon reaches out his arm to stop me.

"Allow me." Some of the tension lifts from his shoulders and erases from his face.

I kiss him. "Go get our son. He's incredibly excited. He's been listening to your new album in the car. He wants to learn all the songs so he can sing along with you when you're on stage."

"Oh God." Ash gulps, slapping a hand over her chest. "I love that little human so fucking much. Thank fuck, he takes after you and not dumbass over there." I wouldn't be too sure about that, at all, but I smile anyway because Ash always brings a smile to my face.

Dillon flips her the bird as he stalks to the entrance and disappears outside.

"Thanks, Viv," Ronan says in a quiet voice.

I drop into the seat beside him. "Don't thank me yet. You know how stubborn your brother is, and he might not ever be able to forgive you." I feel I need to prepare Ronan for that possibility. "I know Dillon disappointed all of you when he concealed so much, but those secrets didn't hurt any of you. Mostly, he hurt himself."

"Whereas, what I did directly hurt my brother." He hangs his head. "I'm so ashamed."

"I can see that." I pat his arm.

"I'm unbelievably sorry for my actions, Vivien. If I could go back, I would never have destroyed the letter."

"I believe you, and I forgive you." At least it explains why he's had trouble looking me in the eye. He stares at me now.

"You do?"

I nod, and I'm proud of myself. I know forgiving him is the right thing to do, but I'm not saying it to keep the peace. I genuinely mean it, and it hasn't been difficult for me to reach this decision. It's completely different for Dillon though, and it will take him some time. I hope, for everyone's sake, they can find a way to move past this. "You were a great friend to me in Ireland, Ronan. I know you didn't deliberately set out to hurt me."

He hugs me, and there are tears in his eyes.

"Hands off my woman," the caveman says as he reenters the plane carrying a little wriggly live wire in his arms.

Ro jerks back as if he's been electrocuted.

"Auntie Ash!" Easton exclaims, sliding down Dillon's body. "I'm coming on tour!"

"I heard, little munchkin." She high-fives him. "We are going to have so much fun."

"Mommy!" he jumps on my lap. "Daddy says I can play guitar on stage with him!"

I look at Dillon through hooded eyes. That is something we really should have discussed together, but I'll give him a free pass. "That is awesome."

"Not every night, buddy," Dillon says, scooping him up and putting him in the seat across from Ronan. "And we'll have to practice."

"Of course." East looks at him like he's being ridiculous.

"Swap with me," Ash says, looking over at Ronan, and he silently gets up, taking her seat. She drops down beside me while Dillon settles into the seat beside Easton. They are whispering with their heads huddled, plotting trouble, most likely.

"Do you ever feel like you live in a real-life soap opera?" she asks, as Leon climbs on board the plane.

"All the freaking time."

"The luggage is safely on board, Vivien," my bodyguard informs me.

"Thank you."

"Make yourself comfortable, Leon," Ash says, pointing at the spare seats behind Jamie and Conor.

The door shuts as the flight attendant appears, advising us to buckle our seat belts and prepare for takeoff.

Easton chatters nonstop until he falls asleep, lulled by the motion of the plane. Dillon reclines his seat and drapes a blanket over him, before offering me his hand. "Can we talk?" he whispers, jerking his head toward the two empty seats behind us.

"I'll watch the treasure," Ash says, lifting her head from her book.

We resituate ourselves in the seats. Leon is across from us, napping, and the others all have their AirPods in.

"I'm sorry for being a jackass this morning," he says, threading his fingers through mine.

"It's okay. I'm well acquainted with your assholish gene."

He grabs my face, kissing me passionately. "In case you weren't aware, I'm over the fucking moon you're coming on tour with me."

"I'm excited."

"I love you."

"I love you too."

"I have a favor to ask," I say, twisting in the seat to face him. "I've decided I would like to get up on stage with you, once, and sing."

His eyes pop wide. "What's brought this on?"

"You. You've encouraged me to overcome my fears. I have always been the truest sense of myself with you. I want to do this. I want to prove to myself that I'm the only one who is in control of my life. I want to be brave and put myself out there knowing how some will perceive it."

"You should sing 'She Moved Through the Fair.' That will bring the most critical of cynics to their knees."

I very much doubt that. "That's an odd choice for a rock concert."

"It's our show, and if anyone dares to question me, I'll punch their lights out."

"Me too," Ash says from overhead. We both look up. "I'll square it with the label."

"Fuck off and mind your own business," Dillon says, but there's no heat in his words. "This is a private conversation."

"There is no such thing as privacy on tour," she retorts.

"Not for you." He grins smugly, sliding his arm around my shoulders. "We've got our own bus."

She flips him the bird before sliding back into her seat as Jamie comes over to join her.

"Are you mad I didn't tell you?" I ask, wanting to clear the air before we step foot on said bus.

"I understand why you didn't, but it raised old fears to the surface. And I reverted to default mode."

"You can't test the people you love, Dillon. What you did earlier was emotional manipulation, just like those early days in Ireland. We can't go there again. We're supposed to be older and wiser."

"You're right, and I've spoken about it in therapy. Maybe I need to do a few more sessions."

"I think that would be a good idea." I wet my lips. I'm slightly nervous to say this, but we've got to be honest with one another, and this needs to be said. "I still think you're triggered by Reeve, a little, and we need to discuss that and properly move past it. Would you be open to couples therapy? Meryl mentioned it to me before, and I'm sure she'd be open to some video sessions while we're on the road."

"I am willing to do whatever it takes to make this work and to make you happy. Line it up, and I'm there."

"Thank you." I peck his lips, resting my head on his shoulder.

He twists my ponytail around his fist. "We fucked up again, huh?"

"We're going to fuck up occasionally, Dillon. We're only human, and well, you're you." My lips twitch, but I fight the urge to laugh. "And I'm me. We're going to argue and not see eye to eye on things, and that's okay as long as we communicate. I was wrong not to tell you. I should've realized it would remind you of the past and cause you to doubt us." He loosens his hold on my hair, and I lift my head, resting my hands on his shoulders. "I just wanted to do something big. You have done so much

627

for me, and I wanted to give something back. I wanted to see the shock and excitement on your face when we showed up."

"We'll do better next time we reach a stumbling block."

"We will because you're stuck with me, in a confined space, for the next seven months." In a way, I'm glad this happened. It has reminded us of what's important and shown us we are not infallible. We have worked hard to get to this point, but that doesn't mean it will be smooth sailing going forward. All relationships require effort and investment. What matters is that we love each other and we're committed to making this work, and that is half the battle.

CHAPTER 46
DILLON

THE PAST SEVEN MONTHS HAS, hands down, been the best seven months of my life. This tour has been the best touring experience of my career. And it's all thanks to Vivien and Easton. Living on the bus with them has been amazing, and we're as close as we can be.

Easton has taken to life on the road like a pro.

Seeing his obvious joy at being a part of my world has meant everything to me. During the day, when we're sleeping and later rehearsing, he does the tourist thing with Ash and Vivien after his schoolwork is done. They've managed to squeeze in tons of activities in the various cities we've visited, and we have mountains of photos for new albums when we get home.

Vivien rejoined social media, and she's amassed quite a loyal following who go crazy for the daily posts and pics she shares. Being on the road has done wonders for her anxiety. She no longer cares what people say about her, and the interest in us has eased off from the intrusive levels of the early days.

She conquered her fears and sang on stage with me in Ohio. It was just me on guitar and her singing to a packed stadium. There wasn't a peep from the audience as she delivered the haunting lyrics with so much emotion I know it came straight from her soul. They were as hypnotized as me, and at the end, they gave her a standing ovation.

I was so fucking proud of her.

Videos of her performing were all over social media the next day, and it garnered a lot of good will.

Tonight is our last night on the US tour, and it's extra special because Easton is joining us on stage. This will be his first time up here, and I'm stoked to be accompanied by my son on guitar. Originally, I had planned on letting him join us more often. Until Viv and I talked about it and she explained her concerns, which were all valid.

She doesn't want him living under a media glare, and she's done her best to protect him over the years. Kidnapping is also a very real worry.

I thought East would throw a fit, but he's happy getting to jam with us on stage during rehearsal, and now he's getting his wish to play before a packed stadium. We've been practicing like crazy to get this performance right, and his perseverance, talent, and determination have impressed me to no end.

Vivien doesn't know I'm about to embarrass the shit out of her, but she's going to find out in a couple of minutes.

"Are you ready to hear our new single, Las Vegas?" I shout into the mic, grinning at the deafening roar of approval from the massive crowd. I pace across the front of the stage, wiping my sweaty brow with the back of my arm. "This is an extra special performance tonight because we have an extra special guitarist joining us."

I turn around, grinning when I spot East standing in the wings with Vivien. We planned this together because I need to get her out on this stage. I want to sing the words to her so she has no doubt how much I love her, and then later tonight, I'm going to propose. "Please welcome my son, Easton, to the stage," I shout, facing him as the crowd whoops and hollers.

Easton struts across the stage like he owns it, and Jamie cracks up laughing at his swagger. He's holding Vivien's hand, beaming proudly at me for playing his part. "Thanks, buddy." I lean down, and we do our special handshake with our elbows and our arms. The crowd goes nuts because he's the cutest fucking kid. He turned six in May, and we threw a special party for him backstage at the venue in DC.

"What's going on?" Viv mouths, looking a little nervous.

"Stay put," I tell her, smirking.

Helping Easton up onto his stool, I fix his guitar around him, and then I reposition his mic so it's at the right level. "Hellooooo, Las Vegas," he booms into the mic, and Jamie almost pisses his pants. Ro nearly falls off his stool he's laughing so hard. Conor is as zoned out as ever. Vivien and I exchange smiles as the crowd screams for our little wannabe rock star.

"I asked my son to help me tonight because this is the first time I'm singing this song in public, and as it's about the love of my life, I wanted to make it personal by singing it to her."

Oohs and aahs echo around the giant stadium, as one of the crew rushes out with a high-backed stool for Vivien.

Vivien's eyes pop wide as I walk toward her. I pull her flush against me. "In case you're confused, that means you." She slaps my chest as laughter wafts around the large arena. I spin her around to the front of the stage, wrapping my arm around her waist. She's wearing a short, tight strapless black leather dress that has panels cut out at the waist and sky-scraper heels that make her slim legs look even longer. I'm on a permanent horn looking at her. "How hot does my woman look tonight?" I ask the crowd. A chorus of catcalls and wolf whistles rings out, and I flash the audience a trademark grin.

"You are so dead," Vivien says, turning around to look at me.

Discreetly, I move the mic closer. "I can't hear you," I mouth.

"I said you are so dead." Her statement projects through the mic, bouncing around the venue, and everyone laughs.

"That means she wants me," I tell them, winking. "This is our version of foreplay."

"Jesus, Dillon!" she shrieks, gesturing toward Easton.

"Shit." I had almost forgotten he was there.

"A dollar for the cuss jar, Daddy Dillon!"

After the laughter has died down this time, I turn her around in my arms. "I love you." Before she has a chance to reply, I lower her back a little and kiss her hard.

"That is just gross, Daddy," Easton says into the mic.

I pull Vivien upright, both of us laughing along with the audience.

"He is such a carbon copy of you," Vivien says into my ear.

"I'll take that as a compliment," I reply into hers.

"I meant it as one." She smiles, and I'm relieved I'm not in the doghouse.

Tucking her under my arm, I maneuver us so we're facing the crowd again. "This woman is the love of my life and the only woman who has ever owned my heart. Every love song I've written from the time I've met her has been about her. She completes me in every way possible."

I hope someone records this and puts it online, and I hope Aoife sees it. Last I heard, she is back living with her folks after she lost everything in court. She had to liquidate all her assets, and she still fell short. She'll be paying us back every year for the rest of her life, and it will be a constant reminder of all she's lost thanks to her jealousy and her greed.

I stand in front of Vivien, taking her hand and bringing it to my mouth. My lips linger on her skin as I drink her in, my heart consumed with love for her. "I only ever want to exist with you, Vivien Grace. This song is for you."

The crowd swoons, and I know once we start the song I'll have them eating out of my hand.

I lift Vivien up onto her stool, planting another kiss on her lips before rejoining my son. East is sitting, so I've chosen to do the same. This song is a little different than most of our stuff, and it lends itself to this acoustic version. I put my lips to the mic, speaking to the crowd. "This is 'Exist with You.'"

I keep my eyes locked on Vivien as I sing the words that have come directly from my soul. A deathly hush has settled over the crowd as they listen. Easton messes up a couple of times, but he catches up, and I'm so freaking proud of him. To deliver a performance like he's just done at six years of age proves this little guy is destined to belong on stage. Whether it's a rock stage or a theater stage remains to be seen.

Vivien is crying by the time we finish to massive applause from the audience. Scooping Easton into my arms, I walk toward her as she rushes across the stage, throwing her arms around us. "Dillon," she croaks. "That was so beautiful." She kisses me before turning her attention to East. "I am so proud of you, Easton. You were awesome! You are every bit as talented as your daddy." She dots kisses all over his face, and he beams, delighted with her praise and high off his performance.

"We're going to wrap this up now," I say, placing Easton on his feet. "Go wait with Ash." I kiss her again because I can't get enough of her tonight. I crouch down to Easton, opening my arms, and he gives me a massive hug. "You did amazing, buddy. I couldn't be prouder of you."

"I loved it, Daddy! Can I do it again?"

I straighten up, chuckling. "The tour is over tonight, and we're going home soon, but there will be more tours and more opportunities to join us, I promise." I ruffle his hair. "Time to go with Mommy."

He steps around me and bows to the audience, and there's a giant collective swoon from all the female fans.

Jamie approaches, grinning. "You are going to be in so much trouble with this little dude when he gets older. He'd charm the knickers off a nun."

"Dillon." Vivien pushes my shoulders, looking up at the corner of the elevator. "There are cameras."

"Don't fucking care," I say, returning my lips to her neck and continuing my upward journey under her dress.

She slaps my hands away. "Have patience. We're almost at our suite."

"Have you seen yourself tonight?" I ask, wrapping my arms around her waist, burying my head in her shoulder. "You're sex on legs, sweetheart, and I've been dying to fuck you from the second you walked out on that stage."

"Is that why you arranged a sleepover for East in Jamie and Ash's suite?"

"It's our last night," I murmur, grazing my teeth along her neck as the elevator comes to a stop. "I want to make the most of it."

We crash into the penthouse, knocking over shit as we devour each other while tearing our clothes off. "Fuck, Hollywood. I need inside you right now."

"I'm ready for you, rock star," she pants, peeling her knickers off and standing before me in all her naked glory. "You're not the only one who's been horny all night." She flings herself at me as I kick my boxers away, grabbing a condom from the pocket of my jeans. "Seeing you on that stage turns me on like you wouldn't believe, and you definitely deserve a reward for that song." I lift her up, and her legs circle my waist as tears pool in her eyes. "It was beautiful, Dillon. I felt every word deep in my soul."

"Good," I growl, nipping at her earlobe as I walk us toward the floor-to-ceiling window. "Because every word was birthed from my soul." I kiss her hard as I slam her against the window, rocking my pelvis against her, moaning into her mouth at the feel of her hot flesh grazing my hard length.

"Fuck me, Dillon. Fuck me really hard. I want to walk around tomorrow feeling that burn for you."

I set her down to roll on a condom before lifting her again and positioning her on my dick. Holding my shoulders, she lowers herself down my length, and we both hiss when she's fully seated. "Love you." I thrust into her, and her head goes back.

"Love you too, baby. So, so much."

She clings to me as I pound into her, holding her up with my arms as I brace her against the window, but I can't drive hard enough in this position, and I need to be balls deep in my woman tonight. Setting her down, I flip her around so her naked front is up against the window.

"What if someone sees?" she asks, jutting her ass up and spreading her legs.

"We're up high enough it's unlikely, but do you honestly care?" Vivien is more carefree and abandoned now, and she has moved past a lot of her fears, but I will never do anything to make her uncomfortable. If she doesn't like this, we'll move away from the window.

She glances over her shoulder at me, biting down on her lower lip. A grin graces her gorgeous mouth. "Nope." Her grin expands. "Zero fucks given." She wiggles her ass as I line my cock up at the entrance to her pussy. "Rock my world, babe."

I slam into her in one thrust and fuck the shit out of her, pressed up against the window, and the thrill of potential discovery only heightens our arousal.

After, we head to the hot tub, which is positioned on a balcony off the bedroom, and we drink champagne while we relax, talk, and kiss. It's blissful, but our night is only getting started, even if it's already past midnight.

"I have a surprise," I tell her when we've showered and dressed. She's wearing a gorgeous red silk negligee, and I'm in sweats with the ring box concealed in the pocket. I wrap my hand around hers, reeling her into my chest. I stare into her eyes before kissing her softly. "Want to sleep under the stars with me, Vivien Grace?"

Her eyes pop wide. "What have you done?"

"Come and see." I keep a hold of her hand as I guide her up to the rooftop terrace.

A gasp of delight escapes her lips, as bile travels up my throat. I haven't been nervous to do this until right now. What if she says no? What if it's too soon? What if she never wants to remarry? It's not like we've discussed it beyond the odd throwaway remark.

"Dillon, this is beautiful." Her gaze takes in the view. Softly flickering candles cover the perimeter of the terrace, but the pièce de résistance is the small marquee in the center of the space. Vivien walks toward it, gasping again when she sees the bed strewn with white rose petals and lavender rose petals. A side table houses a bucket with chilled champagne, two glasses, and a bowl of chocolate strawberries. She throws her arms around me, hugging me tight. "Have I told you how much I love romantic Dillon?"

"Maybe a time or two," I tease.

I step away from her and drop to one knee. My heart is pounding, and my palms are sweaty. I have never been more terrified than I am at this moment.

Vivien clasps a hand over her mouth, and her eyes well up.

"From the moment I met you, I knew you were the only woman for me. Even when I tried to deny you my heart, it was a hopeless endeavor because it was impossible not to fall in love with you. You are everything I never dared to dream of, and I loved you before I even knew you existed. It was always meant to be you and me, Vivien. I cannot exist in a world without you. I know what it's like to lose you, and I never want to experience that again. I love you, and I love Easton, and I want to spend the rest of my life proving that over and over."

Tears are streaming down her face, but she doesn't look like she's going to say no. Yet this woman has been unpredictable before. My hands are shaking as I remove the box and pop the lid holding the ring out to her. "Let me love you forever, Vivien." I'm fighting tears now too. "Marry me."

She sinks to her knees in front of me, laughing amid her tears. "Yes, Dillon. A thousand times yes. I can't wait to marry you."

CHAPTER 47
DILLON

"I'M BETTING Viv didn't think accepting your proposal meant she'd be getting married five days later," Jamie jokes as we stand at the top of the small aisle in the chapel we booked for our wedding ceremony.

"She said she couldn't wait to marry me," I reply, smiling as my parents arrive the same time as Vivien's.

"I'm sure she didn't mean it literally."

I glare at Jamie. "You're the worst fucking best man in history. You're supposed to be calming my nerves not making out like I bullied my fiancée into a rush wedding."

Jamie chuckles. "You are so on edge."

"Don't tell me you weren't the same?"

After Vivien and I announced the good news to our friends and family the next morning, Jamie and Ash admitted they had gotten married last year when they were on vacation in Mexico. I couldn't believe Ash had kept that a secret or that my best mate hadn't told me. They explained they did it on the spur-of-the-moment, and they wanted to enjoy some time as a married couple before anyone knew and the press found out. I'm not mad, just gobsmacked my sister managed to keep it a secret for so long.

"Fact," Jamie agrees. "And I'm only yanking your chain. Vivien loves you. God knows why, but she'll be here."

I elbow my only groomsman in the ribs before I step away to welcome both sets of parents.

Vivien was more than happy when I suggested we stay in Vegas and tie the knot this week. Easton isn't back to school until next week, so there was no immediate rush to head back to L.A. She had a big wedding the last time she got married, and she told me she loved the idea of a small private affair with just our close friends and family. It was a bit of a tight timeline getting my family here from Ireland, but we pulled it off.

Ash, Vivien, and the hotel manager have been pulling long days organizing everything. Honestly, I would have eloped and married her in my jeans with just Easton, Ash, and the band there, but Vivien had a few requests, and I can never deny her anything.

She wanted her dad to give her away.

She wanted both families here.

And she wanted to wear a wedding dress and me to wear a monkey suit.

So, here I am, waiting in a chapel in Las Vegas in a black Prada suit with a black shirt and white tie, shitting bricks because my idiot best man has planted stupid doubts in my mind.

Jamie, Ash, and Audrey are the only other members of the bridal party, along with Easton, because we wanted to keep it low-key.

Before, I would probably have asked Ronan too, but things aren't the same between us. I managed to sidestep my feelings so we could get through the tour, and apart from that betrayal, he's been a good brother. But I can't forget the years I lost with Easton and the part he played. In time, I think I'll get to a place where I can forgive him, but I doubt our relationship will ever be how it once was.

"You look so handsome, Dillon." Ma yanks me down into her arms. "And I'm so happy for you."

"Thanks, Ma."

Dad slaps me on the back. "Looking dapper, son."

"Thanks for being here. Where is everyone else?"

"They are getting pictures outside, but they'll be in in a minute," Ma explains. "I'll be having more words with you and my daughter after the ceremony," she says over my head as Jamie approaches. She let rip at the two of them last night at dinner, but it seems she didn't get it all off her chest.

"You can't still be mad, Cath? You should be happy you got someone to take that wild woman off your hands."

Ma grabs him by the shirt, pulling him into a hug. "C'mere, you scoundrel, and don't be talking about my daughter like that."

"You know I love the fucking bones of her, and I'll take the best care of her."

"Suck-up," I mouth.

Jamie flips me the bird, and I spot Lauren smirking as she takes it all in. She was at dinner last night with the entire clan, so she knows what we're like by now. The two mums get on famously, and Viv's dad even managed to coax my dad into a discussion, which is a miracle in itself because Dad isn't known for his lively conversation. He's more of the stoic silent observer.

"The girls have agreed to a joint wedding reception in Ireland next summer," I remind her. "You can have your day out then."

"That's so far away. What about Christmas?" Her eyes light up.

I bark out a laugh. "Wild horses couldn't get Vivien on a plane to Ireland at Christmas. Are you mad? She'd probably get hypothermia." Ash had suggested a winter wedding to Viv, and the look on her face was fucking priceless. "You have no chance of convincing my Californian princess to get married in Ireland in the fucking dead of winter. No chance. Nada."

The noise level explodes as my brothers, their wives and children enter the chapel. Jamie and my parents move to go to them, but I pull Mum and Dad aside because there is something I need to say to them. "What's wrong?" Mum's brow instantly creases in a frown. "You're not having cold feet, are you?"

"Are you kidding?" My eyes almost bug out of my head. "My feet are about as toasty warm as you can get. I can't wait to marry Vivien. I have dreamed of this day for years."

Lauren's expression softens, and I'm glad I have a good relationship with Vivien's parents now. It's important to me. Not just because of Viv but Easton too. "This isn't about Vivien. There is something I need to say. Something I should have said a long time ago." I take both my parents' hands. "Thank you." Tears stab my eyes, and I swallow over the lump in my throat. "Thank you for taking me in, for loving me, and for always making me feel included. You never treated me any differently, and you never held it against me when I was in self-destruct mode." I hug Mum first. "I love you, Ma. I love you so much."

I rub at the tears leaking out of my eyes. Shit.

Dad comes at me, enveloping me in a hug before I've had the chance to hug him. "We love you, son, and we're very proud of the man you've become."

"Thanks, Da. Love you too." I'm all choked up.

"Who's the pussy now?" Jamie says, and I simultaneously want to punch him and thank him for helping to lighten the mood.

"Oh, I love weddings so much," Lauren says, wiping tears from her eyes. "They always bring out so much emotion. That was beautiful, Dillon."

"I'm not done," I say, improvising now. I had planned to talk to my parents before the ceremony, but I wasn't going to say anything to Viv's parents yet, waiting for my speech. But the perfect moment is now. I bundle Lauren in my arms. "Thank you for giving me another chance and for trusting me with Vivien and Easton. I promise I will love them and protect them for the rest of my life."

"Aw, Dillon, stop." She half laughs, easing out of my embrace. "You're ruining my makeup."

We all laugh, and then she takes my hand, squeezing it. "You have more than proven yourself to be a good man, Dillon. Jon and I know you're going to be as amazing a husband as you are a father. You have put smiles back on my daughter's and my grandson's faces, and that is something we worried would never happen." She tilts her head to the side. "But it's more than that. Vivien has come to life in a way I've never seen before. She literally glows with happiness, and we know that's due to you. Thank you for loving her and Easton, and welcome to the family."

"I am honored to be a part of your family."

"She's here," Ronan calls out, walking into the chapel with his daughter, Emer, in his arms.

The woman conducting the ceremony steps into the room from a side door, waving us forward. "Can everyone please take their seats. The bride will be with us shortly."

Lauren kisses my cheek. "Don't be nervous. She can't wait to marry you. I wouldn't be surprised if she runs up that aisle."

"I should've asked you to be my best man," I joke, shooting a dark look at Jamie. "This one sucks at motivational speeches."

637

"Just keeping it real, bro." Jamie nudges my shoulder, and I grin.

We take our places, and I try to control my nerves as the opening notes to "I Knew I Loved You" by Savage Garden starts playing. I turn to look when there is movement behind us, fighting emotion as Easton walks up the aisle, looking so fucking adorable in his little suit. He insisted on a miniature version of mine, complete with black shirt and white tie. He's carrying the ring cushion, looking proud as punch.

"Mommy was crying," he says when he gets to the top, and I pull him into my side as Ash walks up the aisle next in a gorgeous green silk gown Vivien made. She's carrying a bunch of white roses which makes me smile.

"Is Mommy okay?" I ask East.

He nods. "She said they were happy tears because she's so happy to be marrying you."

A layer of stress lifts off my shoulders. "That's good, buddy."

"I'm happy you're marrying Mom too. Now I know you'll never leave."

I crouch down as Ash reaches the top of the aisle and Audrey starts walking. Easton still misses Reeve, but his life has gone on, and he doesn't get sad as often. This comment reminds me the impact of what he's lived through will always be there, and I hate he still feels insecure. That the tragedy means he probably always will. "I'm not going anywhere, Easton." I hug him. "I love you and your mom, and I'll always be there for you."

"I know, Daddy." He holds my hand as Vivien appears in the corner of my eye.

Everyone turns to look at her, and she's a vision in white as she walks up the aisle on her father's arm. Strong emotion is reflected upon her face, her smile is wide, and her eyes are bright, and I feel like running toward her because I need her in my arms stat.

We only have eyes for each other as she approaches, wearing a strapless knee-length white silk dress with a lace overlay she made herself. It's a pretty simple design but elegant and classy. Just like my bride. Her hair is pulled back in a bun, and her makeup is subtle. She clutches a larger bouquet of roses to her chest.

"You look stunning. I'm the luckiest man alive," I tell her when she reaches me, pulling her toward me before Jon can officially hand her to me.

Screw protocol.

My lips crash down on hers, and I kiss her with all the pent-up emotion racing through my veins.

"Ahem." Jonathon clears his throat. "You're supposed to wait until *after* you're married to kiss your bride." He's grinning when I reluctantly tear my lips from Vivien.

"My daddy is *always* kissing my mommy," Easton exclaims, and everyone cracks up laughing.

"That's 'cause your mom is the best kisser ever."

"Way to go, Mom." East raises his hand for a high-five, and everyone laughs again.

"Take care of my princess and my little prince," Jonathon says, his eyes looking suspiciously glassy.

"Always," I promise.

I take Vivien's hands, and we turn to face the minister as something on the inside of her wrist catches my eye. I flip her hand over, and my eyes widen. "When did you get this?" I ask, running my finger softly over the ink on her wrist. It's still raised and a little red, so it's recent enough.

"Last night," she confirms.

We had separated last night for our hen's and stag's nights. We hit the strip and lost a ton of money in the casinos before enjoying a few drinks in the hotel bar. The girls stayed in Ash's suite, drinking champagne, getting their nails done, and gossiping about us, no doubt.

"I love it." I peck her lips as my heart swells with love for her. "Now every fucker will definitely know you're mine." My name is etched on her skin forever, and damn, if that doesn't fill me with pride. I had a tattoo added to the top of my left arm with Easton's and Vivien's names on it, curled underneath a single rose. There is enough space around it to add more names when we decide to grow our family.

"Are we ready to begin?" the celebrant asks, and I'm sure she's getting fed up of my annoying ass, but feck it. It's my wedding day, and I'm not exactly known for following the rules.

"As ready as we'll ever be," I say, pulling Easton around so he's in front of us. I flash my beautiful bride one of my signature smiles. "Let's get married, Hollywood."

CHAPTER 48
VIVIEN

I GET off the phone with the real estate broker and squeal. "Someone sounds happy," Dillon says, entering my home office, carrying two mugs.

I stand, smiling. "We got it. We got the site."

Since we returned to L.A. from Vegas two months ago, we have been actively looking for suitable plots of land to build our new house. When we got home after our wedding, we talked about where we would live, deciding it was time we looked for our own place. It didn't feel right to start our new married life in the dream home Reeve built for me, yet I wasn't entirely comfortable living in Dillon's bachelor house either. Thankfully, we were on the same page, and we agreed to start looking immediately for a new family home.

We weren't planning on building from scratch, but we'd viewed tons of houses, and none of them were right. Our real estate broker told us about a site high up in the Hollywood Hills with amazing views, and we knew it was perfect the second we saw it.

"That is the best news." Dillon kisses me passionately before handing me a coffee.

"I have good news too," he says, taking my hand and leading me over to the couch. "I spoke to the guys, and they're in agreement. We're delaying the European tour for a year."

"Are you sure, Dillon? You know we would come with you, and now I've decided I'm not going back to my freelance work, I have no commitments holding me back."

I take a sip of my coffee as I consider how fortunate I am that I don't have to work for a living. However, I do like keeping busy, and while, in the past, I enjoyed writing for TV shows and movies, my outlook on life has changed in a lot of ways, and my priorities are different.

I am still working on the book about my life, as well as a few works of fiction, and I'm more interested in dress designing right now. That and I want to be here for Dillon and Easton, and I want to focus on my family. Building the new place will be a mammoth project, even with a full-time project manager on board. I don't want to overstretch myself or make any huge commitments. I prefer to see where life takes me.

"I know, sweetheart, but I want to settle down here and enjoy life with you and East. I'm sick of touring, and I need a break." He drains the last of his coffee, setting his mug down on the table.

"And the guys are genuinely okay with it?"

He nods. "I think Jamie and Ash want to try for a baby, so he's happy to put down some roots for a change."

"She told me they're trying," I admit because I know she wouldn't expect me to keep it from Dillon.

"We should probably discuss that at some point," he says, looking a little anxious.

"Let's discuss it now."

"I know you've said you want more children, but the last time we talked about it, you said you didn't know when you'd be ready. I'm not pressuring you," he rushes to reassure me. "I'd just like to get an idea of when we can start trying."

"When would you like to start?" I ask, drinking a mouthful of my drink.

"Whenever you're ready. You set the pace, Hollywood. You know that." He shoots me a lopsided grin, and I melt on the inside. I love this man so much, and I thank God every day for bringing him back to my life.

"Then I guess we're getting rid of the condoms."

"Yeah?" He sits upright, looking a little dazed. "You mean that?"

I nod, smiling. "I do. I want to have another baby with you, Dillon. I'm ready."

He puts my mug down and lifts me up, swinging me around.

I'm laughing when Charlotte sticks her head in the room. "Sorry for interrupting. I did knock, but—"

"My wife was squealing so loud we didn't hear you," Dillon continues for her.

I swat his chest. "Put me down."

Charlotte smiles, and her delight at my joy is obvious. She was the first to warmly congratulate us when we returned home. She adores Dillon, and he has her wrapped around his little finger.

We posted a selfie on our wedding day, confirming our marriage, wanting to break the news first. Dillien supporters went crazy, and there were the usual haters, but we ignored them.

One of the greatest gifts Dillon has given me is the ability to look at the media intrusion in a completely different light. I don't let it stress me out the way I used to, and I sure as fuck don't let it stop me from living my life.

"You have a visitor at the gate. She's not on the approved list."

I look at Dillon. "Were you expecting someone?"

He shakes his head.

"What is her name?"

"Lori Roberts." Charlotte wets her lips. "She said she's Saffron Roberts' older sister."

Bile churns in my gut. "What does she want?"

"She said she needs to speak to you urgently. She said Reeve told her to come to you if he wasn't around."

Dillon and I exchange looks.

"She gave the security guard this to give to you." Charlotte holds out an envelope with my name scrawled on the front.

My pulse picks up, and my heart beats crazy fast. "That's Reeve's handwriting." I take the envelope with trembling hands.

Dillon winds his arm around my back. "Open it."

I remove the single folded page as nausea swims up my throat. My inclination is to say to hell with this. Reeve is dead, and I want nothing to do with the Roberts family, but I'm stronger than I used to be, and I don't shy away from things as much anymore. So, I open the letter and read my dead husband's words. Dillon reads over my shoulder.

My darling Vivien,

If you are reading this letter, it's because something has happened to me and Lori needs your help. I know you're confused. She will explain, and then she has a second letter for you. Lori is nothing like Saffron, and you need to hear what she has to say.

Please do this for me. You're the only one I can count on.

All my love,
Reeve.

"Oh God." I wobble a little as my knees buckle, but Dillon is there to keep me upright.

"You don't have to do this," he says.

"I do." I look up at him. "I have a really bad feeling about this, but ignoring it won't make it go away. I'll just drive myself demented trying to figure out what's going on." I turn to Charlotte. "Please tell the guard to let her through and send Leon to the gate to collect her."

She nods and leaves.

"What do you think this could be?" Dillon asks, steering me back to the couch.

"I'd rather not guess."

Dillon holds me as we wait for Lori to arrive and explain what the hell is going on. I rest my head against his chest, closing my eyes and breathing deeply, reminding myself I am strong. I'm glad Easton is at school so we can talk to her without disruption.

We move to our formal living room, and she arrives a few minutes later just as Charlotte brings in a tray with refreshments.

Dillon and I stand as Lori enters the room. She is not at all what I was expecting, and she looks nothing like Saffron with her short blonde hair, almond-shaped blue eyes, and pale skin. She is dressed in a navy pants suit with a cream blouse and flat pumps. The only thing they have in common is their short stature, but Lori is a lot thinner than Saffron, and she doesn't have her curves.

"We're half-sisters," she says, and I blush, feeling rude. "We had the same mom but different dads."

Remembering my manners, I step toward her, extending my hand. "Forgive me. I'm Vivien, and this is my husband, Dillon."

She shakes both our hands, and her palm is a little clammy. "Thank you for seeing me. I know you must be confused."

"Please take a seat," Dillon says, gesturing to the couch opposite us.

"Can I get you something to eat or drink?" I ask.

"Some water would be good. Thank you."

Dillon hands her a bottle of water and a glass from the tray.

"I don't want to take up too much of your time, and there is no easy way to launch this conversation, so I'm just going to be blunt."

"Okay. Reeve said in his letter to trust you, so I will give you the benefit of the doubt."

She removes a photo from her purse with shaking hands. I take a closer look at her, noticing the bruising shadows under her eyes, her cracked lips, and little beads of sweat forming on the pale skin of her brow. At this proximity, I can see her suit hangs off her frame, indicating she's lost weight. It's clear the woman is not well, and I wonder if that is part of the reason why she's here.

"I need to speak to you about my son. My husband and I adopted him as a baby." She hands the photo to me. "This is Bodhi."

My vision swims in and out as I stare at the photo in a mix of confusion, horror, and fear.

"He looks like Easton," Dillon says the same time I say, "He looks like Reeve."

"What is going on?" Dillon asks, tightening his hold around my shoulders, jumping into protective mode.

"Bodhi is Reeve's biological son. His and Saffron's."

CHAPTER 49
VIVIEN

WE STARE at her in complete shock, and it's a miracle I don't puke.

"What. The. Fuck?" Dillon says after a few silent beats, and I'm glad he has found his voice because I am still in a state of utter shock and unable to form any coherent thoughts, let alone words.

"Reeve discovered Saffron was pregnant a few months before you were due to return from Ireland," she begins explaining, looking at me.

I grip Dillon's arm as my body begins to shake.

"Saffron set the whole thing up."

That shakes me out of my daze. "Are you saying she got pregnant on purpose?"

She nods.

"How exactly?"

Lori takes a drink of her water. "Saffron has always been troubled, but things escalated after her father was killed in a botched robbery and our mother killed herself six months later. I had just turned eighteen, and Saffron was only fourteen. I dropped out of college and applied for guardianship because I couldn't let her be put in foster care. I switched to the local community college, and I tried to take care of her, but she went completely off the rails. Hanging out with a rough crowd, having sex with guys much older than her, drinking and doing drugs."

"If this is meant to garner sympathy, it's not working," I say. "Your sister did her best to ruin my life, and I will never forgive her for it."

"I know what she did to you, Vivien, and I'm sorry for how she interfered in your life and Reeve's. I'm trying to explain how this is more than just a woman out of control. Saffron has undiagnosed mental health issues. I cut her out of my life when she turned twenty and had that affair with the film director and his wife. She tried to coax him into leaving his wife and marrying her, and when he dumped her instead, she leaked those sex tapes on the internet to cash in on his notoriety."

I remember her discussing this when we were at Laguna Beach. "She told us it was a mutual decision and that it boosted all of their brands." I'm not surprised she told different versions of the story to different people. I wonder if she even remembers what is actually true anymore. The woman is a pathological liar.

"It catapulted her to instant fame, and she became insufferable. I had to cut ties with her because she was dragging me down. I was spending all my time stressing out about her, and Travis, my then fiancé, told me she was an adult responsible for her own actions. He saw how toxic she was and knew she'd only continue to wear on me, so I moved to San Jose to put some distance between us."

"How did you come to adopt Reeve's child?" I ask, almost choking over the words.

Dillon is quietly seething beside me but doing his best to hide it.

"Saffron showed up on my doorstep a few years later, drunk and rambling. We'd had very little contact since I'd moved away from L.A." She takes another sip of her water. "I'm not sure if she meant to tell me everything, or if it was the alcohol in her system, but she told me she'd deliberately manipulated Reeve to break you two up and how she had planned to trap him into marriage by getting pregnant."

"Jesus Christ." Dillon shakes his head while running his hand up and down my back.

"Saffron was an opportunist, and she was essentially lazy. She knew she wasn't a great actress and that her fame was fleeting. She had no intention of working for the rest of her life. Her plan was to find a rich husband and become a trophy wife." Lori slants me an apologetic look. "She set her sights on Reeve. He was young, rich, and naïve. She knew he was going places too, but you were a stumbling block she had to eliminate. Reeve refused to have anything to do with her after she sabotaged your relationship, but Saffron is stubborn and determined, and she bided her time. She knew she'd find a window to make her move, and she did."

"In Mexico," I say, starting to slot the pieces into place.

Lori bobs her head. "She was planning to get him drunk and pounce on him when they were there, because she was ovulating, but he made it easier for her."

I look up at Dillon, not sure if I've ever told him this. "Reeve told me he found out I was dating you when he was in Mexico and he fell apart. He got drunk and took drugs and woke the next morning naked in bed with Saffron."

"She laughed telling me how easy it was to get him into her bed. She'd given him uppers, and well—" She clasps her hands nervously in front of her, not wanting to say it.

"It made him horny, and they fucked all night long," I surmise.

She nods. "Saffron couldn't believe it worked and she got pregnant, but her plan backfired, because when she went to Reeve, he went ballistic. He refused to marry her, so then she asked him for ten million dollars to have an abortion."

"There is no way Reeve would have let her abort his child." I know how he felt about abortion.

"You're right. He wouldn't entertain any notion of abortion. He told her he'd give her five million dollars if she went overseas to have the baby, stayed clean during the pregnancy, signed an NDA, gave the baby up for adoption, and stayed away from both of you."

"And he trusted her to not blab about that?" Dillon asks, disbelief clear in his tone. "Five mil couldn't have meant much to her back then. Surely, she could've sold her story for more?"

"Saffron didn't have good representation, and she was earning a fraction of what Reeve was earning for the *Rydeville* movies. Whatever money Saffron did have was snorted up her nose. She was pretty broke, but that wasn't the only incentive. Reeve played the ultimate card, and that's how she ended up on my doorstep that night."

"What card?" I ask, tucking my hair behind my ears.

"He found a couple of those girls who attacked you in that alley, and they confirmed Saffron had set it up. They also confirmed she'd paid them with drugs. One of them had a real smart mouth, Reeve said, but she was shrewd. She had video footage of Saffron asking them to attack you and a recording of her handing over the goods."

"She would've been sent to prison for selling to minors," Dillon says, pouring me a fresh coffee and placing the mug in my hand. "Drink that, sweetheart. You're shaking like a leaf."

I glance up at him. "Can you believe this?"

"No. I fucking can't," he grits out, and a muscle pops in his jaw.

"That's how Reeve ensured Saffron toed the line. He took out restraining orders in both your names and organized for her to go to a private rehab clinic in Switzerland. But Saff was always resourceful. She charmed one of the orderlies, and he was supplying her with drugs the last three months she was there."

"While she was heavily pregnant?" Horror and disgust wash over me. I knew Saffron was scum of the earth, but this proves it conclusively. What a reckless, selfish bitch.

Lori nods. "Reeve was furious when he found out. It's why she ended up going into premature labor. She wasn't due until the middle of January, but she ended up giving birth on Christmas Day."

"Oh my God." I look at Dillon. "That's why he was sad at Christmas. It wasn't anything to do with me."

"I'd say it was a combination." Dillon kisses my cheek. "Drink your coffee, love." He refocuses on Lori. "How did you end up adopting Bodhi?"

"I reached out to Reeve after Saffron left that night. I explained how my husband and I weren't able to have kids and we had been exploring adoption. Bodhi was my flesh and blood too. It made sense that we would take him in. We had a lot of love to give, and I wanted to take care of my nephew." She sits back, sighing, looking exhausted. "Reeve wasn't sure at first, but he did background checks on us, and we sat down and talked for hours, and gradually he agreed. He bought us a new house, sent a monthly allowance, and he set up a trust fund Bodhi gets when he is eighteen."

I cannot wrap my head around this. "How could Reeve abandon his child? That must have killed him! He suffered with self-esteem issues his whole life because his father was so neglectful. All Reeve wanted was a family of his own."

"With you," Dillon supplies, fighting to control his anger. "Reeve didn't want a family with her, and he knew if you found out you'd leave him for good." He fists his hands at his side. "He sacrificed his kid for the woman he loved. Exactly like someone else we knew." Dillon drills me with a look, and I'm sick to my stomach because he's right. Reeve turned his back on his child for me while Simon turned his back on Dillon because he blamed him for his wife's death.

This is so fucked up.

Lori nods. "That's exactly what Reeve said when I asked him why he was doing this. I knew he had the means to take care of his child, so I didn't understand it, at first."

"I still can't believe he'd give up his child." I bury my head in my hands. "How could he do that?"

"It wasn't easy on him, but he told me there was no choice. He said it was you or Bodhi. He was working to win you back at the time. He told me how lost he was without you, and he said his life was not worth living if you weren't by his side."

"What a fucking crock of shit!" Dillon hisses, losing the tenuous hold on his control.

Tears stream down my face, and stabbing pain settles on my chest. "This is so wrong!" I cry out. "How could both his parents abandon him?" I hate Saffron even more now, but I have no clue how I feel about Reeve. I'm shell-shocked and my head is a mess.

"Would you have left him if he'd told you?" she asks, removing a tissue from her pocket and wiping her brow.

I rub at my tears, leaning into Dillon for support. I don't need to think about it for long. "Yes. Your sister was a very sore subject for me. I was only twenty, and as much as I loved Reeve, I would never have forgiven him for getting my archenemy pregnant, no matter the circumstances. I know I would have walked away."

"If he hadn't been so fucking possessive with you, everything could've been different," Dillon says, standing and pacing the room.

"It wasn't a good situation, and I don't know how Reeve could make that decision because he seemed like a good man. I know he was a good man," she adds. "He wasn't like my sister. My sister would never have considered her baby for a single second, except as a means of extorting money or marriage from Reeve. She was absolutely furious when he went back to you and apoplectic when she discovered he'd married you and you had a child."

"Did Reeve visit Bodhi?" I ask, needing to know how deep the betrayal extends.

She shakes her head. "He held him as a baby when the adoption paperwork went through, but he didn't visit again. At his request, I sent him a letter every year updating him, and he always sent gifts for him in December. One for his birthday, and one for Christmas."

"Does Bodhi know he's adopted?" Dillon asks. "Does he know who his bio parents are?"

"He knows he's adopted, and he knows the gifts he receives are from his bio dad, but he doesn't know their names."

"Has Saffron ever visited him?" I ask.

She shakes her head again, and it's becoming a familiar pattern.

"Never?" I wonder if she even looked at him or held him after she'd given birth. I fucking hate that bitch with every fiber of my being. I hate she gave Reeve a child when I didn't. I dig my nails into my thighs, feeling sympathy for Bodhi. He's an innocent child caught up in this mess.

"She has no interest in him, and he's the most adorable little boy. He has brought immense joy into my life, and I don't see how anyone could fail to love him."

"Does he have any health issues or problems because of the drugs she took during pregnancy?" I ask.

"He was underweight when he was born, and he didn't speak until he was three, and then he had a slight speech impediment. He attended speech therapy for a year, and his speech is fine now. Although, he's a quiet boy who doesn't talk a lot. He's been evaluated by child psychologists and mental health professionals, and there was no long-lasting damage, thank God." Tears well in her eyes. "He doesn't deserve any of this, and I'm so worried what it will do to him if this comes out."

"It seems Reeve and Saffron were well suited after all," Dillon growls, crossing his hands at the back of his head. "Both of them were selfish cunts."

His reaction is perfectly understandable to me, but I can't work out how I feel. "I don't know what to feel. What to think," I admit. "I had no idea Reeve did this or that he was carrying this secret all the years of our marriage." I wonder did I ever truly know him at all, because the man I loved would never give up his own flesh and blood. I feel sick thinking he did that for me.

"Why didn't Saffron say anything after Reeve died? She had a perfect opportunity to sell her story then, and it would have hurt Vivien the most." Dillon flops down on the couch beside me. "What don't we know?"

"Reeve's attorney sent her a reminder of the NDA, which is intact until she dies. Reeve left clear instructions that if she breached the terms his estate would sue her for the full financial penalty. He suspected she would do this, and he planned for every eventuality." She drinks the last of her water. "Her name isn't on Bodhi's birth certificate. Travis and I are listed as the bio parents. I'm not sure how Reeve made that happen, but I know he was worried about someone finding it at a future point and outing the truth."

"Wow. He really thought of fucking everything, didn't he?" Dillon fumes. "I wonder what else he was hiding, seeing as he was such a master at covering his tracks."

Acid crawls up my throat, and I wrap my arms around myself.

"I wouldn't know anything about that," she says.

"Are you sure?" Dillon eyes her warily. "He seems to have confided a lot in you."

"That was about Bodhi because we both had a vested interest."

"Saffron is going to be a problem," I say, knowing her silence will not last long, NDA or not. I might not know how I feel, but I know I don't want this coming out in the media. It will drag everything to the surface again, and I need to protect Easton.

Bodhi needs protection too.

"Saffron is an addict. All she cares about is her next fix. She showed up at my house a few months ago, saying she was going to sell her story because she needed the money. I panicked because I didn't want this coming out now." She hangs her head, exhaling heavily.

"How much did you give the junkie whore?" Dillon asks.

Shame is etched upon her face when she lifts her head. "Ten thousand, but I know she'll be back for more."

"Why didn't you go to Carson Park?" I ask.

"I did afterward when I calmed down. He told me if she comes back looking for more to call him and he'll deal with her."

I thought I had left Saffron Roberts in the past, but it seems she refuses to play dead. I still don't know why Lori is here, and I need to find out ASAP because I would like her to go so I can talk to Dillon about this. I need to talk to Alex too. If he knew about this and said nothing, there will be hell to pay. That will be the end of our friendship, awkward and all as it would be.

"Do you need money?" I ask. "Is that why you're here?"

She balks, and I think I've offended her.

"I continue to receive the generous monthly child allowance from Reeve's estate, and my ex is still paying alimony under the terms of our divorce. This isn't about money."

I make a mental note to rip Carson Park's head off his shoulders for hiding this from me. I'm sure he'll pull the "client-attorney confidentiality" line, but how the fuck could he have kept quiet about this?

"You're not well," I surmise.

She shifts uneasily on the couch. "I have terminal cancer. It was only diagnosed a month ago, but my condition is deteriorating rapidly, and I've only been given a few months to live."

"I'm so sorry to hear that," I say.

She knots her hands in an anxious trait. "I have no one else to turn to. Travis lives in the UK with his new wife, and he refuses to take him. I don't really want to send him overseas anyway. He's a sensitive little boy, and this is going to devastate him."

"What exactly are you asking us to do?" Dillon asks, sitting forward, placing his arm on my lower back.

"Bodhi is your son's cousin, and he's your nephew," she says, turning pleading eyes on Dillon and then me. "I know your feelings toward Saffron, and I know this is hard for you, Vivien, but he's your husband's flesh and blood, and he's an amazing kid. So intelligent and compassionate and caring." She sits up, taking my hands. "Please, Vivien. I'm begging you. Please agree to take Bodhi."

CHAPTER 50
VIVIEN

DILLON BREATHES fire as he reads Reeve's second letter over my shoulder. Lori has just left. We promised her we would talk about it and reach out to her in due course, but we need time to process everything. It's a lot to take in. I lower my eyes to the letter, leaning in closer to Dillon, siphoning some of his warmth and his ever-present support.

My darling Vivien,

I know you are in shock and your mind is reeling at the news I have another son. A son I gave up because I knew there was no way I could keep you both. Giving Bodhi up for adoption was the hardest thing I have ever done. The hardest decision I've ever had to make, but I knew it was a choice between you and him, and I can't lose you without losing myself.

Choosing him would have meant turning into my dad because I would've pined for you, the same way he pined for my mom. I didn't want my child to grow up in that kind of situation. To experience the childhood I had. Letting him go, giving him to good parents who will love him and give him a good life, is the best way I could demonstrate my love for my child.

"That is the biggest sack of shit I have ever heard in my life," Dillon hisses, dragging his hands through his hair. "He didn't even give you a chance to consider it, for fuck's sake. He just made that decision for you too."

"He knew me well enough to know I could never have accepted Saffron's child."

Dillon holds my face in his large, callused palms. "I think you're selling yourself short, Viv. I know you would've been upset, at first, but I think, in time, you would have done the right thing. You have a big heart, and you're a natural mother. I don't think you would've turned an innocent child away."

"You have a much higher opinion of me than I deserve," I admit, not wanting to say this out loud, but we have promised each other complete honesty. "Because even now, I'm wondering how I could consider doing this knowing that bitch's DNA flows through his veins." Shame crashes into me. "What if I look at him and all I see is her?" I squeeze my eyes shut for a moment. Soft lips land in my hair as my husband pulls me close. "You're in shock right now. We both are, and we might feel differently once we've had time to digest the news."

I rest my head on his chest. "I don't know what to do."

"Read the rest of the letter."

I have tried to move on and forget about my eldest son, but it hasn't been easy, no matter how wonderful our life together is. Lori has sent me pictures of Bodhi, and it's hard sometimes not to look at Easton and see my other son. It's hard not to feel guilty when I consider how I've denied Easton his brother.

My chest heaves painfully because that's one of my greatest fears now. I underline that part in the letter with the tip of my finger. "That is very true." I look up at Dillon. "If we don't take Bodhi in, how do we tell Easton we turned him away? We would be no different than Simon."

"Don't talk bullshit," Dillon snaps. "This *is* different. Simon made a conscious decision to give me away and split us up. He either gave no consideration to our feelings or he realized the full extent of his actions and he couldn't care less. You and I haven't made the decisions which have led to this point."

"No, but the decisions we make now will impact Bodhi and Easton. We may not have asked for the responsibility, but it's ours whether we like it or not."

"Is it really though, Viv?" His troubled blue eyes penetrate mine. "Lori is his mother. It's her responsibility. Her and Travis." He scoffs, looking disgusted. "Reeve sure did a great job picking the right parents. Bodhi is only six, and he's already lost his dad due to divorce, and now he's going to lose his mother."

"That's not fair, Dillon. I'm sure Reeve thought he was making the best choice giving him to family. Lori is nothing like Saffron. It was obvious she's a decent parent and a good mother who loves her son. It's not her fault her marriage didn't work out or that she got cancer."

Dillon blows air out of his mouth. "I know it's not her fault, but this is what happens when you give your kid away. You're gambling with their future."

"It turned out okay for you," I remind him.

"I was lucky. So fucking lucky."

I smile, caressing his face. "I love hearing you acknowledge that now."

He presses a kiss to my palm. "I was an idiot for taking it for granted." A dark expression washes over his face. "Finish the letter before I burn the damn thing."

I haven't regretted my decision, no matter how callous that makes me sound.

"I'm glad he realizes what a selfish prick he was," Dillon grumbles. I ignore his little outburst, wanting to finish this so I can call Alex.

❧

*But I **have** suffered huge remorse. My only salvation is knowing Bodhi is loved and well cared for and he's happy.*

I don't know the circumstances under which Lori has come to you. I send her an updated letter every December so she has a way of contacting you if she needs help and I'm not there to support her. If you are reading this, it means she has nowhere to turn and she needs you. I know this is a lot to ask, especially if something has happened to me, but there is no one else I trust more than you.

Please help her. Do what you can for her and Bodhi.

If you can find it in your heart, please forgive me for making this choice and for keeping it a secret from you. Everything I have done was for you, for us, for Easton. I have tried to do right by Bodhi too, but I'm well aware of how it must look. I could never have asked you to take in her son. I know how much I hurt you back then, and I never want to be the cause of your pain ever again.

I love you, Vivien. I have loved you my whole life, and I know I will love you in the afterlife too. You have given me more joy than you know, and I will love you for eternity. Kiss Easton for me, and tell him I'm proud of him.

Until we meet again.

All my love,
Reeve.

I fold the letter and put it in the envelope, flopping back on the couch and sighing. Dillon is quiet beside me. Too quiet. I twist my head, eyeballing the side of my husband's handsome face. "Spit it out, Dil."

He leans forward on his elbows, and I sit up straighter, linking my fingers in his.

"I always thought the way he loved you was obsessive bordering on psychotic, and this confirms it." He turns to me. "That kind of love is not healthy. He was obsessed with you and had to have you at any cost."

"I can't reconcile that Reeve with the Reeve I knew and loved. I just can't believe he abandoned his child so he wouldn't lose me. I feel so guilty. Like it's my fault that child was deprived of his father."

Dillon glares at me. "Don't you fucking dare take that on. That is not on you."

I'm contemplative as I try to organize my thoughts so this comes out right. "Perhaps you are right and the way he loved me wasn't healthy, but it grew from the best foundation. Reeve was my best friend growing up. He was always there for me. It was the two of us against the world, and when we became lovers, it seemed like the most natural progression. I don't remember at what point we acknowledged we were always going to be with one another, but whether we were right or wrong for each other, doesn't take away from the fact he did his best to love me the only way he knew how. I don't condone what he did. He should have told me and accepted the responsibility that came with his actions, but I know he did it because he believed he was protecting me and protecting our future."

Dillon twists around to face me, and his knee brushes mine. "That sounds scarily like some form of Stockholm syndrome."

"You don't get to do this!" I shout. "You don't get to take every single memory I have of him and twist it into something nasty." Tears spill down my cheeks. "This doesn't redefine everything we were to one another or change the happy marriage we had or alter how good of a father and husband he was." I break down, sobbing, covering my face in my hands.

"Come here." He pulls me into his arms, and I cry into his shirt, hating I'm back to this.

"I'm scared, Dillon." I brush the tears from my eyes and look up at him while clinging to him. "I'm scared that this news will do all of that, and I don't want to look back on my memories and feel like they were lies."

"I'm not going to lie to you, Vivien, but the truth is, you have to accept there were things about him you didn't know. How can that not influence the things you did? You say he was protecting you? Well, why the fuck didn't he turn that evidence into the police? Those bitches assaulted you and left you bleeding and unconscious in an alley. They should've been brought to justice. Instead, he used it to bargain with that cow."

"Why did you do any of the hurtful things you did? You showed up here, prepared to ruin my marriage and shatter my heart again." He moves to pull away from me, but I won't let him. "I'm not saying that to hurt you, and I know it in no way compares to what Reeve has done. What he has done is unforgivable."

I let that thought settle in my mind for a minute, and I realize behind my confusion is a lot of anger. "I'm mad at him for using me to shirk his responsibility to his son, and I am questioning everything. But I'm trying to get you to see it's not as black-and-white as you think it is. I know this is personal for you because of your experiences, and I hate that Reeve did this. This revelation has definitely shaken my belief in him, and I don't know how to process all of my emotions."

"I don't want us fighting about this. I don't want him coming between us again."

"We won't, and he isn't."

"We may not see eye to eye on this, Vivien." He stares deep into my eyes. "I know we're not in a position to make any decisions yet, but what if we want different things?"

"You want to do this," I quietly admit.

Dillon stands, pacing. "I'm not sure yet, but how can I abandon my flesh and blood? As much as I am disgusted with my twin, I can't deny the facts. Bodhi is my nephew, and I don't see how I can turn my back on him. The thought of him going into the foster care system breaks my heart." He drills me with a look. "Or worse, ending up with Saffron."

All the blood drains from my face. "She doesn't want him."

"Lori is desperate. If we don't do this, she may go to Saffron. Leave her everything if she agrees to take him in."

A full-body shudder takes control of me. "We can't let that happen, but we can't let it drive our decision either. If we decide to do this, it has to be for the right reasons. That we want to care for him, offer him a loving home, and the same attention and care we give to Easton or any other children we may have in the future."

"I know." He flops back down, burying his head in my shoulder for a few seconds. "We should talk to my parents. They know a bit about this."

"Definitely," I agree. "But let's talk with Alex first. I want to know if he knew about this."

CHAPTER 51
VIVIEN

"I SWEAR TO YOU, Vivien. Reeve never mentioned a word to me. I'm as shocked as you are," Alex says, looking as pale as a ghost.

Audrey and Alex moved back to L.A. in July, and he's coaching football at a local private school while Audrey is getting her new practice off the ground. Renovations are underway on the space Reeve bought for her medical practice, and she's hoping to open for business in a few weeks. I love having my bestie close again, and it meant they were able to come over after Alex finished work for the day.

"I just can't believe he would do that. It goes against everything I thought I knew about him," Audrey says, sipping her glass of white wine.

I was tempted to hit the vino immediately after Lori left, but I abstained until my friend and her husband showed up. My parents were here earlier, and they have taken Easton for a sleepover.

"What did your parents say?" she asks.

"They are shell-shocked too." I cross my feet at the ankles. "Mom thinks we have to accept there were parts of him we didn't know. She believes this is a direct result of the damage Simon caused. This is what abandonment, neglect, and abuse can do to a person."

"I can't believe he had a kid with that whore and he told no one." Audrey's mouth pulls into a thin line. "I remember how stressed he was that summer you were in Ireland, but I put it down to his anxiety over getting you back." She slants a sympathetic look at Dillon. My husband is sipping a beer, perched on the arm of the couch, looking drained. And I get it. It's been an exhausting emotional day.

"I knew she was harassing him," Alex admits, and we all swing our gazes in his direction.

"Sit down and tell us everything you know," Audrey demands, leveling her husband with a look that warns him not to refuse.

"I don't know much." Alex drops onto the couch beside Audrey. "But he did confide that Saffron was hounding him, constantly calling and showing up at his house, and he told me Carson Park was working on obtaining restraining orders for you and him. It had to be done discreetly so the press wouldn't find out, and he didn't want you knowing either." He has the decency to look ashamed.

"Was he having an affair with her the whole time, Alex?" I eyeball Reeve's best friend. "Did he sleep with her on more than one occasion?" It's not that I'm doubting what Lori believes or that Saffron could've gotten pregnant from one night. If she was ovulating and they used no protection, it's totally possible. What I am doubting is whether Saffron told her the truth. And whether Bodhi's existence is the only thing Reeve was concealing.

"No." He vigorously shakes his head. "Absolutely not. He hated her, Vivien. He hated how he let her come between you." He takes a mouthful of beer while I gulp my wine. "She played him perfectly from the start. She was friendly, wanting to know about you, gushing about how amazing it was you two were so close and had such big plans. She stroked his ego, telling him how talented he was and how he was going places."

"And he fell for that bullshit?" Dillon looks and sounds incredulous.

"He was out of his depth, Dillon. He was struggling without Viv. She always grounded him, and he had never been away from her before. He was drowning under the weight of responsibility. He was always trying to prove himself to that prick, Simon, and he wanted to prove to Vivien that he could go it alone and he could take care of her." Alex looks at me. "That's why he refused your mom's help. He wanted to be able to say he'd done it all on his own."

"But it backfired because that bitch stuck her claws in him," Audrey adds.

"She had been acting all sisterly, speaking about her boyfriend, showing no sexual interest in Reeve, but she was gradually planting seeds of doubt, gradually getting more flirty and touchy-feely. By this point, things were strained with you, Viv, and he was seriously stressed and depressed. That's when she started properly manipulating him. He was surrounded by older actors who all made it seem like doing drugs and fucking each other was the norm on sets."

"And you expect me to believe he only kissed her at Christmas and had sex with her that time in Mexico?"

"I can only tell you what he told me, and that was it." He scrubs a hand over his jaw. "By the way, he only told me all this after the fact. If you remember, I didn't see much of him when I first moved to Boston."

"I remember."

"I wish he'd confided in me at the time. I might have been able to decipher the signs and warn him about her."

"And you're sure he was only with her on those occasions?" I ask because I need to know for my sanity.

"One hundred percent, Viv. Oh, she tried to seduce him many times, but he knocked her back."

"I don't know if I believe that anymore," I admit. "And I don't want to focus on that. It will only make me all ragey." I reach out, squeezing Alex's hand. "I just needed to know you weren't keeping it a secret too."

"I'm hurt you'd think I would, but I understand."

"What are you going to do?" Audrey asks, her gaze bouncing between us.

"That's the million-dollar question," Dillon says, and we exchange a look.

"I don't know if I can take him in, knowing he is hers. But he's Reeve's flesh and blood." Tears fill my eyes. "At the funeral, I remember thinking how sad it was that there was no physical part of Reeve left behind. No son or daughter who carried his DNA. Now there is, and I don't know what to do about it." I scoot down on the couch, taking Dillon's hand in mine. "And it's not just my decision. This is something we have to decide together, and it's got to be what's best for our family."

A week passes, and it's hard to think about anything else but the situation we find ourselves in. Lori has called, asking if we want to come and visit. She thinks it might help if we meet him. I agree it makes sense, but how do we meet the child and then let him go if we decide we can't do this? Having met him will make it all the more real.

"We need to make a decision," Dillon tells me when he arrives back at the house after dropping Easton at school. "We are torturing ourselves and going around in circles."

I turn away from the window, clasping my hands around my mug of peppermint tea. I've been staring out the window since I got off my call with Audrey. "I know." Time is something Lori doesn't have, and if we can't do this, she deserves to know so she can make alternate arrangements.

"Let's talk outside." Dillon approaches, and I drink the rest of my tea, setting the cup down on the counter. Bending down, he kisses me. "I love you."

I wrap my arms around his neck. "I love you too." I kiss him softly, and we rest our brows together, just holding one another for a few minutes, both of us understanding the magnitude of our impending conversation—the culmination of many, many conversations we've had this past week. We have spoken among ourselves and talked with Jamie and Ash and both sets of parents. My in-laws spoke about the rewards and the challenges of adopting, and they offered a different perspective.

Dillon takes my hand and leads me out to the memorial garden. My heart is swollen with conflicting emotions as we sit down on the bench.

"You're a prick," Dillon barks, glaring at the wooden plaque he nailed to the tree. It has Reeve's and Lainey's names on it. "How could you do this to your son? To Vivien and Easton? To us?" He clutches my hand. "Now, we're the ones left picking up the pieces." He flips his middle finger up at the sky. "I hope you see that, you selfish jerk."

I shouldn't laugh, because there is nothing humorous about this, but I can't help giggling. I rub his back. "Feel better?"

"A little." He grins.

"I remembered something last night," I tell him. "When we were arguing that last night in the car, Reeve mentioned how he had made sacrifices for me. I didn't understand it at the time, but I know this is what he meant. He must have regretted his decision in that moment, Dillon." I lift my hand, brushing waves of blond hair off his brow. "He must have felt so betrayed. I hate to think he died feeling like that."

"He died protecting you, Vivien. That was his sole purpose in life. Keeping you safe was the last thing on his mind. He died loving you. You can be sure of that."

"I never thought I'd wish for a boring life, but I really fucking do." I stare into his gorgeous blue eyes. "Is it too much to ask for?"

"Life is never dull, that's for sure." He tweaks my nose, grinning when I slap his hand away.

"What do you want to do?" I ask, and his grin fades.

He lifts my hand to his mouth, and delicious tremors whip up my arm when he plants his lips on my skin. "I want to adopt him, Vivien. I want to give him a chance at a normal life. I want the boys to be brothers."

My smile expands. "I want that too."

Shock splays across his face. "Are you sure?"

I nod. "I'm terrified to do this, but I can't say no either." I chew on the inside of my mouth. "I spoke to Audrey before you came home. She and Alex offered to take him."

His eyes pop wide. "Wow. That's a big commitment to make."

"They loved Reeve, and neither of them want to see Bodhi going into the system or being adopted by strangers."

He is silent for several minutes, processing, no doubt, like I was when my bestie made her kind suggestion.

"That is very generous of them, but we can't let them do it."

"I agree." I rest my head on his shoulder. "Bodhi belongs with us. He's Reeve's flesh and blood. I can't turn my back on him, and it's not just because I know this is what Reeve would want. It's what I want." I lift my head, looking my husband in the eyes. "Reeve lives on in this little boy. If I can have a little piece of Reeve with me, then I'm going to grab Bodhi and hold him close." I examine his eyes carefully, to ensure he understands what I mean and that I'm not hurting him.

He stands, pulling me to my feet. "I'm glad we're on the same page, and it's like that for me. I missed out on getting to know Reeve, but now I get to care for and love his son." He bundles me into his arms, and I go willingly. "When should we tell East?"

I lift my chin up. "I think we should tell him when he gets home from school."

"Should we wait and visit Bodhi by ourselves first?"

"I don't think so. We're either all in or we're not. Visiting him should just be a formality because the decision is made. It's not like we get to say no if he doesn't warm to us immediately or it looks like he might have behavioral issues or problems adjusting. All of those things are probably par for the course, and in agreeing to accept him into our family, we are agreeing to love him through the good and the bad."

"I love the fuck out of you, Mrs. O'Donoghue."

"Right back at ya, babe." I plant a loud kiss on his cheek as a trickle of nervous excitement bubbles up my throat. "We're doing this. We're really doing this."

"Yeah. We are." He hugs me tight. "This already feels right." He rests his chin on the top of my head.

"It does. It really does."

"Come on then. Let's call Lori and give her the good news."

CHAPTER 52
DILLON

"DO you think he'll like his gift?" Easton asks as Vivien helps him out of the back seat. I parked directly outside Lori and Bodhi's comfortable two-story family home. At first glance, the large garden at the front is a little overgrown, and all the flowerbeds need tidying. Upon closer inspection, it's obvious someone has been lovingly tending to the garden until recently.

"I'm sure he'll love it," she reassures him. "Who doesn't love superheroes, am I right?" She waggles her brows, keeping the tone lighthearted for Easton's sake, even if she's a bag of nerves underneath.

I'm not exactly Mr. Cool, Calm, and Collected myself.

Since we spoke to Lori a few days ago, I've been dying to meet Bodhi, but we all agreed to tell the boys the truth and give them a few days to process it. We feel it's important to go into this as openly and honestly as possible. So, Bodhi now knows who his bio parents are and who we are. Easton is aware Bodhi is his cousin and he's going to be his brother.

He had tons of questions, as I'm sure Bodhi did, and we did our best to answer them truthfully while protecting him from the harsher aspects of reality. I'm not sure how much of it he understood, because he is so freaking excited over the news he has a new brother. Lately, Easton has been praying to God, and Reeve, and Lainey, to give him a sister or brother, so the timing is kind of perfect.

"Remember what we told you about Bodhi's mommy, Lori," Vivien says, straightening up Easton's shirt.

He blinks profusely as he looks up at his mom. "It's sad she's sick, but I'm glad she will be coming to live with us so I can help my brother to take care of her."

With Lori's agreement, we have decided to transform one of our spare rooms downstairs into a hospice room, and we're in the process of hiring a full medical team to care for her. It's not ideal that we have to speed through this process, but her health is failing rapidly, and we need to get this done as soon as possible.

Vivien and I have already met with Carson Park, and he's getting the paperwork completed. We need to get the adoption paperwork finalized before Lori dies to prohibit Saffron from making a play for him. I have no doubt that bitch would try for custody, if she knew what we were planning, purely to spite Viv.

Vivien places a hand over her chest, audibly gulping as she looks up at me. I lock the car and walk to her side. "That is very kind of you, East." I place my hand on top of his hair, careful not to mess it up and incur my wife's wrath. She has put him in one of his best outfits and styled his hair. She even made me change his socks because they weren't color coordinated. You'd swear we were meeting the queen.

"Can we go in now?" He bounces from foot to foot, and he's practically bristling with excitement.

I slide my arm around Vivien and rest my hand on East's shoulder. "We sure can. Let's go."

"Relax, sweetheart." I press a kiss to Vivien's temple as we stand at the door, waiting for Lori to open it. I can feel my wife trembling with nerves. "It's going to be okay."

The door swings open, revealing a frailer Lori and a little dark-haired boy clinging to her leg from behind.

"Hi. I'm Easton Lancaster, and this is my mommy and my daddy Dillon." East thrusts out his hand, giving her a big grin.

Lori smiles, shaking his hand. "It's a pleasure to meet you, Easton. We've been very excited waiting for you to arrive."

"Are you my brother?" Easton asks, peeking around Lori to where Bodhi is hiding.

Slowly, he emerges from the protection of his mother. Vivien barely stifles her gasp, and I tighten my arm around her waist. I know this is like looking at a ghost. I've seen enough pictures of Reeve as a kid to know Bodhi is the fucking spitting image of him. He has the same brown hair with little blond highlights and the same shape blue eyes. I see none of Saffron in him, and relief is instantaneous. I was a little concerned Vivien might struggle if he bore any resemblance to his tramp of a mother, but he is all Reeve.

"Why don't you come inside?" Lori steps aside with Bodhi still clinging to her side. "We have cupcakes and lemonade."

"Do you have chocolate cupcakes?" Easton walks into the hallway. "Those are my favorite."

Lori beams. "Chocolate cupcakes are Bodhi's favorite too. Isn't that right, love?" She pats his head, and he nods shyly.

"Who's your favorite superhero?" East asks, stepping in front of his soon-to-be brother and thrusting the gift at him. "Mine is Iron Man. I dressed up as him last Halloween, and my daddy had this massive party at his house, and all my friends from school came, and it was awesome. Daddy dressed as Captain America, and Mommy was Wonder Woman, but Daddy wanted her to be Black Widow because the costume wasn't as schmexy and it meant no other men would be cov'ting his woman."

"Oh my God." Vivien looks at me like she wants to murder me in cold blood.

"Buddy, that was supposed to be our little secret." I smile as Bodhi peers up at me.

"But Bodhi is my brother. I can't keep secrets from my brother." Easton loops his arm through Bodhi's. "Open your present. It's Avengers Assemble. Wanna play superheroes?"

"Cupcakes and superheroes. That sounds like a good plan," Vivien says, crouching down a little. She smiles at Bodhi, and I can tell she's fighting her emotions. "Hello, Bodhi. I'm Vivien. I'm Easton's mommy. It's really nice to meet you."

"Hi." His cheeks flush red as he looks at her. "Thank you for the gift."

"You're welcome. I hope you like it."

"This is my daddy Dillon," the little motormouth says, reaching back to grab my hand.

"Hey, Bodhi," I lean down, holding up my hand for a high-five.

His mouth hangs open, and his eyes widen as he stares at me. "You're in a band!" he exclaims in an excited voice. He looks up at Lori. "I saw him on TV! Remember!"

"My daddy is the best singer and the best guitarist in the whole wide world," East says. "And our daddy Reeve is the best actor ever. I've got his movies at home. We can watch them when you live with us."

Poor Bodhi looks a little overwhelmed.

"Let's move out of the hallway," Vivien says, lifting her shoulder in Lori's direction. Lori is clutching the door frame, looking a little wobbly on her feet.

I offer Lori my arm, as Vivien closes the door behind me. "Lean on me."

We make our way into the main living area, and it's a large open space that looks well lived in with comfortable sofas, a colorful worn patterned rug, and tons of pictures of Bodhi on the wall. A packed toy box is open in the middle of the room, and the boys gravitate there after helping themselves to a cupcake. I help Lori to sit in a recliner chair while Vivien pours lemonade into two plastic glasses for the boys. "I should make coffee." Lori moves to stand.

"Don't get up," Vivien says. "I'll make some."

"The kitchen is through there." Lori winces as she points through an archway. Pain lances across her face as she tries to get comfortable in the chair.

"Have the doctors not given you anything for the pain?" I ask when Vivien has left the room.

"I have pain meds, but they make me groggy, and I kept falling asleep. It's only the two of us here, and I need to be alert to take care of Bodhi."

"I know we were going to wait a couple of weeks until we had the room set up for you, but I think you should move in with us ASAP."

"I don't know." She looks over to where Bodhi and Easton are playing with their superhero figures on the floor. "This has all been a big shock for Bodhi. He's been quieter than usual."

"It's only delaying the inevitable. At least at our place, you can take your meds and grab some sleep knowing he's being cared for. Our housekeeper, Charlotte, is an amazing cook, and she'll make all your meals. It will remove the burden from you and give you more time to spend with your son."

"What about school?"

"They have a place for Bodhi at Easton's school," Vivien says, coming into the room carrying a tray with some mugs and a coffee pot, milk, and sugar.

"You have that lined up already?" Lori looks shocked.

"Once we made the decision, we started putting plans in place," my wife confirms, pouring coffee into a mug for Lori and handing it to her. "Dillon made a bed like Easton's for Bodhi, and we added it to his room. We thought it might help if the boys roomed together? Although, we have plenty of space, and he can have his own room or stay with you, if you prefer."

Viv hands me a coffee, taking a seat on the couch next to me.

"Mommy, look what Bodhi got me!" Easton comes bounding over, holding out a Hot Wheels set.

"Awesome. Did you say thank you to Lori?"

"Thank you, Lori." Easton leans down, kissing her cheek. "I love it so much."

"Bodhi picked it out for you."

"My brother made a good choice." He runs back to Bodhi, sinking onto the floor.

"He's a very confident little boy," Lori remarks. "I think he'll help to bring Bodhi out of his shell."

"Reeve was very quiet as a kid," Vivien remarks, sipping her coffee. "Then he got to eight or nine, and it was like he suddenly found his voice."

"How did he take the news?" I ask Lori, watching Bodhi smile at something Easton says.

"He was happy to hear he has a cousin but sad he never got to meet his daddy."

"What did you tell him about Saffron?" Vivien asks.

"I told him she was sick and couldn't take care of him and I was desperate to love him so I adopted him and he came to live with me and Travis."

"Travis signed the paperwork," Vivien confirms. "Carson called this morning to confirm he has legally relinquished all of his parental rights."

"I'm so disgusted with him. It was one thing to abandon me but quite another to walk out on Bodhi. He was only three, so he barely even remembers him now." She purses her lips. "I'm glad he didn't challenge it. At least it makes it a little easier."

"Vivien." Bodhi clears his throat, standing in front of Viv with two red spots on his cheeks and his hands behind his back. He looks to Lori and she smiles, nodding in encouragement. "This is for you." He whips a rose from behind his back—a lavender rose—and hands it to Vivien.

Her hand shakes as she takes it from him, but she keeps her composure as she smiles at him. "Thank you so much, Bodhi. It's beautiful." He flushes, looking at his mum before racing back to join Easton.

Vivien stares at the flower in shock, and I slide my arm around her shoulder. Viv glances at Lori. "How did he know Reeve used to give me lavender roses?"

Lori's eyes widen. "He did?"

Viv nods.

"Well, I'll be damned." A smile graces Lori's mouth. "I'm a keen gardener, and I have a few red rose bushes out in the backyard. Bodhi was playing out there just before you arrived, and it was the strangest thing, but that rose was in the middle of one of the bushes. He stared at it for ages, and then he asked me if he could give it to you." She wipes a tear from her eye. "I think Reeve is looking out for him. Looking out for all of us, and that's his way of saying he approves."

"How much longer is this going to take?" I ask Carson Park, leaning back in my chair, having a hard time not snarling at the guy. I've never been overly fond of the dick, but since we discovered he knew about Bodhi and continued to keep it a secret after Reeve died, I have zero time for him. The only reason we're using him to manage the adoption is because he's been involved from the very start and he has paperwork which was supposed to help speed up the process.

"I'm pushing it through as fast as I can, Dillon, but there is a lot of red tape and a lot of procedures to comply with. These measures are in place to protect children, and we can't cut corners."

"We're running out of time," Vivien says. "Lori may not last the week. I'm concerned about Saffron making a play for Bodhi if we don't get it finalized before Lori passes."

It's been four weeks since Lori and Bodhi moved into our place, and her health has been steadily declining. She can't get out of bed anymore, and we have a medical team watching her twenty-four-seven. Bodhi is getting more and more withdrawn. It's been tough for the little guy.

Easton is helping. A lot. They formed an instant bond, and when Bodhi is feeling sad, Easton always knows how to cheer him up. Bodhi is cautious around Vivien and me, but he's never rude or disrespectful. He's a very well-mannered kid.

"Try not to worry. Dillon is Bodhi's uncle, and Easton is his cousin. You are Reeve's widow. You have the means to take care of him and the support of his adoptive mother. You have passed the family assessment process. Saffron Roberts has had no contact with her son, and she relinquished her rights at the time of the birth. Even if she does try something, I doubt she would get custody. She works in the porn industry, and she's a known drug addict."

"You don't know how manipulative and cunning she is," I say, kicking one heel up onto the table 'cause I know it will piss the dickhead off.

"Or how much she hates me," Vivien adds.

Carson narrows his eyes on my foot as the phone on his desk rings. He gets up from the meeting table and answers the call, listening to whoever is on the other end, nodding. He looks up, his gaze darting between me and Viv as shock registers on his face. I drop my foot to the ground and sit up straighter in my chair as he ends the call and returns to the table.

"Well, we've just gotten one piece of good news." He rests his palms on the table in front of us. "That was a police contact friend of mine. This isn't public knowledge yet, but Saffron Roberts OD'd last night. She was officially pronounced dead two hours ago."

Lori passed away three days before Thanksgiving and two days after we became Bodhi's legal adoptive parents. Bodhi was inconsolable, and it was hard to bear witness to his grief. Watching him go through what Vivien and Easton had endured was hard, but we got him through it.

The four of us built an additional bench in the memorial garden for Lori, and I nailed a plaque up beside the one for Lainey and Reeve. Our project manager has been given strict instructions to ensure it's taken with us to the new house. I've no idea how they'll uproot and replant the tree, but we're paying him enough fucking money to make it happen. He burst out laughing when I told him we want a lake with swans—until he realized I was serious, and then he nearly passed out.

The work on our new family home is progressing well, and we're hoping to be in by the end of the summer because we have a new addition to the family on the way. Vivien surprised me on Valentine's Day with the news she was pregnant, and we're expecting a daughter in early November.

We were concerned about telling Bodhi, worried it would make him more unsettled, but if anything, it has helped. He's seeing a therapist too. The same woman who helped Easton deal with his grief, and gradually he is opening up to her. Vivien or I sit in on the sessions so he has someone familiar to support him as he deals with his emotions.

Easton is very excited for the new baby, and his enthusiasm spread to his older brother, and it helped to distract him from his grief. Every night, the three of us sing to Vivien's expanding belly, much to her obvious delight. Her pregnancy is moving fast, and I can't wait to meet our little girl in four months' time.

"Where are the little monsters?" I ask, stepping into the kitchen when I arrive home from work. We've delayed our European tour indefinitely now, choosing to focus on new music instead. We're still using the recording studio at my house, but I'm having it extended once we get this album wrapped. We have decided to set up our own label when our contract expires next year, and we're going to use my house as the base. We have an architect drawing up plans to remodel it so it's fit for purpose.

"Out in the treehouse," Vivien says, sniffling. She's standing at the window, staring out at the garden with her back to me.

I slide up behind her, circling my arms around her swollen belly. "What's wrong, sweetheart?" She has had some emotional moments recently, and I know she's remembering Lainey and worrying everything will be okay. I'm trying my best to assure her, but I know she won't fully relax until she's holding our beautiful little girl in her arms.

"Nothing," she says, almost choking on a sob. She whirls around in my arms, smiling at me through blurry eyes. "These are happy tears," she adds, seeing my concern.

"Are you sure?" I kiss her softly.

"Bodhi called me Mommy Vivien." More tears fall down her cheeks. "It was the most amazing feeling in the world. I'm so happy."

"He loves you, Hollywood. Just like we all do." I press another sweet kiss to her lips, which is hugely at odds with how I've been devouring her mouth lately. Pregnant Vivien is horny as fuck, and we're going at it like rabbits any chance we can get. I have sex on the brain permanently, and I couldn't be more in love with my wife, or my life, if I tried.

"I love him so much," she says. "I can't believe I was ever worried that I wouldn't. He's the missing piece we didn't realize we needed."

"And our daughter will be the cherry on top." I tilt her gorgeous face up, staring at her in awe, amazed that with every passing day I love her more and more. "Thank you for making my world complete, Vivien. Thank you for letting me love you."

EPILOGUE
VIVIEN - NOW

THE AFTER-PARTY IS in full swing at the plush five-star hotel the label rented for the occasion, and the room is packed with well-wishers, family and friends, and industry heads. I'm proud of our movie even if it was painful to sit in the theater knowing everyone was dissecting some of the most heartbreaking and intimate moments of our lives.

But it feels cathartic too. Everyone knows the truth now. The good, the bad, and the ugly, and they can decide what they want to do with that themselves.

"For the woman of the hour," Ash says, materializing at my side, offering me a glass of champagne.

I shake my head and hold up a hand. "I'm abstaining. That glass I had earlier went straight to my head. That's what I get for hardly eating all week."

"I need to live vicariously through someone," she pouts, running a hand over her growing belly. "Hurry up and get here, little monster, so your mummy can have an alcoholic drink!"

I smile at my sister-in-law because I know she's joking. Ash adores being pregnant, and she is positively glowing. It took them some time to conceive, but her pregnancy has been smooth sailing so far. They are both very excited, and I'm thrilled for them. I can't wait to meet my new niece or nephew.

"I'm happy to help," Audrey cuts in. She drains the dregs of her current glass of champagne, sets it down on the high table behind us, and plucks the fresh glass from Ash's hand.

"I thought you were still breastfeeding," Ash says.

"Nope. Emily is taking formula now, and as it's Alex's turn to do the night feed tonight, this mommy is partying to the max!" Audrey gave birth to their first child four months ago, and Ash is due in three months' time. Our daughter, Fleur Belle Lancaster-O'Donoghue, is twenty-one months old now and the apple of her daddy's eye. I love that my daughter will have a ready-made friend in Emily and her new little cousin, and she has two older brothers who dote on her.

"You must be relieved the movie was so well received," Ash says.

"I am, and I love that it was a true family affair." I wrote the screenplay. Studio 27 made the movie. Dillon and I were executive producers, Mom played herself, Dad directed, and Collateral Damage recorded a number of new songs specifically for the movie soundtrack.

Easton played Reeve in a couple of scenes, and I couldn't stop the tears from flowing during those parts of the movie. We had asked Bodhi if he wanted to share the role of young Reeve, but he is more of an introvert than Easton, and he turned pale at the thought.

"It makes it more special," Ash agrees, glancing over her shoulder to where the guys are chatting.

I look over, and Dillon's bright blue eyes lock on mine. He mouths, "I love you."

I blow him a kiss, admiring how hot he looks in his suit. Waves of white-blond hair tumble over his brow, and nobody would ever believe he turned thirty in January. He is so unbelievably gorgeous, and every time I look at him, I'm reminded of the young guy I met in Dublin who showed me how to let go of my reservations and truly live.

"Earth to Vivien." Ash waves her hands in front of my face before poking her tongue at her brother. "You two are always sending googly eyes at one another. It's disgustingly adorable."

"We have fought hard for our love. I never want to take it, or him, for granted." I'm feeling especially emotional after watching my life with both my loves play out on the screen. "I'm relieved I got through tonight without puking," I truthfully admit. "Dillon will tell you I've been a hot mess all week. I could barely sleep or eat, worrying if I'd done the right thing."

"That's understandable." Audrey knocks back her champagne like it's water. "You have serious lady balls, my friend. I'm not sure I could have opened my heart and my life for the entire world to see."

"It hasn't been easy, and I've been panicking all week that I made the wrong call. I have a responsibility to both my loves and my children to do right by them, and I was plagued with last-minute doubts."

Dillon has been repeatedly talking me off a ledge all week long. He is my rock, and I know I couldn't have done this without his support and his permission. He wasn't sure when I first broached the subject, until he read my book, and then he told me I had to do it.

"That's completely natural. I would've been the same." Ash gives me a quick hug.

"I was shaking like a leaf on the red carpet, and when those women hurled their accusations, it sent me reeling back in time. It was like Reeve had only just died, and I felt the pressure sitting on my chest again."

"I can't believe the nerve of those bitches. I thought that was all behind us," Ash says.

"I knew what I was getting into when I chose to make this movie. I knew it would dredge up good memories as well as bad, and I knew it would bring the crazies crawling out of the woodwork. This is only the beginning too."

"Do you regret it?" Audrey asks.

I don't have to think about it. "No. So much has been said over the years that is incorrect, and I wanted, *needed*, to set the record straight. I know there will be people who won't ever understand, people who will probably hate me more after this, but I didn't do it for them. I did it for me. For Dillon. For Reeve. But most of all, I did it for the kids. I hope when Easton and Bodhi are older they will understand how I came to love both their dads. I want them to know the true story, not the twisted version that will forever remain on the internet."

After we adopted Bodhi, we filed the relevant paperwork to have his birth certificate changed. While Lori will always be Bodhi's mom, and we do what we can to nurture her memory and ensure he never forgets her, his biological parents were Reeve and Saffron, and that needed to be officially documented, for a number of reasons. One of them is so Dillon could transfer his half of the Lancaster inheritance to Bodhi.

At the same time, we got Easton's birth certificate altered to list Dillon as his father.

We had a dilemma then in terms of our family name. The changes we made meant Bodhi became a Lancaster and Easton became an O'Donoghue. But Reeve is still Easton's other daddy, and we promised we would never take that from him. Bodhi and Easton are brothers, in every way that counts, and we didn't want them having different last names. Also, Dillon's US citizenship was proclaimed around the same time, and his birth certificate now confirms Felicia Lancaster and Simon Lancaster as his bio parents. Technically, in the eyes of the law, Dillon is a Lancaster. Which means I'm still a Lancaster too.

For me, the solution was simple: Lancaster-O'Donoghue. But I knew it wouldn't be as easy for Dillon because of what Simon Lancaster had done to him. However, my husband surprised me when he readily agreed. For him, the decision was simple too. He loves our sons enough to put aside his own feelings to do what we both felt was right. Plus, the Lancaster name is a way to remember Reeve and Felicia, and none of us want to forget them.

So, now we are all Lancaster-O'Donoghues, and it feels right. The press and the haters had a field day when that news broke, but they can all kiss my ass.

"Uh-oh." Ash looks over her shoulder, and I turn around.

Dillon is jabbing his finger in Deke Rawlings' face, looking like he's seconds away from punching him in the nose. Deke is the head of security for Studio 27, and he was in charge of security for tonight's premiere. Ultimately, it's his fault those women slipped through the net and were able to harass me on a night that was already going to be difficult enough. I'm not surprised Dillon is tearing strips off him. I'm only surprised my dad isn't joining in.

My parents are around here somewhere, along with all our Irish family. Conor even graced us with his presence, and he brought a date too. He's the only remaining single member of Collateral Damage now that Ro tied the knot.

Ronan shocked the whole family when he returned from a weekend in Las Vegas married to Shania Webster—an up-and-coming name on the country music scene. Apparently, it was love at first sight. The guys had bets on how long it would be

SIOBHAN DAVIS

before they broke up, but it's been seven months, and they seem more in love than ever.

I'm happy for Ronan.

He deserves love in his life after the ordeal he's been through with his ex, Clodagh, over access to his daughter Emer. Things are good between him and Dillon again, but they're not quite as close as they once were, which makes me a little sad.

"I think you should get over there," Audrey says, pulling me out of my inner monologue. "Dillon looks like he's about to commit murder."

My husband has fistfuls of Deke's jacket now, and he's shoving him up against the wall. I spot several security guards getting ready to move in, so I walk toward them to defuse the situation.

As the temporary caretaker of the Lancaster shares in Studio 27, I need to ensure amicable relations continue. From the way Reeve's will was constructed, the forty percent stake in Studio 27 will now pass to Bodhi when he turns eighteen. It's why it made sense to have the company produce our movie. If it's as profitable as the analysts expect it to be, it will significantly enhance the value of Bodhi's investment.

So, it's a win-win all around.

"Dillon." I place my hand on my husband's arm. "This isn't the time or the place." I fully intend to request an investigation into how this happened, but I don't want anything to put a stain on tonight.

"Learn to own up and accept responsibility," Dillon growls, glaring at the man as he releases him. "And if you ever put my wife in that kind of position again, I will punch first and ask questions later."

"I'll find out how it happened and ensure it doesn't happen again." Deke smooths a hand down the front of his tuxedo jacket as he turns to me. "I apologize for any upset, Vivien."

"We'll discuss it next week," I curtly reply.

I don't have a controlling interest in the studio, and I'm not on the board of management, but I will be strongly advising James—the current head of Studio 27—to let the incompetent Rawlings go. James listens to me, and I was thrilled when he agreed to let me adopt a special child ambassador role. It's something I'm working on pitching in a more official capacity within the industry.

Having seen what Reeve went through, and becoming more familiar with the stresses and pressures placed on child and teen actors, I want to help to create a better working environment for kids who act. I also want to ensure that when the Studio 27 shares pass to Bodhi he is inheriting a production company that is not only profitable but one that sets and maintains high standards extolling family values and a nurturing environment where child actors thrive without unnecessary responsibility, stress, or peer pressure.

Safeguarding children within the movie industry is something I am very passionate about, and I've spoken to Dillon about creating a company in Reeve's name. Some kind of governance or regulatory body with a set of guidelines every studio would have to adhere to. It's only an idea right now, but it's something I'm invested in exploring and developing at some point.

Rawlings walks off, feeling the daggers Dillon is embedding in his back, no doubt.

"I can't stand that prick," Dillon seethes.

"I think everyone in the room can see that, and I think the feeling is mutual." My lips twitch. Dillon has been breathing down Rawlings' neck for the past week, wanting to know all the security measures in place. Deke isn't the kind of man who appreciates being put on the spot or being challenged, so they've been butting heads nonstop. "Come dance with me." I take his hand, leading him out onto the dance floor as the song changes, and a slow number begins to play.

I wrap my arms around my husband's neck as he pulls me in close, placing his palms on my hips.

"Are the kids okay?"

I nod. "I just spoke to Charlotte. They are all sound asleep. The boys are in East's room."

Dillon chuckles as we move in sync to each other and the soft, sultry beat. "I don't know why we bothered giving them separate bedrooms when they always sleep together."

"It was important they each had their own space, but I love they're so close. It warms my heart to see them together." When we moved into our new home in the Hollywood Hills, we had adjoining rooms built for the boys, but we put twin beds in both rooms because they love rooming together. Now, they alternate between the rooms, making them happy, and that's the main thing.

"Yeah. Me too." Dillon smiles. "Sometimes, when I look at them, I imagine that's what it would've been like if Reeve and I had grown up together." There are only six months between Bodhi and Easton, and they look so alike they could easily pass for twins.

A veil of sadness shrouds his face, and I feel it deep in my heart too. "I think the same way on occasion." I cup his face. "Are you okay?" This is the first opportunity I've had to speak to my husband alone since we left the theater. Everyone has wanted a piece of us, and it's been exhausting. I'm just about ready to call it a night and go home to my kids.

"I should be asking you that." He leans down, kissing me softly. "I know watching it, with an audience, can't have been easy."

"It wasn't, but I'm glad we did it. I just hope the people who turned on Reeve, after they discovered the truth about Bodhi, understand him a little better now. I want people to see he wasn't a bad person. I want people to know his actions were driven by love. It may have been misguided and wrong, but he was tragically flawed, like we all are in some way. I hope people see the damage that abandonment and neglect can cause. He craved love and acceptance his whole life, and it twisted his reality of things."

"It twisted mine too." Dillon moves us around the dance floor, swaying us in time to the music.

"It did, but you overcame it because you had a loving family to help keep you on the right path and you were more self-aware. When the chips were down, you did what you had to do to be there for me and Easton. You accepted your responsibilities and fully owned them in a way Reeve didn't do."

"Seeing your childhood play out on the screen helped me to put the last few things into perspective."

"In what way?"

"I see what you've been saying all along. He was a part of you the same way you were a part of him. Watching those scenes, rather than just reading about them, really made it come alive. I understand it better now. I understand how it was you came to love each other and how it was he came to rely on you so much."

"I love it out here in the moonlight," I say, nestling into Dillon's side on the stone bench. I tilt my head up. "Look at all the stars."

"It would be so much more romantic with a lake and swans." I hear the pout in his tone and see it on his face under the illumination of the moon and the dim night-lights dotted around the memorial garden.

"We'll have our swans when the kids are older," I reassure him, resting my chin on his shoulder. We decided to forgo our plans for a lake with swans because it's not really advisable to have either when you have young kids. Dillon was really hung up on the idea, so it's a bit of a sore point.

He peers deep into my eyes as he links our hands. "Do you still feel him around?"

I told Dillon how I feel Reeve is still with me, explaining the instances where I've felt his presence. We're both still shocked over Bodhi and the rose that day we first met. I know some people don't believe in an afterlife or spirits or that our loved ones look after us when they are gone, but there is nothing anyone could say that would convince me that wasn't Reeve's work. "Not in a long time." I snuggle in closer to him. "I like to think it's because he sees how happy I am and he knows I don't need that reassurance or comfort anymore."

"I bet it makes him happy too. To know his two boys are with the love of his life, like he always wanted."

"And with you." I clasp his face in my hands, kissing him passionately. "If there was anyone Reeve would have trusted me with, it's you." I lower my hands to my lap, threading my fingers through Dillon's.

"I will always be sad that I never got to know him."

"And I will always miss him, but this is the way it was supposed to be, Dillon. I truly believe that now." I've given it a lot of thought these past few weeks as we prepared to premiere the movie. I don't understand why I had to lose Reeve and Lainey, but I do believe it was preordained. In a lot of ways, that makes me so freaking angry, but in other ways it helps me to accept it. "I think I was destined to love Reeve because his fate was already decided. I'm glad he got to experience my love for the short time he was with us. That he got to experience fatherhood and the kind of family he always craved."

"I'm glad he had you too." He laughs softly. "Man, I never thought I'd ever say those words, but I can't be selfish. Not when I get to spend the rest of my life loving you, Easton, Bodhi, and Fleur."

"Do you think you have room in your heart for one more?" I run my fingers through his hair.

He straightens up, his eyes popping wide. "Do you mean?"

"I'm pregnant again," I blurt, unable to keep the news in any longer. "I did a test this morning and then another one just to be sure."

He places his hands on my belly and tears glisten in his eyes. "You have no idea how happy this makes me. Another kid. Yes!" His eyes light up with sheer happiness. "Thank you, sweetheart." He examines my face carefully. "Are you feeling okay?"

"I'm fine, apart from being tired, but that's more than likely down to not sleeping well all week."

"We should go to bed, but I just need to hold you first." He reels me into his arms, pressing fierce kisses into my hair as he hugs me close. I melt against him, loving the security and familiarity of being in his embrace. If I'm having a bad day, all I need is a hug from Dillon to make everything all right again. "Thank you, Vivien Grace. Thank you for this life we lead. I never take it for granted. I hope you know that."

"I know," I say, fighting a yawn. "And I don't either. I cherish every day with you and our children."

Dillon stands, pulling me with him. "Time for bed. It's been an exhausting day."

"You can say that again." I lean my head against his shoulder as his arm slides around my back.

As we walk away, a subtle breeze appears out of nowhere, swirling around me, moving wispy strands of my hair. The strong, sweet fragrance of lavender roses tickles my nostrils even though there are none in this part of our garden. Invisible fingers sweep across my cheek, and I know he's here. Tears pool in my eyes, but they are happy tears because I know, in my heart and soul, this is Reeve's way of telling me he will always be with me.

It was never a competition between my loves.

I have loved Reeve and Dillon with my whole heart, and it will forever belong to both of them.

They were always destined to be mine, and I will live out the rest of my days safe in the knowledge they are both with me.

My first love.

And my forever love.

675

GLOSSARY OF IRISH TERMS/SAYINGS

Aisling – female Irish name pronounced Ash-ling

Aoife – female Irish name pronounced E-fa

Bandied about - said

Bedside locker – nightstand

Beggars belief – is unbelievable

Bin – trashcan

Biscuits – cookies

Blanked – ignored

Boot - trunk

Chinwag – conversation

Clodagh – female Irish name pronounced Clo-Da

Cooker – stove

Crisps – chips

Emer – female Irish name pronounced E-mer

Feeling peckish – feeling hungry

Gob – mouth

He's a little nutter – he's a little crazy/wild

Hen's and stag's nights – bachelor and bachelorette parties

I was in bits – I was a hot mess

Knackered – tired/exhausted

Knickers – panties

Knocks me for six – knocks me for a loop

Leaving cert – state exams you take in the sixth year of secondary school (senior year of high school)

Letter box – mailbox

Made up for you – so happy for you

Paracetamol – acetaminophen

Permanent horn – permanent boner

Porky – lie

Press – cupboard

Pulling myself away from her is a wrench – pulling myself away from her is difficult

Solicitor – attorney/lawyer

Steady on – calm down/take it easy

Ten-dollar note – ten-dollar bill

Virgin One – a TV channel in Ireland

Wouldn't have lasted pissing time – wouldn't have lasted long

HOLD ME CLOSE

ME

CLOSE

USA TODAY & WSJ BESTSELLING AUTHOR

SIOBHAN DAVIS

NOTE FROM THE AUTHOR

This novella is set approximately seven years after the epilogue in *Let Me Love You*. There is an Irish glossary of words and sayings at the back of this book.

Fair warning – you may need some tissues for this!

Happy reading and hugs from Ireland.

CHAPTER 1
DILLON

"YOU HAVE THE REST," Ash says, dumping the remainder of the bottle of white wine into Viv's glass. "You look like you need it."

My wife arches a brow as she stares at her sister-in-law-slash-best-friend. "Is that your way of telling me I look like shit?"

"Puh-lease." My sister rolls her eyes. "That's a virtual impossibility. You always look stunning, babe."

No truer words have ever been spoken. My wife is a fucking goddess, and she only gets more beautiful with age. I regularly pinch myself. I still can't believe she's mine. That I get to share such an incredible life with her. Viv has given me everything I never dared to dream of, and I love her so fucking much.

We fought hard for our love, and I never take it—or her—for granted.

My heart melts as I look at her, admiring her natural beauty and the elegance she exudes from her every pore. Viv inherited some incredible genes. Lauren, my mother-in-law, is sixty-six and still one of the most stunning women in Hollywood. She has chosen to grow old gracefully, refusing plastic surgery and proudly show-casing the thick streaks of gray lining her jet-black hair. She eats well and works out regularly, and she still has a beautiful figure. Viv's dad is no slouch either. He looks years younger than his seventy-six, and he is fit as a fiddle and sharp as a tack. If they keep it up, they may outlive all of us.

Ash reaches around Jamie to squeeze Viv's arm. "It's my way of telling you you look stressed. You work too hard."

I wish that was all it was.

Viv takes a healthy gulp of her wine as I slide my arm around her shoulders and move in closer to her in the booth. This Italian restaurant is Viv's favorite primarily for the large velvet-backed circular booths that are comfortable and perfect to fit the six of us with ease. It's also tucked away in a quieter part of L.A. and not one of the trendier celeb haunts. No one pays more than a passing interest in us when we come here. The food is also to die for, and they serve this bramble gin cocktail Viv loves.

"I have three words for you. Pot. Kettle. Black." Viv drills Ash with a knowing look.

"The difference is I have one child to look after. You have four."

"And two teenage boys is no picnic," Audrey adds, swirling the wine in her glass.

"Tell us about it," I say, knocking back the last of my Peroni.

"More trouble?" Alex asks, quirking a brow.

"The boys got suspended from school for five days," Viv admits, and I hear the strain in her tone.

Leaning in, I press a kiss to her temple and hold her close, wishing I could absorb all the stress for both of us.

"That isn't like either of them," Jamie says, gesturing at the waiter. "What happened?"

I wait until we have ordered another bottle of wine and three more beers before replying. "Some shitheads at school got their hands on a Saffron Roberts porno, and they printed out stills of it and plastered it all over Bodhi's locker," I explain.

Jamie curses under his breath.

"As if that wasn't bad enough, they taunted him about her, and that's when Bodhi lost it," Viv adds. "He threw the first punch. Then East got involved, because you know he always defends his brother, and it turned into a massive fight in the hallway."

"I hope they suspended the pricks who did this." Alex's jaw is tight, his eyes blazing with the same anger Viv and I felt when we first found out.

"They should fucking expel them," Jamie says. "And Bodhi shouldn't be punished for standing up for himself."

"It doesn't work like that," Alex says. "The school can't be seen to condone any type of violence. If Bodhi threw the first punch, he's equally as culpable in their eyes." Alex knows what he's talking about. Until the twins were born, he worked as a football coach at a local private high school. He understands how volatile teenage boys can be with all that testosterone and aggression flooding their bodies.

"Everyone involved was suspended," I confirm, nodding in thanks when the waiter places a fresh beer in front of me.

Audrey tops up the girls' wineglasses as a waitress appears, depositing our main courses on the table.

"That sucks for Bodhi," Audrey says, lifting her cutlery. "Kids can be so cruel."

"The boys have had to deal with this kind of crap before." Viv twirls pasta around her fork. "But this is a new low. Bodhi isn't handling it well."

That's the understatement of the year. "I have to practically frog-march him from his bedroom to join us for dinner," I say, grabbing a slice of my pizza. "And he has barely said a word to any of us all week."

"He internalizes everything," Viv says. "And that can't be good. I want him to speak to a therapist, but he's refusing."

"You can't force him, sweetheart." I remind her again. We've had this conversation a lot this past week. "At least he's venting some of his emotions through his songwriting. He's been down in my studio most days working on new stuff."

"It's ironic that Bodhi is the one more obsessed with music," Ash supplies in between bites of her ravioli.

"It's not really." Viv pauses eating to reach for her glass of water. "Bodhi adores Dillon, and he's naturally gifted with a guitar. They bonded in those early days over music, and I truly believe it helped Bodhi cope with Lori's loss and the big change in his life when he came to live with us."

"Easton is really fucking talented too," Jamie says, talking over a mouthful of pizza.

Ash elbows him in the ribs, narrowing her eyes at him in that silent way she has of chastising any of us when we don't act appropriately. You'd think after nearly twenty years as our manager that she'd be used to us by now.

"East is a jack of all trades," I say, feeling a surge of pride in my chest as I think of both my sons. "He's a talented guitarist and drummer. He loves drama, and he has a natural affinity for the stage, and he's gifted at sports too."

"Yet he's so down to earth about it all." Audrey smiles and her pride in her godson is obvious.

"E is definitely more laid-back," Viv says. "He feels things as deeply as Bodhi, but he doesn't dwell on them in the same way. Bodhi is more intense but also more focused. He already knows he wants to pursue a career in the music industry."

"As a songwriter," I elaborate after swallowing another bite of pizza. "He has zero desire to be up on a stage."

"That doesn't surprise me." Alex cuts into his chicken parmigiana. "He has always hated attention."

"I think it's great the two boys are so close despite how different they are," Ash says.

"It's the main reason I'm not rocking in a corner this week," Viv explains. "As long as Bodhi has E to talk to, I feel like he'll come through this."

"Are we still coming to your place for Halloween?" Jamie asks before biting a large piece of pizza.

"Of course. It's tradition." I lift my bottle of beer to my lips, taking a quick sip. "Fleur and Melody would throw a hissy fit if we didn't have our annual Halloween party. It's all they've been talking about since Oisin's birthday last week."

"Emily too," Audrey says in reference to her eldest daughter.

"We were putting Oisin to bed after his party, and he was already talking about Halloween," Ash supplies

"Oh, to be a kid again." Alex shakes his head, grinning. "When the only thing you worried about was when the next party was."

"Or what costume to wear at Halloween," Viv says.

Alex chuckles. "I remember giving Reeve such shit about that. He was always such a pussy about Halloween."

"It was the theatrical side of him," Viv says, a faraway look appearing in her eye as it often does when she talks about her first husband and my twin. "He would start planning our costumes in the summer," she adds, turning to face me.

She squeezes my thigh though I don't need the reassurance. I am confident in our love and no longer threatened by my dead brother. In fact, I like when Viv, Audrey, and Alex reminisce over the past. I like learning new things about Reeve because I never got the chance to know him in person. Something I will regret until the day I draw my last breath.

"That's actually how my passion for sewing started. Reeve always wanted us to dress in matching themed costumes, and he wanted to be unique, choosing costumes no one else would show up in."

"When we were in middle school, they would throw these lavish Halloween parties and award prizes for best costume," Audrey explains, eyeballing me across the table.

"Reeve and Viv either won or were runner-up every year," Alex says.

"Reeve was very competitive." Viv kisses my cheek. "I would be up for hours in the weeks before the party putting the finishing touches on our costumes." She runs her fingers through the scruff on my chin and cheeks. "Maybe I can make our costumes this year," she muses.

"That's a sweet thought, Hollywood, but I think you've got enough on your plate making the kids' costumes, managing the foundation, and running the household." I am trying to lift the strain from my wife's shoulders, not add to it. I do my best to lighten the load, but our label has grown a lot in the past few years, and we are still putting out albums, so I don't have a lot of spare time. We hired a nanny when the kids were younger, and we have a housekeeper and a couple of drivers to help ferry the kids to and from school, playdates, and extracurricular activities, but life is still hectic most all of the time.

I make a mental note to talk to Lauren and Jon on the weekend and see if they would be down to mind the kids so I can whisk Viv away for a naughty weekend or even a night at a hotel. She has been working too damn hard lately, and now we are dealing with all this trouble with Bodhi and the shit at school. I'm worried about her, and I want to do what I can to alleviate her stress. A night away by ourselves might be just what the doctor ordered.

Viv sighs, looking like she is carrying the weight of the world on her shoulders. "I wish I could clone myself," she jokes.

"If you discover the magic formula, please share it." Audrey finishes her pasta dish and pushes the plate away. "The clinic is full to capacity every day, and I am maxed out to the hilt."

Alex rubs his wife's shoulders while dotting kisses in her hair. "I wish I could do more."

"You gave up your career after the twins were born, and you mind the kids and run the house. You do more than your fair share." Audrey pecks his lips.

"I thought you were going to recruit a couple of doctors to come and work with you," Ash inquires, spearing the last ravioli and popping it in her mouth.

"I am trying, but the pickings are slim. There is a shortage of qualified doctors, and any I have interviewed would not be a good fit. I need people I can gel with and doctors who have the right kind of people skills. I have met so many who had an awful bedside manner. I have worked my butt off to cultivate a certain vibe in my practice, and I don't want to sacrifice that as I grow."

"What about hiring an agency to recruit on your behalf?" Viv suggests.

"I have a contact who knows one of the directors of Recruit Plus," Ash says. "I am pretty sure they have a medical division. I could put in a call and ask Sheena if you like?"

"It can't do any harm," Audrey agrees. "That would be great. Thanks, Ash."

"Aisling Fleming to the rescue again." I waggle my brows and grin at my sister.

"Is there anyone you don't know?" Viv smiles at my sister as she finishes her food and lifts her wineglass. "I can't think of a single time I have gone to you for help where you didn't know someone you could call."

Ash shrugs, letting the praise roll off her back. "Networking is the name of the game when you manage this lot." She jabs her fork in the air, pointing it at me and Jamie. "And I like to pay it forward. You never know when a contact might come in handy."

Isn't that the truth. Ash has gotten us out of more scrapes and holes over the years, thanks to her smart thinking. "We are lucky to have you. I have no doubt Collateral Damage wouldn't be the success it is without you, and the same goes for the label. We owe a lot to you, Ash."

"Hear, hear." Jamie plants a loud kiss on her lips. "You're the real rock star, babe."

"Aw." Viv clings to my arm, smiling broadly as tears glisten in her eyes. "You guys are so sweet, and Ash deserves all the praise."

"Amen, sister." Audrey lifts her glass, clinking it against Ash's and then Viv's wineglass.

My cell vibrates in my pocket, and I pull it out, frowning when I see who it is.

"Who is it?" Viv asks, tension threading through her tone when she spots my expression.

"It's East." I swipe my finger across the screen, and loud noise accosts my eardrums as I lift the cell to my ear.

"Dad!" East hollers to be heard over the din in the background. "You need to come home."

"What's going on?" I ask, sliding out of the booth and standing.

"It's Bodhi. He's lost his shit, and he won't listen to me."

"We're on our way," I say, pinning Viv with a troubled look as she grabs her purse and scoots out of the booth.

CHAPTER 2
VIVIEN

"OH MY GOD," I say, surveying the wreckage in front of me with disbelieving eyes. Bodhi's room is trashed. The bed is overturned, the mattress strewn across the floor, and every book and item from his shelves is scattered across the wooden floor. The globe my parents gave him for Christmas is smashed to pieces, and the autographed song lyrics Dillon had framed for him, that hung over his bed, is tossed on the floor, the glass cracked and broken. All his drawers are open, the contents upended on the floor, and a line of clothing extends from his walk-in closet to the bedroom, many of them shredded and slashed and unwearable.

None of it matters. Material things can be replaced. All I am concerned about right now is my son and the state of mind he must be in to do something so uncharacteristic. "Where is Bodhi?" I ask E, rubbing a hand along the tightness spreading across my chest.

"Your son is outside," Bobby says, and I spin around on my heel to face the man who was a lifeline for me and Easton in the months after Reeve died.

We have a team of bodyguards on payroll now, but it is Bobby and Leon I gravitate to all the time. I trust those men with my life and my family's lives, and I go out of my way to ensure they are well taken care of so they never leave.

"Leon went after him," he adds.

"I'll go find him," Dillon says, bundling me into his arms.

He holds me close, and his brief strong embrace fills me with much-needed strength. Dillon has been my rock this past week as I struggle to help our eldest son cope with the latest revelations about the past.

"Try not to worry," Dillon says even though he knows it's an impossibility. He kisses me, before letting me go. "Stay here. I will try to calm him down. Talk to East." He levels our son with a knowing look, and I can read the silent communication: Look after your mom.

Dillon leaves with Bobby, and I trail my gaze over the messed-up room as I knot and unknot my hands. Anxiety waits in the wings, ready to swoop in and toy with my insides. "Did your sisters wake?" I ask, worried at what they might have heard tonight. I bend down and start picking up debris off the floor.

Easton shakes his head, drawing a hand through his hair. "No. I made sure to close their doors and I closed Bodhi's too when he started throwing shit around the place."

I glance at him as I move around the room, gathering up the remnants of Bodhi's room. I'm on edge, and I need to do something with my hands to keep myself distracted.

Wordlessly, E starts helping, righting Bodhi's bed and flipping the mattress over, replacing it on top. He is strong from football and weight training, and it's hard to believe he's only sixteen when he's so tall and broad and looks like a grown man.

He looks so much like his father. Like Reeve too. Sometimes, I do a double take watching Bodhi and Easton together because they remind me of Reeve at sixteen, and it's like looking at a ghost. E wears his hair very similar to Reeve in a classic all-American style while Bodhi favors a more edgy look. Presently, he is wearing his hair in a faux hawk with bleach-blond tips.

"Is this a delayed reaction to what happened at school?" I ask after a while, reaching down to retrieve the broken frames from the floor.

E strides toward me. "Careful, Mom. That could cut you."

"Why don't you let me do that?" Charlotte says, entering the room, carrying a dustpan and brush and the cordless vacuum.

My inclination is to keep cleaning, but I also want to find Bodhi and Dillon. I need to see my son with my own eyes to know he's okay. "Thank you, Charlotte. Only clean up the broken things. Sweep anything that might harm him, but leave the rest. Bodhi must take responsibility for his actions. It will be up to him to fix his room."

Charlotte nods, her expression conveying her agreement.

"Thanks, Lotty." Easton gives our housekeeper a quick hug, and her eyes meet mine over my son's tall, broad shoulders. Her face shines with love. She adores all the kids, and she's so good with them, but there is a special place in her heart for Easton, and it's definitely mutual. Charlotte has been with us since E was a little baby. She never married, and she has lived with us for years, helping me to take care of our expanding family. It's safe to say we all cherish her and have happily adopted her as one of our own.

We leave Charlotte to the mess and step out into the hallway, heading in the direction of downstairs.

E slings his arm around my shoulders as we walk the hallway on the ground level, moving toward our casual living room. "It's going to be okay, Mom." He gives me a reassuring squeeze, but I detect the uncertainty in his usual confident tone, and that troubles me enormously. "Bodhi is just going through a rough patch, but he'll pull through."

"I want to believe that," I say, striding into the room. "But this is not like him." Bodhi has always been reticent about speaking his mind, preferring to vent his thoughts and feelings onto the page than speak to me or Dillon about them. I know he has confided in Easton, and that has helped to reassure me, but lately it's as if

Bodhi has pressed some inner self-destruct button, and whatever coping tools he's used in the past don't appear to be working now. I even suspect he is being more guarded with his brother, and that worries me greatly.

It's one of the main reasons why I'm so concerned.

"What happened?" I ask, turning around to face my son.

Easton wets his lips, dragging a hand through his brown hair. It's threaded with natural blond highlights, just like Reeve's hair was, from the California sun. "Don't get mad, but we watched the movie."

Shock races through me as my jaw slackens. "You did what?" I splutter as shock instantly gives way to anger. "We agreed if either of you wanted to watch it, we'd watch it together!" Pain spears me through my heart at the thought of how they both must be feeling.

Shortly after the movie premiered, some kids at school started talking shit to Bodhi and Easton about Reeve and Saffron. We went to the school immediately and handled it, but it forced us to revisit the topic of them watching it. They were only eleven at the time, and we felt that was too young to see it, but how could we protect them from other kids? That any parent would let an eleven-year-old watch an adult movie was shocking but not a surprise. A lot of parents suck at parenting.

Dillon and I had decided to let them watch it when they were thirteen. We felt that was old enough for them to be able to grasp the basics of our messy past, and we chose to stick to our guns. Yet when thirteen rolled around, the boys didn't want to watch it, and we didn't force the agenda. We told them when they decided they were ready to see it, we would watch it with them.

It wasn't optional.

It was a rule.

I know the emotional tsunami that movie will unleash in both my boys, which is why I'm livid they watched it without saying a word and without letting us be there to discuss it with them.

"I'm sorry, Mom. It wasn't planned. It was spontaneous, and you were out with Dad. I know you've been freaking out over the school thing, and I didn't want to worry you."

I sense there is more to it than this, but E is loyal to Bodhi to a fault, and I can't ever find it in me to criticize him for it. Easton has looked out for Bodhi from the minute he came into our lives, and I know he will always have his back. I love how close they are. I love how much they support one another, and I hope this movie won't do anything to damage their relationship because that would kill me.

"I didn't want you to learn the truth like that." Tears prick my eyes as I close the gap between us. I take his hands in mine. "Are _you_ okay?"

A shuddering sigh leaves his chest. "Honestly, Mom, I'm pissed."

I nod, understanding why that would be the case.

"How could Reeve do that to you? How could he be so fucking stupid?"

A look of disgust crosses his face, and I hate seeing it there. But I won't criticize my son for reacting naturally to the truth or tell him he is wrong to feel the things he is feeling. "He was young and naïve, and he made mistakes."

"You told him she was a gold-digging slut! You warned him, and he refused to listen! I had him on this pedestal all my life, but he didn't deserve it."

"Don't let what you've discovered erase the happy memories you have of him, Easton. You loved Reeve, and he loved you. Every interaction between you was born of love. It doesn't excuse his actions, but he had a difficult childhood, and he felt abandoned his whole life. That made him vulnerable, but it doesn't mean he was a bad person. He was a good man who made some poor life decisions, and those decisions hurt the people he loved."

E shucks out of my hold and paces the room. "I don't know how you can defend him. I don't know how you could have taken him back after what he did to you."

"I loved him, and I forgave him. He was a good husband and a good father."

A bitter laugh rings out behind me, and I freeze as I turn around. My eyes meet Dillon's over Bodhi's shoulders. "He was a piece of shit, and my mother was a whore." Bodhi sways on his feet, slurring his words, and I'm appalled and concerned in equal measure.

"You were drinking?" I move toward my troubled son with my heart jackhammering behind my rib cage. I'm not naïve. I was a teenager once too, and things are even more advanced nowadays. Kids rarely remain kids, and they grow up way too fast. Since the boys started attending parties a year ago, we have suspected they might be drinking.

We have talked to them extensively about alcohol and drugs and encouraged them to make the right choices. Neither of our sons have given us reason to actively worry about it.

Until now.

Bodhi is obnoxiously drunk and only remaining upright because Dillon is propping him up.

"Anyone would after watching that fucking movie." Bodhi pins me with tortured blue eyes. "Why did you do that? Why the fuck did you make that movie?" Dillon grabs him when he lurches forward, stopping him from toppling to the ground. "That shit should have stayed buried with both my parents. No good comes from knowing that. I would rather you lied to me."

Pain eviscerates me from the inside out, and I'm struggling to hold on to my emotions. But I do. Because this isn't about me and my feelings. This is about my sons. They are both hurting, and it's our job to support them.

"We won't ever lie to you," Dillon says, hauling Bodhi back against his chest. "Your mother wrote that book, and we made that movie, to set the record straight. As much as all of us might want to bury the truth, it's impossible when we are celebrities and this all played out against the backdrop of Hollywood."

"We didn't want you learning about the past from the internet because so much of what was said was wrong," I say, stepping closer to him. "We didn't want you learning this without us there either. You should not have watched it without your father and me."

"It doesn't change the facts," he slurs. "I've been passed around like a sack of worthless shit. You only took me in because you had no choice."

"No, Bodhi." Tears leak from my eyes as he attempts to push Dillon away, but he's too inebriated, and Dillon is strong. "That is not the truth."

"I don't care," he shouts, struggling in Dillon's arms. "Get off me!"

"Bro." East steps up alongside me. "Don't do this. They're only trying to help. We all are."

Another bitter laugh tumbles from Bodhi's chest. "I don't need or want your fucking help!" he yells, fixing his brother with a hostile look. "I don't fucking care! It's all bullshit! No one wants me, but I don't care. I don't need anyone. People only let you down." Dillon stumbles as Bodhi continues to struggle in his hold. "My whole life has been one big fat lie."

"That's not true." Easton shakes his head. "I'm your brother. We're your family. That's not a lie."

"You're not my brother," Bodhi snarls, looking like a stranger as he fixes Easton with an ugly look. "You're my cousin." He jabs his finger in my direction. "Like she's not my mom and Dillon's my uncle, not my dad."

He pierces me with bloodshot eyes, and his face contains a world of pain I wish I could wipe away.

It's not like any of that is a secret.

Bodhi has always known who we are to him, but learning the full truth of the past has clearly twisted things and warped his way of thinking. I know it's hurt speaking. The alcohol sloshing through his veins doesn't help either. I try to remember all of this as he lashes out.

"I don't know how you can even bear to look at me after what my mother did to you. Or how you could take that piece-of-shit sperm donor back after he cheated on you with her. What is wrong with you? Why would you do that? Have you no self-respect?"

He might as well have driven a stake straight through my heart. Pain has a vise-grip around my internal organs, squeezing and squeezing until it feels like I can't breathe. I swipe at the hot tears coursing down my face as I observe the angry expression on my eldest son's face. His pain cuts me deep, and right now, I hate myself. Why did I think making a movie was a good idea? Why did I think this would help? All I have done is hurt both my boys and potentially damaged our relationships forever.

I couldn't hate myself any more than I do in this moment.

"That's enough, Bodhi." Dillon's sharp tone cuts through the tension in the air. "You will not speak to your mother like that. She loves you, and I know you love her. I know this is hurt speaking, but I won't stand by and let you talk to Vivien like that."

With more strength than I figured he could muster, Bodhi rams his elbow back into Dillon's stomach, catching him off guard. Dillon loosens his hold on our son, and he wrangles himself free.

"You are one to talk!" Spit flies from Bodhi's mouth as he whirls around, pointing his finger in Dillon's face. "You're almost as bad as Reeve. You purposely set out to deceive her, and then you showed up and stressed her out when she was pregnant." I can't see the look on his face from this angle, but I don't need to see it to know it's ugly.

East wraps his arms around me, and I don't realize I'm shaking all over until he holds me and I feel myself trembling against him. Unshed tears fill Easton's eyes as he stares at his brother, looking utterly lost, just like he did in the aftermath of losing

Reeve and Lainey. I rest my head against his shoulder and circle my arms around him, holding him as tight as he's holding me.

"I am not proud of the things I did," Dillon says. "I will regret my actions for the rest of my life, but I love your mother. I love you, your brother, and your sisters. This isn't the time to discuss it. It's late, and we all need to sleep, but I don't want you going to bed thinking you don't mean the world to us, Bodhi, because you do."

"You are our son in every meaning of the word," I add, silently beseeching him to turn around. "I hate that you're hurting. I hate that we're the reason you're in pain." Easton lets me go, and I walk up behind Bodhi, wanting to envelop him in my arms but terrified to do anything else to set him off. Dillon pulls me in front of him, wrapping protective arms around my waist as I stare up at Bodhi. "I know you are confused, but we love you, Bodhi. Whatever you are thinking about how we came to adopt you, know we did it because we wanted you to be a part of our family, and from the minute I met you, I loved you with my whole heart."

Tension is heavy in the air as he stares at me, a myriad of emotions flitting across his handsome face. "I think you're the one who is confused, Vivien."

My heart thuds painfully against my chest wall at his use of my first name. I prayed for months for him to call me Mom, and it was one of the happiest days of my life when he did. If I have lost that now, I will be inconsolable. Though it's nothing less than I deserve. I rue the day I ever made that damn movie. Bodhi already lost one mother, and I don't want him to feel like he's lost me too because that will never happen. As long as there is blood flowing through my veins and air in my lungs, I will be his mother. Easton, Fleur, and Melody's too.

"It is *guilt*, pure and simple." He hisses the word, and I flinch. "Why the hell else would you take Saffron's bastard in?"

"You can't say that to Mom!" Easton cries. "Why the hell would you say that?"

"Don't, Bodhi. Please," I whisper, trembling against Dillon.

"Don't do this, son," Dillon says. "Go sleep it off, and we'll talk in the morning."

"I don't know why you think anything will change," he slurs, knocking into Dillon as he brushes past him. "It's all a stinking pile of lies, and I'm done with it."

CHAPTER 3
DILLON

VIVIEN HOLDS it together long enough to say goodnight to Easton, offering reassuring words that most likely sound hollow to her ears. The second East's bedroom door is closed, I scoop my wife into my arms and race down the hallway, past Bodhi's closed door and the girls' bedrooms, heading toward the stairs at the end that leads to our master suite on the next level. Vivien snakes her arms around my neck, burying her face in my shoulder as she clings to me. Her body shakes as she cries silent tears, and my heart is aching for her. For Bodhi too. Though I'm furious at him as well for the things he said to her.

Vivien is already predisposed to blame herself for this.

The last thing she needs is Bodhi cranking the guilt-o-meter to the max.

A sob erupts from Vivien's mouth when I reach our bedroom door. I hold her tight as I fumble with the door handle, eventually opening it. She bursts into loud, anguished tears as I carry her into the room, slamming the door shut with my foot. The dam breaks, and my wife falls apart in my arms as I stride toward our bed. I sit down and scoot up to the headboard, leaning back against it as I cradle my heart-broken wife in my lap.

Vivien is full-on blubbering, and every agonized cry that tumbles from her mouth tears another strip off my heart. I hug her close, dotting kisses into her hair as she fists my shirt and presses her body flush to me, clinging to me with a desperation that equally hurts and soothes.

I love that my wife turns to me in times of need, but I hate that we are here at all.

I don't offer platitudes or fake reassurances as she cries. I won't lie to her like that. The truth is, we are at the start of a harrowing journey with no specific destination and no end in sight, so I won't tell her everything is going to be okay when we don't know if it is.

My shirt is soaked by the time Viv stops crying. Tipping her face up, she peers at me with red-rimmed, bloodshot eyes and the most forlorn expression. "I have failed him, Dillon," she croaks over an errant sob. "I should never have made that damn movie. What the hell was I thinking?"

"Sweetheart, don't beat yourself up over this. I know you're upset, but you aren't at fault here. We made that movie for the right reasons, and they still count." I brush my lips against hers, hating to see her in so much pain. "You have not failed him. You have loved Bodhi with your full heart and given him a happy, secure family life." I push damp, matted strands of her long brown hair back off her face. "We knew it would come to this. We knew the truth would be hard for the boys. But it's better than them discovering a warped version of reality via the internet. We'll support them as they come to terms with it. We'll answer their questions honestly and continue to shower them with love."

"What if it's not enough?" Her gorgeous hazel eyes widen with fear and pain as she slants me with a pleading look.

I wish I had a magic wand to solve this, but it will have to be done the hard way. "It might not be, but there is only so much we can do, Viv," I softly say, swiping the dampness from her cheeks with my thumbs. "Bodhi is drowning in self-loathing and a multitude of other negative emotions. He is going to lash out at us because we're the easy targets. He is going to resist any offer of help we suggest. He won't see what is right in front of his eyes. He won't want to accept the truth that the past really doesn't fucking matter. He won't be able to see it like it is, Viv, because he's in too much pain and he's too young to process it."

I clasp her face in my hands, peering deep into her eyes, which look more green than brown today. "Or maybe he is more mature than I was at his age. Maybe he'll see through the bullshit quicker than I did. Maybe he'll cling to us more, knowing he's so fucking lucky he has us and it doesn't matter who his bio parents are when he's surrounded by people who love him like we do." I shrug though my body is wound up tight, and I'm every bit as concerned as my wife. "We don't really know how he will react, and we must prepare ourselves for anything and everything."

"You had a family who loved you, but it didn't matter. You refused to accept it at face value. You didn't even tell them when Simon approached you and offered you money in exchange for your silence. You kept it all bottled up inside for years, Dillon. *Years.*" More tears leak out of her eyes. "What if Bodhi does the same? He is like you in so many ways."

"He's also not like me in a lot of other ways. He's his own person, and we can't know how he'll react based on my circumstances and how I dealt with things."

"You've got to admit there are a lot of similarities." She winds her fingers through my hair, and I feel her touch everywhere. It helps to ground me, like always. "Maybe he'll listen to you," she continues, hope glimmering in her eyes. "If you explain how you felt and the things you wish you'd done differently, maybe you can get through to him."

"You know I will try." I tilt her face up, running my thumb along her lower lip. "I will do everything in my power to get through to him, but you have to face the fact he might not listen to any of us. He might completely break. All we may be able to do is continuously reassure him of our love and be there to pick up the pieces."

"God, Dillon. Don't say that!"

She cries, and I hug her closer again. "This isn't going to be easy, Viv. You need to prepare yourself for it. There is Easton to consider too. This won't be easy on him either."

"No." She sniffles, sitting back and lifting her head. "There is much for him to process too, and I know him. He'll downplay his own feelings because his brother will be dealing with so much more. He won't want to add to our worries, but we can't let him bottle his feelings up either. He has a right to his anger and his grief too. We need to ensure we look after both boys and that we protect the girls from any fallout." A hint of determination glints in her eyes.

There's my girl. There's my fighter. The woman who would burn the world down to protect those she loves. Viv is going to need all her inner strength to get through the difficult times ahead. And I will be there, right by her side, battling to protect our family and safeguard everything we have built over the years.

Lifting her arm, I bring her wrist to my lips and press a tender kiss to her sensitive flesh. "We are in this together, Vivien Grace. We have an amazing family, and we won't let this derail us. We will come out swinging and fighting to hold on to what we have built, and that is a rock-solid fucking guaranteed promise."

"Oh, Dillon." She repositions herself on my lap, circling her arms around my shoulders as she smiles softly at me. "I love you so much. I couldn't do this life thing without you."

"Ditto, Hollywood." I tweak her nose. "There is no one else I would want to navigate life with than you." My hands land on her hips, and I give them a gentle squeeze. "We are facing some tough times ahead, but we'll survive. We will get Easton and Bodhi through this."

"We won't ever give up on them." Steely determination underscores her tone, like I knew it would when she got over her initial pain.

"It's going to get really rough, Viv. He is going to say horrible things to us. I know, because I did. You need to remember he doesn't mean it. You need to remember you're the best fucking mother and you have given your all to these kids. Remember how much trust Reeve placed in you. He always wanted you raising Bodhi, and I know he's looking down with pride when he sees what a great job you've done. This is no measure of you or Bodhi or any of us. It's a necessary process to deal with the shit hand we were dealt by others. But we will get through this." I tuck a piece of her hair behind one ear. "What doesn't kill us will make us stronger."

She presses her lips against mine in a brief soft kiss. "I love you, Dillon. So fucking much. You are my rock. My world. My desire to keep fighting when things get tough is because you have given me the strength to be the best version of myself."

"I love you too, Vivien." I hold her face in my hands. "You have given me everything just by breathing, and I won't ever stop fighting for our family because I love our life and I will move mountains to ensure we never lose it."

She stares at me with blatant adoration and the potent need that always lingers at the back of her eyes. "Make love to me, Dil. I need to feel our connection now more than ever."

Gripping her hips harder, I dart in and peck her lips. "You never have to beg, Hollywood. You know that. I'm as insatiable for you as I always have been."

Our sex life has suffered over the years with kids and work and the crazy chaos that is our lives, but we always make time for one another, no matter how stressed or tired we are. We may not have the time to fuck nonstop like we used to or engage in the kinky sex of our youth, but we still have regular sex, and it's always out of this world. I am so hot for my wife, and every time just gets better and better.

Viv climbs off my lap and stands, moving her hand around to the zip on her dress.

"Let me." Lust deepens my voice as I crawl off the bed. Standing directly behind her, I run my hands over her gorgeous body through her dress, loving how easily my hands fit to her curves, like they were made to perfectly slot against her. Brushing her long hair to one side, I plant a slew of feather-soft drugging kisses along her neck as I slowly lower the zip down her back. "You are so beautiful. You still take my breath away."

"Mmm." She moans softly and angles her head to the side, granting me more access to her neck as she presses back against my growing erection.

I slide the dress off her shoulders, letting it pool on the floor at her feet, while my hands wander over the silky smoothness of her tan skin. Unclasping her bra with a flick of my fingers, I drag the straps down her arms before tossing it away. I look down at her from behind as my hands reach up to cup her heavy tits. I fondle them with urgent hands, tweaking her nipples with my fingers as I grind my hard cock against her lower back and suction my lips to her neck.

Twisting her head around, I claim her lips in a passionate kiss as one hand glides down her body and under the band of her silk panties. Two digits push smoothly inside her wet heat, and she bucks against my hand as I fuck her with my fingers. "Always soaked for me," I murmur against her lips as I roughly grab one tit while pumping my fingers in and out of her pussy. Rotating my hips, I rock against her from behind, rewarded when she moans into my mouth. I slip my tongue between her lips and worship her mouth as I angle my hand so I can fuck her faster with my fingers while my thumb rubs circles against her clit.

It doesn't take me long to work her into a frenzy, and then she's crying and calling out my name as she grinds on my hand when an orgasm rips through her. I band my arm around her waist as she milks her climax, holding her up when her limbs turn floppy, and she sags against me. My cock is leaking precum behind my boxers, and I'm dying to drive inside her and fill her to the hilt.

Lifting her up, I gently place her on the bed with her head on the pillows. I drag her wet panties down her legs and toss them aside before standing at the end of the bed, staring at the gorgeousness that is my wife.

My wife.

My woman.

My soul mate.

My goddamned reason for living.

"Spread your legs, Hollywood, and show me my pretty pink pussy," I demand as I start unbuttoning my shirt. I take my time undressing as she widens her legs, her chest heaving and cheeks flushed as she stares at me. "Lift your knees up to your chest. I want to see all of you."

She bites down on her lower lip, and I growl as I fling my shirt aside before moving to my jeans. I pop the button and rub my aching cock through the denim as I drink her in. Both holes are visible from this angle, and I would love nothing more than to fill each one tonight. But that's not what she needs. My wife needs a loving touch tonight, and I plan to deliver. "Touch your tits," I tell her as I shove my jeans and boxers down my legs, freeing my straining cock.

I strip out of my jeans, boxers, socks, and shoes, stroking my dick as I watch my wife fondle her tits while exposing her pussy and her ass to me. I am salivating and straining with the need to come as I climb up between her legs, but my needs can wait.

I want my wife to be thoroughly fucked and sated so she sleeps without trouble tonight.

Our problems can wait until tomorrow.

Right now, there is only me and Viv and our matching need for one another.

Everything else can take a hike.

Sliding on my stomach, I press my face to her delectable pussy and feast on it with my fingers and my mouth. Using her slickness, I coat my fingers and tease her puckered hole as I drive my tongue inside her cunt with relentless determination. I silently fist pump the air when she comes all over my face a few minutes later, her back arching off the bed, her nipples hard enough to cut glass, and her hips bucking, as she writhes and moans for me.

I waste no more time because I'm all out of patience and I need to be inside my woman. I push inside her in one long deep thrust, both of us groaning with mutual pleasure when I fill her up. I lean down and press a tender kiss to her lips. "I love you."

Her arms wind around my shoulders. "I love you, Dillon. You anchor me in all the right ways."

"I never want you to forget how much you mean to me. How much I worship and adore you," I say as I slowly pull out before shoving back inside her. Her legs wrap around my waist as I move in and out of her.

"I could never forget. Not when you show me in so many ways," she rasps over a moan as her tight, hot walls hug my throbbing cock.

Those are the last words we speak for a while. Both of us get lost in our lovemaking, relishing the caresses and kisses as I slide in and out of her, taking my time, bringing her to the edge and back, over and over, until we come before collapsing in a tangled heap of sweaty limbs, sated and exhausted, and bolstered by the knowledge we are a true team in every sense of the word.

As I spoon her from behind, grateful for the soft murmurings of contentment that slip from her plush lips as she drifts into sleep, I know as long as we stick together, we will weather the approaching storm and come out on the other side of it.

CHAPTER 4
EASTON

"BABE, WHAT'S WRONG?" Hollis asks, a frown marring her pretty face as she tugs at my sleeve.

"Nothing," I lie, not wanting to tell my girlfriend how bad things are between me and my brother at this point. I close my locker on autopilot as I stare at my brother down the hallway.

"Is it Bodhi?" she asks, sliding her arms around my waist as she follows my troubled gaze. "What's he doing hanging around with those guys? I didn't know he was friends with Otis and Mahlik."

"He's not." Easing her arms off me, I bend down and peck her lips. "I'm gonna catch up to him. Go to class. You don't want to be late."

She grabs the sleeve of my uniform jacket, halting my forward trajectory. "You don't want to be late either. Bodhi has gotten you into enough trouble lately."

Hollis's parents found out about our recent suspension, and to say they weren't happy is an understatement. Her family comes from old money, and they live by old-world values and traditions. They are super strict with her. She isn't allowed out on school nights, and they impose a curfew on weekends. I might respect that if it didn't limit our time together and the opportunities to hookup and if her dad wasn't a giant asshole.

He looks down his nose at my parents because of their celebrity status and how they made their money. I couldn't give two shits what Mr. Astor thinks really, except it matters to my girlfriend, and I'm crazy about her. We got together at the end of summer break, and we have been pretty much inseparable since then.

Best two months of my life.

"Stop worrying." I kiss her again, hating I can't linger. "I'll see you at lunch."

She palms my cheek and smiles sadly at me before turning around and walking in the direction of her first class. I sprint down the hallway, calling out to Bodhi as he

701

starts walking off. He ignores me, and I clench my fists at my sides as familiar annoyance bubbles to the surface.

I am so sick of this bullshit.

I wish to fuck we'd never watched that damn movie.

"Wait up!" Grabbing a fistful of his shirt, I yank Bodhi back. Otis and Mahlik slow their pace, turning to look. "I need a word with my brother—*in private*," I say, hoping they get the hint.

They don't. Leaning against the wall of lockers, they stab me with hostile looks that might scare some people, but not me.

"Fuck off." Bodhi wrestles out of my grip and turns to glare at me.

"You can't keep ignoring me forever." I eyeball my brother, pretending like the two assholes aren't listening to every word.

"I don't want to talk to you." Bodhi purposely shoves me, and I can't get over how much he has changed in such a short span of time. Unless he was hiding this part of his personality for years, stewing over the past, and now it's all come rushing to the surface, like a dormant volcano sprung to life.

Bo works out with Dad in our home gym, and he's bulked up a lot this past year, but he's still not a match for my strength, and I don't so much as flinch when he shoves me. Coach puts us through our paces every morning before school and most evenings at practice, and my body is a solid block of muscle. "I'm your brother, and this shit isn't cool. I'm not the enemy, Bo." I lower my voice as I lean in closer to him. "Why are you shutting me out? We need to talk about this. Turning on one another is not the way to handle it."

Bo has always been quiet and introspective. Except with me. We always tell each other shit, and it hurts that he's pushing me away and refusing to speak to me. This past week has been a total shit show. Mom is crying all the time but trying to hide it. Dad is attempting to break through Bo's walls and get him to open up, but he's getting nowhere. My little sisters have picked up on the tension, and they're acting out. "You're not the only one hurting. It's hurt me too."

He snorts out a laugh and levels me with a look that can only be described as hateful. "Of course, you would make this about you." He shoves me again, and I'm starting to get angry now. "You are so fucking selfish and so self-centered. What the fuck do you have to be angry about? You're not the one who was dumped on and abandoned his entire life. But poor E. The attention is on me this time, and you don't know how to handle it, so you try to make it about you. Fucking typical."

Otis and Mahlik laugh, and my hands clench at my sides. I want to knock their two ignorant heads together and unleash some of the burning frustration racing through my veins. I am literally speechless. I cannot form a single word in response to the utter bullshit that has just streamed from my brother's mouth.

I grind my teeth to the molars as I stare at the stranger in front of me. This is not my brother. I don't know who Bodhi is anymore, and he's really starting to scare me.

We need to have this out but not here.

"We'll talk at home."

"Are you deaf?!" Bodhi moves to shove me again, but I step back.

If he pushes me one more time, I will not be responsible for my actions, and I really don't want to fight my brother.

"I want nothing to do with you," he hisses. "Leave me the fuck alone."

Pain spreads across my chest as I watch him walk away, and I hope it's not prophetic.

"Okay, spill," Hollis says from our table tucked into the corner of the cafeteria. "What is going on with you?" Usually, we eat at the jocks' table with my teammates, their girls, and some of the cheerleaders. But I'm not in the mood for company today. Hollis didn't protest, readily letting me drag her to the quietest spot in the place so I can lick my wounds in relative obscurity.

I shrug, wanting to talk to her but not wanting to broadcast my family problems to anyone outside the house either. "Just some shit at home," I say before stuffing the last of my sandwich into my mouth.

"I am a good listener if you want to unburden." She pierces me with a concerned look as she slides her arm around my shoulders and presses into my side.

Her gorgeous big blue eyes radiate sincerity as she stares at me, and I loosen the hold on my tongue, deciding I need to talk to someone about it before I explode. "Bodhi and I watched the movie about our parents last week. Now, he's pissed and taking it out on all of us. He won't talk to me at all, and I'm worried about him."

Her eyes pop wide. "You only watched the movie now?"

I nod. "My parents asked us if we wanted to watch it the day after my thirteenth birthday. I wanted to see it, but Bo was adamant he didn't want to know. It was an all-or-nothing situation, so we told our parents no."

"Let me guess, all that shit at school started this." She rubs her hand up and down my back, and her touch is comforting.

"Yeah. It flipped a switch in Bo, and he was moody and withdrawn all that week we were suspended. My parents were out at dinner when I discovered him watching it in his room. I freaked because we'd promised we would watch it together with my parents, but Bo refused to turn it off, so I watched it with him, and then all the shit hit the fan."

"I'm sorry, Easton. I can't imagine how much that must have hurt."

"Have you seen it?"

Slowly, she nods. "I don't say this to make you feel bad, but I reckon most kids at school have probably watched it. Your mom is the daughter of Lauren Mills, and she's totally stunning. Reeve was a famous movie star, your dad is a rock legend, and they're both seriously hot."

I shove her arm away and glare at her. "That's my fucking dad, Hollis. You can't say shit like that about him."

She holds up her hands in surrender. "I take it back. I didn't mean anything by it, just trying to explain why people have a vested interest in watching the movie. You and Bodhi are two of the most popular guys at school. I could name countless girls who would kill to be in my shoes, and Bodhi has that moody, broody, bad boy vibe going for him that has tons of girls lusting over him. You two are a big deal around here, and your family history only adds to the appeal. My mom said it was quite the scandal when it was revealed your mom was in love with twins and that you were actually Dillon's son and not Reeve's."

"Jesus, Holl. Could you say it any louder?" My head whips around, but thankfully no one is paying us any attention.

"No one is listening," she says, deliberately lowering her tone this time. "I felt sad for your mom watching the movie. You could tell she really loved Reeve, and I was crying when Saffron broke them up. But then she met Dillon, and oh wow." She rubs a hand across her chest as a dreamy expression appears on her face. "He was amazing, and you could tell they had this epic kind of love, and then when she went back to L.A. and Reeve was waiting for her, I couldn't help but think how lucky she was to have found that kind of love twice."

I think my girlfriend might be a little bit insane or delusional, or maybe it's a bit of both. "I don't think my mom's intention was to romanticize everything she went through. Both my dads put her through hell, and we will be dealing with the fallout of all their shit for the rest of our lives. There is nothing amazing about that."

She purses her lips, looking like she's ready to argue with me, but I'm done. "It almost sounds like you're in love with my dad. Are you using me to get to him?" I half joke because I'm getting a weird vibe off her now. Or maybe it's just me because I'm having a shitty day and I haven't slept properly in weeks.

"Don't be ridiculous. I'd have to be invited to your house to use you to get close to your dad, and you still haven't asked me to meet your parents."

I stare at her like she's grown an extra head. "Are you for real right now?"

She shrugs, looking at me like maybe I'm the crazy one, and I give up. I don't have the mental capacity to deal with this shit at the moment. I bury my head in my hands. It's that or strangle my girlfriend. I know she's only trying to help, but she's making it worse with every word that comes out of her mouth.

"I'm sorry, East," she whispers, linking her fingers through mine under the table. "I suck at this. I don't know the right thing to say, and I don't want to hurt you. Of course, I'm not in love with your dad. I'm in love with *you*. So completely and utterly totally in love with you."

I curl my fingers around hers and lift my head, kissing her softly, as her words melt my frustration. "I love you too." I nuzzle my nose against hers. "I know you mean well, babe, and it's cool. Don't mind me. I'm just extra sensitive right now."

"I get that, and I understand. I am here for you, and I have an idea." Her eyes spark to life as she tosses her long blonde hair over one shoulder and leans in, pressing her warm mouth to my ear. "I know how to relax you. I can hang around after cheer practice and wait for you. I'll tell my mom I'm studying at the library. Meet me under the bleachers in our spot, and I'll make it up to you."

"I love you," I whisper, lifting Hollis to her feet and planting a hard kiss on her mouth. I can taste myself on her lips as I kiss her while tucking my cock back in my boxers and pulling my zipper up.

"I love you too," she rasps in a breathless tone as I back her up against the wall in our spot under the bleachers.

"I needed that," I say as my fingers creep under the short skirt of her cheer uniform.

Her fingers wind around my wrist, stalling my upward trajectory. "You don't have to do that. I like looking after you."

I dart down, pressing my lips to that sensitive spot under her ear. "As I like looking after you. My dad would kick my ass if he knew I let you blow me first. He told me to always look after my girl's needs before my own."

"Your dad seriously gave you sex advice?" Her face contorts into a funny expression, like she can't decide if she likes it or is disgusted by it.

I chuckle as I caress her outer thigh. "You said it yourself. My dad is a rock legend, and he's blunt as fuck. He doesn't hold back, and he always tells it to me straight. My mom was with my dad when they gave us the sex talk at ten, but she doesn't know Dad spoke to me and Bo again when we were fourteen. He gave us condoms and the safe sex speech but also spoke to us about respecting women, ensuring it was fully consensual, and to make sure we treat them right."

"I guess I have your dad to thank for your magic fingers then," she purrs, letting my wrist go.

"Don't start that shit again," I growl, only half joking. "The only person you can thank for my magic fingers is me," I say as I push her panties aside and slide the magic inside her slick warmth.

"Call me later," Hollis says, leaning through the window of her BMW to press one final kiss to my lips. "And don't forget we are picking up our costumes tomorrow after school." Her best friend is throwing a Halloween party at her place, and most everyone from school is going. I am looking forward to it. I need to release some of this pent-up frustration, and losing myself in my girl and a gallon of beer sounds like the perfect solution.

"Drive safe," I say, blowing her a kiss. I watch her drive out of the mostly empty school parking lot before I walk toward my SUV.

I decide to stop at our local bakery on the way home to pick up some treats for Mom and my sisters. It's a French bakery, and Mom adores their almond croissants and lemon tart meringue. I pick up some of them along with a box of macaroons for Fleur and Melody, an éclair for Dad, and cinnamon apple pies for Bo and me.

I know what Bodhi said earlier, but I'm not giving up on him. He's my brother. We're as close as twins. Hell, most of the kids at school think we are twins because we look so alike. I know that was only anger speaking earlier. Maybe the pie will soften him up and he'll agree to at least sit down and talk to me. Despite what he said, I don't give a shit about me. Bo is the one who was crapped on by Reeve, and I need him to know I am here for him. That I get it and he can vent to me. A part of me understands why he might not want to talk to me about it, but that's exactly why he should.

We aren't responsible for the things Reeve did.

It doesn't change who I am to Bo or who he is to me.

I need him to know I always have his back and he's my brother through and through.

It doesn't matter that I can't reconcile my memories of the man I called Daddy Reeve with the knowledge I have of him now.

I swallow over the messy ball of emotion as I unlock my car and set the cake boxes down on the passenger seat.

It's a cluster fuck of epic proportions, and I still can't process how I feel about the fact Reeve chose Mom and me over Bodhi. It's wrong on so many levels. My heart aches for my brother as I start the engine and glide out into traffic. I have only gone a few blocks when I spot my brother's truck, parked at the curb, outside a bar that is a known hangout for bikers and career criminals.

An ominous sense of dread tiptoes down my spine as I park my SUV and get out to investigate. It's almost sunset, and the darkening clouds casts gloomy shadows on the pavement as I walk toward the bar. A noise from the alley to the left of the bar claims my attention, lifting all the fine hairs on the back of my neck. Cautiously, I pop my head into the alley, crouching down as I spot three indistinct figures up ahead. Keeping low and tucked in tight to the wall, I creep up the alley, stopping a few feet from the men and hiding behind a smelly dumpster.

Panic sluices through my veins when my brother's voice rings out loud and clear. "Thanks, man."

There's a rustling sound before a man with a deep unfamiliar voice says, "Nice doing business with you, dude."

I flatten my back to the wall at the sound of approaching footsteps, hoping I blend into the shadows, as a figure walks by. Bodhi's expression is grim, his body rigid with stress as he strides past me without noticing.

My heart slams against my rib cage as I watch him shove the packet of pills in his back pocket and exit the alley.

CHAPTER 5
BODHI

I THRUST into the busty blonde from behind, rubbing her clit as I drive into her one final time before spilling my load in the condom and roaring my release. The brunette underneath her moans and writhes on the bed as blondie licks her pussy. I'm guessing it's still slippery from my dick because I fucked the brunette first before moving on to her friend.

I'm high as a kite, a mix of narcotics and alcohol sloshing through my veins, but at least I remembered to wrap my dick before I took these two girls up to one of the bedrooms in Otis's house. That is one good thing Dillon taught me. I shudder at the thought of ever knocking a girl up. That is something that will never happen.

I'm never having kids.

My DNA is way too fucked up to consider bringing more mini-Reeves or mini-Saffrons into the world.

My blood boils, like it does anytime I think about Reeve or Saffron or Mom or Dillon. To think I used to look up to my dad. Want to be like him. Hung off Dillon's every word like he was some kind of god.

What a fucking joke, I think as I pull out of blondie and flop down beside her on my back. I grab my joint where I left it on the bedside table, light it up, and take a toke, inhaling deeply as my mind wanders over the shit show that is my so-called life.

Adults suck.

Every single adult in my life has either screwed me over or let me down. Dillon included.

He's as selfish as the rest of them. If he hadn't been such a cunt the night Vivien left Ireland, my entire life could have been completely different. If he had claimed his woman, Vivien never would have returned to Reeve. Maybe Reeve wouldn't have abandoned me then. I don't harbor any delusions he would have been with Saffron. That whore was one seriously crazy bitch. He clearly regretted letting her mess with

707

his life in such a destructive way. He never would have gotten with her if she permanently ruined things for him with his childhood sweetheart.

Saffron Roberts was a lying, cheating, stealing, whoring, good-for-nothing, gold-digging slut, and I hope she is rotting in the fiery pits of hell. It is nothing less than she deserves. That bitch didn't give a shit about me. I was a means to an end for her. When her blackmail backfired, she was willing to terminate her pregnancy without giving her baby, *me*, a second thought. Then she took drugs while pregnant, uncaring how that might impact the baby growing inside her.

She truly was a selfish bitch.

"Babe." The brunette slinks over to me, pressing her nonexistent tits to my side and pinning me with fake doe eyes. "I need your cock again."

I shake my head and swat her hand away when she reaches for my dick.

"Ah, come on," the blonde says, getting in on the act again. She crawls between my legs, pushing them apart. "It's not every day we get to screw a rock legend's son. We need to make the most of it."

I explode, venting all my aggression in the wrong direction. "Get the fuck away from me, you slut." I shove her shoulder with my foot, pushing her back, and swing my legs around, planting my feet on the edge of the bed. Looking over my shoulder, I glare at both of them. "You're both whores and lousy lays. All women are gold-digging sluts with ulterior motives." I jab my finger in their direction. "You have just proven that fact." Blondie scowls, opening her mouth to retaliate, no doubt. "Shut your skanky mouth, and get the fuck out."

"Fuck you, asshole," she says, climbing to her feet.

"I told you we should've held out for the other twin," the brunette says, flipping me the bird as she scrambles to her feet, hurriedly pulling her slutty dress back on.

Her words roll over me like water off a duck's back, but I know they might register and hurt when I'm sober. "My brother wouldn't touch either of you even if you paid him," I say, turning around on the bed and sitting up against the headrest.

"Doesn't say much about you, does it?" Blondie retorts, squeezing her massive tits into a bra that looks way too small to contain them before shimmying into a tight black dress.

"No underwear. How classy," I snarl, pulling my boxers and jeans on. Reaching down, I swipe my T-shirt off the floor and yank it over my head.

"Loser," Blondie says, glowering at me as she yanks the door open, and the two girls storm out into the hallway.

"Good riddance," I mumble as I stand, thrusting my hand out to hold on to the wall when my body sways and the room spins.

"Holy shit," Otis says, appearing in the doorway a few seconds later. "What the hell did you say to the girls? I have never seen Nellie so angry. Mahlik will kick your ass if you hurt his sister."

"Which one is his sister?" I ask, not realizing one of the girls was related to my new friend.

There is a hierarchy at the snobby private school I attend with my brother. The token scholarship kids stick together and don't usually mix with the rich kids. Not sure where I fit in the scheme of things. Or life, in general, anymore. I only hung around with the popular kids because of my brother. But they are his friends, not mine. It's time to change things up, and the truth is, I feel more at ease around Otis, Mahlik, and their crew than I do my so-called own kind.

Mahlik lives in a foster home and Otis lives in this rundown two-story three-bed two-bath house in a less than desirable part of LA. Mom would throw a hissy fit if she knew I was here, but she thinks I'm tucked up in bed, licking my wounds and nursing my sore feelings.

Well, fuck that shit.

I'm done wallowing. Done letting the sins of the past impact me.

I'm singing my own song now, and if my parents and East don't like it, tough shit.

Otis and Mahlik are good people, and they keep it real.

"The brunette," Otis says, halting the rambling thoughts in my head.

"She has no tits," I blurt, shoving my feet into my boots and trying to ignore the way my eyes can't focus. "And they were both shitty lays."

Otis barks out a laugh. "You are way more talkative when you're trashed, man." He slams his hand down on my back. "We should definitely do this again."

"For sure."

Somehow, I stumble out of the house and manage to call an Uber to take me home.

I have lost all sense of time, but I don't care. My head is buzzing, my body is tripping, and I feel alive. Grabbing a bottle of JD from the liquor cabinet in the living room, I wander out to the garden, casting a quick glance at my cell phone as I stumble across the grounds at the back of our house. I have a shit ton of missed calls and messages from my brother. A pang of longing slaps me in the face before I wrangle that shit back into a lockbox where it belongs.

Easton is not my brother or my friend or even my cousin.

He is nothing. He can be nothing to me.

He is the physical representation of everything I will never be, and I can't stomach looking at him.

Opening the whiskey with my teeth, I swallow a large mouthful, welcoming the burn as it glides down my throat. I keep drinking as I head in the direction of the memorial garden, growing more and more angry as my thoughts churn and rage reignites in my veins.

"You're an asshole," I roar when I reach the garden with the tree replanted from our old house and the bench Dillon lovingly carved from wood. Two plaques are nailed to the bark. One with Reeve's and Lainey's names on it and the second one is in remembrance of Lori. My first mother. "You're both assholes," I amend, leveling a glare at Lori's name. "You lied to me until you were forced into telling me the truth," I snarl, tipping my head back and shouting at the stars, hoping wherever she is Lori is hearing this. "You let this happen. You were too soft on Saffron. You let her get away with too much, and then you passed me off to Vivien like a sack of old clothes when you could no longer care for me. You left me too!"

My head whips around, and I narrow my eyes as I glare at Reeve's name. I advance toward the tree, trampling the flowers underfoot. "But you." I jab my finger into the wood, wishing I'd had the forethought to bring a screwdriver with me so I could chisel through his name and erase it in the way I wish I could erase it from my brain. I try to pry the plaque from the bark, but it's nailed in tight, and it doesn't budge, no matter how hard I tug at it. "You were a pathetic, weak prick who cheated on the woman he professed to love and abandoned his baby son. Why?!" I roar before knocking back more whiskey. "How could you give me away? I was just an innocent baby."

A sob rips from my throat, but I shut that shit down. None of them deserves my tears. Only derision. I bark out a laugh as I glance down at the colorful flower beds, remembering how East and I helped Vivien to plant this memorial garden after we moved into our new house. Fleur was young, but she helped too. What a joke. To think I used to find solace coming out here and talking to my dad and Lori. Now I know neither of them deserved it.

Fueled with a fresh layer of rage, I let out a roar as I flip the bench and drop to my knees. I dig up the flowers with my nails, ripping out roses and shrubs and other colorful flowers, mashing them between my hands until they are completely destroyed, growing more enraged with every passing second as I remember how I used to draw comfort from coming out here and talking to them. I hate how fucking gullible I was.

But no more. My eyes are fully open now.

"Stop!"

My head jerks up at the sound of my brother's voice. Easton is jogging across the grass in sleep shorts with his feet shoved into untied sneakers. His fist is closed around something in his hand, and the expression on his face is a mix of pity and anger. I sit back on my butt and lift my knees, bringing the bottle of JD to my lips as I survey the carnage around me with a satisfied grin.

"What the fuck is wrong with you?" East yells, and I feel a sense of pride I got him to raise his voice. He's always so fucking happy and amicable and far too laid-back. It's good to see him rattled.

"What the fuck is wrong with *me*?" I snap, champing at the bit for this fight that's been brewing for days. I clamber awkwardly to my feet, still struggling to focus, and it's an effort to remain upright.

"Look at the state of you, bro. You're totally wasted." He dangles my bag of goodies from his fingers. "How could you do this? This will kill Mom. You know what she went through with Reeve, and Saffron was a known junkie." He takes a step toward me, pain comingling with concern on his face. "This isn't the way to deal with things. This is a one-way trip to hell, and I'm not going to stand by and watch you throw your life away."

I laugh. He still doesn't get it. "You don't get a say."

"The hell I don't. I'm your brother. You might have forgotten what that means, but I haven't."

"I hate you," I roar, throwing the bottle of JD at his head. He ducks down, and it soars over him, landing somewhere in the grass behind him.

"You don't."

"I do." I march toward him, putting my face all up in his. "I hate you. If you didn't exist, if Vivien didn't exist, he wouldn't have abandoned me."

East sucks in a sharp gasp. "You don't mean that. Take it back."

"No." I shove his shoulders, understanding I am in no fit state to fight my brother but uncaring. I need to hit something, and his smug face will do. I swing my arm around, but he easily blocks me, wrapping his hand around my fist and staring at me in shock.

"What the fuck, Bo? Stop this."

With my free hand, I punch him in the stomach, but it lacks power because my limbs aren't cooperating and I can't pack any strength behind it. "I am sick of you always coming first," I hiss.

"C'mon, bro. That is not true, and you know it. Mom and Dad have always treated us equally."

I swing for him again, glancing the side of his jaw with my fist before he pushes me away. "Stop trying to fight me."

"He chose *you*!" I yell, wrapping an arm around my middle as intense pain jumps up and slaps me from within. "He gave me up without any hesitation because he loved you and he loved Vivien. I was nothing to him!" I roar, not even aware tears are rolling down my face until salty moisture trickles over my lips. "It's a miracle he didn't agree to let Saffron abort me. He would have done the world a favor if he did."

"No, Bo. No." East lunges toward me, and I seize the opportunity, thrusting my fist in his face and landing a decent blow to his nose. East stumbles back, losing his footing as he trips on one of his laces, tumbling to the ground.

I jump on top of him, pummeling him with my fists. "I hate you. I hate he picked you. I hate I will always be second best. That I'm never good enough for anyone." I lash out with my words and my fists, and East just takes it. "Fight me, you coward!" I land a particularly vicious punch to his temple, and his eyes darken as murderous rage finally sweeps over his features.

Features I hate are so similar to mine.

Then it's on.

We roll around the garden, punching, kicking, and grappling with one another, and it's the most alive I have felt in weeks. Pain rattles around my skull and spreads across my stomach as East enters the spirt of things, but I don't care, continuing to throw punches and shout insults at my brother.

"What the fuck are you doing?" Dad says, appearing out of nowhere and grabbing me off Easton.

I thrash about in his arms, continuing to expel insults and expletives as I watch Vivien help East to his feet. My brother is clutching his side as Mom inspects his swollen nose and the bruise mushrooming on his cheek. I'd say I fared the same, if not worse, but I don't care. It felt good to do that.

"This has got to stop," Mom says, imploring me with her tone and the pleading expression on her face. "Please, Bodhi. Please stop this."

"He was fighting me too!" I yell, struggling to get out of the vise-grip Dad has me in. "But, of course, you take his side! Everyone is always on his side."

"That is not true, and you know it," Dad says.

"Bullshit! I always come last! Reeve sacrificed me so he could have Vivien and

SIOBHAN DAVIS

Easton. He didn't give a shit what happened to me. Abandoning their baby was so easy for him and Saffron."

"We need to talk about this—properly talk about this," Mom says, walking closer to me. "There is so much you don't know. Things you need to let us tell you."

Tears stream down her face, and for a second, I hate I'm the one who put them there. But it quickly passes; incinerated by the raging anger that burns continuously through my veins. "I know you took me in out of pity and guilt. Did it make you feel less foolish, Vivien? Was it your way of proving you were better than them? Take in the poor orphan and appease the knowledge you were the reason my father gave me away. Raise me with the golden boy and pretend like you weren't the catalyst for all of this."

"That's enough," Dad snaps, tightening his hold around my body, but I'm only hitting my stride now.

"You were such a dumb bitch, Vivien. You let both of them play you, and you continuously forgave them. You're as weak as Reeve."

East pulls his mom into a hug, tugging her back as he glares at me with something akin to loathing.

Good.

At least the feeling is mutual now.

"This isn't you," she says, hastily swiping at the tears coursing down her face. "This is anger and whatever drugs you pumped into your body because I see your eyes rolling in your head. I know you're on something, and it's okay. It will be okay."

I laugh because she is so fucking delusional. "I'm just living up to my birthright. Reeve threw you under the bus for a high, and so will I. I might not look like her, but Saffron's blood flows through my veins. I was always destined to be a junkie. Nothing was ever going to save me from this fate."

"No one believes that bullshit," Dad says, turning me around and grabbing me by the upper arms. "Least of all you. You are your own person, Bodhi. You are not the sum of the people who gave you life."

"You're such a fucking hypocrite!" I yell. My stomach churns, and nausea crawls up my throat. "You turned to sex, drugs, and booze when you discovered the truth, or did I misinterpret that part of the movie?"

"Don't make the same mistakes I did. You are smarter and more focused than I was at your age."

"I'm worthless," I admit, all the fight leaving me as nausea washes over me in heady waves. "No one wants me. Everyone is destined to leave me or push me away. You guys took me in out of pity. You don't really care for me. I'm a way to assuage your guilt. Nothing more. So just leave it alone. Nothing any of you can say will ever make me believe otherwise."

My gaze bounces between them, and I feel numb inside, which is weird because I'm a giant mass of pain. Every cell in my body is drowning under the torrent of anguish obliterating me from the inside out.

I want it to stop.

All of it.

"You know I'm right, so let me accelerate this next part of the process," I say before I jerk to the side and puke my guts up all over the ruined memorial garden.

712

CHAPTER 6
VIVIEN

"THAT'S the last of the trash," Audrey says, entering the kitchen with Ash in tow. They are carrying black sacks filled to the brim with dirty paper plates and plastic silverware from the kids' party. In addition to our gang, we had twenty boys and girls from Fleur's and Melody's classes this year, and it was absolute mayhem. The guys are supervising the trunk-or-treat taking place in our driveway, and then it will be time for all the outsiders to leave. I can't say I'm sorry. It has been hard to enter into the spirit of Halloween this year with the way things are with Bodhi.

It's hard to function, period, right now.

I am not sleeping well, and my appetite is virtually nonexistent. I am so worried about Bodhi and worried about Easton because he's pushing his own feelings aside to try to be there for his brother, and I know he doesn't want to add to our stress. That only compounds the guilt and the fear. The only saving grace is the girls seem oblivious. Bodhi is acting normal with them, and I'm grateful for that small mercy.

My children are the only reason I get out of the bed each morning, and I won't stop trying for them.

My husband is the other reason.

Dillon is my rock, holding me and loving me every night as we confide our fears in one another. I crawl into bed a wreck each night, collapsing in his arms, and we lose ourselves in one another, needing kisses and touches to remind us of who we are and the things we have overcome already. Then we sit and talk for hours, and every night, my husband papers over the cracks in my heart, reminding me I'm not in this alone.

We haven't even spoken much to anyone outside the family. One, I don't want to worry them either. And two, I think it's hard for anyone to relate unless you are living with this. Dillon and I are even closer now. A feat I never thought possible because we're as close as a couple can be, but in a weird way, this situation is strengthening our bond on an even deeper level. I love how he is the strength I need to get through this, but he's also not afraid to be vulnerable with me, sharing his fears and concerns and letting me bolster him in the same way he's doing for me.

It's how I know we will survive this. We will get our boys through this. Love has to be enough. And we won't ever stop fighting for our family.

I have never been more in love or more in awe of my husband.

"Are you getting work done in the garden?" Ash asks, interrupting my inner monologue. She squints in the direction of the memorial garden as she peers through the window.

Dillon laid a temporary fence around the area until we have time to repair the damage Bodhi wreaked on the space. "Bodhi destroyed the memorial garden a couple nights ago when he was trashed," I calmly explain as I open the refrigerator and grab a fresh bottle of white wine. "Dillon and I had to pull him and East off one another in the middle of the night. They were throwing punches and wrestling on the ground like they weren't as close as twins."

"Shit." Ash dumps her garbage bag at the door to the laundry room and walks toward me with concern shining in her eyes. "That's a bloody nightmare, and so unlike my nephews. I take it things aren't any better on that score?"

I shake my head, swallowing over the thick, painful lump in my throat, as Audrey removes three clean wineglasses from the overhead cupboard. "Things are terrible, and Bodhi won't speak to any of us. It's like I don't even know my own son anymore. It's like a stranger is wearing his skin. My sweet, intense, deep thinker has disappeared, replaced with a boy who is so angry he has forgotten how much he is loved." A strangled sound rips from my mouth, and my lower lip wobbles as I struggle to contain my emotions.

"Ah, Viv. Don't cry, babe." Ash drapes her arms around me as Audrey pours the wine, pinning me with sympathetic eyes.

Audrey knows more than most because we sought out her advice. We needed her knowledge of mental health and the law to understand our options. That was a depressing conversation for sure.

"I saw him outside with the girls a few minutes ago," Audrey says, handing me a glass of wine. "Melody was on his shoulders, and he was holding Fleur's hand as they went from car to car, so all isn't lost." She hands a wineglass to Ash when she eases out of our embrace. "That sweet boy is still in there. You can still get through to him. Try not to lose all hope."

We take our glasses and head to the living room to wait for the guys. Dillon has some surprise lined up, and he told us to wait here until we were called. I really am not in the mood this year, but Dillon insisted we party it up like usual, and I'm glad he was so pushy. It's important to keep things normal for the girls, and a night of wine and catching up with my girlfriends is just what I need.

"Did you talk to that therapist I recommended?" Audrey asks when we are settled on the comfy couch.

I'm wearing the Sandy costume I made—a tight off-the-shoulder black top, matching black leggings, a belt with a gold and black center clasp, and open-toed red sandals with a high heel—while Audrey and Ash are dressed as Frenchie and Betty from *Grease*. I curled my hair and temporarily dyed it blonde with one of those wash-out color spray cans, to really look the part.

Dillon is wearing a tight black T-shirt, black pants, and boots—it didn't take much for him to transform himself into a white-blond version of Danny Zuko. Jamie is dressed as Kenickie, and Alex is Doody. It's the first year all three couples have coordinated outfits, and I have a sneaky suspicion this is all tied into my husband's surprise.

Did I mention how much I love him and what a lucky bitch I am to call him my man?

Audrey peers at me expectantly, and I try to focus my wandering mind. "Yes. Dillon and I met with her yesterday. Bodhi is still refusing to see her, but she is going to come over one night next week and see if he'll talk to her then." She also recommended a therapist for Dillon and me to speak to, and we have an appointment arranged for next week. We need all the help and support we can get because we're floundering, so I'm willing to try just about anything if I think it will work.

"Good luck with that plan," Ash says, kicking off her heels and pulling her feet up onto the couch. "I remember how much of a nightmare Dil was when he went off the rails. My parents tried everything to help him, but it was like talking to a brick wall." Her brow puckers, and her nose scrunches up. "Actually, it was worse than that. A wall doesn't have an attitude and lie to your face."

"We can't sit by and do nothing. He's doing drugs, and he's drunk every night. He's full of self-hatred, and I'm so worried about him."

Ash sits up straighter, leveling me with a troubled stare. "You don't think he plans to hurt himself, do you?"

"He's already hurting himself, Ash, and yes, I'm worried about suicide." I set my glass down and bury my head in my hands, drawing deep breaths as I try not to descend into a full-on anxiety attack. I can scarcely swallow over the messy ball of emotion clogging my throat, and I'm clinging to my sanity by my fingernails.

Audrey runs a soothing hand up and down my back.

"Can you force him into rehab or therapy?" Ash asks. "If you are genuinely worried he might try to kill himself, are there legal measures you can adopt?"

"You'd think there would be," Audrey says in a clipped tone as I lift my head and try to compose myself. "California law states minors over twelve can be forced into rehab; however, if a professional determines the child is mature enough to participate in the decision, they often defer to the kid. Most kids don't want to go to rehab, so they say they didn't mean it and they're not addicted. There is a seventy-two-hour emergency hold for a minor if they are gravely disabled, like when there is an acute medical event. I have seen cases where kids have OD'd several times, some were even clinically dead for a short period, and the courts still refused to sanction the hold order or let the parents sign them into rehab. I understand why some of these measures were put in place, but the whole system is wrong. Parents' hands are really tied in these situations."

It's not anything Audrey hasn't told us already. She was the first person we called the morning after the garden incident. What she explained left us feeling so impotent. Powerless to do anything to help our son. At least if there was something we could do, it would feel like we were trying and maybe making some progress. But there is little we can do except sit and watch this unfold—however it's going to unfold —and it's killing me slowly.

715

I feel like I'm dying inside.

My kids are my world, and to know one of them is suffering and in so much pain and I can do nothing to stop it or help him is unbearable. Easton is hurting too, but he's trying to put a brave face on, and I hate that for him. His feelings matter too, and I'm trying to be there for both my boys, yet I feel like I'm failing them.

There is no rulebook or parental guidebook for dealing with this. Winging it is not in my nature, but we have little choice. We are ambling around in the dark, blind and terrorized, unsure if we're going the right way or heading toward a black hole we won't be able to crawl back out of.

"I could try talking to him," Ash offers. "You know my past. I tried to kill myself, and I regretted it almost instantly. Maybe my experience might help."

"I don't know, Ash." I swirl the wine in my glass. "It might just put more ideas in his head." I knock back a mouthful of wine. "Or maybe it would help. Maybe he might open up to someone outside our immediate family." I shrug because I have never felt more helpless or more clueless. "It's hard to know what the best thing to do is. We are walking on eggshells around him. Dillon has tried to break down his walls. Out of all of us, he can relate the most to what Bodhi is going through. But Bodhi is angry with Dil too, and he just doesn't want to hear it. He won't even go into the studio if his dad is there."

"Mom."

We jerk our chins up at the same time, the three of us looking over at Easton standing in the doorway.

"Hey, love." I force a smile on my face, hating that smiling no longer comes naturally.

"Can I talk to you for a minute?"

"Absolutely." I set my wineglass down and stand.

CHAPTER 7
VIVIEN

"YOU STAY," Ash says. "We'll go see what the guys are up to."

Easton shakes his head. "Dad said if you even attempt to peek he's locking you in the laundry room for the rest of the night so you'll miss out on all the fun."

"Your father is going to get a swift kick in the arse when I see him," Ash replies.

"Let them do their thing," Audrey says, topping off Ash's wineglass. "It's not often we get time to ourselves without the kids or the guys. I say we make the most of it."

"I won't keep Mom long," Easton says as I walk toward him.

"Enjoy your party," Audrey says, waving at him.

"Don't do anything I wouldn't do!" Ash calls out.

"I have a license to do whatever I want, so…" East quips, waggling his brows at his auntie.

Ash barks out a laugh. "That's my nephew!"

I appreciate they keep it light and neither of them references the large purple bruise on East's cheek or his swollen nose. Thankfully, it wasn't broken, and though both of them walked away with bruises and cuts, no one suffered serious injury. For that, I'm grateful. "I hope that costume comes with a mask," I say when I step out into the hallway, tugging on the black cape flowing over my son's broad shoulders.

East closes the door behind me. "It does, but it's creepy as fuck, and I didn't want to scare the little kids." He lifts a shoulder. "Can you walk me to my car? I'm already late, and Hollis is a stickler for punctuality."

I'm not sure I like the sound of his latest girlfriend. All of her family are snobs, and she sounds a little too controlling for my like. She has lasted longer than most of them, and I get the sense he's more serious about Hollis than any girl that has come before. And there have been a lot. E is a serial dater, and there seems to be no shortage of girls willing to go out with him.

Bodhi is the complete opposite. He hasn't had a girlfriend, at least not to our knowledge, though I am sure there are girls or maybe guys. He's too handsome not to garner interest. We are very open about sexuality, but neither of our sons have come outright and said they are hetero or otherwise, and we would never ask. They are entitled to their privacy, and if there's something we need to know, I'm sure they will tell us in time.

"What is Hollis dressing as?" I ask, keeping step beside my son, which is no easy feat with his long-legged strides. East is as tall as Dillon now, and if he keeps growing, he will end up taller, something he loves teasing his dad about.

"She's an angel to my devil." He grins, waggling his brows as he grabs a scary demonic red mask with horns and a tall black pitchfork from inside the hall door.

"Will your brother be at this party?" I ask, my stomach churning with anxiety at the thought of the mayhem Bodhi could indulge in on a night like tonight.

"That's what I wanted to talk to you about," East says, looping his arm in mine. "Bo will be at the same house party. He left already, but you don't need to worry. I won't drink, and I am going to watch out for him."

I slam to a halt, peering up at my son with tears in my eyes. "You are such a good son, Easton. And a good brother, but this is not your responsibility. It's not your job to keep Bodhi in check. You have your own life to lead, and we want you to live it."

"I know, Mom, but I can't not do it. I will always have his back, especially when he's hurting so bad. I am worried about him but super pissed too. The stuff he said to you the other night is not right, and it made me so angry, but I know he doesn't mean it. Like he doesn't mean the shit he said to me. He might have abandoned me, but I won't abandon him."

I fling myself at Easton, bundling him into a tight hug. "You are so loyal and so strong." I lean back and raise my hand, palming one side of his cheek. It's still so weird to feel a hint of stubble on his face. In my mind, Easton and Bodhi are still my little boys. "You make me proud every day, East. I know this isn't who Bodhi is, and he needs us to be strong for him. But we are here for you too. I know the truth has upset you as well."

"It's worse for my brother."

"It's not a competition. You are entitled to your feelings, and they matter to me and your dad. You can talk to us about it. You have always idolized Reeve. I can only imagine what you must be thinking and feeling now."

He shrugs, and a muscle clenches in his jaw. I rub his hand, and maybe we shouldn't have started this conversation now, but I need Easton to know we are worried about him too. I know I asked him to be strong, but he has a right to be mad or upset or confused or all of those things.

The situation with Bodhi doesn't negate what Easton is going through.

"I feel guilty, Mom," he says, almost in a whisper. "Bo was right when he said Reeve gave him up for us. That was wrong on so many levels. How could he do that? Especially after the way Simon treated him and Dillon. I just don't get it."

I squeeze his hand. "Reeve isn't here to tell us for sure, but I think he knew I wouldn't have been able to take Saffron's child in at that time in my life. I think he was afraid if he kept Bodhi, he would lose us, and he feared he would come to resent him and neglect him the way Simon did to Reeve."

"He didn't even give you the chance to consider it though. You're a good person, Mom. I know you wouldn't have turned Bodhi away. Dad thinks so too."

"You spoke to your father about this?" Dillon hasn't said anything to me, which isn't like him.

"We talked briefly while we were outside with the kids."

Ah, that explains it. "I'm not sure what I would've done. I hated Saffron, and I was very confused over my feelings for Reeve and Dillon. I like to think I would have taken him in, but Lori was there. She was his flesh and blood too. I might have considered that the best option."

Easton shakes his head. "You wouldn't have, Mom. You knew Reeve inside and out. If you'd known Bodhi existed, you would have taken him in. You loved Reeve more than you hated Saffron, and I know you'd never have turned an innocent baby away."

Tears prick my eyes, and I have never felt prouder than in this moment. "I love you, E. I am so proud of the man you are becoming."

Easton envelops me in a warm hug. "I love you too, Mom. Bodhi loves you as well. He's too angry to do anything but lash out now, but I know what's in his heart. He loves you and Dad. He loves our family. We just need to remind him of that."

"We will, son." I ease back, smiling up at him, needing to get these words out because I don't want Easton paying the price for Reeve's sins. "Reeve loved you so much, Easton. I don't ever want you to doubt that. I know it pained him to give up Bodhi. I know he never stopped thinking about him. It doesn't make it right, but I don't want you carrying misplaced guilt. Reeve always wanted a family. It had been denied to him growing up, and he'd led quite a lonely existence, outside the times he was with me and your grandparents. His greatest wish was to be a father and to have a family of his own. You gave him that. *We* gave him that. I hate what he did to Bodhi, and I don't know if I can ever forgive him for his actions, but I am glad Reeve got to experience family life with us before he died. He wasn't a bad person. He was a good person who made bad decisions, and a lot of that was because of the neglect he endured as a child. He craved love, and it often blinded him to the facts. The best way we can honor Reeve and support Bodhi is to love Bodhi with all of our hearts and to be patient and kind as he struggles to deal with the truth."

"I know, Mom. I am trying to be there for him even when he makes it hard."

I lean up and kiss his cheek. "We can't ask any more of you, Easton, and you are not shouldering this alone. You come to us anytime with anything. All we want is what is best for both our sons."

CHAPTER 8
EASTON

"WOW, your brother sure seems determined to party hard," Lewis says, as we stand at the corner of the room watching Bodhi knocking back beers like they're water. A posse of girls from school surrounds him, fawning over him and vying for his attention. His bruised face and the shiner he's sporting—thanks to yours truly—only seem to add to the appeal. Some girls are weird.

Otis, Mahlik, and the rest of that crew are lapping up the additional popularity Bodhi has brought to their door, looking like their shit doesn't stink. I honestly couldn't care less, except for theyscene they have introduced my brother to. "I don't like it. It's not him. Bo has been strictly antidrug, and now it's like he's forgotten every single code he lived by."

"It's probably just a phase."

Lewis slaps me on the back, oblivious to the turmoil churning in my gut. Although he's my best buddy, I haven't told him what's going down at home. The only person who has a clue is Hollis, but she hasn't pried since that day in the cafeteria, and I haven't volunteered any more information. She didn't need to ask me to know it was Bodhi I got in a fight with. I'm pretty sure the whole damn school knows just by looking at our faces.

"You should cut loose," he adds. "No point in both of us drinking soda. You can leave your car here tonight, and I'll pick you up tomorrow to come get it."

Lewis is on the football team with me, and he takes it very seriously, rarely partying, even after a win. I like a few beers, as much as the next guy, but I try not to overdo it. I work hard to keep in shape so I'm at the top of my game, and being healthy is important to me. I had plans to go a little crazy tonight, but that was before Bodhi and I got in a fight and beat the crap out of one another.

Now, I can't drink. Not when Bo is already smashed and showing no signs of slowing down. One of us has to remain sober. "Thanks for the offer, man, but I need to remain sober. I told Hollis's dad I'd drive her home, and I promised my mom I would watch out for my brother."

"Bodhi is lucky to have you because I gotta say it. He's asking for trouble hanging around with those dudes. I hear they're into all kinds of shit."

"I don't doubt it." I just hope Bodhi has enough sense left not to get mixed up with worse shit. However, I'm not feeling overly confident as I watch him smoke a joint while a hot redhead grinds on his lap, practically dry humping him in front of everyone.

"Let's go find the girls," I say, needing a few minutes reprieve.

We move into the next room, and I find my girl in the middle of the dance floor, shaking her tempting booty and curling her fingers in my direction. Lewis's current fuck buddy happens to be Hollis's best friend and the girl hosting the party. Chelle is dancing in the same circle as Hollis, so we join them.

"Baby, you're here at last," she slurs, flinging her arms around my neck and pressing her tits up against me. "I thought you'd ditched me."

"Never, babe." My gaze roams over her gorgeous body, both loving and hating how much skin she's showing. If it was all for me, no problem whatsoever. But the tight bra top shows way too much cleavage, and the little tutu skirt barely covers her ass. She has glittery white angel wings strapped to her back, and she went heavy on the makeup tonight. I prefer her when she wears less, but I can't deny she looks hella hot. "You look gorgeous," I whisper in her ear, swaying my hips and rocking against her.

"And you're wearing far too many clothes." She pouts, running the tip of her finger up over the red muscle top covering my chest and arms.

"You picked this, remember." I circle my arm around her slim waist.

"We could always go to the bathroom and strip you of a few layers." She waggles her brows in a flirtatious manner as she simultaneously stumbles on her feet, and I have to steady her to keep her upright. She is still slurring her words, and her eyes are a little blurry.

"How much did you have to drink, babe?" I ask, moving us in time to the beat.

"Just some wine coolers. Oh, and a few vodka shots." She flips her fingers up. "Maybe four or five." Her brow puckers as she continues flipping fingers up. She giggles. "Possibly it was more like six or seven." She shrugs, like it's no biggie.

"How the hell did you drink that much in a couple hours?"

"I have been here since four. I came over to help Chelle get everything ready."

That makes more sense. She's clearly drunk, and though I'd love to take her upstairs and fuck her, I'm not having sex when she's not in a position to make any such decision.

She seems to have forgotten about it anyway, so we dance for a few songs, bumping and grinding against one another, kissing and making out, and I finally feel myself relaxing.

A while later, I head outside to the patio area to join my buddies. I pop my head into the main room on the way, checking to ensure Bo is okay. He has a girl draped on either side of him on the couch, and he's taking turns kissing and groping them. Bo isn't usually one for PDAs, and I have never known him to have a threesome.

Sure, he's hooked up with girls, but it's always singular, and he's never shown any interest in girls other than sex.

His eyes open as if I called him, and his head lifts, our gazes locking. A new, familiar snarl curves the corners of his lips as he flips me the bird. Pain dances across my chest as I push my way through the room and head outside. The fresh air is a welcome balm to my troubled soul, and I walk in the direction of my buddies, grateful to be away from the stifling atmosphere inside.

We leave our girls dancing inside as we sit around the pool, drinking beer and shooting the shit. Talk mostly centers around our next game, which is against our biggest rival. They beat us last year, and we are determined to nail their asses to the wall this time.

"What's up with you and Bo?" Niall asks, blowing smoke circles in the air as he passes the spliff to the guy beside him. "I thought you two were close." He gestures toward my face. "We all know you two got into it, but we don't know why. What went down?"

"It's none of your business," Lewis says, taking a quick drag of the joint. "Just drop it."

"Is it about Hollis?" Niall asks, arching a brow.

"Why the fuck would you think that?"

He kicks his legs out, crossing his feet at the ankles. "I saw them eye fucking one another in the hallway at school on Friday."

"Shut the fuck up," Lewis says. "You just love stirring shit." My best friend turns to face me. "Ignore him. He's an idiot."

"If you say so." Niall smirks at me like he knows something I don't.

His words piss me off enough that I get up five minutes later to go and check on my girlfriend. I head into the main room first, but Bodhi is nowhere to be seen. I storm over to his friends, folding my arms across my chest as I level a look at Mahlik. "Have you seen my brother?"

He looks me up and down, leaning back in his seat and crossing one leg over his knee. The redhead who was grinding on my brother's lap earlier is tracing her tongue up and down his neck, and I guess my brother's new sharing habit is a result of hanging out with these guys. I don't want to be judgmental when I don't know the guys, but I see how my brother is changing, and I don't like their influence on him.

"Answer the question," I snap, all out of patience.

"I don't know where Bo is, but even if I did, I wouldn't tell you." Mahlik turns to the redhead, claiming her lips in a hard kiss as he blatantly dismisses me.

Asshole.

I exit the room and head into the next one in search of Hollis. My heart crashes around my chest as I inspect the dance floor and the rest of the room, finding no sign of my girlfriend. I gulp back bile as a feeling of dread washes over me. Rubbing the back of my neck, I take a final scan of the room, spotting Chelle on my second inspection. I stalk toward her and press my mouth to her ear. "Where is Hollis?"

She pins me with bloodshot, unfocused eyes as she giggles, clinging to my arm. "I thought she was with you," she slurs, trying to drag me into dancing.

"Where did she go?" I ask, rapidly running out of patience.

"Try the guest bedroom," she says. "She usually stays in the pink one."

I maneuver my way out of the packed room, taking the stairs two at a time, while trying to ignore the acid crawling up my throat.

He wouldn't do this.

I know things are shit between me and Bodhi right now, but he wouldn't cross a line.

I'm not sure I could say the same about Hollis. She's drunk, and she was horny earlier, and I've been getting weird vibes off her all week.

I reach the long hallway on the second level, which I assume houses the bedrooms. I open and close doors, apologizing to the couples I interrupt. I'm down to the last two doors, one on either side of the hallway, when a familiar voice curses out loud, lifting all the hairs on the back of my neck. The sound came from the room on the left, and my hand flies to the door handle.

Without hesitation, I fling the door open and barge inside, pain tightening my chest when I find my girlfriend stark naked on the bed with her mouth gliding up and down my brother's cock.

"What the actual fuck?" I roar, clenching my hands into fists at my side.

Hollis shrieks, releasing Bo's cock from her mouth with a loud pop. Her red lipstick is smeared all over her face, and saliva pools around her mouth and dribbles down her chin.

"East," Hollis whispers, scrambling off the bed and walking toward me. "I can explain," she slurs, almost tripping over her feet.

My arm darts out to steady her before she takes a fall. I am so disappointed in her. I really liked her, and I thought she felt the same. Now, I'm wondering if she wasn't using me to get to my brother all along.

"She is drunk and not thinking clearly," I shout at my brother. "You shouldn't have come up here with her." I want to believe Hollis wouldn't have done this if she was sober, but I can't say that for sure. Bodhi knows better though. Dad drilled this into us. What's to stop her turning around and claiming he forced himself on her when she's so drunk I doubt she even remembers her own name?

"Tell yourself whatever you must to feel better, *brother*." Bo sneers as he wraps his hand around his dick, giving it a few pumps. "She's been coming on to me for weeks. Hollis was the one who came looking for me tonight. She knew exactly what she was doing."

"Baby. It's cool." Hollis runs her hand up my chest, and though my inclination is to push her away, she is completely smashed, and I won't hurt her.

She doesn't have such qualms though.

"It's true. I want him, but I want you too." She licks her lips and attempts to bat her eyelashes, and it's pathetic. Slowly, I peel her hand off me and step back. Bo is still on the bed, stroking his dick, and I'm disgusted with him and so fucking angry at both of them.

"I don't share," I snap at her. "And I don't date cheaters either."

"C'mon, babe." She makes a grab for me again, swaying on her feet, and I curse under my breath as I reach out to steady her again. "It'll be fun. I've always wanted to do twins." Her eyes light up, and I wonder what the hell I ever saw in this girl. "Don't pretend like you're shocked. It's practically your legacy."

Anger surges through my blood, and the vein in my neck pulses violently as I see

724

red. "What the fuck did you say?" I roar. "I bet Daddy would love to hear this. He thinks his little girl is such a good girl, but I know the truth. You're a self-serving slut, and I don't know what I ever saw in you."

Bodhi barks out a laugh, but I see the rage in his eyes and the tension in his jaw. He's as pissed at her comments as me, but his stubborn need to hurt me overrides his true feelings and doing the right thing. He narrows his eyes at Hollis. "If anything goes down, it goes down on my terms." Shifting his attention to me, he shoots me a sneering look. "Reeve and Dillon shared Mom. Maybe we should see what all the fuss is about?"

My blood boils as I glare at him. "You take that back." I prod my finger in the air, working hard not to lose my shit. "You can't say shit like that."

"I can say whatever the fuck I want."

"This whole fucking nightmare started because our dads both wanted Mom!" I shout. "Don't you dare make light of this or attempt to glaze over it. Be careful what you say next, Bo, because I'm all out of patience with you."

He glares at me, and tension bleeds into the air as we stare at one another with so much emotion and so many things left unsaid filling the space between us.

If you'd asked me even a month ago if anything could ever tear me and my brother apart, I would've laughed in your face and told you to stop saying stupid shit.

I cannot believe we are here and that things have sunk to a new low. In the grand scheme of things, Hollis doesn't matter one little bit. Except for what she represents. I don't know if I can ever forgive Bo for this. If our relationship will ever recover.

I know he's hurting, but that doesn't give him a free pass to betray me.

Bo breaks our staring contest first, ignoring me as he gestures toward Hollis. "Slut, get over here and finish sucking my dick."

And he's made his choice.

Pain mixes with frustration and anger inside me, and I'm close to the edge.

This was the time to pull back on the bullshit, and he made the wrong choice.

Hollis glances between Bo and me, biting on her lower lip in an obvious tell. Drunk as she is, she's not oblivious to the clear tension between me and my brother, and it's evident she's torn over what to do.

I decide to help her out because I'm not torn over this decision. "I'll make this easy for you," I tell her. "We're done. I want nothing more to do with you."

Bodhi barks out a laugh. "This wasn't your decision, and you know it, but you just can't bear to lose face, can you, *brother?*"

He's so full of shit. Even if Hollis does want him, there's no way he actually genuinely wants her and no way in hell her parents would let her date Bodhi with his current attitude.

His eyes roll back in his head as Hollis makes her decision and climbs up on the bed. Bodhi grabs her arm and pulls her to him. She giggles, kissing his neck as he purposely gropes her, deliberately trying to hurt me. "Tell me, Easton. How does it feel to take second place to me? How does it feel knowing I have taken something that belonged to you?"

"If this is some fucked-up form of revenge, you lose. Hollis doesn't matter." I grind my teeth to the molars, struggling to hold myself in check.

Hollis *doesn't* matter, but Bodhi does.

I can't believe he is doing this.

How can a person change so much so fast?

Where the fuck has my brother gone, and do we have any chance of ever getting him back?

"Really?" He quirks a brow as he lifts her up, positioning her over his body. "Little slut, ride my cock. Show my brother how much you matter."

I should walk away. My head screams at me to do that. To be the bigger man, but I can't make my limbs move. It's like I'm frozen in place, watching in horror as my brother drives the knife in deeper.

There will be no coming back from this.

His eyes never stray from mine as she lowers her pussy down over his cock. She moans, throwing her head back and rocking on top of him as rage becomes a festering inferno in my veins. Bodhi sits up, keeping her on his lap, sucking her tits and grinning at me like a maniac as he tugs her nipple with his teeth.

"Holy shit!" someone says from the open doorway behind me. "You guys, you gotta see this."

Hollis is so out of it as she rocks up and down on my brother's dick, she doesn't realize they have gained an audience. Bo laughs as he thrusts up inside her while glaring at me like he hates me. Laughter rings out behind me, and humiliation mixes with anger and pain as the hold on my control snaps, and I lunge across the bed, wrapping my arm around my brother's neck and dragging him away from my ex-girl-friend as Hollis screams.

CHAPTER 9
DILLON

"DIL." Vivien shakes me, and I slowly rouse from slumber as my phone vibrates across the top of the bedside table. "Babe, wake up."

"I'm awake," I mumble, reaching my arm out for my phone as I blink my eyes open.

"That's the second time it's rang in succession." She sits beside me as I haul myself upright and lean my back against the headboard.

I stifle a yawn as I swipe my finger along the screen, not recognizing the local number. I glance at the time. No good can come from an anonymous phone call at three a.m. I brace myself for bad news as I wrap my free arm around my wife, press the cell to my ear, and answer the call.

"Dad!" Easton's panicked tone greets my eardrums.

"What's going on?" I ask while mouthing "East" at Vivien.

"Bodhi and me got arrested. We need you to come get us."

A muscle clenches in my jaw as I instinctively tuck my wife closer to my side. "Where are you?"

"We're at the Hollywood station on Wilcox Avenue."

"I'll be there as soon as I can," I say, removing my arm from around Viv and flipping the covers off.

"Thanks, Dad." His voice sounds meek in a way that is not characteristic of my son.

The call ends, and I grip the phone tight in my hand as I swing my gaze to my worried wife. This is going to kill her, but there is no way to sugarcoat it. "The boys got arrested. I need to go get them."

"What?" she splutters, her eyes popping wide. "Why?"

"I don't know the details." I pull her into my arms and hold her. She's shaking, and I hate what this is doing to her, especially at a time when the foundation is growing at an unprecedented rate and she's so fucking busy. She should be enjoying seeing her hard work come to fruition, but instead she takes no pleasure from it because she's so worried about the boys. Bodhi in particular. "Stay here." I lean down and kiss her. "Try to sleep. You have a big meeting tomorrow."

"Fuck the meeting, and fuck staying here." She climbs over my lap and off the bed. "We're in this together. I'm coming with you."

I stand and pull her into my body because I'm very needy these past few weeks. I always have to be near her. To reassure myself she's okay. To offer what little comfort I can with my touches and my kisses. If I could take on all of her pain, I would because I hate seeing her so upset. "Are you sure?"

"One hundred percent. Let's go get our sons."

"I see the word is already out," I say, over a resigned sigh, when I drive up to the entrance of the Hollywood station, spotting a handful of paparazzi hanging around outside.

"I think those guys always hover around police stations hoping to land a juicy story."

"It's widely known cops are paid to leak tips to the vultures." I maneuver our car into a free spot at the curb alongside the drab redbrick building and kill the engine. Bobby and Leon pull up behind us in one of the security SUVs.

"Either way, there's no avoiding this."

I stretch across the console and kiss her. "We'll get the PR people on it in the morning and spin the narrative the way we always do." Lifting her hands, I kiss her fingers. "Don't stress it, Viv. The media are the least of our worries."

"I don't want this to make it harder for the boys."

"There is nothing they can say they haven't already said over the years. Fuck 'em, Viv. They don't matter."

"You're right. Let's go."

We exit the car at the same time, and I run around the hood to reach my wife, clasping her hand and keeping her close as we stride toward the entrance. Bobby and Leon exit their car and come up either side of us, shielding us from touch. The bloodsuckers notice us immediately, lifting their cameras and snapping pics as we make our way inside. We ignore the questions they throw at us, keeping our gazes firmly fixed ahead. As soon as our feet hit the ramp with the star-studded overlay, they hang back and leave us alone.

Inside, we talk to an unfriendly jackass behind the desk until Carson Park, the Lancaster family lawyer, shows up and takes control. Viv had called him when we were en route. His arrival is timely as I was seconds away from punching the unhelpful asshole glaring at me like I have committed some crime.

"Take a seat, and let me handle this," Carson says, pointing over our heads at the waiting area. "Keep your head down and your mouth shut, Dillon."

I glare at the dick. "Last I checked, you're not my father and I'm a grown man who knows how to control himself. Go do your job and get my kids." Sliding my arm around Vivien's shoulders, I turn us around before I land one on his annoying face.

I still hate him, but he's a damn good lawyer, and it made sense to retain his

728

services rather than having to move all our business to a new firm. We sold most of the assets in Simon Lancaster's portfolio to raise funds for the foundation Viv set up in the aftermath of Reeve's death, and Carson ensured that everything went through smoothly.

The Reeve Lancaster Foundation for Child Actors now boasts tons of famous donors including actors, directors, producers, movie studios, and other personnel involved in Hollywood. Along with the funds we raised, there is a decent pool of money to execute Vivien's vision for the foundation. Child advocacy consultants are the new norm on movie sets, with most of their salary being paid by the foundation.

The meeting Vivien is attending tomorrow afternoon is with the heads of most of the top studios in Hollywood to get their sign-off on the new governing rules for child actors which they have all agreed to support. It is the culmination of years of hard work to get to this point, and I am so proud of her.

She is truly making a difference.

Viv is ensuring child actors are kept safe and protected on movie sets with rules around the number of hours they can work per day. Guidelines are being implemented so that each actor is assigned a qualified tutor on set, ensuring their education doesn't fall behind. A list of restrictions on promotion and other activities that expose them to the seedier side of the industry has been drawn up. The advocacy consultant has a team of experts to call on should additional support be required, like therapists, doctors, trainers, and a whole host of medical and health specialists to ensure all their needs are being catered to while on set.

Not every studio is on board, and there is still a lot of work to do, with fundraising being an important ongoing activity. Viv, with help from Ash, has built a team of people around her to help to manage the foundation, but her personal workload in recent months has been extreme, and I can tell she is struggling to cope right now.

This is the very last thing she needs, and I am going to knock those boys' heads together when I get my hands on them.

We take seats on the hard, uncomfortable chairs in the waiting room, with Bobby and Leon flanking us, and settle down to wait.

Carson returns thirty minutes later with a surly Bodhi and a remorseful Easton in tow. Vivien rushes to hug the boys, and I want to slap sense into Bodhi when he stands there like a statue, refusing to hug his mother back. I don't know how much more of this behavior I can tolerate.

He can rant and rave at me as much as he likes, but he sure as shit is not going to disrespect his mum.

These past few weeks have made me realize, all over again, how much of a little prick I was to my parents back in the day. I even called Mum to apologize again. I didn't tell her how bad things are with Bodhi because I know she'll worry and there isn't much she can do from Ireland. She thinks it's normal teenage bullshit we're dealing with, and she even joked about karma biting me on the ass.

If only it were that simple.

"Are they being charged?" I ask Carson, in a low voice, as I watch Easton hug his mother, holding her for longer than usual to make up for his brother's failing.

Commendable as it is, that boy has got to stop taking on everyone else's responsibility.

Carson shakes his head. "I wrote a check to cover the damages and secured an agreement from the Peltzes' attorney that they won't be pressing charges."

"What did they do?"

"They were at the Peltz house attending a Halloween party. Apparently, they got into a fight over a young lady, and then others joined in. It got vicious, and someone called the police. There was a lot of damage to the bedroom and the upstairs hallway." Carson leans in close, talking into my ear. "Bodhi resisted arrest and refused drug and alcohol testing. He's lucky because he is clearly on something, and he smells like a brewery. If we hadn't arrived when we did, they most likely would've gotten a warrant to take a blood and urine sample."

I doubt much would've happened if it was confirmed he's high and drunk, but he doesn't need a record or the media spinning the bullshit they would if they discovered this truth. I can just imagine the headlines now and how they'd tie his behavior to Reeve's and Saffron's addictions.

"Thank you." I mean it sincerely. Carson might be a pain in the ass to deal with, but he's a shrewd, skillful pain in the ass.

He nods. "You know I value your family business, and I apologize if I was out of line earlier. You're not always known for your restraint."

"I know, but I'm not an imbecile either. You need to give me some credit."

"Noted. You and Vivien should stop by the office soon. I'll be retiring next summer, and my son is taking over the practice. I'd like to introduce you to him and start handling the transfer."

I quirk a brow. "I thought you'd retire the day they carted your dead ass out on a stretcher."

He chuckles. "So did I." He clamps a hand on my shoulder. "But it was either that or get a divorce, and I love my wife. I think she has suffered enough. Besides, none of us are getting any younger."

Isn't that the truth.

"I will leave you to take these young men home. I trust they'll have learned a lesson."

That's highly debatable in Bodhi's case, but I don't articulate the thought.

We walk in silence outside, all of us keeping our heads down and ignoring the larger throng of paps on the sidewalk as we make our way to the car.

"I'm sorry," East says when I have pulled away from the curb.

"What happened?" Viv swivels in her seat, staring at our sons in the back seat.

I glance at Bodhi through the mirror. He's staring out the side window with a newly familiar apathetic look on his face, but he's not nearly as indifferent as he'd like us to believe. He holds himself stiffly, and a muscle throbs in his cheek as he grinds his jaw while glaring at the outside world like he's pissed at everything and everyone.

And I get it. I haven't forgotten those feelings. I just wish I knew how to get through to my son. I wish my experiences could connect us in a way where I'm in a position to support him and help him. But nothing I could say will get through to him. Tough as it is to accept, he needs to process these feelings and go through the pain in order to come out on the other side.

All we can do is let him know we love him and that we are here for him.

I return my attention to the road, casting a quick glance at my other son. East is equally as tense and ignoring his brother too. His brow puckers, and he scrunches his nose, like he always does when he's thinking. I only noticed recently how I do the same. Genetics are fascinating.

"Is someone going to answer me?" Vivien says, a hint of her anger and frustration breaking through.

I reach across the console and squeeze her hand. "Maybe we should wait until we get home to have this conversation."

"He fucked my girlfriend," Easton blurts, shocking both of us.

"Hollis?" Viv says, her gaze bouncing between East and Bodhi.

"She's a slut," Easton adds. "Which makes her perfect for *him*." He snarls as he glares at Bodhi.

Bodhi turns his head, smirking at his brother, and I'm tempted to stop the car and take both of them outside to beat some sense into them.

"Shrinks would have a field day with you and all your mommy issues," he adds as Vivien says, "Easton! That's enough."

Ignoring Vivien, he continues. "And that's before they get to the daddy issues. You're just like them. Selfish, an addict, and incapable of loyalty. I have done nothing but watch out for you from the moment we met."

His voice elevates a few levels, and Viv and I exchange a troubled look. I want to tell him to zip it until we get home so we can discuss it fully when I'm not driving, but East has been bottling shit up for weeks, and I don't get to dictate the timing.

If he needs to get this off his chest, I'm not going to stop him.

In a way, having this conversation in the car is perfect. It's not like they can avoid it when we're trapped within such tight confines.

Pain stabs me through the heart as I see how East is literally trembling with anger.

He jabs his finger in Bodhi's direction. "My parents took you in and treated you as an equal part of this family. All they have ever done is loved you and supported you. They have given you everything, and you don't get to treat me or them like this!" he shouts.

"Pull over," Viv says as I'm already slowing down. I pull off to the side of the road and kill the engine. We aren't far from home, but East is on the verge of a meltdown, and it can't wait.

"You're a disloyal prick, and I hate you!" Easton roars as Vivien climbs out of the passenger seat and opens the back door.

Bodhi has an impassive expression on his face, and I don't even know if his brother's words are registering.

"As long as I live, I will never forgive you for this," East says. "From now on, you're dead to me."

CHAPTER 10
VIVIEN

"HOW ARE YOU HOLDING UP?" Audrey asks as I pile more pancakes on the plate on autopilot.

"I'm not," I truthfully admit. "Bodhi is even more withdrawn. It's been a week since they were arrested, and he hasn't spoken one word to Dillon or me. Easton is still mad at him, and they aren't talking. Not that I blame E. It was a huge betrayal, and he has every right to his anger. The therapist came on Tuesday, and that was a shit show."

I pour more batter into the mold on the skillet, staring into space as I recall one of the worst weeks ever.

I've endured a lot of heartbreaking things in my life, so I don't say that easily.

"East spoke with her but didn't want to talk about it with us after, which we had to respect," I explain. "He was withdrawn and quiet the rest of the night. Then Dillon frog-marched Bodhi into the living room where he sat in silence for a half hour while the therapist tried to coax him into talking to no avail."

"Jesus, Viv."

"He refuses to eat meals with us. He leaves for school early and doesn't come home until after midnight most nights. He removed the GPS tracker from his truck and his cell so we have no clue where he is or what he's up to. He's either drunk or high when he returns or sometimes both. Last night, Dillon confiscated the keys to his truck because we're terrified he's going to wrap it around a pole and kill himself or hit an innocent person."

My hands shake as I flip the pancakes over. I'm still a nervous passenger and I cross myself every time the boys leave in their cars. I think I will always worry about car accidents after what I lived through, but there is a very real possibility of it happening now with Bodhi because he has become reckless and shown he has little value in living. "I can't concentrate at work. I was a total basket case presenting at the meeting last weekend though thankfully I had already done the groundwork and all the studios signed off on the new child advocacy rules."

"That's a big win, Viv. You should be so proud. I know Reeve would be."

"Gawd, don't mention his name because I'm so fucking pissed at him." I lift the pancakes out of the skillet and drop them onto the plate. "He started all of this, and I'm angry at him all over again." I glance at the clock. "Is eleven thirty too early to hit the vodka because, I swear, I want to drink myself into blissful numbness and pretend like this is all just a nightmare."

"Breathe, Viv." Audrey takes my hands and rubs them. "Let me finish brunch. Go take a bath, and we'll go for a walk then."

I shake my head and retract my hands. "I'll finish brunch. I'm trying my best to keep things normal for the girls." Emily, Fleur, and Melody attend a dance class at ten a.m. every Saturday morning, and it's tradition for them to come back here and have pancakes and strawberries.

"Who's hungry?" I say, in my loudest, cheeriest voice, as I lift the plate and head toward the large wooden kitchen table where our three princesses are currently coloring while they wait to be fed.

"Me, me, me!" they respond enthusiastically as one.

"I want the biggest pancake 'cause I'm the oldest and it's my birthday in ten days," Fleur says, licking her lips as she watches me approach.

"I want the biggest pancake 'cause I'm the youngest and I've got the most growing to do," Melody chips in.

"What about you, Emily?" I ask Alex's and Audrey's eldest daughter, who at seven is slap bang in between my two girls. "Don't you want to stake a claim?"

"Nope. I don't care what size pancake I get as long as there are lots of them." Her goofy grin is adorable, and I love that little girl as much as if she was my own.

I lean down and press a kiss to her cute blonde head. She is the sweetest child and so affable. "Don't ever change," I tell her, my voice cracking a little.

"I hate to break the news to you, girls," I tell my daughters as my gaze darts between them. "But all the pancakes are the same size because I got a new pancake mold." I set the plate down in the center of the table.

"Everyone gets the biggest!" Melody says, clapping her hands as I watch Fleur grab three pancakes and dump them on her plate. That girl has the appetite of an elephant, but she's as skinny as a rail, and I have no idea where she puts all the food she devours. Not that I'm complaining. For a kid, she's very adventurous and willing to try anything. Melody is a picky eater, and I have to sneak vegetables into sauces and blitz them until they are hidden so I can get some goodness into her. If I left it up to her, she'd live on a diet of chicken nuggets and grilled cheese sandwiches.

"Can I have a chocolate cupcake after my pancakes?" Fleur asks in between bites as I place a few strawberries on all their plates while Audrey sets a glass of freshly squeezed orange juice down in front of the three girls.

"You can have a cupcake later. You don't want to make yourself sick."

"I love chocolate cupcakes," Emily says before popping a piece of pancake into her mouth.

"My brothers loooooove chocolate cupcakes," Melody says over a mouthful of pancake. "But Mom hasn't made them in ages."

It's true. The foundation has kept me super busy, especially this past year, but recent weeks were a lesson in prioritizing what's important. I'm interviewing for an operations director at the moment—Ash is helping with it—and once I have someone in the role, I plan to take some time off to focus on my family. Going forward, I aim to work only while the kids are at school. I want to have more time to devote to my family. That has always been my goal, but lately it's been hard to stick to it. The foundation needed more of my time, but now it will have to take a back seat.

My kids and my husband take precedence.

I haven't been able to sleep properly for weeks, so I have been getting up early and baking. I find it therapeutic. The boys loved chocolate cupcakes when they were younger, and it's silly, but I thought it might help to remind Bodhi of his youth and help him to remember all the fun times we had as a family. I leave a bag for him and Easton at the door every morning with a homemade smoothie and a cupcake in each one. Both bags are gone every day, but I don't know if Bodhi is taking his and dumping it in the trash or if E is taking both so as not to hurt my feelings.

"Your mommy is very busy," Audrey says, leaning around her daughter to grab a strawberry.

"Like you." Emily picks up another strawberry and hands it to her mom.

"My daddy is crazy busy finishing his album," Fleur says, already on to her fourth pancake. "It's going to be awesome."

The girls love hanging out at the studio with the guys. Sometimes Dillon takes them there on the weekend when they're not on such a tight deadline. It is housed on the grounds of Dillon's old home. He ended up completely remodeling the place after they moved the label to a trendy high-rise in downtown L.A. Now the house is a fully equipped commercial recording studio with several plush apartments on the grounds so bands signed to the label can live and work there in privacy. He added a new bar, enlarged game room, inside pool with a sauna and jacuzzi, and a state-of-the-art gym. It's like a mini luxury resort for rock stars, and it's a big hit with his artists.

"He wanted Mommy to sing on it, but she said no." Melody makes a face at me. "Daddy would be sooooo happy if you sing with him, Mommy. Please do it." She glues her hands together and lifts them up in a pleading gesture, tilting her head back and fixing me with big doe eyes. "Daddy would love you forever if you did it."

Ever since Dillon, Jamie, and Alex set up our *Grease*-inspired karaoke the night of Halloween, the kids have been begging me to sing on the album. The guys decorated the room with themed memorabilia and banners, and they set up a makeshift stage. We all took turns singing, individually and as couples, and the girls got a huge kick out of watching me and Dillon sing together.

Dillon being Dillon, he used it to his advantage, recruiting the girls to help in his campaign to get me to sing on the latest Collateral Damage album. My husband has been trying to get me to sing on a track since Vegas, but I repeatedly tell him that was a one-time thing.

"Daddy already loves Mommy forever," Fleur says, looking at me with a big, dreamy expression on her face. "When I grow up, I'm going to marry a rock star just like my Daddy and make smoochy faces at him all the time just like you do, Mommy."

Audrey snorts out a laugh. "What's a smoochy face?" she asks as warmth floods my chest, briefly eradicating the constant pain.

Fleur smiles and widens her eyes, tilting her head to the side and staring dreamily into space.

"I do not look like that!" I protest, smothering a laugh.

Audrey giggles, and my lips twitch.

"Just like that, Auntie Rey." Fleur straightens up and returns to stuffing herself with pancakes.

"I think you might have a little actress in the making," Audrey says.

"I think you might be right." Our eldest daughter is definitely theatrical, but Melody is too. Easton loves drama as well, and I wonder if any of them, or all of them, will follow Mom and Reeve into acting.

"I'm going to be a singer," Melody announces. "And I will sing with my daddy on every track."

"Daddy would love that," I say, darting down to press a kiss to her soft cheek. Both our girls have Dillon wrapped around their little fingers. He adores them as much as they adore him.

My husband is an amazing father. He somehow manages to be both playful and strict. If I want the kids to do anything, I usually have to ask repeatedly and raise my voice for anyone to take me seriously. Yet Dillon only has to say it once, in his stern disciplinarian voice, and they jump to obey. Even though he's the fun one, I'm actually softer. Together, it works, and we get the balance right.

Or we used to.

These days, I don't know if we're getting much right at all.

"Mom." Melody looks up at me with her big blue eyes, flinging her arms around my neck. "Please sing with my daddy. He loves you sooooo much, and you're the best singer and the best mommy in the whole wide world."

Her words bring tears to my eyes, and she can't know how much I need to hear and feel her love.

"Do it, Mom." Fleur clings to my arm and peers up at me with a matching pleading expression. She is the only one of my children to have my hazel eyes. The other three all have their fathers' blue eyes.

In the face of such devotion to Dillon and the excitement I know it will ignite, I relent. "My two princesses have convinced me." I kiss both their cheeks. "I'll do it. We can tell Daddy together when he gets home tonight."

There is much celebration and cries to call Dillon and tell him immediately, but I know they are busy now that Ro is back from Ireland and they can finish the album, so I don't want to disturb him.

CHAPTER 11
VIVIEN

IT'S AFTER SIX, and Dillon still isn't home. He called to say they were finishing up a track and to keep some dinner for him. The kids are bathed and happily watching cartoons in the playroom as I make my way outside. I'm not due at Ash's until eight, and I feel a strange compulsion to visit the memorial garden. Or what's left of it.

The flowers Dillon ordered arrived a few hours ago, coinciding with Bodhi's emergence from his room. It's the one and only time I have seen him today, and I stupidly saw it as a sign. I asked him to help me to replant the garden. I thought it might help him to remember and to begin to heal, but I should've known it was asking too much too soon.

I'm grasping at straws now. I'm terrified I'm losing my son forever, and I can't cope. I can't stand it. I can't bear to watch him self-destruct knowing I am powerless to do anything to stop it.

Pain lances through my chest as I hurry across the grass, rubbing at the pain as if that will make it go away. My path is guided by the illumination from the moon hanging low in the dark night sky.

I saw a flicker of something in Bodhi's eye when I asked, but it was gone so fast I can't be sure it wasn't wishful thinking. He shook his head and returned to his room without uttering a word.

"My heart is broken, Reeve," I say when I reach the cordoned-off area. I hop over Dillon's makeshift fence and plonk my butt down on the bench. I'm grateful Bodhi only flipped it over, that he hadn't broken it. The plaques nailed to the bark are intact as is the tree. Those are the most important parts. The rest we can replace, but I refuse to do it until Bodhi is ready to replant the garden.

When we moved to our new home in the Hollywood Hills, we had the tree professionally relocated from our old home. As a family, we planted this garden, and it meant something to me. Which is why I refuse to replant it until every member of our family participates. I don't care how long I have to wait.

"Help me. Help us!" I beseech, tipping my head back and looking at the smattering of stars lighting up the sky. "We love him. We love him as much as we love Fleur, Easton, and Melody. He's our son. He owns an equal part of our hearts. He's an integral part of our family. He's the only part of you still with me, but it's way more than that. I love him for the person he is. I love the quiet introspection he gives to every decision. I love the intensity on his handsome face when he's scribbling songs in his journal or playing his guitar. I love the adoration in his gaze when he watches his sisters and the joyful laugh he emits when he chases them around the playground. I love the respect shining in his eyes when he speaks with Dillon and the fierce way he protects his brother when Easton doesn't even notice it. I love his intelligence and his fight and his focus. I love how he hugs me. I love when he calls me Mom."

A sob tears from my throat, rippling through the still night air. "He's the sweetest boy, Reeve. You would have been so proud of him, and you'd be so worried now if you knew how messed up he is. A lot of that is your fault, and I'm pissed at you, but I can't get mad at you without turning that lens around on myself. I have tried to be the best mother to him and Easton, to my daughters too, but I'm failing. I'm failing my boys. They are both floundering, and I don't know how to help them!"

Tears spill from my eyes and I let them fall even though it feels like I've shed enough tears to fill an ocean recently. "Easton will be okay. I know he will. It doesn't stop me worrying about him, but I know he'll get through this. With Bodhi, I am genuinely terrified, Reeve. I know he is still the same sweet boy deep down inside. I know he is hurting and lashing out, but I'm so scared."

I get up and walk to the tree, running my finger over Reeve's name carved in the wood before doing the same with Lainey's. "I can't lose him too, and I'm fearful he's following a path he won't return from. It's a path I can't follow, and that hurts so bad. I'm supposed to hold my kids' hands and be with them for everything. But I can't follow Bodhi down this particular path, and I am terrified. If anything happens to him, I will die!" Wracking sobs rip from my chest as I drop to my knees, pressing my brow to the bark. "Help him, Reeve. I know you're still out there. Please help our son. Help me and Dillon to do the right thing. Just…help."

A gentle breeze lifts strands of my hair, and the lightest touch sweeps across my cheek. I whip my head back as my breath stutters in my chest. My nostrils twitch as a familiar spicy scent tickles the back of my nose. Tears stream unbidden down my face as I bring my fingers to my cheek. "Reeve," I whisper, lifting my hand to my other cheek as I feel a light touch brush against it. "You're here." I tilt my head back, staring up at the stars as the breeze wraps around me, cocooning me in the illusion of safety. Warmth infiltrates my body as I half laugh, half cry, surrounded by the ghosts of my past.

Some might think I'm crazy, but kneeling in the ruined garden, with memories of my first love playing in my head and the feel of his love winding around me, I feel at peace for the first time in weeks.

"I think your brother is considering having me committed," I joke a few hours later, stretching along Ash's comfy velvet couch as I knock back another glass of wine.

"Nonsense." Ash kicks her feet up on her coffee table. "He knows you used to feel Reeve around, and he made his peace with that a long time ago."

"I haven't felt him in years, Ash." I sit up a little straighter, turning on my side to face my sister-in-law. Audrey was supposed to be joining us for a girl's night in, but Lake and Kylo, her two-year-old twins, both came down with a fever this evening and she didn't want to leave them. "Do you think he's really there or is it my imagination conjuring him up at times of need?"

She shrugs, looking contemplative as she stares off into space. "The brain is a complex organ, and we still don't know enough about it. Perhaps it's a coping mechanism for times of high stress, or maybe he really is still there. If any man could stay anchored to the mortal realm, it would be Reeve Lancaster. That man was obsessed with you, and he loved you so fucking much. If there was a way to stay around you, I know he'd make it happen."

"Dillon has been incredible these past few weeks. I would be hanging from the cray-cray tree by my fingernails if it wasn't for your brother. I don't need Reeve to cope. I have Dillon."

"This has brought everything to the surface again. It's understandable you might feel drawn to Reeve at a time like this."

"Something compelled me to go out to the garden tonight."

"Whether it was Reeve or your brain tricking you isn't really the issue though. What matters is it helped, right?"

"Yeah, it did, which is kind of silly, but—"

"Nope, not silly." She vigorously shakes her head. "Take the wins where you can, Viv, and don't ever feel bad for it."

"I love you," I tell her because it's the damn truth.

"I love you too." She grabs the bottle of wine and tops off both our glasses. "I know someone else who loves you extra special tonight."

I grin at her, and it's a miracle I can smile. "Let me guess. A tall, sexy, super talented rock star who is currently at my house with your husband and your brother perfecting the lyrics to the last track on the new Collateral Damage album, the one I am going to sing alongside him?"

"Ding, ding, ding!" She beams at me. "He was so excited when he called to tell me."

"I should have said yes years ago. I like making him happy. God knows we both need more of the happy stuff right now."

"Nope." She shakes her head and wags her finger in my face. "We're not going there tonight. You left your problems at the front door, remember?"

Thoughts of Bodhi and Easton instantly flood my mind, and it's hard to hold onto my previous happy thoughts when concern forces its way into my brain, but I try. I swore I wasn't going to be a Debbie Downer coming over here. "Right," I say with more determination than I feel.

"I love who my brother is when he's with you. Growing up, watching him battling his demons was so hard. All I ever wanted was for him to be happy and you make him so damn happy. I love the way you two love one another. It makes me want to break out into song whenever I see you making googly eyes at one another."

"You're ridiculous." I roll my eyes even though a massive grin spreads across my face. "But not wrong. I love the way your brother loves me." My expression turns more serious. "He loves me good, Ash, and I don't have the words to describe all the ways I love him back. I always wanted the kind of marriage my parents have, and I got it."

"Aww. I love that."

"You have your own epic kind of love too."

"I know." She beams from ear to ear. "We're lucky bitches."

"We are." I pull myself upright and knock back a mouthful of wine. "Have you given more consideration to adoption?" I ask because we haven't spoken about it for a while. Ever since this stuff blew up with the boys, I've been a bit of an absent friend.

"We're doing it."

"Oh my God!" I squeal, setting my glass down and hopping up. I run over and grab her into a hug. "That should have been the first thing out of your mouth tonight, instead of letting me ramble on about ghosts."

"You've had a lot on your mind."

"All the more reason to tell me. I'm so happy for your guys."

"Me too. Oisin is seven now, and we want to give him a brother or sister. We have tried everything to conceive again and it's time to accept it's not going to happen."

"You couldn't have tried harder." They have been through several rounds of IVF, attempted the surrogacy route, which turned into a disaster, and tried a couple of experimental procedures, none of which produced results. "You two have a lot of love to give so I'm thrilled you are adopting."

"Me too. It feels right, and the timing is perfect now."

"I need updates every step of the way." I grab my wine and sit cross-legged on the floor beside her. "I don't care what shit is going on in my life, I want to know it all. You hear me?"

"You will know everything first. I promise."

"A toast," I say, raising my wineglass. "To families and kids and love, lots of love."

"Amen to all that."

We are in the kitchen making tea and toast a few hours later when Dillon walks into the house, instantly raising all my hackles.

"What's wrong?" I ask, spotting the panic he's trying to hide on his face.

"I got a call. Bodhi is in the hospital."

"Oh my God." My lower lip wobbles, and I sway on my feet. "Is he okay? Is he…alive?"

Dillon bands his arms around me and hugs me tight. "The nurse I spoke with said he was in surgery and he was stable."

"Surgery?" Ash asks, and I suspect her mind went to the same place mine did, but you don't need surgery if you've overdosed. At least, I don't think you do, but my brain is malfunctioning right now as panic races through my veins and blood thrums in my ears.

Pain is etched across Dillon's face as he tilts my chin up and looks me straight in the eye. "He was stabbed, sweetheart. That's as much as I know, but we've got to go."

"Take me to my son," I say, clinging to my husband as we race out of Ash's kitchen and down the hallway.

CHAPTER 12
BODHI

"ARE THE GIRLS OKAY?" Mom asks in a hushed tone.

"They're fine. Jamie took them over to their place after breakfast. They'll keep them there as long as we need to stay here," my dad replies.

"I need him to wake up," my brother says in a tormented voice that hurts me. "The last words I said to him were horrible. I need him to know I take them back."

Pain rattles around my skull as I try to move my head, but it won't cooperate.

"He's going to be okay," Dad says. "You'll get a chance to tell him."

"So why isn't he waking up?" Easton says. "He's been out of surgery for hours."

Warmth spreads from my hand up my arm as I wage an inner war with my eyes, willing them to open. I try my body next, but my limbs refuse to move. Awareness creeps into my consciousness as pain radiates from my side, up over my chest, and higher. A painful tightness stretches across my ribs and around to my back, and I feel the darkness calling me back to slumber, but I don't want to sleep.

It all rushes back to me like a movie on fast-forward, and I want to wake. I need to tell my family I'm sorry and I love them.

"His body needs time to rest and heal." Mom's voice cracks, and a different kind of pain rips through me.

I caused that anguish in her voice. The anguish in all their voices. And I couldn't hate myself any more than I do in this moment.

My body jerks as I fight to regain consciousness.

"Bodhi." Mom's soft tone is like a comfort blanket swaddling me. "Honey, are you there? Can you hear me?"

I feel her hand squeezing mine as my eyes slowly blink open with an exhaustion that threatens to reclaim me if I don't fight it. My eyes shutter again as my fingers close around hers.

"Bro." Easton's voice sounds closer. "You're in the hospital, but you're going to be okay. The doc says you'll make a full recovery. It's okay to wake up. We're not mad at you."

"He is squeezing my hand," Mom says as I battle the tiredness and force my eyes to open again.

Slowly, my vision comes into focus, and I see Mom, Dad, and East all standing over me with concerned expressions on their faces.

It is so unbelievably good to see them. There was a point where I thought I never would again, and every horrible mistake I made flashed before my eyes as I lay bleeding out on the dirty ground of the alley thinking I was dying.

"Mom," I croak as wetness seeps over my cheeks. "I'm sorry."

"Shush, honey." She brushes hair back off my face. "There is plenty of time for that. Don't worry about it now. Do you want some ice chips?"

I peer deep into her troubled face, and I hate I have caused her so much pain. It shouldn't have taken me almost dying to realize the truth. For weeks, I have struggled to clear the fog from my head and see what has always been right in front of me. I couldn't see it, hear it, or think it because I was consumed with pain, writhing in agony with every conscious moment I lived, and I just wanted it all to stop.

"I love you," I rasp, the words scraping over the raw ache in my throat and the dryness in my mouth. I move my head, looking at my dad and my brother. "I love you all, and I'm so sorry."

Mom's sobs filter into the solemn silence as her arms go gently around me and she cries against the side of my face.

Dad moves around my bed to comfort her. "We love you too, son," he says, his voice thick with emotion. "Thank fuck, you're going to be okay. You gave us quite a scare." He holds my hand as he rubs a soothing hand up and down Mom's back.

"I didn't mean what I said," Easton says, hovering by my other side.

I lift my gaze to his.

"I don't hate you. I never could. You're my brother. You mean more to me than some stupid girl who tried to come between us."

Shame washes over me as I think about all the nasty things I have said and done to East. He deserved none of them. He has always had my back, and it was a shitty way to repay him. But I'll make it up to him. I swear. "Bros before hoes," I croak, attempting to smile. "I'm sorry, East. That was a shitty thing to do. I wish I could take it back. I was just hurting so much, and I wanted you to feel some of that pain."

"I get it."

"You didn't deserve it. I know you liked her, and I'm sorry I ruined your relationship."

"I'm not. She had an agenda. I'm not going to say what you did was okay, because your betrayal cut deep, but in a weird way you actually protected me."

If I hadn't been so smashed and so determined to hurt my brother, that bullshit the bitch spewed would have made me seriously mad. At least we won't have to worry about Hollis coming between us again; her father has sent her to an all-girls reform school in Switzerland. An asshole at school recorded some of the events that night, and the video found its way into her father's inbox. He shipped her out of the country two days later. Can't say I'll miss her. She was nothing more than a tool to hurt my brother. A fresh wave of shame crashes into me and I hate what I did to East.

"Let's sit you upright a little so I can give you some of these ice chips. The nurse didn't leave any water, only these." Mom tenderly cups my face. "I'm so glad you're okay. We were so worried."

"I'll let the nurse know you're awake," Dad says, as East presses a button on the side of the bed and it slowly elevates. Dad leans down and kisses my brow. "It's good to have you back, son."

His words carry a double meaning, and they linger in the air as he leaves to get the nurse. The gentle whirring as the bed raises is the only sound in the room.

I am sitting propped up in the bed with Mom feeding me ice chips when Dad returns with a nurse. She makes a fuss over me, checking my vitals and promising to send a doctor in to talk to us and some food if he gives me the all-clear. She reappears a couple of minutes later with a large glass jug of water and some plastic cups. Mom holds my hand while she helps me to take small sips as if she is terrified to let me go.

I guess I fell asleep after that because when I blink my eyes open the room is brighter, and little rays of daylight filter through the gaps in the blinds.

"Hey." Mom's beautiful face swims in my line of vision as she looms over me. "How are you feeling?"

As soon as the words leave her lips, I'm acutely aware of all the aches and pains ricocheting through my body. "Sore," I truthfully admit. "Can you help me to sit up?"

"Let me," Dad says, and I move my head around, watching him enter the room holding two paper cups.

My brother is asleep in a chair alongside my bed, his head thrown back, his lips slightly parted as he softly snores. The sound is like music to my ears. For years, East and I shared a bedroom until we became teens and he started snoring, waking me continuously during the night, and it became apparent I needed to start sleeping in my own room. Occasionally, when we stay up late watching TV or playing video games, I crash in his room. It always reminds me of the closeness we share and how much of a support system he was for me when I first moved in with them and it felt like my entire world ended when Lori died.

Dad hands a cup to Mom before setting the other one down on the bedside table. Then he elevates the bed and fixes the pillows behind my back.

"Where am I?" I ask because I have no recollection after I passed out on the sidewalk outside the bar, having crawled from the alley.

"You're at Southern California Hospital at Culver City," Mom explains.

"What do you remember?" Dad takes his cup and sits beside Mom. They pull their chairs in closer to my bed.

"All of it." I wince a little as I sit up straighter in the bed. "Unfortunately."

The nurse shows up then to check me over, but I refuse her offer of more pain meds for now. I want to talk to my parents and my brother. I have so many things I need to get off my chest and it can't wait any longer.

I have put them through hell, and I need to fix it now.

She leaves after promising to send a light breakfast in for me, but food is the last thing on my mind. East is still asleep, but I don't want to wake him or delay this conversation.

"Do you feel up to talking about it?" Dad asks, sipping his coffee as he watches me with laser-focused eyes. "The cops have been around, but they weren't able to tell us much other than you were found in front of a dive bar in West Adams, bleeding out and beaten up."

A strangled sound erupts from Mom's mouth, and tears glisten in her eyes. I squeeze her hand, only imagining what she must have felt when she heard the news.

Dad circles his arm around Mom and holds her close. I don't even know if he realizes he has done it. It just comes automatically to him. When I'm older, I hope I find someone to love as much as they love one another. It's couple goals for sure.

"They will be back to take a statement from you, most likely at some point today," Dad adds.

"You're awake," East says in a hoarse voice, and we all turn to look at him as he rubs sleep from his eyes.

"He just woke a few minutes ago." Mom stretches across the bed to hand him her undrunk coffee. "You look like you need this more than me."

"Thanks." He accepts it without protest, immediately taking a mouthful and forcing himself more upright in the chair.

A woman enters the room with a tray holding two pieces of toast, a glass of juice, and a Styrofoam bowl with some chopped fruit. Mom insists I eat all of it before I begin explaining. They fill me in on my sisters and how worried they were when they got the call from the hospital while I eat.

"I'm really sorry you were worried. I know I've been horrible to everyone." Tears prick my eyes, but I don't fight them. If I'm going to do this, I'm doing it right. That means no more shielding things from my family.

Dad removes my tray, setting it over by the window ledge before reclaiming his seat by Mom's side. Mom clings to one of my hands while my brother holds the other.

"It hurt so much," I whisper, my eyes blurry.

"We never should have made that movie," Mom says as tears roll down her cheeks.

"I'm glad you made the movie," I truthfully tell her, unsurprised to see shock materialize on her face. I squeeze her hand. "It wasn't a secret that Reeve gave me up, Mom. I've known that since Lori told me the truth, but I purposely didn't think about it until the movie forced me to."

Agony transforms her beautiful face, and I push on even though it's hard for me to talk about this stuff with anyone. But I owe it to my parents, to my brother, to tell them the raw truth, no matter how much it might hurt to hear some of this stuff.

I thought I was going to die and I'd never get to tell them these things, so I'm not chickening out now.

"This was always bound to happen, Mom." I brush the tears from her cheeks. "What happened recently has been years in the making."

"It is better we heard the truth through your eyes, as the people who lived it, rather than the shit that's on the internet," East agrees.

I nod. "East is right. The movie put some things into perspective, but it still hurt.

It forced me to confront things I have tried to bury. I'm embarrassed I didn't handle it well. Instead of pushing you away, I should have confided in you, but my head was a mess. It still is. All these thoughts keep going round and round in my brain and they are driving me mad. I was so angry at everyone for lying to me, and then I got angry at myself for believing you took me in as anything other than pity. I couldn't get it all to stop, and I just wanted it to stop." I fist my hand in the bedsheet and avert my eyes. "Numbing the thoughts and the pain with booze and drugs was the only thing that worked."

I lift my eyes slowly, knowing what I will see when I look at my parents and my brother. "I couldn't talk to you. All I saw when I looked at you was pity and guilt, and I hated that." I eyeball my brother. "All I could see when I looked at you was everything I wasn't. He chose you. My dad picked *you* over me. I have always felt like I've been in your shadow. You are amazing at everything and one of the best people I know. I could live a million lifetimes and never be as good as you."

"Bo, that is so wrong. We're different people, but it doesn't make you better or worse than me. You're a good person too. I'm sorry if I ever made you feel like you weren't. You're my brother. The best brother a guy could have. If I've done stuff to make you think you're in my shadow, I am so fucking sorry. That's not how I feel. It's not how I want *you* to feel."

Tears well in his eyes and it pains me to have hurt my brother. I squeeze his hand. "It's not your fault. You have never done anything to make me feel inferior. No one has." I look over at my parents. "You have treated me fairly and equally and with so much love. The way I feel is on *me*. It's not because of anything any of you have done. Please believe me."

745

CHAPTER 13
BODHI

"WE LOVE YOU SO MUCH, BODHI," Mom says through her tears. "When Lori first came to see me and your dad and she told us about you, we were in total shock. I didn't know if I could love Saffron's child."

Agony is etched upon her face, and I know it's hard for her to say these things to me, but I appreciate her honesty. It's not anything I don't know from the movie now anyway.

"We spent a week talking and reflecting on it, running through our options," Dad explains.

He runs a hand through his bleach-blond hair, and the strain on his face is obvious. The scruff on his chin is thicker than he usually wears it, and he has dark shadows and pronounced bags under his eyes. He looks exhausted. I know him, and I bet he didn't sleep because he wanted Mom and Easton to sleep, and he watched over me in case I woke.

"We independently reached the decision to adopt you because we wanted to give you a home, Bodhi. We wouldn't have reached that decision if we couldn't have treated you as an equal member of this family." Dad leans over and grips the side of my head with a gentle touch. "My flesh and blood runs through your veins, Bodhi. You're as much my son as Easton is. It kills me that you would ever think that couldn't be true." He presses his brow to mine for few seconds before easing back, not wanting to hurt me, I'm guessing. "Having you in my life helped to assuage some of my guilt with regards to Reeve. I never got a chance to know my brother. Some of that was my fault, and it's something I must live with for the rest of my life. I have made my peace with it because continuing to beat myself up over something that is in the past, something I can't control or change, is pointless. It took me years to accept that realization, so I understand some of what you're going through. Getting to raise Reeve's son was a way for me to feel connected to him, but, my God, Bodhi, you are so much more than that."

Tears drip down his face as he reclaims his seat, placing his hand over Mom's hand on mine. Mom is still crying too, and Easton is swiping at a few errant tears leaking from his eyes.

Hell, I'm an emotional mess as well.

But that's nothing new.

What is new is the fact I'm not hiding it anymore.

"You are *my son*, and I love you for the person you are. Not because you are Reeve's son or a way for me to connect with the brother I didn't know. Like your brother said, you're a good person. Smart, compassionate, caring. I watch you jotting down song lyrics in your journal, and my heart bursts with pride knowing we share the same passion. I listen to you composing songs on your guitar in the studio and I'm blown away by your talent and your commitment. I see how you dote on your sisters, look up to your brother, and every time you call Vivien Mom, I feel it in here." He thumps a hand over his chest.

"I cried tears of joy the first time you called me Mommy," Mom says. "I was pregnant with Fleur, and it was about four or five months after Lori passed. We were really worried about you. You were so quiet. You kept so much locked up inside. You called me Mommy Vivien, and I seriously thought my heart would burst."

She leans in and kisses my cheek. "Like Dillon, at first, I thought adopting you would be a way for me to keep a piece of Reeve with me always, and it is. Some days, you say something a certain way, or make a gesture that reminds me of your father, and it takes me back." She looks over at Easton. "I see reminders of Reeve in you too. You both look so alike it's not hard to see it at times." She kisses my dad on the lips. "I see elements of you in the boys too."

He kisses her back, nodding.

She returns her attention to me. "But, Bodhi, you are so much more than that. It's like Dillon said, you're your own person. A truly wonderful, amazing, inquisitive, thoughtful, deep thinker. Watching you blossom and grow has been one of the most rewarding experiences of my life." She reaches across the bed for Easton's hand. "That goes for you as well. We are so blessed with both you boys and we love you very much." A cry filters from her lips. "It kills me to think you might not feel that."

"No, Mom." Ignoring the searing-hot pain the motion produces, I lean forward and hug her. "You have done nothing wrong. I know you love me. It's me who feels unworthy of all of you, not the other way around."

Dad and Easton sit on the edge of the bed, carefully draping their arms around us as we embrace in a group hug.

And it's everything.

It would be virtually impossible for me to ignore their love when they surround me with it all the time. Even when I was putting them through hell, they never gave up on me.

"I hate that you feel unworthy," Mom says when we break our embrace and everyone reclaims their seats. She softly cups my cheek. "You are so worthy, Bodhi, and we are lucky to have you in our lives." She peers at me with so much love in her eyes it would be impossible to deny the truth. "I know you have a lot of emotions to process. I know the things you have to deal with are things no boy your age should ever have to face. But you aren't alone. You have us. We will help you to get through this. But please don't shut us out again. Let us help you. Let us love you. Let us be there for you the way a family should, because we love you and we hate to see you in so much pain."

"I know it won't be easy," Dad says, piercing me with that no-bullshit look of his. "I went through something similar when I was your age, and I can relate to some of how you are feeling. We can't make this right for you. You need to process this yourself, and you are going to get mad, sad, and every other emotion in between. Just promise us you'll lean on us. You can talk to me at any time about anything, and I won't judge."

He leans back, exhaling with a wry smile. "I was an absolute asshole back in the day. I treated my parents like shit. I didn't tell my mum I loved her until I was in my twenties. I lashed out at everyone, and I fixated on revenge instead of trying to heal myself. If my mistakes can help you to avoid making the same ones, I will gladly tell you everything. But only you can do the hard work, buddy. We will support you however we can, but the hard slog is yours. It won't be easy and there is no quick fix."

"You are entitled to your feelings, Bodhi," Mom adds, dabbing at her face with a tissue. "Just like East is entitled to his." Her gaze dances between us. "Both of you need to work through them. Don't ever feel guilty for how you feel but let us help you figure it out."

"I will try," I admit, meaning it with my whole heart, as East bobs his head.

"Why were you in West Adams?" Mom asks. "I need to understand how you ended up there and who did this to you because those assholes are going to be behind bars even if I have to scour the streets searching for them myself." Fierce determination glimmers in her eyes along with righteous anger.

"Steady on there, GI Jane," Dad says, his lips tipping up at the corners. "You won't be stepping foot in that hellhole. We'll hire a PI and find these scumbags ourselves, doling out some vigilante justice of our own before we hand them on a silver platter to the cops." His eyes burn as he stares at me. "Mark my words, those assholes will pay for this."

"Yes, Dad." Easton nods in agreement. "I want in on the vigilante justice part. Those fuckers hurt my brother, and I want to make them pay." He cracks his knuckles, looking ready to bulldoze the world for me.

A lump wedges in my throat. How could I ever have thought the things I thought about my family? All they have ever done is love me and take care of me. I know I have a long road ahead to deal with things, but I make a silent vow to myself to not take it out on my family anymore.

They are the heroes in my story. They are not my enemy.

"I saw you out in the garden," I blurt, staring at Mom. "I heard some of the things you said. I heard you begging Reeve to help." The lump thickens in my throat, and I swallow painfully. "I couldn't handle it. Knowing how much I was hurting you, and I was so confused. I needed to know more about the past. To see it with my own eyes, so I took the spare truck keys, drove out to San Jose, and I visited the house I lived at with Lori." I rub at the tight pain in my chest that has nothing to do with my physical injuries. "I can hardly remember her anymore," I admit in a low voice.

"I can relate." East leans forward in his chair. "I barely remember Reeve anymore. The memories I have are fleeting and fading."

My natural instinct is to lash out, to tell him at least he still has some memories. Or even if he doesn't, it doesn't wipe out the fact he had five years with my father when I got no time with him.

But I force that instinct aside. It's not my brother's fault that happened. The blame squarely lies with Reeve and Reeve alone. He made that decision, and he's the only one who deserves my scorn and my hatred, so I promise myself I will direct all that aggression and hostility in his direction. I won't blame my parents or Easton for Reeve's sins.

"Lori loved you so much, Bodhi," Mom says. "She was in a lot of pain those last few months, but she worked tirelessly to ensure you were taken care of before she died. She was a great mother and you adored her."

"I have been mad at her for abandoning me too, which is unfair when it wasn't her fault."

"You can't force yourself to feel a certain way and emotions are there to be felt and understood. It seems like you have dealt with that one," Dad says.

"I'm not sure I have dealt with any, but things are starting to look a little clearer. I just wish it hadn't taken a near-death experience to reach this point."

"You're alive, and you'll make a full recovery. You have some cracked ribs, a mild concussion, and the gash on your side is nasty, and it'll leave a scar, but the knife missed all your vital organs," Mom reassures me, patting my hand.

"The doctors cleaned the wound and stitched it, and they have you on antibiotics, as well as pain meds, to ward off infection. You should be allowed to go home in a couple of days," Dad says.

"That's good, but I wish I could leave now. I miss my sisters. I want to hug them and tell them I love them too."

"We can bring them over later," Dad says. "I know they'd like to see you."

"I'd like that." I clear my throat, and Mom instantly reaches for my water. I take a few sips before continuing, knowing this part is going to devastate my parents. "I wanted to know more about Saffron," I blurt, watching Mom's face pale and Dad's arm automatically go around her shoulders. "I needed to know she wasn't all bad because if she's all bad there's a good chance I'm the same too, right? I mean, neither of my parents were saints, and both were addicts."

"Your father beat his addiction, and you will too." Mom's voice resonates with supreme confidence, and I hope I am strong enough to not let her down. "And there isn't a bad bone in your body, Bodhi. You have always been a good kid."

"Being troubled doesn't equate to being bad," Dad says.

"But the choices you make from here on out will largely dictate that," Easton says, sounding way older than he is. But that's my brother. "You lost your way, bro, but you'll find it back."

"What did you do?" Mom asks, chewing on the corner of her lip.

"I found a guy online who went to school with Saffron. I had reached out to him, and he suggested meeting up. I wasn't sure if I wanted to go there, but after hearing you in the garden, I knew I needed to find out if I was to have any chance to move beyond this. I met him at Lori's and Saffron's childhood home. It was in a shitty neighborhood, and the house is abandoned now. It was all boarded up and overrun with weeds."

That was the first wake-up call. Staring at the poverty they grew up in showed me how fortunate I was to have grown up in nice neighborhoods never wanting for any material thing. "I actually felt kind of sorry for her," I truthfully admit. "It's like she never stood a chance."

"Saffron had plenty of chances," Mom says. "She threw them all away including an acting career and all the money she made from it."

"And Lori grew up there, and she was a decent person," Dad adds. "We all have choices in life, like Easton just alluded to. No matter our circumstances, the decisions we make shape the people we become and the lives we lead. I'm so fucking lucky I got the opportunity to make up for my mistakes, and I choose to live my life more openly now. Not everyone gets that chance. I'm grateful I had so many people around me who cared enough to help set me straight. You do too, Bodhi."

"I know," I whisper, biting on the inside of my mouth. "I was clutching at straws, wanting to see something good in her, but there is none." My voice sounds hollow to my own ears as I continue. "Dirk took me to the bar. He said there were some other guys there who knew Saffron." I gulp back bile. "They were cool at first, and we shared beers. But gradually the masks came off, and I saw them for what they were."

My chest heaves, and I squeeze my eyes shut as I remember all the horrible stuff they said about my bio mom. I know they weren't lying, but I didn't need to know all the gory details. I was trying to cling to an illusion she was a drug addict who was incapable of making any decision when it came to her child, but the truth is, Saffron Roberts was a cold, heartless, selfish bitch her entire life. It wasn't the drugs that made her like that. It was just her.

"They said horrible things about her," I admit, forcing my eyes open. "But it wasn't lies. They told stories of week-long drug and booze orgies where they all shared her. She routinely broke up relationships, and she had at least three abortions those guys knew of." A shuddering breath escapes my lips as I pause to take a minute. This shit is hard to say.

"You don't have to continue if it's too painful for you, honey," Mom says.

"Yes, he does," Dad counteracts. "If Bodhi is serious about facing up to his issues, he can't bury his head in the sand any longer."

"He's lying on a hospital bed, bruised, stabbed, and concussed, Dil," Mom replies. "We can cut him some slack until he feels better."

"No." I shake my head. "Dad is right, Mom. There'll be no ideal time to face up to this shit. Hiding behind my injuries is no different than hiding behind my shame and my fear." I rub her arm. "I'm okay. I want to get this all out."

"I'm here for you," East says, his voice projecting strength. Strength I know I'll need to lean on in the coming months.

"It became clear I'd made a big mistake," I continue. "A few of the guys turned nasty, and they told me Saffron had OD'd owing them money. It was obvious they expected me to repay her debts and I'd been baited into a trap. I tried to run. Got outside to my truck when they caught up to me. They hauled me into an alley and started punching and kicking me. I tried to fight back but there were six of them and only one of me. I'd brought a knife with me."

I'm not completely stupid or confused to the point I didn't care at all about my safety. Though I've been going around acting like I have a death wish, deep down I

751

have never wanted to die. I just wanted the noise in my head to stop. The pain in my heart to go away.

"I tried to use it to get away, but they overpowered me, took the knife, and one of the guys stabbed me with it. The other assholes went crazy. They knew who I was. They knew they would get heat if anything happened to me."

"It still didn't stop them from leaving you there," Mom says, and her voice sounds all choked up again.

Dad kisses her temple and wraps his arms more tightly around her.

"They panicked and ran," I explain. "They stole my truck, my wallet, my cell, and they took Reeve's golf watch." I can't look at her as I admit the last part. I know my parents won't care about the truck, my cell, or the wallet. They are replaceable, but Reeve's watch isn't.

"What?" Easton blurts, looking confused, and I guess he hadn't noticed it was missing from the top drawer of his bedside table. "Why did you have my watch when you have your own?"

After I came to live with my family, Mom gave me some things of Reeve's. She had given Easton some after he died, and she wanted me to have a few of his treasured items too. She gave me the watch she bought him on his twenty-fifth birthday, but I always secretly wanted the golf watch as she gave it to him when he was seventeen and he barely took it off. I know because I've seen it on him in so many of the photos in the albums Mom keeps in the living room.

"I stole the watch from your room."

Easton stares at me in shock.

"It was an asshole move." I eyeball my brother, hoping he can see the genuine remorse on my face. "I know how much you loved that watch, so I stole it to fuck with your head. I honestly don't know why I wore it that day. Something compelled me to put it on. I begged them not to take it when they untied it from my wrist. I knew it would devastate you and Mom to lose it. I'm so sorry, East."

His Adam's apple bobs in his throat, and it guts me when he looks away. Mom has a hand over her mouth, and I hate I have disappointed her again.

"It's okay," Easton says after a few beats of silence.

"No, it's not."

"Your life is worth more than a watch, Bo."

"Reeve would say the same if he were here," Mom says.

"This is going to sound hella crazy, but I think…I think he was there with me in the alley."

You could hear a pin drop in the room. Dad and East look shocked as hell, but Mom is smiling. "I don't think that's crazy, honey. You know I used to feel him around me in the aftermath of his death. I haven't sensed his presence for a long time. I don't know if you stuck around in the garden to see, but I felt him that night. I was crying to him for help, and he answered." Tears roll down her face again. "What did you experience?"

My heart is beating superfast, thumping against my rib cage, adrenaline coursing through my veins at the thought my bio dad might have actually been with me in some way. My mind wanders back to that night. "I was on the ground in the alley, and the wound in my side was gushing blood. I had my hands pressed to it, but it wouldn't stop bleeding."

I look down at my hospital gown, placing my palm over the bandaged wound. "I tried to get up. I knew I needed to get back out onto the street, or I would die in that alley because no one would've found me in the dark in time to save me." I draw a deep breath. "I couldn't get up. My legs wouldn't cooperate. I think it was a combination of shock and blood loss." I wet my dry lips. "Then I heard someone in my ear urging me to get up, telling me to fight. I went rigidly still, looking around in confusion for the owner of the voice, but there was no one there."

Mom is practically bouncing in her seat, and Dad is as white as a ghost—no pun intended. Easton looks riveted and intrigued.

"Then I felt someone nudging me. Reeve's image popped into my mind, and I freaked. I'm not sure I connected the dots at first, but I was scared enough that it jolted my body into action. I managed to get to my feet, and I hobbled out of there as fast as I could. The last thing I remember is collapsing in front of a couple on the sidewalk before I passed out."

"Oh my God. Oh my God." Mom repeats it over and over again before a laugh bubbles up her throat. She leans in and kisses me before doing the same to Easton and Dillon. Then she graces us with the biggest smile. "Reeve listened. He helped you." She clasps both my cheeks, taking care to be gentle. "Your father saved you, Bodhi. He came through for you when you needed him."

EPILOGUE
DILLON – 18 MONTHS LATER

"ARE YOU CRYING?" Vivien whispers, leaning into my side as she scrutinizes my face.

"Yes," I readily admit, circling my arm around her slender shoulders. "I'm so fucking proud of our boys and secure enough in my manhood that I can cry in public and own up to it."

"God, I love the hell out of you, Dillon Lancaster O'Donoghue." She stretches up and smacks a loud kiss on my lips. When she pulls back, she's grinning. "I'm secure enough in our love and proud of the husband and father you are to kiss you in public and not give a flying fuckity-fuck who saw or what they think about it."

"That's my girl." I slap her ass.

I feel disapproving, disbelieving eyes around us, and I'm tempted to flip them the bird, but that would be immature. Considering I'll be forty in eight months, I figure I should probably try to act my age. Besides, it's our sons high-school graduation, and nothing should steal their thunder.

The long ceremony ends, thank fuck, and our boys make their way over to us.

"I'm so proud of you," Vivien squeals, flinging her arms around both boys and hugging them to death. "I love you, I love you, I love you." She peppers their faces with kisses, and both boys wear similar amused adoring grins. They love their mother, and it makes me happy to know it and see it.

"Control your woman," Easton teases, eyeballing me over Viv's shoulder when she shows no sign of stopping.

"Women should never be controlled, son." I reel Viv back into my arms. "You should only ever want to free their wings and give them room to fly."

"Spoken like a true poet," Bodhi says, grinning at me.

"Takes one to know one." I waggle my brows as another surge of pride swells in my chest. "I won't be the only fool in our house writing love songs for a living. Come Monday, that accolade will be passed to you."

"Now, I feel left out," Easton pouts.

"Don't talk stupid." Bodhi wraps his arm around East's neck, grinning. "You're going to play ball for the Bears. I'm proud of you little brother."

"Hey. I'm not the little one in this combo." East wrangles out of his hold, straightening up and puffing out his chest as he wags his finger in Bodhi's face. He has a couple of inches in height over Bodhi, and he's much broader and more muscular too. He loves to tease his brother over it any chance he gets. "And we're both eighteen now."

"I'm still six months older than you. Last I checked that makes me the eldest and you the little brother."

"You two would fight over air," Viv says, fiddling with the settings on her Nikon. She insisted on bringing the big guns out today.

"Are we going to the restaurant yet?" Fleur asks, looking bored. She turned ten on her last birthday, and she's already entered the tween phase. God help us all.

"I want to get some photos of the boys with their friends and then we'll leave."

"Auntie Ash is outside," I say, mussing up my eldest daughter's hair. Predictably, she scowls at me, before rushing to fix it. "You can join her and wait there for us," I suggest.

"I'll come too," Melody says, instantly threading her fingers in her sister's.

"We'll walk them out," Lauren offers, beaming at her granddaughters. "Just give me one second to congratulate your brothers." She moves over to hug Easton and Bodhi.

Fleur grumbles, deepening the sound when Jonathon musses up her hair again.

We share a chuckle and a knowing look. My father-in-law and I have grown very close over the years, and he's a man I admire a hell of a lot. Lauren and Jon now spend half the year in Italy, at the home Reeve bequeathed them in his will. We joined them for a few months last summer, and it did wonders for Bodhi's mood.

Our boy has tried hard to deal with the ghosts of his past this last eighteen months. It hasn't been plain sailing. He relapsed at the start of senior year, but he came and told us, allowing us to get him the support he needed. We discussed him going into rehab, but Bodhi didn't want to defer senior year, so he attended an outpatient program for a couple of months around school, and he managed to get through it and graduate on time with his brother. Something which was important to him.

Bodhi is itching to leave school behind him and come work with me at the label. He has no desire to be front and center stage, but he wants to learn the industry from the ground up and he wants to be a songwriter and producer. He certainly has the talent, and I couldn't be more excited he is joining the CD label next week.

Lauren and Jonathon leave with our girls while Viv gets the boys to pose for her.

"Why is Ash outside, or do I want to know?" she asks as she snaps some pics.

"Did you really expect my sister to wait patiently at the restaurant for us to arrive? You know she adores these guys. Hell if I know why," I joke, flashing them a grin. I'm deflecting on purpose. The whole O'Donoghue clan is outside, having flown in from Ireland to be here to celebrate with us. I wanted to surprise everyone, so I made my sister and Jamie keep it a secret.

"Funny, Dad. Not." East nudges me in the ribs, and I tackle him playfully.

Viv takes a ton more photos, grabbing some of the guys' friends into pictures.

Lewis's mom takes a few shots of the four of us together, and then I finally manage to get Vivien to leave. Ash has been blowing up my phone the last fifteen minutes. My sister is not known for her patience.

We walk out of the dwindling auditorium together with my hand wrapped around Vivien's and one son on either side of us. When we reach the hallway, I stop them before we head outside to complete bedlam. My Irish family are not known for being subtle or quiet, but I wouldn't have them any other way.

It took me a long time to appreciate the value of family, and now I have so many different variations of family and so many people I love. I never take it for granted.

"Stop for a second," I say, moving us over to the side. "I want to say something before we go outside."

"Oh damn. Dad's about to get totes emote. Prepare yourself," East says, snaking his arm around his brother's shoulder.

I am glad they were able to put that horrible stuff behind them and repair their relationship. If anything, I think they are even closer now.

These next few years will be a test of their bond as they each make their own way in the world.

Easton is going to live on campus, like Viv did, but we aren't far away, so I expect we'll still see a lot of him. Easton is a home bird at heart, and he loves his family too much to not make time for us.

Bodhi has chosen to stay at home for now, and we were both relieved to hear it. Though he has made a lot of progress, he is still not out of the woods. We want him close, so we can continue to support him. It helps to soften the blow too. Our boys are grown up and spreading their wings. It's a confusing time full of joy at the men they are becoming and the paths they are forging in life, and sadness because they are moving on and leaving home and we're going to miss them.

"You're not too old to knock the shit out of," I joke, narrowing my eyes at my son. "Punk," I add, so he knows I'm just messing.

"Get on with it, Dad. We've got dinner and a party to get to," East retorts.

"I just want to say your mother and I are super fucking proud of you both. It's an honor to be your parents. Watching you grow up has been a privilege and the most rewarding experience of our lives. I know things haven't always been easy, but you've faced your challenges head on, and we love you both very much." I grip Bodhi's shoulder and then East's.

"No matter how old you get, we are always your family," Viv says, emotion threading through her tone. "We are always here for you, for anything you need."

"Like condoms," I quip, lightening the mood.

"Dillon!" Viv thumps me in the arm.

"What?" I hold up my hands and plant an innocent expression on my face. "We should encourage them to wrap it before they tap it."

"Oh God." Viv buries her face in my neck. "I do not want to think about my babies' sex lives."

"Ugh, Mom. That sounds so wrong," East says as Bodhi and I share a grin.

Viv lifts her head and grabs Easton's cheeks, smushing them together. "You will always be my baby, Easton." She lets his face go to grab Bodhi's in the same way. "You too, Bodhi." Releasing his face, she slides back into my arms where she belongs.

"Even when you're fifty, you'll still be my babies. And we will always be here for you."

"Always." I pull the boys into a group hug, holding them close. "Family forever."

"Family forever," they chorus as one.

It's a mantra I will follow with my whole heart and soul until the day I die.

GLOSSARY OF IRISH TERMS/SAYINGS

The explanation given is in the context of this book. Also includes pronunciations.

Aisling – female Irish name. Pronounced Ash-ling.

Arse - ass

Oisin – male Irish name. Pronounced Ush-een.

Plain sailing – smooth sailing

Tops up (as in wineglass) – equivalent of tops off.

Zip - zipper

BONUS CONTENT

BONUS SCENE – REEVE

This scene shows Reeve's reaction to news of Vivien's attack and hospitalization.

"I GOT YOU A COFFEE, *movie star.* Just how you like it." Saffron thrusts a paper cup at me, waggling her brows and grinning. "You can thank me later," she adds, pressing up against me and smirking suggestively as we stand to one side of the set, waiting for the director to call us.

"Thanks," I reply, faking a smile and purposely ignoring her blatant innuendo. We have been on set since six a.m., over nine hours so far, and I'm in a shitty mood. It's been a long day and we still have two scenes left to shoot. I'm dying to call it a wrap and head back to my hotel to sleep. I sidestep her, leaving a gap between our bodies. Since all that stuff went down a couple of weeks ago with Viv and the drunken video, Saff is getting more touchy-feely with me. I have told her to quit with the flirting and reiterated I am only interested in her as a friend, but I'm not sure the message is getting through to her.

Taking a sip of the lukewarm black coffee, I almost spit the bitter-tasting liquid back into the cup.

Just how I like it, my ass.

Most everyone on set knows I take my coffee with cream and sugar.

"Don't tell me you're still moping over your ex?" Closing the distance, she sidles up close again. "I know you're hurting, but you'll see it's for the best." She bats her lashes at me as she clings to my arm. "Vivien doesn't belong in your world. Your breakup was inevitable."

I grind my teeth to my molars as I step away from her again. "For the last time, we haven't broken up."

I think. I hope.

I haven't talked to my girlfriend since it went down because Viv is ignoring my calls and my heartfelt texts. I even tried calling the house, but Lauren told me in no uncertain terms to back off and give Viv some space.

She laid into me, and I could do nothing but listen and accept it. I know I have made a mess of things, but Viv hasn't exactly helped either. It wasn't on purpose, but she knows better than to entrust intimate details of our relationship to anyone outside our inner circle. What was she thinking getting drunk and blabbing to that asshole?

Still, it's behind us now, and the media has already moved on to another scandal. It's made me realize I need to protect Vivien more with the press, and I've decided to hire my own publicist. His or her role will be to look after my interests, and that includes Viv.

I know we can fix our relationship and get it back on track, but we need to talk for that to happen.

Our last call was eighteen days ago, and it was painful. I know I overreacted. I'm ashamed that I lashed out at my girlfriend before giving her a chance to explain, but in my defense, the video was pretty damning. Bianca and Cassidy gave me hell, and I got some heat from the studio. After a grueling day on set, the last thing I needed was to deal with that shitstorm. I was also majorly pissed watching Viv dancing with other guys at the frat party. She gives me hell if I'm even sitting beside Saff in a photo, yet it's okay for her to dirty dance with random strangers?

That is still a touchy subject for me.

I shouldn't have accused her of cheating on me though. That was a low blow. I know Viv would never do that to me, like I'd never do it to her.

We are just going through a rough patch. It happens to all couples in long-term relationships. These movies put a big strain on our relationship, but I can't lose Viv. I won't. I'll be home soon for Christmas, and my sole mission is to make things right between us. I know this has been hard on Vivien. My pretending to be in a relationship with Saff has hurt her, but it's only temporary, and she knows it's fake. I have zero interest in Saffron outside of friendship, and lately, I've even begun questioning that. I'm starting to see a side of her I don't like.

I think Viv was right, and she's had an agenda all along.

"Movie star!" Saffron pinches my arm before waving one hand in front of my nose. "Don't ignore me when I'm talking to you!"

"Back off, Saff." Removing her hand from my arm, I sidestep her again. "And cut me some slack. I've got a lot on my mind."

"I know you do." She tilts her head to one side, piercing me with puppy-dog eyes. "I just want to help." She glances around before stepping up closer, shoving her tits against me as she presses the front of her body into mine. "I know you're not sleeping, and it's showing on set." She slides something into the front pocket of my jeans. "These will help."

Grabbing her wandering hand, I remove it and the small packet of pills from my pocket. "Quit with that shit," I hiss, stuffing the packet in her hand and taking two steps back. "I told you I'm done with that stuff. And stop crowding me."

"Hey, man," Rudy says, coming up on my left. I'm surprised to see him as he has no filming today and I know he went partying last night. Although it's after three, I didn't expect him to surface on set at all today. The fact he is here instantly raises my hackles. He must have sought me out for a reason, and I'm immediately wary. His gaze bounces between Saff and me. "Am I interrupting?"

"Wouldn't you like to know?" Saff says, licking her lips and grinning at our costar and my best buddy on set.

Rudy barks out a laugh as I scowl.

"You're not interrupting. What's up?" I ask.

"Can we talk in private?"

Saffron giggles. "Reeve and I have no secrets from one another. Isn't that right, movie star?" She waggles her brows and links her arm in mine as if I haven't just told her to quit that shit.

"Stop insinuating there is more between us." I rub a tense spot between my brows. "I sound like a broken record around you all the time, and it's exhausting."

Saffron feigns hurt before throwing her hands in the air and moving away from me.

Finally.

"Everyone knows I'm a big flirt and I mean nothing by it. You are seriously tense, Reeve. You really need to get laid." She winks at Rudy before flouncing off.

Rudy chuckles. "She's not wrong on all scores."

I'm not even touching that. "What's going on?"

"Not here." Rudy lifts one shoulder. "Director's office is free. Let's talk in there."

We walk silently side by side to the small office off the set, and I close the door when we're both inside the room.

"I know you haven't been online, so I wanted to be the first to show you this."

Goose bumps sprout on my arms as trepidation instantly sets in. Social media is a curse. It's an evil necessity in my line of work, and something I have come to dread. "What now?" I ask, accepting his cell when he hands it to me.

"It's Viv. The reports aren't substantiated yet, but if what they are saying is true, she's been attacked."

All the blood drains from my face as I silently listen to the woman from CNN reporting from a dark alleyway beside the yoga studio Viv attends. The reporter claims a woman was attacked there last night and a source in LAPD has suggested it was Vivien Mills. "Fuck!" I toss the cell at my friend and storm out of the office, searching for my assistant.

I need to use my phone, and Wen holds it for me when I'm on set. I had no messages or missed calls when I last checked it at five thirty this morning, which is strange if the reports are true and this happened last night.

Maybe it wasn't Viv. Perhaps the media got it wrong.

I hope so because the thoughts of anything happening to her terrifies me. Pressure sits on my chest, making breathing difficult, as I stalk around the set, seeking out my assistant. From the corner of my eye, I spot Saff trailing my movements with an intense gaze that is off-putting.

I find Wen flirting with one of the set engineers in the coffee area, and I'm ready to rip into him. Why is my friend the one to bring this information to me? Wen should have been all over this. He's a weak assistant, and if it was up to me, he'd have been fired in the early days. But the studio hired him, and they pay this salary, so I'm forced to put up with the moron.

"Phone," I snap, holding out my palm.

"Has something happened?" he asks, his brow puckering when he notices the look on my face.

"Shouldn't you be telling me that?" I bark, grabbing my cell from his fingers and opening it. Or Cassidy for that matter. Or my agent. Why has no one thought to contact me on set if it's true?

Just as I've convinced myself it must be a case of mistaken identity, I spot the slew of missed calls from Lauren and Jonathon, and I curse.

Ignoring my idiot assistant as he shouts after me, I race back into the director's office where Rudy still waits. He sits patiently in a chair in front of the desk while I call Vivien's dad. Jon picks up on the fourth ring as I pace the floor. "Is it true? Has Viv been hurt? Is she okay? Where is she? Can I talk to her?"

"Calm down, son. Breathe. Vivien is going to be okay. We're at Cedars-Sinai, and she's getting the best medical care."

Air whooshes out of my mouth in strangled spurts. "What happened?" My voice cracks, and pain lays siege to my insides. It must be bad if she's at the hospital.

"We don't have the specifics as Vivien hasn't woken yet, but she was found last night by the owner of the yoga studio unconscious and lying bloody and bruised in an alleyway that leads to the parking lot."

An inhuman sound tears from my throat, and Rudy sits up straighter in his chair. "How badly is she hurt?"

"She has a concussion, three broken fingers, and a broken wrist, and a couple of her ribs were fractured."

"Oh my God. That sounds serious." I rub at the shooting pains spreading across my chest, and knots twist in my gut at the thoughts of the agony my girl must be in.

"The doctor has said her injuries are not life-threatening and she'll make a full recovery."

"If this happened last night, why hasn't she woken yet, and why didn't you contact me yesterday?" I could've been there with her now if I'd been informed immediately.

"She woke briefly, but we weren't there, and she fell back asleep quickly according to the doctor. He's not concerned. He said the CT scan shows no permanent brain damage and sleep is the body's and brain's way of healing. As for your second question, Lauren and I weren't sure if Vivien would want us to call you, so we held off, waiting for her to wake up. When the media broke the story this morning, we called."

"I want to see her. I need to be with her. I'm on set, but I'll make arrangements straightaway." It's almost a seven-hour flight to L.A. Which means it'll be tonight before I reach my love, so there is no time to waste.

"Do what you must," Jon says, "but if Vivien doesn't want to see you, Reeve, you know we'll have to respect her wishes."

"I understand." That doesn't mean I won't pull out all the stops to see her, and it's not something I need to worry about now. "I'll see you soon," I say before hanging up.

I fill Rudy in and then call my dad. I hate asking that bastard for anything, but he's my best hope of getting to L.A. quickly. Studio 27—the production company he co-owns and is the CEO of—has a fleet of private jets at their disposal. Dad promises to find me a jet and tells me to make my way to Logan International and he'll text me the details as soon as he has them.

Then I talk to the director, telling him I need to go. He refuses to release me before I've filmed the last two scenes, citing a whole slew of reasons why I can't just walk off the set.

"I don't care," I say, crossing my arms and leveling him with a dark look. "My girlfriend is lying unconscious in a hospital bed after a brutal attack. I need to go to her now."

"I'm not unsympathetic, Reeve, but you can't hold up production like this. You know how tight our schedule is."

"Just add the scenes on to the last day of shooting." They aren't anything special so they can easily be moved. "I'll pay whatever it costs to reschedule them."

"I know you're worried, Reeve," Saffron says, walking forward from the spot where she was clearly eavesdropping. "We all are. What's happened to Vivien is terrible, but surely, she wouldn't want you to relinquish your responsibilities? She's probably sleeping anyway, and she won't miss you if you're a few hours late."

"Saffron talks sense," the director says. "My assistant will organize a car and a flight while we get these scenes down, and you can leave the instant we are done."

"No." I shake my head. "I couldn't concentrate even if I wanted to stay, which I don't." I take a step back. "I'm sorry to let you and the crew down, but Viv needs me. She's the love of my life, and I won't forgive myself if anything happens to her and I'm not there. I've got to go now."

"You can't just walk off without consequences," the director hollers after me, but I ignore him, heading across the lot toward the exit.

"Reeve!" Saffron's heels tap noisily on the floor as she runs after me. "You're making a mistake. They're going to punish you if you do this!" She tugs on my elbow, slowing my progress.

"Do I look like I care?" I shuck out of her hold. "It's not like they're going to fire me this late in the game."

"They will hit you in the pocket. You know that's how they do things."

I shrug. "They can take every penny they have paid me for all I care. Getting to Viv is the only thing that matters."

She scowls, planting her hands on her hips and thrusting her tits up. "She doesn't deserve you, and you're making a mistake. She's going to ruin your career, Reeve, and you'll have no one to blame but yourself."

The driver drops me off at the entrance to Cedars-Sinai, and I hop out, pulling the hood of my black hoodie up over my head to avoid detection. But it's a feeble attempt. A throng of paparazzi, at least three rows deep, surges behind the barricade facing the entrance to the hospital, jostling and pushing one another as they vie for the perfect shot. "Reeve! Is it true Vivien was attacked by Reeveron fans who want her dead?" some asshole shouts just before the doors glide open, and I step inside, shutting the vultures out.

I checked my feed in the car en route from the airport, and I'm up to speed on the latest speculation. The LAPD has made no comment except to confirm a young woman was attacked in the alleyway behind a yoga studio on Saturday night, but shit is blowing up online with plenty of commentors stating the attack was made by my fans and Saffron's fans. I am waiting to speak to Lauren and Jon before jumping to conclusions, but if the reports are correct, I will never forgive myself for putting Viv in the line of fire.

A woman with a pixie cut and an austere black skirt suit steps out in front of me, introducing herself and offering to escort me to the private suite where Viv and her parents are.

We ride the elevator in silence with only my frantic thoughts for company. I didn't get a wink of sleep on the plane because I couldn't stop worrying about Viv. Worrying about how much pain she's in and torturing myself trying to figure out how this could happen and who would want to hurt my girl. I panicked non-stop wondering if she is awake or still unconscious. Terrified the doctors got it wrong and there is permanent brain damage, and that's why she hasn't woken up.

Trailing the woman out of the elevator and along a corridor, I ignore the heated stares and excited whispers that follow me. She swipes a card at a set of double doors and ushers me inside a large private suite. Jon is standing in front of a large window, looking out over the views of the city at night. He glances over his shoulder when he hears us enter. The bruising shadows under his eyes match my own and are testament to his lack of sleep too.

The woman leaves while my eyes skim over the luxurious waiting room with a cream leather couch, glossy black coffee table, and a small matching dining table with three chairs. To the left is a small hallway, which leads to the guest bedrooms, I'm guessing. Details of these luxury suites have been widely documented in the press, thanks to its celebrity clientele.

"You're here," Lauren says, closing the sliding door to Viv's room behind her as she slips out.

I move toward Viv's room. "I want to see her."

"We need to talk first," Viv's mom says, narrowing her eyes. "And she's sleeping."

"She's still sleeping?" Lowering my hood, I drag a hand through my messy hair. "That's over twenty-four hours. That can't be good. Not with a concussion."

"She woke earlier for a few minutes," Jon says, moving around to the coffee machine.

"It's a misconception you shouldn't sleep with a concussion," Lauren adds. Her eyes rake over me, and her features soften. "You look like shit. When did you last sleep or eat?"

"I ate on the plane, and sleep wouldn't come."

Lauren pulls me into a hug. I cling to her like a lifeline, feeling drained and overemotional and completely wound tight. She eases back, momentarily gripping my arms as she inspects my face. "What are you doing to yourself, Reeve? What are you doing to my daughter?" She chokes up at the end, and Jon slings his arm around her shoulders as he hands a mug of coffee to me and gives one to his wife. "I'm so mad at you," she adds, letting her husband steer her to the couch. "But that doesn't mean I don't worry about you."

"You shouldn't worry about me. I'm fine," I lie. I'm the furthest from fine a person can be. "Reserve your energy for Viv. She's the one who needs it." I take a sip of my coffee, and it's perfect, exactly how I drink it.

"Sit down, son," Jon says. "You look dead on your feet."

I walk silently to the couch, sitting on the other end. "Tell me what you know."

"This wasn't a random attack," Jon says. "Vivien was targeted."

I gulp over the messy ball of emotion clogging my throat and it's an effort to force the words from my mouth. "Targeted by who?"

"Who do you think?" Lauren snaps, and Jon tugs her in tighter to his side.

I hang my head in shame, squeezing my eyes closed as my hands circle my mug, and I try to siphon some warmth into my icy bones. Tears prick my eyes when I open them. "Fans of the movie did this?" I quietly ask, needing them to confirm it so I can add it to the list of my sins against the woman I love.

"Viv said they were Saffhards. Young girls, but they were vicious." Lauren's voice cracks. "They scratched her face, pulled out clumps of her hair, kicked her, and spit on her. One of them even stood on her." She bursts out crying, burying her face in Jon's chest as she sobs.

"Please tell me they have them in custody?"

Jon shakes his head. "Viv was found alone at the scene, and the cops are investigating, but we have heard nothing so far."

Pain rushes through me, filling every cell, nook, and cranny until it's all I know. Thinking of my Viv, lying unconscious on the cold hard ground, beaten and broken, destroys me. It's killing me inside to visualize her like that. How could someone who claims to be a fan of me or Saffron do this to an innocent woman and just leave her there? When I get my hands on them, I am going to reenact everything they did to my love and see how they like it. My heart hurts as pain lays siege to my body. This happened to Viv because of her association with me, and I am so ashamed my decisions have led us here. "This is all my fault."

"Damn straight it is." Lauren lifts her head and glares at me. "Your actions have led to this. You never should have signed that bullshit contract or agreed to any of those awful terms. You haven't done right by Vivien, Reeve, and I'm so disappointed in you."

"I'm disappointed in myself," I truthfully admit.

"You need to fix this," Jonathon says.

"Or the next time, they might kill her." Anguish is etched upon Lauren's face.

"I'll hire her a bodyguard. A whole team of bodyguards, and I'm already in the process of hiring my own publicist." I take another mouthful of my coffee as my brain conjures up ideas of how to proceed from here. I know what I need to do. Something I should have done that summer when we were negotiating the second contract. Something I was too stupid to insist on. I've been so naïve, and it's time I grew up and showed I have balls.

"Good, that's good, son."

"You need to do more." Lauren straightens up as she swipes at the moisture under her eyes. "You need to put that Roberts bitch in her place, and I really think you need to cut Bianca loose. She's not a good person, Reeve. I know you don't want to hear this, but she has manipulated you and the entire situation. She does not have your best interests at heart. All that self-serving bitch cares about is herself. Just say the word, and I'll talk to Margaret. She'll take you on and you will be in much safer hands."

"I'll handle Saffron, and I'll think about Margaret," I say, setting my coffee down and standing. "But now I need to see Viv. Please." I pin pleading eyes on her parents, praying they are not going to block me from her. I need to see my girl with my own eyes to know she's okay. I need to hold her and tell her I love her and beg her to forgive me.

"Don't do anything to upset her," Lauren warns, narrowing her eyes on me again.

"That is the last thing I would do, and you should know that. You know me."

"I used to think we did," Lauren says. "But I honestly don't know any more."

"No heavy talk, Reeve," Jon says. "Vivien can't handle anything like that right now. She's already in a lot of pain, so just let her know you are here for her, but don't pressure her to talk about anything she doesn't want to talk about."

"I won't. I promise," I say, curling my fingers around the sliding door and pushing it back.

Entering the room, I close the door softly behind me. Lifting my head, I stare at my love with a mix of relief and anguish. Pain rattles around my chest as my gaze roams over her. Viv is sleeping, lying perfectly still in the elevated hospital bed, looking tiny and vulnerable under the sheets with her dark hair fanned out on the pillow. She is hooked up to a drip and a machine, and she looks so young and so broken but still so beautiful. My heart pounds painfully behind my rib cage as I drink her in, hating to see her like this. Guilt slaps me in the face.

I did this to her.

My failure to protect her, to put her first like I always promised I would do, led us to this moment.

As long as I live, I will never forgive myself for letting her down.

Scratch marks mar her pretty face, and bruising is evident on her exposed lower arms, hinting at what she's endured. I sway on my feet as my legs threaten to go out from under me. A lump the size of a ball wedges at the back of my throat, and tears sting my eyes as I walk toward the bed.

Pulling the seat up close to her right side, I sit down and take her hand gently in mine. It is warm to the touch as I lift it to my lips, pressing a soft kiss there. "I'm so sorry, baby," I whisper, not wanting to wake her but needing to get this out. "I'm so sorry for failing you. I swear I will fix things. I will do what I should always have done." Lowering her hand back to the bed, I stare at her gorgeous face as my heart swells with a mixture of pain and longing. "I love you so much, Viv. I hate that you haven't felt that recently, but I promise I will do everything in my power to rectify that. You are my everything, and I let you down, but never again."

She stirs ever so slightly in the bed, and I hold my breath, waiting to see if she wakes, but she doesn't. I don't whisper to her after that, letting her sleep, hoping she is finding some peace in slumber. I stare at her while holding her hand and making plans and promises in my head. I guess at some point I must have nodded off because I wake later as slivers of buttery sunshine trickle through the blinds in the room.

I don't want to leave her, but I need to take a piss, so I head to the adjoining bathroom and attend to business. When I return, Jon is by her bedside, crouched over Viv as he presses a soft kiss to her brow. He glances up at me. "Lauren is showering," he whispers. "I'm going to order breakfast. What would you like?"

I shrug. "Order me whatever," I say, glancing at the time on my watch. It's a little after seven.

Jon squeezes my shoulder before exiting the room. I sit back down by Viv's side and retake her hand.

A few minutes later, Viv moves onto her side, murmuring quietly, and I sit up straighter, clutching her hand a little tighter. Her eyes blink open, and she winces at the light filtering into the room.

"Viv. I'm here," I say.

She turns around, whimpering, and her face contorts in pain.

It kills me. "Baby, I'm so sorry." I kiss the back of her hand as tears fall silently down my face. I don't try to stop them. I want her to see how devastated I am. "Sorry this happened to you, and sorry I wasn't here immediately. I got here as soon as I could. The plane ride was the most excruciating journey because I was terrified, Viv." Raising our conjoined hands to my cheek, I lean into her warm touch. "You were still unconscious when I got on the plane, and I didn't know what I'd find when I arrived."

I quietly sob as she watches me, saying nothing, and I wish I was a mind reader so I could hear her thoughts. She probably hates me. I know I would if I were in her shoes. Shame washes over me as I recall the last words I spoke to her on the phone. And now this. She knows this is all my fault, and I have never hated myself more than I do in this moment. I need her to know I'm sorry and I love her, and I can only pray I haven't fucked us up for good.

"I was so scared you were dead, Viv. Scared I would never get to hold you again or tell you how much I love you. Scared I wouldn't get the chance to apologize for all the ways I have let you down. Scared I wouldn't get an opportunity to make up for all the wrongs."

Her chest heaves, and pain engulfs her bruised, scratched face. "Your fans hate me, Reeve. They want you with her, and it seems they'll stop at nothing to make that happen." Tears stream down her face, and I hate seeing them.

I hate that she's hurting, and it's my fault. "Your parents filled me in." I grind my teeth, my tears quickly transforming to anger. "I know this is my fault. I haven't prioritized you or your needs, and I've been a selfish asshole, but it stops now." I peer deep into her eyes, hoping she can see the resolve there. "I'm going to make this up to you." Carefully, I reach out and touch her cheek, mindful to avoid her injuries. "They will pay for what they did to you, and I'm going to make sure no one ever touches you again."

Leaving the hospital for home is a shitshow. The entrance to the hospital is swamped with reporters, paparazzi, and my fans. Lauren tells me my presence here is making things worse, which only adds to my guilt. I know she's right. Like I know she is furious with me. Viv isn't the only one I have hurt with my careless actions. Lauren and Jon mean the world to me too. They have been there for me when my father wasn't, and this has been a shitty way of repaying them for their love and affection.

I have a lot of groveling to do, and I intend to do it.

Back at the house, after I carry Viv to her bedroom, Lauren shoves me toward the kitchen, telling me to fix something for Viv to eat while Jon goes to retrieve her bag from the car.

Lauren pulls out a tray table and gives me instructions on what to prepare. I don't argue, doing what she tells me because I'm in the doghouse and I don't have a leg to stand on. She fills a glass with water and strides out of the kitchen a couple of minutes later.

I heat up some chicken noodle soup and cut a few slices of crusty bread before adding them to the tray table. I head upstairs and enter Viv's room for the first time in months, a rush of nostalgia slapping me in the face. I have so many happy memories of time spent in this room. Viv is tucked into bed, sitting up, propped against a mountain of pillows, as I place the tray table over her lap.

"It's good to have you home, princess," Jon says, coming into the room behind me. He drops Viv's bag on the floor and smiles softly at his daughter.

"It's good to be home, Dad." Viv offers her dad a smile in return, but her face is tense with pain, and she looks pale and exhausted.

Lauren and Jon leave, shooting me abject warning looks on their way out. As soon as the door is closed, I kick off my shoes and carefully climb onto the bed beside my love. Lying on my side, I face her, my eyes flicking to the tray. "Eat, babe."

I watch her sip her soup, looking like she has the weight of the world on her shoulders. There is so much I want to say to her, but this isn't the time. She's tired and hurting, and her dad wasn't wrong when he warned me about keeping things light. Viv can't handle any of the heavy right now, and I won't add to her pain.

When she finishes eating, I lift the tray off her and set it down on the floor on this side of the bed. Viv lies down, and I crawl under the comforter and reach for her hand. The instant my fingers link with hers, a comforting warmth seeps into my bones. Without stopping to think about it, I press a light kiss to her lips. It's been too long since I felt her mouth and her body moving against mine. I scoot closer, happy when she rests her head on my chest.

Very carefully, I run my fingers through her hair, closing my eyes and savoring the moment. Viv is back in my arms where she belongs, and everything feels right with the world. Her familiar scent and touch wrap around me, and when we are together like this, I feel invincible. Like I can fix everything I have broken and get us back to the place where our love was everything and nothing else mattered.

Her eyelids flutter, blinking open and shut, and I can tell she's fighting sleep. "I love you, Viv," I whisper, pressing a feather-soft kiss to her damaged cheek. "I know I've done a piss-poor job of showing you recently, but I'm going to do better. Almost losing you has put everything into perspective. I can't lose you, Viv. I won't. You're the other half of my soul, and nothing matters more to me than you."

She falls asleep, and as I feel my eyelids drooping, I set my alarm for later so I don't miss my flight.

I don't want to return to the set.

I want to stay here with her. To nurse her back to health and care for her as she heals.

But I've been fielding angry calls all day, and everyone is livid with me. Filming ground to a halt today because I wasn't there, and the studio threatened to bring in the lawyers if I'm not back on set tomorrow. I spoke to Lauren about it earlier. I asked for her advice, and she told me to go back. Viv wouldn't want me jeopardizing my career, and there isn't much I can do to help. Viv needs rest, and her parents will be here to take care of her.

I hate having to leave her.

I don't want to return.

I want to stay here where I belong, but I'll be home shortly for Christmas, and I will be spending every single second with Viv then. It's the only way I'm able to convince myself to return to Boston.

My alarm goes off way too soon. I forego a shower to stay in bed, not wanting to waste a second of precious time with the only girl who has ever mattered. I can shower on the plane later before we land. When I can't leave it any longer, I dot soft kisses into Viv's hair before reluctantly getting out of bed.

I take a piss and brush my teeth before coming back into the bedroom.

I'm bent over her, gently sweeping hair from her face when she stirs. I don't like waking her, but I won't sneak out without saying goodbye. Her gorgeous hazel eyes are soft and unfocused as she blinks them open. "I've got to leave, baby," I whisper. "But I meant everything I said. I know we need to talk too, and I promise we'll do that when I come home for Christmas." I kiss her plump lips, wishing I didn't have to go. "Don't give up on me yet. Let me make this right, and everything will go back to the way it was. I promise."

"How?" she asks, disbelief threading through her tone.

It guts me, but what did I expect? "I've hired my own publicist, and I'm issuing a video statement later today. When I return to the set, I'm telling the studio I'm publicly 'breaking up' with Saffron. And I'm setting her straight too. I know she harbors ideas of us, but I'll tell her again that it'll never happen." I have told her countless times, and the message isn't getting through, but I'll just have to drill it home. Saffron needs to back off and stop interfering in my relationship.

"That will only make her more determined," Viv murmurs.

She isn't wrong. Saffron is like a dog with a bone when she wants something, but she can't have me. I have let her get away with too much shit. Been too trusting and too blind. That stops now. I never should have let her manipulate me into doing drugs, as it only compounded the situation. But I'm not holding her responsible for that.

That's all on me.

I have lost sight of who I am.

The old me would never have gone down this road, and I'm so fucking angry at myself.

For so many things, but especially for letting myself get manipulated by Saffron Roberts. I didn't listen to Viv before, but I'm listening now. If Saffron won't back down, there is no room for her in my life in any capacity. The movie is wrapping up soon, and I won't have to deal with her for much longer. I have no problem cutting her dead. If that is what Viv needs, she's got it.

I don't belong to Saffron, and I never will. Viv is the only woman who will ever have a claim on my heart. "It doesn't matter. I love you. I know I've let her come between us, and it ends now."

As I walk out of the house, I am more determined than ever to reset my life and restore my relationship with the woman I love.

BONUS SCENE – DILLON

This is the scene in Whelans pub in Dublin when Dillon meets Vivien for the first time.

"SHE'S FUCKING GORGEOUS," Jamie says to Ronan as I return to our usual table in Whelans with fresh beers. Aoife scowls and scoots in closer to Jay's side.

"Who is?" I ask, setting the tray with the drinks down on the table before sinking into a chair.

"The Yank," Jay replies.

"Is she here?" I ask, sitting up straighter and looking around the crowded bar for any sign of my pint-sized feisty sister and her new sidekick. I'll admit I'm curious. Ash hasn't shut up about Grace since they met at Trinners.

"Not yet," Ronan says, staring at his phone. "They are on their way."

"I bumped into them in The Buttery during the week," Jay supplies. I'm surprised this is the first time he's mentioned it.

"She's not that gorgeous," Aoife pipes up, sulking and scowling because the risk of competition threatens her perceived position within the band.

She hasn't gotten the memo yet that her place is temporary. It's not like any of us would settle down with a girl who openly shares herself among us. I'm not judging her. I think it's cool she owns her sexuality, and I love she's down for anything, but she's not exactly girlfriend material.

Not that I ever want one of those.

Love is for pussies and fools.

"Do I detect a hint of the green-eyed monster?" Ro asks, grinning before he knocks back his beer.

Jay slides his arm around Aoife's shoulders. "I didn't say I was going to bang her. Just acknowledging she's a real looker."

"Depends on your taste," Aoife replies through tight lips and gritted teeth.

Her attitude is starting to grate on my nerves. I was fine to keep her around when she seemed satisfied with casual sex, but she's getting needy, and I'm thinking the time to cut her loose may be approaching.

I can't stand clingy women. Especially when we have always been up front with her. We told her it would never be more than sex, and she agreed.

I stand, deciding to check things with Ron before our set, to ensure everything is in hand, rather than sit here with the pouting possessive groupie now climbing into Jay's lap.

"Hey, Dillon." A vaguely familiar brunette sidles up to me, brushing her hand against my chest. "It's been a while."

Aoife shoots daggers at the woman as she pushes her tits into my chest, and I'm not having this.

"It has," I lie because I have no fucking clue who this girl is, but I'll go along with it. I think it's time Aoife learned a valuable lesson. "What's up?"

"Hopefully you." A seductive smile graces her full lips as she discreetly slips her hand in the gap between our bodies and palms my cock through my jeans.

"Is that an offer?" I flash her a smile all the ladies love, inwardly chuckling as her eyes pop wide, her cheeks flush, and her lips part with longing.

She snaps out of it fast. "Absolutely." Her smile expands as she gently squeezes my hardening dick.

"It'll have to be quick. We're on soon," I say, grabbing her hand and pulling her with me as I force my way through the crowd, heading for the staff door at the rear of the main room.

"Thanks for the blowjob," I say fifteen minutes later as I lead the girl out from the back into the main area of the pub. Still don't know her name, and I have no interest in learning it. It was a pretty shit effort, but I least I got to blow off some steam before we go on stage. I kiss her quickly. "See you around," I say, pretending I don't notice how her pretty face twists into a frown as I walk away.

I'm an asshole. I readily admit it, but it's not like these women don't know what they're getting into. Everyone on the indie scene in Dublin knows I'm not into commitment.

I am making my way toward our table when the strangest sensation washes over me. All the hairs on the back of my neck stand to attention, and an electrical charge coasts along my skin. My heart picks up pace, thumping quicker, as butterflies swoop into my stomach.

What the fuck?

Then I see her. Standing beside Ash. The girls have their backs to me as they face a clearly excited Ronan. He's still seated, staring up at the Yank as if the sun shines out of her arse. I roll my eyes. My little brother is so obvious. He knows it and refuses to change. He wears his heart on his sleeve and carries lust in his eyes without shielding it from the object of his affection. He rotates through girls almost as fast as me. Unlike me, he likes having a girlfriend, and he usually has a different one every month. He falls in and out of love as fast and as often as Taylor Swift.

I hang back on purpose, drinking Ash's new friend in, wondering if she's the source of my weird reaction. Her dark hair hangs in waves down her back, looking shiny and thick and perfect to wrap around my fist if we were fucking. She's tall, even accounting for the added height from her black and gold stilettos, making Ash appear even smaller than her five feet three inches. I can't see much of her body as she's got a coat on, but the ripped black jeans she's wearing are molded to slender legs I already know would look good wrapped around my head. My dick perks to life as I walk toward them, wanting an introduction.

Ash already warned us off her new best friend, and while I probably should keep it in my pants, I suspect that's going to be problematic. "If it isn't my favorite sister," I say from behind Ash, cutting across the conversation she's having with Grace, Cat, and Ro. "About time you showed up."

Ash whirls around and smacks me in the upper arm while her friend remains oddly rooted in place. "I'm your only sister, clown, and that joke's getting real old."

"Is this the Yank?" I ask, wanting to get a look at her face. If Jay says she's gorgeous, she must be. He's a fussy fucker, and he only likes 'em pretty.

Ash thumps me again. "Be nice, Dillon," she warns as Grace slowly turns around.

Shock renders me mute when our eyes lock and I get a look at her face.

No. Fucking. Way.

She's gorgeous all right. Even more so in the flesh. With her flawless skin, expressive big hazel eyes framed by long thick black lashes, perfect nose, high cheekbones, and fuckable lips, she is smoking hot. My fantasy woman in more ways than one. The pictures I have seen of her online have not done her justice at all.

She is the most beautiful woman I have ever laid eyes on.

That weird electric current I felt a few minutes ago pulses and strains in the small gap between our bodies as we stare at one another.

I'm guessing shock is registering on my face when I spot the panic in her eyes.

Interesting. Does she suspect I know who she is? Or is there a more sinister reason for her reaction. My eyes narrow, and admiration gives way to anger as I think about why she is here and whether her meeting my sister is a coincidence.

That fucking asshole Lancaster.

I grind my teeth to the molars and clench my fists at my sides as I consider the very real possibility this is a setup.

Every few months that asshole who spawned me reaches out, reminding me of the offer he made. It's not like I've forgotten. That meeting with him when I was seventeen is imprinted in my brain, no matter how badly I wish I could scrub it away. The contract resides in a secure hiding place at the back of my wardrobe. Not sure why I don't just rip that shit into pieces, but my gut tells me to hold on to it. It's a decent amount of money, but I refuse to give the sperm donor or my brother what they want.

Fuck them both.

Let them stress over it.

I have zero desire right now to let anyone know Hollywood's new golden boy is my twin. I don't want that kind of attention. But they don't know that, and I'll use it to my advantage. There may come a time when I need that ammunition, and I'm keeping my options open.

Besides, I don't want that prick's money. He can shove it up his pompous ass and choke on it.

A muscle clenches in my jaw, and Vivien Mills, my twin's precious girlfriend, takes a step back, fear and confusion clouding those stunning greenish-brown eyes. The table rattles, and some of the drinks spill.

"Watch it," Jamie snarls, drilling her with a look. "Or the next round's on you."

"Stop complaining," Ash says to Jamie while yanking on my arm. "A little drink got spilled. Big deal."

Why is she here? And why is she masquerading as someone else? Did Simon put her up to this? Is that why she looks so terrified? Is she afraid I have already figured out who she is? If she thinks she's going to influence me into signing that contract, she can think again. And if she thinks she's going to use my sister to get to me, I will fucking ruin her. Fuck the freaky connection simmering between us, and I don't care how gorgeous she is. No one gets to hurt my sister. That shit will never happen again on my watch.

The skin on my knuckles blanches white I'm clenching my fists so tight. I glare at her, pouring all my venom into the look so she gets the message loud and clear. If Vivien is here to cause trouble, I'll be the one bringing it to her. The Lancasters will rue the day they tried to manipulate me. If she's a part of whatever game they are now playing, I won't hesitate to take her down too.

What if she is here to spy on me? To report back to Simon on whether I'm being a good boy and keeping the news of my bio family to myself?

Ronan gets up and shoves me a little, leveling me with a warning look. "You're being rude."

Ash snorts. "Are you even surprised?"

"I'm Ronan," my brother says, smiling at the spy with stars in his eyes. "Ash and Dillon's brother, but please don't hold that against me."

"Grace." She smiles back at him, and a snarl builds at the back of my throat. "Nice to meet you."

I'm not buying this sugary-sweet act. Not for a single second do I think she is being genuine. Reeve Lancaster's bitch doesn't randomly show up in Dublin. That girl's got an agenda, and I need to figure out what it is ASAP. I sharpen my eyes and drill her with a lethal look that usually has grown men shitting their pants. "Why are you here, *Grace?*" I hiss, trying and failing to rein my hostility in. I'm sure it's projecting from me in waves, but I don't care. Let her see I'm onto her.

She thrusts her shoulders out, brazenly staring me in the eyes, and I'll give her some credit for that. "Ash invited me." Her husky voice is confident and alluring, and it's doing strange things to my insides.

It only makes me hate her more.

"In Ireland," I add in a clipped tone. Bitch knows what I mean, and if she wants to play this game, I'm more than up for the challenge.

Her brow puckers. "What does it matter why I'm here?"

"Just answer the question," I snap, my eyes briefly flickering around the space, wondering if her jerk of a boyfriend is here too. Then I remember he's promoting his new movie in the US, and it's most likely she is here alone.

She squares up to me, narrowing her eyes. "I don't owe you any explanation, and is this how you always treat new people you meet?"

"I'm suspicious of anyone who comes into my sister's life." I lean down, putting my face all up in hers, trying to ignore how utterly exquisite she is up close. "Especially nosy Americans." If that doesn't make it clear, I don't know what will.

"Wow. Generalize much?" She crosses her arms over her gorgeous rack and glowers at me like I'm the devil.

Close, sweetheart. Real close.

"You're pissing me off now, Dil." Ash's nails bite into my arm as she yanks me away from her friend.

"Fact." Ronan nods.

"What's going on?" Aoife asks.

I wondered how long it would take her to interject herself into the conversation. I knew her anger at me for disappearing with a girl who wasn't her wouldn't last long. "Nothing." My jaw is tense as I circle my arm around Aoife's shoulders before dropping into the empty seat bedside Jamie and situating her on my lap.

Aoife babbles shit in my ear as she feels me up, but I'm not paying her any attention. My gaze is laser-focused on the American spy. I tune my surroundings out as I try to figure out why she is here. Ash evidently doesn't know her true identity. Rage spikes in my blood. How fucking dare she try to pull the wool over my sister's eyes? What the fuck has Ash ever done to her?

I snap out of my angry haze as Vivien removes her coat and scarf, exposing a revealing outfit. My dick hardens as my gaze roams over the figure-hugging jeans that showcase her slim legs and shapely ass to perfection. She's wearing a sheer black lace top that exposes her bra and a sliver of tantalizing tanned skin.

Straightening up, she turns around and fixes me with a heated stare. My eyes drink her in as if she isn't the enemy.

Fucking hell.

She is sex on legs.

Her bra is fully on display underneath the risqué lacy top, leaving little to the imagination. Her chest heaves under the underwired cups as we stare at one another. My gaze dips lower, over her flat stomach, toned waist, and the soft curves of her hips. I hate my bio brother, for many reasons, but I've got to begrudgingly admire his taste in women because Vivien Mills is a bona fide knockout.

Every guy within our vicinity is looking at her with lust in their eyes, and my little brother is about to bust a nut in his pants.

Aoife's arms tighten around my neck, like a choke hold, and I feel the hatred oozing from her pores. Aoife isn't the smartest chick on the block, but she's not dumb either. She knows competition when she sees it, and she won't like this girl one little bit.

I may be able to use that to my advantage.

"Wow. You're beautiful," Ronan says because he has no chill. His words break whatever shit was going down between Vivien and me, and she ends our stare, looking away and smiling at my brother.

I tune them out, focusing my attention on Jay and Conor. The latter looks as disinterested as ever, and I wonder how long it will take him to nuke all his braincells with weed. I don't know if the guy is ever sober. Not that I care. As long as he gets up on that stage and performs, I couldn't give two shits if he's stoned or drunk.

"Told you," Jamie says, waggling his brows and grinning. "Sexy, feisty, and her tits are the real deal."

Aoife is peppering kisses along my neck as she grinds against the semi in my jeans, thinking it's all for her. I actually wish it was. I don't want to get hard for the Yank. She is the enemy, and I need to find a way of conveying that to my sister without admitting the truth. No one knows who my bio dad and brother are, and it's going to stay that way.

Whatever the reason behind Vivien Mills' relocation to Ireland, she is not going to succeed.

Hell will freeze over before I let Simon and Reeve Lancaster trample all over me.

If they are using her to achieve their goal, they are going to regret it.

I'll send their precious princess back to L.A. a broken shell of a woman, and they'll wish they never crossed me.

BONUS SCENE - VIVIEN

This scene is set three weeks after Viv has returned to L.A. from Ireland. It is the start of her junior year at UCLA.

"UGH, I CAN'T EAT THAT." Audrey pushes her salad bowl away and groans as she rubs her tummy.

"Is something wrong with it?" I ask, frowning as I peer into my own chicken salad bowl. "The food is usually good here, but it tastes a little off to me too." Setting my knife and fork down, I slide my food to one side and lift my bottle of water.

Noise surrounds us in the packed cafeteria as students catch up over lunch. I sip my drink as I glance around the crowded dining hall, taking it all in. Junior year is off to a busy start, and we are both already inundated with assignments and reading lists. It's enough to keep me distracted, but I can't stop thinking about Trinity, my friends back in Dublin, and...Dillon.

"It's not that." Audrey tosses her gorgeous red hair over her shoulders as she leans back in her chair. "I'm having the period from hell this month, and my stomach is too sore to eat." She shoots me a sympathetic look. "I'm getting a taste of what you go through every month."

"My periods have been a lot less painful this year," I admit, stalling with the bottle of water perched against my lips. My stomach plummets to my toes, and blood rushes to my head as the thought lands in my mind. "Shit." Putting my water down, I grab my cell and pull up my calendar. All the blood leaches from my face when I scroll backward through the dates and read the note staring back at me.

"What's wrong?" Audrey sits up straighter in her chair, instantly alarmed by whatever she is reading on my face.

My heart is racing, blood is pounding through my veins, and an uneasy fluttering feeling is skittering across my chest. Clutching my phone tightly, I fix panicked eyes on my best friend. "I'm late," I whisper.

Audrey's eyes pop wide. "How late?" she asks a few seconds later.

"A week." I squeeze my eyes shut for a moment. "I can't believe I didn't notice."

"I can." My bestie reaches across the table, placing her hand on top of mine. "You've had a lot on your mind, and we were busy settling into our place and getting everything ready for the new school year."

"I'm never late, Audrey." Terror pulses through my veins as my mind trawls through the events of the last three weeks. "My periods have always been regular. Like clockwork. Fuck." Hanging my head, I blow air out of my mouth in an attempt to calm myself down. I draw deep breaths, in and out, as I contemplate the potential situation I could be in. My chest heaves painfully as I lift my head, pinning her with a stark look. "I can't be pregnant, Rey. I just can't be." My entire body is trembling at the mere thought of it.

"At the risk of sounding cliché, how could this have happened?"

"Dillon and I stopped using condoms those last few weeks, and Reeve and I never used them as I was always on birth control. I still am, but...oh, fuck." I rub a hand across the tightness spreading across my chest as I realize exactly how this could have happened. "I threw up a couple times." I stare, horror-struck, at my bestie. "Once in Dublin and then again after I slept with Reeve. I was too traumatized to even consider the implications, let alone think about getting a Plan B pill."

She purses her lips, looking contemplative. "Come on." She squeezes my hand before grabbing her stuff and shoving it in her book bag. Her chair scrapes along the floor as she pushes it back and stands. "We need to get to the pharmacy and see what, if anything, we are dealing with."

I gather my things in a daze as my brain conjures up the impending shitstorm I could be facing.

Audrey leads me out of the cafeteria with a firm grip on my elbow, and I'm in autopilot mode. "Breathe, Viv. There's no point worrying yet. It could be a false alarm. You've been under a lot of stress. That will have messed with your hormones and could have impacted your cycle. You might be panicking for nothing."

Audrey is premed, so I choose to cling to her words like a lifeline as we head toward the pharmacy on campus. "Wait," I say a few minutes later, slamming to a halt on the path. "I can't be seen buying a pregnancy test."

I glance all around me as I rub at the tight pain sitting on my chest. I don't see any paparazzi, but it doesn't mean they aren't here somewhere, skulking around campus waiting for the money shot. Since some asshole with a long lens took shots of Reeve and me on his apartment balcony the day I returned to L.A., celebrity photographers have been following me everywhere.

Dad spoke to Doug—his friend and the current UCLA president—and he added extra security on campus to keep the paps away. Reeve insisted on hiring a bodyguard for me, something my parents wholeheartedly agreed with. Now, Leon follows me everywhere. I thought it would be a major inconvenience, but he's discreet, and most times, I forget he's even there.

Interest in me is at an all-time high, and I'd be lying if I said it didn't make me break out in a cold sweat. Reeve's Oprah interview aired a few days ago, and I'm already dealing with an upsurge of paparazzi and online trolls. It only makes me miss Ireland more. I loved being anonymous there, and I hate being back in this fishbowl. At least this time, there are fans coming out in support of me, and there is more of a balance, but I still hate it. I hate all the attention and the intrusion into my privacy, and I don't know if I'll ever get used to it.

"I'll get it," Audrey says, dragging me out of my head. "Go home with Leon, and I'll meet you there."

"What about class?"

"Screw class. We can get notes later. This is more important."

The walk home flies by in a daze, and I'm pacing the floor in our living area, trying to keep calm, as I wait for Audrey to return, when my phone pings with an incoming call.

Reeve's handsome face stares at me from the screen as my cell vibrates upon the coffee table. I'm tempted to send it to voice mail, but Reeve knows my schedule and that my next class doesn't start for ten minutes, so he'll just keep calling.

Finding an opportunity to talk daily is challenging for him now he's back on the promo circuit, but he's making the time. I'm not sure he truly understands the meaning of giving me space or if he's still panicking at the thought he may have lost me.

My head is a mess, and my heart is split down the middle over the two guys I'm in love with.

Guilt is ever present whenever I think about how I slept with my ex the instant I arrived back in L.A. However, I can't find it within myself to regret it. Because I needed Reeve, and he has always felt like home. He wants me back, and he's pulling out the big guns, determined to reclaim his place in my life even if I have asked him to give me some breathing space.

I haven't seen him in over a week as he's busy doing promotion for *Sweet Retribution*—the last movie in that damned *Rydeville Elite* series—and I've been tied up with classes and schoolwork. But he makes a point to call me every day, and our apartment is overrun with lavender roses, expensive chocolates, and other gifts.

Reeve returned the photo album he made me for my birthday before he left, and flipping through the pages is only adding to the turmoil in my heart. Reeve is so embedded in my life, and I'm not sure I could cut him out even if I wanted to.

Which I don't.

Ugh.

I don't know what to do, and I'm consumed with conflicting emotions.

The ringing stops as I stare at my cell in my palm, feeling confused and dazed and a multitude of other sentiments.

I haven't heard a peep from Dillon, and that has been hugely disappointing. Crushing pain squeezes my heart like every time I think of my Irish lover. I haven't even heard from Ash, and I've been too chicken to call her. I know those balcony images of Reeve and me made headlines around the world, and I can only imagine what she must be thinking of me. What Dillon must be thinking. It's no wonder he hasn't called. Or maybe it's because he's too busy fucking Aoife to even care.

Pain shuttles through me at that thought` just as Reeve calls again. I pick up this time, praying I can get through this call without alerting him to my underlying panic. "Hey."

"Hey, beautiful. Have I caught you at a bad time?"

"I have a few minutes to talk."

"I miss you," Reeve says, going straight for the jugular.

"I miss you too," I truthfully admit. "What are you up to?"

"I'm over at Universal Studios with some of the cast. We're being interviewed by Kelly Clarkson today."

I'm so glad that bitch Saffron Roberts is in rehab and not involved in the promo tour for this last movie. I wouldn't be able to handle all that shit again. "Oh, get me an autograph. You know how much I love her music." I'm not usually one for fangirling or autographs, but there are a handful of exceptions, and Kelly is one.

Reeve chuckles. "I already have it in my pocket along with a few goodies she gave me for you."

My heart melts at the affirmation of how well he knows me, and I love seeing my Reeve again. That version of himself that hurt me these past few years is no longer evident. Reeve is the boy next door again. My best friend and the man who first captured my heart. His thoughtful gestures, dedication to winning me back, and his loving words are chipping away at my resolve to keep my distance until I've worked out what I want. "Thank you."

"Anything for you, babe. You know that."

The door opens, and Audrey enters our place. I shake my head and point at the cell. "You can stop sending flowers now," I say, dropping onto the couch as Audrey quietly approaches. "If you send more, there won't be any room for Audrey and me."

"I need to show you how much I love you, Viv. I need to remind you of who I am and who we are. I need you to remember all the good times because there were way more of them than bad. I know we can be amazing together again if you'd just give me a chance to prove it."

"I'm not disputing any of that, Reeve, but you can't pressure me. You need to give me space to sort through my feelings."

"I'm scared of losing you, Viv," he says in a soft tone, his voice cracking in parts. "I can't live without you."

A pregnant pause ensues as Audrey sets the paper bag down on the coffee table, and fresh pressure sits on my chest.

Reeve clears his throat. "Are you talking to *him*?"

"No. I haven't heard from him since I left Ireland."

A loud sigh of relief echoes down the line. "I love you, Viv, and I want you by my side. I want our dream to come true. The one we talked about endlessly as kids. We have the resources to make it happen now, and I want that with you. I want our forever. I'm ready for it."

"I wish it was as easy for me, but we can't just pick up where we left off, Reeve."

"Why not?"

"Because too much has happened, and we still have stuff to work through."

"Let's work through it then because I'm not letting you go, Viv. Never again."

This is too much of the heavy when I already have a potential bomb to deal with.

"We'll talk when you get home in a month. This isn't the kind of conversation we can have over the phone."

"Just remember I love you, Viv. I have loved you since I was a little boy, and I never stopped. I never will."

"I love you too, Reeve, but you need to give me some time."

"I'm trying, my love. I am trying to be patient, but it's hard when I've been without you for so long."

I want to say try harder, but another part of me doesn't want Reeve to pull back. When he is fully invested, Reeve loves me so completely and thoroughly that it surrounds me like a security blanket at times when I need it the most.

"I know it's coming from a good place," I say.

"If you just give me a chance, I will make it up to you."

"You agreed we'd rebuild our friendship first. It's all I can offer you right now." That may be all I can offer him for some time if it turns out I'm pregnant.

"And I'm grateful for it and for your forgiveness. But you can't blame a guy for trying for more with the only woman he has ever loved."

"I don't, but it's making it harder for me."

"That's not what I want, but I can't stay away, Viv. Please don't ask for that because it'll kill me."

"Just back off a little, Reeve. That's all I'm asking."

Air whooshes out of his mouth and down the line. "Okay. I will try."

"Thank you."

"You're my entire world, Vivien. Don't forget it."

"I won't, but I've got to go," I say, needing to end this conversation because I refuse to discuss such serious matters on a call. "Have fun at the interview, and give Kelly my love."

"I will. Have a great rest of the day. Love you, baby."

"Love you too."

I hang up and flop back on the couch, scrubbing my hands down my face. "What the hell am I going to do if I'm pregnant, Rey?" Turning my head, I eyeball my friend. "I won't know who the father is." She is aware I slept with Dillon and Reeve within a short time frame of each other.

"Let's take it one step at a time." Audrey helps me to my feet and hands me the brown paper bag. "Go piss on a stick, Viv, and remember, whatever happens, I am here for you."

I head into the bathroom on shaky legs and do what I need to do. There were three different tests in the bag, and I used all three of them. Might as well be sure of the outcome. After leaving the tests on the counter in the bathroom, I wash my hands and return to the living room.

Sitting on the couch beside Rey, I pull her in for a hug. "I love you. You're such a good friend, Audrey. I can always count on you to come through for me, and I want you to know how much I appreciate it."

"It works both ways, chica. You held my hand when I broke up with Alex, and you supported me when my parents divorced. I couldn't have survived either of those things without you."

I rest my head on her shoulder, purposely not looking at my watch as I know not enough time has passed yet.

"I was thinking about what you said while you were in the bathroom," she says, resting her head alongside mine. "There are ways to prove paternity while pregnant or after the birth. You will be able to confirm which one of them is the dad."

"I know." I pick at the pretty pink varnish on my nails. "Only I could get myself into such a mess. Dillon clearly doesn't want anything to do with me now. I haven't forgotten his harsh words and cold treatment of me that last night. He's probably shacked up with that bitch Aoife now. How do I even call him up and tell him I'm pregnant?"

A strangled sound rips from my mouth before I bury my head briefly in my hands. Pain lashes me from all sides as I struggle to maintain composure. My eyes are stinging as I straighten up and stare at my friend's concerned face. "How would I tell Reeve I'm pregnant and the baby might not be his? It would devastate him."

"You'll find a way of dealing with it, Viv. Like I said, you have options, and you don't have to rush into making any decision. We don't even know if you are pregnant yet. It could be a false alarm. Stress could have delayed your period."

Glancing at the time on my watch, I rise to my feet. "I guess we're about to find out." I pull my bestie to her feet. "I need you with me for this part but only if you are okay to keep this from Alex. If I'm pregnant, you'll need to keep this strictly between us until I've figured out what I'm going to do. Alex can't know because he'll feel obligated to tell Reeve immediately. If you're not okay with that, I understand. I don't want to come between you and Alex, not when you have only gotten back together. If you need to bow out here, I am cool with it."

I'm not really. I can't imagine carrying this burden alone, but I would do it for Audrey. I won't cause problems in her relationship.

She loops her arm in mine. "I don't like keeping secrets from Alex, but this situation is unique. You can trust me to keep your confidence. I won't let you go through this alone. I promise this'll remain between us until you decide otherwise."

"Thanks." I give her a quick hug, and then we walk to the bathroom.

Stopping in the doorway, I count to ten in my head, willing my errant heart to stop beating so frantically. My palms are sweaty, and my ears are ringing as I approach the counter.

"You've got this," Rey says, squeezing my arm as we come to a stop.

The three tests are lined out in a row on the counter, and they all confirm the same thing.

PREGNANT.

We stare at the tests in a state of numbed shock, and multiple emotions are flitting through my head. Panic, guilt, grief, and fear are there, for obvious reasons, along with a healthy dose of trepidation. But there is also joy and warmth and excitement, which I wasn't expecting. No matter what the outcome, or who the father is, I know this baby was conceived with love. I already want this child, and my heart swells with instant love and protectiveness as I make a silent vow to adore and cherish him or her, irrespective of how this all plays out.

I won't let my failings impact my innocent child.

Even if I end up raising him or her alone, I will ensure they want for nothing. My extended circle will ensure that too. My parents will adore their grandchild, and I know Audrey will be there for me every step of the way. If this baby is Dillon's, Ash, Cath, and the O'Donoghue family will warmly welcome my child and make sure he or she is included.

If I must go it alone, I won't ever be truly alone. The same goes for my baby.

These thoughts slice a layer off my anxiety, and it settles something inside me.

My hand gravitates to my flat stomach, and I lay my palm on my toned flesh as tears prick my eyes and resolve beds deep in my bones.

Audrey pulls me into a hug, and I appreciate she is letting me process my thoughts before we start discussing the situation. My bestie knows me well. I'm sure she's already aware of the thoughts flitting through my head, and she knows where I will focus my energies.

My baby's needs come first, and that will remain my priority. Every decision and action I make from now on will be guided by the unflappable love in my heart for my child and my determination to do what I feel is in his or her best interests.

I didn't plan for this or anticipate it.

But it doesn't feel wrong.

On the contrary, despite the painful situation I find myself in, this feels utterly right, and I'm choosing to follow this gut feeling and pray that everything works out okay in the end.

Want another emotional, angsty romance to sink your teeth into? Check out *Insepa-rable*, *When Forever Changes*, *Still Falling for You*, *Incognito*, *Always Meant to Be*, *Holding on to Forever* or *Surviving Amber Springs*. All are stand-alone romances and currently **FREE** to read in Kindle Unlimited.

ABOUT THE AUTHOR

Siobhan Davis is a *USA Today, Wall Street Journal,* and Amazon Top 5 bestselling romance author. **Siobhan** writes emotionally intense stories with swoon-worthy romance, complex characters, and tons of unexpected plot twists and turns that will have you flipping the pages beyond bedtime! She has sold over 1.8 million books, and her titles are translated into several languages.

Prior to becoming a full-time writer, Siobhan forged a successful corporate career in human resource management.

She lives in the Garden County of Ireland with her husband and two sons.

You can connect with Siobhan in the following ways:

Website: www.siobhandavis.com
Facebook: AuthorSiobhanDavis
Instagram: @siobhandavisauthor
Tiktok: @siobhandavisauthor
Email: siobhan@siobhandavis.com

Made in the USA
Middletown, DE
11 October 2023

40601399R00440